# VESSEL OF WOVEN NIGHT

## ROWAN BLOOD VOLUME 4

### KELLEN GRAVES

*For Mo,*
*I would follow you*
*into the woods any day.*

# CONTENTS

**Author's Note**

This novel is Fantasy-Romance for a New Adult audience, and contains tropes commonly found in that genre. Such tropes include but are not limited to:

- Brief scenes of sexual harassment
- Descriptions of trauma around terrorist events
- Descriptions of abuse, imprisonment
- Descriptions of paralysis via magical means, vulnerable while in a state of partial nudity
- References to previous sexual assault; no explicit acts described on-page
- Themes of anxiety, depression, ptsd
- Themes of gaslighting and manipulation
- Crude language
- Themes of fantasy-based bigotry
- Descriptions of blood, gore, and death
- Descriptions of excessive drinking/drunkenness
- Explicit scenes of consensual sex
- Descriptions of (fantasy-based) terrorism at crowded/public events

## Pronounciation Guide
### (Fictional & Inspired)

*Ailir* (fictional) *eye-leer*
*Ailinne (fictional) aye-lin*
*Aodhán (Irish-Gaelic) ey-ohn*
Asche (fictional) *ash*
Beantighe (irish-gaelic) *ban-tee*
Cylvan (fictional) *sil-van*
*Erelaine (fictional) air-ah-len*
Fiachra *(irish-gaelic) fee-kra*
*Fjornar (fictional) fyor-nar*
Gaeilge (irish-gaelic) *gwel-gah*
Kyteler (irish-gaelic) *kite-ler*
Naoill (Fictional) now-ill
Shamhradháin (irish-gaelic) *sham-ra-dien*
Sídhe (irish-gaelic) *shee*
Sionnach (irish-gaelic) *shun-nah*
Tuatha dé Danann (irish-gaelic) *too-ha de
    dan-an*
*Vjallrod (Fictional) vyal-rod*


## Title Reference (fictional)

*he/she/they*
Lord/Lady/Gentle
King/Queen/Danae
Prince/Princess/Daurae

AND BECAUSE HIS MOTHER FEARED THAT THE SONS OF MORNA WOULD FIND HIM OUT AND KILL HIM, SHE GAVE HIM TO A DRUIDESS AND ANOTHER WISE WOMAN OF CUMHAL'S HOUSEHOLD, AND BADE THEM TAKE HIM AWAY AND REAR HIM AS BEST THEY COULD.

SO THEY TOOK HIM INTO THE WILD WOODS ON THE SLIEVE BLOOM MOUNTAINS, AND THERE THEY TRAINED HIM TO HUNT AND FISH AND TO THROW THE SPEAR, AND HE GREW STRONG, AND AS BEAUTIFUL AS A CHILD OF THE FAIRY FOLK

⸻

*The High Deeds of Finn and other Bardic Romances of Ancient Ireland*
T. W. Rolleston, 1910

# 1

## THE COFFEE

Lavender leaves at the base of the porcelain cup. A spoonful of maple syrup. Fresh honeysuckle picked from behind Muirín Dormitory, where flower sprites nipped at Saffron's fingers like he foraged in the Agate Wood and not a manicured high fey garden. Where signs of wild things encroaching past the school's barrier were proven by the missing flowers, berries, leaves.

He gently rolled fresh blueberries beneath his palm until soft and fragrant, staining his skin crimson. Pouring steamed milk into the cup last, it swirled at the bottom like a golden purple storm. Like the color of Cylvan's amethyst eyes during a dark, overcast day.

*What's it like to have all your memory threads pulled out?*

Saffron glanced over his shoulder, knowing there would be no one seated at the counter at his back. Still hoping he'd spot Asche's long ,cornsilk-blonde hair braided over one shoulder like Cylvan always wore his at night; to see their dark horns and golden eyes, that mischievous look like they knew they were being rude but didn't know any other way to assert authority as Alfidel's Daurae. Just like the first time, in Danann House.

Exhaling through his nose, Saffron brought the tea to his mouth and took a boiling, burning sip.

There was no one else in Muirín's kitchen so early in the morning. The sun was still an hour off from rising in the distance. Beantighes wouldn't be arriving until lunchtime, since all those remaining at Mairwen were assigned to the main kitchens for the foreseeable future. A result of so many fleeing with the silver-tongued man who offered them magic and freedom.

Saffron only imagined the daurae's voice behind him, because it had been the last thing echoing in his mind as he woke from a restless sleep; Asche's calls from the depths of that black nightmare, begging for Saffron to find them. *Help me, find me; I'm right here, I'm not far. Please come, please come for me.* There was a reason he barely slept any more.

Saffron had come to prefer the silence that fell over Avren in the week since the Midsummer Games—it gave him time to think. With classes on pause and every noisy high fey in the city hiding in their homes except to run the most important of errands —his mind never stopped.

The kitchen in Muirín dorm was different than that in Danann House. They were also exactly the same. They stocked the same foods and herbs and spices and loose leaf teas and other daily essentials, in the pantry and on shelves tucked cleanly away behind doors. There were other staples like eggs and meats and fruits in the ice box, though left to fester as any magic meant to maintain a chilly temperature in perpetuity had been snatched in the ashen state. Sugar, flour, molasses, corn meal lined the cabinets in dark places, where only those who knew better would think to look. Unfortunately, *bwcas* and other wild things knew where to look, scavenging the dry goods as they were not being left loaves of bread by beantighes in exchange for their nightly work. Saffron might have baked them something had he had the chance—would it not have been so strange for someone to stumble upon him, presumed high fey lord, baking bread for wild inhabitants of the dormitory.

*"Teach the fox lord to bake bread. Make him useful for something."*

"The fox lord has a name," Saffron mumbled. By then, he'd grown used to hearing Taran mac Delbaith's voice ghosting through the back of his mind, usually muttering something condescending, or scolding him for how he chose to do things. It used to unsettle him, knowing someone he used to despise so much was always there to watch and listen to everything Saffron did—but even in only a week since the Midsummer Games, even Saffron could find a pinch of comfort in having someone there. Always there, a companion, another presence to fill the lonely gaps festering in his soul. "But even then—foxes are notoriously bad at sifting flour."

Saffron could *feel* Taran's hesitance at that, confused and frustrated, wondering what in gods' name that meant, before scoffing like he didn't want Saffron to think he didn't understand. Saffron just smiled to himself.

"Do you want me to pour a bowl of tea for you? I'd have to serve it on the floor, since I don't want to teach you bad manners for begging at the table."

*"Oh, fuck off."*

He was getting better at sensing exactly when the wolf stirred to the surface of their shared consciousness, like a common area of a shared mind. More often than not, his presence drifted away again, into nothingness, into the ether, where even Saffron could forget he was there—though he always came whenever Saffron searched for him. He didn't hesitate to float back in again whenever he had something to say. A perpetual companion, whether Saffron liked or not.

He would have hated the constant sense of surveillance more had the beast not been at least minimally helpful while poring over books and notes all night, night after night, trying to figure out a solution before any oracles could. Trying to figure out what to do with Ryder Kyteler, before any oracles could. Taran never had any of the right answers, either—but they shared a muted, frenzied desire to rescue the daurae, and that was common ground enough to exchange more than disguised insults back and forth.

Since his dog wasn't interested, Saffron scattered a small handful of remaining berries across the counter, clicking his tongue at Fiachra who perched sleepily in the open window meant for the passage of messenger robins. The owl yawned, cracking open her dark eyes that reflected the light with an unsettling red flash. Spreading her wings and descending to the counter, her trimmed talons clacked on the wood as she lazily pecked at the berries that rolled away from her. Resorting to smashing a talon down to catch a particularly stubborn one, like trapping a mouse—only for it to squish beneath her foot with a gruesome pop.

Sipping his tea again, Saffron closed his eyes. He let the taste spill over his tongue, burning still as it went, but that time not from the heat. From the rawness of his throat. He was far done crying, at least in a waking state. He still woke in tears more often than not, glad he at least didn't cry out for anyone to hear. He'd cried enough. He wasn't sure he would ever cry again, for as long as he lived, with the amount he'd sobbed in private and in Cylvan's arms and in front of his friends in the past week alone.

One week out of the two he'd promised himself to get his friends back, already gone. Already gone, as every day further brought new dread that what Ryder Kyteler had done was going to be more difficult to replicate, to solve, to undo than anyone ever anticipated. Tearing open the broad field amidst the Midsummer Games, swallowing earth and grass in the center, and more—at least two dozen high fey attendees in the stands. Tearing that rift through reality as Saffron refused to obey him, as Ryder insisted on sending a message to the kings, to Cylvan, to all of Alfidel—and successfully doing just that, when he took Asche through the veil with him. As he took all of Avren's opulence, through the resulting ashen state.

He hated that most—but in ways he couldn't explain. He

hated being outwitted. Saffron hated thinking there was anything that man could do that he couldn't figure out.

Ryder Kyteler was no smarter than Saffron—only more experienced. That was all. He hadn't accomplished the same things Saffron had, magic wise—he didn't have access to the same resources Saffron did, knowledge wise—which meant Saffron just had to keep looking. He had to keep trying. Once he figured it out, surely, he'd be able to fix everything he'd caused.

The only solace he could take as the days passed without progress, was the knowledge that time moved slower in the human world. He didn't know exactly how long, except by what Sunbeam had once told him long ago in the Kyteler Ruins outside of Morrígan—that one week for Alfidel was little more than two days in the human world.

Saffron knew how much harm could be done in only two days, though. The peace he felt with every self-reminder was always short-lived.

Royal oracles spoke to him more than once, to the point of demanding to know the truth. Accusing him of lying when he said Ryder used pixie rings to tear open the veil, but never explaining why they refused to believe him. When he said there may have been a giant veil circle in the grass, too, they really sneered at him, like that was what proved he only had an over-active imagination. '*But you just said he used pixie rings,*' they'd said, as if catching him in his lie. He just stared at them in confusion. In growing frustration. He might have cried in front of them, too—if he hadn't instead leapt to his feet and screamed insults in all his overwhelming frustration. King Tross was the one to quickly grab and steer him away before he could truly say or do something worth arrest.

Only later did they realize it was strange for Saffron to know anything about veil circles to start—and sore-throated, puffy-eyed, and pissed off, he had to tell them the actual lie he'd already practiced for that exact moment. *My mother in Alvénya used to tell me stories of Oisín and Niamh. Oisín passed to the human world by a circle Niamh drew in the grass...*

All the while, Taran's voice never left the back of his mind. That warning he'd given in Cylvan's bedroom the night after the games. A warning that Saffron should be wary of who he trusted, even the royal oracles. There wasn't a soul he should trust unwaveringly, in fact—including the people he held closest. Perhaps because Saffron cussed the oracles out during the interview was the only reason the wolf didn't later scold him for being so forthcoming with what he knew.

It was torturous, having to pretend like he didn't know better. To pretend he didn't know who Ryder Kyteler was; to pretend he didn't know why that man did what he did. To pretend it hadn't partially been for Saffron's eyes to see, to pretend he hadn't originally been the biggest piece of Ryder's plot, had he not come to his senses in time.

To then also pretend he had no idea why beantighes were disappearing from their jobs before the veil event—and how they vanished even faster after. In just that week since the games, the staff at Mairwen had dwindled by nearly half. Enough that they couldn't maintain dormitory kitchens. Enough that students were asked to tidy up their own rooms—which nearly sparked a riot on its own. Saffron, meanwhile, cleaned his dorm and the shared space every single day in his restlessness; he would have scrubbed Copper's room clean, too, had the fox lord not refused. Insisting he could do it on his own, even though Saffron knew he wouldn't.

In so many ways, it was thrilling to think humans finally rebelled how they wished, to escape the leash of beantighehood.

In others—it was gut-churningly harrowing, to know they were only able to do so on the word of Ryder Kyteler—who was not anything like he claimed. Only half-human. Half-fey. Capable of compelling humans who weren't expecting it. Coming from a place far north, where oracles loyal to Queen Proserpina once learned to become witchhunters. The same place where Eias Lam learned how to manipulate memory threads, where Taran mac Delbaith was given the bones of the Wolf King. Where Ryder must have learned to twist memories, himself, as he'd done to Saffron—perhaps even more times than Saffron knew.

*What's it like to have all your memory threads pulled out?*

When Asche first posed him that question in Danann House's kitchen, Saffron had smiled to himself. He didn't know. He didn't think he'd ever know. If he thought too closely about how he would be able to answer it while standing in Mairwen's kitchen in comparison—he might actually, finally snap through the thin barrier of sanity keeping his real emotions at bay.

"Beantighe, can I get a coff—oh."

Saffron straightened up—the way a fey lord was supposed to stand—resisting the instinct to turn and bow and offer whatever the visitor wanted. He just glanced over his shoulder to whoever poked their head inside, recognizing messy red hair spilling over shoulders, a shock of white strands hanging between two golden-brown eyes.

"Good morning, Copper," he said with a relieved chuckle. "I can make you a coffee if you want."

"Oh, uh," Copper stammered, straightening up and scratching the loose hair on the back of his head as he shuffled a few steps inside. "That's alright, Saff. Feels rude, considering you're... and all... Oh, shit, I called you *beantighe*, but I didn't mean it like—I really just thought you were—I wasn't tryin' to insult you or anything, considering—"

"I'm already pouring the water," Saffron said, hooking the kettle he'd used for the tea over the spigot and turning the knob. Even boiling hot water had become a hands-on chore in Avren with the ashen state. No longer could they charm a little flame to keep water boiling at all times, without ever having to feed it more sticks beneath the stove. He briefly wondered if the fey who'd lost beantighes in the human exodus even knew how to start a fire to cook their oatmeal and boil their drinks.

"You sure?" Copper asked still, though he shuffled in a little more. Dressed in his hurling practice uniform, still dirty from the last time since he refused to let Saffron wash it. Pretending like Saffron didn't know that hurling practice had been long cancelled for days—Saffron constantly wondering why his friend still insisted on going to the field every morning as if things were normal. Perhaps not having to wonder, at all. There had been too many of his own sleepless nights spent in his dorm, where he could hear Copper shuffling around in the common area. Trying to keep quiet, like Saffron wasn't equally wide awake. Even the fox-lord struggled to sleep.

"I already ground the beans," Saffron lied. "Come on, or else it will go to waste."

He hadn't ground anything—but just getting Copper into the room was be worth the fib. The fox-lord had not outright ignored him since he and the others learned of Saffron's past beantighehood and future kinghood, but he'd skirted all of Saffron's attempts at talking about it at the same time. And while a week wasn't very long in the grand scheme of things, to Saffron it felt like an eternity. Especially when there was nothing else to keep his attention on campus. Not while Cylvan was constantly busy at the palace dealing with the political fallout of the games and navigating aid for the fey affected by the ashen state; not while classes were cancelled as the administration worked out a way to navigate the ashen state of all their professors; not while Saffron was encouraged to remain on campus unless he had a chaperone to the palace, meaning all there really was for him to do was sit and read and take notes and obsess over how he could fix everything he'd broken.

Despite his desperation for friendly companionship, Saffron had determined it best to give Copper whatever time he needed to process whatever feelings he had. But Sionnach was running thin from their own stress of it all, and Saffron's constant need for company, even just while sitting silently in the library together. Cylvan was too busy with responsibilities as the prince, and even the perpetual companion in Saffron's head wasn't exactly his *first* preference. Even Maeve was pulling her hair out as a dorm prefect, having to run around all over Mairwen resolving issues with everyone else.

Copper made a sound like he meant to say something else, but Saffron interrupted again:

"We don't have to talk about anything you don't want to," he said outright, and the awkwardness in the room intensified, before popping and deflating. Copper looked at him in disbelief, like he wasn't used to anything being said so bluntly. "Come on. It'll take two minutes. I'm very good at making coffee, you know, even without any kitchen charms to help. I once learned how beantighes make it for even the pickiest of high fey."

Thankfully, Copper finally chuckled. He stepped fully into the kitchen, even leaning on the counter in the center. As if none of the resting stools would be able to brace beneath the size of him; though he more likely was bracing for a quick getaway. Just in case.

"You coerce the prince into doing what you want like this, too?" He asked.

"The only way to get Cylvan to do anything is coercion." Saffron threw him a coy smile. "How else do you think I got into this position?"

That might have been a little too close to the unspeakable topic, and Saffron bit his lip in regret. But Copper smirked.

"He secretly loves being told what to do, doesn't he?"

"Only by me."

"Nasty."

Saffron could feel Copper's eyes on his back as he set the kettle to boil on the stove, before scooping a cup of whole coffee beans from a canvas bag beneath the counter and pouring them into a metal cylinder. Sliding the top into the center, he handed it to Copper behind him.

"Press down on the top and turn at the same time. Like you're peppering something. Oh—have you ever had to pepper your own meal?"

"What's this?" Copper asked in lieu of answering that question.

"A bean grinder."

Copper wrinkled his nose, then groaned once he realized he'd been caught in Saffron's lie. Still, he made a show of pushing up the sleeves of his hurling uniform, flexing his arm muscles until Saffron laughed, then going to work like instructed.

"How's everything going for you?" He asked as Saffron pulled a carafe of heavy cream from the ice box, still just cold enough to be good. Next, Saffron snagged a sprig of vanilla bean from a ceramic jar on the counter. He scraped vanilla seeds from the shell with the back of a knife as Copper watched with rapt interest.

"As well as it could, I guess," Saffron answered, trying to keep his tone as light as possible. "Hard to find things to keep me distracted without any classes going on, and since I'm not really allowed to leave campus, I'm limited in the kind of research I can feasibly do..." He didn't mean to mention his research habits, either, but didn't realize until it was too late. It was all he ever thought about, anymore.

"Yeah, me too," Copper said. "Less about doing research, but... I never thought I'd miss having class to go to. There's no fun in skipping a lecture to run around in the woods when there's no lecture to skip, you know?"

"Have you been running around in the woods without me, fox?" Saffron asked with a little hiss, and Copper put his hands up.

"Not so loud... *beantighe.*" He tested the word. It escaped him like air between two squeezing hands, only relaxing when Saffron laughed.

"Good thing our glamour charms still work despite everything else, hm? Otherwise we'd both have some things to explain to everyone."

"Daurae Asche would be having the time of their life if they were here," Copper said, once again speaking carefully, as if he wasn't sure Saffron was ready to talk so casually about Asche. He had no idea exactly how desperate Saffron was to speak *casually* about the daurae, as never mentioning them at all felt too much like they really were lost for good.

"I've actually been writing down some of the more interesting things to tell them about once we see them again," Saffron said with a grin. "Like how our glamour charms are working fine, but all the professors' charmed notes are completely blank. Or how some of the access tokens work like normal but others are broken, depending on where someone is trying to go. I heard all the charmed lanterns around campus aren't working anymore, either, which is why they've had beantighes out lighting them by hand every evening."

"Oh, that's why the path from the hurling field was dark when I left around midnight last night..." Copper said, extending a leg to show a gnarly scrape of dried blood on his knee.

Saffron had to resist scolding him for staying out that late in the first place, while also biting back a comment of: *'they probably don't have enough beantighes on staff to light all of them, anymore.'*

"The barrier around campus and the woods isn't working very well either," Copper added. "Been seeing more wild things wandering around after the sun goes down. Even just last night, I thought I saw a unicorn munching on some wild roses on the other side of the stands—"

"A unicorn!" Saffron practically shrieked. "Really?! Oh, *damn you, fox!*"

"Why d'you think I was rushing back to the dorm so late! I was trying to make it back in time to grab you!" Copper laughed, a boisterous sound Saffron didn't realize how much he missed until it rang in his ears again. "Don't hate me too much —might not have even been a real one. Probably just a mimic that was really eyeballing me. I guess it makes sense, considering how it kept whinnying in this really unsettling way, like it wanted me to go over and pet it... might've bit my whole hand off...":

"Mimics have to drink the blood of the thing they copy,

though, don't they?" Saffron argued. "They drink opulence from the creature's blood and use it on themself."

"That's what I'm saying. If I hadn't split when I did, you might have two of me to deal with."

Saffron grinned. "Maybe two of you could really put your heads together and clean up that pit of a bedroom."

"Alright, *beantighe*, listen here—"

But Saffron laughed, and Copper grinned.

"Mimics having to drink the blood of what they copy actually makes me have some questions about you and your fox form, you know," Saffron went on, grabbing a mug for the coffee before taking the ground beans to brew in the boiling kettle.

"I can assure you, my fox form is nothing more dastardly than a family curse from the forest."

"Because of your family's ancient feast."

"Careful—mentioning my family's feast is a quick way to get my dad's ears ringing. Really don't want him trotting into the city, now more than ever."

Saffron laughed, Copper laughed—and for a moment, everything felt *normal* again. Even though that *normal* was still so very different from the life Saffron had known before arriving at Mairwen, even though his *normal* at Mairwen had only been a few months long—he was beginning to learn to appreciate those small windows of peace he was allotted, as they always came to a crashing, inevitable end. He wouldn't take that brief moment of peace, there in Muirín's kitchen, pouring his friend a cup of fresh coffee for granted, either.

"Wanna come to practice with me?" Copper went on as Saffron finished mixing a spoonful of cream into his cup. "Really need someone to hold the body cushion I tackle. Promise I won't hurt you too badly. Maybe we'll even see that probably-not-a-unicorn again..."

"Gee, that sounds like a *lot* of fun, but... Why don't you try asking Madame Hutter if she needs anything like that in her self-defense lessons? I hear other students are still scrambling for open slots."

"Oh—you mean 'cause they can't compel humans anymore?" Copper smirked. "No, I opted out of that days ago. Personally, if they deserve it, I think a high fey getting their ass walloped by a beantighe would be hilarious."

"You're not worried about your own ass, in this uncertain time?" Saffron asked sarcastically.

"Nah. Beantighes aren't gonna start a fight with me."

"There are plenty of beantighes who could take someone as big as you."

"No—I mean, because I have a beantighe name. You know. They wouldn't pick a fight with one of their own. Just like you never did, either. Wait—was *'Saffron'* your original beantighe name? Seriously? Cylvan couldn't come up with something else for you fast enough?"

Saffron snorted. Before he could tell Copper all about it, the soft clopping of hooves approached the kitchen entryway, where a frazzled-looking Sionnach shoved their head inside with a worried flush.

"Oh, thank the gods!" they groaned, throwing the door open and hurrying inside. "I was worried sick as soon as you weren't in bed, your high—! Erm!"

"Good morning, Sionnach," Saffron said, lifting his drink as a way of inviting them over. Sionnach hesitated, chocolate-brown eyes flickering to Copper, before they stepped in a little more to join them at the counter.

They intentionally stood an arm's length from Copper, like they thought he might try something wicked even so early in the morning. Saffron couldn't exactly blame them, especially with how Copper looked them up and down more than once. Not even trying to hide it, before scoffing something and sipping at his drink.

"Were you up late again last night?" Sionnach asked, thanking Saffron for the cup of coffee he poured them.

"Copper invited me to watch his hurling practice this morning," Saffron changed the subject, feeling himself mentally recoil from the mention of his worthless research and the lack of sleep he made as payment, "but Maeve finally has some free time to take me to the palace this morning. Copper says he needs someone to —what, hold your tackle-cushion? Even promised it won't hurt. Why don't you go with him instead, Sionnach?"

"No. I don't think so."

"Not even a polite second to think about it, huh?" Copper chuckled, only partially in disbelief. He threw back the rest of his coffee, before planting both hands on the counter and getting to his feet. "Well, if you change your mind, *goat*, there's a lot more grass to munch on in the field than in the library. Or do you eat the corners of the books you read? No wonder you're so smart."

"Goodbye, Copper," Saffron said in warning. Copper grinned, then laughed, smacking a big hand against Sionnach's back as a sign of *'I'm only joking.'* The satyr clopped forward a few steps, scowling as Copper made his goodbyes and saw himself out. Saffron just smiled to himself, pouring another coffee, that time for himself. Knowing he would need it; wanting to be aware, and available, and—*awake*, during his first chance in days to finally spend time with Cylvan again. Hoping, for once, *for once*—he might be permitted just one morning with a slightly lessened sense of dread.

2

———

# THE HORN

Sitting across from one another in Morrígan's Grand Library, when Prince Cylvan first told Saffron about ashen states caused by violent manipulations of the veil, Saffron had pictured it to be much different.

He imagined flowers wilting. The color of the grass fading, pixies losing their sparkle, even the sky turning ruddy. He wondered if the inherent beauty of the high fey made ashen would dim somewhat, even pondering if that was how humans first came to be. Before he ever learned about Baba Yaga's teacup circles; those small epithets Cylvan, at the time, only had the courage to call *folk magic*.

But Avren's trees remained verdant and vibrant, with leaves fluttering in the summer wind as they always did. The flowers in Mairwen's gardens remained bright and fragrant, even if fewer people passed by to appreciate them during daylight hours. Perhaps the plants even appreciated the break in ogling; from what Saffron scribbled in his sketchbook, they might have even spread their petals wider to soak up as much sun as possible. No longer afraid of being plucked and given to someone as a romantic gesture, then left on one of the benches to wilt.

Or, more contemptuously—as if the constant cloud of

opulence over the city, before then, had kept their blooms from fully unfurling. As if, with it gone, they felt the same sudden, unexpected, overwhelming blanket of relief Saffron did once the initial hysteria gave way. That cloud of opulence, dissolving into the sky and allowing the sun to beam through, just for him. The relief of a rowan witch unencumbered by opulence he didn't realize had been weighing on his chest in all the time since making his oath. Finally allowed a chance to breathe in fully—only to realize, in a new fit of anxiety, he didn't actually know how.

With so many students fleeing Mairwen, it meant Saffron had the library all to himself more often than not; it meant he could wander the school gardens, the archer field, the paths between buildings in peace. Sionnach joined him more often than not; they were the reason Saffron even left his room more often than not. They were the reason he remembered to eat, to bathe, to step out into the sun and breathe in every once in a while.

The air that morning was crisp and fresh as ever, as Saffron inhaled a deep offering and hurried from Muirín dorm. He passed other students milling about on campus, only a scant few remaining as most had returned home to wait-out the school's temporary hold on classes. To wait-out such a sudden, detrimental change to their daily routines. Suddenly forced to bathe as often as humans did, without charmed stones or cloths or palm-sized gold eggs to rub over their skin to perfume them. Forced to write their own letters by hand, without magic quills to dictate every word spoken aloud. They had to stir their own coffee, and wipe their own shoes, and use actual keys to open the doors to their rooms because access tokens didn't always work anymore. Perhaps it was no wonder so many fled the moment they were permitted. Meanwhile, Saffron was writing long dossiers in his head about how high fey, apart from the sidhe, had long forgotten how to perform any sort of magic that didn't involve making themselves beautiful. More than once he asked Sionnach if it would be more scandalous to publish it under a human or fey pen name. Sionnach always just grimaced at the idea, though they also always scribbled down at least a few of the things Saffron rambled on about while lying on his back in the grass.

That morning, Maeve waited for Saffron at the campus stables, looking more intimidating than ever in her all-black ensemble that matched the color of Saffron's. As was expected of all citizens in Avren during that time of grieving, both for the loss of those at the games and the loss of their inherent magic. The fey lady was paused mid-task in untangling the reins of her horse, gazing off into the trees lining the other side of the barriers, and Saffron paused as he approached. Smiling to himself as a cluster of sparkling pixies buzzed around a knot in one of the trees like swarming bees, he knew right away.

"Did they steal anything from you?" He asked, closing the distance between them. Anyone else would have jumped, but Maeve turned calmly as ever. She wore a face similar to the one Cylvan always did when confronted by the glittering pests. A slightly wrinkled nose, corners of her mouth downturned just enough to show her displeasure.

"I think one of them was in my glove. It bit me when I pulled it on."

Extending her hand to show, Saffron nodded. Pixies bites always swelled up in an instant, red skin surrounding a tiny, pearlescent spot where teeth had sunk.

"That's a pixie bite, for sure. It was probably just surprised."

"It tried to steal one of my rings right after."

"Did you give it to them?"

"Of course not," she scoffed, before sweeping her long braid over one shoulder and shaking her head. "Come on, let's get going before the streets get too crowded."

Saffron eagerly agreed, seeking out the dark bay horse in her stall. Boann rattled the gate with her chest as he approached, as eager as Saffron was to get a break from Mairwen's banality. He pet her over the white star on her forehead in greeting, before grabbing the lightweight day-saddle from the cubby assigned to him, throwing it over her back with a grunt and tightening the belts around her belly as she skirted her feet back and forth slightly in anticipation. When a stable beantighe suddenly hurried over, breathlessly apologizing for not being there to do it for him, Saffron just smiled and assured them it was no bother.

"I've already had to learn to pull on my own tunic, what's any different about this?" He said like a cool, charming fey lord. The beantighe just smiled awkwardly, like they weren't sure they were allowed to laugh. Saffron just reiterated it was fine, nodding for them to return to what else they were doing. God knew they had a thousand other chores to finish with hardly anyone left to help out.

As they went, Saffron couldn't help but wonder why that beantighe, specifically, hadn't gone with them. Neither wishing they had, or glad they'd stayed. Only—curious.

One week had passed since the Midsummer Games; since the ashen state fell upon Avren, and gossip writers from across Alfidel swarmed the city for every opportunity to publish whatever they thought would stoke the biggest, most explosive response. Never mind that most high fey chose to remain indoors ever since; never mind that, perhaps for the first time in Avren's history, human beantighes hurried up and down the streets in greater numbers than high fey did, running errands for their patrons who were too afraid to go on their own.

And all the same—every morning, there were new calls for missing beantighes in the same gossip pamphlets delivered to high fey doors at the same time before sunrise. None of them ever realizing that, perhaps sending their servants out on their own, to pass by others on the street, allowing them to chat and vent with no one to watch, only made it easier for Ryder's witches to extend a crimson card from beneath a cloak. Printed words on the front inviting them to bigger and better things, than rushing to pick up breakfast for their terrorized patron families. *Wouldn't they rather be the ones stoking terror, instead?*

There was a reason Saffron remained on Mairwen's campus more often than not, when he wasn't visiting the palace. There was a reason he always passed through the streets of Avren with his hood pulled up, never meeting eyes with the people he passed. Never accepting any offered gossip leaflets, or even acknowledging when someone recognized him as a friend of Cylvan's and attempted to stuff letters for the kings into his hands.

The kings wouldn't read them. The kings were too busy writing correspondence to everyone else in Alfidel, and beyond. As the Danae of Alvenya demanded to know if Alfidel's red witches would soon spread overseas, to wreak havoc on their shores. As sidhe families within Alfidel demanded to know what Ailir and Tross intended to do, to ensure what happened at the Midsummer Games never happened again—when they weren't pressuring them to pass new laws that severely punished any beantighes found attempting to flee to the other side. Demanding arrests, demanding well-publicized court hearings for abandonment of their beantighe-duties. Demanding a better way to track their humans wherever they went, until eventually—perhaps *inevitably*—the mac Delbaith name began appearing in gossip pamphlets, beneath bold headlines advertising the miracles of their opulent silver. Unaffected by the ashen state, but the ancient rite of their blessed abilities. Always printed right alongside long opinion columns calling for formalized witchhunter training to be reinstated in Alfidel. Desperate to cut the red witches off at the root. Desperate to keep their houses fully staffed, so they still had someone to heat their baths and wash their clothes.

The kings were able to keep those demands specifically at bay —but even Saffron knew, it was only a matter of time. As more and more noble families, courtiers, even sídhe families would continue to grow frustrated and restless.

Meanwhile—it was only a matter of time before Ryder decided it was time to cause another scene. Which would only put remaining beantighes at a higher risk. Which would only drive them more willingly into his arms.

It was only a matter of time—and the constant, looming uncertainty was the reason Saffron never slept anymore.

The streets of Avren were quiet again that morning, with only the occasional beantighe hurrying by. Always throwing Saffron little looks that made his heart thump, like he thought they might stop and say something to him. Still not entirely sure exactly how many knew who he really was, the extent of what Ryder had revealed to his witches, who might then whisper rumors to beantighes still unsure about defecting. But they never did, especially so early in the morning. Too busy rushing to pick up their patron fey's breakfast, while it was still hot. With no charms to keep trays steaming all the way back home, they had no choice but to nearly sprint in both directions.

The only other sign of life amongst beantighes scurrying like fieldmice—were the occasional city riders who cantered by where Saffron and Maeve passed. Always offering them the smallest nod of greeting, but nothing more. Clearly hurried in their own morning tasks; more than Saffron had ever seen before at once, as well, though perhaps only because the street was otherwise so vacant. Passing each other on the street, only occasionally pausing to exchange a few quick words. Sometimes halted when a messenger bird swept in behind them, and they took the note to read right away, before turning and racing in the opposite direction. Saffron tried not to think about it; perhaps high fey had simply given up on slow beantighes on foot, resorting instead to personal riders to ensure their meals were delivered hot.

That day's gossip has already been posted on every bulletin board they passed on the road, swollen to the brim with fluttering leaflets printed by at least two dozen different presses, while a gossip crier announced the day's most scandalous headlines. By then, they may have had more money than was stored in the palace treasury, by how much each press was willing to bid to be the one shouted up and down the street.

*KINGS LIFT STATE OF EMERGENCY IN AVREN TO A STATE OF WARNING; REQUEST ALL SUSPICIONS TO*

*BE REPORTED TO THE PALACE BY ROBIN OR PERSONAL BIRD...*

*MAC DELBAITHS MAKE GENEROUS OFFER OF OPULENT FAMILY SILVER TO THOSE AFFECTED BY AVREN'S ASHEN STATE; Civilians Can Make Requests Through Family Or City Oracles...*

*LOVING PARTNER OF LADY LOST IN MIDSUMMER EVENT BEGS HUMAN REBELS TO FIND MERCY IN THEIR HEARTS, ELSE THEY SHOULD ANTICIPATE HARSH PUNISHMENT ON THOSE BEANTIGHES LEFT BEHIND...*

*PRINCE CYLVAN REQUESTS ALL INFORMATION AVAILABLE ON MISSING BEANTIGHES; Comments Can Be Submitted Via Messenger Robin To The Palace. Some Wonder His Intentions, As Old Rumors Of His Seelie Nature Come Back To Light...*

Saffron tightened his hands on his reigns. He didn't allow his eyes to linger too long, just like every other time. He was too easy a victim to every single bold headline, exactly the type of pedestrian gossip pamphlets hoped to grab the attention of. Even if he despised each and every word—instinctively, he felt compelled to know exactly what was being written, even if it made no difference. Even if Cylvan told him there was no point, to just ignore them, it would save Saffron an infinite amount of grief if he would just let them fade into the background. He did his best— but still, his eyes trailed.

*DID PRINCE CYLVAN THROW AWAY DAURAE ASCHE IN FEAR FOR HIS THRONE? Knowing How Little The People Of Alfidel Think Of Him, And How They Adore The*

*Younger Gentle—Some Ask, Did Prince Cylvan Intentionally Sell The Daurae To Human Rebels...?*

That morning, at the very least, there wasn't so much vitriol directed at Cylvan. The prince had told him, essentially *promised him* that efforts would soon shift, and the harsh things they wrote about him would soften; especially as he spent most of his time out of the public eye, hidden away in the palace, eventually the people would lose interest in favor of something else a little more visibly tempting. Saffron was glad to see it slowly shifting that way —while also infuriated that Cylvan was so familiar with the patterns of gossip that he could even promise such things without a doubt.

Maeve glanced over her shoulder to him, as if she could sense how Saffron's anger grew in his chest. But if there was anything Saffron knew how to do—it was keeping stark emotions off his face. He'd spent his entire life beneath a veil pretending to feel nothing for anything that ignited flames in his blood.

Not unlike the rest of the city, the palace had gained a sense of solemn soundlessness, though it was far more tangible in those grand hallways than on the streets. Even as they approached the gatehouse, Saffron felt it pressing on him, for more reason than just the black flags dangling from the peaks of the gatehouse towers; the aromatic scent of constant garlands of burnt pine signifying a loss in the royal family, a passive prayer that the smoke would bring the missing back home.

Only the occasional rider or guard passed them on the bridge, all offering Saffron and Maeve a polite nod—except one, that came racing with hooves slamming on the stone, echoing off the valley walls below. Saffron nearly leapt from his skin as they flew past him, even Maeve straightening up on instant alert. Saffron normally wouldn't have thought anything of it, once his heart started beating again—but that time, noticed the rider was one of the same sort that had passed them so many times in the street. Whatever was so urgent wasn't for them—and Saffron forced himself to breathe again.

The remainder of the crossing was silent, though something rumbled in the back of Saffron's mind the moment they approached the second gatehouse. He turned at first, thinking it another horse racing up behind them, but then the sound emerged again, and he realized it was only Taran.

"Something on your mind?" Saffron asked in a whisper. Maeve barely glanced over her shoulder, like she wasn't sure she heard it or not. Saffron pretended to be far too busy gazing over the side of the bridge to have said anything. Not that it mattered, as Taran didn't respond. Saffron let it go, knowing it to be a lost cause to try and force the beast to speak—but once they crossed into the cobblestone courtyard at the opposite end of the bridge, Saffron understood.

Parked off to the side, emblazoned with the family crest of a silver-foiled wolf, a carriage of the mac Delbaith family sat. Saffron reeled back on his reins on instinct, a rush of panic flooding his body and freezing his skin, not helped by the additional rumbling and pacing of the wolfish presence in his mind. Whether or not Taran's reaction fed into his own, making it worse, or perhaps even keeping him calmer than he would have been otherwise—the thought of any member of the mac Delbaith family stepping foot within reach of Cylvan had his heart pounding harder than racing hooves on the stone bridge.

Perhaps he should not have been so surprised, considering the headlines that very morning mentioning the continued offerings of mac Delbaith silver—but until that point, it had only been rumors. It had only been gossip, discussing if the cursed objects would be useful in staying the slow bleeding of beantighes from Avren. Surely the kings weren't actually considering...?

*"Don't overreact yet,"* Taran grumbled in warning. *"Opulent silver is a common offering in times of ashen states, to high fey more than beantighes. Don't cause a scene. It will only embarrass you."*

Saffron's hands on Boann's reigns were so tight they nearly compacted into stone.

*But why would they have come here?* He mentally asked, even knowing it sounded stupid. Like a child asking something obvious, because he simply didn't want to accept the truth—that there were political, diplomatic benefits to the kings making nice with the mac Delbaiths, and vice versa. Like vultures over a massacre, like wolves over a lamb, the mac Delbaiths had likely been licking their lips all week, waiting for just the right amount of time to pass before paying a visit to Avren. As if waiting, specifically, for the first organic mention to appear in the gossip leaflets, before deciding to make their move. Even Taran just grunted in response, like he couldn't deny the possibility.

"Tacky," Maeve muttered like she could read Saffron's mind, instantly popping the swelling panic in his body. Not so much surprised she would agree with his feelings—but that she agreed *so much* to be willing to risk the wrong person overhearing. Saffron just bit his lip, unsure if it was to hide a smile or to keep his own string of insults at bay, focusing on taking Boann to the stables so they could actually make their way inside. The beantighe working them did not appear to be wearing any controlling silver, at the very least. Saffron tried to take it as a good sign.

Leaving the horses, Maeve followed Saffron up a back stairway to avoid any unwelcome, observing eyes, especially those belonging to descendants of the wolf king. Saffron even opted to show Maeve through a beantighe passage behind one of the walls, then through another side corridor. The fey lady just appeared silently intrigued while never arguing, though she had to constantly adjust the sword on her hip so it didn't scrape along the narrow walls. As they went, Saffron blabbered on about how those passageways had been shared with him by Asche, who had every nook and cranny of the palace memorized as a means of escaping parties they had no interest in.

Cylvan was not in his room, nor in any of the libraries where he normally liked to hide; he wasn't eating a meal in the dining hall, nor in the upper greenhouse where he practiced his violin when lost in thought. Saffron even searched the outer gardens from a high balcony, then each and every private sitting room he could think of; the prince's personal study, then the king's personal study, then even risked a glance into King Tross' work-room to ask if he knew where the dark raven was hiding.

King Tross had cordoned himself off in his workroom since the first night after the games, rarely emerging even to make nice with the palace's constant stream of visitors, both personal and political. Never once did he appear bothered when Saffron poked his head into the room, at least, a few times even holding him hostage to show off some of his work or insisting he try a few things on. That time, though, even the king appeared apprehensive, which did nothing to ease Saffron's growing nerves.

"I believe Cylvan is currently with Lady Anysta in the family infirmary," the king said, confirming Saffron's suspicions, then adding: "Ah—I see that look on your face. Remember, *diplomacy*, dear Saffron." Even he emphasized the word through a tight jaw, sarcasm as thick as the sincerity of the recommendation.

Saffron pressed his lips into a pout, but swallowed back the rude words he wished to share about the palace's newest visitor. Something told him King Tross would have loved to gossip about that specific guest more than anyone, but Saffron resisted the urge. He might be there all day otherwise if he broke the seal of Tross' politeness.

Wishing the King luck with the project spread over his desk, Saffron slipped back out where his face instantly twisted up in annoyance. If he wasn't so focused on getting to the infirmary straight away, he might have told Maeve all about exactly *how* well he knew Anysta mac Delbaith, despite never being formally intro-duced. Despite never exchanging a single word with one another. But there might never be enough time in the world to explain how he once romped through Taran mac Delbaith's memory threads in the first place.

. . .

ANYSTA MAC DELBAITH HADN'T CHANGED AT ALL FROM what Saffron remembered in said memories. That morning, her long, dark-brown hair was pulled back from her eyes with two clips, with tawny skin and eyes a pretty hazel-green that matched her brother's. She and Taran might have even passed as twins, if Saffron didn't know any better.

She wore the garb of a Dagdan priestess just like Saffron had first seen of her, hating how it reminded him so much of the vestments donned by witchhunters, though admittedly the same could be said for every high fey wearing black during the city's mourning period. He still didn't know anything about what it meant to be a Dagdan priestess, either, let alone where they practiced, what they practiced, or how—which only made his new, additional misguided sense of annoyance brew hotter at the thought of her standing there. Wearing those clothes, dedicated to some fey religion he personally wasn't familiar with. Knowing only that the Dagda was the highest of all gods to both arid humans and opulent fey—even more aggravated to think someone like Anysta mac Delbaith had the arrogance to don the mantle of someone regarded so highly. Why hadn't the Dagda struck her down yet? It would have saved them all a lot of trouble—

"*Focus,*" Taran mumbled. Saffron inhaled sharply, but held it. Forcing himself back into his body. Back to where his foot stood planted in the infirmary entryway.

Still, despite his best efforts, the sight of the lady was enough to make Saffron's blood bubble—only for furious panic to tip into near-boiling the moment he recognized exactly how close she stood to Cylvan on the edge of the bed in front of her. Cylvan, who had long already noticed Saffron enter, while Saffron stood there and attempted to set the fey lady on fire with his eyes. Perhaps that was why he hadn't yet called out a greeting—like a part of him hoped Saffron might actually be able to do it.

Beneath Anysta's deft fingers, the prince's broken horn had been replaced with a silver replica; a perfectly matching prosthetic, down to even the carvings he'd once had. Even Taran in the back of Saffron's mind reeled, and the sound of an agitated beast almost broke from Saffron's mouth in tandem.

He mentally shoved Taran's presence back. He shoved his own feelings back, scolding himself for being so emotional. As far as Anysta knew, they had never met. Technically, Saffron, the fey from Alvénya, had never even met Taran mac Delbaith. He didn't know what opulent silver was, or what it was for. For him to know anything at all would be a dangerous bit of intrigue to lay at Anysta mac Delbaith's feet, like a rabbit under the nose of a dog.

"Good morning, your highness," Saffron managed instead of what he really wished to say, smiling politely as Lady Anysta glanced his way. Cylvan's own expression flickered through a handful of emotions all at once, but most visibly—his own amusement tempered the moment Anysta turned to perceive Saffron fully. Watching her with a flash of his eyes, as if attempting to read her every movement, to observe every twitch of her face. Protective and possessive, in an instant. He really was no different from Saffron, after all.

"You must be Lord Saffron," Anysta said, flashing Saffron a pretty smile while turning to properly offer him a low bow. She moved with a practiced grace, one that reminded Saffron of how Maeve did when on high alert on her horse, or with a hand resting on the hilt of her sword. It also reminded him too much of how Taran used to smile when being intentionally charming, hiding something, and smug at the thought of being the only one who knew—and Saffron's hackles raised impossibly higher. "His highness said you might come by this morning. My work will be finished shortly, and I will be out of your way."

"Your *'work'*?" Saffron asked as innocently as he could manage, but failed right at the end when the slightest flicker of sarcasm edged in. A muscle in Cylvan's jaw twitched, like he didn't know whether to laugh or clear his throat in warning. "Oh! I was just reading in the gossip columns this morning about 'mac Delbaith silver'—is that what you mean? I assumed by all the pamphlets it was more of a pretty toy than anything else."

"My family works in opulent silver, yes," Anysta answered with ease, ignoring Saffron's comment at the end. Assuming he was only a simple countryfey from Alvénya, like everyone else. Of course he wouldn't know any better. Cylvan had his lips pressed together again, at one point having to softly clear the amusement from his throat. Meanwhile, Anysta motioned to the cap replacing Cylvan's missing horn. "Blessed objects imbued with natural opulence to fill gaps where ashen states leave high fey in need. Admittedly we are still trying to source something that can help mitigate Prince Cylvan's missing sídhe gift, but in the meantime wished to provide something else to ease his hardship."

"Ah," Saffron smiled, speaking the first thing to come to mind that wasn't *'get your hands off him before I bite them off'*: "What a relief. I'm glad. He *was* looking a little unbalanced, wasn't he?"

Cylvan cast him a venomous smile that whispered *'I'm going to remember that.'*

"Are there any opulent gaps I can ease for you while I'm here, Lord Saffron?" Anysta went on, and Saffron shook his head.

"None for me, as generous as that is," he spread the polite tone on as thick as any other beantighe receiving an offer that made their stomach turn. "I've been ashen since the day I was born, and I have never wished otherwise, to be quite honest."

Cylvan bit back another little smile while Anysta's back remained turned. The fey lady responded with a musical little laugh. "Well, hardly more than a beantighe without any opulence to prove otherwise, aren't you?" She said like it was a common joke, and Saffron barked an off-putting laugh in response.

"Seems Avren no longer has a shortage of beantighes, then, by that logic. Even Prince Cylvan ought to pick up a broom."

"That's enough," Cylvan interrupted with an exasperated little smile, like he could sense Saffron's self-control reaching a breaking point.

"If you ever change your mind, my lord, Prince Cylvan knows

how to contact me," Anysta said, offering a smile to Cylvan over her shoulder before bowing in finality. Saffron managed another stiff little laugh, though even the wolf in his head muttered for him to keep it together.

Anysta excused herself. The instant the sound of her heels disappeared down the corridor, Saffron rushed Cylvan with an arm extended, only to be swept up in Cylvan's arms and kissed instead.

"You're going to start a war between our families by Sunday," he said, squeezing Saffron's face as Saffron writhed and flailed his arms, attempting to snap the silver horn right back off his head. Before he could make any progress, Cylvan swept him off his feet to throw him on the bed behind him. Saffron hissed, attempting again to yank the silver away as Cylvan scolded him through a smile, playfully commanding him to *behave* and *remember himself*. Finally, he pinned Saffron's arms down on the pillows, before leaning in for another kiss.

"Good morning," he said, properly, as if trying to start over.

"Why didn't you tell me she was going to be here?" Saffron asked, squirming beneath Cylvan's grasp as Maeve just rolled her eyes and wandered over to the window. "I don't like that you were all by yourself with her—!"

"She surprised us," Cylvan answered with a sigh. He lowered down, resting on a bent elbow and brushing fingers through Saffron's hair with his opposite hand. Combing his bangs like he thought Saffron had used too much pomade to slick them down that morning. "And I can handle myself, púca. She wasn't going to do anything to me on palace grounds. Not even the mac Delbaiths are *so* desperate."

"I've seen how far their desperation can take them," Saffron argued back. "It ended with one of them living in my head." The entity in the back of his mind circled and growled at the mention, and Saffron imagined Taran's paws carpeted in sharp thistles to silence him back down again. He wasn't in the mood.

"I'm sure that wretched dog in your head was equally

displeased at the sight of her," Cylvan said, pressing a finger to Saffron's forehead like he was knocking on the door of a squirrel's winter hollow. "Tell me I'm wrong."

"You're wrong."

"Lying to your favorite prince?" Cylvan asked with a threatening laugh, before baring his teeth and feigning a bite to the tip of Saffron's nose. "I should have known. No human can resist their nature."

"Seems the palace is seeing plenty of unexpected visitors today," Maeve interjected, summoning both Cylvan and Saffron's attention to where she gazed out the window. "Looks like one of the High Keepers just arrived by carriage. Tapestries, maybe?"

"A what?" Saffron asked as Cylvan immediately pulled away, practically leaping to his feet to rush to the window and see for himself. Saffron sat up on the bed behind them, about to repeat the question, but Cylvan returned to take his hand and pull him to his feet, first. Saying nothing else, just leading Saffron for the door, hurrying down the hallway as Maeve jogged to catch up behind them.

"Cylv—" Saffron attempted, but King Tross suddenly appeared at the top of the stairs they were headed for, looking apprehensive.

"Good," he said at the sight of Cylvan already on his feet. "Come, now. Something's happened."

3

___________

## THE CIRCLES

Saffron had only heard of 'memory tapestries' a handful of times before, the very first being when Cylvan mentioned them during the early days of their time in Morrígan's Grand Library. A comment he'd made off-handedly when discussing how even he didn't know Queen Proserpina's true name, despite her being long dead. *'One day I'll tell you about tapestries...'* he'd teased, perhaps thinking nothing of it. Saffron hadn't, either, until it came rushing back after only a few sentences exchanged between the kings, the prince, and the person Maeve had called the High Keeper of Tapestries.

Saffron wasn't allowed in the room where the discussion continued following introductions, leaving him to pace back and forth on the other side of the door, while Maeve stood with her arms crossed against the wall alongside Saoirse. It was grueling, being forced to wait on the wrong side of it all, none of them speaking as if equally restless despite Saffron being the only one so obviously so.

"What's so important about memory tapestries, again?" He asked. "That they need an entire High Hall dedicated to them? Aren't they just—fabrics woven to depict scenes from a person's life?"

"They're a sort of funerary rite, especially amongst fey nobility," Maeve corrected, showing Saoirse the pixie bite on her hand as she did. "Far more than just visual depictions of 'scenes from a person's life,' too—There's a brief window of time following someone's death that their mind, their memories, remain intact enough that the family oracle can unthread them. Taking every single memory the deceased ever made, and unspooling them onto the floor to be picked back up and woven into what we call 'tapestries'."

Saffron stopped pacing. He stared at her for a long moment, as if waiting for her to smile and admit she was only joking—only for her to raise an eyebrow at him in question. Reminding him that Maeve was not the kind to make things up just to make fun of him.

Saffron didn't know how to feel about her explanation, either way—it was both morbid and poetic, at the same time. He'd found most high fey poetry to be rather morbid, though, so perhaps it shouldn't have come as any surprise.

"So what's the purpose of the tapestry hall, then?" He asked. "Just to store them all?"

"Avren's Hall houses the tapestries of some of the most prestigious fey in history, including members of the royal family," she said. "Hence why someone causing trouble inside is a little more alarming than, say, when a common cemetery's tapestry-mausoleum is vandalized. *Especially* in this time of so many new arid witches coming out of the woodwork... Anything *you* feel like confessing, *witch?*" She gave him a sharp, amused little smile, and Saffron stiffened. Quickly shaking his head, he went back to pacing.

"They rarely store actual memory threads of the most important fey folk in the tapestry hall for anyone to pay respects to," Saoirse added, like she misunderstood Saffron's antsiness. "So even if someone managed to destroy or steal one on display—they would be sorely disappointed to learn it was only a recreation."

"... Oh, I'm going to go fucking mad," Saffron groaned after those words settled, only prickling his nerves more. He turned on heel and going straight for the door. Glancing up and down the corridor, he met Saoirse's eyes for a moment, then glanced to Maeve. The guard gave him a narrowed, warning look, but Maeve looked curious, which was enough to embolden him to dig into his shoulder bag for a piece of charcoal.

Saoirse released a small, guttural sound when she realized what Saffron was doing, but neither she nor Maeve stopped him as he scribbled the smallest arid circle manageable on the door. Adding hatchmarks for *'hear inside'*, the low voices of the conversation inside emerged through the wood, loud enough for Saffron to press his ear and listen. Even Maeve and Saoirse stepped a little closer, curious even if they wouldn't admit it.

*"Do we have any proof it was a human witch who did it?"* Cylvan asked, and Saffron's heart thumped. *"You mentioned multiple arid circles all over the city—are you to tell me there are dozens of capable arid witches in Avren who have gone unnoticed all this time?"*

Saffron's ears rang. Arid circles reported throughout Avren? Multiples of them, not even in the tapestry hall alone? He thought of all those official messengers they saw racing by in the city on their way to the palace, and panic instantly flooded him. Fearful at first that another part of the veil had been torn open— but there would have been news of that. He would have heard it. He hadn't heard anything, in fact—not a single knock, for the entire week since the games.

It had to just be a trick, then. Some of Ryder's witches—or even humans unrelated to him—playing some sort of trick to try and scare the high fey who didn't know any better. Ryder was not known for doing things *quietly*, after all. If it had been him behind it, there would have been far more of a show. He would have sent Saffron a personal invitation to watch.

If Saffron could get his eyes on one of the reported circles or another, he would be able to tell for sure if they really were *just tricks.*

"*No one ever said they were* capable, *your highness,*" the voice of the High Keeper responded. "*Seeing as none of these circles appear to have had any magical effect.*"

"*That you know of,*" Tross added, sounding like he was in the middle of sipping tea.

"*Tell me again exactly where all of them have been found, apart from the High Tapestry Hall.*" Cylvan went on.

"*Well—the National Library, the High Hospital, in an alleyway off the city square, reportedly outside a handful of courtier homes—*"

"*And you're certain these are markings left by* arid witches, *not simply high fey children playing pranks?*" The prince interjected, and Saffron bit back a smile, even flushing a little bit in pride. As if Cylvan read his mind. "*Even you say you don't recognize the markings as, how did you put it? A 'standard arid circle'? Yet you can tell they performed no successful spell? By what authority do you know if taboo is 'standard' or 'successful', High Keeper...? Have you been training as an oracle without our knowledge? Considering the delicate nature of the sacred objects you oversee, you can understand my concern.*"

Saffron wanted to kiss him. Saffron would show Cylvan all there was to know about *arid spells* later, with how eloquently he spoke. Meanwhile, the High Keeper only cleared their throat. "*Even if I cannot identify each exactly, the markings simply resemble arid magic circles, your highness. I am not sure who else it could have been. Even a young fey playing tricks would not have been able to create something so convincing.*"

"*Anything can be made convincing to those who don't know any better.*"

"*Are young fey drawing fake arid circles often, as pranks?*" King Tross asked with a flutter of conspiratorial curiosity. "*How many times before now has that occurred and not been reported?*" Even Ailir let out a small breath that time, and Saffron could picture the old king placing a hand on Tross' in an attempt to keep him focused. "*I only ask so that we might better know if these circles truly are something to be concerned about, or simply the hijinks of young fey that are being taken far out of proportion due to recent events. Not that I am accusing you of fear mongering, High-Keeper. Of course."*

*"Of course,"* the keeper answered, but it sounded flat. *"Whether or not it is only the hijinks of young fey, your highness, I thought it best to alert you. Like you said, particularly due to what has occurred recently, I think it better to consider them a real threat rather than merely jokes. What the humans did at the summer games were also unprecedented, until now. It should come as no surprise that their antics may continue to escalate. While most young fey tricks consist of a randomly drawn circle here and there, waking to find these all across Avren, even in the High Hall where I oversee—you understand how it was alarming."*

*"You said nothing was taken,"* King Ailir spoke, next. Clearly having taken his time to consider every possibility—or perhaps just to ensure both King Tross and Cylvan had their chance to pinch and appraise every side of the claim first. To ensure the keeper told enough of the truth to survive it. *"How can you be sure if you only found the alleged arid circle a few hours ago? I'm sure with the number of tapestries stored in the high hall—"*

*"We have our ways of keeping track of tapestries kept in our care, your highness."*

*"Opulent means?"* Cylvan asked, still polite but ever so coy, like he secretly enjoyed making the high keeper sweat. Even Saoirse over Saffron's shoulder groaned quietly, like she wished Cylvan would behave better. *"Do you know if anything else was stolen from any of the other locations, yet? There are some very dangerous books stored in the National Library's archives, for example."*

*"I'm sure you're performing checks by hand as well, just to be safe?"* Tross chimed in with the same tone as Cylvan, like even he enjoyed making the official sweat. To be on the receiving end of two sardonic Tuatha dé Danann, Saffron couldn't fathom. *"Have you consulted with the others heads of the high council to ensure the*

*same could be said for the library? The hospital? The reformatory...?"*

*"Of course, your highness. Messengers were sent before, and even still as I made my journey here to inform you."*

*"Should we have all high council members gather for a meeting, father?"* Cylvan went on. *"Until then, we have these copies of the circles found. We can show them to the royal oracles and have them determine which are real and which may only be pranks. Lugh pray they're only pranks."*

*"Lugh pray, indeed..."* Tross hummed in the same tone.

Saffron knew Cylvan's composure was only in performance—a master of remaining calm and collected, even if the news unsettled him as much as it did Saffron. The result of a lifetime of royal training, to never let anyone see the cracks. A skill Saffron both admired and despised, whenever Cylvan had to implement it.

The pleasantries continued a few minutes longer, and Saffron finally swept his own arid circle from the wood once the conversation ebbed and he knew they would be making their way out soon enough. But in what could have only been a minute or two of silence between stepping back and when the door would open—it passed like an eternity as Saffron's heart raced, making him feel flush in his fine doublet. Suddenly feeling tight, claustrophobic in even a hallway as broad as where he loitered. Thoughts turning, tangling. Each one as disorganized and dismayed as the cloud of pixies that had nibbled on Maeve's finger.

Two days after the games, Saoirse and a small troupe of trusted guards had been sent in secret—by Cylvan's order, but Saffron's anxious request—to search the Finnian Ruins for Ryder and his witches. They returned to report them as empty as the day they were first abandoned, with no sign of life from anyone—specifically wording their report as if it had been foolish to ever suspect human activity there at all. Cylvan took it as an insult, but Saffron understood it differently—as proof Ryder knew what he was doing, knew how to cover his tracks.

Wholly cleared out, the only possible sign of recent activity came in the smell of charred wood and stone on the air, as well as a few that had fully crumbled since scouts previously passed through decades prior. Though even the report stated neither of those things were indisputable proof of life.

When Cylvan specifically asked Saoirse which buildings had been destroyed, Saffron was unsurprised as she described the main cathedral, then the smaller building he, Cylvan, Copper, and Taran had once passed through while fleeing the ruins. That unassuming building with the door at the very end, that transitioned through a veneer into the King's Keep, all the way in the Winter Court. Where they'd crossed between the buildings and into the surrounding woods, where the same veneer carried them back into the forest outside the ruins. Back in Avren. Ryder must have been beside himself with fury when he realized.

News of the abandoned ruins had itched at the back of Saffron's mind since. Haunting him when the nights hunched over books at his desk stretched long. Buzzing constantly in the back of his mind the few times he attempted to sleep. Begging the question: if Ryder and his witches had long cleared out of the Finnian Ruins—where had they gone instead?

And with the reports that morning, a new question hooked into him—wondering if they remained hidden in Avren; more than just those few who continued recruiting beantighes from the shadows. Who may indeed have had something to do with the circles left around the city. Hating that he would only get an idea once able to see the circles for himself.

Gazing down at his feet, Saffron rubbed the toe of his boot into the palace's polished floor. Ahead of him, voices and footsteps approached the door from the other side, forcing him to straighten back up again. Returning to the present, where he was needed far more.

The doors finally opened, and those inside emerged. The High Keeper looked slightly less stately than when they first arrived, belted robe slightly askew and the long silver braid down the center of their back free of a few fine hairs over their forehead.

As if discussing anything with the kings and the prince always took a decade off their life. They didn't bother meeting eyes with Saffron or Saoirse as they emerged, though did offer a slight bow to Maeve.

Cylvan, meanwhile searched for Saffron right away, and Saffron smiled at him with innocently-fluttering eyelashes. Wordlessly informing his raven that he had absolutely been up to some dirty work while forced to wait outside. Cylvan should have known better—and he did, proven by the sly smile he gave back.

"I eagerly await your next report on the situation, High Keeper," Cylvan said, turning back to the old fey whose lips were pursed and pale, clearly displeased with how the discussion had gone. "I'm sure King Tross will be able to provide a time for the council meeting."

"Perhaps dinner," Tross said thoughtfully, though directed neither at Cylvan nor the keeper, instead turning to flutter his own eyelashes at Ailir who just shook his head with a weary smile and wrapped an arm around his harmonious king.

"Now—I hope you don't mind," Cylvan went on, "I promised one very handsome friend of mine a private brunch. Have you decided what we should eat, flower?"

"There are so many options," Saffron sighed lazily, stepping in close to Cylvan to wrap his arms around the prince's waist and smile up at him. "Whatever you think I would like, your highness."

"Then you'll excuse us," Cylvan said in finality to the others, putting his arm around Saffron in return.

"Oh—how could I have nearly forgotten?" the keeper said, just as Cylvan turned away with Saffron on his arm. "Lady mac Delbaith happened to be in the courtyard when I arrived; after briefly discussing this morning's events, she offered to send a bird to the oracles of Fjornar, requesting they come at once. Many still practice in the old ways, so if there is anyone who would be able to recognize the intent of the spell in the Tapestry Hall, or any of the others, I'm sure it would be one of them. I imagine they may be able to assist in the recovery of the daurae as well, should they be needed... I've heard word of the royal oracles struggling to connect with the veil, something about it not responding to their calls, closed off from opening for even them after the harm caused at the Midsummer Games... If there is anyone in Alfidel who may know better, it is those from Fjornar, your highness."

Cylvan's eyes flashed to Saffron, showing the briefest flicker of uncertainty, just as Saffron's eyes snapped to Cylvan in return.

"I think... that is a wise call to make," Cylvan finally answered, as even the kings waited to see how he would respond. "In the meantime, however, let's avoid *discussing* this morning's events with anyone else, shall we? We wouldn't want a panic over something that may be nothing more than a prank. Should I read about this in the morning gossip, High Keeper, I will know exactly whom to call back to the palace for an explanation."

"Of—of course!" the keeper stammered, loud enough to echo off the ceiling.

"Good," Cylvan answered, before smiling at Saffron. "Shall we go enjoy our meal, then?"

Saffron fluttered his eyelashes again, lifting his hand demurely to his mouth and letting his eyes sparkle in adoration as he asked, *"Was your discussion important, your highness? You're so handsome when dressed so formally,"* as sweetly and vapidly as he could. Cylvan playfully bared his teeth like Saffron was something to eat, putting an arm back around his shoulder to finally walk away with him. Maeve and Saoirse followed on their heels.

"I thought of you the entire time," Cylvan whispered, leaning close so only Saffron would hear. "Though I'm sure you managed to eavesdrop on every word yourself, so you can fill in any gaps I missed while fantasizing about your mouth."

"I suppose I could provide that service, amongst any others you need from me," Saffron smiled, pulling Cylvan down to playfully kiss him just as they rounded the corner. A small moment of lightheartedness, stolen like a loose thread from a fraying blanket draped over all of Avren. Plucked and hidden in that brief moment between their mouths, until Cylvan pulled a leaf of paper from his pocket, donning illustrations of the arid circles found around Avren for Saffron to look over. As Saffron silently took it from him, the sweetness faded as quickly as it came. The weight of apprehension returned, an unwelcome presence Saffron had long come to accept a constant companion over his shoulder.

4

## THE EVENT

With the new developments, and to Saffron's quiet disappointment, Saoirse thought it best to remain in the palace rather than journeying out for their morning date—so Cylvan asked for something just as lavish to be prepared and served on the private garden terrace. Saffron could not complain, because everything that came from the palace kitchens was as delicious and decadent as he could ever ask for—but having to remain there, especially with the page of drawn arid circles for him to look over, he couldn't help but feel like it was more of a political meeting rather than a romantic morning spent with his raven.

But he would not show it on his face. He would appreciate any and all the time he could get with Cylvan, even if it wasn't as carefree as he hoped. Someday again, soon. Just not yet.

With the leaflet of illustrated circles in front of him, Saffron's heart finally stopped pounding, at least.

"Most of these are nonsense," he said, pointing to a few in particular as Cylvan leaned over to look with a curious eye. "This one at the National Treasury, this one at the Hospital, this one at the Library, and these three found in the random alleyways. These ones here," he pointed to the ones labeled *Council Office, Observa-*

*tory*, and *High Oralcry*, "... are legitimate circles, but not nearly as scary once you can actually read them. I think they just used so many hatchmarks to make them more intimidating. For example, this one at the Observatory, just says, *'release all enslaved nightjars from their roosts'*... I'm not going to say that means *nothing*, but it's certainly not an arid spell for destruction."

He trailed his finger over the rest, pausing at the last remaining circle he hadn't mentioned specifically. The only one with a purpose that wholly escaped him. Two circles within one another, feda hatchmarks scrawled around the edge of the exterior circle like any other arid circle—but in that one, additional lines extended from a few strategically-placed markings to extend past the edges of the circle, cutting through the middle to meet matching marks on the opposite side. Three points extended past the outer edge, one on top and two on the bottom, connecting to one another to form a triangular shape. His thoughts writhed at the sight, hating how that particular shape reminded him of the witchhunter's symbol. Off to the side were additional notes—the only circle to include such a thing:

*'Drawn in what appears to be charcoal mixed with red paint.'*

*'Found: red apple in circle of yew twigs,'* with an arrow drawn to indicate the center of the circle.

The yew tree was to rowan witches what rowan was to high fey—so to find it included in the center of such a strange arid circle made Saffron's mind buzz with far more questions than answers. But it wasn't even the inclusion of the yew that bothered him most—it was the apple that had apparently been nestled within them. Prince Cylvan's apple allergy was no secret in Alfi-del; and yew branches were used commonly to repel arid magic and witches, even by those who had never seen an arid epithet in their lives.

"This one..." he trailed off. "Is... interesting."

"What does it say? Around here," Cylvan urged Saffron back in the right direction, using one of his sharp nails to outline the illustration.

*"Proclaim self... shelter soul... disgrace,"* Saffron read under his breath. "Those are proper arid spell terms, unlike the others I described. But this epithet, the shape of it, and these lines that cut through the middle, and outside the edge, I've never seen anything like them before..."

"More nonsense then?" Cylvan asked with the smallest flicker of relief, like he was beginning to get worried with how intrigued Saffron was. Saffron couldn't confirm or deny that, instinctively offering his prince a wary smile as if to say *'yes, maybe.'* If it would ease Cylvan's nerves, Saffron would say anything. Even if something else nibbled at him, telling him it wasn't exactly true.

"Have you had a chance to send word to Luvon about what happened at the games?" Cylvan asked next, clearly eager to change the subject with the new reassurance. He stabbed a stalk of herb-and-buttered lettuce with his fork and crunching into it.

"Yes—Fiachra actually brought back his response just the other day," Saffron said. The bird in question sat perched on the balcony bannister wrapped with pine garlands, pecking at the needles and squawking every time they poked her back.

"That's why she's been so clingy lately," Cylvan commented with a little smile. Saffron grimaced, pushing the eggs and honeyed ham around on his own plate while determining the best way to describe the contents of Luvon's letter without being too obvious what he was really saying. Not sure who might be listening, within the palace walls or somewhere in the trees around them.

"He doesn't remember how we ever found those ruins in the mountains—" *He's lost track of the natural veil tear where he used to pass through to the human world, since he stopped going to make deals and collecting changeling babies.* "I'm not sure I'll ever be able to see them again. Apparently it was so long ago, he's certain the road has been lost to the weather." *He won't be able to take us there to pass through that way. I'm sorry.*

Cylvan nodded, picking at his food. Saffron hated that silence, even if it was only a few moments long. The brief threads of lightheartedness from that morning, even from their time in the ruins, were slipping through his fingers faster than he could catch them. Especially with how their excursion had resulted only in more questions, rather than any answers. Still no leads. Still no resolution. Saffron could see exactly how it weighed on Cylvan's shoulders, how by that point, his prince was struggling to maintain the same level of composure, let alone the same positivity, as what he'd demonstrated with the High Keeper and beyond. Being forced to watch as Cylvan's lightened mood slowly dimmed beneath the crushing, silent yoke of frustration was enough to suffocate Saffron right alongside him.

"I asked if he could show me how he used to find *old ruins*, though, so that I might be able to do it myself. I think I might be especially cut out for it, since... you know..." Saffron went on clumsily, watching as Cylvan stirred his tea. "Luvon says the landscape has changed too much in the Winter Court that he doesn't think any of his other places will be accessible anymore, but it's impossible to really know. He apparently never did anything special to find those places years ago, just knew how to read the environment. So perhaps he could do it again, if we ask..."

"That's understandable," Cylvan answered, but said nothing else despite his lips parting like he meant to. Saffron squirmed in his seat. He sipped at his own tea, before picking at the garnished steak half-eaten on his plate. He wished to tell Cylvan more of the things he'd tried in private in an attempt to find a solution himself —eating as many rowan berries as he could, hoping it would increase his magic enough to see something that would help him, only to puke them all back up again; searching the woods behind the beantighe dorms at the palace for that abandoned doorway he'd once passed through the veil to the ruins with Ryder, though no matter where he looked, he never found it again. As if someone, either by Ryder's orders or the Kings', had already gone and knocked it down.

God knew Saffron had dozens of other ideas, possible leads, all scribbled down in his sketchbook, but he suddenly worried it would only dampen Cylvan's mood further. Saffron's own guilt crashed relentlessly whenever he secretly wished Cylvan could be more confident in him, all things considered. Despite what everyone else seemed to think, Cylvan was not meant to always look so sad—and Saffron hated knowing it was all his fault.

"Asche... will be so angry to know they weren't here to see the strange magic circles reported around Avren..." Saffron attempted with an uncertain smile. Cylvan's eyes flicked up to him, before, to Saffron's relief, he chuckled and sat back in his chair.

"Oh, they'll be fuming. Good thing we have these to show them when they get back, hm?" He said, touching the page with the illustrations.

Saffron nodded, taking a bite of his food. Doing everything he could to act natural—until Cylvan asked another question.

"How much time has passed?" He asked, sipping at his tea again as if the question was the most unassuming thing in the world, not five words that made Saffron's stomach sink like a rock. Cylvan wasn't asking about how much time had passed since the Midsummer Games—at least, not in terms of Alfidel's clocks.

Gazing down at his hands, Saffron hated to be reminded. One week in Alfidel.

"A little more than two days," he whispered. A muscle twitched in Cylvan's jaw, saying nothing at first, only nodding. They sat in silence for a while longer, listening to the sound of morning birds, servants hurrying by in the garden below, the sound of the ocean a few blocks away and the late-summer breeze that carried it.

"Has Sunbeam's bird returned with anything else?" The prince continued. Saffron having to shake his head was torturous.

"No," he said quietly. Yama had come to deliver Sunbeam's only message the night after the games, three words on the strip of paper: *Found them. London.* He hadn't even gotten the chance to send anything back before the fairy wren was gone again. He'd never forget the sound Cylvan made when they realized, like he'd been gutted on a knife.

"Well," Cylvan finally spoke again, clearing his throat then dabbing the napkin to his mouth. Something was clearly on his mind; perhaps still ruminating on the news of that morning, while Saffron had made the mistake of thinking it wasn't anything to worry about just yet. But a new sense of restlessness had infiltrated his raven prince's movements, and Saffron noticed the shift in an instant. "Perhaps the oracles from Fjornar coming to assist will be a blessing, rather than something to dread. If anyone can find a way through the veil, it's them."

Saffron had already asked a hundred times if any progress had been made with the royal oracles working around the clock—but Cylvan never quite knew how to explain what, exactly, the problem was they were having. Something told Saffron even they weren't entirely sure. It was as if, at least from Avren—the veil had simply refused to answer the calls of anyone, even those most experienced in weaving it.

"Is your mother still in Avren?" Saffron asked, hoping to change the subject to something more lighthearted. He hadn't gotten the chance to be properly introduced, yet, but had been hoping to do so, as Gentle Naoill dé Fianna rarely left the Winter Court for Avren. Despite the circumstances of their visit, Saffron was eager to finally be introduced to his future—

"They actually left late last night," Cylvan said, and Saffron wilted again in an instant. "Our conversation did not go... *well*. I think they were eager to return to the Winter Court as soon as possible, afterward. Ah, that reminds me, I should pray for their safe travels while there's still time. I should make my way to Lugh's altar now, while the weather still permits; if Maeve is no longer in the palace, I'll ask Saoirse to ride with you back to Mairwen, púca."

"Oh, I thought..." Saffron started, but closed his mouth as Cylvan was already standing. *I thought I might spend the day with you*, he wished to say, but swallowed every word back like pieces of sharp ice. Not wanting to make Cylvan uncomfortable, not wanting to pressure him into something he wasn't in the mood for. Wishing to give him the space he needed to grieve, to pray, to do what he needed to feel better after all that had happened—even if praying was all he did when not caught up in bureaucratic responsibilities. There were many reasons Cylvan spent most of his time in the palace since the Midsummer Games—and one of the few Saffron never commented on, was how his prince prayed to their family god endlessly. Whenever a moment allowed itself. He'd hoped that morning, with even a single day away from bowing on his knees, Cylvan might wake up the following morning without so many bruises on his pale legs—but it seemed even Saffron couldn't provide the comfort Cylvan sought from old king Lamhfada, to bring his missing sibling back from the ether.

WHEN HE WASN'T THINKING ABOUT HOW TO GET through the veil, Saffron was thinking about how he might still pass a message to the other side; when he wasn't thinking about what sort of message he would send, he ruminated over when Ryder would inevitably come back for him, considering Saffron had been the single thing Ryder was convinced he needed in order to fully win the favor of all the humans he was saving.

Only in the briefest of moments, in the earliest hours of the morning, when his mind finally wore itself too thin to carry thoughts any longer, did Saffron allow himself a chance to sleep—but rarely was it ever anything more than tangling in those same thoughts like a withered net. Tangled until he choked; until he kicked himself free of his blankets and went back to work.

That night, Saffron woke a second time to the sound of screaming. It echoed through a faint vision of kneeling before a great bird, wings spread over him, interspersed with a rhythmic *knock, knock, knock, knock, knock, knock*—sensations already too thin to fully grasp in sleep, and whisked away the moment his eyes opened.

Staring at the dark ceiling of his dorm room, his ears rang as sweat dampened his forehead and chilled his skin. Again, those screaming pleas for help, echoed off his eardrums, even if the vision thinned like watercolors into nothing. *Come find me, I'm lost, come find me*—those cries, that voice that resembled Aschewing far too closely. Enough to bring panicked, exhausted tears to Saffron's eyes. Nearly filling the back of his throat with vomit.

But sitting up in his dark bedroom, the terrible cries faded beneath wakefulness as swiftly as the brief images of the dream had. He was in his Muirín dorm room. There was no one calling out to him. There was no bird spreading its dark wings over his bed as he slept. Even Fiachra remained curled up in her nest of Copper's blazer and stolen trinkets on the mantle. Only one other presence joined him there, the dark shadow of a great beast seated on the floor at the end of Saffron's bed.

"Your nightmares are loud enough to even bother me." Taran's voice was low, ghostly in the low light, but brought an unexpected sense of calm to Saffron's frantic nerves.

"Sorry," he muttered, putting his face in his hand before dragging fingers back through his hair, damp with sweat. "Do you normally listen in on my dreams?"

"I do not," Taran growled. "Hence my annoyance."

"And what am I supposed to do about it?" Saffron asked tightly, before throwing the blankets off and kicking his legs over the side. "If you have any suggestions for keeping nightmares at bay, I'm all ears. In fact, as my familiar, I think it's your responsibility to take care of me even while I sleep. Hm?"

"I don't think you know what a familiar is meant to do."

"And you do?"

Taran's red eyes narrowed in exasperation, but he said nothing. He had as much idea as Saffron did, when it came to how exactly he was meant to perform as the familiar to a rowan witch.

Making his way to his desk, Saffron sank into it with a deep sigh. He struck a match and lit the oil lamp within reach, glass still warm since he'd only just put it out a few hours prior in that futile attempt to sleep. Slotting it back within the disordered piles of books, parchments, spilled ink, worn-down quills in front of him, he silently vowed to give up on sleeping altogether. Clearly it was no longer meant for someone like him, and only a waste or time to try.

Flipping open his sketchbook to the list of ideas for getting through the veil, the beaded unicorn bookmark gifted to him by Asche after Ostara reflected the light of the lamp as it always did. Saffron rested his chin in one hand and stared down at it in silence, before forcing his eyes to travel to the written list that never changed. Next to him, Taran's presence lingered, even pawing over to sit and take stock of the words with him.

*~~Ask Luvon if he can get me through the veil~~*
*~~Ask Luvon if he'll teach me how he used to pass through~~*
    *(says all his old tears are closed)*
*~~Eat enough rowan berries to speak directly to the veil~~ (puked*
    *them all back up)*
*~~Check the veneer of the Finnian Ruins again~~ (guards*
    *reported the building destroyed/burned with the rest)*
*Find books about the veil in the library (ha ha.)*
*Go back to Morrígan's Kyteler ruins and see if Sunbeam's*
    *veil circle can be made viable at all*
*See if Prof Adelard would be willing to explain anything*
    *~~(threaten him?)~~*
*Find Eias Lam ?? (Learned oralcry in Fjornar like Ryder)*
*~~Ask Baba Yaga about the knocks again~~ (too dangerous)*
*~~Go back and check the tear in the veil behind the royal~~*
    *~~beantighe dorms~~ (cannot find it <u>anywhere</u>)*

*Wait for Mabon and make Cylvan my bridge partner?*
~~*Go back to where they tried to sacrifice Fiachra*~~ *(nothing
    there)*
*Fjornar? (Where Ryder is from)*
*The King's Keep in the Winter Court*

Exhaling through his nose, Saffron scribbled another idea at the bottom, before groaning and knotting fingers in his hair in his endless frustration.

*Find out where Ryder and the other humans from the ruins
    went ?*

"Is this really all you've come up with?" Taran asked.

"Icarus, *go,*" Saffron growled back in irritation.

Taran rolled his eyes, but obeyed, vanishing into the air with nothing more than a faint burning sensation in the scars of Saffron's arm. And like every time before it, Saffron gazed down to where they looked back up at him, visible and ugly and pink when not wearing his glamour. He ran fingers down the markings, feeling each and every one, as if he could summon a resolution from them. From that moment on Ostara when he was pure magic, pure rowan-veil magic, where he doubted nothing and would have gotten what he wanted with his teeth if forced to.

He tried to assure himself that part of his soul wasn't lost—just tired. Just tucked away. Such a vicious thing wasn't safe to let loose too often, anyway, hence why having Taran there to keep the wildfire at bay was actually a good thing. He only wished he could figure out how to tap back into it again on his own will, at his own control. He'd gone from his magic running out of control, to seemingly stretching so far out of reach he didn't know how to reel it back again. Constantly battling between wishing to let loose with it once more—to reminding himself, the events of the Midsummer Games would have been far, far worse, if Ryder had gotten his way with Saffron doing exactly that.

. . .

Washing the night-sweat away in a few inches of bathwater, Saffron emerged into the dorm's common area just as Copper did from his bedroom, offering good-mornings and then good-byes as his roommate hurried off to hurling practice that wasn't actually practice.

Waiting in Muirín dorm's common room for Sionnach to join him, Saffron paused a moment at the bulletin board where half a dozen of the morning's newest gossip columns had already been pinned. Each and every one displayed large, bold titles crying out about the human attacks around Avren the day before—making Saffron smile bitterly, as he knew as well as anyone that such a thing was never going to be kept a secret—though only one of the pamphlets was printed with a gallery of every one of the found circles illustrated for all of Avren to see. Surrounded with paragraphs decrying the kings and their seemingly 'uncaring' attitude; pleading with the 'red witches' to come forward in favor of peace over chaos, followed by an illustrated gallery of new 'missing beantighe' notices lining the bottom, as if he was the only one in all of Alfidel who could see the irony. He had to resist tearing it down and throwing it in the trash—also well aware it wouldn't do any good. There would be dozens more scattered around Mairwen, alone.

Sionnach finally approached from behind, breathless and apologizing for running late. Saffron told them not to worry about it, reaching out to fix the collar of their blazer and making their face go bright red in reaction. The sight alone was enough to ease Saffron's growing agitation, bringing him back to earth with a teasing smile.

Outside, the sky was overcast with thick clouds, but a rain had no yet punctured the air, and Saffron breathed in a deep lungful of it. Attempting to steal the buzzing, electric-energy from the possibility of thunder like it could replace the perpetual exhaustion in his blood.

They barely made it through the front door and down the courtyard when a professor suddenly rushed up on the other side of the gates, throwing their hands up and shouting. Commanding Saffron to stop, to wait, even shoving him back through the gate and into Sionnach. She slammed the metal shut with a deafening *bang* that shook every bar.

"Professor?" Saffron asked, but Sionnach tugged on Saffron's sleeve and pointed over the professor's shoulder to where Maeve appeared on the pathway, hurrying toward them with a shared look of deliberation. The professor, meanwhile, just looked pale, clutching a piece of paper in her hand and stammering as she spoke quickly. Saffron saw Mairwen's official letterhead printed at the top, and the briefest string of words including 'overnight' 'event' 'Erelaine'.

"All students must remain in their dormitories until further notice!" The professor exclaimed as Saffron attempted to search Maeve out again on her heels. "A formal announcement will be sent via house birds within the hour, so please return to your room for now—"

"Excuse me," Maeve said as she reached the gate. Her dorm-prefect badge was displayed front-and-center on her blazer, catching the eye of the professor in an instant. "Let Lord Saffron pass, please. I'll take responsibility for him."

"What's going on?" Saffron asked again while shimmying through a gap in the gate, keeping a tight grip on Sionnach's hand to ensure they passed through with him. Maeve said nothing, just taking Saffron's opposite hand and roughly pulling him away before anyone could stop them. "Maeve!"

She still said nothing—but handed Saffron a piece of paper, a copy of the same one the professor trying to lock the gate had crushed in her grasp. Sionnach hurried to match Saffron's pace, reading it over his shoulder, though the both of them came to a halt once the words struck in order.

TAKE IMMEDIATE ACTION UNTIL FURTHER NOTICE: MAIRWEN ACADEMY AND ALL SURROUNDING AVREN INSTITUTIONS ARE TO IMMEDIATELY LOCK DOWN.

OVERNIGHT OCCURRENCE AT THE MORRÍGAN'S TEMPLE IN ERELAINE: SECOND VEIL EVENT REPORTED.

5

————

# THE TEA

They went straight to the palace. Still in their school uniforms, with Maeve riding alongside Saffron and Boann, and Sionnach clinging to Saffron's waist from behind in their shared saddle. Thankfully, Avren's streets were still relatively quiet—all the way until they approached the palace, where Saffron barely reeled back on Boann's reins just before crashing into a small crowd gathering to pound on the gatehouse doors. Shouting. Demanding the kings come and address them, to address what was already written and published in the paper even so early in the morning.

Saffron realized too late that at least half of them held parchment and pens in their hands—and they were the first to turn at the sound of Boann's hooves racing up the road. Gossip writers, who, the moment they laid eyes on Saffron—turned and shouted his name. Rushing to where he barely managed to keep Boann calm in all the growing chaos.

*"Lord Saffron! Have you seen the news?"*

*"You were there during the games—do you think it was the same human rebels who tore open Erelaine?"*

*"Have you heard of the arid circles found all around Avren? Do you think they're related?"*

*"Are they trying to send a message? Do you have anything to say to the human witches behind this?"*

"L-let me pass!" Saffron attempted, having to wrap Boann's reins around his fists as the horse reeled in discomfort.

*"Will Prince Cylvan be sending any aid to Erelaine?"*

*"Do you have anything to say about Daurae Asche? Do you have any message for the humans who are doing this?"*

"I said—!"

The gatehouse doors suddenly banged, opening as everyone turned to look. Saffron didn't recognize the guard who appeared, but they lifted an arm and waved him to come. Two others rushed out, then Saoirse emerged on the back of her horse, wearing full plate armor as if prepared for war. The moment she spotted Saffron and Maeve already there, she shouted for the crowd to part, loud enough that even her own horse reeled back in agitation.

Bodies separated just enough for them to pass through, and Saffron rammed his heels into Boann's ribs the moment he could clear through. Hands clawed at his clothes, smacking against Boann, even pulling at Sionnach's legs as Saffron forced his way through. A hundred crying voices demanding answers all at once, when they weren't calling out everything they wished for him to pass on to the kings. Sentiments of both fear and anger—sentiments of bloodthirsty, and cries for them to repent to The Morrígan for what had apparently occurred at her Erelainian temple. Sionnach just clung to Saffron's waist as they passed through the horse, face pressed into his back as if terrified of being torn off and eaten alive.

Saoirse turned her horse the moment Saffron was within reach, and he followed with Maeve on his heels. Galloping across the long bridge, Boann snorted and whipped her head from the effort, but never slowed as Saffron urged her to keep pace with Saoirse ahead. The second gatehouse opened just as they approached, slowing to a breathless lope while passing through.

Right on the other side, Cylvan was just reaching the bottom of the stone steps, rushing to throw his arms around Saffron the instant Saffron kicked his foot over the saddle. Saffron clung to him in return, sensing Cylvan's mounting trepidation by how tightly his prince's arms locked around his body, how his heart pounded hard enough for Saffron to feel it in his own chest.

"It's alright," Saffron told him breathlessly. "You're safe, it's alright. We're all here."

Cylvan clung to him a moment longer, before finally pulling away. He placed a firm arm around Saffron's waist, and they hurried across the courtyard with the others on their heels toward the stairs.

Inside the palace wasn't any calmer than the bustling crowd outside the gates—as servants of every background and status raced back and forth, barking commands at one another when they weren't tripping over each other's feet. Most kept out of Saoirse's way as the guard hurried Cylvan, Saffron, and the others through the hallways—but Saffron couldn't help noticing every human they passed, specifically. All of them, looking far more pale, far more frightened and apprehensive, than their fey counterparts.

King Ailir stood with King Tross in one of the upper floor libraries, an arm holding his harmonious partner behind the back as they gazed out the tall window together. From that vantage point, the bridge over the valley was visible, as well as the growing crowd at the first gatehouse. Saffron knew more folk had gathered without having to see for himself. It was evident enough on the kings' faces. He just kept a grip on Cylvan's hand as they entered in tense silence.

Saoirse entered the room last, where she closed the door and remained in front of it. Lady Éoine, King Tross' sister and the mother of Cylvan's half-siblings, sat in a chair in the center of the room with an infant bundled in her arms. Two more guards hovered out of the way, but always within reach of the kings at the window. A final stranger Saffron didn't know sat in their own chair at the back of the room, shoulder-length hair dark and wavy like Cylvan's, though it was the cutting edge of their eyes that resembled the prince most. The stranger teased the the tip of a dagger against a finger while looking intently at him, and Saffron quickly averted his eyes again.

"We are still waiting to hear more from Erclaine's city oracles," King Ailir finally broke the silence, turning to address the gathered group as Tross remained facing the window. Ailir never took his hand from his partner's, and Saffron realized Tross' grasp trembled slightly. "Once we have a better idea of what exactly happened there, we will be able to decide how to proceed in sending aid to the people. Particularly—should there be lives lost."

He didn't have to utter it for Saffron to hear what the king meant to add—Lives lost, *again.* His heart pounded. He clutched Cylvan's hand so tightly, the prince's nails burrowed into the side of his palm.

And then—King Ailir looked at Saffron. Not with the same cold intensity as the stranger seated at the back of the room, but such a gaze was still enough to reduce any man or fey to stone when on the receiving end of it. Saffron was no exception, stiffening beneath those eyes like bright gold coins.

"Saffron," he said, pausing for a moment to press his lips together before parting again with a soft sound. "Do you know why they would have done this again?"

"No!" Saffron exclaimed right away, before forcing himself to pull the emotions back. Everyone in the room jumped with his sudden cry, and embarrassment toiled in his stomach. "I mean— No, I don't, I... I was thinking about it the whole way here, wondering if it had anything to do with the circles reported in Avren yesterday, but... It's hard to say, who... or why..."

"Could it have been someone else, then? Someone other than Ryder Kyteler," Ailir asked. Saffron didn't know how to answer that time either, lips parted like he wished a confident response would come. When none did, the shame grew heavier in his chest. All he could do was shake his head in uncertainty.

"Your majesty—do you think it has any connection to the arid circles left around the city?" Maeve asked next, reiterating Saffron's point as everyone turned to look at her.

"We are wondering that as well," Ailir said calmly, before his eyes traveled back to Saffron. "Considering what has been reported, we must consider it related."

"The oracles from Fjornar haven't had a chance to arrive yet," Cylvan said, almost like an argument, though it lacked his full confidence. "We still don't know anything about the attempted arid magic, and Saffron assured me himself the circles around Avren are nothing to worry about. There's no reason to believe—"

"Perhaps," Ailir interrupted, in agreement but voice firm. His golden eyes reached for Cylvan, and even the prince straightened up slightly beneath them. "But it is foolish to pretend like they were still anything *other* than human magic, whether worrisome or not. Just like it will be foolish to believe this attack on Erelaine is in no way related to what befell Avren a week ago."

Cylvan stiffened slightly. Saffron quietly squeezed his hand again.

"Whether or not they are related, it may still be a few days before the Fjornaran oracles arrive," Ailir went on. His eyes returned to Saffron once more. "For now, we will focus on what we are able to do with certainty. We must do what we can to ease the worries of the people—and see if there is any way to anticipate additional veil events that may come."

"More..." Sionnach whispered, and Saffron's stomach sank in turn.

"For now, we will send half of our royal oracles to Erelaine to help assess—" Ailir continued, but Cylvan interrupted him.

"No!" He exclaimed, earning a sharp look from the king. But Cylvan didn't back down that time—in fact, he released Saffron's hand, stepping forward. His breaths came quickly, voice strained as he visibly panicked for exactly what he wished to say. "If we send them away now, who will look for Asche until those from

Fjornar arrive? We can't pull any of them away from their work. Not now."

"What do you suggest instead, Cylvan?" Ailir asked. A pointed question, one brimming with implications, as if he really insisted *'do not defy my command unless you have a better one.'* And Cylvan—didn't. His mouth opened, then closed, pressing into a hard line as Saffron could see the growing dread behind his prince's expression. Desperation mixing with uncertainty, mixing with shame for having nothing else to propose.

"I'll go," Saffron said without thinking. Desperate to ease Cylvan's burden. To be of use to him—however possible. "I'm not as experienced as an oracle, obviously, but—I can read arid circles. I can tell you what's there, and if Ryder was involved."

The air in the room tightened in an instant. A step ahead, Cylvan had turned to stare at him. Still pale, apprehensive, with nerves muddying the color of his eyes. Saffron looked right back at him, lips parting in the briefest moment of hesitation, before hurriedly insisting before Cylvan could refuse. "It's just—if Ryder Kyteler is behind this veil event, too, I want to see it with my own eyes. If anyone can figure out, first, if it really was him, then why he did it, or if he plans to do more—I can. He might even still be in Erelaine—and if so, I might even be able to find him before—"

"Or draw him out—!" Cylvan exclaimed. "Or drive him to something worse—!"

"Or *stop him* from doing anything worse!" Saffron argued back, instinctively squeezing his hand—but it was not longer held within Cylvan's. Unable to help feeling like he'd lost anchor in a rough storm. "Whether he did this to hurt more people, or cause another big scene, or even just to get our attention—even if he only did it to draw me out of Avren—it doesn't matter. Ryder Kyteler is—he's my fault! His actions are my fault, he's my problem! He's also..." Saffron's throat flexed, heart swelling in his chest and nearly choking him. "He's also the only person I know who can manipulate the veil like that."

The atmosphere encircling him tightened further, making it

even harder to breathe. Still, Saffron flared his nostrils, forcing air into his lungs. He straightened up, extending his hand in an effort to claim Cylvan's back again—and to his relief, Cylvan wordlessly offered his back. Anchored once again to his raven, his prince, whose eyes danced in bright apprehension.

"If we can find him before he runs, again—that might even be our best chance at forcing him to tell us where Asche is. Even to take us to them," Saffron continued, calmer that time, though with his voice no less heavy with emotion. "To Letty and Hollow and Nimue, too. Because even if the oracles here are able to find a way through—there's no promise they'll know what to do after that. No one knows for certain, except Ryder. I —" His voice cracked. The rest of the room fell away into a humming blur, and Saffron saw only his anguishing prince in front of him. "I don't have anything else, Cylvan... I haven't been able to figure out anything else..."

The silence rang loud, bouncing off the ceiling, the books on the shelves, echoing back and striking him like the ocean striking weathered cliffs.

"Saffron is right."

All heads turned, though King Tross still hadn't pulled away from the window. Saffron watched his reflection in the glass, eyes keeping on the gathering crowd at the far gates. "I think we ought to listen to what he has to say, as the one who knows the man behind this better than anyone else."

"I'm not about to put Saffron directly into Ryder Kyteler's reach—" Cylvan started, but King Tross finally turned, interrupting him.

"There are many things I wish I could suggest otherwise, Cylvan, I can assure you," he interjected. Saffron had never heard such firm coldness in his voice. "There are many things I wish to say about Saffron's flippancy when it came to navigating that man's intentions, as well—but I do not think it will do any of us much good, at this point."

Saffron bowed his head, flushing with shame. Tross continued: "In fact, the only good to possibly come out of his show of glaring ignorance is that Ryder Kyteler may still believe it. He may still believe Saffron to be as nescient as when they spent all their time together in the Finnian Ruins—"

"How do you know—" Cylvan attempted, but Tross cut him off.

"I do not need to know the details of their day-to-day to imagine exactly how every conversation went," Tross snapped. "I also know Saffron. I know how he was raised, where he came from, and the environment he was thrust into at Mairwen—things I thought you would have been more aware of, yourself, Cylvan. You both carry pieces of responsibility for the situation we've found ourselves in, even if there is nothing in the world you could have done to stop it."

"How dare you—" Cylvan flared.

"Cylvan," Saffron whispered, pulling Cylvan back. "Don't. He's right."

King Tross' nostrils flared, before closing his eyes. He released a long exhale, with it seeming to expel most of the tension locking his body upright. His tight posture slacked, shoulders falling, even the wildfire burning in his eyes pulling back when he opened them again. They returned to Saffron, that time heavy with sleepless nights and the weariness only a king could carry.

"I think King Tross has a fair point," Ailir said next, his tone remaining as calm as the start. "I also agree with Saffron. I think it may be wise for you both to travel to Erelaine to assess the damage, and determine what aid they require from Avren. At the very least, it would reflect kindly on your image, Cylvan. As Alfidel's future king."

Cylvan stood stiffly, wooden, head bowed slightly.

"Yes, father," he finally uttered, but the words were empty.

"I'll begin preparations for Prince Cylvan and Lord Saffron to leave as soon as possible—" Saoirse said from the door.

"Me as well," Sionnach interrupted, though their voice squeaked slightly with nerves. "I'll accompany them as well."

"Me, too," Maeve sighed, but slumped into one of the cushioned chairs as she did. "Might as well."

"I'll have a carriage prepared, then," Saoirse corrected. "As well as horses."

Saoirse motioned to the other two guards in the room, who bowed to the kings before excusing themselves. The stranger sitting at the far side also rose to their feet, sheathing their dagger and following Saoirse out. Saffron turned to Sionnach, who immediately stepped forward upon meeting his eyes.

"Would you go back to my dorm and get a few things for me?" he asked wearily. "If you can find Copper, he should let you in. I'll need my shoulder bag and sketchbook, specifically. They should be on my desk. Fiachra, too, you can find her travel carrier—"

"You should go with them," Cylvan attempted, but King Tross cleared his throat.

"I would like to speak to Saffron alone, if I may."

They all stared at him for a moment, before eyes flickered back to Saffron, who had gone still as stone. Sionnach was the first to speak again, reassuring Saffron they would bring everything they could think he might need. Excusing themself, Maeve followed behind, but Cylvan remained. Perhaps having no choice, as Saffron's hand was locked around his.

"Father—" He attempted, but Tross raised a hand, and Cylvan went quiet again.

"I won't cause your beloved any harm, Cylvan, I can assure you," he said, finally offering a tired smile. "I only wish to speak to him alone, before you all depart."

Cylvan glanced to Saffron, but Saffron remained petrified where he stood. When he did manage to give Cylvan a look back, it was to wordlessly beg for rescue, even if Cylvan knew better than to argue any further. He lifted Saffron's hand to his mouth, kissing the back of it.

"I'll make sure everything is prepared for us to leave before noon," he said. "Don't rush, púca. I'll see you again soon."

"Alright," Saffron managed, hardly more than a nervous rasp. Cylvan hesitated a second longer, throwing Tross a look like he hoped the king would change his mind, but Tross just lifted a hand to wave Cylvan away.

Cylvan obeyed, closing the library door behind him and leaving Saffron alone with the Harmonious King of Alfidel.

A part of Saffron truly did believe Tross didn't intend him any harm, though his certainty wavered slightly as the room emptied. Especially as the king said nothing else at first. Even as he went to the wall by the door and tugged on a little rope that rang a bell somewhere in the belly of the palace.

"Some tea, Saffron?" he asked upon returning to the couch in the center of the room and taking a seat. When he patted the cushion in invitation, Saffron had no choice but to join him, though he silently gave a little prayer to Ériu as he did.

"That's a fine cloak, you know." The king said casually, and Saffron only then realized he still wore the covering over his school uniform. Something about it was immediately embarrassing, though he couldn't explain why. "I believe an excursion such as this one will require something a little more... fitting, however. I'll have something ready before you leave. A whole wardrobe, even. Finally, a chance to dress *someone* in a little color. The constant black of Avren's grieving period is so depressing, isn't it? As if the gods care what color our clothes are in such a time..."

Saffron barely heard it, too busy stripping the cloak off and tossing it over the back of the couch, just as the main doors opened and two beantighes with a tea cart rattled their way inside.

"In all this time, you and I have never sat down for a private chat, have we?" Tross went on as the beantighes finished placing the table in front of them then saw themselves out. King Tross casually crossed one leg over the other, allowing the fine fabric of his skirt to drape at the long slit and reveal the dark skin of his leg underneath. As he reached to take the teapot and pour a cup for Saffron, Saffron lurched forward, moving faster so he could do the honor. God—for King Tross to pour him a cup of tea, Saffron really might have a deathwish.

"You've been nothing but welcoming and cordial to me from the start," Saffron said, choosing his words carefully. "Never once did I feel like your grace wasn't extended to me, even if we've never had a private chat."

"Hmm," Tross said with a considerate smile, sipping at his cup after Saffron handed one to him. "I'm curious whether that perfect of a response comes from being a beantighe, or being *Master Luvon's* beantighe."

Saffron flushed red, avoiding the king's eyes while claiming his own cup and saucer.

"I wasn't trying to give the perfect response," he said meekly. "I'm being honest. Although—if anything, it was Madame Catrín who would have taught me how to respond properly to such things."

"Madame Catrín and Master Luvon make quite the indomitable pair, don't they?"

Saffron didn't know what *indomitable* meant, but he still nodded. King Tross helped himself to one of the macaron cookies on the tray, enjoying himself a moment and leaving Saffron to sit in apprehensive, tortured silence.

"I have had many conversations about you with your patron master, you know," he said, that mischievous smile returning to his face. Saffron nearly grimaced, the mental image of King Tross and Luvon gossiping about him over wine making his stomach flutter in embarrassment. "Even long before you ever became Cylvan's chosen king. Who would have thought my own dear friend's favorite beantighe would woo my darling, brooding son. If I wasn't so sure of Luvon's disbelief, I would have thought you and him planned it as some sort of coup."

Saffron's hand jolted as he stammered out reassurances that that had never, ever been the case, and Tross only laughed again.

"I know, child, you can catch your breath. Luvon isn't the type to ever wish to be king, anyway. I'm not sure how thrilled he is for you to be in this position, either, though not because he thinks you incompetent—rather, I think he worries Cylvan isn't good enough a partner for you."

Saffron let out a stiff exhale, but chuckled at the end. "I'm aware. Though I wonder how a prince could possibly not be impressive enough for a patron-child. A changeling baby, marrying the crown prince..."

"It's like something from a myth," Tross said. Saffron's heart flipped, unsure if the king really meant it—or only said so because he knew of Saffron's favorite books.

"To be quite honest, ever since I heard the long story of how you both really met—the honest story, which took two bottles of wine to wring out of my son," the king continued. "I believed you would make for a fair Harmonious King. Especially that little trick of yours when you first met. In the forest clearing, I think it was, with the pixies at the hollow. You made Cylvan cut his hair."

Saffron's ears rang. He wasn't sure he was still seated. He must have been floating along the ceiling, especially with the gutted wheeze that puttered out of him.

"Oh," he croaked. "Y-yes, I did..."

"Cylvan says they sleep in piles." Tross continued, sipping his tea, then raising an eyebrow when Saffron didn't respond. "The pixies, I mean."

"O-oh, yes!" Saffron replied. Mind continuing to spin as he couldn't seem to grapple with how casual all the chatter was turning out to be, all things considered, after such a heavy morning. Perhaps that was exactly what made King Tross so dangerous, after all. Saffron continued to brace for a trap to spring at any moment. "Erm—except the ones meant to stand guard at the front of the hollow. But most times I found them fast asleep with the others."

"I've never heard of anyone to successfully find pixies sleeping —let alone keep their eyes afterward," Tross smiled, turning the stem of his cup around on the saucer until it hummed. "One semester at Ambegun, there was a pixie infestation in one of the dorms. At least three students lost an eye, though they were later found hanging from a tree on the edge of campus. One of them was successfully popped back in, but the other two were frozen solid. I'm sure you know how Winter Court pixies are far more ruthless than Spring or Summer ones—they love to steal fleshy bits from their prey and hang them to freeze from branches."

"Oh, yes," Saffron grimaced. "Not to mention impossible to see in the true season, when they all turn white as the snow. When I was a child, a small pack of them even stole one of my loose teeth while I was sleeping. Right out of my mouth."

Tross made a face of interest, before furrowing his brows. "I always forget human childrens' teeth fall out... Is it true some patron families keep them? For all of their beantighes? Perhaps for charms, or tracking spells... I wonder if Daurae Asche has ever thought of that..." he hummed, turning the cup on the saucer again. "High fey babies just slowly grind down the sharp points they're born with."

Saffron choked. "Excuse me?"

"Have you never seen the mouth of a young high fey?" The king smiled, showing all of his own white teeth. That morning, as if on purpose, his canines were capped with sharp golden points that would certainly, definitely, break skin if he tried. "Every tooth is sharp as a knife. Carryover from our wild ancestry. Did you not notice the shape of Asche's? They still have the smallest bite to them."

"That's..." Saffron almost called it a lie, stopping himself short of accusing the king of being capable of such a thing. He'd never looked particularly close at Asche's teeth, either, though picturing them with slightly-pointed fangs rang true. Recalling how Luvon's girls used to leave bite-marks on Saffron's arms as a toddler suddenly made sense, too. "Prince Cylvan must have been a menace. Even more than I've heard, at least."

"Oh, for *many* reasons, as you already know," Tross grinned. "But his menacing nature has... diminished somewhat, since he met you. It's never fully gone, of course, but it does seem like he tries his best to hide his sharp teeth whenever you're nearby. I did always hope Cylvan would find someone with a little more lust for life than Lord Taran, at least, to show him not everything had to be so miserable all the time," Tross mused freely, unfurling a napkin as he claimed one of the finger-sandwiches lined up on the tray. "You may have come with your own hurdles for him to jump, but at least you have a sense of humor."

If Taran hadn't been paying attention through Saffron's ears up until that moment, he certainly was the moment his name was mentioned. Saffron subconsciously rubbed his thumb over the scar on his arm beneath his sleeve.

"Did you... not like Lord Taran, your majesty?" he asked, much more willing to discuss that branch of conversation over the aforementioned hurdles he himself came with.

"I cared plenty for Lord Taran," Tross said, though his smile was flat with the insistence. "Lord Taran and Cylvan were close friends since they were young—but as they grew, and the unfounded rumors circulating my son grew along with them, the mac Delbaith Family started planting seeds of their own into that poor boy." He spoke so casually, Saffron almost didn't realize exactly what he was saying. To King Tross, those words were hardly more than gossip to share with new ears; to Saffron, they were the slightest peeks into Taran's past, normally withheld from him as much as the wolf-lord possibly could. All the while, Taran himself remained silent in the back of Saffron's mind, though Saffron could still sense him lingering. Perhaps because he was apprehensive to hear what the king would reveal—or, perhaps more innocently, there was a part of him that wished to know what King Tross actually thought of him, all along.

"What sorts of seeds?" Saffron dared to ask. Tross' mouth quirked at the corner as he sipped at his tea, as if glad Saffron asked.

"Telling him he would be the only one who could stop a Night Court, of course." Tross's bright eyes lifted from the rim of his teacup, striking Saffron so suddenly with the gaze that even

Taran shied away. "But, seeing as you spent all that time in Danann House under that deal you made with him, in order to protect my son—I'm curious what *you've* come to think of him, yourself, Saffron."

Saffron bit his lip. He sipped at his tea, watching his reflection ripple in the surface of the dark drink before absentmindedly rubbing his hand against his scarred forearm again. The wolf attached to his soul stirred again, as if perking up. As if—a part of him, while he would never admit it—was curious to know, as well.

"There are many things I despise about Taran mac Delbaith," he said with all honesty, knowing it wouldn't come as any shock to the wolf in his head. King Tross nearly responded, but Saffron continued, first. "But... But I've learned a lot since my time in Danann House. About him, and about Cylvan, and about what it means to be... a person raised with such harsh expectations placed on them. You said yourself, Taran's indoctrination started when he was only a child, which is no different from Cylvan in so many ways. So... I guess I could say I 'understand' why he did the awful things he did, but not in any way of extending forgiveness. Not yet."

*Not yet.* He didn't know why that final sentiment escaped him, but the words lingered between himself and the king.

Tross' eyes sparkled, staring at Saffron, unblinking, like he wanted nothing more in the entire world than for him to say more. But Saffron knew better than to share too much with a king prone to gossip, especially when it was his own words being shared.

"That is very harmonious of you," Tross finally conceded, giving Saffron a satisfied smile before plucking another pastry from one of the tiered plates and slathering it in jam and honey. "Not that I ever doubted you—a beantighe is a perfect fit for a harmonious king, when one considers it past the initial shock."

His eyes flickered upward to meet Saffron's again. The way the sun shone through them reminded Saffron of King Ailir;

reminded him of Asche. Cutting and warm and searching all at once. Perhaps the Daurae got their insatiable curiosity from King Tross.

"If I may be honest with you, Saffron," the king went on with a sense of finality. "While I once worried Lord Taran lacked the capacity to comfort my son in his darkest moments... a part of me worries you will lack the same in quarrel." He let those words hang between them, until they sank and rooted in Saffron's bones. "I know how deeply you care for the prince—for my son. But I think it has blinded you both to what waits on the horizon. A Night Court that has haunted him since the day he was born. An era that will be difficult to navigate, only made more treacherous now with what occurred at the Midsummer Games.

"It is still long before Cylvan takes the throne, Danu bless it be, yet his reputation already carries the blame. He will have his own decisions to make, and they will come quickly—Decisions for the better of the people, though with a human harmonious partner, high fey will no doubt wonder *which* people. An ancient game of survival that I am far too familiar with, as King Ailir's Harmonious King, having had to watch the one I love retract his claws time and time again in favor of keeping the peace amongst courtiers far older than he. I worry, when the time comes that you two truly clash in what you think is best for Alfidel—true harmony will be hard-sought, if you are not able to see past your feelings for Cylvan, and stand up against him for the things you believe to be right, and vice-versa.

"Considering the hand Cylvan has been dealt since the day he was born, and the fate he is destined to receive, knowing my son better than most—I can tell you right now, when backed into a corner, Cylvan's instinct will be to survive rather than to fight. Especially if the people he cares about, and the people who care about him—as few as there are—are threatened. He will bow first, and consider his ethical responsibility second. Do you understand?"

Saffron stared at him. His stomach turned, spilling the tea and sweet pastries and bites of fruit he'd swallowed over one another, until there was only nausea.

"If there is one word of advice I can give to you now, Saffron, it is this: Use this journey to Erelaine as a chance to witness what, exactly, you have in store for yourself as the harmonious king to a coming storm. Decide if it is a storm you are truly prepared to weather—or a storm you are prepared to clash against, as the only way to balance the wind and rain.

"I know you care deeply for Prince Cylvan. He cares deeply for you as well. But that love you hold for one another will either be a strength, or a curse. You will have to be prepared to make your decisions not only for yourself—but for the sake of all the people who may suffer if you choose wrong. Including Cylvan, whether he will recognize it or not. Should affection cloud your judgement, allowing Cylvan to choose survival over the good of those who need him—Alfidel may, with certainty, suffer beneath the very Night Court swiftly arriving over the horizon. But in ways none of us could ever imagine."

"I—" Saffron spoke without thinking, not knowing what he wished to say. His mind was blank, feeling only the nervous pound of his heart in his chest. He'd always known being a harmonious, human king in a Night Court would not be easy— but Tross' words of warning filled him with ice. Flooded him inch over inch, until his hand twitched on his lap as if instinctively searching for warmth. But Cylvan wasn't there; Cylvan wasn't right within reach. Saffron would have to internalize that warning, and every eternal, potential consequence—accepting that it was for him and him alone.

6

———

## THE CREST

Restless after his conversation with King Tross, restless with the sudden change of plans for the day and the days that would follow, Saffron made his way through the palace hallways as quickly as he could without drawing too much attention to himself—though it wasn't hard, with how people continued to rush by in every direction. Guards hurrying by in groups or alone; servants, human and fey, dashing away carrying armfuls of clothing or fabric, valuables, trunks of hidden goods as if ordered to take them into the palace vaults for safekeeping. Saffron would not be sick. He would not allow himself to be sick.

Escaping through one of the passages Asche once showed him, he escaped into the back gardens. He disappeared beneath the thick-flowering wisteria trees and willows, hiding from the coming rain beneath one tree easily older than he was within the dome of its weeping vines. Leaning against the trunk, he pressed a hand to his chest, fighting to catch his breath. Breathing in the smell of the blossoms, the fresh air, the creek that snaked down the center of the grounds, the distant scent of the ocean. His heart wouldn't slow; it refused to allow him a moment of solace. He worried it would beat right through the cracked scar of his sternum.

When someone slipped a hand between the veil of willow branches and slipped in to join him, anyone else would have been startled by the tall and broad shadow—but Saffron sighed in instant relief, falling into Cylvan's arms and holding him.

"You made it out in one piece," Cylvan said, clearly only half joking. Saffron groaned, pressing his face into Cylvan's chest and breathing him in. He wasn't wearing his perfume that morning; he hadn't had any chance to do his makeup or his hair, except to pull the long strands into a simple side ponytail. Even his clothes were simple, which felt wrong for him—but at least made it easier for Saffron to bury his face into his chest without the prodding of beads or sculpted buttons.

"Are you alright?" Saffron asked, finally pulling away just enough to look up at him. Cylvan let out a sigh of his own.

"King Ailir spoke to me while Tross spoke to you; and now I have to meet with both of them to discuss what I'll say on the platform to the crowd," Cylvan said. "What a morning it's been..." he trailed off, combing a few stray hairs from Saffron's forehead. Saffron sensed how his touch trembled slightly. He wanted to ask what Cylvan was thinking—but the prince shook his head, first, reaching into the inner pocket of his doublet.

"I was meaning to give this to you later, but now seems as good a time as any," he said, presenting the gift wrapped in beautiful gold-embroidered fabric. Saffron glanced up at him in surprise, before carefully taking it. "I had to sneak it into my blouse from my room, between all the chaos. Had anyone found it on me before speaking in private to my father—gods, I do not want to think what sort of wild stories they would spin about my intentions."

Untying the fabric knot, Saffron unwound the covering over the object, holding his breath when a sheathed knife half the length of his forearm was revealed. Intricately crafted with a black leather exterior, the shaft was inlaid with faceted rubies and beaded rowan leaves, making Saffron's breath catch as he trailed his thumb over the polished gems.

"It's beautiful," he said. Cylvan smiled unevenly, placing his hand on Saffron's to encourage him to pull the blade from its leather case. Saffron expected to find silver inside—but instead, a shining black blade emerged.

His eyes went wide in appreciation, fully grasping the weapon by the handle to pull it free for a better look. Noticing first how, even in that overcast light, the slightest amount of sun passed through the semi-opaque body when held up to the sky. *'Like glass obsidian,'* he nearly exclaimed with a grin, but something else caught his eye first. Within the depths of the blade—subtle, swirling embellishments were visible, as if carved into the stone before being polished down into such a sharp edge. To anyone else, the designs would have been nothing more than a charming detail—but Saffron knew, the moment he saw them.

"This is—!" He choked, immediately clutching the blade flat to his chest. Staring at Cylvan in wordless disbelief, his heart pounded as he fully understood. "This is made from—!"

"My lost horn, yes," Cylvan smiled. His silver replacement shined in the low light as he did, as if taunting. "It was Saoirse's idea, actually. The blacksmith did a stunning job, didn't he? 'Like nothing he'd ever made before,' he said. Don't let first impressions fool you, either—it should be strong and sharp as any other fey-forged steel."

"It's..." Saffron gazed down at the blade one more time, before gently tucking it into its sheathe. "God, I've already cried enough, haven't I?"

Cylvan chuckled, as Saffron threw his arms around him once again.

"It's beautiful, Cylvan," he said upon returning back flat to his feet. "It's—it's the most unique thing I've ever seen. Just like you."

"Use it liberally," Cylvan said. "If ever there is a moment you need me, but I'm not there—you can still defend yourself, and I will take the blame."

Saffron pulled him down into a kiss, holding Cylvan's face in one hand, clutching the knife to his chest with the other.

"Everything is going to be alright," he said. "I know it. We'll have a safe trip, I know it, but..." He trailed off, closing his eyes and pressing their foreheads together. "Thank you. I'll carry it with me everywhere."

"Good," Cylvan smiled. "A small reassurance, for me. Despite it all... I want nothing more but for you to remain safe, púca."

His voice grew heavy with unspoken intensity, those words pleading far more than just what Saffron could use a blade against. Locking his arms around Saffron and pulling him tight, he pressed his nose into Saffron's hair and breathed him in. Whispering about the smell of rain and willow and wisteria.

Saffron didn't know what else to say; he didn't know what else to do. He just held Cylvan back, hoping it was enough to reassure him. *Everything will be alright.*

THEIR MOMENT TOGETHER WAS BRIEF, HARDLY MORE than a few minutes—but was just enough to reinvigorate Saffron with enough energy to finally make his way to the front courtyard, while Cylvan left for one final private meeting with both King Ailir and Tross, before they would depart.

Sneaking into the stables while everyone else was busy with tasks before their departure, he went searching for Boann, grabbing a brush from a shelf on the way in case anyone spotted him and asked what he was doing. The beast was clearly still agitated from the excitable morning as Saffron stepped into her stall, nudging her nose into his side as if to ask where he'd been. But Saffron just threw his head back with a groan, collapsing onto his haunches and burying his face into arms crossed over his knees. Forcing himself to breathe, balling his hands in and out of fists as his fingers tingled in anxiety. He clawed at his hair, tugging at the roots until his scalp burned, as if he could pluck out every worry like oracles plucked out memory threads. If he just pulled hard enough, he would unravel and weave his own memory tapestry, but only of things he didn't wish to keep for himself. Someone else could find use for them.

All he'd wanted—was one peaceful, romantic summer with his prince. And even that had been too much to ask.

Boann's teeth found his fingers in his hair, nibbling and making Saffron yelp. Falling back, his landed on his ass with a sigh, allotting himself exactly ten more seconds of feeling sorry for himself before shaking his head and forcing himself back to his feet. He collected the brush off the floor, then snagged a few fresh vegetables from the bucket reserved for the royal horses.

He was in the middle of open-palming a thick slice of pumpkin for Boann when Saoirse suddenly hurried in. Startling one another, then startling Saffron a second time when the guard let out a bark of laughter. It wasn't so much the volume that surprised him, rather the sound itself, as Saoirse had always been so stern and stoic since they first met.

"I worried his majesty might eat you alive," she said, surprising Saffron further. He stepped out of the way as the guard approached Boann to look her over for the journey.

"King Tross is not all that scary," Saffron reassured, even if it was mostly a lie, as if Saoirse didn't already know. "He reminds me so much of Master Luvon, honestly, which definitely keeps my nerves at bay."

At some point during Saffron's time with King Tross, Saoirse had removed her plate armor, perhaps for the ease of movement while hurrying back and forth performing so many chores in preparation for the journey. Saffron had always been aware of her size, but for the first time had a chance to really appraise her without all the silver plating that made her look even more intimidating.

She stood as tall as the tips of Cylvan's horns, upper body easily as broad as Copper's with thick, burly muscle. Saffron spotted sun-warmed skin beneath the cuffs of her long sleeves, though her face and hands were tanned even more from the sun, spotted with freckles across her cheeks and the backs of her knuckles that also donned years of scars, both faded and recent. She was clearly older than Cylvan, with the fine lines beneath her eyes and around her mouth, though that could have simply been from a long life of hard work. The wrinkles blended into faint scars that criss-crossed over her facial features, the most notable one cutting down through one of her dark eyebrows and warping the shape of her right eyelid.

That morning, her red hair was pulled back in a series of braids and knots that, when let down, might have reached to the middle of her back. She wore a single stroke of gold eyeliner over her top eyelids, with a tiny added accent on her lower lashes, the color matching a pierced ring in her nose that flashed slightly whenever caught in the light. One of her pointed ears was notched, missing its tip, and Saffron couldn't help but wonder if she'd lost it the same way Hollow had lost his.

"How long have you been Cylvan's personal guard?" he asked, hating the silence, hating just standing there while someone else worked in front of him. Saoirse gave him a brief glance, holding back her answer until she'd grabbed Boann's travel saddle and lifted it into place on her back. The new one was freshly polished, donning the crest of the royal family on both sides.

"I was his mother's guard first," Saoirse said with a grunt, adjusting the saddle before bending down on one knee to cinch the belts around Boann's middle. Saffron knelt to help. "When the prince was born, Gentle Naoill asked me to keep an eye on him. Once he was old enough to move to Avren for school, they asked me to go, too."

"So you've known him his whole life," Saffron said with a little laugh. "Was he really always as troublesome as he says?"

"I don't know what exactly he's told you, but you can double it." Saoirse smirked. "I cannot possibly put into words what a handful that little storm has been since the moment he first opened those damned eyes. You know—most sídhe fey develop their powers in adolescence, but Prince Cylvan had storm clouds brewing on the ceiling even as the nursemaids were wiping him down."

"It's unfair, isn't it?" Saffron said, at first without thinking, then adding: "When I first met him, I didn't think he was as scary as everyone else does. I just thought he was rude."

Saoirse chuckled. "Cylvan tells me you're not afraid of anything."

"Does he?" Saffron grimaced. "He's only being polite."

Saoirse said nothing else, just smiling to herself as if reminiscing on a personal memory.

They continued working in wordless silence for a few minutes, Saffron feeding more vegetables to Boann as Saoirse made sure the saddle was properly tightened in every place. Not much longer passed before the quiet was interrupted by a voice calling the guard's name, and they both turned just as someone stepped into the stables.

Saffron thought it was Cylvan at first—before realizing, it was only the dark-haired stranger from the king's library. The one who had regarded Saffron with cold eyes at the start, then followed Saoirse out when excused. They stopped in the opening of Boann's stall, looking Saffron up and down before a catlike smile crossed their face, laced with mischief. The curl of their mouth was familiar, resembling how Cylvan's lifted when he had naughtiness on his mind. Draped over one arm, they held a crimson-red cloak, and Saffron had a sneaking suspicion they were there to give it to him.

"Well, good morning," they said, stepping in and offering Saffron a little bow for the very first time. "I don't think we've been properly introduced, Lord Saffron. No better time than now, seeing as I'll be accompanying you on your journey."

"I thought we decided last night you would be heading back home today?" Saoirse muttered like a warning, like she knew exactly what trouble edged in the stranger's voice.

"Well, Erelaine is on the way, isn't it? Besides..." The stranger's eyes never left Saffron, and Saffron refused to avert his own that time.

Instead, he memorized their appearance, trying to put a finger on what, exactly, felt off about it. Shoulder-length, wavy black hair; pale skin; blue eyes accentuated with dark, smoky pigments; plum-colored lips that reminded Saffron of how his own looked after working too long in Luvon's cold orchards. The fey wasn't particularly tall or muscular, but seemed sturdy at the same time, somehow. Saffron could tell right away, there was certainly more to them than it seemed—why else would their closeness make his skin buzz in apprehension? "Besides, what you've got going on sounds far more interesting. You might even need my help keeping an eye on the prince and his entourage, Saoirse, don't you think? This one especially seems to invite trouble. Ah, that reminds me. Here. The rest of your new things are already packed up in pretty luggage bags, *your highness.*"

They extended the folded cloak, just like Saffron expected. He accepted, holding the covering by the shoulders and letting it unfurl. Sewn from deep, blood red fabric, Saffron didn't know if the fluttering in his gut was apprehension or appreciation. Tross had never been known for designing any piece of clothing that could be called *simple*—but that cloak, meant just for Saffron, very much was. Red, with some subtle crimson embroidery up the edges, imitating rowan branches. How long had he been holding onto it? Perhaps it was technically unfinished, in that state—but for Saffron's tastes, it was perfect.

"Lord Saffron, why don't you go see if the others have returned from Mairwen yet?" Saoirse asked, interrupting Saffron's awed silence. Her tone was flat and irritated. "I'll need to prepare their horses, too, as soon as they arrive."

"Oh, sure," Saffron said, throwing the cloak over his shoulders and pinning the front. The stranger wrinkled their nose like they hated how Saffron hadn't reacted to their little jab—but admittedly, Saffron had already forgotten what they'd even said.

"It was nice to meet you—" He attempted, and the stranger interrupted again.

"Gentle Aodhán," they introduced themself, offering a hand

to shake. Saffron took it, realizing with that small motion, they must have originated from the Winter Court. Folk from other courts rarely shook hands like cold northerners exchanging warmth.

SIONNACH AND MAEVE WERE JUST MAKING THEIR WAY through the gates when Saffron emerged from the stables, but more surprisingly, Copper rode up behind them. It made unexpected emotion flutter in Saffron's chest, and he hurried to hug Copper tightly the moment his friend kicked his legs from the saddle.

"What's going on?" Copper asked, throwing Maeve and Sionnach a dirty look like they'd both refused to tell him anything, like they both couldn't believe he insisted on riding all the way back to the palace with them despite it. "Everyone's losing their minds on campus right now. Had to use my hurling shoulder on a professor to let me through the dorm gate."

"There was another veil event in Erelaine. We think it may have been Ryder who did it," Saffron said, and Copper's face dropped in an instant. Before the fox could fully shut down, Saffron added: "We're getting ready to go see for ourselves. Will... will you come with us?"

"Wh—Of course!" Copper exclaimed, grabbing Saffron's arms. "To Erelaine? Gods, of course—I'm not gonna let you go anywhere that prick might be without me to take care of you."

Saffron grinned, not expecting that emphatic of a reply, hugging Copper again before reaching out for the reins of his horse. "Saoirse is in the stables changing out riding tack..." he turned just as Boann was lead out by Aodhán, who handed her reins to Saffron before raising an eyebrow at him in terms of Copper's. Saffron nearly handed them over, but Copper stopped him suddenly, snatching them back.

"Oh—" he said, eyes lingering on Boann's new saddle

donning the royal family crest. "Er—is this a crown-sanctioned thing?"

"What do you mean?" Saffron asked. He thought Copper was joking, but the furrow in his friend's brows insisted otherwise. "Is something wrong?"

"No, nothing wrong," Copper said, but his frown remained. "I just, uh... I assume if everyone is going to be riding with tack printed with the royal crest, then... there's going to be a lot of attention on the party, huh? Everyone's going to be watching. Everyone's going to be writing about it in their gossip columns, about how the kings are sending the prince to check the damage at Erelaine..."

"Copper..." Saffron argued. He didn't mean it, but a flicker of irritation bubbled in the back of his voice, like long-brewed carryover from the first time Copper hurried out of the room while King Ailir asked for their combined help and discretion. That had been 'sanctioned by the crown' too, in its own way, requiring Copper to closely associate himself with the future king of Alfidel. And that same look of pale uncertainty, anxiety was evident on the fox-lord's face as he stood there in the palace courtyard.

"I just—don't really wanna wrap myself up in political stuff," Copper said, though his voice lacked any resolve. He pulled the reins fully from Saffron's hand, even taking a step back and leaving Saffron standing there. "Erm... well, I can just keep an eye on Avren for you while you're gone. Send a bird if anything else strange happens, you know?"

"Copper!" Saffron exclaimed in frustration, but Copper just offered him an uneven smile, then turned to pat the side of his horse's neck.

"Let him go, Saffron," Sionnach appeared, offering the reins of their horse to Aodhán, instead, who took them, but didn't turn away just yet. Like they wanted to see how the tension resolved, intrigued and curious. Saffron gave them a look, and they must have realized how rude it was to linger, because they turned and pulled Sionnach's palomino horse into the stables as

Sionnach went on: "He made it clear last week, he doesn't want to associate himself with anything honorable."

"Sionnach," Saffron interjected in surprise, and even Copper looked shocked. But the half-satyr appeared more irritated than Saffron had ever seen them, like there had been more words exchanged between them and Copper before they ever arrived at the palace. Or perhaps even before then—as if Sionnach had confronted Copper about his response to King Ailir's request at the very beginning. Only when Sionnach straightened up and pressed their lips together, though, did Saffron realize—it might have been more disappointment, rather than irritation, they felt toward Copper's decisions.

"*'Honorable'*? You're one to talk, goat," Copper said stiffly, clearly bothered, clearly—*overwhelmed* by the flooding emotions inside of him. "Ironic, considering you wouldn't even exist if your mother had done what everyone thought was *'honorable'* years ago…"

"*Copper!*" Maeve snarled that time, making Copper jump. But Sionnach didn't move, just staring at Copper as the tight line of their mouth shifted, then trembled. Their chin wrinkled as they fought against how they wished to respond, before turning and hurrying away toward the stables. The second they were gone, Saffron whirled back on Copper, but the fey lord's shoulders had slumped. He looked miserable, in an instant, like a fresh candle taken to heat.

"I should go," he said, grabbing the horn of his saddle and pulling himself up. "Good luck, Saffron. I'll see you again soon."

"Copper, wait, please—!" Saffron attempted, but Copper was already pulling on the reins and turning away to gallop toward the bridge.

Saffron stood there, staring at the gates, hoping his friend would re-appear. Laughing and insisting it was only a joke. Of course he'd join them. He would apologize to Sionnach, there was nothing wrong. There was nothing wrong at all.

But only a light rain returned to shift the air, sprinkling the crown of Saffron's head. He didn't notice, until someone pulled the hood of his cloak over his hair, and he stiffly turned to find Cylvan gazing down at him. Looking as solemn, as lost as Saffron felt.

"Should we go?" he asked. Saffron bit down on his tongue, swallowing back his own swelling emotions, putting his arms around Cylvan and holding him close for as long as they had left. Until the gates would open, and they would emerge to be perceived by all of Alfidel again—and he couldn't any longer.

# 7

## THE ADDRESS

"I know you're not eager to go on a long trip, Maeve, but the new chill in the air is a little much, don't you think?" Cylvan asked as they made their way across the bridge to the first gatehouse, an unexpected attempt at lightening the mood considering his own demeanor after everything that morning. Ahead of them, the kings rode in their carriage far more decorated and impressive than the mac Delbaith one had been, and Saffron made sure to mentally note every single thing that was more luxurious about it for that reason alone. He adjusted his new cloak as he did, at the reminder of King Tross seated inside.

"Speak for yourself, storm-lord," Maeve argued back, adjusting her hood as a playful wind whistled past each of them so high on the bridge. "If anyone is the cause of the rain, it's you and your curse to always be unlucky."

"Nothing about the rain is unlucky. Some people prefer it to hot days, anyway, don't they Saffron?"

"Sure," Saffron answered without thinking. Perhaps Cylvan's attempts at keeping conversation light were actually only meant for Saffron's sake, so realizing Saffron was distracted by something else irked him. He leaned his horse a little closer to Boann, pinching at the bright-red fabric of Saffron's cloak.

"At least if it gets any worse, we won't have to worry about losing you in this, will we?" he asked, and Saffron huffed, tugging the fabric away in embarrassment. His face only went hotter when Cylvan added under his breath: "Though it's a suitable color for a witch of your stature, I suppose."

"Careful Cylvan, you wouldn't want to start any new rumors so close to recent news," Maeve added, smirking that time as she trotted up a little closer, too, sandwiching Saffron between her horse and Cylvan's. She, too, reached out to pinch at the fine fabric draped over his shoulders. "I wonder, do all rowan witches wear crimson, Lord Saffron?"

"It—it was a gift from King Tross!" Saffron insisted, but the two fey daemons continued to purr over him.

"Red suits him," Cylvan said. "Don't you think? It brings out the color in his cheeks, the green of his eyes..."

"It makes him so intimidating, like I would gladly follow him into the woods to see what he could give me."

"And what would you give to someone like me, Lord Saffron?" Cylvan asked, sliding a finger beneath Saffron's chin to pull it toward him. "Will you feed me wine while casting spells over my body?"

"Will you bathe in my blood while I beg to feel the edge of your knife again?" Maeve touched Saffron's hand on Boann's reins, drawing his attention back to her. "Or will I get drunk on herbs and incense, first?"

"Perhaps we'd perform another spell together on your whims, like once in that woodland henge," Cylvan said.

"S-stop!" Saffron finally snapped, face hot enough to practi cally melt. "That's enough!"

Both fey bothering him laughed, pulling back and allowing Saffron room to breathe. All he could do was put his hand to his chest, exhaling a long breath before meeting Sionnach's eyes that were turned back to him. He offered them a weak smile, and they offered one back, but said nothing.

Saffron wanted to ask if they were alright; he wanted to ask what Copper meant, with that comment about their mother—but instead, he just nudged Boann ahead, fleeing the sídhe harassing him in favor of trotting in line with his friend. Sionnach gave him another little smile, and Saffron nodded back.

He wouldn't ask about Copper's words, he wouldn't comment on how Sionnach's eyes were red and a little puffy, like they'd cried in the stables after Copper left. Instead, he asked if Sionnach had brought any textbooks to keep up with their readings despite Mairwen being closed, chuckling when Sionnach immediately cleared their throat and listed off every single tome they'd packed for exactly that purpose. A small moment of peace, a distraction, that time for his friend, he hoped.

THE CROWD AT THE MOUTH OF THE FIRST GATEHOUSE had grown, erupting once again into cries for an explanation, unending demands for answers, none caring that even the kings may not yet have them. Saoirse led at the front of the line, with Aodhán and a handful of additional palace guards riding in a perimeter around the carriages and horses. It kept hands from grabbing, but was unable to stop the abusive words thrown as easily as rocks. Most of them were directed at Cylvan, who remained perfectly upright and gazing straight ahead despite some of the things said. Calling him a beast, a wicked thing, the bringer of Alfidel's fall and calamity. The Night Prince come early, darkening his father's Day sooner than he was meant to. How it should have been him, not Asche; the humans should have taken him, and left the golden daurae in his place.

Saffron could only white-knuckle Boann's reins to keep from shouting back. To resist even turning his head, either toward the crowd or toward Cylvan. He had to pretend like there was nothing to see, nothing to hear, to keep whatever peace remained. There was no telling how even the smallest twitch in the wrong direction might be intentionally misconstrued in written gossip the following morning—a sentiment that only grew more incessant as they travelled through the heart of the city, where the people of Avren gathered to observe the kings' procession toward the train station.

The station platform was not much better, even with a handful of guards already dispatched ahead of the rest of the group to clear off a portion of the boarding platform so they would not be crowded upon arriving.

Leaving their horses with baggage attendants, the train was already on the tracks and waiting for them, delayed slightly for the arrival of the prince's travel party so they would be able to arrive and board without having to wait. The haste of it all made Saffron's heart race, doing his best to keep up as Saoirse hurried them onto the platform and toward the doors to the train cars. He held Sionnach's hand as they went so there was no chance of being separated. More than once, Saffron turned to look for Copper, as if his friend had only fallen behind—only to bite his lip in embarrassment and turn forward again.

Had the circumstances been any different, Saffron would have been thrilled. He would have been overwhelmed with excitement at the thought of traveling outside of Avren, to see more of Alfidel, to visit a new town and breathe in all the parts of the world he'd never gotten the chance to while working as a beantighe, or even during his few uneventful months at Mairwen. Ériu help him—the thought that the previous few months had been *uneventful* with his new perspective made the world turn under him.

At the last moment, he turned to look for Cylvan, but the prince had remained near the edge of the cordoned-off section of the platform, exchanging words with King Ailir as Tross stood slightly off to the side. The harmonious king was looking at Saffron, meeting his eyes and offering a reassuring smile, before motioning for him to board.

Saffron didn't want to go without Cylvan, but everyone else was waiting on him. Still holding Sionnach hand, he stepped into the train, but rather than turning toward the sleeping car where he'd been instructed, he paused. He turned back toward the exit, biting his lip, hesitating just a moment longer—before hurrying the opposite way, into the neighboring passenger car. Sionnach whispered his name in confusion, but followed even as Saffron let go of their hand.

Only a few heads in the passenger car turned as they hurried in, but the interest didn't last long before turning back toward the windows. As Saffron thought—Cylvan was approaching the growing crowd outside, adjusting the cuffs of his sleeves before flattening the front of his tunic. Preparing to address them like he'd mentioned in the garden. Saffron instinctively pulled the amethyst pendant from down his tunic, squeezing it. Hoping Cylvan felt it.

Moving carefully, not too quickly, Saffron found an empty seat just a few rows away from where Cylvan stood on the platform with his back to the train. The crowd in front of him gathered closer, and Saffron couldn't help but taste bile in the back of his throat when he realized the first two rows of bodies all clutched quills to paper, eager to write down every word spoken. Did they have to rush him onto the train that way? Saffron would have liked to be there, right behind him.

Kneeling on the seat, Saffron cracked the sashed window as Sionnach shuffled in behind him. Cylvan's voice wove into the train car as they settled, just loud enough for Saffron to hear.

*"The events that befell Avren, and all of Alfidel, at the hands of the arid terrorist during the Summer Games have not gone unmourned by your kings, myself, or any of Danu's people. After endless discussion held with my fathers, our most trusted oracles, and many people of Avren, I, myself, fear the growing threat of humans dabbling in illegal magic, and what exactly they intend to do with that magic. Manipulating the veil, wreaking havoc upon innocent high fey, disrupting the peace we have worked so hard to cultivate since the War of the Veil, there is no telling what may come next. Now, with news of a second veil event occurring in Erelaine, where high fey of all stature go to worship our gods with prayers of*

*peace, these are threats we can no longer address without the utmost priority."*

Saffron's heart had stopped beating.

*"As your crown prince and future king of Alfidel, today I depart to not only witness the aftermath of last night's attack on Erelaine, but to observe the needs of the people there and on her outskirts. I will see for myself exactly the damage caused, and how far the curse of ashenness has spread from it. I wish to look into the eyes of the people suddenly without their lifeline to our inherent opulence, to offer comfort and promises of the return of peace. Your kings' Day Court has not come to an end, as Danu provides. I will ensure Alfidel remains illuminated by the sun for as long as the goddess will allow it."*

Cylvan inhaled a long breath, like he felt every quill scratching away on paper. As if the nibs dug each word into his own skin.

*"As I tread the path of the gods in Erelaine, I will also seek the spiritual guidance of my dear Great-Grandmother, Queen Aryadna. While many things are different now than they were then, there is no denying the depth of her work and experience with the veil reaches farther than even our most practiced oracles. I plea with Danu to touch me with some of her wisdom with what we shall do next, to keep any more harm from befalling Alfidel, her people, and the veil itself. I know there is a peaceful resolution on the horizon for us, for both high fey and humans alike, and I will do everything in my power to draw that resolution swiftly. I ask that all of you pray for Alfidel in these uncertain hours.*

*"May Lugh watch over my passage and ensure it a safe one, both for myself and my companions. May Lugh watch over Daurae Asche and the other missing high fey where they may be, and may the veil take pity on their plight, returning them to our waiting arms soon..."*

Saffron's ears rang. He stared at the broadness of Cylvan's back, though no longer heard any words the prince spoke. Sionnach's hand had slipped into his at some point during the address, but Saffron hadn't noticed, until that moment when his skin flushed hot and he suddenly felt *everything*. Every trickle of breeze through the open window, the warmth of Sionnach's skin, how his stopped heart had come back to life and pounded relentlessly against the inside of his chest.

How could Cylvan say such things? How could Cylvan beseech Queen Proserpina for her wisdom, despite everything she did? Despite everything that still went on even after her death, the stains she left on Alfidel and its treatment of humans, not even those performing arid magic? Even if it was to put on an act, to plead for leniency from the people of Alfidel on his reputation, or their expectations of him, or as some sort of reassurance that their best interests were in his hands—how could he say such things, knowing he would next board the train to where Saffron was waiting for him?

It was no wonder he waited for Saffron to go before speaking. He'd intended on making that announcement using the veiled queen's name, before joining Saffron in their reserved cab to pretend like nothing had happened. Saffron wanted to believe Cylvan only spoke those words because they were handed to him at the last moment and he had no choice but to—but being unsure even of that was more upsetting than what had actually been shared.

Something dark in the corner of Saffron's eye caught his attention, and he turned to look, blood running cold at the sight of four black-veiled witchhunters hovering behind the line of the crowd, on the side where Cylvan stood with his back to them. Speaking amongst each another, one clutching the silver pendant of their work like something precious, like a protective totem. But that wasn't what paralyzed Saffron—it was the way one of them had their head tilted toward where he stood on the other side of the window.

Their face was hidden beneath the veil, but he knew. He could feel the knife of their eyes, looking him up and down, memorizing him. Reminding him how it felt to be incapacitated by yew branches, a silver coffin, to be thrown into a pit in the earth by hands wishing to bury him. To give him a rowan witch's death, as Queen Proserpina would have encouraged. Witchhunters had once tried to bury him, but failed. And those ones knew his face, just as Ryder did.

"Why don't we go to the sleeping car?" Sionnach asked, not having noticed the looming shadows in the corner of the platform. Or maybe they had, but chose not to acknowledge them for Saffron's sake. Saffron's ears just continued ringing.

Rising a little too quickly to his feet, he followed Sionnach out of the passenger car. They passed the door right as the four witchhunters on the platform stepped into the cab to join them, pausing to allow Sionnach and Saffron room to pass. Saffron didn't give them a second glance. If they knew who he was, they'd already recognized him. He wouldn't give them the second thrill of looking directly into his eyes.

8

-------

## THE TRAIN

The last four sleeping cars of the train had been reserved for Cylvan and his travel party, though they only needed two for everyone to have a place to stay. That left two empty cars between Saffron's friends and the witchhunters who boarded after them, at the very least—but even that didn't seem like far enough.

Had his mind not been overwhelmed by the sentiments shared by Cylvan with the crowd, followed by the knowledge of witchhunters there on the train with them, Saffron might have been able to appreciate the amenities extended. Like small apartments in their own right, clearly the most luxurious options reserved for the prince; the car at the very end was far fancier than even Saffron's dormitory, with a plush full-sized bed, washbasin, buffet of fresh fruits and wine, attached restroom, cushioned seats at the windows for sitting and watching the landscapes go by. There was even something strangely charming about the gold-foiled signs posted about indicating how their experience may differ due to the ashen state. Fruit would no longer remain perpetually chilled and fresh due to the loss of the charm on the silver tray; windows would no longer remain perpetually clean, and may carry residue from weather or other external factors as they traveled; the ice in their buckets of chilled wine would inevitably melt; passengers would be able to hear the clattering of the tracks beneath them, but earplugs would be provided upon request.

Maeve and Aodhán of all people were in Cylvan's assigned car helping themselves to the table of food when Sionnach and Saffron made their way back, Saoirse standing by the door with no care to stop either of them. She clearly had better things to worry about, looking restless as Cylvan was still on the platform addressing the crowd.

At her feet, Fiachra squirmed and screeched in her cage, flapping her wings and biting at the thin gold bars in demands to be released. Saffron hooked a finger through the top loop of the cage to carry her into Cylvan's cab, letting her out where she swooped over Aodhán's head before perching on the mantle and shaking herself out.

The prince joined them not much later—and the way he bypassed everyone else without a word to collapse straight into Saffron's arms, wrapping him in a tight embrace with a long exhale, made any resentment burning in Saffron's chest tighten, then loosen again. He circled his arms around Cylvan in return, closing his eyes and burying his face into his raven's soft hair. The natural scent of his skin and fine clothing made all of Saffron's nerves ebb in an instant. Even if tangled emotions still knotted in and out in his chest, he still found instant comfort in Cylvan's arms.

"There are witchhunters on the train," Cylvan said quietly, and Saffron nodded, squeezing him tighter.

"I know," he whispered. "I saw them." *One of them looked right at me.*

Before the anxiety could grip Saffron around the heart any tighter, Fiachra shot suddenly from the mantle like a drawn arrow, arching toward the ceiling and spreading her wings, then making sure to scrape her talons over Cylvan's silver horn before sweeping to Saffron's shoulder. Landing in a ruffle of feathers, she clacked her beak and flared her wings as Cylvan snapped at her to behave. Even Cylvan's raven Balor sqwaked from his cage in the corner, as if complaining how it wasn't fair that Fiachra would be let out while he remained imprisoned.

Any remaining tightness in the atmosphere popped with the rush of frenetic energy, allowing Saffron to breathe easily again. He cooed at his bird, petting under her beak as she purred and melted into hardly more than a well-mannered, winged housecat.

With the broken tension, Cylvan turned to regard the rest of the room, only then realizing his table of complimentary snacks was in the middle of being raided.

"Out! Everyone out!" He barked, throwing his hands up as Maeve and Aodhán scrambled out of reach with arms full of goodies. He shoved Sionnach out first, then attempted to do the same with Maeve, but the fey lady gave him a narrowed look of *don't you dare* that halted him in his tracks. Still, he waved her away. "Let me have at least one moment of peace alone!"

"But I was hoping for a chance to get to know your Alvényan lord a little better," Aodhán announced from the hallway, earning an eyeroll from Saoirse and a kick in the ass down the corridor, though they added as they went: "Come on, Lord Saffron, I promise it'll be a lot more fun than watching Cylvan brush his hair!"

"People think you brush your own hair?" Saffron asked, receiving a pained look from Cylvan. Even Saoirse hid a muffled little laugh before bowing and sliding the cabin door shut. Cylvan went straight to lock it in their wake, intent on maintaining the peace he'd demanded.

He swept a plate of fresh fruit from the table and collapsed onto the bed. Plucking a strawberry from the silver platter, he held it out in offering, and Saffron took a bite before sighing and sliding onto the soft blankets alongside him.

Cylvan reclined on his back with one arm bent behind his head, closing his eyes as Saffron was occupied with Fiachra hopping around them, first pecking at the adornments on the duvet before taking interest in the fruits on the tray. Using one of the cheese knives, Saffron cut away the peel from a bright yellow pear slice, offering it to the bird who bit off the end and munched away with squeaks of delight.

It would have been the perfect time to mention Cylvan's speech to all those people—but Saffron couldn't bring himself to utter the words. Not when Cylvan looked so comfortable on his back, eyes closed like it was the first moment he'd had to truly rest with any semblance of peace all morning. Obvious by the dark circles under his eyes, by the way his handsome mouth parted slightly as he relaxed.

Saffron found himself too enchanted by his person to find the strength to break the silence, even as bright amethyst eyes opened to gaze at him in return. Beneath them, the train rumbled, and a wave of goodbyes and wishes for safe-travels sounded off from the crowd on the platform. Saffron couldn't help but lift his head to look, but the windows facing the platform had the curtains securely drawn so no one would be able to look inside as they passed. Reassured, he glanced back to Cylvan again, finding the prince's eyes still on him.

"What is it?" he asked, embarrassed. "Stop looking at me."

"You can remove your glamour while you're in here," Cylvan answered, far from what Saffron expected. "No one will see."

Saffron smirked, offering another piece of pear to Fiachra as the bird nibbled on his fingers demandingly. " I don't know, your highness. I hear there are black-veiled wraiths aboard this train, who knows if they're in the walls watching us as we speak..."

"Don't joke about that," Cylvan chuckled, though it sounded a little miserable. He sat up, turning on his side and resting on his elbow. He regarded Saffron for another long moment, the tiniest smile curling the corner of his mouth. Reaching out, he gently brushed the back of his knuckles down Saffron's cheek. "I haven't seen you without it for a while."

Saffron's cheeks flushed at Cylvan's touch, turning his eyes down as he wasn't expecting how the rest of his body warmed at such a soft sensation. It had only been a week since the

Midsummer Games, but even long before that, it had been some time since he and Cylvan had been intimate in a way that felt safe, reassured, with as much freedom as they would have liked to indulge in one another. Between the chaos, the emotions, the grief. Saffron didn't realize exactly how much he'd missed Cylvan's touch until it reached for him with such gentleness again, hating how his heart twisted greedily with want for more.

Undoing the top few buttons of his tunic, he once again down to grasp at the pendant that resembled the color of Cylvan's eyes so perfectly. Pulling it over his head, the magic faded from the back of Saffron's hands, revealing the uneven, scarred skin of his fingers and knuckles. He couldn't imagine what his face must have looked like after so many days without sleeping, without eating as well as he should have, certain the comparison between the perfection of the glamour was enough to even make Cylvan reel. He never understood how Cylvan could stand it, to witness such a stark difference between the perfectly smooth, pretty features of the fey glamour, to those of a tired, plain human beantighe.

But hardly a moment passed before slender, pale fingers encompassed Saffron's scarred hand, holding it as if carved to perfectly fit within one another. Saffron let out a small breath, smiling at the perfect being gazing back at him.

"Are you nervous?" Cylvan asked.

"This actually isn't my first time," Saffron answered back in a whisper, and Cylvan threw his head back with a laugh.

"Oh, nasty thing. You know what I really mean."

Saffron laughed, too, finally relaxing on a bent elbow and offering Fiachra the last bit of pear before grabbing another to peel with the knife.

"I think I should be the one asking you that," he said, letting the words linger as he thought back once more to Cylvan's statement on the platform. He bit his lip, still debating whether it was worth to bring up, or if he should just let it go. Spinning and spinning and spinning, even Cylvan may have sensed it, growing dizzy enough to reach out and touch Saffron's cheek to draw him back again.

"What's on your mind?" he asked. Saffron grimaced, offering the next pear slice to Fiachra to buy a moment of time.

"It's... nothing," he finally decided in the moment. He didn't want to ask about it. He didn't want to think about it. He didn't want to come across like the nervous wreck he really was beneath the numbing exhaustion of so many sleepless nights. Instead—he just wanted to trust Cylvan, knowing nothing the prince ever did for the public to see was easy for him. God knew Cylvan had blindly trusted Saffron in countless ways before—once even at the cost of losing his own sibling. "Do you think we should be worried about the witchhunters on the train?" he asked instead. "I assume they're also going to Erelaine to inspect the damage, maybe..." He trailed off as Fiachra nibbled on the pear slice, nicking his finger with the sharp end of her beak. He barely felt it.

Perhaps Ryder really would still be there. After all, he had an association with the witchhunters, in one way or another. It would make sense for some to travel to Erelaine to see him, wouldn't it? Perhaps he'd even called for them. The thought made Saffron's stomach sink —but then his heart squeezed the other way. The thought of confronting Ryder scared him to death, but at the same time—there was a part of him bloodthirsty enough to use the opportunity to get what he wanted back from that man who'd stolen so much.

"I have nothing to be afraid of with such a powerful witch by my side," Cylvan answered with all the seriousness in the world, breaking through Saffron's distracting thoughts. Saffron rolled his eyes, but couldn't resist smiling. He plucked a strawberry from the fruit tray and offered it to his other favorite bird, letting Cylvan kiss his fingertips once they reached his lips. "Mmmh... Especially in my weakened, ashen state, what else could a withered sídhe lord ask for?"

"'*Withered,*'" Saffron laughed, leaning down to press his face into the side of Cylvan's neck, breathing in his skin, unable to resist combing fingers through the hair draping long over the blankets from the nape of his neck. Rich with verdant perfumes that brought images of ferns and oak trees swathed in golden chains, a welcome respite from the reality. "You're still a fearsome sídhe lord to me, your highness. Even if you can't summon the winds, for now."

"Or compel you to do whatever I please. For now."

"Oh, are you sure?" Saffron pulled back with a coy smile. "Here so many gossip pamphlets gave me the impression the all-powerful sìdhe fey could still compel those weaker than them, despite their ashen states. Perhaps you should try. Maybe I am enchantable, yet."

Cylvan's smile curled into something wicked. *"Kiss me,"* he said, honeyed and tempting, making goosebumps grow over Saffron's skin even without any real compelling magic to sweeten the command. He knew as well as Cylvan did, though, that the gossip pamphlets were technically right. His prince was only being a tease.

He leaned down to obey, sliding a hand beneath Cylvan's ear to cup his jaw and tangle fingers back in his hair. He kissed Cylvan softly at first, then with more intention, until Cylvan's hands found his face in return and pulled Saffron closer. Fruit on the tray skittered off and over the blankets, onto the floor as Saffron bent his leg over Cylvan's hips, straddling him, kissing him with all the hot breathlessness of someone who'd missed the taste as much as a person suffocating missed breath.

Cylvan's hand locked against the back of Saffron's head, holding him in place, pinning their mouths together as his opposite hand trailed up Saffron's hip, then slid beneath the bottom edge of his tunic. Warm fingers teased the skin of Saffron's stomach, making his breath catch slightly.

"I'm not afraid, either," Saffron exhaled against Cylvan's demanding mouth, as sharp nails slid further up under his tunic and grasped at his waist. He pressed his hips into Cylvan's, holding his prince's face like it would disappear if he didn't. "I'm not afraid of anything, if you're with me."

Cylvan lifted beneath him, hooking an arm around Saffron's middle and turning him onto his back. Pressing him into the pillows without ever pulling their mouths apart. His knee slid between Saffron's thighs, pinning him as Saffron rolled his hips in response.

"You're mine," he promised, his hungry mouth pulling away to travel down Saffron's jaw, to his throat, sucking and biting at the thin skin and leaving blossoms of heat in its wake. "You're mine, *you're mine,* Saffron—no one will ever lay a hand on you, ever again, for as long as I live. No matter what happens next—nothing, no one will ever take you from me."

"Cylvan?" Saffron whispered, sensing the slightest hitch in the prince's voice. But Cylvan's arms remained locked around him, holding him close, his face pressed flush into the side of Saffron's neck. No longer kissing him, breaths growing shaky. "Hey..."

"You have nothing to be afraid of, with me," Cylvan said in a breath. His hand cupping the back of Saffron's head flexed, before tangling fingers in Saffron's hair. "No one will take you away. I'll keep you safe, I'll protect you, for as long as I live—I won't lose you too, I won't—I won't—"

"Cylvan...!" Saffron attempted again, heart pounding in concern. He attempted to sit up, but Cylvan held him firmly against the bed. His muscles tightened all over, clinging to Saffron so unflinchingly it soon became hard to breathe—and all Saffron could do was wrap his arms around Cylvan in return. Cylvan, who began to tremble. Who held his breath before releasing all the emotion in a shaking exhale, like he desperately fought to keep it at bay.

Saffron pet the back of his head; he held Cylvan close, whispering reassurances, kissing his cheek, the side of his temple, all while stroking his hair. *I'm alright; you're alright; I'm right here, you haven't lost me. You're not going to lose me.*

Cylvan never sobbed, not like Saffron did—but the train was already well on its way, with its rhythmic clanging over the tracks, the steady swaying of its cars, before his raven finally fully relaxed again. All the while, whispering apologies, but never pulling away. Holding Saffron close, closer, never loosening his grasp. Like he truly believed it would take one only moment of loosening his embrace, and Saffron would sink through the floor. He would vanish into the ether, swallowed by the veil as easily as Asche had been. Saffron could only repeat the reassurances that everything was fine, he was right there, Cylvan would not lose him—and as he uttered them, again and again, hoping they offered his raven any peace at all, there was only a growing indignation in his chest. A sparking flame, a wrath in his bones that had burned ever since he first learned Ryder was not fully human like he'd always claimed.

All Saffron had wanted was a romantic summer, to enjoy at Cylvan's side—and even after all the destruction he caused, even long gone where Saffron couldn't find him, Ryder continued to steal even the smallest moments of bliss out from under Saffron's feet.

Saffron would never forgive him for it; and Ryder would know it for himself, soon enough.

9

—————

## THE STABLE

E relaine, the 'Mount of the Gods,' emerged from the landscape like a castle from the sea. Built up the steep slope of a mountain, not unlike that of Avren, it was visible from the windows of the train even with another hour to pass before they arrived at the station. As the city emerged from the horizon, Saffron sat in the quiet car, stomach full of food and rum after Cylvan finally caught his breath.

The prince himself sat in a chair opposite Saffron with a pile of missives on his lap, provided at the last moment in Avren and describing in better detail oracle observations from Erelaine's event. Every now and again he would share one or another with Saffron, but otherwise remained quiet. He occasionally glanced up, but only when other passengers walked by. There wasn't a single hint of his previous emotions anywhere in his demeanor, except the small flickers Saffron alone could recognize. At the very least, none of the witchhunters Saffron had watched board in Avren were anywhere to be seen, allowing him to relax.

He didn't realize Erelaine emerged at first, silently wondering why other passengers suddenly crowded against the window to look. Making the motion of beseeching a Day Court as they did, many praying in whispers that the stop at Erelaine's station would go without delay so they could continue their journey along. So they wouldn't have to linger too closely to the newest city cursed by *red witches*. Those words were what finally grabbed Saffron's attention, closing his book and getting to his feet.

The closer the train drew to the mount, the more detail every structure demonstrated, until even Saffron had his nose pressed to the glass like just another tourist. Most of the structures collected around the base of the mountain, built from marble and polished stone; painted with gold and inlaid with gems; draped with multi-color fabrics and hanging incense pots, glass lanterns, strings of bells, flowers that came fully into view as they approached.

Saffron had only a passing knowledge of the city, mostly that Erelaine was called the Mount of the Gods for a reason, though it wasn't nearly as sacred a place as Mag Meall or Ailinne further north. A city for high fey to visit when they wished to make offerings to household deities, family deities, any god who might listen to one particular plight or another. Even Luvon's family would make the journey at least once a year to pray to Cailleach Bhéara of the Winter Court, and any other number of names who might offer him a fruitful frostfruit crop and keep his wine from turning to vinegar. Saffron himself had never joined them on the trips, but he knew enough just from the stress of the annual preparations and complaints made once they returned back home.

Built up the height of the mountain, layered on top of one another like decor on a tiered cake, temples steadily grew taller, more ornate, some topped with gold shingles that reflected the light of the sunset, others swallowed by ancient trees as tall as the buildings themselves. Clustered all the way up to the peak, the altar-buildings grew more lavish, until at the very top, a single structure sat with a carved marble statue overlooking what Saffron could only imagine to be a view of all of Alfidel from the height.

That was when Cylvan sidled up behind him, resting against an elbow on the window, partially caging Saffron against it in order to see what had him so interested. As he did, the other passengers huddled nearby took one look before quietly scoffing and turning away. Cylvan followed them with his eyes, but said nothing.

"It's a tiered arrangement," he said, touching a sharp nail to the glass and drawing a slow spiral upward while explaining. "Smaller, more common deities—demigods, figures of myth, and so on—have their temples built on the lower tier, at the bottom. Niamh, Derdriu, Oisín, folks like those. Any fey, high or low, are allowed to pay respects to those as they please. The goat is most likely to have all of their satyr-gods located in that tier. Don't look at me like that—I didn't design it." His finger inched upward on the glass. "The middle tier venerates more powerful gods, particularly family gods to the sídhe. Such as Lugh, technically, though he's at the highest point just before the entrance to the upper tier. Generally, only sídhe and special guests are allowed entry there. The highest tier, of course, deifies the most important of Alvish gods—direct descendants of The Dagda, for example. Even Bríghde has her place."

"But Bríghde is a human goddess," Saffron whispered. "Isn't she?"

"Yes, but—still a child of The Dagda. You know, before the War of the Veil—even humans were allowed in the Mount of the Gods. I imagine rowan witches visited the uppermost tiers, too. The Dagda was considered a god of both human and fey, equally." He leaned closer, whispering just for Saffron to hear. "Myths say The Dagda even preferred humans over fey, which was why they gifted them with magic, then the ability to converse with the veil before ever offering the same to the rest of us."

"Oh," Saffron breathed, flushing a little bit, but unsure why. He just peeked over at Cylvan with a sheepish grin, and Cylvan smiled back like Saffron was something to eat.

"Maybe I'll toss you to The Dagda while we're here, just to see if they have something to say about it," he threatened under his breath, trailing his nail over the glass to indicate the temple at the very peak of the mount. "Perhaps they will be able to offer us some advice for our current predicament, hm?"

"I don't think I'm ready for that," Saffron gulped, and Cylvan laughed.

"You're right. We'll get our chance later, anyway, on our coronation day—the only time Erelaine opens The Dagda's temple for visitors. I wouldn't want to send you in alone, without me by your side to declare you mine—what if they try and take you for themself? I would have to go to war with a god. And once I defeated them, I would be a Night *God*, rather than just a prince... Can you imagine the headlines?."

"You'd defeat a god for me?"

"I'd flatten an entire pantheon for you with just the word, *my prince*."

Saffron flushed hotter, nudging him, but couldn't resist grinning. The other passengers keeping their distance had no idea exactly what sort of blasphemous, treasonous things their coming Night loved to whisper to his beantighe pet.


SAFFRON HAD DONE A DECENT ENOUGH JOB KEEPING HIS nerves under control from the moment they left the palace in Avren, even after overhearing the words Cylvan spoke to the people crowded on the platform, even knowing there were witchhunters somewhere on the same train where the landscape passed them by; but all of his tempered anxieties came rushing back within a few steps of disembarking the train onto Erelaine's platform. Illuminated by lantern light in the growing darkness of sunset, a throng of people fought to board the train and flee the city, not caring who they shoved or elbowed or shouted at. His heart jolted in his chest, halting his feet before he could claim more than a few steps, instantly intimidated by all the shouting and flying limbs. Sionnach tripped into him from behind, grappling for Saffron's shoulders to remain upright. But Saffron's ears rang too loudly to hear anything they said.

The platform was technically situated just outside the gates of the lower tier of the mount, though equally adorned with wreaths of flowers and bells, trinkets, flags that flapped in the wind and illuminated by rows of hanging lanterns in every color, matching more colorful lights on the other side of the gates, as if according to whose-ever altar one sought to worship at. The air was rich with every type of incense possible to burn—enough that the stench was more nauseating than inviting.

It was a place Saffron could tell had once swelled with opulence—but as he stood there, the once-sumptuous mount rang only with the shouts and cries of high fey attempting to leave. Made ashen by the veil event unleashed upon it just the night before—despite reportedly so small in its actual destruction that it had taken a search party to even find where it occurred. From where Saffron stood, he couldn't see any sign of the event ever happening—but that brought him no peace. He didn't want to think that Ryder could open the veil with those six banging knocks wide enough to swallow entire throngs of people—or so narrow that they would simply go unnoticed, except the ashen state left behind.

If Ryder was still there, for whatever reason—Saffron would find him. And watching as the four witchhunters left the train and made their way toward the front gates with the rest of the crowd—Saffron was certain, it wouldn't be very hard. Even if they told Ryder he was coming, Saffron would not let him get far.

*"My sister may likely be here as well,"* Taran's voice ghosted, making Saffron jump. *"To shill our family silver to those newly affected by the ashen state."*

Saffron scoffed under his breath. *How honorable of her. Do the mac Delbaiths anxiously await disasters like these in order to make money?*

*"They certainly don't mourn them."*

Saffron noticed Taran's choice of words, *'they'* rather than *'we'*. He wasn't sure how he felt about that.

*"Either way,"* Taran went on. *"I'll let you know if anything seems amiss."*

*How would you know?* Saffron thought back, before frowning and adding: *And why should I trust—*

*"Because you own me, remember?"* the wolf responded, bitterly, sarcastically. Saffron could imagine exactly how Taran's face would have twisted and sneered if spoken out loud. *"And because I don't want Cylvan getting hurt because you're not paying attention. Especially since Anysta already found her way into the palace once."*

Saffron glanced over his shoulder just as Cylvan emerged from the train, with Saoirse and Aodhán on his heels. An unexpected uproar of voices overtook the platform in an instant, reminding Saffron too much of the shouts heard as they passed through the crowd gathered outside the palace gatehouse. From those who clustered on the train platform in Avren. Cylvan's silver horn flashed in the lanternlight as he emerged, and even Taran's mood soured further.

*Do you think...?* Saffron started, unsure how to ask without sounding foolish. Unable to think as clearly as he wished with the sudden cacophony from the crowd. *Could the horn have an opulent ability that we should be worried about?*

*"I would not be surprised if it did,"* Taran answered. *"However —I also would not be surprised it if truly is just meant to help aid regrowth. My family is not known for playing such tricks, especially through their silver."*

Saffron wasn't sure if that reassured him, or made him more skeptical—but the ruminations of Taran and the witchhunters and everything else whisked away the moment Cylvan spotted where he stood, and made his way over.

"Come," he whispered, placing a cordial hand on the small of Saffron's back to lead him into the lingering crowd, many of whom held their quills and parchments. "Stay close, I fear what will be left if any of us fall into this sea of sharks."

Saffron grimaced, but did as he was told, walking close as Saoirse took the lead of the group and barked orders to *stay back* while approaching the crowd that called out insults and demands for Cylvan. The noise of the throng mixed with the shrieking of the train's whistle, the groan of the steam engine as the metal beast shuddered on the tracks. It conglomerated with the thick, sticky cloud of incense in the air that didn't help Saffron's growing headache, nor how, despite their best attempts at parting the crowd, they were still constantly knocked this way and that, more than once almost entirely off their feet as more and more demands were made, growing in vitriol as Cylvan bowed his head and hurried through the wave rather than stopping to address them like he had in Avren.

*"Prince Cylvan, Prince Cylvan!"*

*"Have you come to bear witness! Have you come to plead to Queen Morrigan for deliverance!"*

Saffron turned his head, but Cylvan's hand on his back drew him forward again.

*"You've brought this with your Night Court, Seelie Prince!"*

Saoirse shoved someone away ahead of them, who'd lunged forward, red-faced and spitting curses. In their hand, they clutched a fistful of a printed gossip column from that morning.

*"May Queen Morrigan swallow you whole, sluagh!"* They screeched. *"Do not bring your cú sídhe from her academy to the ruins of her temple, beast!"*

*"Get gone, seelie sluagh! Do not bring your curse upon us!"*

*"Stay clear of our gods, else you damn us all!"*

*"Go! Be gone!"*

Something whistled through the air—then crashed against the side of Cylvan's head, sending glass and wine raining down over him and Saffron by his side. On instinct, Cylvan threw his arm up over Saffron, covering him with the side of his cloak and pulling him closer as Saffron nearly lost his footing in shock. Aodhán rushed the undulating crowd that time, drawing their sword as Saoirse did the same at the head of their group, compelling the unruly fey back with threats of each blade.

Gazing up through the bend of Cylvan's arm, Saffron could see the prince's face—with his jaw clenched, and eyes wide. Like even he hadn't anticipated such a violent reaction to his arrival; all the while clinging to Saffron so tightly, he would surely leave bruises on Saffron's ribs.

Arriving at the carriage house, the stablemaster waved the group inside before closing the door behind them, effectively cutting off the rush of people who attempted to follow. Fists slammed against the wooden doors, faces appearing in the glass windows, shouting and demanding Cylvan witness them and their grievances. Every time Cylvan turned to look, pale and unsure what to do, Saffron felt the instinct to reach up and touch his face. Drawing him back, meeting his eyes. There was nothing for him to say. And if he went out there to address them—Saffron didn't know what he would do. The sight of Cylvan's hair soaking wet and stinking of wine, the small cuts on his forehead from where the glass nicked him, was enough to make Saffron want to tear open the veil and swallow the crowd on his own. If they were given a chance to do something worse—Saffron might swallow Alfidel entirely.

"Stay with me," Saffron whispered instead, voice tight as Cylvan's face remained turned toward him, but his anxious eyes continued to flash in the direction of the doors, the windows. "With me, Cylvan..."

Saoirse worked with the stablemaster to organize getting their horses off the train and into the paddocks. Aodhán and Maeve positioned themselves near the doors that rattled against the beam holding them closed, just in case. Even Maeve had her sword drawn, holding it like she was prepared to skewer anyone who pushed through.

"Just ignore them, don't listen," Saffron continued, touching Cylvan's face once more before gently picking small shards of glass from his dark, wet hair. "I need you more than they do."

"Right..." Cylvan breathed, closing his eyes and furrowing his brows for a moment. "I'm here, Saffron."

The stablemaster barked at his beantighe to take everyone to the back office where they could sit in peace, offering Cylvan his apologies for the people's behavior as they passed. Cylvan just lifted a hand with a polite smile as the fey man insisted the excitement would die down as soon as the last train left for the night, after which they should be able to move safely to their lodgings in the city.

All the while, Saffron just kept his arm wrapped through Cylvan's, not caring if it looked too intimate. He couldn't get the shouted words out of his head, he couldn't stop seeing the look on Cylvan's face when the prince's instincts begged him to turn and defend himself against the slander being thrown. As if he thought another address would cure the ire storming in a tempest on the other side of the door. Worse than anything that had ever thundered in Avren. Cylvan must have sensed Saffron's own urge to shove through the doors and fight anyone who shouted such terrible things, because he kept a firm grasp around his waist in return. A silent plea to stay with him, even if everything else barked at him to get up and do *something*.

Settling into the cramped stable office, the master's beantighe was eager to give Cylvan and the others anything they wanted, offering hot tea and whatever snacks they had on hand—which weren't many, but she seemed equally willing to run to the nearby shop to buy anything they requested. It wasn't hard to guess why when, every time Cylvan politely smiled and accepted her offerings, she blushed bright red and hot enough to practically change the temperature of the room. It was almost enough to mask the bruising around her eye, the puffiness of her cheek. Even her arms were bruised, hands bandaged as if her knuckles had been lashed. Saffron shifted uncomfortably where he sat, trying not to stare as he was certain everyone else noticed as well.

"What's your name?" Saffron asked instead as she poured cups of tea for them all, seated in a circle around the makeshift table. Cramped in close enough that Maeve and Aodhán constantly elbowed one another, and Sionnach flinched when Saoirse accidentally stepped on their tail. The beantighe girl's eyes flashed to Cylvan, then back again before meekly answering:

"My name is Moth, my lord."

"That's a pretty name," Saffron said with a smile. "Is the stablemaster your patron fey?"

"Yes, my lord."

"How long have you been a beantighe for him?" Cylvan asked next, while sipping at his tea.

"Oh—only a few months. Before this, I worked for another family in Avren."

Saffron had to resist asking if Ryder's business in Avren had anything to do with Moth being sent away. The temptation was so great, he had to physically bite down on his tongue to keep it at bay. Instead, he found something else to take its place: "Moth, did you happen to see what happened last night?"

"Oh!" she exclaimed, jolting back and nearly burning herself with the pot. Even Cylvan tensed next to Saffron, his hand moving on instinct to block any boiling water from splashing him. "No, no! I can't—I'm not allowed to share anything I might overhear, of course. And beantighes aren't allowed past the gates except when running errands for their patrons, and the stablemaster has never asked me for anything like that..." she trailed off, glancing up at Cylvan again, before looking away. Like every one of her instincts fought to obey her master, while also wishing to appease the prince. "Erm, but... I suppose... in the middle of the night, I woke up to this this tremendous sound. Like drum beats, one after another. Then the earth shook, and another sound like the train had gone off its tracks. At first I thought that was exactly what had happened, except there were no trains expected until morning."

"It happened in the middle of the night?" Cylvan asked, despite already knowing. Clearly wishing to encourage her. "Do you know what time?"

"I-I'm not positive," she stammered as soon as Cylvan addressed her. "A little after midnight, maybe? I had just put the horses down and finished my other chores. I was already asleep when the drumming started, so I can't be more specific..."

"The gossip papers say it occurred in The Morrígan's Temple," Sionnach spoke up from the other side of the table, and Moth turned to look at them. "Where is that, in relation to here? Do you know?"

"I don't," Moth said with a nervous smile. "I apologize."

"Was it particularly crowded yesterday? With people visiting the temples," Saffron went on. "Erm—even just from what you could see from here."

"The stables were all full, so I assume so." She nodded. "The fey were eager to leave first thing this morning, that's for certain."

Saffron's eyes trailed over the beantighe's bruises again, but Cylvan spoke first: "Were they rough with you, in their panic?"

No one expected him to even be so straightforward, even Saffron, who looked at the prince in surprise. Not realizing Cylvan had even noticed them, as it was more of a beantighe instinct of his own. Moth herself stared at him like she thought she'd only imagined it, before closing and opening her mouth with stammering reassurances that everything was fine, there was nothing wrong, then apologizing if her appearance was off-putting. Cylvan only put his hand up with a polite smile.

"I did not mean to make you uncomfortable," he said. "I was only wondering, though..." his voice went low, holding Moth's eyes with an intense look Saffron was far too familiar with. "If you find your time here to be *unpleasant*, you should know you can always send a bird to the palace. Patrons are not allowed to abuse their servants—but the servants have to be the one to report it."

Moth stared at him. All the color in her face had drained, as if once again wondering whether or not she'd only imagined that. Saffron, meanwhile, slid his hand under the table to spread over Cylvan's thigh in acknowledgement. A silent thank you, in a way. He hadn't been expecting to hear anything like that, either, but—it made his heart race.

"Your tea has been a welcome comfort, Moth. I will be sure to remember it," Cylvan added lastly. The girl blushed hot all over again. She blabbered, stammered, then raced off to brew more. Immediately, Maeve teased Cylvan over his clear preference for cute little humans, to which Cylvan sneered and teased her right back. Back and forth, across the table, Saffron's companions chuckled and chatted like everything had finally settled back to normal again—but Saffron only sipped at his own tea in silence. The surface twitched with his unsteady hand. It wasn't anxiety that buzzed in his muscles—but returning anticipation.

WHEN THE CROWD STILL HAD NOT DISSIPATED BY THE time the last train left the station, Saoirse decided it best to remain where they were in the stablehouse. There was a single bed that belonged to the stablemaster to the side of the office, which would be reserved for the prince, and the rest of the traveling party would have to make do elsewhere for the time being. There was hardly an expression not draped in annoyance once the head guard made the call, but no one outright complained. Especially as shouts continued calling through the doors.

Saffron particularly didn't mind finding the stall where Boann lazily munched on straw, throwing down his cloak and curling up on the ground. Imagining the look on Tross' face if he knew exactly how Saffron used his beautiful cloak as a bedroll; knowing at the same time, it was surely crafted well enough that a little straw dust wouldn't hurt.

It reminded him of sleeping in the loft of the barn in Beantighe Village, or piling up old blankets and pillows in the attic while resting his head on Hollow's bare chest after an hour of stolen intimacy. Even Fiachra had no complaints, unsurprising considering her nest at Mairwen consisted of one of Copper's school blazers and other stolen trinkets from every corner of campus. She even kept herself busy chasing field mice up and down the walkway on the other side of the stalls while Saffron cobbled the little bed together for himself. Never once swooping over them like a proper hunter, insisting on chasing on foot with the sound of her talons on the wood intermingling with the crunching of horses.

Eventually, even the pounding on the front doors ebbed into silence, though Saffron's nerves told him it didn't mean the people had gone. The thick smell of incense never ceased, the distant sound of bells and flags in the wind never died out, either, as if the gods forced a constant breeze in order to revel in their offerings. Perhaps there was a reason Erelaine closed its gates once the sun went down—that was the period when the gods emerged from the mounds to inspect the offerings made during the day. To dole out blessings to any patrons who had come to give gifts and beg on their knees.

"Remind you of home?" Cylvan's ghostly voice emerged from the shadows, making Saffron lift his head in surprise. Squinting through the darkness, he smiled at the faint silhouette of a leanan sídhe hovering at the gate of Boann's stall, clearly having snuck away from his chaperoned cot.

"A little bit," Saffron answered in a whisper, not wanting to alert anyone else. "It's missing something, though."

"Hmm, let me guess," Cylvan smiled, unlatching the gate and inviting himself inside, just as Fiachra clattered by on the walkway.

As Cylvan knelt to the stable floor, Saffron lifted a corner of his cloak, inviting the prince to crawl in alongside him. He moved over so Cylvan had somewhere to lay his head, though the pillow wasn't any more than a pile of loose straw. Cylvan didn't complain, still smiling as he slid close and wrapped his arms around Saffron beneath the makeshift blanket.

"Are you alright?" Cylvan asked under his breath.

"I meant to ask you that, first," Saffron answered, pinching a piece of Cylvan's hair still damp from rinsing the wine out. "Does your head feel alright?"

"I'm alright," he said, bowing his head to demonstrate. "I think it bounced off my horn rather than my skull. You think my head is hard enough to break glass?"

"Yes, actually."

Cylvan feigned insult, making Saffron laugh. He scooted closer, until their chests and stomachs and legs pressed together, pulling Cylvan down to kiss him on the forehead.

"Those things you said to Moth, earlier—that was kind of you."

Cylvan was quiet a moment, chin tucked into the curve of Saffron's shoulder. He pressed a soft kiss to the side of Saffron's neck.

"It reminds me of you, when I see beantighes like that," he whispered. "At least—it reminds me of what I should be looking for, when I interact with beantighes. That I should be aware of what they show me, even if they can't speak it. I hate that I cannot do anything unless she herself requests an investigation, but I couldn't stop myself from sharing at least that much..."

"Why can't you?" Saffron whispered. He brushed fingers through Cylvan's hair, picking out pieces of loose straw. "I wonder if a stern implication to the stablemaster might change his behavior."

"A stern implication from the visiting Night Prince—"

"From the future king," Saffron corrected softly. Cylvan considered that, before exhaling a sigh that made goosebumps grow over Saffron's skin.

"Perhaps you're right," he whispered. "I'll speak to the stablemaster in the morning, before we leave for the city gates."

Saffron continued brushing fingers through Cylvan's hair as silence, darkness enveloped them. Fiachra continued hunting up and down the walkway; a few stalls over, Maeve and Sionnach were whispering to one another about the best way to layer a sleeping cushion over a bed of straw, while Aodhán smoked something aromatic by the far window.

"I'm sorry," Saffron whispered, though not sure exactly what for. Cylvan didn't ask, just closed his eyes and buried his face further into the side of Saffron's neck. Breathing him in.

"Thank you," he responded in the same way—not clear

exactly what for. Saffron didn't ask, just smiled to himself. He held his arms protectively around his raven, keeping him right where he was. Warm, safe, comfortable, even when sleeping on straw.

SAFFRON HELD CYLVAN CLOSE WHILE THEY SLEPT. Closer than he'd been able practically since the Midsummer Games, nearly having had it again while curled up on the train, but still not as entangled as he craved to be. Like they used to. Perhaps their souls inched slightly nearer than even the day before, but Saffron could still feel it. That distance Cylvan kept himself at, whether he knew it or not. A distance Saffron felt like a valley as deep as the one that separated the royal palace from the rest of Avren—except there was no ribbon-thin bridge to carry Saffron to where Cylvan hovered out of reach.

The prince had hidden it away so well, even Saffron couldn't find it. He'd moved all the ways anyone had ever been able to cross into him—so desperate to protect himself, he'd accidentally cut Saffron off as well. Whether he knew it or not. Compelled by the constant vitriol and insults thrown whenever he passed in public, even bottles of wine thrown in hatred. Saffron had always known the people had a distrust of Cylvan, but never to such an extent—never to the point of needing an armored guard to guide him through a crowd, else they tear him apart limb from limb.

And while Cylvan tried to act like it didn't bother him, he was used to it, it was simply part of his role as the crown prince—Saffron saw every tiny shift in his expression. The shared anger, vitriol, resentment. Even as they laid there in the straw over his fine cloak, wrapped in each others' arms, Saffron could sense every time his raven's heart beat a little out of rhythm. Every time his breaths changed. He could sense when something was off about his prince, no matter the distance, no matter how small, and Cylvan was left hardly functioning in his body.

But Saffron would never say that. Saffron would never let

Cylvan know. He would just hold him, all of his pieces, keeping him together as best he could, in hopes it was enough to maintain his shape. Saffron only needed to find Ryder. To find Asche. To bring the daurae back, and all of Cylvan's misplaced pieces would click right back into place. Just like he'd once faced the wolf in Danann House, as his prince crumbled into pieces in front of him —Saffron only needed to face the new beast that tormented them.

His arms tightened around Cylvan at the thought. His heart thumped steadily. He hoped Cylvan could hear it. Even in his dreams, he hoped Cylvan could hear it. Saffron was there, he was close, holding him. Prepared to do whatever it took to keep his raven's own internal Night at bay.

Saffron wouldn't let Cylvan lose anything else.

## 10

### ERELAINE

The mass of the crowd had dissipated by morning, though a handful of straggling bodies remained outside the stable doors holding quills and pads of paper. Wishing to be the first ones to see how Prince Cylvan fared sleeping with animals in pens. Saffron could already imagine the headlines without having to read them, deciding perhaps gossip writers should try to be a little more creative.

Getting dressed in the stables was no issue for Saffron—he was used to it—which meant he had plenty of stamina to assist the others while they struggled to keep straw out of their hair, off their expensive clothing, even Maeve nearly having a silent meltdown as her horse continually attempted to munch on her hair for breakfast.

Moth was eager to show the group a way out the back where far fewer predatory eyes would know to look. Cylvan offered her a slight bow as they went, and she blushed bright red in the doorway, petrified, the entire time they left after. Not knowing that Cylvan had just finished requesting the stablemaster treat his servant better, in the same terrifyingly calm way he and King Tross had spoken to the High Keeper of Tapestries. Saffron hoped things got better for the girl thanks to it.

From what Moth made Saffron believe about the sanctity of Erelaine's gates, he was admittedly impressed by the height of the stone archway that opened its wide mouth over the road, where Saffron and the others passed through on foot. Decorated with the same multi-colored lamps, flowers and flags, and Old Alvish writing he didn't have a chance to read and ask about. *Blessed be the gods*, or something, he was sure.

What he didn't expect, however, was the sudden rush of noise and offerings—seemingly made to *them*, right on the other side. First came a fey that jangled with every movement, shoving an offering bowl into his chest and requesting—demanding—a token of appreciation for the safe arrival of him and his party; flower crowns were tossed onto their heads from the opposite direction, someone else appearing to ask if they needed a guide through the temples, expecting payment up front with hands outstretched; handfuls of candy, pieces of bread, beaded necklaces were tucked into their hands as 'first offerings' to the gods as it appeared they hadn't brought any of their own. One pair of hands even yanked Fiachra off Saffron's shoulder to draw a half flower on her pale forehead—surprised when Saffron shouted at them and physically shoved them to the ground while stealing his bird back. In the chaos he turned and pitched the owl into the sky, where she rolled over herself before taking wing and arching into the clouds.

Aodhán was the one to sweep Saffron forward again, hooking an arm around his back and forcing him through the rabble. They barked at anyone else who attempted to shove objects into Saffron's hands, to drape him in flowers or spray him with perfumes, even lashing out when one person lost their balance against them and yanked Saffron's tunic open.

Had there not been other tourists filing in behind them through the archway gates, Saffron might have thought all the excitement to be over Cylvan's arrival specifically—but it appeared to be a common greeting from the people of Erelaine. Perhaps even more desperate than usual, considering how many of their previous patrons had fled for the train the night prior, leaving the city essentially abandoned.

"There is a reason no one described Erelaine to be a particularly *spiritual* place," Cylvan said with a wry smile, as they made it through the initial mass of people. Saffron knew how disheveled he must have looked with how Cylvan chuckled, then approached to help fix the collar of his tunic pulled open, the mess of his once-nicely-combed hair.

"I suddenly understand how worms caught between two birds feel," Saffron grumbled, stepping back from Cylvan to scramble fingers through his hair and fully dislodge all sorts of confetti faster than Cylvan could pick them out one-by-one. Fiachra lighted down on his shoulder again once he straightened back up, looking equally irritated to have been man-handled in such a way.

"At the very least, it appears they still don't allow reporters through the gates," Cylvan sighed, putting an arm around Saffron's shoulder to try and reinvigorate him. It helped, for the briefest of moments—until Saffron noticed a familiar carriage tucked off to the side of the road, donning the mac Delbaith crest. In front, someone was already there conversing with visiting fey about an array of silver for sale on the table in the front of them. Cylvan noticed Saffron looking, nudging him back to look ahead. "Don't mind them," he breathed. "They won't bother us. Just taking advantage of an opportunity, like everyone else."

"Erelaine used to have a better reputation," Maeve added from behind, her tone equally as annoyed as Saffron felt. Further emphasized by how she ripped fingers through her messy braid in agitation, plaits littered with more small flowers and strings of beads stuffed inside. Petals and bells and polished gems tumbled to the ground as she undid the strands, then stepped right over them again while re-braiding. "A wonder so many willingly travel in every day just to pretend to serve one god or another. While folk dressed as priestesses trick them out of their money."

"Are all the temples going to feel like that?" Saffron asked wearily, as Cylvan pulled him into his side and turned to continue up the road.

"The *really* emphatic types tend to stick to the front gates," he reassured, to Saffron's relief. "There *are* real temple-keepers who live and work here full-time, too. You'll be able to tell them from the grifters easy enough, once we make it past these small-time gods on the lower tier."

"'Small-time'..." Saffron repeated, glancing at the temples on either side of them as they made their way up the road. Once free of the cacophony, able to breathe and think clearly again, Saffron was able to relax and fully regard what was in front of him. Altars lined both sides of the street, flooding his senses with the sounds of bells or other god-specific instruments; different kinds of incense and scented candles burned depending on who the offering was meant for; other infrequent visitors to Erelaine stopped in front of one altar or another, making an offering of something from their pocket or pulling a stick of incense from the hanging bowl to breathe in the smoke then whisper something for only the individual god to hear.

*"I'll let you know if I sense that man nearby,"* Taran ghosted in the back of Saffron's mind. Perhaps sensing his perpetual, low-burning anxiety, witnessing how Saffron's eyes constantly flicked back and forth around the street so restlessly it made him dizzy. Gulping back the nerves, he tried to stay in the moment. He didn't want Cylvan, or anyone else for that matter, to notice how anxious he was and begin to feel the same. More than they already did.

"Is it usually this quiet?" Saffron asked, knowing how ironic it was to ask after what they'd just passed through. But once the initial frenzied crowd was gone down the street—the atmosphere was peaceful. Relaxed, respectful. Other pedestrians spoke in soft tones, barely raising their voices even to call out to one another. Even Saoirse ahead of them kept one gloved hand on the grip of her sword so it wouldn't clatter so loudly on her belt.

"You saw how many people fled last night," Cylvan said under his breath. "I imagine fewer have opted to come and visit, all things considered. The ones who have may be here out of curiosity more than actual intention for prayer."

Saffron glanced at the nearest tourist couple as he thought about it, frowning when they were definitely watching Cylvan's party pass by. Whispering to one another. Despite what Cylvan said about reporters prohibited from entering, too—one of them undeniably had a pad of parchment in one hand, a quill in the other.

He had to constantly remind himself they were in Erelaine for a real reason, and he should have been more on his guard considering that reason—but Saffron couldn't help losing himself in every altar they passed, no matter how small. Sometimes he recognized the names of the deities from the myths he loved so much, sometimes they were strangers that Cylvan was more than happy to explain. Some, he was surprised to learn, were even appropriated from human myths, like the temple to a goddess called *Athena* and another to *Odin*. It made Saffron wonder if there were any altars to the likes of Ériu, like there was apparently to Bríghde, both being generally worshipped by human beantighes.

"Even Avren had an altar to Ériu," Saffron muttered in disappointment while sipping wine from a shallow dish at the temple of a god called *Sucellos*. "Even if it wasn't very well taken care of."

"When I'm king, I'll build an altar to Ériu in every town," Cylvan said, making Saffron roll his eyes.

When he spotted a little altar for Niamh further up the road, Saffron couldn't help but step to it as well, followed by Cylvan who barely let Saffron out of reach for a moment. Saoirse and Aodhán paused on the road with them, though Maeve and Sionnach politely continued on their way. Curious to seek out altars of their own, while there was a chance.

"You mentioned Niamh on the train, but I never expected her to be considered a *goddess,*" Saffron said, appreciating the tokens on display for her. Golden threads woven with bells, bowls of sea water, flowers and shimmering pieces of polished mirrors dangling from strings between the two marble stone columns. The priestess was clearly too busy behind the tent to tell him anything else, but luckily, the Prince of Alfidel was the best informant Saffron could ask for.

"Outside of Alfidel, she isn't," Cylvan said, reaching down to pluck two mirrors tied together with a string, letting them dangle from the hook of one of his nails. "But the fey love deifying all beings of myth. Can you guess what she represents?"

Saffron gazed over the minor altar again, before flicking one of the mirrors hanging from Cylvan's finger and watching it spin.

"Beauty?"

"Hmm, almost," Cylvan smiled. "Think about her story, beantighe. I know you have it memorized by now."

Saffron frowned, watching the mirror pieces spin before swaying to a halt.

"Love."

"That's it," Cylvan smiled, taking Saffron's hand and tucking both mirror pieces into his palm, closing his fingers over them. "*Eternal* love, to be specific. She blesses couples with shared protection, so one might never be without the other. They say mirrors touched by her grace allow you to always see your beloved in the reflection, even when apart."

Saffron's cheeks flushed, peeking at the two mirrors in his hand, but seeing only himself looking back.

"A trick of Erelaine," he said with a sigh, remembering what Maeve said. Cylvan just tucked his fingers closed again.

"Who knows. Perhaps you only need to win her favor."

"Or perhaps it's the ashen state."

"Bold of you, to assume something as simple as an ashen state could keep Lady Niamh from charming these little trinkets to bless two eternal lovers."

Saffron rolled his eyes, tucking the mirrors into his pocket—only to jump when someone wearing priestess garb barked at him to put them back. Cylvan gasped, dramatically accusing Saffron of being a thief, laughing loudly as Saffron scrambled to toss the mirrors back on the table and bow to the priestess in apology. He punched Cylvan in the gut and shoved him back down the road, face bright red as Cylvan howled in amusement.

Meeting back up with Sionnach and Maeve before passing into the upper tier of the gods, Saffron was in the middle of rambling on and on about the altars he and Cylvan had passed by and the random gods he'd recognized—when Maeve suddenly put out a hand, stopping him.

"You have to be shitting me," she muttered. Saffron petrified, turning slowly, afraid of what he'd find—but melted in an instant at the sight of red hair visible a ways down the unoccupied street. Clearly attempting to blend in at one of the altars, despite being one of only five people loitering around.

"Is that...?" Sionnach asked, squinting.

"Copper!" Saffron gasped, shoving Cylvan out of his way and hurrying into the street. He didn't have to move much closer to know for sure, especially once Copper's golden-brown eyes met his, and the fox-lord grinned ear-to-ear.

"Oh, Lord Saffron!" He exclaimed. "What a coincidence! Was it *Erelaine* you said you were visiting? Huh, I could have *sworn* it was Morlaín..."

Saffron hugged him, which seemed to catch Copper off guard, before laughing and hugging him back. Like he wasn't sure what kind of reaction he would get upon showing himself. The fact he ever worried Saffron wouldn't be thrilled only made Saffron hug him tighter—even if Copper really was the biggest idiot he knew.

"How ironic..." he went on, like he'd spent all morning scripting exactly how it would go when they *accidentally* crossed paths. "Here I just wanted to get away from Avren, thought I might visit some of the ol' family gods and pray for good favor... huh... Hey, where are you guys staying? I'm still looking for an inn that has a room open... Oh, good morning, your highness, funny running into you here—"

"What do you think you're doing?" Cylvan asked as he approached. "Do you think I'm some kind of idiot?"

"Because of something right now, or in general?"

"You followed us here?" Sionnach asked, eyes narrowed.

"What? Of course not—like I was just saying to Saffron, I totally misunderstood what exactly you all were doing—"

"Copper, just—*shut up,*" Saffron groaned, squeezing his friend one more time. "I'm glad you're here."

"Well—it's not for any of you, of course," Copper reiterated, wrapping his arms around Saffron again and squeezing until Saffron wheezed. "Definitely not for any kind of royal mission or whatever, either... Definitely on my own volition, by my own choice... I'm not here to help with whatever King Ailir asked for, so don't go telling anyone—"

"God—*shut up!*" Cylvan hissed, grappling for one of Copper's hidden ears and yanking on it. "You're goddamn insufferable! Why does everything have to be so godsdamned dramatic with you!"

"Speak for yourself, dragon prince," Copper argued, bumping Saffron away to accost Cylvan instead, throwing him in a head-lock until they were fighting in the middle of the street. Saoirse was the one to clear her throat, while Aodhán just hissed at Cylvan for letting Copper overpower him so easily.

Releasing Cylvan in a flurry of curses and rumpling Cylvan's clothing, Copper pushed hair from his eyes and let out a casual sigh.

"Well, since I ran into you all... might as well spend the afternoon together too, huh? Have you had a chance to check out the event site yet? I've been keeping my eye out for anything suspicious, you know... nothing to report, for now. They've got some great food in the upper tiers, though, Saffron, you're gonna love it. I assume the prince is paying."

"Are you sure you can stomach a meal afford by the crown?"

Cylvan sneered, grabbing Saffron's arm and yanking him close, like they were fighting over a toy. Saffron swallowed back a laugh.

"Aren't all meals afforded by the crown? Seeing as you all oversee imports into Alfidel, and... whatnot..." Copper attempted, clearly overwhelmed by his own uncertainty as the insult petered off. Cylvan just stared at him like he'd grown a second head, as even Copper shifted uncomfortably on his feet before clearing his throat. "I'll eat whatever you wanna give me, yeah. Used all my money on the train ticket, anyway."

"Useless," Cylvan muttered, turning with a whip of his hair and furl of his cloak. "Come, Lord Saffron, we have more temples to see this way... Let us see what's waiting for us in the second tier, as obliged by the *Primary King of Alfidel, Ailir dé Tuatha—*"

"Alright, don't be a dick about it," Copper muttered, nudging his toe into the pit of Cylvan's knee and almost making Cylvan trip. Had Saffron not burst out laughing and pulled Cylvan forward again, it would have definitely resulted in more fist-fighting on the cobblestones.

COMMISSIONING A WAGON TO TAKE THEM TO THE higher tiers of the mount, and long before they arrived at the site of the veil event—Saffron felt it. The words in his mouth, in the middle of chatting idly with Sionnach, dried up into a rasp as his throat tightened. His blood buzzed, skin flushing hot, then cold, as he tasted iron at the back of his throat.

Turning to look, the number of pedestrians in that area of the city had grown compared to the lower temples, likely due to what Cylvan had said about curiosity around what had happened—but even with the added activity, Saffron noticed the fruits first. The smallest little bulbs of pink fairy fruits spawning from cracks in the street, though scattered figures with shovels and netted bags on their hips were in the process of hurriedly scooping the sparkling plants up to toss them out before they could mature.

The only thing to possibly make Saffron's already-buzzing

blood boil was the sight of silver cuffs and veils on those working. Realizing right away, they were beantighes who scraped the berries away. Beantighes, seemingly allowed into the city just for the special occasion of cleaning up after Ryder's most recent mess. Saffron wondered if Ryder was aware—but knew, even if he was, he wouldn't care.

Saffron also knew without having to ask—the cuffs they wore were opulent. It was obvious by their shape, the ornate designs embellishing them, not to mention how they'd passed a mac Delbaith carriage on their way in. Sellers of mac Delbaith silver had already arrived, had already distributed accessories for control long before setting up their stall at the mouth of the city. He thought he might be sick; he thought he might not be able to resist the urge to set fire to the carriage on their way out again.

*"They're fireproof,"* Taran informed him lazily, and Saffron mentally cursed him back into his cage.

Hardly a single part of him wanted to get too close to The Morrígan's temple ruined by Ryder's actions—but Saffron also knew he had no choice. Maybe more pointedly, he knew *Cylvan* had no choice. Considering it was his duty to walk the site and observe the damage per King Ailir's request, Saffron was not about to leave him to do so alone. Not when there was still the chance of Ryder remaining nearby. Ryder, or one of his other red witches, as the fey passengers on the train had called them. Saffron clenched his fists on his thighs, fighting to keep the apprehension off his expression.

Despite having just snapped at Taran to *go away*, Saffron returned to mentally dig around in the back of his mind, like combing fingers through stalks of wheat. Searching for where a shadowy beast might be crouching amongst the grains.

*Do you sense anything?* He asked upon finding it, that small sense of a presence other than his. *Specifically—do you sense Ryder? Or anything else with veil magic?*

The dog stirred, clearly still annoyed to have been told off only moments prior.

*"No,"* Taran answered simply. *"Not right now."*

*Tell me if you do.*

*"I already said I would. Don't bother me again."*

"I'll bother you all I like, mutt," Saffron grumbled as the wagon slowed to a halt at the base of the ruined temple, and he rose to his feet to step out before anyone could stop him.

Saffron knew enough about The Morrígan from myth to know exactly why the destruction of their temple was alarming for the people of Alfidel, even when not considering the means in which it happened. The goddess of war and death; sometimes referring only to Queen Morrígan herself, sometimes to her and her sisters, Macha and Badb, the crow. For one of their temples to burn down, of course it would be considered an omen of death, destruction, catastrophe to come. Then to be visited by the coming Night Prince, himself, to observe the damage—it was no wonder those fey fleeing Erelaine the night before had been so bold to shout such terrible things.

Originally built from marble, with columns stacked every few feet around the perimeter of the great building, only half remained standing from how the earth had split beneath it. Stone crumbled from what remained of the interior, where Saffron noticed another handful of beantighes crawling around in the debris attempting to recover anything they could. Donning the same veils and cuffs as those on the road.

A flock of crows gathered on the remaining stone roof overhead, cawing and opening their wings wide whenever someone passed, as if to warn all from coming too close to such a desecrated place. Fiachra made sure to flare her wings at the birds in response, but when challenged back, just tucking in close to the side of Saffron's neck.

Where the temple had been devoured on one side, the earth beneath was equally churned and turned over itself. It resembled the field of the Midsummer Games almost exactly, though instead of grass, stone mosaic flooring jutted out from the rent soil like a neglected graveyard. All of it, beneath a thick blanket of veil magic that both suffocated and energized Saffron to a nauseating degree, having to put his arm over his mouth while no one else seemed to notice. It called out to him, to the magic in his blood—and he suddenly recalled that thin dream of crying off in the distance. Someone calling to him for help.

"Your highness," a familiar voice greeted once everyone disembarked the wagon, turning as Anysta mac Delbaith approached with a small box in her hands. Saffron instinctively took a step forward, but Cylvan put out a subtle hand to stop him. "I heard you may be coming to witness the destruction, here. Funny how our paths have crossed a second time; I am glad your journey was a safe one."

"You as well," Cylvan said with as polite a smile as ever, before glancing to Saffron like he could sense the indignation emanating from him. "Lord Saffron, you remember Lady Anysta. We met her a few days ago, at the palace."

"I remember," Saffron said, forcing himself to be good. Forcing himself to be as polite as Cylvan was, though he had no idea how persuasive his tone could possibly be in that circumstance. "I also saw your salesperson on the road in the lower tier— did they not permit your silver offerings this far up the mount?"

Anysta's smile tightened slightly, but she had no grounds to snap back at him. As far as she knew, he was still just a naive countryfey who didn't know when he was being rude.

"I much prefer to offer our family silver in charitable donations, when possible," she said, motioning with her hand to the beantighes who cleaned out the interior of the temple, no different from those who picked fairy fruits off the street; donning silver cuffs to ensure they didn't wander further than allowed.

A high fey appearing to be the keeper of the temple hurried over to Cylvan, next, taking the prince's attention to show him the damage a little closer; to go into detail about what had happened the night of the event, which wasn't too different from what Moth had told them. It happened during the night, where temple guardians only pass through every few hours to ensure things are in line and nothing is amiss. Even then, due to the temple's history, guardians never had any reason to pass through that one, specifically.

The comment made Saffron glance back to the destruction, wondering if The Morrígan were so frightening that no one ever made offerings even during the day—but then he realized, there was fire damage on the interior of the walls. A barricade had been set up at the mouth of the entrance, but the closer he looked, the more Saffron realized it was far older than only a few days. Possibly years, maybe even decades, or even longer, by how the bells and tapestries appeared faded from the sun and weather.

"Sionnach," Saffron asked in a whisper as Cylvan and the keeper of the temple continued their conversation, turning to make their way toward the temple itself. "Is there a reason no one would be allowed inside this temple? Maybe that's the only reason Ryder chose to do it here..."

"Well... he may have chosen this one for its state of abandonment, yes. But also..." Sionnach said thoughtfully, standing next to Saffron and taking a moment to observe the crumbling remains for themself. "This location comes with some notoriety regarding Queen Proserpina."

Saffron raised his eyebrows, noticing how Sionnach's voice grew quiet as they spoke. As if it was to summon a storm just to speak of it.

"This was technically The Morrígan's *first* temple here in Erelaine; there's a new one a little higher up the mount. Some call this one, specifically, the 'Profaned Temple of The Morrígan,'" Sionnach explained in a conspiratorial whisper, and Saffron's eyes widened in curiosity. "Because this was the final place on Queen Proserpina's coronation route, before she became queen. She prayed here very last, before entering Avren, beseeching The Morrígan for a court protected from destruction and misfortune like other crowned rulers had before her. Except—it burned down the same night she and King Clymeus were crowned a week later.

Perhaps Ryder thought it a good place to bring attention, to destroy it while everyone's eyes were on Cylvan most after what happened at the games..."

Saffron pressed his lips together, gazing back at the temple with a frown and furrowed brows.

"What's a 'coronation route?'" he asked first.

"When a new ruler wasn't raised in Avren, they would make a spectacle of traveling from their home city to the capital, stopping at small towns and sacred sites along the way to greet the people and pray and give offerings in exchange for a peaceful rule. Queen Proserpina was from the Winter Court—erm, at least, the Winter Court was where she passed through from her home in the human world, so hers started from there." Sionnach explained thoughtfully. "You know, when this temple burned, people say the flames were 'so fierce that they rearranged the stars.' Enough that the queen's Night Court was anticipated long before her Court of Expectations."

"Oh," Saffron exhaled, not expecting the squeeze in his chest. Resisting the impulse to acknowledge how familiar that sounded, as his eyes traveled to where Cylvan stood at the mouth of the damage with the temple keeper, extending his hand toward where the beantighes worked inside. Saffron's heart thumped as the prince clearly waved the beantighes toward the exit, while sharing a tense conversation with the keeper. Demanding the servants be relieved of their duties, due to the instability of the temple over their heads.

"Ryder really must have been trying to make Cylvan look bad again, like you said," he finally spoke again, like a curse. Hoping that, if Ryder was still nearby, he would feel the intention ricochet through him like a burning arrow. Saffron knew what Ryder was thinking, which meant he was closer to finding him. He'd already taken enough—and Saffron would get back what was stolen from him, with his prince still intact. In fact—he would scour every inch of that profaned temple, for as long as he had to, to figure out exactly where Ryder had gone next.

# 11

# THE TEMPLE

The rest of the afternoon was spent walking the streets of Erelaine, where it seemed everyone had a bone to pick with Cylvan and how the kings chose to address their newly-found ashen state. Complaining that it took far too long for Cylvan to arrive—despite boarding the train within hours of hearing the news. They complained that the prince visiting without bringing aid in-hand meant they would be forced to suffer even longer for no purpose—despite there not being anything, particularly, for Cylvan to bring them.

Saffron managed to keep his growing anger at bay throughout it all, by the almighty grace of Ériu and every other damned god on that mount—until someone spit at Cylvan's feet, exclaiming his visit was a waste of time, as Anysta mac Delbaith had already offered more than they would ever receive from a coming night prince. Saffron nearly lunged at the word, but Sionnach threw their arms around him first, hooves clopping against the cobble-stones as they struggled to hold him back.

As night fell, Saffron's venomous mood did not lift, despite Cylvan's constant reassurances that everything they heard was normal. Everything he'd been expecting. He hadn't had any false idea about what awaited him once he arrived, and so far everyone had met those expectations. That didn't make it fair—but it was better for the response to be unfair than unpredictable. Saffron hated that—but he would swallow his temper for Cylvan's sake. By the end of the day, as they finished dinner and separated for bed, Cylvan looked exhausted from it all. Saffron was not going to add to that weight on his back.

He never anticipated being able to sleep, just like every other night, but Saffron kept it to himself. He didn't want to keep Cylvan awake, either, if the prince managed to steal a few hours in the darkness.—though even Cylvan proved as restless as he was, stepping from bed to briefly pace the room before claiming his cloak from the hook by the door and whispering something to Saoirse on the other side. All the while, Saffron said nothing. His raven had moved so quietly, as if he thought Saffron was fast asleep alongside him, too. If it would settle his nerves, Saffron would allow Cylvan to believe that. If anything, it meant he was free to slip away himself, to address the impulse eating at the back of his own mind.

Waiting until he was certain Cylvan and Saoirse were no longer lingering in the hallway, certain they'd gone for a walk in the quiet streets to settle Cylvan's nerves, Saffron followed suit. He slipped from the bed, kicking his feet into his boots, then grabbing his red cloak before hurrying out on his own.

Fiachra followed on silent wing as Saffron snuck through the inn and out the door. The moment the moonlight outside hit him, mixing with the faint glow of surrounding lanterns and flickering lamps, a dark shadow manifested by his side, and Saffron released a low exhale through his nose.

Perhaps because they were already in an unfamiliar setting— but the sight of Taran looming alongside him that night was more unsettling than usual. He seemed bigger than Saffron remembered, more intimidating, more—unnatural, to the deepest of his human instincts. But then, catching the red eyes of the beast in the moonlight, Saffron was reassured all over again that it was still the wolf he commanded. The one whose name he'd carved into his arm.

Pausing just a moment longer, he grabbed a stick of charcoal tucked in the pocket of his cloak, wetting the end with his tongue before drawing an ogham stele down his forearm that read *'without trace.'* A spell to keep him from being spotted, as much as possible, especially if Cylvan and Saoirse truly were on a nightly walk. The last thing he needed was for one of them, or even worse, one of the stalking gossip writers, to see and start questioning why the Alvényan was scouting out The Morrígan's defiled temple in the dead of night.

Tucking the charcoal back into his cloak, he gave Taran another glance while the wolf hovered just a few feet away.

"Don't look at me like that," Taran muttered, ears flattening slightly before trotting forward. Saffron followed, with Fiachra hovering just far enough overhead to sweep away at the last second if she had to.

"Can't help it," Saffron muttered. "Especially in the dark. Not that I care much for the sight of you during the day, either."

"You're the one who trapped me like this."

"I didn't like your high fey face much, either."

The wolf growled lowly from the back of his throat, annoyed. He picked up his pace, making Saffron huff in his own annoyance as he hurried to keep up.

"Remind me why we're doing this, despite Ryder being long gone?"

"I want to be sure," Saffron said under his breath, instead of a more stubborn *'we don't know he's long gone'*-sounding reply. "I want to be sure he only chose this place to embarrass Cylvan. Because if there's any other reason, it means he may do the same thing again somewhere else—and if that's the case, I want to know now."

They slipped between temples glowing beneath multicolored lights, and by then Saffron could even figure out a few of them by the smell of their strong incense alone. No one they passed spotted any movement thanks to Saffron's little arid trick, which seemed to naturally extend to Taran's form like he hoped it would. Though imagining how folks might react to the ghostly form of the wolf king made him smirk with possibility.

Without the bustle of other visitors, the overwhelming mash of smells and sights to distract him, Saffron sensed the damaged veil sooner than the first time. That low buzzing sensation in his bones, the taste of mint and rust on the back of his tongue, a ripple of magic that teased the rowan threads in his blood. He swallowed the spit growing in the back of his throat and instinctively wiped his hand under his nose, relieved to see there still was no smear of blood left behind.

Approaching the burned temple from the side, Saffron slipped behind one of the tall pillars, into the shadows as a group of temple guardians passed by with lanterns. Taran watched them go with the same alertness, ears perked up straight and eyes trained like an attack dog.

When they didn't catch sight of him, Saffron's heart thumped in annoyance. Perhaps it was no wonder the temple's most recent, destructive visitor was able to slip in unseen, after all. Once again reminded that Ryder Kyteler was merely a man, not a wraith. Not a ghost. Nothing Saffron couldn't put his hands on, when he got his next chance.

"Come on," Saffron whispered, hurrying between the rows of columns and the polished stone wall of the temple's antechamber, around the front corner to where the entrance was barricaded with ancient rows of candles, woven ropes, garlands of dried herbs and flowers, and plaques indicating where patrons could find the new temple dedicated to the goddess instead. Saffron passed beneath the crossed ropes and herbs with ease, though Taran's fur bristled and he sneezed upon following, like he'd inhaled a plume of dirt and smoke. It made Saffron smirk, reaching back to scratch the wolf's snout, making Taran yank back with a snarl of warning.

The inside of the temple smelled of stale smoke, due to what

Sionnach had described to him earlier in the day. It reminded Saffron of the scent of the charred remains of the Kyteler School outside of Morrígan. He had to press the edge of his cloak to his nose in an attempt to smudge it out, but the feelings of swirling apprehension were already making his chest tight.

He focused on the interior in front of him—burned dark and crumbling from centuries of slow decay. Clearly untouched from the very day it all burned down, like the morning after the flames faded, all the people could think to do was close it off in an attempt to trap any lingering misfortune inside. To build something new a little higher on the tiered mountainside, as if demonstrating a little more respect would keep the queen's ire at bay from returning.

"When it first burned, I wonder what sparked the flames?" Saffron asked. Even speaking in a whisper, his voice bounced off the silence and skipped along the floor, like spirits joined him in conversation. "Why didn't they do anything to stop it from spreading and destroying the entire place?"

"They likely thought it a direct message from The Morrígan, herself," Taran grumbled, tracing his nose along the floor and kicking up tiny clouds of dust with every exhale. "I'm sure they thought if they tried to stop it, she would only curse them more for defying her will."

Saffron grumbled under his breath about that, thinking once again about the burnt Kyteler School, even about the burning of Beantighe Village by Taran's own hand. Apparently high fey both feared fire and had no qualms about using it to cleanse anything they didn't like—which, perhaps, further explained why everyone in Avren was so keen on Asche taking Cylvan's place, what with their fire magic. Fire magic they were afraid to use, risk hurting someone or something they cared about. The irony cut so deep, Saffron had to resist snorting with bitter laughter.

"There," Taran spoke next, drawing Saffron back into the moment. He turned, squinting in the darkness, unable to see as clearly as the wolf could. Taran noticed, rolling his eyes and taking a mouthful of Saffron's cloak to physically drag him to the opposite side of the burnt room, having to crawl over upturned chunks of the mosaic floor on the way. Fiachra met them there, perching on the edge of upturned stone.

He could hardly inhale a full breath upon standing within touching distance of what he'd hoped—but also dreaded finding inside. Black charcoal mixed with bloody red markings on one of the overturned stones of the floor, torn apart by the opening veil performed after the initial circle was drawn.

Even amongst the broken pieces throughout the debris— Saffron recognized the wide arc of a strange, nauseatingly, newly-familiar arid epithet. Specifically, the elongated lines that cut through the center, crossing over one another before split amongst the broken mosaic flooring. Just like what Cylvan had shown him of the arid circle found in the Tapestry Hall. *Proclaim self—shelter soul—disgrace.*

It left Saffron paralyzed where he stood, ears ringing as he swallowed the confirmation he'd been looking for, but never fully considered the implications of finding. Whoever had placed that epithet in the Tapestry Hall, was the same person who'd done it there, in The Morrígan's profaned temple. And Saffron was certain, only Ryder knew how to rend open the veil in the way the floor beneath his feet indicated—which meant, Ryder must have been the one to first draw it in the Tapestry Hall, too. The random circles discovered around Avren actually had been him and his red witches—though for what purpose, Saffron still couldn't fathom.

"Look there," Taran mentioned, pulling Saffron back into his body. He quickly spotted what the wolf indicated, raising his eyebrows and carefully shuffling through the upturned flooring to get a closer look. Hardly any bigger than Saffron's fingernail, a pink fairy fruit missed by searching beantighes shimmered in the moonlight, stark against the darkness of the burnt floor. He couldn't resist crouching on the balls of his feet to regard it even closer, having to frantically whip Fiachra away the moment the owl landed and attempted to gulp it down for herself.

"Here, beantighe," Taran went on, having already turned to continue his search. "Another one, here."

Saffron followed the wolf's calls through the darkness, plucking every fruit as he went on an impulse he couldn't explain, more than just an effort to keep his bird from swallowing them whole. Down a short corridor to the side, Saffron kept on Taran's heels into a secondary room far less crumbling than the main hall, but still equally neglected.

Immediately, he jumped back with a startled yelp when something massive flared its wings toward him in the darkness—only for an intricate crow statuette carved from dark wood to come into view as his eyes adjusted.

"Good god," he wheezed, clutching his chest. "For what goddamned reason would... they..."

He trailed off, mind racing when he realized, he knew the shape of that bird. He'd seen it before, vaguely, only for a moment —but joined by those crying pleas for *help*. For rescue, to be found, that nightmare of Asche wailing and begging for Saffron to find them.

Instantly, Saffron perked. He searched the room, breathing fast as for a split second, he wondered if the daurae would be hidden somewhere inside, even if it was a foolish thing to believe. But just for a moment, it consumed every inch of him, until reality crept back in and reclaimed his nerves. Asche wasn't in a burned-out, cordoned-off room in The Morrígan's old temple in Erelaine. As much as he wished it would be that easy, he couldn't allow himself to lose focus.

Taran indicated another weak bushel of fairy fruits, and Saffron approached to claim them, adding them to the front pocket of his shoulder bag in silence.

"What is this place?" He asked, only once he was sure his voice wouldn't tremble from the adrenaline, then the disappointment.

"There's likely a room similar to this in her new temple, too,"

Taran said from the opposite side of the carving, just as Fiachra swept into the room and landed on one of the bird's outstretched wings. "Look at the base of the bird, there—worshippers used to leave scrolls tucked inside, hoping the crow would carry their plea to The Morrígan."

Saffron did as Taran invited, crouching on the balls of his feet to examine exactly how many little notes were tucked within the base of the statue. But more than that, he realized—there were hundreds, thousands more stuffed into notches of the walls, into cracks between the floorboards, some even in the plastered adornments along the ceiling. An uncountable number of scrolls, individual pleas for The Morrígan to answer or ignore, from centuries of patrons who passed through before the main chamber burned and those notes were left to time with the rest of the building.

He couldn't resist gliding his palm over the nearest cluster stuffed within every tiny nook and cranny of the wall, biting back little laughs whenever he accidentally knocked a few loose. The majority of notes were written on plain parchment, as if scribbled and tucked away in the moment, though others were clearly planned ahead of time. They donned wax seals on their ends, little golden strings that spilled out from the cracks, and one, even, reflected light off a golden scroll-cap shaped like the head of a unicorn. Saffron knew that was the universal symbol of the royal family, and couldn't resist intentionally plucking it out to see. Taran grumbled something about daring to show disrespect, considering whose temple they stood in, but Saffron shushed him, popping off the golden endcap and unrolling the tightly-wound paper.

"From some courtier, surely, to be bold enough to decorate their little note with the unicorn of the Tuatha dé Danann..." he mused, flattening the scroll and squinting through the darkness to read it. "Don't make me laugh... I'm sure they're begging for riches or more power, if that were even possible, or maybe..." he trailed off as the golden ink shined up at him, ears ringing as, first and foremost, he saw the name written at the bottom. Swallowing against the new, sharp lump in the back of his throat, his eyes dragged back to the top of the scroll to read from the beginning.

> *Beloved Badb, I humbly beseech thee to deliver this plea from one to-be-crowned queen to another.*
>
> *I ask for no power, influence, or protection, more than I am already blessed to have. I ask only that you may shelter those I love left behind through the veil; my dearest Adone and Deimne, and those who watch over them.*
>
> *Yours in perpetual worship,*
> *Princess Aryadna dé Tuatha dé Danann.*

A low chuckle rumbled from the wolf at Saffron's side, the only thing that could bring him back into his body again. Only then did Saffron realize his hands trembled, to be holding something once written by the veiled queen, herself. It was a wonder his skin didn't burn, that the paper didn't erupt into flames, to dare be touched by a rowan witch like those she would later come to despise so deeply.

"It's no wonder the temple went up in flames the day she was crowned," Taran mused. "The queen was here begging for The Morrígan to watch over those who had no right to her grace."

"Adone was Proserpina's human lover," Saffron said. His voice cracked, and he cleared his throat. He didn't know what else to say, there was nothing else to add to that comment—but speaking the name out loud was enough to sense a new chill in the air. "She asked The Morrígan to protect her human lover, just days before she would be crowned alongside Clymeus... to then do what they did, to all of those humans, both arid and not... to destroy the veil the way they did, when she'd pleaded for the protection of her own human lover just before..."

The words spilled out of him; a mix of confusion, resentment, practically a plea to understand. His next instinct was to crumple the paper between his hands, to tear it into a thousand pieces; to desecrate it just as the temple had been, just as the Kyteler School, Beantighe Village had once been—but his fingers disobeyed.

Instead, they gently pinched the edges of the smooth paper, rolling it back into place. He even returned the gold unicorn-shaped caps to either end, though there was no repairing the broken seal on the front. Taran only watched as Saffron then tucked the note into an inner pocket of his cloak, then turned to leave.

He didn't know why. He had no reason to keep it. Had Taran asked for an explanation, Saffron didn't know what he would say.

Only that something about the title *Princess,* followed by her full name, filled him with a strange dread—perhaps because it reminded him so much of how Cylvan's name looked when he once wrote it in Morrígan's Grand Library for Saffron to see.

Returning to the inn, Saffron's mind looped over a hundred things at once, resulting in hardly more than a buzz of thoughts that went nowhere, started with nothing, culminating in unhelpful nonsense. Only one thing remained clear above the rest, and it was the constant sound of Sionnach's words repeating from their earlier explanation of the queen's coronation route. How it'd originated in the Winter Court, where she must have come through the veil from where she originally lived in the human world with her lover. With Adone. Her human lover, who she'd left in the human world when called to become queen alongside Clymeus. She must have still loved Adone so deeply, to still plead for his protection while away...

Something in Saffron's gut couldn't let it go. Wouldn't let it fade into the rest of the noisy cacophony of ideas and fears and anxieties swarming him from every angle.

Even as he snuck back into Cylvan's room, where the prince waited for him. Wide awake with a book on his lap. Candle burning, regarding Saffron with annoyed exasperation like a worried parent, as if he himself hadn't been the one to sneak out first.

Even so—the knotting in Saffron's gut never faded. He walked straight into Cylvan's arms, straddling the prince's lap in the chair and snuggling into him before Cylvan ever had a chance to scold him. Pressing their mouths together before Cylvan could gather himself to remember what he was so worried about.

Cylvan seemed just as willing to let it go, as worn-through as Saffron was from the journey, too much to spare the strength to discuss it. At least until morning. Saffron was grateful, kissing the side of Cylvan's next before sinking into the shape of him with a deep exhale. Closing his eyes to vanish into his warmth, for as long as he was allowed.

ONCE OFFERED ANOTHER CHANCE, SLEEP STILL CAME AS hesitantly as every night prior—only to be stolen out from beneath Saffron's attempts, once again by the shrieking call of someone begging for his help. Echoing off the inside of his skull as if cried directly in his ear; pleading with him. *Find me. Please, save me. I'm lost. I'm here.* That time, surrounded by a brightly-lit forest; a henge of stones, a black and red arid circle painted in the grass beneath his feet, *knock, knock, knock, knock, knock, knock*— deafening until Saffron woke with a shuddering gasp. Heart pounding as only one thought met him on the other side—a harrowing sense that Ryder had done it again.

## 12

# THE VISION

"I was standing in the middle of this grassy clearing," Saffron said, sipping his coffee as the rest of their party listened with curiosity from around one of the inn's meal tables. Other patrons chattered away in the dining area, creating just enough background noise that Saffron didn't feel too anxious about being overheard. Not to mention—the cacophony of high fey demanding the prince's attention and apologies had dwindled into almost nothing overnight, meaning they could enjoy their meal in relative peace. "There were these stones jutting out of the ground around me, and an arid circle in the grass that looked just like one that was reported in Avren recently... the trees looked like they were starting to change, too, for fall. I guess that's proof it was only a dream, since we're still at least a month away from summer ending."

"Trees are pretty much always golden in the Fall Court," Copper corrected, mouth stuffed full of food and making both Cylvan and Maeve wrinkle their noses in disgust. Cylvan muttered something like, *'they never should have let you in here, fox,'* referring to how Copper's own rented room was located down the street. Copper went on like he didn't hear it. "'Specially in the old wood."

"The stone circles, did they have anything on them?" Sionnach asked next. "Any markings or runes or anything?"

"I don't remember." Saffron gazed down at the half-eaten breakfast cake on his plate, prodding it with his fork. Trying to recall any other details, having to push past the sound of Asche's voice crying out for him, the distinctive six knocks that rang out with the veil being torn open. "I think... there were white flowers growing around the stones? Little ones, maybe clover flowers? One of the stones might have been a little bigger than the others, too, but I don't remember if there were any markings on them."

Sionnach stirred their soup with a matching thoughtfulness. "Were they oak trees?"

"I think so."

"Hmm..." They sighed, before shaking their head. Saffron had to nudge them to get a little more of what they were thinking. "It just—sounds a little familiar. There's a henge similar to that outside the satyr borough where my father comes from. In the woods near where I grew up."

"There is?" Saffron asked, unable to help the sudden swell of his voice. He pushed it down, forcing himself to recline back in his chair, swallowing down the sudden rush of emotion. Sure he'd sound like a mad fool if he suddenly started blabbing about his dreams as anything more than random images, even though... Even though... Sionnach implying he may have witnessed a real place, especially when he'd even apparently dreamed of the crow carving in The Morrígan's burned temple the night before they left Avren, it made him think... Perhaps...

"Saffron?" Cylvan urged gently, and only then did Saffron look up and realize everyone around the table had gone silent again. Watching him, like it was obvious exactly how badly he wished to blab about his dream that—may not have been entirely his imagination.

"It's just..." he didn't know how to explain. He looked to Cylvan in that moment of need, hoping it would give him some courage. "I've had more than one dream like this one, lately, where... in them, someone is calling out to me. Asking for my help, crying... And—and... I swear the voice, it... it sounds like Asche."

Cylvan started slightly. Behind him, Saoirse straightened up as well, and so did Aodhán, who stared at Saffron with a look of curiosity.

"Like Asche?" Cylvan prompted under his breath. Saffron nodded, biting his lip as Cylvan quickly added: "Do you think Asche is there?"

Saffron nearly choked.

"I don't know—" he blurted, not wanting to get Cylvan's hopes up. "I —I don't even know if it's really Asche's voice, or if it's even anything more than just a dream, but—! It might just be nothing, but since we have no other leads on what to do next, I figured it wouldn't hurt to mention—"

"We should go," Cylvan declared, eyes bright and unblinking on Saffron. There was a tiny flicker of something hopeful in the depths of his purple irises—and Saffron didn't know whether it made him glad, or made him sick. The thought of being wrong made his stomach turn, knowing what would happen to that little flicker of hope the moment they found nothing where Sionnach believed Saffron to be describing. But—the temptation of keeping that look in Cylvan's eyes was impossible to resist. To be able to give Cylvan anything at all to cling to, even temporarily, might be worth it. So, he nodded.

"I think so, too," he said, before glancing around to everyone else, then to Sionnach. "Even if it's nothing, maybe going to visit would ease my suspicions, at the very least."

"E-even if it's nothing," Sionnach mimicked, perking back up. "Um, at the very least, at home, in my room, I have a large collection of books that might be useful to us. Erm—" they lowered their voice, leaning forward slightly. "Books you wouldn't be able to find on library shelves, that is... Lots of history books, specifically. I, erm... wasn't immune to snagging a rare copy from a library cull when the opportunities arose, myself, you know, and the satyrs have their own ways of getting old books from around Alfidel whenever I asked..."

"Oh?" Cylvan's interest turned to the satyr in an instant. "Stealing old books from library culls, goat? Even more reason to go. Maybe it would be in my best interest to see what sort of taboo literature you've collected..." he spoke with more life than Saffron had seen all morning, as if the mere mention of Asche resurrected him. Another pinch of reassurance that there was no harm in just going to see, even if it was nothing. Even if it only gave Cylvan something to look forward to.

"That's not—!" Sionnach leapt up in a panic, but Saffron grabbed their arm, pulling them back down.

"He's teasing you," Saffron cooed, not without throwing Cylvan a look. Cylvan just smirked mischievously, dabbing at his mouth with a napkin. "His highness also is not immune to collecting old, taboo books, though I don't think he's ever waited for them to be in a library-cull before taking what he pleased."

"Speak for yourself, *beantighe.*"

Saffron threw him a sharp, threatening smile. Cylvan smiled in challenge right back.

"So we're going to visit the satyrs in the Autumn Court?" Copper asked after finally gulping down his mouthful of food. "'Been a while since I ran around naked in the woods."

"Oh, you run around naked in the woods?" Cylvan asked. "Are you hairy enough under those clothes to blend in with wild satyrs, you beast?"

"You're one to talk with those horns on your head."

"He's descended from dragons, Copper," Saffron inserted before Cylvan could, though his tone remained rich with sarcasm. Behind them, Aodhán sighed as if exasperated. Like they would have offered their own opinion, had they not been relegated to keeping guard of the table in favor of sitting at it.

"Have you considered the chances of sharing ancestry with dragon-satyrs, Cylvan?" Maeve asked cooly next, and Cylvan simply wiped his mouth and got to his feet to excuse himself. The table erupted into laughter, even Saffron unable to help it as he leapt to his feet to chase the prince down and bring him back. Cylvan didn't argue, just huffed and pouted in his chair as Saffron offered him fresh fruits to ease his suffering.

While Saffron already brought a handful of books with them on their journey, with the decision to extend their trip a little longer, he was able to convince Cylvan to let him peruse Erelaine's bookstore before they boarded the train. Pretending it was for nothing but curiosity, when really, his discoveries during the previous night's excursion to the profaned temple continued ringing bright and *agonizingly* loud in Saffron's mind even long after they finished breakfast with the new plan in place.

Specifically, Saffron turned over the names of those who Proserpina had begged The Morrígan to protect—Adone and *Deimne*. He knew that name, he was sure of it. He'd read about it somewhere in a book. And when even Taran just mentally shook his head when Saffron asked if he was familiar with it, Saffron knew it would eat him alive until he had something to spark his memory.

With a stack of new books tied together with string, Saffron gathered with the others on the platform, where that time Copper did not make such a big deal about joining them. Still, though, he insisted on purchasing his own ticket. On standing in a different ticket line. On requesting a seat far away from the prince's private car, though he promised Saffron he would *'stop by to visit'* once the train got on its way. Saffron might never understand what went on in Copper's head—though a part of him no longer cared. He was just happy to have his friend there with him again.

To add to his improving mood—it seemed the crowd willing to harass Cylvan had diluted even outside the inn's dining area, while they shopped around at the bookstore, then even allowing the prince's travel party to mill about waiting on the train platform in peace. No more shouting, no more clawing hands or thrown objects to get his attention—at worst, most folks were simply back to looking over their shoulder and whispering to nearby companions. Perhaps, as infuriating as it was, Cylvan's efforts the day prior had proven himself a caring and compassionate prince that the people could be grateful for—

Or so Saffron thought, until a news crier waded through the throng waiting for the train to come, offering Saffron one of the gossip leaflets for a coin. In big letters across the top, Saffron read the headline that actually explained the sudden appeasement, and it turned his relief right on its head.

*PRINCE CYLVAN OVERHEARD DISCUSSING FAIR ALLOCATION OF OPULENT SILVER WITH LADY MAC DELBAITH IN LATE ERELAINE RENDEZVOUS; Sources Say The Crown Has Offered To Front The Cost Of Distribution To Affected Residents Of The Mount Of The Gods...*

*"That explains where he slipped off to last night,"* Taran said flatly in the back of Saffron's mind, as if Saffron hadn't figured it out on his own. He crumpled the leaflet in his hand, whipping around just as Cylvan approached to inform him the train would be arriving in another minute. Shoving the crumpled paper into Cylvan's chest, Saffron turned away and went to find where Sionnach waited, instead. On the verge of boiling over, and at the very least knowing better than to blow up in front of all those people.

HE MANAGED TO AVOID CONFRONTING CYLVAN ALL THE way up to boarding the train, then while settling into their private rooms, then even half an hour into the journey while he distracted himself with the landscape, with something strong to drink. All the while, Cylvan clearly knew what had Saffron so agitated, considering the prince kept the gossip leaflet in his front pocket. Flattened out from Saffron's crumpling, a little corner peeking out like he wanted Saffron to know he intended on addressing it when he got the chance.

He took that chance while Saffron sat reading *Alvish Myths New and Old* in the quiet car, while the others found their own entertainment elsewhere to help time pass. Cylvan got Saffron's attention by grabbing the back of his chair and shaking it slightly, smiling down at him as Saffron craned his neck back.

"Hello," he said simply. "I'm reading."

"Oh, come on," Cylvan sighed, the tail end of it verging on begging. "Haven't you punished me enough? I am suffering immensely."

"I think you could stand to suffer more," Saffron said as Cylvan claimed the seat alongside him, though he extended a foot to rest on Cylvan's knee as a sign he didn't actually want the prince to leave. His initial anger had subsided enough, already, to stand to be in his presence again. Cylvan's hand found Saffron's ankle, teasing under the cuff of his trousers and rubbing his thumb over bare skin.

"I was going to tell you once I got the chance," he said. Saffron just raised an eyebrow to encourage him along. "I hadn't even considered speaking to her about anything until we'd already gone to bed, either. I wasn't keeping secrets from you, púca. I swear it."

"What made you decide to do it, then?" Saffron asked.

"It was... a moment of weakness," he said, and Saffron's heart thumped mercifully when Cylvan couldn't meet his eyes. "I couldn't sleep. I kept thinking about all the trouble I went to trying to speak with the people in Erelaine, and how none of them were receptive. I got in my own head about what sorts of things the gossip papers would write about it. I couldn't stomach the thought of being humiliated when I genuinely was trying my best. I thought... going to Anysta might help mitigate that chance. And—I was right."

Saffron bit his lip. He finally closed his book, resting it flat on his lap. "I guess... that makes sense," he whispered. "Even if I don't like it."

"I don't like it either," Cylvan said. He squeezed Saffron's ankle, making Saffron's leg twitch. "But I want you to know, I didn't make any sort of long-term agreement with her. We did not make any kind of secret alliance, no matter what sort of wild things will be published over the next few days about it."

"You haven't secretly proposed marriage to her or anything like that?" Saffron teased. "So when the gossip columns inevitably claim—"

"Absolutely not." Cylvan said declaratively, squeezing Saffron's ankle again. "*Ab-so-lute-ly* fucking *not.*"

Saffron chuckled, then sighed. He brushed his palm over the smooth face of the book on his lap, before reaching out to briefly take Cylvan's hand on the armrest and squeeze it.

"I understand," he said in a whisper. "I don't blame you, either, even if, like I said—I don't like it..."

"Thank you," Cylvan whispered. He visibly relaxed in his chair, before sitting forward with a fresh look of intrigue on his expression. "Now. *You* are going to tell me where *you* went last night, while I was gone."

"Hm?" Saffron hummed innocently, fluttering his eyelashes and smiling at his prince like he simply had no idea what he could possibly mean.

"Oh, don't act dumb, you demon. Not only were you gone by the time I returned—but even Aodhán told me they saw you sneaking out less than an hour after I did. I've already told you who I was meeting with in secret—now it's your turn."

"Seems we're both prone to late-night meetings."

"Don't try and distract me. Answer the question, beantighe."

Saffron groaned, throwing his head back dramatically before sitting forward, reclaiming his leg so he could properly lean over the edge of his seat.

"I was going to tell you eventually, too, you know," Saffron assured him. "I wasn't keeping it a secret for a reason, either."

"Secret enough to sneak out while I slept."

"Speak for yourself, Night Prince," he shot back through a tight smile. Cylvan smiled back in threat.

"You were saying?"

Saffron huffed again. He leaned slightly closer, and Cylvan did the same, until they were hardly more than a few inches apart.

"After we finished touring the site of the veil event yesterday... I decided I wanted a closer look, without so many eyes to see me."

"Oh, Danu help us," Cylvan rasped, hand snapping out to hook over Saffron's thigh and claw into it. "What did you do, witch?"

Saffron smirked, grabbing Cylvan's knee in return and squeezing until the prince flinched. "I just wanted to see if Ryder left any clues behind," he explained as simply as he possibly could. Cylvan gaped at him in disbelief, and Saffron sensed the moment a string of reprimands swelled up the back of Cylvan's throat, interrupting him first: "I was gone less than an hour—you know that—and Taran was there to make sure no one bothered me. Even Aodhán, apparently, didn't see where I went. No one saw."

"And?" Cylvan insisted next, catching Saffron by surprise. He tightened his hand over Saffron's thigh again, making Saffron jump and stifle a sharp giggle.

"And—there were some remnants of the same reported specifically in the Tapestry Hall. Also a few bunches of fairy fruits left behind, though I took care of those."

"And what else?"

Saffron fluttered his eyelashes again. "What do you mean?"

"You think I can't tell when you're hiding something from me? You're like an open book to my knowing gaze, you little thief. What else did you take?"

"You definitely know me too well," Saffron conceded with a nervous smile, throwing a quick glance over his shoulder before pulling his shoulder bag to settle between his feet on the floor. Digging into the front pocket cinched tightly closed, he slipped out the queen's ancient plea to The Morrígan. Cylvan audibly grunted when he saw it, jolting forward to clap his hands around Saffron's. Staring at him with wide eyes—but not out of protest, so much as shock.

"You little—!" He wheezed. "You—damned púca thief!"

Saffron grinned, hiding the scroll within the shell of Cylvan's rounded shoulders, popping off the two golden caps on the ends so the prince could unroll the aged paper. He watched in tense silence as Cylvan read the words once, then twice, then a third time, before his pretty eyes flickered up to meet Saffron's again.

"You look a little disappointed," Saffron started weakly, only for Cylvan to clamp their hands together again and aggressively shake his head.

"No, no, not at all—I'm—I simply—I think I'm still in a bit of shock, is all. I'm also praying The Morrígan doesn't come back and curse me for this, too."

"What else could you possibly be cursed with at this point, Your Seelie Night Prince Highness?" Saffron teased in a low voice. Cylvan looked like he was going to eat him alive.

"What made you think it was worth stealing?" Cylvan clarified. "I want to know what *you* think of it."

Saffron tried to explain the feelings he'd been sorting through all night long, and in the background all morning. That feeling of sadness and loss over Proserpina having to leave her human lover behind—despite everything that would come to pass, later. The way she specifically named Adone in the note, as well as someone else called *Deimne*.

"I know that name from somewhere, but I can't remember exactly," Saffron sighed, rolling the scroll back up and tucking it securely back into his bag. "That's part of the reason why I asked you to buy me so many new books. I'm certain it's from a myth, but I haven't figured out which one, yet..."

Cylvan glanced down to the book of Alvish myths on Saffron's lap, before smirking the most wicked, foxlike smile Saffron had ever seen.

"You recognize the name but not where it's from, do you,

beantighe? And here I thought you were better versed in myth than even I—"

Saffron grasped the book in both hands, smacking Cylvan on the thigh with it.

"Will you just tell me if—!"

*"'Did you eat of the salmon, lad?'"* Cylvan interrupted theatrically, grabbing Saffron's arm and shaking him as he quoted the lines. *"'Did you eat of the salmon that feasts on hazelnuts of the nine trees? Before even I could, despite being the one who caught it...!'"*

Saffron stared at him as the thoughts swirled behind his eyes, knowing those words, knowing where it came from, barely skirting past the recognition until Cylvan reached out to twirl a finger through Saffron's hair, made blonde by his fey glamour.

*"'Fionn is your name, for the fairness of your hair—'"*

"Fionn mac Cumhaill!" Saffron exclaimed, before throwing a hand over his mouth in embarrassment when other passengers turned to look. Cylvan burst out laughing, and Saffron swatted at him, then grabbed one of his horns to yank him back in embarrassment.

"Fionn mac Cumhaill was born *'Deimne'* before the poet Finn named him otherwise," Saffron reiterated before Cylvan could tease him further. The prince finally nodded, but couldn't stop grinning, like the blood filling Saffron's face was strong enough to even show through the glamour. "But why would Proserpina refer to him in her note? Unless it was actually referring to someone she knew... A friend? Maybe a pet..."

"It does seem strange, considering how little else she left behind," Cylvan agreed once the amusement chuckled out of him. He sat back in the chair, gazing out the tall window at the passing landscape in thought. Saffron just watched at him in the meantime, disappointed, but not surprised, to hear even Cylvan didn't know who, what *Deimne* could have meant in the context of Queen Proserpina. "Perhaps it's no surprise after all that the temple burned down once she became queen... perhaps she regretted ever writing anything so personal and leaving it in a place where anyone could find it."

Saffron's heart thumped. He gazed back down at his own handwriting that had copied the words into his book.

"Do you mean—she was the one who set the fire? But Sionnach said..."

"Let me guess—*'the flames burned fierce enough to rearrange the stars,'* right?" Cylvan mimicked, like it was a common phrase taught in class. Saffron nodded.

"If she did know about the fire, then she either didn't think it would matter to burn down the temple, or perhaps..."

"Didn't care?" Cylvan asked, but it wasn't so much to finish Saffron's thought, rather than to consider the idea for himself. A wild, outrageous thought, Saffron believed—but the look on Cylvan's face, the face of the next to likely receive declaration of a Night Court—was a little more unreadable.

Saffron didn't know how much time passed in contemplative silence across from one another, only that even the sound of Cylvan's clothing shifting as he turned back was loud as lightning.

"Well," he said, calm smile so very different from the bright amusement of only moments before. As if weighed down with what Saffron had shared with him, and filling Saffron with a miasma of guilt. "It's a compelling mystery, that's for sure. Once we finish what we've started here, I'm sure Daurae Asche will be more than eager to help you solve it, Lord Saffron."

Saffron's heart twanged heavily, but he smiled back with a nod. Right. There was no use distracting himself with something else, when he was already running short on time trying to bring his friends back home. He had to focus on the dreams he was having, and if they meant anything. He had to focus on Ryder Kyteler, alone. If they found Ryder—they would find a way to the others. And that was most important, above all else.

13

———

# THE SEARCH

"*W*ake *up, wake up!*"

Saffron's thoughts were heavy from a restless sleep, eyes cracking open first to darkness, then the faint light of a candle being quickly struck. Between the bunk beds, Sionnach was quickly pulling on a robe over their sleeping clothes, while Maeve and Copper crowded the doorway. The curtains were drawn over the window, too dark to see outside —except for a slow-moving, bobbing line of lantern light that slowly passed by. Only then did Saffron realize the train had come to an unexpected stop.

Cylvan was suddenly there, pushing his way between Maeve and Copper in the doorway and moving straight to where Saffron was only just beginning to sit up. Saffron had no chance to ask what was going on before Cylvan's hands were under his arms, fully lifting him from the bed and pulling him to the floor. He said nothing, moving quickly to ask Sionnach where Saffron's dressing gown was, while Saoirse and Aodhán appeared in the corridor outside carrying a lamp of their own.

"What's going on?" Saffron finally asked. Cylvan didn't meet his eyes, just grabbing the robe from Sionnach's hand and quickly dressing Saffron in it. "Cylvan—!"

"Witchhunters," he said, quick and low. "The ones who rode with us to Erelaine—they must have followed us. They've stopped the train." His voice trembled. "They're checking any human beantighes registered on board. They may search the rooms for any others who may be hiding."

"What?" Saffron's voice cracked, grabbing Cylvan's shoulder. "Cylvan!"

"It's going to be alright, Saffron, come," Cylvan insisted, putting his arm securely around Saffron's waist and leading him toward the corridor.

"Passengers are gathering in the drinking car. The rest of you as well," Saoirse instructed.

Saffron walked quickly in line with Cylvan, who held him close in an arm that never loosened. The brief moment he glanced up to his prince's face, his jaw was locked tight enough to flex the tendons in his throat, staring straight ahead as they passed swiftly between the cars.

As they went, any passengers who stepped aside averted their eyes, before making the motion of beseeching a Day Court. Saffron wished he could put his arm around Cylvan in return, wished he could take his raven's hand and reassure him it was going to be alright, everything was going to be alright, this wasn't the first time they'd had to slip unnoticed beneath the gaze of searching witchhunters—but even he wasn't sure how much he believed it.

But even if he himself could go unbothered by the privilege of his glamour and the company he kept—what about the other humans on board? What if there were any who had been dabbling in arid magic, who had eaten rowan berries, who had been swept up in Ryder's sweet promises, like all those others?

He wanted to say something, he wanted to quietly beg for Cylvan to do something, knowing if anyone could, it would be him—but for the first time, Saffron's mouth remained clamped shut. His voice might not have come even if he'd tried with how fast and hard his heart pounded in his chest, either, the moment he was reminded—witchhunters knew him, proven by how they once tried to give him a rowan burial. Those on the train, there, knew him specifically. One of them had looked directly at him on Avren's platform. Would they be bold enough to accuse him there, in front of everyone? Even with his glamour, even with no indication he was anything other than another fey lord...?

They arrived in the dimly-lit drinking car, where a small group of beantighes gathered near the opposite end while their patron families gathered at the bar, where the bartender worked to keep up with the sudden rush of midnight orders. With the humans, one of the witchhunters stood waiting for all to be accounted for. Their face remained hidden beneath the veil, but Saffron felt their eyes the moment he and Prince Cylvan appeared with the rest.

"Please do not worry, ladies, lords, gentles, we will not keep your beantighe servants long," another witchhunter announced in a calm, reassuring voice. Making Saffron jump, as he didn't realize exactly how close they were with how they blended with the low light of the car. Nearly within reach, had he taken another few steps forward. "The train will return on its way momentarily."

"What is it you're looking for?"

Cylvan's hand tightened on Saffron's shoulder. The faces of every person in the train car turned toward him—and only then did Saffron realize, he'd been the one to ask. Without thinking, numbed by fear yet simultaneously emboldened by Cylvan's nearness. Even the witchhunter's gaze lingered on the prince's hand evident where it held Saffron close, as they folded their own hands politely over their stomach.

"Considering what we lost at the Midsummer Games, my lord," they answered, speaking slowly, edging on condescension, "... it is in the best interest of the people of Alfidel to ensure we cut this human resistance off at the root. We mean no harm to anyone found innocent. We only mean to question what they may know."

Saffron nearly asked what, exactly, they could possibly be looking for—something that a handful of spring witches *at best* would be able to share, especially if they already had Ryder who always had an answer to everything—but something else prickled at the back of his throat, first. That question, exactly. Why not ask Ryder directly—unless...?

"Members of the resistance would not be on this train with their patron families," Saffron said instead. That time, more curious than accusatory. Wondering if they would be uncoordinated enough to answer what he suddenly suspected.

Murmurs rose from the groups of high fey standing around the empty bar, looking a mix of annoyed at him for speaking up, and intrigued by the point he made.

"There is no way of knowing exactly how far this recent growth of red witchcraft has spread," the witchhunter replied, and that time, Saffron had to purposefully bite his tongue. Once again fighting the impulse to snap back: *you know exactly how far-reaching the resistance is, considering your closeness to Ryder Kyteler...'* but again, he swallowed it. Another suspicion clogged the back of his throat, feeding the first. If the witchhunters could get whatever they were looking for from Ryder directly—they never would have any reason reason to put on such a large show for such a small crowd.

To follow Saffron and the others from Avren to Erelaine, the site of the veil event—then to continue with them from Erelaine into the Fall Court, despite no reports of anything else on Ryder's heels—

Saffron questioned—if even the witchhunters didn't know where Ryder Kyteler had gone, or where he might appear next.

"If there are arid-magic practicing humans on this train, living amongst their patron families, then there are a far few more you should be taking with you for questioning, witchhunter," Saffron said, next. His eyes flickered to the cluster of high fey, who shifted uncomfortably on their feet. Cylvan's hand on Saffron's shoulder locked tight enough to bruise. A silent command for him to *be quiet*.

"Your interest in defending these beantighes makes me think perhaps *you* are the one who should be brought for questioning, Lord Saffron," the witchhunter countered, but Saffron didn't flinch. A clear, threatening reminder that those on the train were well aware of his secret thanks to their allyship with Ryder—but Saffron knew, especially if they were also looking for the man, that causing trouble with Saffron would only be a distraction.

"Am I defending the beantighes, or their patron families?" Saffron asked. Unfazed by the veiled threat. Cylvan's grip on him tightened—but then loosened. Catching on to exactly what Saffron was trying to do.

"Am I to believe there are potentially high fey on this train who are patronizing magic-practicing humans?" Cylvan spoke as the Prince of Alfidel, commanding and authoritative. It gave Saffron chills, and he had to resist turning to smile at him. "Perhaps Lord Saffron is right—the fact so many of you are silent despite such serious accusations makes me wonder what you're hiding, using your servant as a shield..."

A brief moment of silence—followed by Copper, of all people, who scoffed loud enough to even make Cylvan jump.

"If some witchhunter accused me of patronizing an arid human, I'd tell 'em to kick rocks, personally..."

Saffron bit back another smile, unable to help it as Copper's delivery wasn't nearly as polished as Cylvan's. It seemed to do its job, however, as the gathered fey looked between one another uncomfortably, some shuffling away from their neighbors, straightening up to look judgmentally down at those standing next to them. Saffron could practically see the cloud of gossip forming along the ceiling.

"As if I would trust some out-of-date trial to determine the loyalties of one of my own servants, anyway," Maeve interjected with a disapproving sigh. "Who knows what sort of agenda they have behind the scenes."

"Would be real easy to accuse some noble family of harboring arid humans, huh?" Copper added.

"Makes me wonder, considering how few of us there are on this train as it is."

Silence rang like an echo. Discomfort, as those words lingered, as the passengers surrounding them looked between one another again, shifting back and forth on their feet. Finally, someone spoke up. A fey lady who cleared her throat, airing herself with the feathered fan in her hand.

"It's as I said in the cabin—this is an outrageous thing to do in the middle of nowhere. We've nearly entered the Fall Court—we could be robbed blind while sitting here, playing this theater."

Copper muttered something at that, but Sionnach elbowed him to be quiet.

"Do they think us such poor patron fey that we wouldn't know if one of our own beantighes is acting out?" Another snapped. "Preposterous—return my beantighe at once! I will not stand for this blatant disrespect."

"Mine as well. Come, Flicker. You must light the heater in my cabin again."

One beantighe in the group wasted no time shoving free of the others, hurrying to where their patron lady extended an arm to possessively pull them in and lead them away. As they passed, they met Saffron's eyes. Full of silent gratitude. Saffron pretended not to notice, though his stomach knotted.

"If they wish to investigate my property, they can send me a formal letter," came another. "They can't just come and search my things without warning. And expect me to just bow and accept it! Come, Dandelion!"

"You as well, Cotton!"

The beantighes huddled at the head of the car scattered, all hurrying back to their patron families as the volume of voices in the car rose to near-deafening. Saffron had to stumble back into Cylvan to avoid being crushed by the sudden swell, but Cylvan kept a steady, protective grasp on him the entire time. Soon, even the witchhunters at the head of the car scowled, turning and hissing orders to one another before disappearing through the doorway into the upper car.

Only once they left did Saffron's confidence wane like water from a broken glass, legs buckling beneath him but caught in Cylvan's arms before he reached the floor. He helped Saffron to one of the nearby chairs, as if Saffron was merely lightheaded from the cramped confines of the car. Kneeling in front of him, he touched Saffron's face, before asking Copper over his shoulder to get Saffron something to drink.

"Whiskey," Saffron croaked. "God, as much as is in the bottle."

Copper chuckled, lumbering over to the drink counter like he was told. Behind him, Aodhán's eyes lingered on Saffron in an indiscernible mix of confusion and intrigue, before they turned to join Copper at the bar counter.

Cylvan, meanwhile, never pulled back, just touching Saffron's face again and again, pushing hair from his eyes with such a soft expression—like he wanted to ask if Saffron was alright, but not confident those would actually be the words to leave his mouth. Saffron avoided the prince's eyes for as long as he could, knowing that once he met them, he wouldn't be able to keep it together any longer—and he was right.

The instant he accidentally met Cylvan's gaze, the emotional dam inside him broke, tears filling his eyes and streaming over. At least he cried silently, quickly drying them with a kerchief offered by Sionnach. He kept his composure, just looking at Cylvan and letting the emotion come while shaking his head.

"Thank you," he whispered, taking Cylvan's hands and bowing his head to kiss them. "Thank you, thank you, for saying something."

"You spoke up for them first, Saffron," Cylvan whispered, squeezing Saffron's hands in return. "You were very brave. Those beantighes may owe you their lives. They may owe Copper and Maeve, too, but don't tell them that. Especially not Copper,"

Cylvan smirked, lightening the mood. "He will undoubtedly never shut up about it."

Saffron laughed weakly, lifting his watery eyes to look for Maeve, who hovered nearby, but her attention remained on the head of the car where the witchhunters had disappeared through the door. When Copper came with Saffron's golden drink, he carried a second one for himself, declaring it all the thanks he needed before downing half in one go. Saffron did the same with his, only for the glass to be snatched away by Cylvan who took his own massive gulp of what remained.

Saffron saw how the prince's hand shook as he threw it back, making his insides squirm with something that felt like guilt, or shame, or relief, he didn't know. Only that he wasn't sure how long he'd be able to keep the alcohol down, especially if they stayed out there in the open for anyone to see. Where those who hadn't returned to their sleeping cars with their beantighes still lingered, some looking their way, others gazing out the windows, all whispering softly to one another.

The cloud of gossip lingered near the ceiling, invisible but nearly tangible. Perhaps Saffron was simply learning how to recognize when moments were colorful enough to be worthy of discourse. Perhaps he subconsciously noticed something out of the corner of his eye, otherwise hidden behind the edge of someone's cloak. A quill quickly scribbling over parchment.

14

—————

## THE GARDENER

Breakfast was served on the train before they would disembark for lunch at the station, and Saffron was more than aware of the continued looks and whispers carrying over from the night prior. He just ate his meal in silence, as normally as he could manage, while the others bantered around him. Copper especially let his voice boom out, as if emboldened by being back in his home court. Sionnach, on the other hand, seemed smaller than normal, movements stiff and nervous like they were only just realizing what it meant that the prince's traveling party would be visiting their hometown. At the same time Saffron did, Copper seemed to notice, opening his mouth with clear intent to verbally harass them—but a sharp look from Saffron shut him down in an instant, and he went back to teasing Maeve for the way she wore her hair, instead.

While watching the landscape pass in the quiet car, Saffron quickly lost interest in his book as Summer Court greenery gradually gave way to the golden blanket of the Fall. On its surface, The Fall Court even reminded Saffron of the Winter Court more than he expected; while the Winter Court had its four seasons just like all the others, there was always a perpetual chill or layer of snow and ice depending on where one visited, even during the hottest days of the summer.

The Summer Court was similar, where it never got particularly cold even in the deepest months of winter. The Spring Court experienced a little bit of every season, perhaps because it was nestled comfortably between the two extremes, and Saffron had expected the Fall Court to be the same—but as they crossed the valley that separated the Summer from Fall, Saffron realized the trees of that golden forest were nothing like any of its three seasonal cousins.

The Fall Court, as its name implied, and as Copper once described, flourished in a near-constant state of golden leaves and honeyed, dappled morning sunlight. Copper clearly noticed the awe on Saffron's expression as he gazed out the window, explaining that the only time leaves actually died and fell, then regrew green, was during a brief period at the end of of Alfidel's winter, and beginning of spring. And even then, that greenery rarely lasted longer than a few weeks before it shifted back to its warm oranges and yellows and burnt reds. When Saffron asked how that was possible, when the trees that passed them weren't otherwise any different from the ones that grew in the Spring Court's Agate Wood, Copper just smirked like he was thrilled to answer.

"Y'know the Autumn Court is the oldest one of all?" he asked. "The forests were here even before the oldest mountains in the Winter Court. They were planted by the Aos Sídhe themselves, when they first emerged from the mounds. That's why the Autumn Court's also called the Court of First Opulence. Some believe even The Dagda's mounds are supposed to be in there."

"If you're a tourist, maybe," Cylvan scoffed from where he sat, looking less than happy that Copper was monopolizing all of Saffron's attention.

"He's not entirely wrong," Sionnach interjected, before shifting uncomfortably in their seat when everyone turned to look at them. "I mean—it's no secret the forests of the Autumn Court have more natural magic than anywhere else."

They way they slipped into that vernacular—calling it the Autumn Court rather than the Fall Court, as most from the Fall Court did—Saffron realized there was a sense of pride even Sionnach held for the place they came from. He couldn't help it, stepping back to lean against the arm of the chair where they sat.

"What do you mean by natural magic?"

"Well—the veil is thinner, here," Sionnach explained, adjusting the reading glasses they wore. "The Queen spent more time in the Autumn Court closing tears than anywhere else in Alfidel. That, and because it's the biggest court compared to all the others, means you're more likely to cross paths with wild things that otherwise live isolated from high fey society."

Saffron's heart danced excitedly.

"Like what?"

"We may catch ourselves another show of nymphs, beantighe," Cylvan teased under his breath, laughing when Saffron's head snapped around to him.

"R-really? Nymphs!"

"And satyrs, of course, proven by the one sitting right in front of you."

"Of course!" Saffron exclaimed.

"Don't forget unseelie shapeshifters and the like, too," Copper added with a sly smile. "Plenty of wild fey who would love to steal your voice or your toes, Saffron."

"You certainly will not be wandering out into the wilderness all alone like you used to at Morrígan, that's for sure," Cylvan added flatly. "I'll tie you to my waist if I have to."

"That's unfair," Saffron whined. "Tie Copper to your waist. He gets into way more trouble than I do."

"We'll get in trouble together," Copper promised. "There are plenty of things I can show you in the woods that I know you'll love, Saff. No rope can stop me."

"I'll kill you," Cylvan growled. "Don't you dare."

Copper and Saffron exchanged a look, making Cylvan bark at them to '*stop that!*'.

Arriving at the train platform, Saffron and Copper continued dramatically whispering to one another, casting fleeting glances over their shoulders to Cylvan who walked behind them, only for Cylvan to puff up even bigger in annoyance. On the verge of grabbing Copper's glamoured tail and ripping it off, or maybe swinging Saffron into his arms and forcing through the ashen state in his body to throw them both up into the sky. Saffron shouldn't have enjoyed teasing him so much—but it was hard to resist.

Stepping off the train, the platform was more crowded than Saffron anticipated, though perhaps he should have known, considering it was as far as the rails went into the supposed ancient-magic woods of the Fall Court. Before he could help it, the pressing crowd separated him from Copper, and then the others, though he could see them over the heads of the passing pedestrians.

He worked his way off to the side, first, so he could gather his bearings. Barely pressing himself against the exterior of the station office, he took in a breath before a hand landed on his shoulder, spinning him around.

He expected to find Saoirse, or Cylvan, or someone else there to take him back to the group—but instead it was a stunningly dressed fey lady, thick makeup on her eyes and golden hair twisted into a tall up-do that nearly brushed the bottom of the hanging station-sign. Behind her, a few other members of the crowd shoved through to reach where she stood, and for a second Saffron thought she'd mistaken him for someone else—until he saw the pad of parchment in her hand. The quill she had to hold physically, as she had no opulence to charm it to transcribe automatically. A writer from Avren, obviously. Who had followed them all the way that far.

Saffron's heart sank, but the beantighe in him surged to the surface in tandem, a defense mechanism he would never quite shake. He offered her a polite smile, shaking his head and putting a hand up to imply he didn't wish to speak with her. Despite the effort—he turned to find a few more gossip writers clustering at his back. Surrounding him like a pack of wild dogs.

"Ah—" he attempted, but the first fey lady interrupted him.

"I don't mean to keep you for long, Lord Saffron, especially after such a commotion on the journey here. I only wanted to ask —what exactly are your thoughts on how the witchhunters are handling the scourge of red-witch rebels? You seemed so passionate about their work last night, not to mention about ensuring the protection of patron fey over their beantighes."

"Huh?" Saffron blurted before he could stop himself, turning back to her with slightly-furrowed brows. Somewhere over the commotion of the crowd, someone called out his name.

"You showed those on the train some surprising deference— and it's not the first time you've extended such grace to beantighes you perceived as being mistreated, is it? You once assaulted a fey lady courtier at one of Prince Cylvan's courting galas, did you not? What will you do if word spreads amongst beantighes that you will show them sympathy in their times of need?"

"What?" Saffron asked again, sharper than he meant to. Growing annoyance pinched at the back of his throat, and despite how hard he tried to swallow it back, the frustration and exhaustion combined into a response. "Well—I think—I think perhaps it should be more telling that no other patron fey spoke up in favor of their own servants, who they're responsible for—" By some miracle, he cut the words off as all around, pens scribbled on paper. The rational part of his brain begged him to just *shut up*, to shove his way out of the circling vultures as soon as he could, but they must have sensed his urge with how tightly they formed ranks and entrapped him.

"You were there at the summer games, when those human witches attacked," a high-pitched voice came from someone else behind him. "Doesn't it worry you how it might look for humans to see you as a friend?"

"Yes—didn't it frighten you to witness what power humans have over the veil? How can you still choose to show them deference?"

"Aren't you worried how your actions might reflect on Prince Cylvan? Even as he is working so hard to sow calm both in Avren and, most recently, Erelaine."

"You've grown rather close to him in recent weeks, haven't you? How do you feel about his recent midnight affair with Lady mac Delbaith?"

"Do you discuss Alfidel's treatment of beantighes with him often? Have you heard how some people call him a 'seelie prince'?"

Saffron shook his head, blocking out the wave of questions suddenly drowning him. Even Taran growled something in the back of his mind, but Saffron pushed the words away in a panic before he could hear them. To his right, he recognized the sound of Saoirse forcefully parting the crowd in order to reach him, to rescue him.

"Lord Saffron, what are your thoughts on the human rebels and their infiltration of beantighe dormitories? Where do you think they've all gone after the events of the Midsummer Games?"

"Is it true the palace has only a dozen servants left?"

"You were at the games the day it happened, right there in the middle of the field—can you tell us exactly what you saw? What did that human man say just before stealing those innocent fey through the veil?"

"Do you think humans are justified in wreaking havoc on the veil as a form of rebellion?"

"Don't you have any words to condemn their actions? How do you feel after seeing a human manipulate the veil like that?"

"I think—!" Saffron snapped, just moments before Saoirse could reach him. "I think—! Perhaps all of Alfidel should reflect on why humans felt the need to go to such lengths! And whether or not that has anything to do with why the veil responded to a human witch but no high fey in such a long time!"

Saoirse's gloved hand on Saffron's wrist was instantly *tight*, turning and pulling him into her armored back as her voice boomed out and commanded every high fey circling him to step away. Saffron pressed himself back against the train station, staring at his warped reflection in the silver armor and hating the face that stared back at him—nostrils flared, brows furrowed, lips pressed together like he was either on the verge of bursting into tears or ripping a hole in the veil, himself. The whole time as Saoirse barked at the crowd to back off, then pulled Saffron swiftly through the bodies—Saffron just recalled his own demeanor. His face, that wasn't his. Glamoured and unnaturally beautiful—and wasted on someone as stupid as him.

WITH THE INFLUX OF TRAVELERS ARRIVING BY TRAIN, they wouldn't have access to a carriage until the next town on such short notice. Saffron wouldn't have wanted to sit in one, anyway. He wanted the fresh air. He wanted to stew in frustration and self-loathing in the privacy of his own saddle, as guilt and nausea roiled like a storm in his gut. Replaying his words over and over again, and dreading how they would certainly be used against him as soon as the next morning.

He hoped Saoirse didn't tell Cylvan too much. He hoped she hadn't overheard what Saffron had accidentally blurted in his rush of overwhelm. He would deal with the consequences of his fool-ishness when the time came. He would apologize to Cylvan for being so goddamned stupid and reckless and—selfish.

Almost grateful for how equally irritable and anxious Boann was when Saffron finally heaved himself up into the saddle, it meant he could distract himself with patting the side of the horse's neck, speaking gentle compliments to soothe her nerves as the others chattered amongst themselves while making their way down the packed dirt road.

Cylvan and Copper teased Sionnach for the type of stirrup they used to accommodate their hooves, while Sionnach attempted to fight back by commenting on how worn out Copper's saddle was. Copper and Cylvan went on to entertain themselves by trying to kick the other out of their saddle any chance they got. All while Saffron just lingered near the back, riding alongside Maeve, who was silent and stoic as ever on her tall white horse as perfectly proportioned as she was. Only when Copper actually managed to dislodge Cylvan and send him tumbling to the road with a heavy *thud* did she crack a smile, shaking her head, then accidentally meeting Saffron's eyes. Saffron quickly turned away, not realizing he was looking. She sidled a little closer.

"You're quiet," she commented, but added nothing else. Saffron didn't know whether it was actually meant to be a conversation starter, or just an out-loud observation. He watched Cylvan scramble back onto his horse and chase Copper up the road while formulating a response.

"Have you ever visited this part of the Fall Court?" he asked, giving up on addressing her initial sentiment.

"Of course. My family has a holiday estate just a few hours west of here."

"Of course they do," Saffron sighed. "I think the Tuatha dé Danann do too."

"We used to spend time visiting the dé Bricríu estate nearby as well, back when the three of us were much younger. Taran even joined us often too, for a while. Until Cylvan made fun of Copper's ears at the dinner table, one night, and Renard said he was never welcome back again."

"Ohhh," Saffron grimaced. "How old were you?"

"Hmm... I think we were just a few months from our last year of primary school."

"So young!" Saffron laughed, surprising even himself. "I guess it doesn't surprise me, considering all the other stories I've heard about Cylvan as a child."

"I spent a few weeks with Lady Étaín a few years ago as well," Maeve mused, a weak smile on her face. At the mention of the name, Sionnach threw a curious glance over their shoulder. "Sionnach's mother, that is."

"You—really?" Saffron asked, clicking his reins to keep up with the long strides of Maeve's horse. "What for?"

"Advice," Maeve answered simply. "There was a time I second-guessed turning down the opportunity to become Cylvan's harmonious queen. Étaín mac Carce was the only high lady I knew who had experienced something similar..."

"What?" Saffron nearly choked, but Maeve burst out laughing when, ahead on the road, Copper's horse skid out from under him and sent him reeling into the trees. Cylvan absolutely howled with laughter, grabbing the newly-abandoned horse by the reins and just barely keeping it out of Copper's reach once the fox-fey scrambled back to his feet and took chase. Saffron couldn't stop himself from laughing, too, as Cylvan's own amusement rang out loud and bright for the whole forest to hear.

SAFFRON DIDN'T KNOW WHAT TO EXPECT OF Sionnach's home, except that it was a bit of a ride away from the nearest town. The full distance, though, he never imagined, as hours passed from the last face they saw, the road growing more and more unused and overgrown until even Saoirse grew visible restless like she thought they were being lead into a trap. But Saffron, even if he was the only one, trusted that Sionnach wouldn't be the one to have intentions like those, and did his best to distract by pointing out plants he recognized, or chatting light-heartedly about the wild fey he used to see and sketch in the Agate Wood. Every time Sionnach grinned and shared a similar anecdote, and then Copper tried to one-up with his own, time passed a little more without anyone in the party fully snapping and asking where in god's name they were going.

Sionnach said they would know they were close when they

could smell the flowers—and Saffron didn't give them enough credit, until the wave of thick florals crashed into him like the sweetest wave he could imagine. He practically lifted from the seat of his saddle with how delightful the scent was, prodding Boann forward a little faster in anticipation.

The house itself, two stories tall and, while once easily as grand as Luvon's townhouse, the age of it simplified much of the adornments of the facade, with cracking plaster and a few missing shingles on the roof replaced with stones or carpets of grass. Even so, any flaws were near impossible to see through the ocean of flowers in a lovingly-curated garden, overflowing with blooms Saffron knew and others he'd never seen before.

To the side of the house, a vegetable garden was visible past the aromatic blooms, with fruit trees planted around the back corner in a variety of kinds, as even wild berries and planted grapes grew side by side along the fenceposts.

Cylvan must have noticed the pure thrill on Saffron's expression, because he made a little sound before commenting: "Seems Lady Étaín took some inspiration from the palace gardens for her own..."

"This is mostly my father's work," Sionnach corrected, clicking their reins to continue toward an opening in the fence. Saffron eagerly followed, mouth hanging open slightly in appreciation as they made their way up the lengthy drive that cut right up the center of the bountiful life. Bees buzzed between the flowers, bumping into one another drunk on pollen; pixies glittered amongst the fluffiest bundles, giggling like they could feel every time Saffron's eyes skimmed over them. He wondered if there were any flower sprites sleeping in the rosebuds or iris pockets, too, just like he knew from Morrígan.

On the path, songbirds pecked at seeds scattered on the dirt, barely flapping out of the way so they wouldn't be flattened beneath the arriving horses. Fiachra peered at them and shifted on her feet on Saffron's shoulder, curious but apprehensive, only opening her wings to get a closer look once Saffron nudged the back of her talons in encouragement. It wasn't long before she was sweeping after a cloud of sparkling, chittering pixies, and Saffron grimaced, hoping the rowan magic he gave her was enough protection from even the hungriest of sprites that might notice how pretty her feathers and eyes were.

Reaching the end of the path, Saffron was distracted by the thick blanket of flowering vines along the brick exterior of the house when the front door flew open, and a melodic voice called out loud enough for all of them to hear. It exclaimed Sionnach's name, and Saffron barely turned in time to see a cornsilk-haired fey lady rushing from the house with arms extended to wrap around Sionnach, shaking them back and forth with enough enthusiasm their hooves clacked against one another.

"Mama...!" Sionnach attempted, face going red in embarrassment as their mother pulled away. She grinned, stunning in its sunny beauty, squeezing Sionnach's face in her hands before planting a thousand kisses all over them. Only when Saffron's feet met the earth did she finally turn to address the remainder of the travel party, and her gaze was striking enough that Saffron jumped when she looked to him, first.

Étaín mac Carce, the high-fey side of Sionnach's parents, was as beautiful as any other Saffron had ever known—but in a way he hadn't seen before. She wore no makeup, her hair was pulled back in a messy-but-controlled knot on the back of her head, there was even a little dirt on the side of her face. She wore a simple dress beneath an embroidered pinafore, and stood there in the drive completely barefoot. Wild and beautiful and not at all what Saffron expected when he thought of a high fey lady—not to mention, his friend who was so careful to always look their best no matter the circumstances.

"You must be Saffron," she said, turning her hugging arms on him next. Sionnach whined for her to wait, but Saffron welcomed the embrace in an instant, like something told him every ache and pain in his body would heal the moment she held him. He wasn't entirely wrong. Étaín was like walking sunshine, smelling of fresh-cut herbs and rising bread. He would have kept holding her if there weren't half a dozen others watching.

When Cylvan approached, she offered him a bow that belonged directly in the center of court, a well-practiced movement, even if rarely used so far out in the woods. She smiled as bright as ever, even giving the prince a hug. Cylvan seemed surprised by it, but wrapped his arms around her in return, too.

"You look handsome as ever, Prince Cylvan," she said, pulling back and fixing Cylvan's braid knocked askew by their embrace. "I hope the journey wasn't too long. We have plenty of food and beds for everyone, though I hope some of you won't mind sharing."

"I hope the sudden notice was no trouble," Cylvan said with a polite smile, glancing over his shoulder at the strange collection of guests he'd brought along with him.

"None at all! Sionnach's never brought friends to stay—especially so many of you all at once! Such a handsome gallery of faces —oh, and some familiar ones, as well!"

"Hello, Lady mac Carce," even Copper greeted, approaching like a pet eager for a hug, too. Étaín didn't hesitate, though her arms barely met around Copper's strong middle. Saffron saw the way his smile lit up as soon as she greeted him back, like a part of him wasn't sure she would. "I hope my brothers haven't been causing you too much trouble while we've been at school."

"Your brothers are naturally gifted with the ability to cause trouble," she answered. Saffron wanted to ask what that meant, but Maeve stepped up behind them, next, like they really were all in a queue to receive some much-needed affection from the bare-footed sunshine in front of them.

"Lady Étaín," Maeve said, and Étaín swept Maeve into a tight hug before touching her hair, the fancy buttons of her doublet, complimenting her all over like they were long-time school friends. For the first time since Saffron could remember, Maeve even smiled and complimented the lady back, though it was intermingled with teasing about how she looked about as wild as her husband. Étaín just continued grinning, before clapping her hands together and motioning for them all to join her inside where she would brew some tea and make something to eat.

The inside of the house was only slightly more of what Saffron expected of a high fey's living space; similar to the outside, the interior matched what he knew from Luvon's various dwellings in many ways—the most prominent difference being the clear scarcity of beantighes milling about. There was no handful of human servants to mop the floors or polish the wooden furniture until it was glossy; to repair curling wallpaper that peeled from the ancient plaster beneath it. But even with such small imperfections scattered all over, the house was far from dirty, let alone even unkempt. In fact, it reminded Saffron more of Cottage Wicklow than any of Luvon's townhouses, enough that he couldn't stop grinning.

Étaín showed where everyone was welcome to sit, but Saffron followed Sionnach toward the kitchen, where even the simplicity of the setup there made him practically giddy. He offered to help brew tea, and Étaín thanked him, though gave a mischievous look that made him wonder how much she knew about his background. Just to be safe, he did his best to ask silly questions about tea-making like any other fey lord would, but perhaps offering to help at all already gave him away as having a secret.

He was in the middle of pretending like he didn't know how to stoke a wood stove when the sound of clopping hooves on the floorboards entered the kitchen. Saffron barely glanced up, thinking it was only Sionnach walking around—instead finding himself face-to-face with a tall, broad-chested, broader-shouldered satyr who grinned ear to horned ear at the sight of Sionnach in the kitchen.

"Saw all the horses outside!" The satyr-man boomed, and even Sionnach jumped before whirling around and sighing. Saffron assumed the newcomer had to be their father by the features they shared—excluding the obvious—and he stood slowly, eyes wide in curiosity while definitely taking a little too long regarding every inch of him.

Devilishly handsome in a way high fey never could be. Rough and rugged like a wild thing, with hard-wrought muscle stretching across his tanned chest and bulking his arms. His face was the most fey-like thing about him, with bright green eyes and an even brighter smile, the mild points of his teeth making Saffron's heart race in every way but intimidation.

His fur was a pretty dark reddish-brown, covering his muscular thighs and legs in a thick layer that made it impossible to see the skin underneath, despite wearing no pants for modesty. The fur coated his arms and shoulders as well as a majority of his back, though thinned to reveal his fey-esque chest and even a bellybutton at his navel, and a small peek at his spine and the strong muscles of his back. His tail was longer than Sionnach's, as well as thicker and more intimidating with the weight it swung around, jingling with decorative rings at the end that matched gold shimmer around his hoofed ankles and wrists. His hair was long and curly, the same color as his fur, matching stubble hiding the bottom half of his face and neck. His ears were thicker and longer than Sionnach's as well, and they flicked with every sound of movement from both inside the house and through the open door he'd just entered through. Two curling horns emerged from either side of his temples, looping a total of three times in a spiral, making Saffron wonder if Sionnach's would curve around themselves that many times someday, too, as they grew older.

"Sorry, what?" Saffron blurted when he realized Sionnach and both parents were looking at him, as if waiting for him to say something. Carce just smiled—in a way that made Saffron's insides shiver, unearthing many long-buried fantasies he used to indulge in while wandering the Agate Wood alone.

"I said you must be Saffron. Sionn has told us plenty about you in their letters home. You two have become fast friends, haven't you?"

"Erm, yes, I guess we have," Saffron smiled and nodded.

"They made it easy, though. Sionnach's the only reason I didn't completely fail every one of my classes last semester. Though I didn't exactly pass them, either."

Carce grinned, nudging Sionnach with his elbow. "No judgement from me. Never had a day of 'formal' education in my life, and still turned out just fine, didn't I?"

Sionnach mumbled something in embarrassment, shrugging away from their father's playful prodding to return to helping their mother put together plates of finger-foods.

"Saffron was appreciating your garden when we rode up," they went on, anyway. "Saffron, do you want him to show you around?"

"Oh!" Saffron and Carce both exclaimed, Saffron nearly leaping off his feet. "I would love that, if you have time!"

"I always have time to chatter on about my plants, c'mon," Carce said, waving his hand for Saffron to join him back out the door. Saffron barely resisted sprinting.

"Sionnach's letter said you were visiting because of something to do with what happened during the Midsummer Games, right?" Carce asked. Saffron tried not to think there was a reason he waited until they were speaking-distance from the house to do so. "Traveling with so many sídhe fey in close confines... sounds miserable, if I do say so."

Saffron chuckled, watching how Carce's feet left prints in the dirt, embossed with swirling leaf and filigree designs.

"It's not so bad," he answered. "Maeve never causes trouble unless it's to get a rise out of Cylvan or Copper... and even they seem to behave better than normal when I'm there to scold them. Even Sionnach has gotten a little bolder with telling them off, when they deserve it."

"You must be very convincing to be able to do so, especially with the Prince of Alfidel. Even more impressive as only a human, hm?"

Saffron came to an halt. Carce grinned over his shoulder in

return, but it wasn't malicious, let alone even mocking. His demeanor remained pleasant as ever.

"Don't panic, Saffron, Sionnach hasn't revealed a thing. Satyrs can see straight through fey glamour magic, especially when it's made with a charm."

"O-oh," Saffron rasped, suddenly inundated with the mortifying thought of Sionnach seeing right through him from the first day they met. Surely they hadn't, right? They would have said something sooner, wouldn't they have? Carce must have noticed his panic, but said nothing—just continued smiling to himself.

"More satyrs than high fey for a long ways in every direction, here. And even more wild things than that." He said, stopping to look Saffron fully up and down all over again. Flicking his ears and momentarily captivating Saffron with the color of his eyes, bright and green as the plants behind him. "Welcome to the Autumn Court, little witch. I'll be sure to show you all the wonders we have to offer, maybe to even keep you here for ourselves, if you like, by the end of it all."

Saffron's face boiled. Carce definitely noticed, just smiling to himself again before turning to begin the tour of his garden.


ALMOST THREE HOURS PASSED BY THE TIME SAFFRON and Carce made it just around to the front of the house, halfway through every inch of the garden, chatting endlessly about the different kinds of buds, fruiting trees, rows of vegetables that had been planted there, even discussing the pixies and flower sprites that made homes in the flowers. Saffron meekly suggested using honeycomb to gain the allyship of the pixies against the sprites if Carce was worried about such things, and even blushed some when Carce grinned and thanked him for the advice. Even if it was obvious the satyr already knew such tricks.

They were crouched alongside a stunning hybrid of roses and tulips in the front yard when an exhausted Fiachra flapped over to perch on Saffron's shoulder, initially nipping at Carce when he reached to pet her, before purring and chittering once he let her have a little taste of blood.

"Pretty thing," he smiled. "Well loved, I can tell."

"Thanks," Saffron chuckled, reaching up to pet under the bird's beak with a flush of pride.

"Was she a gift from the kings? Since their reigning symbol is the barn owl."

"Erm, not exactly," Saffron said with an awkward smile. He described the human rebels' intentions behind using barn owls sacrificed and nailed to the palace gates as a way of sending warnings to the kings inside. He didn't mention the specifics of how he rescued Fiachra, though a part of him wondered if Carce already had an idea the extent of his magic, considering he'd already casually referred to Saffron as *witch*. Carce never interrupted as Saffron spoke, absentmindedly pruning the bushel of flowers in front of them while nodding along in consideration.

"I knew something was amiss," he finally muttered. "I could tell Sionnach wasn't telling the whole truth in their letters home. Not to mention the shift in the air. Wild things acting strange, lately. Didn't want to think it had anything to do with the veil, at first, but—perhaps even it knew what was coming long before being opened during the games. We felt the reverberations all the way here, hitting like a wind on the trees. Whole forest went silent in an instant, every bird and magic thing alike. Woke me from a rather pleasant nap, too."

"That's actually why we came," Saffron said sheepishly. "There was a second veil even in Erelaine a few days ago—"

"Felt that one too. And the one that occurred last night? Pretty close this time. That's the real reason you're here, isn't it?"

Saffron stared at him a moment, mouth hanging open before Carce gently reached out to nudge it closed.

"Don't fret, little witch," he said in a low voice. "Satyrs are friends of the veil as much as you are. We'll help you figure out what's going on, however we can. In fact, I'll take you to visit

Síomha in the borough tonight. She'll be able to answer any questions you might have."

Saffron pressed his lips together. He nodded in gratitude, but still struggled to find the words to properly thank him. To say anything at all. Too wrapped up in the understanding that he had, indeed, dreamed of a third veil event the very night it happened.

Finding it difficult to swallow the understanding that Ryder attacking the temple of The Morrígan in Erelaine had not, in fact, been for the sole purpose of making Cylvan look bad, especially if that third event occurred so far out in the woods, not a single high fey knew any better. Having to accept, perhaps—there really was more at play, and Saffron had still only scratched the surface of what it would take to find Ryder Kyteler and put an end to him.

## 15

# THE BOROUGH

Saffron anticipated Cylvan not being particularly *thrilled* to visit the satyr borough so soon after arriving, but the prince clearly had enough training to keep it off his face. His demeanor, however, was an open book. He wrinkled his nose the entire time they walked; adjusted his gloves a hundred times despite going on foot rather than horseback; he fidgeted with his hair until Saffron sighed and pulled him off to the side of the road to braid it for him. He waved for the rest of the group to go on ahead, partially not to keep them, partially because he knew he had to give his prince a chance to de-pressurize before they got even closer to the destination.

"I have nothing against satyrs," Cylvan insisted once Saffron accused him of acting strangely. "But I already know what they are going to say to me, and I am not looking forward to it. Didn't I already do enough *listening* in Erelaine? *Ugh.*"

"Well, if you already know what they'll say, then you should have a response prepared," Saffron countered. "What exactly are you expecting to hear?"

"They're going to ask why neither of the kings have come to hear their demands in some century or so," Cylvan muttered. "But they're a sovereign people, why would the kings come to see them? What good would it do to make an audience with them? Especially since they always refuse to travel to Avren, insisting someone come to them."

"Oh, boy," Saffron breathed with a weary smile, and Cylvan *hmph'd* in annoyance. "I promise to be there with you throughout it all."

"What's that supposed to mean?"

Saffron laughed. He finished braiding Cylvan's hair, smoothing his hands over the handsome doublet he wore, pinching a fallen leaf from his shoulder.

"I'm here to be your balance," he said. "You chose me because I can help you better understand those who aren't high fey. Right?"

Cylvan wanted to argue—it was in his nature, and painted on his expression—but instead, he just closed his eyes, and sighed. He reached into an inner pocket of his doublet, producing the carved hair-pick Saffron had given him the night after the games. Saffron was surprised to see it, eyes lifting to Cylvan in question.

"I carry it with me everywhere," he said gently, "but don't get many opportunities to wear it. I don't know how to put it in so it will stay, like you do. If you could perhaps help me out, since you've already braided my hair for me, beantighe..."

Saffron smirked, plucking the pick from Cylvan's fingers. Beneath his own, he was reminded of how rough the texture of the wood was, a reiteration of how amateur his carving work had been, a reminder that the gift was nowhere near suited for a prince as perfect as Cylvan was—but as he adjusted it in his hand, his thumb brushed over an unexpectedly smooth spot on the carved moon, and Saffron realized it was worn down from constant rubbing. He bit his lip, imagining Cylvan's thumb gliding back and forth over the shape absentmindedly, under the table, behind his back, without Saffron ever knowing he had it with him.

Cupping the braid in one hand, Saffron carefully threaded the long end of the pick in and out of the plaits a few times, making it visible from the front. Like a needle pricked through multiple ruffles of a collar, holding them in place.

"There," he said softly. "A little spot of handcraft to balance how pretty the rest of you is. To prove you aren't so pompous as they think."

"You believe they already think that?" Cylvan muttered. His hand trapped Saffron's against where the prick nestled within his dark hair, stealing it to leave a brief kiss against the back of Saffron's fingers. "Thank you."

"It's going to be alright," Saffron reassured one more time. "Dealing with satyrs can't be any worse than courtiers. At least they aren't all trying to marry you."

"Hm," Cylvan exhaled, before throwing his head back with a louder, more dramatic sigh, and turning with his hand in Saffron's to continue up the road. Saffron followed close, holding Cylvan in return.

SAFFRON DIDN'T KNOW WHAT TO EXPECT OF A SATYR borough, since his only familiarity came from spotting a few wandering around the Agate Wood where he would scribble down sketches as fast as he could, knowing satyrs vanished into the trees as easily as nymphs. He was also always warier about crossing paths with a playful satyr over a nymph, in many ways. In other ways, a part of him always secretly wished he would, the idea reinvigorated upon laying eyes on Carce the first time. A thought he hadn't ever shared with Cylvan, and would definitely never with Sionnach or Copper. Not wanting them to know there was a part of him that wondered what exactly it was like to be stolen and used on the unpredictable whims of a wild satyr in the middle of the woods.

There were plenty of wild things Saffron had the same sentiments about—but god help him if the wrong people found out. Especially considering his closest circle of confidantes at the moment, three of whom could pass as those sort of wild fey if

Saffron squinted. A wild fox, a satyr, a leanan sídhe. He had to resist shivering; he had to shove that realization far, far away before he flushed so bright even they noticed.

While he certainly didn't imagine them to have streets as houses as decadent as those of the high fey, Saffron also didn't expect how particularly *simple* the small satyr community was, either. It made his heart flutter in curiosity the moment they found the others at a spot in the road that branched off into a thicket of trees, passing through a veil of hanging vines and wild wisteria into a dark corridor of foliage on the other side—and emerging into a wide open meadow, flush in every direction with flowers amongst grass and scattered stones arranged in spiraling designs, others marking a path into the center of the clearing where a massive tent the size of Carce's entire garden ten-times over stretched. From it, multiple spirals of smoke emerged through openings in the fabric, smelling of spiced meats and herbs and incense, combining with the natural aroma of the forest into something that made Saffron's mouth water.

Encircling the tent, garlands pierced with leafy twigs of golden oaks, maple trees, pines swayed lightly in the wind, adorned with ribbons braided from what Saffron realized was hand-pressed paper and woven strips of fabric that matched the fabric of the tent canopy. The center mass of the tent was made of a creamy-white spun wool, sweeping out from a towering tree in the center and extending like fingers to a circle of trees along the outer edge. The flared fabric whispered with every breath of wind that strained its anchor points, while the dangling edges ruffled with a patchwork of additional fabrics, some embroidered, some decorated with beadwork, others dyed in unique ways or stamped with flowers like Saffron used to do with his friends in Beantighe Village.

The borough whistled lightly with flutes dangling from strings, some forged from iron while others were carved with expertise from pieces of wood, some even woven from grasses in such a way they created a buzzing whistle when the wind passed through. More buzzing flutes could be heard off to the side of the open field, combined with chatter and laughter, and Saffron spotted a cluster of furry things racing each other up and down the treeline. They banged sticks with bells along the trunks as they went, leaving one of a hundred markings behind in the bark. Up and down they ran, only stopping when a pair of sparrows finally had enough of all the noise and emerged from their nests to screech and swoop down at them. The furry daemons waved wooden baskets through the air whenever the birds dipped close enough—until soon they captured one, half a dozen shrill voices howling and shouting in celebration.

"They're sparrow-catching," Sionnach said, noticing how Saffron stared.

"For a snack, right?" Copper interjected, but Sionnach ignored him.

"Sparrow feathers are used to fletch light arrows for hunting. Children are always trained with that kind, first."

"Those are children!" Saffron gasped, making Sionnach laugh.

"What did you think they were?"

"I—! I don't know, god! Look at them! I thought they might be wild *grogoch* or something—since there are all those decorative stones at the head of the road, I just... Ah, please don't tell anyone..."

But Sionnach just kept laughing, shaking their head. "They're much cuter up close—but tend to have a mouth on them. Try not to take offense to anything they might say, they love trying to get a rise out of visitors." Their eyes specifically skimmed over to Cylvan, who grimaced, before turning his nose up like he of all people were immune to being insulted by a bunch of children. Saffron squeezed his hand in emotional support.

Following the path to the main entrance of the tent, Saffron could hardly keep the interest off his face, and knew it was obvious by how the satyrs they approached turned to look back at him. With matched interest, at first, even a bit of reservation, until they noticed Carce and Étaín led the way. Until they spotted the

Crown Prince on their heels, and then suddenly every satyr within shouting distance was suddenly upright to hurry over.

Satyrs were as diverse in appearance as humans or high fey, particularly with so many varying shades of fur, patterns of growth, how much actually covered their bodies; the length of their tails, the shape and curl of their horns; even the spots on their ears and how they hung. Some wore their hair long, braided out of their eyes, while others kept it cropped short; they painted symbols and other adornments on bare skin, while patches of fur were shaved away in swirling or leafy designs down their legs, around their navel. Saffron knew it was rude to stare as they approached—but he couldn't help it.

Even so, it quickly became clear that the sprawling community of satyrs beneath the tent were no more *wild* than beantighes with far too much time off from chores. Chatting away in the cool evening air, knitting scarves and ankle-cuffs and headbands for each other; smoking wild herbs they picked from patches of the scattered gardens, or maybe found deeper in the woods; playing games with squares of painted bark no differently than beantighes played with cards. In reality, to a high fey, any living thing that didn't mind a little mud on their feet was wilder than they could fathom.

Perhaps that was why Saffron fought so hard to hold his tongue. Overcome with the urge to pull out his sketchbook to draw them lounging; to ask why some shaved designs into the fur, while others used paints or adorned with jewelry; then why some adorned with jewelry, while otherwise naked; even as others wore random pieces of clothing, like beautifully-beaded waist belts that cinched over their hips, or bracelets and anklets made from hammered-gold. Saffron wanted to ask, he wanted to know all of it, he wanted to sketch them onto paper like he did other beautiful things found in the woods—but not like a high fey trying to study them. Like a human who wanted to be eaten alive by every mouth at once—but not even so literally. He wasn't sure there was a string of words to properly explain. So he just kept his mouth shut.

"Ah—there she is, right where I thought. Good morning, Síomha," Carce drew Saffron's attention back as he led them through the center of the tent, toward a satyr perched on a mossy log on the opposite side.

"My prince," the old satyr woman smiled at Carce from where she sat, a swathe of beaded fabric draped over her lap. Cylvan made a sound to answer—but Carce spoke first, and the rest of them had to stand there and silently comprehend exactly what had just been revealed so casually.

"I've brought some special guests here to see you. Specifically —ah, Saffron, come on, come a little closer. Síomha's eyes aren't what they used to be."

"I can see a glamour charm from across the field just fine, though," she smiled wickedly, like when Baba Yaga would tease. Saffron hurried forward, offering the old woman a bow, only for her to take his hand without warning and turn it over in her own. Her nails were grown long, but well taken care of, filed into almond shapes and even painted with a springy green tone. "Saffron, your name is? Looks to me like you're due for a long and happy life."

"Sorry?" Saffron said, before realizing she was reading the lines on his palm by how she traced the tip of a fingernail along one of them. Rather than pulling away, he crouched on the balls of his feet, having to resist shoving his hand a little closer for her to continue.

*"Your dad's the prince of the satyrs?"* Copper meanwhile muttered from the back of the group, followed by a nervous sound from Sionnach.

*"It's different from how the fey do it."*

*"That makes you like, what, satyr royalty?"* Copper continued anyway. *"Or was the honor stripped from you like how your mom was stripped of her nobility when she chose—hrk!"* Out of the

corner of Saffron's eye, Maeve elbowed Copper in the gut before slicing him in half with a cutting look.

"Saffron was hoping you might show him the stripped henge," Carce went on as Síomha continued tracing lines up and down Saffron's palm.

"Dangerous place to go, right now," she answered, but it wasn't a refusal. Her round green eyes lifted to look at Saffron directly, and Saffron straightened himself up.

"Has anyone heard anything strange coming from there recently? Something to do with the veil," he asked. "Carce mentioned having sensed something as recent as last night...?"

The old woman smiled, tilting her head in curiosity. "And how did you know about that, child? Not even the fey in Tyara felt it. Some rogue entered the henge and tore the veil open right over it."

Saffron's heart pounded loudly in his ears. Ringing loud, like those sparrow-whistles shrieked all around him. All he could do was nod, before answering: "I... saw it in a dream, last night."

"A dream?" Síomha asked, matching Saffron's curiosity with the look on her face. "Well—I can't remember the last time I met a human as in tune with the veil as that. Did it call out to you itself, child?"

Saffron jumped. His stomach turned, but he managed to keep the nausea at bay. "I—I hear a voice when I dream of it, yes, but— I don't know if it's the veil. I sounds... it sounds like someone else I know, but... I don't know."

Síomha gazed at him for a long moment, observing him closely, or like she read the lines of his face as well as she'd read those of his palm.

"Must have been the very end of the war when I last read the hands of someone like you, you know. Touched by the veil as you are; I think his name was *Virtue*, but it was so long ago, perhaps I'm mistaken. I'll never forget that tired look on his face, though —the same exhaustion you wear on yours, beneath that glamour.

He'd just lost his sister, and was trying to decide what to do with himself next. What have you lost, Saffron?"

The satyr woman waited for a response, even as Saffron felt the earth tilt beneath him. Finally, he managed to wobble out a quiet answer.

"There's a man abusing the veil as he pleases; maybe even the same one who came to your henge last night. He took some very important people from me, and is hiding them on the other side," he said. "I thought the person calling out to me in my dream might have been one of them, but... like I said, I don't know, I— I'm just trying to find them, or find him, I don't know..."

"Do you intend on opening the veil, yourself? To chase after him?"

Saffron hesitated, unsure how to answer that, either. The mere thought made his heart race with anxiety, with—*fear*. A fear he'd held for a long time, since he was a child; one he hadn't resolved even after making his oath, and especially after witnessing exactly how much damage the veil could do when misused.

He let the answer come on its own, allowing his instincts to dictate for him: "I don't want to, if I don't have to."

"What has the veil advised of you?"

Saffron shook his head. "Nothing. I haven't heard anything from it."

Síomha tilted her head in curiosity again. "So you can sense shifts in the veil, enough to dream of them—but you do not communicate directly with it?"

"I... didn't know that was something I should have been doing," he admitted, voice hitching in a rush of embarrassment. "I spoke to it once when I first made my oath, but—nothing else since then, really..."

The humiliation mixed with shame in his gut, but Síomha didn't taunt him for it. She didn't even smirk. The old satyr just released his hand, rising to her hooves and grabbing a nearby cane leaned against the sitting log.

As she turned, her long tail whipped out and snapped against

Saffron's shoulder, making him jump back with a yelp, though she clearly hadn't noticed. The appendage was longer than any he'd seen on other satyrs—possibly even twice as long as she was tall. He quickly rose to his feet to avoid getting whacked a second time.

"Come, come on, then," she said out as she hobbled away from the log, moving faster than Saffron anticipated. He hurried after her. "I'll show you what's come of the stripped henge. Veil might even be willing to chat with you there, too, if you're patient enough. Ah, not all of you—just this one."

Copper, Sionnach, Maeve all exchanged looks, coming to a halt—but Cylvan pressed ahead, grabbing Saffron's hand possessively and locking himself in place. Refusing to be left behind. Saffron clung to him in return, grateful for something to hold and keep him grounded.

"Really?" He asked while hurrying after her, even Cylvan struggling to keep up through the cramped tent arrangements. "You can—you can help me talk to the veil?"

"Sure. S'not that hard, if you know how. Even calfs know how to solicit the veil for the smallest things. You've already made an oath with it, anyway, haven't you? Should have no reason to ignore any beseeching, so long as you haven't done anything to upset it."

Saffron grimaced. What a thought.

Leaving the shade of the community tent, Síomha led them into a nondescript edge of the trees, into the thickest undergrowth Saffron had ever seen. He managed to navigate the upturned roots, reaching vines, thorny brambles well enough, but soon had the thought to glance behind him to see how his raven fared through the same.

As if Cylvan had sent him a mental plea for help, Saffron barely threw out his hand to pull the prince back upright as he almost twisted an ankle on the uneven ground. It nearly knocked them both off their feet, and Saffron couldn't help but chuckle as he brushed Cylvan off. Keeping hold of his hand again while continuing forward.

"I assume you made your oath via the traditional arid way?" Síomha asked as they went, though it took Saffron a moment to respond, that time busy untangling the heel of Cylvan's book from a cluster of weeds snaking around his ankle.

"Yes, ah—are there other ways?"

"Every type of magic user has their way of making oaths," she answered without looking back. "High fey, humans, satyrs, even the wild fey, though they don't require so much pomp and ritual to do so. The veil tends to offer its benefits to the wildest of creatures without demanding trade—as they're the least likely to use it for selfish reasons."

"That... makes sense," Saffron breathed. Cylvan squeezed his hand.

No different from approaching the crumbling temple in Erelaine, Saffron could sense the moment the site of the torn veil came within reach. That buzzing under his skin, the warm goosebumps that flushed his arms, even the minty-sweet taste of the air. There in the old woods, though, there were no temple guardians hurrying in every direction to scrape up any fairy fruits sprouting from the earth—they grew wild as ever, uninhibited, almost suffocating the surrounding flora.

Crossing into the clearing, Saffron had to stop for a moment and take it all in. Exactly like how he'd seen it in his dream, though with the earth tilled beneath their feet, the henge of stones circling the center knocked on their sides and turned upside down.

"Did the satyrs in the borough experience any ashenness from this?" Cylvan asked first, and Síomha gave him a funny look.

"Not that I know of, your highness. That's a high fey curse."

Cylvan frowned. Síomha noticed, adding: "No need to pout. Make amends with the veil and it'll stop biting back."

Saffron had to bite back a little smile, just squeezing Cylvan's hand and pulling him forward to observe the damage closer. Síomha hopped up onto a tall churn of soil, fresh and damp beneath her hooves that left half-moon prints behind. Saffron wasn't brave enough to get that close, but he did lean over to gaze into the remains, unsure if he was unsettled or relieved to see they resembled what had been left behind at The Morrígan's temple in Erelaine, too. Even down to the same strange arid circle hand-painted with charcoal over the grass. No surprises, at least; no explanations, either.

Síomha, meanwhile, bent her furry legs to pluck a handful of fat, pink blackberries from the tilled earth, casually popping one into her mouth before extending the rest toward Saffron. Saffron shuffled his way over, accepting the offering in hands that immediately went clammy.

"If you wish to communicate with it, the fruits help," she said. "I recommend doing so now, while they're still ripe. Once the veil starts healing from this damage, the fruits will wither off quickly."

Saffron stared down at the morsels, blackberries candied pink by the magic of the veil; once again unsettled by how something so violent could result in such pretty, glittering remnants. Síomha's instruction reminded him of Ryder right before the summer games, and how the man's eyes had been as bright and pink as the berries in his hands. He must have eaten so many, before tearing open the veil with such ferocity.

Saffron glanced back to Cylvan in uncertainty. The prince immediately stepped into Saffron's reach, placing a hand on Saffron's back.

"Do you want to try?" he asked in quiet encouragement. "I won't let anything happen to you."

Whether or not he *wanted* to—Saffron didn't feel like he had much choice. But, at least, he would be able to make the attempt there in private. In the quiet safety of that henge, with both the ancient satyr woman and his prince watching over him.

"Strange to be holding these so casually, considering they were the reason you and I ever made our geis," Saffron whispered, attempting to relax his nerves. Cylvan smiled at him with months and months of lovingly-nurtured affection for those memories, the sight of him so handsome and familiar and *safe*. Saffron would be brave enough to try anything, if Cylvan was there next to him.

"How many should I have?" he asked Síomha before committing. She'd taken a cross-legged seat on her perch, watching a cluster of robins pecking at worms wriggling free of the upturned earth.

"As many as it takes," she said. "As many as you need, little witch."

Saffron gulped. He closed his eyes, then glanced back down at the fruits again. His hands trembled slightly, but he wouldn't be a coward. He'd done it before. The veil wasn't going to hurt him— if it wanted to, it would have, already. It wouldn't have made an oath with him in the first place.

Stepping away from the churned soil, Saffron wandered like a lost cat for a moment, unsure where exactly he wanted to engage the veil while drugged on the fruits. By the trees? In the clearing? Would it be best in the center of the ruined earth, or off to the side? Would it matter? Would the veil have a preference? He followed the edge of the tilted henge stones while Cylvan followed in silence.

Saffron nearly asked what he thought a good place would be —but then Fiachra swooped in from where she'd been exploring the grass between the feet of the others, landing straight ahead on the tip of the tallest henge stone at the head of the circle. Saffron exhaled a breath, following her lead. There was a patch of smooth grass at the base of it, facing the tilled earth but not directly within it. That was good enough for him.

Cylvan took the initiative, sitting first and putting out his hands for Saffron to join him. Saffron crossed his legs, seated between Cylvan's thighs and leaning back into his chest. Wrapped gently around the waist in the safety of Cylvan's arms.

"If there's anyone who can do this, I know it's you," Cylvan whispered, making Saffron's heart flutter. He looked at Cylvan over his shoulder for a moment, before biting his lip. He gazed down at the fruits in his hands again. They left specks of dark red juice on his palms, like flecks of paint.

Swallowing back the apprehension, Saffron tilted his head back and put two in his mouth to start. As he did, Cylvan reached for a small handful more within reach of where they sat.

The taste made Saffron gag—but only because it reminded him of all the artificial fruits he'd ever been forced to eat at fetes, while cornered on campus, after being dragged into the woods for a prank. But the flavor also reminded him of when he first made his oath, that night in the burned out library of the Kyteler School. Guided by the beannighe, who offered the end of her long life in order to open the door for conversation. Allowing him to save Cylvan; to save everyone he cared for. At least for the time being. Having no idea what would come next.

The bittersweet sensation on his tongue, sparkling and fizzing like champagne, sugary-sweet and minty blackberry that blanketed his tastebuds, finally slid like warm syrup down the back of his throat. In the Kyteler library, the effects of the berries had taken a few minutes to fully settle in, creeping like a rising tide, shifting so gradually he never felt the sensation fully swallow him —but there, at the edge of Ryder's most recent chaos, they hooked into Saffron's being in an instant.

The world grew brighter, more vivid; his ears rang, his thoughts spun like petals caught in a summer wind; every smell of the woods struck his nose, laced with a thick coat of the same sugary-mint aroma of the fruits. Overwhelming him, overtaking him, a cacophony of sensations that rang wildly at first, before slipping into step with one another. Finding the music only they could hear, his thoughts, the flickering colors and lights, the hum of the wind in the trees, the undulating scents in his nose, soon it all found rhythm with one another, and Saffron's spirit stopped reeling.

It slowed, attempting to match the pace, until soon enough— there was more than just his brightened senses. Saffron could see something shifting in his vision, flashes of colorful light, like reflections cast on the wall from polished glass in the sun. His hand lifted, and he nudged a few more berries between his lips. Knowing he needed them without actively having the thought. Like every dancing sense compelled him to continue chasing a little closer.

Those undulating streaks crawling like spiderwebs over the tilled earth—were tears in the veil. Minuscule cracks through the intangible fabric of magic that draped all of Alfidel, all of the fey world. Only then did he understand the first line of Baba Yaga's knocking rhyme: *split knocks are memories.*

Those tears were the remnants of what Ryder had done, open wounds slowly stitching themselves back together like a bleeding cut on the back of Saffron's hands.

"It's... awful," he whispered. He didn't know the word—it was beautiful, it was painful. He didn't have to feel it then to know how badly it hurt; he'd been subjected to moments of the same agony after made drunk on the same artificial taste that coated his tongue. Torn apart, explored against his will, so that a stranger might climb through to get what they wished on the other side. And while Saffron had never been physically torn to shreds in the process—he understood the shimmering ribbons left behind. Scattering seeds for fruits that were never meant to exist except as proof of the suffering, like patches of memories that remained no matter how much weaverthistle tea he drank afterward. It was no wonder why the veil shrieked every time, loud enough to ring through his dreams—and before he realized he did, Saffron began to silently cry.

*Have you brought me... your bridgepartner, witch?*

A chill raced down his spine, striking through the wavering emotions. His hand lashed out, gripping Cylvan's wrist and holding it tight.

"No," he answered in a rasp, emotion still thick in his voice. *Don't take him from me.* "Not yet."

*Ahh...*

The voice came from the ruined earth—from the trees—from the sky—from every glittering scar undulating in front of him. From far, far off in the distance, Cylvan's voice joined it, asking if Saffron was alright. Saffron just clung to him without answering.

*Have you come... to split me open as well, then?*

"N-no," Saffron repeated weakly. His grasp on Cylvan loosened, just slightly. "No, I haven't, I—I keep hearing this call coming through you, someone who needs my help—"

*There is no thing that calls through me without me knowing.*

Saffron's mouth dangled open, unsure if the emotion paralyzing him was more disappointment or embarrassment.

"Then..." he croaked, still wishing to keep the veil's voice nearby, feeling like he had to continue prompting it in order to do so. "Then... I want to find the man who keeps doing this to you."

*He is near. But not for much longer.*

"What?" Saffron jumped. His head snapped to one side, then the other, in search, but everything moved slowly around him. The sun was too bright, everything was too vivid to properly see, and moving so quickly made his vision swirl like trying to see clearly through a bowl of milk. "Why—is he doing this?"

*He's searching.*

"For what?"

*Can you not read the spell he uses?* The veil's voice came harsher that time, reminding Saffron too much like Asche when they were being intentionally condescending. *Have I really made an oath with someone who cannot even read the spells required to—*

"I've read it," Saffron croaked. "But I didn't understand it. It —was strange. The feda markings, the lines were—strange."

The veil ribboned in consideration around him, as if trying to decide whether that admission was worth more derision, or perhaps something they could extend patience to. Saffron closed his eyes, hoping it would take pity on him.

*It's a very old epithet, yes,* it whispered. *From The Dagda's own book. Older than oaths, older than rowan witches and yew mancers. Even older than me, even if he requires me to carry it...*

"The...?" Saffron started, but was interrupted.

*He is searching for something, calling out to a lost thing.*

"What?" Saffron insisted. "What is he looking for?"

*By the nature of it... the old power of the magic... even I do not know. That is between the deliverer and the most innate parts of me I cannot fathom. But—he thinks himself a ghost's most precious thing. Precious enough to hear its call. Perhaps that is what you've heard calling out to you; but it is not me.*

"A ghost?" Saffron fought to keep the frustration out of his voice. His hand on Cylvan's arm tightened again, a flash of pure panic freezing his veins at the thought of the veil calling it a *ghost*, when the voice resembled Asche so much—

*I care little for him and his pleas,* the veil spat. *He begs to kiss my lips so often, but until the day the Dagda draws me back, I will not submit to him.*

Saffron forced his nerves to settle. Through the thick milk of his thoughts, he recalled what Breton had once said, about how the veil refused to speak to Ryder. To make any oath with him.

"If he's trying to find something through you, I think..." Saffron croaked. "He's going to open you again, until he does."

*If he is as predictable as the last—he will seek his missing ghost next where the earth's minerals heat the rocks.*

"What?"

*He is not the first to unhook me in this order. From these places. One by one, like buttons.*

Saffron wanted to ask again what the voice meant—but forced himself to be silent. When the veil's words began to drift, he blindly pawed at Cylvan's hand holding more berries, pressing them between his teeth.

"I'm trying to stop him," Saffron tried to tell it. It didn't hear him, or it didn't listen. It didn't want to, as it only grew more agitated.

*Pull enough of my seams, and I will unfurl entirely. What then, when all opulence curls in on itself and dies?*

Saffron had to force himself to blink. His eyes burned from staring ahead.

*What then, when I turn inside out? When both sides collide? When human and fey become one; when life and death become one; when the mounds split open and The Dagda wakes from their long sleep to wipe the earth and begin anew. Then there will be nothing left of any of you. Maybe then I will be allowed to rest. Perhaps I should allow it. Perhaps my suffering will finally cease. Only then can none violate me any longer.*

*Please*, Saffron wanted to say, but his voice was whisked away with each attempt. The veil did not want to hear it. He wasn't sure the veil recalled him listening, if it perceived him there speaking any longer, or if the pain of its ribbons slowly drove it mad. He didn't know if the wetness on his face was tears—or blood dripping from his nose. He wanted to let go, he wanted to pull away. The agony roiling in his body wasn't his—or perhaps it was. Perhaps the veil gave it to him, perhaps it simply unlocked a lifetime of his own suffering so that it might have a companion to weep with.

Saffron closed his mouth, then his eyes. He let the veil's agony sink into him, through his skin, around his bones, until it touched every inch. If that was as close as someone like him could come to embracing something that suffered so much pain—he wouldn't pull away. He would let it weep for as long as it needed, with the first person who could hear it in centuries.

# 16

## THE PARTY

Saffron wasn't sure if he fell into a full sleep, or just some sort of veil-induced meditative state—but whichever, it was the most rest he'd had in days. A welcome rest, despite sinking so deeply into it he wasn't sure he would ever open his eyes again; a welcome rest, even if he felt as if intangible fingers combed through every inch of him out of curiosity, like a mortician slicing open a human body for the first time. Wishing to see how it worked. Wishing to see what things he hid inside. Fingers leaving behind bright, colorful, sparkling scars with every tear through his skin.

When he did stir, it was on a bed of earthy-smelling blankets and pillows. Bodies shifted around him constantly, as the rest of the borough continued through its day as if nothing had changed; only the occasional hand or voice entered the part of the community tent where Saffron laid, touching his face or combing hair from his eyes, as if checking to see if he continued breathing. Somewhere in the distance, he overheard Cylvan conversing with many others at once, sometimes with amusement, sometimes with harsh and stern discussion. Had Saffron not been so exhausted, he might have gone to join him. Knowing he was addressing of grievances of the satyr community by himself, even though Saffron had promised to join him.

When Saffron finally roused fully, it was already dark. The moon was high in the sky, air rich with smoking meats and fresh wheat breads, warm sugar and roasted fruits. The occasional flute or string instrument plucked off toward a clearing back in the woods, and Saffron, for a moment, though he was back in Beantighe Village overhearing the sound of distant satyr festivities that were so unbearably difficult to ignore. Calling out to him, wishing for him to join them, despite how well he knew what would happen if he listened. If he didn't lose his way in the woods, first.

But then Sionnach came to check on him, hands soft with scented lotions to do away with the callouses of riding horseback for so long. Saffron cracked open his bleary eyes to regard them, not realizing a lazy smile infected his mouth until it was too late once he noticed how they were dressed. Essentially naked, except a collection of beaded chain jewelry that draped from their hips and shoulders, a crown of leaves and twigs in their hair, more vines woven up their legs from ankle to mid-thigh. Due to being only half-satyr, they didn't have the same thickness of hair from their navel and lower, so they covered their bare skin with a patch of embroidered fabric to protect any modesty they had left. Something told him they normally didn't bother—but considering the company of that night, they felt it the wiser choice.

Their face burned red hot when they realized Saffron was definitely staring, grabbing his face to look him over every inch and determine if he was still fairy-drunk, or finally sober again.

"Father insists on throwing a party for you all," they explained as Saffron finally found the strength to sit up with a grunt.

"You look cute," he complimented them. "Do I get to wear something like that, too?"

"My mother offered a few things for you," Sionnach said, producing a small handful of garments that were far more modest than the outfit Sionnach wore. Saffron frowned, holding up a tunic better fit for a *fey lord* than a human dancing around with a clutch of half-naked satyrs; when Sionnach noticed, they sighed like they should have known better.

Providing him with an outfit as scant as their own, Saffron was far too amused with how he jangled with every movement, how the wrong bend of his legs or his waist exposed his bare ass or other parts for all to see.

"Are you sure?" Sionnach asked, like they truly believed Saffron was only trying to be polite to satyr traditions—but Saffron just gave them a look.

"Humans dance naked in the woods all the time," he reassured, swaying his hips sensually before swishing back and forth more aggressively and grinning as the jewelry whipped at his bare skin. "Do you think they'd mind if I draw some of them while they party?"

"Oh—I think they would like it a little too much, to be quite honest..." Sionnach politely declined, and Saffron followed their eyes to see why. On the other side of the tent, a scattered gallery of satyr faces were angled toward him, watching in curiosity. Perhaps more than that, as their eyes trailed up and down his exposed skin. Saffron was the one to flush that time, laughing sharply as Sionnach grabbed his hand to lead him away.

On their way out of the tent, Saffron grabbed at whatever snacks or drinks he could find—starving after sleeping through dinner—and soon enough, satyrs were even happy to oblige him. Offering candies, pastries, goblets of special wine that tasted of spiced herbs and pressed apples. Saffron made sure to remind Sionnach to keep Cylvan away from those drinks, even as another was poured sensually into his mouth, and he had no choice but to swallow it back or else he choke. All while the feeling of a satyr's strong hand cupping the back of his head was as enthralling as he ever thought it would be.

"Has Cylvan been behaving himself?" he asked as he really

thought about it, hand-in-hand with Sionnach as the world already buzzed with wine, making their way down an illuminated, winding path toward the satyrs' festivity clearing. Where the sound of energetic music, the smell of more foods made Saffron's mouth water.

"They have all been surprisingly well-behaved," Sionnach told him, grabbing a goblet of their own to throw back in order to keep up with Saffron's relentless pace. "I admit, even though his expression is sourer than ever, Prince Cylvan has sat and listened to every grievance every satyr has brought to him. Even had Saoirse taking notes of it all, though he can't make any promises of anything…"

"What sort of grievances do satyrs have for fey kings? The borough seems pretty self-sufficient," Saffron went on, pausing at the edge of the brightly-lit clearing just long enough to untangle his amethyst necklace from the other strands of jewelry around his neck.

"Yes, but that doesn't mean help shouldn't be offered," Sionnach answered. At first, their tone bordered on agitated, like they instinctively thought they had to go on the defensive against another ignorant fey lord—but eventually it softened again, especially once Saffron managed to pull his amethyst free of the other chains. Reminding them he wasn't just another fey lord acting ignorant on purpose. "Satyrs are unique, in that we have such a long history and relationship to the oldest forests of Alfidel—but because we look so much different from high fey, we're still considered more *wild fey* than citizens. So while we might be offered most of the same protections and benefits of the high fey —they're never eagerly given. We're never prioritized when there is a disaster nearby. If a forest fire burns down a borough some-where, Avren is slow to send aid. They assume because satyrs live off the land normally, they don't need help from the cities."

"Did something happen recently?" Saffron asked, before grimacing. "I mean, other than the obvious, I guess…"

"There have been issues around here for a while, especially with the fey town nearby. And, well... other long-time residents..." Sionnach's eyes drifted off, and Saffron followed, finally spotting Copper amongst the crowd. Standing near Maeve at the edge of the clearing, the fox-lord was shirtless, as naked as Saffron, and shimmying his hips back and forth to show off how his body chains jingled. Saffron had to take another drink, realizing he and his roommate really weren't all that different.

"The dé Bricríus?" Saffron asked to clarify. "Maeve mentioned Copper's family also lives outside of Tyara."

"More reason why the kings have been slow to do anything about their harassment," Sionnach muttered. "Renard dé Bricríu is one of the oldest sídhe heads-of-house in Alfidel—and has a long history of despising King Ailir. Essentially leaving him and his sons to cause whatever trouble they wish, without consequences. Destroying the borough's crops, damming up creeks used for drinking water, strong-arming contracts from Tyara claiming they own pieces of the forest where satyrs have historically lived... such things rarely stick, but they still cause problems until sorted out."

"I'm sorry," Saffron said, pressing his thumbs together as guilt chewed on the inside of his stomach. He recalled what Ryder had once said about King Ailir's weak grasp on the throne. How there were many people who were just waiting for him to do something they could use to get him out of power. He searched for Cylvan again, hoping to spot him nearby, sighing when his raven was still hidden somewhere amongst the crowd.

"Sorry, I didn't mean to ruin the mood," Sionnach went on with an awkward laugh. "It's complicated, like most things."

"Yeah," Saffron breathed, then shook his head, before glancing to his friend over his shoulder. "Well—let's try and have fun tonight, despite it all. This is the closest I've ever gotten to a satyr borough—though not for their lack of trying. Spring Court satyrs occasionally followed me around the Agate Wood, trying to lure me away with them… almost went a few times, too. I probably would have enjoyed myself, at least at first."

Sionnach blushed again, shaking their head. "I'm glad you didn't. I promise no one will try anything strange with you tonight—unless you really want to."

"Don't tempt me. According to what I've read in books, like I said… I probably would have enjoyed myself."

"Just at first."

"Who's to say."

"Well—don't believe everything you read about satyrs in books. Gods, I don't even want to imagine what kinds of ideas you're getting right now."

Saffron's smile spread wider. "You mean they're not going to make a feast of me? One by one? Or even all at once?"

Sionnach's grimace deepened. "Once again—not unless you let them." They watched Saffron's expression, perhaps hoping he would finally break and laugh and promise them *no, of course not* —but Saffron couldn't think of a better way to really experience wild satyrs than allowing them to do whatever they pleased to him.

"I mean—with the prince here with you, I doubt any will be so bold," Sionnach added quickly, face going bright red as rowan berries. "They wouldn't want to offend him—"

"Well then, even better for me," Saffron sighed, running his fingers down the delicate chains that decorated his chest, dangling down to his stomach, where only that one strip of cloth covered him. "I always like it when Cylvan gets a little jealous."

"Naughty," Sionnach whispered, like they couldn't believe it. Saffron just continued smiling at them.

Whistling pan flutes and the rhythm of hands on drums filled the clearing as Saffron and Sionnach made their way into the thick of it, interspersed with songs that every satyr seemed to know; even Sionnach hummed along as they made they way to where more wine and snacks were spread on a table for anyone to take as they pleased. One satyr woman hovering around the area was more than happy to offer Saffron what he was looking for, inviting him to lean forward and open his mouth for her to pour the wine directly. He obliged, laughing when it spilled down his chin and into his hair, pretending like he didn't notice how half a dozen eyes turned toward him when he straightened up again.

Saffron followed Sionnach to the center of one of the grassy circles with the fewest bodies, where they took hands and Sionnach showed him how to dance like a satyr. On the balls of his feet, extending his foot without too much movements in the ankles, circling around one another not unlike some of the fey dances he'd learned from Catrín while preparing for Cylvan's suitor galas. Satyr dances never maintained that relaxed pace for long, though, always picking up before slowing down again, circling one another before lifting and bowing their partner over their head. Sionnach didn't have the strength for anything like that, but they still danced back-to-back, or chest-to-chest, hooking legs together with each turn and using one another's weight to counterbalance so they didn't fall while turning.

The dances were easier once a little drunk, where Saffron managed the steps well enough for another satyr to step in and ask to dance with him. Then another, and another, until soon there was practically a crowd circled around where he and Sionnach started, all watching him, one by one slipping in when they got the chance. Always smiling, pressing their nose into the side of Saffron's neck, trailing fingers up the length of Saffron's spine or tucking a soft, furry knee between Saffron's thighs with each turn, until soon Saffron was hardly more than drunk, melting wax to be spun and turned and passed around between whichever satyr had their hands extended for him to fall into.

Upon stumbling onto a stump for a chance to catch his breath, Saffron politely declined any other offers to dance—or other amusement—wishing instead for a glass of water amongst it all. Étaín mac Carce of all people came to his rescue, offering a ceramic cup filled with crisp, fresh water. She wore even less than Saffron did, fully nude with only anklet chains donning little bells that twinkled as she moved. Saffron only stared for a moment, before swiftly glancing away again with a drunk apology.

"Nothing to apologize for," she said, kneeling in the grass alongside where he sat. "It seems you fit right in, yourself. There's no shyness here."

"It's a lot of fun," Saffron said, gazing over at her again, appreciating her appearance—but not necessarily her nudity. She wore her hair long and loose, golden-blonde strands braided in an out of a leafy crown of twigs similar to Sionnach's. Sionnach definitely took after their mothers soft features, particularly her eyes and mouth. "You look like there's nothing you regret leaving behind."

She raised an eyebrow at him in question, and Saffron attempted to remember exactly what words he'd just said. "I mean —you're beautiful. Like—one of the most beautiful high fey I've ever seen."

"Oh, honey, you're drunk."

"Yeah, I'm—I'm wine-soaked. This satyr-made stuff doesn't hesitate, does it? I guess—what I'm really trying to say is—you look really happy, despite being covered in dirt."

She smirked, reaching up to nudge the bottom of Saffron's water cup back to his mouth. He obediently took a big swallow.

"I think I understand what you mean."

"Most high fey don't enjoy running around in the woods," Saffron attempted to clarify anyway, motioning with his cup toward where he suddenly, finally, spotted Cylvan hovering alongside Maeve at the opposite edge of the clearing. The prince remained in his dark clothing from earlier in the day, to Saffron's disappointment, while Maeve freely entertained herself with a gaggle of pretty satyrs clustered around her, feeding her snacks and pouring wine in her mouth while braiding her hair. Cylvan, meanwhile, just watched Saffron. Saffron smiled at him.

"The youngest dé Bricríu is certainly an exception, isn't he?" Étaín asked, and Saffron followed her eyes to where Sionnach was stiffly, awkwardly trying to show Copper the steps to the dance happening around them. Being nearly twice Sionnach's size, the two of them standing hand-in-hand looking almost comedic, but Saffron could practically see the fox-lord's tail swishing back and forth in amusement. His eyes certainly lingered on Sionnach's bare skin and legs more often than their face—though he wasn't the only one, Saffron also noticed, as other satyr gazes dwelled on Sionnach as well. He suddenly wondered if they ever had to worry about suitor galas like Cylvan did, considering they were the unpartnered daurae of the Fall Court satyr prince.

"I'm glad they're being nice to each other," Saffron said with a sigh. "They normally don't get along."

"That does not surprise me. Sionnach is slow to make friends," Étaín said, before her eyes returned to Saffron, smiling at him. "This is the first time they've ever brought anyone home—I'm so grateful for you, your highness, more than you know. I'm more aware than most how difficult it can be to keep friends with non-high fey when you yourself are being watched at every turn. You've even convinced Copper and Prince Cylvan to show a little bit of kindness to my child—you must indeed be a very powerful witch."

Saffron flushed. He finished drinking his water.

"Um, a few days ago, Copper mentioned something that upset Sionnach a lot—I don't know the context, but it was something about being *honorable,* and how Sionnach wouldn't even exist if their mother—erm, you, I assume—had done the 'honorable thing'...?"

"Did he?" Étaín asked. Her mood instantly soured, and Saffron put his hands out, but couldn't think of anything to say to save what little wisp of respect she held for Copper in the first place. "And you would like to know what he meant by something like that? I'm surprised Prince Cylvan hasn't already told you all about it."

Saffron smiled awkwardly. Someone passed by and offered him a new goblet of wine. He gladly accepted it.

"I was King Ailir's first fiancée," she said, reaching down to pluck a clover flower from the grass by her knees. "We'd been good friends since school, and it seemed a natural fit. But then, one afternoon while staying with friends in the Fall Court, I twisted my ankle while gathering flowers in the woods... and Carce found me." She sighed, like the memory was enough to make her swoon. "He wrapped my injury and carried me all the way back to the house. He was so gentle and careful with me, like he thought I'd break—I only realized exactly how possible that was the first time we... well, his arms aren't even the strongest part of him, if you know what I mean..." she giggled. Saffron wanted to know. But he didn't press it. "The morning after carrying me home, he even left the basket of flowers I'd dropped by my window, with a written apology for taking a few to remember me by. Any chance of me becoming Ailir's Harmonious Queen was lost, that easily."

Saffron's cheeks burned a little hotter, searching for the prince of the satyrs in the crowd, spotting where he'd kicked Copper out of the way to dance with Sionnach properly.

"I get it," he said without thinking, making Étaín laugh. He shook his head, sipping at his wine again before allowing his eyes to trail back over to Cylvan, who no longer sat near Maeve. Saffron exhaled a little breath, worried the prince wasn't enjoying himself enough to stay. "That... must have been very hard for you," he said, still searching the crowd for his horned daemon. "Since we first left Avren, we've been followed at every turn by these gossip writers... it's been horrible, and so stressful, but... we haven't even done anything all that scandalous yet. I can't imagine what they must have written about you."

"I can assure you, it was indeed *horrible*," she sighed, but a little smile remained on her mouth. "I came from a noble fey family, you know—so to not only deny my right to the throne, then to accept disownment from my family for choosing a satyr as a husband, it was world-ending in so many ways. But the more time I spent with him, and with all of them, away from the pomp and circumstance of Avren, the sooner I realized—my world my have ended, but it was never a world I wanted. The one Carce offered me, instead, was a much better fit."

Saffron's head spun. "So Sionnach is not only... a satyr daurae, technically, but they also have noble fey blood...?"

Étaín laughed, musical and charming. "Perhaps technically, but they are more satyr than noble fey, I can assure you. Their lineage isn't nearly as rare as their life is, either—a satyr and high fey conceiving a child in the first place is about as near-impossible as you can get."

"I think they're rare for plenty of reasons," Saffron added with a smile of his own, before looking at Étaín one more time. "Sionnach is very important to me, Lady Étaín. I won't let anything happen to them, for as long as I live. I promise that."

"I think you'll be a fine king one day, Saffron." Étaín touched Saffron's hand, before tucking the clover flower between his fingers. "If court life ever becomes too much for you, you're always welcome to come and visit. For as long as you'd like. Your prince, too, if he ever wishes to let go a little bit."

"Cylvan is more than capable of getting messy," Saffron said like a promise. Étaín smirked, before getting back to her feet. She encouraged Saffron to not overdo it, and Saffron responded by raising his glass and throwing it back.


Eventually, a dark shadow swept into the firelight where Saffron danced again, taking him for itself, sharp nails burrowing into the flesh of his back and hip in a way that promised he would not be taken away again. Saffron grinned, immediately tumbling into Cylvan's arms, allowing his heels to flatten back to the grass as the demands of the satyr steps vanished to offer him a break. His sore calves almost gave way beneath him entirely, not helped by the strong wine that had long replaced his blood. Cylvan's amused chuckle was the only thing to keep Saffron from spinning all the way into the sky.

"I realized one of them would sweep you away for good, at

some point," he breathed, pulling Saffron closer to whisper it, before pressing a kiss to the skin beneath his ear. Saffron giggled, placing one hand on Cylvan's shoulder and wrapping the other under his arm. Holding him close, breathing in his familiar smell mixed with the burning spiced logs and sugar in the air. Greatly disappointed at the prince's lack of bare skin, like even he knew better than to let a little too loose in front of such wild festivities.

"And what would you have done then?" Saffron smiled, words slurring slightly as he stood on his toes again, though even with the added height, stood no chance against the Night Prince looming over him.

"I would have chased you both down into the trees," Cylvan answered without hesitation, lips hardly an inch from Saffron's and eyes bright. Saffron blinked up at him, awed by how anyone could be so breathtaking even in just the glow of firelight, alarmed and distressed and unworthy to know that something so frighteningly beautiful could possibly be his.

"Would you really?" Saffron asked. Cylvan gazed at him, thoughtfully, possessively, a wicked half-smile lifting the corner of his perfect lips. In his drunkenness, in the low light, Saffron could almost fool himself into thinking the prince was something wild enough to don sharp teeth.

"Would you like to find out?" he breathed into Saffron's ear, pulling him closer, spreading the size of his large hand flush against the small of Saffron's back and making Saffron shiver. "I am tired of allowing all these satyr to lay eyes on you like this, none nearly as hungry as I am to take a bite. I'll hunt you down the moment you're out of the light, little witch. Careful you don't wander too close to the edge of the trees."

Saffron's mind spun, his insides shivered, he knew to anyone witnessing his nakedness that it was likely obvious exactly how hot those whispered words made his wine-drunk blood race. Especially with Cylvan's hand on his back, the size and demand of it, how the tip of one nail teased the base of his tailbone. All he could do was stare wantonly up at Cylvan with his wobbly vision, like he still fought to determine whether or not the unsettling, dark thing holding him was real or only a fantasy.

"I'll make sure to be careful, then, your highness," he whispered. "I wouldn't want to be caught unawares by something with ill intentions in the woods."

Cylvan's playfully dark smile softened just for a moment, just long enough to press a soft kiss to the center of Saffron's forehead, before passing him on to the next satyr waiting. But even as his partner changed, Saffron turned his head to look for where his prince went, surprised as how easily he vanished into the darkness when he wished to cease from the mortal realm. As if he controlled shadows instead of the wind; as if he really was the god of the underworld, and Saffron was the flower he wished to pluck and pull under just for himself.

When Saffron did finally escape the dancing circle—quickly realizing if he didn't bow out on his own, the line of satyrs who wished to do as they pleased would never end, whether he liked it or not—he stumbled his way over to where Sionnach sat on one of the side-laying trees alongside Copper, of all people, who looked a little stiff with his drink. They sat turned slightly away from one another, as if attempts at conversation had happened, but snuffed, though Copper's eyes kept undeniably flickering Sionnach's direction like a part of him wished to try again. Or, perhaps, just to continue gazing over every inch of their body nearly as naked as Saffron's.

"Where's Maeve?" Saffron asked, losing his footing at the last moment in a thick clump of grass and grabbing Copper by the shoulder to catch himself. Copper threw his hands up to steady him, before tilting his head sideways to where the icy fey lady was sitting on a stump a few yards away, drinking her own gratuitous amount of wine from a wood cup with cheeks flushed and hair littered with flowers and beads.

"Good, that's good, everyone is accounted for," Saffron mumbled, more for himself, before patting Copper on the shoulder. "I'm going to go get lost in the woods. And maybe turned inside out by a night lord for the first time in weeks, if you two don't mind."

"What?" Sionnach wheezed, but Saffron just patted Copper one more time before stumbling back through the grass toward the dark treeline.

**17**

---

# THE ENCHANTMENT

Saffron was already flushed enough from the wine and dancing around the fire—but stumbling toward the tree-line, then into the encroaching darkness of the surrounding Fall Court, his body still boiled hotter. In anticipation, in suspense for what Cylvan had enticed him with. Like it was more obvious than Saffron let on exactly how much he liked the thought of being caught off guard by something greedy and sensual between the trees; and there was nothing, no one he'd want to bend beneath more than an insatiable night lord.

The air outside the firelight was expectedly colder, making him shiver as he tripped over a lump of grass and caught himself on the side of a tree with a little laugh.

*"It's not often a human stumbles this way."*

Saffron jumped, turning quickly, but Cylvan hadn't stepped from the shadows where he hid. For the briefest moment, in his inebriation, Saffron even second guessed it was Cylvan who said it at all—having to remind himself of mimics. Creatures who could copy voices, even appearance. Oh, perhaps it wasn't such a good idea, after all.

"Cylvan?" He asked. No answer came at first, except a little whistle of wind.

*"Calling for help so soon?"*

Saffron turned again, that time certain something hovered just behind him. When there was still nothing, he let out a little laugh, claiming a step back from the tree. He hesitated where he stood, before turning and hurrying in the way he thought the bonfire to be. Not to retreat so early—but hoping to at least keep the light within reach. Just in case.

*"This way."*

Saffron stopped. He bit his lip, taking a few steps in the direction the voice beckoned. It sounded like Cylvan. Saffron had no reason to believe otherwise.

*"Come this way, little witch."*

"Cylvan?"

A low chuckle wafted from the shadows, and goosebumps rippled over Saffron's arms. Branches reached out to trail over his bare shoulders and across his chest as he wandered between the trees, tugging on the beaded chains he wore. Once—he was certain a clawed fingernail even reached out to hook beneath one of them, making Saffron turn quickly again, still only finding darkness on the other side.

He'd long wandered too far from even the ambient light of the bonfire, deep into the ancient wood where his human eyes fared poorly compared to wild fey, high fey. He bit his lip again, pausing to try and listen for the music, the singing. But there was only the wind, the sound of crickets and distant chirping of night birds.

"Are you lost?"

Saffron jumped. That time, when he turned on heel, his breath caught as something stood silhouetted in the overhead moonlight. Broad-shouldered and standing bare, pale skin translucent and as white as the moon. Black hair draped in waves down his naked chest and back, two horns curving from the crown of his head. Two black horns, neither donning the silver cap the prince had been wearing. It made Saffron take a nervous step back, heart thumping in uncertainty. The smallest twitch passed over Cylvan's expression, though Saffron couldn't see well enough to know exactly what for. He extended a hand, sharp nails flashing in the moonlight.

"Come with me," he said. "I'll show you where to go."

Saffron understood in that moment, more than ever, why there were so many stories advising humans to mistrust the fey. *Don't give them your name, don't make any deals; don't accept their help, don't follow them down a path you don't already know.* Still—Saffron's heart fluttered. His eyes flickered back up to the horn that should have been capped in silver, swallowing against the nerves tangling in the back of his throat. It may have been only a trick of the light. It may have been a glamour. He didn't know—but his heart raced in flushed misgiving, compelling him to extend a hand and accept the one offered to him. Wanting to know what the creature of shadow would do with him, after all.

The daemon pulled him closer, and Saffron felt the heat of his warm skin through the darkness. Interweaving their fingers together, he held his breath as Cylvan's sharp nails teased over the engagement ring Saffron wore, before his amethyst eyes flickered up to look at him.

"Is this alright?" He asked in a whisper, the smallest peek through a crack in their game. Though sídhe fey could still compel with their ashen state, making Saffron's ring still a protective charm—Cylvan technically owned it, meaning he could have compelled Saffron all along, whenever he wished. But Saffron's heart still raced faster, face flaring hot at the implication. The game, the fantasy. He nodded, still a little drunk, overtaken with how beautiful his raven was up so close.

"I trust you," he whispered. Wishing to kiss him, wishing to touch Cylvan all over. Like it was his first time seeing him so clearly; unable to resist pressing his opposite hand to Cylvan's bare chest, then trailing it down the muscles of his stomach. Bare and captivating, like it truly was his first time seeing him.

Cylvan pulled the ring away, tucking it onto his own finger

for safe keeping. He then pulled Saffron closer, whispering, *"Tell me what you'd like me to do with you."*

Compelling him in a way that was terrifying and—erotic. Setting Saffron's nerves on fire and made colors brighter, made him taste every scent on the forest air, to feel every inch of Cylvan's warm skin beneath his hands. Speaking without being able to stop himself, fully giving his trust to the dark creature who could dominate him, body and mind.

"I want you to use me how you please," Saffron said, gazing up at him. "Show me what an ancient fey might have done with a lost human in the woods—for their own self-centered amusement."

Cylvan smirked. He took a handful of Saffron's hair, tilting his head back slightly. In the same compelling tone, he added: *"You will tell me honestly the moment you're no longer enjoying yourself."*

Saffron nodded. Cylvan's hand tightened in the back of his hair, before pulling him close again.

*"Get on your knees for me."*

Saffron obeyed. Even if he hadn't been enchanted, he would have obeyed. Lowering slowly, he held Cylvan's eyes as he did, trailing his hands down the length of Cylvan's chest, his stomach, over his hips as his cock hung half-erect between his legs. Without having to be compelled, Saffron pressed his mouth to the skin just beneath Cylvan's navel, still holding his gaze. With Cylvan's hand still grasping the back of his hair, he pressed Saffron into the curve of his hip, and Saffron instinctively parted his lips.

"Go on," Cylvan purred, stroking fingers through Saffron's hair. "Show me what you're good for, apart from scrubbing floors or casting spells."

Saffron wrapped his fingers around the base of Cylvan's length, feeling how it twitched with an instant rush of arousal. Stiffening as Saffron aligned the end of it to his mouth, kissing the tip before teasing it with his tongue. He closed his eyes as Cylvan exhaled a satisfied breath, rolling his hips slightly as Saffron took his time stroking and lapping at him, before finally sliding it fully between his lips and over the back of his tongue.

Cylvan curved both hands behind Saffron's head, pulling him closer, until Saffron's nose pressed flat against his stomach. It made Saffron jolt, swallowing against the gag reflex that clenched at the back of his throat, reveling in how Cylvan released a tight breath of pleasure at the sensation. Digging his nails into the prince's thighs, Saffron bobbed his head over the length, thrilled by how Cylvan's thigh flexed beneath his hands, how the muscles of his stomach clenched and he couldn't help but roll his hips in and out over Saffron's tongue. Pressing into the back of his throat and making it tighten every time, summoning a growing desperation from Cylvan as he fought to maintain a rhythm of control. But that wasn't what Saffron wanted—he wanted to be run ragged, left threadbare by the time Cylvan was done with him. By the time the ancient fey who'd found him wandering the wood was satisfied.

Cylvan tightened his grip in Saffron's hair as he suddenly thrust his hips forward, making Saffron choke as the prince groaned with gratification, spilling down the back of Saffron's throat. Dripping in long strings as he pulled away and Saffron looked up at him, eyes half-lidded and still wishing for more. Still too much in his right mind, wishing to come undone.

Cylvan knew it—he could see it, that look in Saffron's eyes that begged. He said nothing, dropping to a knee to roughly grab Saffron's face and wrench him closer, kissing him. Kissing him with devouring intent, teeth scraping across Saffron's lips and leaving them raw, reveling in tasting himself over the bump of Saffron's tongue.

He stole all the breath from Saffron's lungs, until Saffron had to pull away and gasp—only to be grabbed again.

*"Bend yourself over,"* Cylvan commanded in a low voice. *"Present yourself to me, witch—show me why you are something I might enjoy."*

Saffron obeyed, sinking backward and catching his breath for a moment, before turning onto his knees. Angling his hips upward, curving his spine to display the roundness of his ass.

Clawed hands took ownership of him; one carved into the soft flesh of his hip, the other reaching to graze up the center of Saffron's chest. Hooking under his chin and tilting his head backward. Saffron blinked through the bleary darkness of the trees, cursed by his weak human eyes, left to only know who touched him by their breath, the sensation of their hands. The shadow that loomed over him, long strands of black hair draping like a curtain over his back, across his shoulders. Enshrouding him as a mouth tilted into his, and he closed his eyes to kiss it back. Hungry and aggrieved for satisfaction—as the hand on his hip squeezed, before thumbing his ass apart, allowing a thick shaft to slide against him, the tip teasing his tailbone.

Saffron arched his back further, narrowing his waist, allowing him to stretch his neck a little longer to press into the mouth that bit at his lips; desperate for that sweet pressure, the pinch of pain that would leave residual throbs up his spine, down his legs for days to come. He'd been patient, he'd resigned his desire for so long—and if that daemon who'd captured him didn't give him what he wanted, he would surely become as wild and mad as a beannighe washing bloody clothes in the creek.

"You want me," the broad shadow purred, clutching Saffron's hip again while rolling his own, gliding his length up and down the center of Saffron's ass. "You've been left wanting for too long, haven't you?"

"Yes," Saffron exhaled, vision glazed and desperate.

"Are you so eager to be made use of?" A sharp thumb pressed into Saffron's bottom lip, stretching it downward as a mouth hovered, so close to kissing him again. Saffron attempted to reach it, but he was being teased. "Has it been so long, that you crave the feeling of being split apart? Pressed open wide, until your legs are splayed and trembling?"

"Yes," Saffron begged in a whisper. The daemon chuckled, trailing a thumb over Saffron's waiting mouth again.

"You so eagerly wandered into the night—like you hoped to be found, to submit to the aches of someone like me. I think you may come to learn what happens to such soft, pretty things as you, when you don't dare to heed the darkness."

The hand on Saffron's hip slid around to his stomach, fingers splaying over his navel, before trailing lower to grasp at his cock. He jumped, gasping just as the teasing mouth finally pressed down into him again. Flattening their lips against one another, demanding in its movements, in stealing every one of Saffron's hitching breaths as he was stroked and played with. Until his legs trembled, until he dripped pre-cum over the daemon's hand. All the while, the wild darkness complimented him, calling him sweet and lovely, as pretty as a flower to be plucked and enjoyed.

The hand between his thighs left his arousal dangling between two quivering legs, sliding fingers from his tailbone to his entrance, where it teased inside. Making Saffron squirm, bending onto one elbow as the invading force was enough to make his heart leap after so long without a single touch.

"D-don't wait—" his voice shook. "Don't tease me—"

"Arrogant to think this tight hole of yours can take me so easily," Cylvan whispered, casting goosebumps over Saffron's skin. "Especially with how you clench around only my fingers—I would tear you apart, the moment I pressed inside."

"Tear me apart," Saffron begged. "Please—I want you. God, I want you, don't make me wait any longer—open me with your cock, not your fingers."

Cylvan's breath scattered over the bare skin of Saffron's back, before his warm mouth pressed into the peak of Saffron's spine. A hand soon replaced it, pressing down on Saffron's nape until Saffron had to submit to the strength of it, flattened facedown into the dirt with his hips still raised, his back still arched.

"Look how you bend toward me," the daemon said, as his length returned between Saffron's legs. "Begging for it, desperate to be used by me—by any wicked thing that claimed you, first. Is that it?"

Saffron had no chance to respond as the head of Cylvan's cock nudged his opening, stretching his rim and forcing the air from his lungs. Saffron's mouth gaped wide, clawing at the dirt and moss beneath him as Cylvan's opposite hand held him pinned down into it.

"Mmmh," Cylvan breathed, edging himself inside another inch. Saffron's legs clenched tight, toes curling as he bit back a groan. *"Tight,* like an obedient beantighe—you keep yourself this way on purpose, don't you? To better please that prince of yours. It's no wonder—he prefers to fuck humans. Tight, and warm— brave, despite themselves—desperate to please, even if the cock stretching them wide is enough to stop their heart."

He bent forward over Saffron's spine, the angle of it pressing his length deeper inside and making Saffron clench.

"You'll tell me if it's too much to bare, won't you?" He asked, voice smooth and alluring as ever. "I'll gladly tease you until you're ready, beantighe—until I can fully sheathe myself in your warmth, until you feel it pressing through your stomach."

His hand spread over Saffron's navel again. Saffron couldn't find the words to speak—he didn't know how to explain that Cylvan was indeed splitting him in half, but the pain of it was ambrosial. The sensation of it, white hot and sharp, turned his thoughts into milk and honey, swirling more deliciously than any wine could ever compare.

"Fuck me—until it's easier," was all he could manage. *Fuck me until your pleasure loosens inside; until you're all I know, or will ever know again.* Kissing him until he could no longer support the weight of his head, arching backward as Cylvan eased out, and back in again. Moving slowly, intentionally, despite all his sensual threats of dominating Saffron in every way, until the tightness subsided. Until Cylvan's own pre-cum allowed him to slide with more ease, in and out, until he could press all the way to his hips. Taking Saffron's hand to press into his stomach, where Saffron blinked through watering, hazy eyes, with a drunken smile when he was certain he indeed felt the prince's length piercing him all the way through.

A hand returned to Saffron's front, stroking him with a hand while fucking him from behind, until Saffron trembled all over. Clutching at handfuls of wet moss and leaves, crying out in pleasure against the earth, hips pinned upward by Cylvan's arm when he could no longer support himself on his knees.

*"Don't cum until I give you permission,"* the daemon cooed, just as Saffron's insides were beginning to clench—and he audibly moaned, writhing and gasping as Cylvan's pace never slowed; as his deft touch drew the growing orgasm closer to the surface, right to the edge, right at the tip—but Saffron's body wouldn't cross the precipice. Despite how he begged, internally and vocally into the ground, Cylvan's enchantment kept him obedient. Kept him fuckable, tight and warm and wanting, until tears filled his eyes with a sweet agony he'd never felt before. Sparking like lightning in his veins, setting him on fire as he begged and begged.

"Please, let me cum," he sobbed. "Oh, god—please, please, let me..."

*"Not yet,"* Cylvan cooed, pressing his mouth to the nape of Saffron's neck, before biting down hard enough to leave half-moon bruises on his shoulder. "Gods, beantighe—you feel so good. You're impeccable—truly a feast, for every part of me— groveling to be fucked, used up, suppliant and beautiful." His strokes drew out slow, slamming in deep before easing out again. "I could fuck you like this for an eternity—so greedy of you to beg, knowing how it drives me mad. What will you give me—if I let you finally cum?"

*"God,"* Saffron moaned. The enchantment wore off just enough to flush him with heat, dripping between his legs as the climax inched ever closer. "Anything—anything, please, let me—"

*"Then show me, exactly how unraveled you've become."*

Saffron's entire body clenched, flooded with ecstasy as the climax rocked through him, from his hands to his chest, up his legs and into his hips. Spilling out of him into the leaves, as

Cylvan buried himself deep as ever from behind. Throwing his head back, a strained cry of sweet reprieve escaped Saffron's mouth, pulled upright until his back pressed flush into Cylvan's chest.

Cylvan pinned him there, one hand on Saffron's stomach, the other cupping the front of his throat, still fucking him at an uncompromising pace. Pressing against his stomach until Saffron's eyes rolled back, mouth hanging open as his head sank limply over Cylvan's shoulder. Biting back another gasp of delight as a second wave of orgasms filled and flooding out of him, just as Cylvan slammed into him a final time. Breathing heavily as his thick, warm satisfaction filled Saffron to the brim, immediately slipping out and down his leg the moment Cylvan pulled free.

Saffron slumped instantly, evoking a sharp sound from Cylvan who caught him before he could collapse fully to the dirt. Through the haze, Saffron heard him chuckle—before gently lying him back on a patch of fresh moss, pushing hair from his sweaty forehead and kissing him gently.

"I think I'll keep you," he whispered. "I'll come to you every night to satiate myself, for the rest of your human life."

Saffron smiled, weary and barren of any remaining strength. He meant to say something coy in response, but couldn't find the words, let alone his mouth to speak them. He just groped into the darkness for Cylvan's body again, kissing him once more, before opening his legs and inviting the prince to settle between them. To press himself back inside, to fuck him as endlessly and mercilessly as he pleased, until he was satisfied.

# 18

# THE FOXES

Saffron eased in and out of a hazy sleep, draped over Cylvan's chest in the chilled grass. At some point, the prince had carried his exhausted body back within the light of the bonfire, lying them down just out of reach of anyone spotting them from the party. Allowing Saffron a chance to rest before stumbling back in, covered in sweat and bite marks. At the very least, Cylvan had thought to wipe Saffron's legs down with some icy creek water, though Saffron just groaned and whined the entire time.

Feeling like a living, breathing person again, Saffron sat up from where he laid on Cylvan's tunic, rubbing his eyes and running fingers back through his tangled hair. He glanced down to where Cylvan reclined next to him, wearing his undershirt and pants, though they remained undone at the front. Like he was willing to do it all over again, if Saffron had the strength. Mentally, emotionally, Saffron could continue a thousand times over—but physically, he had gotten what he asked for. To be used up by a greedy fey in the woods.

Perhaps that was why Saffron couldn't stop smiling down at him. He couldn't stop trailing fingers over Cylvan's collarbones, drawing circles on his chest within the low cut of his undershirt, thrilled with how he'd even painted his silver horn black in order to better play his role. Saffron's finger followed the arch of Cylvan's brow, then down his nose to his lips, trailing over them before leaning over to kiss them softly. Obsessively. Wishing to know him better than was humanly possible. Wishing to find the perfect way to experience every inch of him, to all the extents magic would possibly allow.

But there would be no time to explore his options—as something suddenly crunched within the trees behind them. Loud enough for Saffron to lift his head, and even for Cylvan to sit up and turn. They both sat in silence to listen, holding their breaths —and Saffron inhaled sharply when two watching eyes briefly reflected the light of the bonfire.

"Cylvan—" he gasped, but Cylvan was already moving.

"Come," he said, grabbing Saffron's arm in one hand and his doublet in the other, handing it to Saffron once on their feet. Saffron shoved his arms through the sleeves, before Cylvan took his hand and hurried with him through the bushes, into the warm firelight.

"Copper!" Cylvan hissed from the edge of the trees the moment they were within speaking distance. Copper jumped, turning to see who growled his name, grinning like an idiot at the sight of Saffron and Cylvan spotted with twigs and moss and lovebites—but the smile faded once he also heard what came from the darkness. The whispered chittering of animals, bounding through the undergrowth. More than just one; at least a small handful.

"We should—" he started—just as a pack of shrieking, cackling foxes suddenly burst through the treeline, nearly three times bigger than was natural and heavy enough to nearly make the ground shake. Three, then four of them suddenly appeared from the veil of darkness into the firelight, and the sound of satyrs shouting and screaming as they scrambled away cut through the festivities.

Cylvan took Saffron's arm again, swiftly tucking him behind

his back before pulling him away from the trees and toward where Copper and Sionnach leapt instantly to their feet. One of the animal intruders noticed them, shrieking with blood-curdling laughter and pouncing in their direction. The beast might have snapped its sharp teeth straight down onto Sionnach's arm had Copper not suddenly leapt forward, putting himself between them and the beast, releasing a guttural snarl Saffron never expected from someone not already in animal-shape. The attacking fox giggled again, barking and yipping and whipping its tail back and forth, corners of its mouth flecked with hungry foam and spit like the half-satyr trembling behind Copper's back was the most mouthwatering thing it had smelled in months.

"Fuck off, Callem!" Copper barked, and the fox's grin spread wider, before finally flicking its tail and skittering off to crash through the rest of the party with the other three. Only then did Cylvan pull Saffron forward again, meeting Copper's eyes with an intensity that demanded answers while simultaneously accusing him of having something to do with it.

"You know them?" Saffron asked, before realizing, the answer was obvious. "Are they—!"

"Your brothers!" Sionnach finally gasped, voice cracking before stumbling back again as two of the foxes collided over one of the fires, yelping and rolling through the flames before taking chase to a cluster of satyrs attempting to flee. Saffron wanted to shout for them to stop, but Cylvan sensed it, grabbing his arm and giving him a stern look to *stay quiet.* Saffron's mouth clamped shut again, turning down his eyes and pulling the front of his borrowed doublet together to try and hide his nakedness as much as he could.

A flaming arrow whisked by, landing in the center of the clearing where the four foxes tore up the earth, erupting into sparks and earsplitting whistles that even made Saffron throw his hands up to cover his ears. The foxes themselves threw their heads back with teeth bared, ears flattened down and tails bristling in annoyance. The moment the sound waned, they turned to search for the archer who shot it; Saffron followed their eyes, spotting Carce standing tall and unamused at the head of the party.

Before he could speak, to command the foxes out—three more riders appeared from the darkness, on the backs of tall horses. Pale and intimidating in stature alone, their matching red hair told Saffron who they were without having to ask. The fey lord at the front, particularly, commanded a cold esteem first by the obvious age of his face, and second by the potency of his aura. Strict and domineering, gazing down his sharp nose to observe the chaos his brood sowed across the party. As his sons snapped sharp teeth at satyr tails and pounced after them, chittering, laughing, snarling and barking as the wild fey fled into the nearby woods. Even as one of the foxes drew blood from one satyr by the leg, the imposing Renard dé Bricríu on his horse did not flinch.

The prevalent red hair was where the lord's resemblance ended with Copper—and Saffron was glad for it. He could not fathom how someone as carefree as Copper could have possibly shared an ounce of familial relation to that high fey whose eyes were sharp as glass blades.

But it wasn't solely Lord dé Bricríu's presence to chill Saffron to the his core—as Anysta mac Delbaith appeared on her own horse behind him, smiling calmly as she surveyed the wild party scrambling to regather itself. The moment her eyes landed where Cylvan stood on the edge with Saffron, the amusement shifted, and Saffron stiffened to resist stepping in front of Cylvan, between them. That curl of her lips looked *excited*, like she'd hoped to find Cylvan amongst the flock.

"You and your skulking brood are not welcome here, Renard," Carce announced. For the first time since arriving, Saffron heard the power in his voice—the unwavering, intimidating strength of a leader, a prince of the satyrs, that hooked deep into even his own nerves. He couldn't help but shy away slightly—only to feel the firm snout of a beast suddenly behind him. Sniffing on him, even nibbling on the fine fabric of Cylvan's doublet; and Saffron turned fast, slamming his elbow into the fox's mouth before thinking.

The animal reeled back with a yelp, before shaking off the surprise and wrinkling its nose, baring and snapping its teeth. Only then did Saffron spot the silver collar it wore, but not one to silence it—perhaps to allow all those siblings to shift into their animal form despite the recent ashen state. Emboldened by the fury the sight filled him with, Saffron lifted his arm again in warning—only to be yanked back a step by Cylvan, who growled his name in disapproval.

"I'm not here to cause any trouble, satyr," Renard answered, voice gravelly but commanding with age. He never once glanced Carce's way, golden eyes instead skimming the crowd until finally coming to a sharp halt where Cylvan stood in front of Saffron. "Lady mac Delbaith paid a welcome visit to my home this afternoon, and informed me my youngest was traveling through the Autumn Court with His Highness. Ah—what a pleasant surprise to find Lady dé Bhaldraithe here as well."

Saffron threw Maeve a brief look, not expecting the blank, polite expression on her face. It matched Cylvan's—like to show an expression in either way was more dangerous than speaking out of line. Saffron wanted to grab Cylvan's hand on instinct—but even he felt a rush of anxiety over it. Never needing that hard gaze to fall over him to sense it. Even if it did, something told Saffron Renard dé Bricríu would not actually see him.

"It is a pleasure to find you well, Lord dé Bricríu," Cylvan finally broke the tense silence, using that voice Saffron hated, the one meant for good impressions and practiced from years of having no choice but to learn it. "I see your sons are healthy as ever, as well."

Renard smiled in return, but not with any sincerity—like a person offered something they knew they were owed. Saffron's frown deepened. He extended his hand slightly, wanting to touch the back of Cylvan's undershirt—but a tiny sound escaped the corner of Maeve's mouth from a few feet away. When Saffron glanced her way again, though, she still had her eyes on Renard.

"I thought I might invite you and Lady dé Bhaldraithe back to my home for the night, your highness," Renard continued, approaching a few more steps on his horse. "I could not bear to allow you to sleep in the dirt with these wild fey."

"That is very generous of you," Cylvan responded with a small nod. "I hope you did not think we intended to pass through without sending you greetings, in fact Lord Copper and I—"

"Copper seems to fit in so well with these satyr-folk, don't you think?" Renard interrupted, turning his eyes to his youngest son for the first time since arriving. Copper stiffened, but didn't dare lower his own gaze from his father's. "I imagine he'd prefer to play in the dirt with them for the rest of the night, anyway. I am sure you and Lady dé Bhaldraithe would prefer to indulge in finer things, however, with us more-refined folk."

"Cylvan," Saffron whispered in disbelief, not expecting the ancient fey lord to hear it. His words cut short in an instant, and suddenly his icy gaze was on Saffron. Saffron stared back at him, trapped in its intensity, unsure if he held it because that's what everyone else did—or because he feared what would happen if he were to glance away, first.

"I see," Renard finally uttered. "This must be your visitor from Alvénya. Lady mac Delbaith told me you'd come to visit, as well. I nearly lost you in the crowd, child. I see the prince draped your nakedness in his finest doublet—how polite of him. Careful that you do not allow these wild fey undo everything you've learned of propriety since arriving in this country."

Saffron's face went hot, a mix of embarrassment and an unexpected wash of annoyance.

"I'm afraid I've yet to see any of the Fall Court propriety you speak of. Though we haven't been here long yet."

Cylvan's head snapped around, eyes wide, nostrils flared in a flash of rage. Saffron glared back at him, but Renard just scoffed with a bitter smile from the back of his horse.

"Ah, apologies for my surprise. I am merely impressed to hear a country-fey use such large words."

"I could say the same for a skulk of foxes—"

*"Saffron."* Cylvan's voice was colder, darker than Saffron had heard in a long time. It froze his throat closed in an instant, leaving him with his mouth dangling open in surprise, only able to barely close it again when Cylvan turned back to address Renard once more.

"I'm sure I speak for Lady Maeve when I say your offer is very kind, Lord dé Bricríu. While an evening with you and Lady mac Delbaith sounds delightful, we wouldn't wish to impose on your house. Prince Carce has been very welcoming to myself and my companions—"

"Your highness." Another voice hissed from behind them, one Saffron didn't recognize until he turned. The last person he expected to offer any kind of disapproval, let alone a reaction, was Aodhán, but the guard gave Cylvan a look that spoke only a language Cylvan seemed to know. Though Saffron could fathom a guess. Cylvan then glanced at Maeve, who glanced back at him. She gave him the smallest flinch of a nod. Cylvan looked ahead again—and the way he never once glanced back to Saffron made Saffron's irritation only flare hotter.

"It is a generous offer, Lord dé Bricríu. As for our other companions—"

"I would hate to take them from their festivities, of course." Renard smiled. "Besides, I'm sure the conversations of sídhe fey over dinner would be of no interest to them. They would much rather stay here and drink and dance. Isn't that right, Lord...? What was your name, Alvényan?"

"My name is Saffron," Saffron answered flatly. Cylvan threw him another look of warning, but Saffron's words were already rolling off his tongue: "And I cannot agree more, that satyr festivities sound far more entertaining than even the finest dinner shared with a brood of animals. I've heard how most *dé Bricríu feasts* go."

*"You have a deathwish!"* Taran snarled suddenly, as Cylvan turned to him fully that time. One last time—where he grabbed Saffron by the arm, hard enough that Saffron jerked back in surprise, but didn't break the grip. The prince's expression made his heart stop, flushed with fury, exasperation, disbelief, reminding Saffron far too much of how he once looked at him in the yarrow field when they first met. Behind him, even the austere Renard dé Bricríu appeared momentarily affronted—though it disappeared just as quickly as it came.

"You can't actually be considering leaving with—!" Saffron attempted in a hiss.

"I am," Cylvan growled in return. Maeve took up conversation with Renard at that moment, as if to distract him away. Anysta kept her gaze toward them all the same. "And you will be sure to reflect on how you're meant to behave while I am gone."

Behind him, the two fey lords flanking Renard kicked off their horses, and Saoirse approached to claim the reins in order to hand them over to Cylvan and Maeve. The brothers then shifted into fox-beasts right there in the center of the clearing, shaking out their fur before touching noses, then snarling at the nearest group of satyrs.

Cylvan, still gripping Saffron's arm, shook him. Demanding his attention back. But Saffron didn't want to look at him— Saffron didn't recognize his raven prince standing in front of him. Like a wild animal in a trap, gnashing its teeth and resorting to frightened instinct. Saffron didn't want to see Cylvan looking like that—and he refused to concede to being on the receiving end of it, either.

"Then go," Saffron muttered at the very least. "Enjoy your dinner. Make another midnight deal with Anysta mac Delbaith while you're there, since that comes so easily to you."

"You—" Cylvan snarled. "For once, can you act how I expect you to!"

"And how is that!" Saffron snapped. Cylvan lurched closer,

and Saffron stepped back, tripping onto one of the logs. Cylvan never let up on him.

"Harmoniously," he growled between his teeth, loud enough for only Saffron to hear. "Like you're *meant to,* damnit!"

"Get off of me," Saffron said. "Being harmonious has nothing to do with being stubborn!"

"Perhaps I should have left you a beantighe, then, if you're going to keep acting like one!"

Saffron stared at him. Cylvan stared back. His shoulders rose and fell with the effort, color gone from his face, eyes wide in a mix of anger and pleading and something else Saffron couldn't read. Even if he could—he didn't want to.

"Morrígan is only a train ride away," he said. "You can drop me off on your way home."

Cylvan furrowed his brows, closing his eyes and groaning from the back of his throat.

"Gods help me. I don't have time for this."

"Enjoy your dinner, *my lord.*"

Cylvan gave him a final look, before turning. He went to where Saoirse had emerged from the sidelines to stand with the horses, Maeve already in the saddle of hers and watching where Saffron had been left behind. Cylvan gave Saffron no second glance as he kicked his foot into the stirrup and heaved himself into the saddle, and even still as he said something to Renard and they turned to cross back into the trees.

He didn't look back—but Anysta did. She offered Saffron a single nod of acknowledgement, which was nearly enough to summon blood to gush from his nose. He fantasized about summoning Taran right in that moment, to demand Cylvan back. To make Renard pale in the face of the black wolf. Maybe to make Anysta faint off her fine horse into the mud.

But he didn't. He remained on the log, watching as the uninvited guests melted back into the trees.

Only once nervous chatter resurrected back into scattered

notes of music, carefully reviving itself in an attempt to summon the energy of the festivities back, did Saffron's insides sink heavily with regret.

**19**

———

# THE ROUTE

Saffron didn't know if Fall Court wine really was stronger, or if he just didn't realize how much he'd had to drink. It seemed Copper wasn't entirely sure, either, because soon enough he was speaking nonsense and stomping off into the woods. Saffron might have thought he was going to chase after his father and brothers, before realizing through his own wobbly haze that the fox-lord was headed in the opposite direction. He would not be any help should either of them get lost—but Saffron followed, anyway. Better to be lost together than all alone.

Copper didn't realize Saffron followed him until they crossed a boulder that Copper scaled easily, leaving Saffron behind until he resorted to calling out for help. Copper poked his head over the crown of the rock, narrowing his eyes like he questioned whether or not Saffron was real, but Saffron just told him to stop looking so stupid and help him up, already. Whether or not Saffron was a figment of his imagination, Copper complied, throwing an arm out and physically dragging Saffron over the mossy, scratchy rock on his stomach. It left green stains and scuffs across the shiny fabric of Cylvan's doublet, but Saffron didn't care. If it wasn't so much colder away from the party's bonfires, he might have thrown the doublet down a ravine altogether.

"What did you think of him?" Copper asked, words slurring together, half a moment before losing his footing in a slick of mud and crashing to the earth with a pathetic grunt.

"He's a massive prick," Saffron said as he attempted to help Copper up, only to immediately slide off his feet on the same spot. "I should—cut off all his fucking hair and make him eat it!"

"I meant my father." Copper hooked Saffron under the arm, hauling him back to his feet with an exhale.

"He's a prick too," Saffron corrected, before sighing. "I can't believe how quickly Cylvan did everything he said..."

Copper snorted, keeping one hand in Saffron's as he continued walking, as if he didn't realize. "Cylvan's a coward. Thought you knew that."

"You didn't exactly stand up to him, either," Saffron argued. "You're no braver than Cylvan is."

"Never said I was. You're braver than all of us—but don't take it as a compliment. Especially not with him. Don't think anyone's ever talked back to Renard like that. Cylvan's probably fighting for his life over there right now—and for yours."

Saffron grimaced. Taran attempted to say something to add to it, but Saffron imagined kicking the dog off the side of a cliff, and he went silent again. "And why not? He's just another sídhe lord, who cares—"

"What? My father's at least as old as Queen Proserpina was."

Saffron stopped short. He stared at Copper in the darkness, his hair illuminated from behind by the moon in a thin halo of orange.

"He's...? How?"

"What d'you mean, 'how'? High fey live for a long fucking time. Especially sídhe fey. Especially sídhe fey who everyone'd prefer dead. How d'you think Cylvan's survived this long? Ah—sorry. That was kinda dark, huh? I'm a little drunk. I didn't mean it."

"Well—how much older, exactly?" Saffron steered the fox back to the point.

"Like, he was friends with King Elanyl."

"Proserpina's son?!" Saffron choked. "The one who—who became king? After the war? *Ailir's father?*"

"Yup," Copper clucked his tongue. "Renard's sister, my Aunt Una, was even King Elanyl's Harmonious Queen. You know that? I mean, technically she was, but not for long considering Elanyl kicked it after like a month... Real messy, all that. Renard's still burnt about it."

Saffron recalled again what Ryder once told him about King Ailir, though it came in wobbly, blurry waves of broken sentences as the satyr wine remained in control of his mind.

"But that means she would be... But I thought King Ailir's mother was a...?"

"A whore?" Copper grinned. "Yeah. Elanyl died before he could get my Aunt Una pregnant with a true heir, but Ailir's mother was already carrying him when Elanyl died. Meant my side of the family didn't get any of the benefits of siring the next king. Una even refused any offers of such—almost like she knew my father didn't need that kind of closeness with any sort of real power... Think she found the circumstances more of a blessing than anything, I dunno..."

Saffron didn't know what to say to that. He just stood in the darkness, letting the Fall Court breeze tangle fingers through his hair, across his bare skin beneath the doublet.

"Oh," he said finally. Too drunk to fully piece together every single nuance of what Copper was saying—but knowing enough to conjure an idea. An idea, at least, of why Cylvan bent over for everything Renard said; an idea of what exactly made Renard such a harsh, intense man even on first introduction. There was a reason why so much bitterness emanated off him, strong enough to make the trees shiver. Not to mention why Cylvan felt so much pressure to appease him. It was to protect Ailir. Not to mention his own future rule, assuming Renard lived another hundred years or however long it took. Oh, Saffron nearly puked at the thought.

They walked in silence for a bit longer, and Saffron could only trust Copper had an actual destination in mind as they went. His mind was too busy recalling what Ryder once told him, about King Ailir, about his birth, about how developing sídhe magic was the only reason they ever let him be king at all.

"Ryder..." he started, but didn't know exactly what to say. He just wanted to get some of the thoughts out of his head before it popped. "Ryder once said King Ailir was barely made king in the beginning, and even now, he has to try really hard to stay on other sídhe families' good side or else they could remove him."

Copper nodded, like he knew what Saffron would say, next.

"Your father is one of those sídhe lords eager to find fault in Ailir and do just that, isn't he." There was no question.

"Yeah," Copper answered after a long pause. It was spoken hoarsely. "Also exactly why I was so hesitant to agree to anything the king asked me back after the Midsummer Games. Erm... I'm sorry about that, by the way. Sionnach was right—it wasn't 'honorable' of me, but I... I was scared, is all. Felt backed into. Corner. Of course I was going to keep you safe, it was just—"

"It's alright, Copper. I understand. You don't have to explain. I never held it against you, anyway. I always assumed there was something else and you'd tell me when you were ready."

"Guess Renard demonstrated the reason well enough."

"God, he did..." Saffron meant to be playful, but could only scowl like he'd taken a bite of something rotten. "I hope Cylvan is alright..."

"Cylvan could have been a little more pushy, himself," Copper grunted. "But I imagine he's been trained for a long time to bite his tongue in front of someone as old and influential as my father. Hate to say it, but don't be too angry with him. I wouldn't want to be him right now, at least... Renard could turn the whole Fall Court on Ailir tomorrow if he wanted. And folk would listen, I think. Especially after everything that happened at the games..."

"I'm going to puke."

"I'm sure you and Cylvan will be back to normal by morn—

oh!" Copper jerked his hand away as Saffron turned and vomited into a nearby bush, groaning once his stomach emptied and the world spun.

"Satyr wine is stronger than I thought."

"Yeah no shit, Saff—didn't anyone tell you it's charmed?"

"N-no," Saffron moaned, spitting another wet mouthful into the dirt, glad he'd emptied his insides mostly all in one go. "I guess they meant it, when they said the Fall Court was full of the good and the bad. Ériu help me."

"Even Ériu can't protect you from Renard. Or satyr wine, apparently."

"Godddddd help all of us," Saffron cried, shaking his head and pushing away from the tree that supported him. "Where in the goddess' name are you taking me, anyway? Please don't tell me we're lost."

"We're not. My family's estate isn't actually that far from here, so I know these woods like the back of my hand. C'mon. I'm headed this way on purpose."

"We're not actually going to your family estate, are we?"

"Gods, no, are you out of your mind?"

Saffron followed without another word. Emptying the contents of his stomach, while flooding him with spinning nausea drier than the hottest day in summer, helped to at least clear his head some of the drunken fog. It allowed him to fully taste the sweet air of the trees, to listen as nighttime creatures scuttled around the forest floor beneath their feet, or through the leaves overhead. Saffron searched for them as they walked, whenever he was sure he wouldn't trip on something in the path, though rarely caught sight of anything more than a mouse or rabbit. He wanted to know what other wild fey things roamed out there—but, perhaps, he was also content to wait until morning to explore any deeper than he already had.

Copper finally came to a halt in a spot indistinguishable from the rest of the thickness around them, and Saffron was half a breath from accusing him of actually being lost when the fey lord suddenly crouched to the balls of his feet—and crawled into the gaping end of a fallen tree. Saffron choked on a laugh, hurrying over to see for himself, just as a match struck within the wooden tunnel and lit a broken lantern nailed into the ceiling.

"Oh!" He gasped in delight at the illuminated interior, realizing quickly it was more than just a fallen tree—it was a hiding place. Childish drawings covered the curved inner walls, with old blankets lining the floor and becoming one with the bark and moss from age. Jars of dusty hard-candies lined an uneven inlet carved into a thicker part of the tree's wall, and Copper even lit a second lantern a few more feet down the way, allowing Saffron enough room to crawl inside and join him.

"I used to come here when I was a kid," Copper explained. He shuffled around the surprisingly cozy space with knowing movements, though it was clear the last time he visited he was half the size he'd grown into. Every time he bonked his head against one of the hanging lanterns, Saffron had to resist laughing. "My days at home weren't exactly *great* all the time, so I, uh, spent a lot of time exploring the woods. Sometimes I'd come out a little too far, or just didn't feel like going home, so I'd spend the night in little nooks like this one. Here, look—this is where I tracked pixies hollows within walking distance."

Saffron grinned, running his fingers over the amateur drawings and hatchmarks carved into the inner bark.

"Reminds me of how I used to do the same in my sketchbook, on my days off."

"Huh?" Copper asked, before grunting. "Oh, right. When you were a—a beantighe. At Morrigan. Almost forgot."

"I can't blame you—I make a very good fey lord, don't I?"

Copper smirked. "Not really. You're always sayin' *sorry* and bowing and stuff. Weird."

"Whatever," Saffron sneered, reaching up to grapple where he knew fox ears hid beneath the fey lord's glamour. "I can think of weirder things."

Together they worked to carve layers of moss and lichen from the walls to uncover more of child-Copper's drawings, and every time Saffron was able to identify what was what, Copper grinned bigger than Saffron had ever seen of him.

It was easy, it was simple, to chatter on and on about the wild things in the woods, more than once even earning a look of disbelief while regaling him with all the things he'd witnessed in the Agate Wood on his own. How Saffron swore he once saw a unicorn in the distance, but it disappeared into a beam of sunshine before he could know for sure; how he used to appease the pixies of the hollow in the yarrow field before reclaiming objects stolen from beantighes; he even told Copper about how Cylvan had taken him to see nymphs at the lake in the mountains, once, and that was where they first kissed. Copper teased him plenty about that, though gave Cylvan credit for being such a romantic.

When a voice suddenly called their names in the distance, their mouths clamped shut simultaneously, staring at one another and sharing a single string of thoughts listing everything that could possibly be trying to get their attention—but then the pleas rich in desperation and yelps of someone losing their footing in the dark compelled them both out of the log, calling back out to the voice they recognized as Sionnach's. When the satyr eventually stumbled through the bushes, they donned a long streak of mud up one side of their changed clothing, pine needles and leaves littering their hair and wild blackberry thorns poking out from the fur of their legs.

"Thank—the gods," they wheezed, bending over their legs to catch their breath. "I thought those damned—brothers had come and eaten both of you. What... hey! What are you doing in there!" They cried, racing over to where Copper was still crouched partially in the mouth of the nook, grabbing him by the back of his shirt and yanking him onto his ass.

"*You* know about the log?" Copper accused after flailing his arms like a turtle stuck on its shell. "You mean *my* log?"

"*Your* log? I'm the one who filled it with blankets!" Sionnach argued, pushing Copper out of the way a second time to get a better look for themself. "You both tracked mud all over them!"

"I think the blankets have been there longer than I've been alive, Sionnach," Saffron commented. "There was already mud on them."

"And you scraped all the pretty clover off the walls!" They went on, ignoring him and crawling into the mouth of the gutted tree. "The flowers used to be so pretty!"

"Tasty too, I bet, for someone like you," Copper muttered. Sionnach whirled so fast their horns smacked against the inner wall, making the whole log vibrate.

"Yes, as a matter of fact!" they argued. "Clover flowers are edible for everyone, anyway!"

"That's also true," Saffron sighed. Copper muttered something that sounded like *'Of course I knew that, too…'*

Chuckling under his breath, Saffron approached the mouth of the log to peer inside where Sionnach was busy undoing everything Copper had done to rearrange, only for Copper to look inside over Saffron's shoulder and immediately start bickering. Back and forth, they argued like two roommates fighting over where a couch should go or what kind of place settings to use, until Saffron couldn't take it anymore and laughed until he couldn't speak.

Copper was disappointed to not return to the party, but Sionnach seemed relieved when Saffron asked to go back to the house where he could properly lay down. By then, he was thoroughly chilled with only Cylvan's doublet over his shoulders, feet hurting, heart hurting, ready for the night and all its ups and downs to finally be over.

Saffron remained quiet as they made their way—though neither of his companions particularly noticed, set on continuing to squabble with one another. Saffron didn't know how to explain it, and he would never say it out loud—but something about their arguing felt different, that time. Closer, more personal, without so much bite behind the words. It reminded him a little bit of how he used to argue with Cylvan, when they were first learning how to navigate one another—which made him smile for his friends' sakes, but regret turned in his stomach for his own.

After arriving at the dark house, Sionnach hesitantly permitted Copper to make a bed on the floor of their cramped second-floor bedroom, offering him an armful of blankets before showing the way. Copper's foot caught on the corner of a stack of books immediately past the door, crashing to the ground and shaking the whole house. Sionnach berated him for being so damn clumsy and nearly putting a hole through the floorboards, and Copper sniped back at them for being such a damned pack-rat, all while Saffron was overtaken by Sionnach's overflowing personal library.

Reminding him far too much of how Cylvan once stored his own books at Morrígan, it was clear Sionnach didn't have the shelf space to offer their endless collection, more towers of books stacked on the floor than Saffron could count. Accidentally knocking one over was apparently the only thing to get Sionnach and Copper to quit bickering, as Sionnach jumped and then hurried over to see if Saffron was alright. Saffron was certain they were actually more concerned about the old, rare books that tumbled to the floor beneath his feet.

He disappeared into one, then another, then another with ease, sitting cross-legged on the floor as Sionnach hurriedly scrambled to make their room a little more presentable, constantly reasserting that they weren't used to having guests inside, they didn't normally live in such clutter—but Saffron hadn't noticed any of the things they apologized for. Copper obviously didn't, either, but made sure to tease about whatever Sionnach fussed over in the moment.

Most of Sionnach's books were far too academic for Saffron to comprehend, even their titles alone making him squirm and quickly tuck away again, until one did catch his eye, and he flipped through the pages while recalling something Sionnach had told him while in Erelaine.

"Sionnach," he said, interrupting another spat between the satyr and the fox, that time about Copper stealing pillows straight from Sionnach's bed. "What's 'Ailinne'?"

"Ailinne?" Sionnach asked, in the midst of cramming one of the pillows in question against Copper's face, clearly attempting to suffocate him. Copper played dead just long enough to evoke a moment of panic from the satyr trying to commit murder. "It's a town a little bit north from here. Why?" Their eyes trailed to the book Saffron held on his lap, curiosity piqued as they finally released Copper from the pillow, summoning a choked gasp from the fox lord in reply. "What are you reading?"

"'*Traditions of the Tuatha dé Danann—Festivities, Family, and Reigns.*'" Saffron answered, showing Sionnach the cover without losing his place. "I wanted to see if it said anything about that stuff you were saying before, about Queen Proserpina's coronation route. Did you know she stopped in the Fall Court, too, before going to Erelaine?"

"Not specifically, but it makes sense that she would. What does the book say, exactly?" They crawled on their knees to where Saffron sat, making sure to smack Copper in the face with their tail as they did. Copper grappled for it, yanking it back and earning a swift kick to the shin from Sionnach's cloven hoof.

"It mentions she stopped for the night 'somewhere in the Fall Court while traveling to Erelaine from Ailinne'..."

"Ohhh, the hot springs," Copper mused. "'Course the queen would stop there on her way. Don't even care that people say they're sacred, they're a godsend on a sore ass after sitting in a saddle for hours at a time." He met Saffron's eyes, then Sionnach's, barely lifting his head off the pillow. "Er... most high fey go there to soothe their humors, or whatever..."

"Their what?" Saffron asked. "Jokes?"

"Nothing, just outdated nonsense," Sionnach huffed, summoning Saffron back to the book. "But yes—the queen stopped in Ailinne on her route. The springs are said to be connected to the spirit realm, so it's common for high fey to go there to try and reconnect with natural gods. The minerals in the water are said to help with some ailments, too, which is true, but not to the extent people say."

"I bet it's overrun right now," Copper muttered, sinking down onto the pillows with a sigh. "Flooded with Avren folk thinking they can bathe their ashenness away..."

"Minerals?" Saffron asked, shaking his head and forcing the conversation back. "Minerals, from natural springs...?"

The veil's voice shot through his mind like a loosed arrow. *Where the earth's minerals heat the rocks...*

"I don't think they can cure you of your human-ness, Saffron, sorry," Copper joked, earning another sharp look from Sionnach. "Or *your* weird goat feet, Sionnach..." He mumbled.

Sionnach *thwapped* him with their tail again, sparking another argument, but Saffron just gazed down at the book. At the illustrated map on the page. Showing every place where Proserpina visited on her journey from Vjallrod in the Winter Court to Avren. Moving in reverse, he thought again about what the veil had told him. He thought about where Ryder had already been. He thought—it couldn't only be a coincidence.

"Avren, to Erelaine... to somewhere in the Fall Court, to Ailinne, then Vjallrod..." His breath caught, finger hovering over the name printed nearest to Vjallrod at the top. Fjornar.

Ryder had started in Avren, a few days prior. He went to Erelaine, next; then the stripped henge outside the satyr borough. What if those locations weren't random at all? Clearly the veil even thought so, which meant—

"What is it?" Sionnach asked again. It took Saffron a moment before he could remember how to speak, forcing himself to pull the thoughts back. To re-center, to refocus.

"I think... Ryder's next target is in Ailinne."

"What?" Sionnach jumped, and even Copper sat up again. "Really? How? Why do you think—?"

"You have another dream earlier, Saff?" Copper asked.

"No, it's—it's something the veil told me," Saffron tried to explain as simply as he could. "When I spoke to it in the stripped henge earlier today. It said Ryder was opening the veil to look for something, or—I don't know, exactly, but even it seemed to anticipate where he'd go next. Said he wasn't the first to follow this path. All it told me was *where the earth's minerals heat the rocks,* and from what you've told me... that sounds like Ailinne."

Sionnach's eyes lowered to the map in the book, before back to Saffron. "You think he's following the queen's old coronation route?"

"What's he looking for?" Copper added, but Saffron could still only shake his head. He didn't know. Even the veil didn't know. The only thing Saffron possibly understood was that, whatever it was, may have been what called to him in his dreams. Begging to be found, reaching out to him—each time Ryder tore the veil open in search.

SAFFRON SETTLED INTO SIONNACH'S BED ALONGSIDE them, while Copper remained on the floor. Already fast asleep and snoring, though it wasn't the reason Saffron remained wide awake. Staring at the ceiling, thoughts racing.

"I don't know how you can possibly sleep in the same dorm as that creature," Sionnach hissed in regard to the fox-lord's noise, glaring at the ceiling. "First he is rude as can be to every person he comes across, then he bitches nonstop to me about *my* hideaway in the log, then he snores loud enough to shake the house!"

Saffron bit his lip, before deciding he was too tired to resist. "You know, when I was a beantighe, I had three roommates. Well —technically seven, but only three at night."

Sionnach gazed at him with big, curious brown eyes, laying so close on the pillow next to him that Saffron could hear every breath they took.

"Really?" they asked. "Seven whole beantighes in a single cottage? That sounds so—what?"

Saffron did his best to bite back the laughter, but eventually snorted, shaking his head. "Seven in one cottage, I wish! There were five other rooms in just Cottage Wicklow, which was even one of the smaller houses. When we'd have a meeting with everyone, we'd fill the entire front room, the kitchen, down the hallway, even up the stairs, where everyone would have to crowd in close..." he trailed off, recalling specifically that meeting Baba Yaga had held when the wolf's attacks in the woods were at their peak. How he'd held Hollow's hand the entire time—and how Hollow had defended him when someone tried to imply Saffron had something to do with it. He rubbed his fingers over the scars on his forearm, an unconscious movement, like a reminder that there was nothing so evil stalking any of those people any longer.

"How did you learn to read?" Sionnach's voice broke through Saffron's growing cloud of worry, puncturing and exhaling through his nose.

"Well... at first, I would read through the practice books Master Luvon's daughters had from when they were in primary school. I practiced so much, in secret, and eventually learned how to read... not very well, of course, but I got better over time. I used to steal books off Morrígan's campus, too, if I found any left behind on benches or in class while cleaning up after lectures." Sionnach's eyes widened in alarm, and Saffron grinned. He paused another moment—before mentioning the Grand Library. How, for the longest time, all he ever wanted was a single chance to step inside, to see the paintings on the ceilings, to peruse the books, even if they were too complicated for him to understand.

How the Grand Library was the reason for his first ever geis with Cylvan, though describing how he and the prince *actually* first met in the yarrow field nearly had Sionnach launching out of the bed with a shriek of disbelief. They hissed about how absolutely, undeniably *idiotic* Cylvan was to give his true name away so easily, how cruel it was for him to expect to just kill Saffron right after or to take his tongue, then to ever agree to their deal again after that despite Saffron still knowing his true name—but all the while, never stopped listening whenever Saffron continued. As Saffron couldn't help but share a little more, and a little more, until the sunrise peeked over the horizon and they'd both been awake all night long.

Recounting every moment of his time spent with Cylvan, all those memories that were sweet, lovely, avoiding any discussion of what went on in Danann House afterward, just regaling Sionnach with every perfect, romantic, honeyed thing that happened before things truly became complicated—it made Saffron wistful. It made him miss the simplicity of it, the simplicity of his secret romance with the prince of the high fey, the simplicity of the danger it put them both in should they be found, even the simplicity of arid magic at the time. How, back then, it was nothing more than drawing circles with hatchmarks on teacup saucers.

He never imagined he would think such a thing—but for the briefest moment, Saffron wished he could go back. Whether or not there was anything he could have done for things to end differently, he didn't know, but—he wasn't sure he would have, even with everything that came after.

20

## THE SHIFT

Reminiscing made Saffron soft for the rising sun, knowing Cylvan would be returning from the dé Bricríu estate soon enough. He wanted to apologize; Saffron wanted to share what he'd learned, and where he thought Ryder would be going next. He hoped Cylvan would be excited to hear it. He hoped Cylvan would be impressed with him, despite how they'd separated the night prior.

All throughout breakfast—eggs and sausage, pancakes with garden jam and raw maple syrup, biscuits with butter and garden herbs—Saffron smiled, and laughed, and looked constantly over his shoulder to the door wondering when Cylvan would finally make it back. He kept conversation with Copper with Sionnach, with Étaín and Carce who returned from the satyr festivities with the sun, looking exhausted but more than happy to host their guests just a bit longer.

When a knock came at the door, Saffron turned in his seat, grinning at the sound of horses nickering on the other side. It was Saoirse who stepped inside with a slight bow of greeting, asking if Saffron and the others were ready to go. Saffron got to his feet a little too quickly—even Carce commenting on his eagerness with a teasing smirk, making Saffron's face go red and turning to offer his own bow of thanks and words of appreciation for their hospitality. Étaín just elbowed Carce in the side, ordering him to stop embarrassing the Harmonious King-to-be, which struck Saffron on the back of the head harder than any tease ever would.

"Go on, Saff," Sionnach said, rising to begin gathering the empty plates. "Go make sure Prince Cylvan made it out alive."

"I'll come with you—" Copper attempted, grunting when Sionnach shoved the stack of plates into his chest with a sharp *'I don't think so, fox.'*

Étaín offered Saffron a final hug, squeezing him tight and wishing him luck in what he was looking for, as well as safety on the rest of their journey, as well as a reminder of her perpetual invitation to come and visit whenever he wished. Saffron hugged her back, attempting to steal as much of her comforting, sunshine-like warmth as he could, before giving one last bow of thanks and hurrying past Saoirse out the door.

Cylvan stood by his horse on the drive outside, brushing her black coat with repetitive strokes like his mind was far from where he stood. Further proven by the way he jumped when Saffron approached and said his name, then how caught off guard he was when Saffron threw arms around him, pulling him close before standing on his toes to kiss him.

He expected Cylvan to hug him back, to kiss him back—but when he didn't, Saffron flattened back to his heels, smiling up at Cylvan awkwardly in question.

"Good morning," he attempted. "Sorry, I didn't meant to startle you—"

"You only caught me off guard," Cylvan interrupted with a brief chuckle, shaking his head. "You can't imagine the night I've had. I hardly slept at all."

"Me, too," Saffron laughed lightly, letting himself feel relieved with that little flicker of the person he expected breaking through. "I hope Renard dé Bricríu didn't harass you too much."

"Far too much, I can assure you, him and Anyst—... Ah, well, at least my diplomatic obligation is fulfilled for the next decade, we can only hope." Cylvan sighed. The smile remained on his lips, but he turned his attention back to brushing his horse. Saffron noticed how he'd cut himself short at the mention of Anysta, almost asking why, before stopping himself. Cylvan clearly didn't want to talk about it, and Saffron wasn't particularly eager to do so, either. Perhaps nothing of note actually had happened, perhaps they really had only discussed obvious things like Cylvan's time in the Fall Court, or other topics as dull as how school was going for him, how the kings were in their health, hardly anything different from what Étaín and Carce asked while they sat at the breakfast table an hour earlier. At least—he wanted to hope. He wanted to believe Cylvan would tell him if there had been anything more alarming.

"I'm glad you're back," Saffron said. Cylvan glanced at him. "And—I'm sorry for how I behaved last night. At the party, when the dé Bricríus arrived. I... think I'll abstain from speaking when drunk on satyr wine, for a bit."

"'Abstain' is a fine word for a beantighe," Cylvan smirked, before it twitched, considering the things he'd said in his own heated anger the night before. But instead of apologizing back, he just cleared his throat and continued: "Did sleeping in Sionnach's room crowded with books rub something off on you? Or did they run vocabulary lists with you as part of their tutoring sessions?"

"Oh—something like that, actually," Saffron laughed awkwardly, unsure how to explain everything he'd learned about Queen Proserpina's coronation route, how he thought he knew the next place Ryder would try and open the veil. Still, he did his very best, though his confidence didn't improve any as Cylvan just stared back at him with blank politeness.

"So, you wish to travel to Ailinne?" he asked. Saffron nodded, biting his lip, unable to help but sense something else Cylvan meant to say—but didn't. He just returned to brushing his horse for a moment, clearly deep in his own thoughts, before nodding slightly. "Perhaps we should consider..." he began, still. His hand on the brush stiffened, before returning to its strokes. "Perhaps... I suppose there's no avoiding it, then... But only if you're absolutely sure—"

"Yes," Saffron tried to reassure, especially with Cylvan's clear hesitance, the uncertainty bubbling beneath his expression. He tugged on Cylvan's sleeve to draw his attention back. "I'm certain, especially after what the veil told me yesterday. That thing about *'where the earth's minerals heat the rocks'*..."

"Then Ailinne makes perfect sense. We'll make our way there right away," Cylvan smiled back, before turning sharply as Copper's sudden, booming laugh from the house made both him and Saffron jump. Saffron snapped around just as Copper was physically kicked out the front door by Sionnach's cloven hoof.

"You should ride in the carriage today, if we're able to rent one from Tyara," Cylvan summoned Saffron's attention back. "Especially if you didn't get any sleep last night. It will be more comfortable than in the saddle."

"Alright," Saffron smiled as the others finally joined them, already chatting about the route they'd be taking to Ailinne assuming Cylvan agreed, like Copper of all people couldn't resist blabbing the night's business the first chance he got. Cylvan confirmed that Ailinne sounded like a good place to try, next, though didn't say much else except to ask Aodhán to ride into Tyara to see if there were any carriages to rent. Maeve offered to join them, leaving together as Étain invited Cylvan and Saoirse inside to eat breakfast before they left.

Saffron reached to take Cylvan's hand, to walk with him back to the house—but Cylvan heaved himself suddenly onto the back of his horse, nodding Saffron to go ahead and return to the house.

"I just remembered, there are a few things I need to pick up before we go as well," he said. "I'll hurry to join Aodhán and Maeve. Don't miss me too much while I'm gone, púca, alright?"

"Alright..." Saffron said in uncertainty, as even that flirtation felt—unnatural. Cylvan offered him a nod, before turning and kicking his horse to trot down the road after the other two up ahead. Saffron just watched him go. Trying to deny the lump forming in his stomach, trying to reassure himself that—Cylvan would have definitely told him if something more alarming had happened while staying the night with the dé Bricríus.

To KEEP HIMSELF FROM OVERTHINKING IT, FROM driving himself mad when there were already so many other things in the world attempting to do that for him, Saffron did as he was told. He rested in the carriage once Cylvan and the others sent a robin inviting the rest of the traveling party into town where they had managed to find one.

Saffron would not overthink it; he would let the anxiety wash out of him as easily as the creek used to wash mud from his veil. He would enjoy the simple luxury of riding in the back of a carriage over another day in Boann's saddle, listening as the wheels bumped over hardened dirt roads through the Fall Court woods. Sionnach sat with him, as well as Maeve, though she mostly just gazed out the window as Sionnach drifted in and out of sleep on Saffron's shoulder.

When he wasn't fighting the urge to sleep alongside his friend, tempted by the constant, rhythmic clattering of the carriage, Saffron had his sketchbook on his lap and a tin of charcoal on the seat next to him. He scribbled quick gestures of the trees they passed by; he sketched Sionnach's legs crossed neatly on the seat next to him; he copied the designs of the stitching of the carriage cushions, and the hand-painted genre scenes of fey enjoying picnics and frolicking through meadows on the walls and ceiling. He drew Maeve, nervously, as she gazed beautifully and intimidatingly out the window, hardly moving except to blink and tuck a piece of hair behind her ear.

He couldn't tell if she had something on her mind, or if that was just how she preferred to pass the time, but he never bothered her. Her stillness was welcome as a drawing subject, at the very least. He would have gladly kept his drawings a secret just for himself, too, if her icy-blue eyes hadn't suddenly flickered his way, raising an eyebrow the next time he glanced at her while trying to get the shape of her jawline right. It made him go stiff, before smiling awkwardly and turning the sketchbook to show her. He didn't expect her to look so surprised, raising her eyebrows and sitting forward.

"Can I see more?" she asked. He nodded meekly, handing the sketchbook over, grimacing when she immediately flipped through the previous handful of pages once finished looking over her own portrait. "You're very good. Better than I expected."

"Uh, thanks. I think."

She smirked, handing the sketchbook back.

"Cylvan told me about your drawings a few days ago, really had me thinking you were some kind of hidden master. I don't think I'd go so far as to say *that*, but you definitely have a talent for it, your highness."

"Cylvan told you?" Saffron asked, embarrassed, never considering that Cylvan actually thought about Saffron as much as Saffron thought about him when they weren't together. Which was a foolish thing to believe, considering everything Cylvan had ever said to promise otherwise—but with the strangeness of his behavior that morning, Saffron couldn't help it.

"You're the only thing he talks about," Maeve sighed. "You or some old book he's reading or bought underhanded from a seller dealing in taboo goods..."

"Saffron is sort of a walking taboo good, if you think about it," Sionnach mumbled sleepily, before slowly lifting their head and rubbing their eyes.

"You're not wrong," he said, settling back into the seat with the sketchbook returned to his lap. That time he gazed out the window, sketching gestures of Copper on the back of his horse, then Cylvan who rode next to him. They shared what appeared to be an intense conversation, lacking the same sort of juvenile laughter and attempts to kick one another out of their saddles as before. Saffron knew it likely had something to do with what happened at the satyr party. Then what happened at the dé

Bricríu home after; and how Copper hadn't been invited to join them.

Exhaling through his nose, Saffron tried to smother the growing nerves, but instead the emotions just showed in the stiffness of the lines on the page.

"Sionnach, Maeve…" He specifically felt Maeve's gaze without having to watch for it. "Back after what happened at the games, after we were done talking with the kings, and then Copper hurried out—you both said his reaction to learning all those things about me wasn't a surprise. Erm, and that his family situation was 'complicated.' When we wandered away from the party last night, after you and Cylvan left with Renard, he did tell me a little bit about how his Aunt Una was King Ailir's mother—erm, at least, she was supposed to be. She was King Elanyl's Harmonious Queen, but he had King Ailir with a prostitute before he died, and she agreed to raise Ailir as if he were her own, and… you know. I'm sure you both already know all that." Saffron's brows furrowed in frustration, hating how quiet they both were while listening, hating how complicated everything about it all really was. "I guess what I'm asking, is… What I'm wondering, is—"

"You want to know if that was what we were referring to," Maeve finally offered an escape, and Saffron sighed with a nod. She too glanced back out the window to where Copper and Cylvan rode alongside each other, considering her answer for what was only a few moments, but felt like an eternity.

"There are seven sídhe families, including the Tuatha dé Danann." She said. "Cylvan has told you at least that much."

Saffron nodded.

"Then you also know that the Tuatha dé Danann family name is as much a title as it is a lineage, right? Sídhe families who marry into the Tuatha dé Danann can become Tuatha dé Danann, themselves, at minimum in benefit if not wholly by name. But that requires having children born under that name. For example—in order to be a rightful heir to the throne, a child has to be born a sídhe fey, which is promised to happen if both parents are also sídhe fey. Which is why Cylvan and Asche have a progenitor mother, Naoill, from the de Fianna sídhe family."

"Right—but they also have siblings with King Tross' family. Asche mentioned his sister, Éoine, is also a progenitor for their family."

"That's right—because Tross' family, the mac Cadáin family, are not a sídhe family, but they earn a chance to have sídhe heirs with King Ailir by marriage. If any of the children between Éoine and Ailir develop sídhe powers later in life, and neither Cylvan nor Asche are eligible for the throne for whatever reason, they could technically take their place, and the mac Cadáin family would become the new Tuatha dé Danann."

"Technically Gentle Naoill could introduce themself as a Tuatha dé Danann—at least, they will be able to once Cylvan becomes king," Sionnach added. Saffron's head spun.

"And why is it a requirement for heirs to be sídhe fey, exactly?"

Maeve smirked. "Why are humans only allowed to be beantighes? Old rules declared by old kings that have not been reconsidered in centuries. Something else to add to your list of things-to-do, your highness."

Saffron grimaced. One thing at a time.

"So then, going back—the fact that Elanyl and Una didn't have an heir between the two of them is a sore spot for Renard. Who is Una's brother," he reiterated.

"That's right. And the fact King Ailir developed sídhe magic despite having only one sídhe parent. Because if he hadn't, the dé Bricríus would have automatically adopted the Tuatha dé Danann name—and therefore the ruling power—by Una's marriage to Elanyl."

"God," Saffron groaned. "Alright, that old fey lord's attitude suddenly makes so much sense."

"Not to mention how he only invited Cylvan and Maeve home with him," Sionnach muttered, before fluttering their lashes and flipping their hair theatrically. *"Only sídhe fey are welcome to break bread at my table, no Alvényan countryfey or half-satyrs shall cross my threshold.*"

"But then why not invite Copper? He's as sídhe as Cylvan and you, Maeve," Saffron added in annoyance. "Though I think I can guess, considering how he talked down to him in front of everyone."

"You're correct that Copper is as sídhe as Renard and all his siblings—but that doesn't mean Renard has to love him any."

Saffron's heart squeezed in disdain, especially as Maeve said it so easily. "If Renard resents Ailir that much, and therefore Cylvan, or anyone else who's part of the royal family—then the reason Copper was so hesitant to agree to anything Ailir asked of him is perfectly clear. And what else is perfectly clear—is that I'll be taking back my apology to Cylvan for how I talked to that old fey. He deserved it."

Maeve grinned, helping herself to some wine from the carafe in the center between the cushions. "I can assure you, *that old fey* will not forget you anytime soon, Saffron. The foul-mouthed, drunk Alvényan who dared talk back to him. You may already be first rowan witch in centuries—but even more impressively, you may also be the first creature to walk away from disrespecting Renard dé Bricríu like that, too."

"Did he mention it at all over dinner?"

Maeve scoffed. "Of course not. But everyone could tell he stewed the whole time."

"Good," Saffron muttered. "I'll claim Copper for myself, too, while I'm at it. Since Renard wouldn't care anyway..." He trailed off, biting his lip and glancing out the window to where Cylvan still rode ahead of the carriage alongside Copper, though they no longer spoke to one another. He couldn't resist, asking: "What did you all talk about at dinner, anyway? Anything that might... might put Cylvan in such a bad mood?"

"Nothing specifically that I can think of," Maeve said. "It was tense, and terrifying, in a way only sharing bread with Renard could be—but there wasn't anything notable that I overheard."

"What about with Anysta, then?" Saffron encouraged. Maeve considered it for a moment, twirling a piece of hair around her finger.

"Anysta was mostly quiet during the dinner," she said. "Though I think she and Cylvan may have had a private conversation sometime after dessert. Before he went to bed. I don't know what about, though—maybe just discussing her family silver, again..."

Saffron't stomach turned over, though he didn't know if it was in a sense of betrayal or further concern. Cylvan promised him there wouldn't be any more deals made with Anysta in private; he promised there wasn't anything long-term formed with her during their first secret meeting in Erelaine. Had he purposefully misled Saffron about it?

"Did any of Copper's brothers attempt to flirt with Prince Cylvan while you were there?" Sionnach asked, clearly sensing the shift in mood and attempting to remedy it. Maeve shook her head, mid-sip from her drink.

"Too proud for that sort of act," she said. "If Renard decides to try and get the crown for himself again, it won't be through marriage. Seeing as that already burned him once. Not to mention, it wouldn't matter—none of his sons are able to have children."

"What?" Saffron raised his eyebrows. Maeve's perfect mouth curled into a sly smile.

"That's right," she said, leaning forward. "Family curse, bestowed by the forest itself after that trick he played with his feast all those years ago."

"It's not just a story, then?" Saffron leaned closer, too, eyes wide.

"Who knows?" she purred. "That's a closely-held family secret, exactly what happened. Exactly the terms of their curse."

Sionnach snorted under their breath.

"It's just..." they said, eyes flashing to where the scars on Saffron's forearm were hidden beneath the glamour. "Funny that the arrogance of two sídhe families earned them a curse that withstands generations, is all."

Saffron touched his hand to his arm, realizing Sionnach was referring to Taran, to the mac Delbaiths, and their family curse of ashenness. How ironic, too, their eagerness to marry into the Tuatha dé Danann compared to Renard's refusal to let such a thing hurt his pride. Taran's presence grumbled something at that thought, too far for Saffron to hear, but enough to make him smirk to himself.

"Every sídhe family has a curse or two," Maeve went on coyly. "Even mine. Even the Tuatha dé Danann, I'm sure."

"What's your family curse, Maeve?" Saffron asked, but Maeve just smiled at him slyly again and shook her head.

"Maybe I'll tell you after you've earned your crown, Lord Saffron. I don't need a rowan-blooded arid-witch-beantighe knowing my family's biggest weakness, hm?"

Saffron's face went hot, jumping forward to declare an apology, which made Maeve throw her head back and laugh. She put her hand up to brush him off, before offering the remaining wine from her glass, and he took it. He even took it gladly, finishing off what was left before returning to his sketchbook.

"All of the sídhe family names, what are they again?" he asked, pressing charcoal to paper. At the very least, Maeve was happy to spill that information, until the page was littered with names both familiar and new. He didn't want to have to go through what he did at the satyr party again, ever again—and knowing exactly who he was dealing with, exactly which members of Alfidel he must reckon with, was one way to start.


BREAKING FOR LUNCH IN A SMALL FALL COURT TOWN on the way, Saffron was happy to get out of the carriage and attempt once more to tease Cylvan back into a better mood— only for a gossip crier to grab him on the corner, stuffing the morning's most recent column into his hands. Saffron attempted to give it back, desperately *not* wishing to know what was printed, especially considering his mistake the morning prior with the reporters who crowded him outside the train—but he couldn't avoid it, and the bolded text summoned bile up the back of his throat.

*FLOWER OF ALVENYA BELIEVES FEY AT MIDSUMMER GAMES DESERVED THEIR HORRIBLE FATE, INCLUDING WHAT BEFELL DAURAE ASCHE; Folk Are Beginning To Wonder If The Flower Isn't Influencing Prince Cylvan's Seelie Ways, Fearing What The Prince May Do Next Regarding Red Witch Scourge...*

21

———

## AILINNE

*Believes fey at Midsummer Games deserved their horrible fate...*

*... influencing Prince Cylvan's seelie ways...*

*... the red witch scourge...*

Saffron didn't realize he leaned too far out of the saddle until it was too late, barely jerking back to life, but not in time to keep from crashing to the road with a grunt. It even startled Boann, who stamped her feet and jerked forward, dragging Saffron a few feet with his boot caught in the stirrup. Copper raced up on his horse to block Boann's way, allowing Saffron a chance to untangle himself. He just managed to yank his foot free when Cylvan was suddenly there, moving so fast a gust of wind kissed Saffron's face even without his magic. It was just enough to knock some sense back into him, as Cylvan touched all over his head and face, asking if he was alright.

"I'm fine," Saffron muttered, shaking his head and brushing Cylvan's hands away. Only half a lie, as his head throbbed and his hands were scraped. "Just lost my balance, it's fine—"

"Come here, sit up," Cylvan insisted anyway, pulling Saffron upright before cupping either side of his face and really looking into both of his eyes. Behind him, the others were stepping off their horses to get a closer look, and Saffron flushed hot with embarrassment.

He already felt self-conscious enough after the news that morning. Especially knowing everyone else had read it, too. They'd all acted like it wasn't anything to worry about. Maybe Saffron knew it too, but—he couldn't help the swirling nausea in his gut.

And more—he couldn't stomach anyone fussing over him for something else, especially not when he already felt so anxious. Agitated. Especially not Cylvan, who, out of all of them—had not reacted to the headline at all. Not even to chuckle, or to reassure Saffron like everyone else it was nothing to worry about. Just reading it, then turning in favor of finishing his meal. Without a word.

"I said I'm fine!" Saffron insisted, freeing himself from Cylvan's hands and hurrying back to his feet. He brushed himself off, nearly tripping over the prince still kneeling in front of him. Boann trotted over next, keeping her head low and bumping him in the side as if to apologize. He just put a hand on her snout, before turning back to everyone else standing in a half-circle around him. Looking a mix of worried and perplexed—which only bothered him further.

"What?" he asked, grabbing Boann's reins and yanking himself back up into the saddle. The leather rubbed against his scraped palms, making his jaw clench. "I just wasn't paying attention to what I was doing. Stop looking at me like that! Come on."

His audience glanced briefly between one another as Cylvan finally got back to his feet, too, before returning to their own horses. Only Cylvan hovered a moment longer, before scoffing and turning to do the same. Saffron had to resist the urge to kick him in the shoulder.


NOT ENTIRELY UNLIKE ERELAINE BEFORE IT—THERE was a line of horses, pedestrians, high fey patrons attempting entry at Ailinne once they reached the long wooden bridge that stretched over the tree-filled valley below toward the front gates. The rich smell of natural springs hung in the air like petrichor during a hot summer rain, fusty with the smell of eggs and hot stone in a way that made Saffron's nose tingle and goosebumps grow on his skin.

Most of those queued in line held thick paper tokens in their hands, a tassel dangling from a hole in the top, some green, others bronze, others silver. The occasional gold tassel jostled amongst the crowd, and Saffron didn't have to wonder long to himself before Sionnach noticed him watching.

"It designates one's access to which pools," they said, patting the side of their palomino's neck as the horse bumped noses with Boann. "There are different tiers of pools here, like there are tiers for the gods in Erelaine."

"If it belongs to the high fey, there's going to be some kind of hierarchy," Saffron mumbled. Sionnach grimaced, but didn't disagree. "Do we need tokens like those to get inside?" He went on, just as Aodhán trotted by, passing the line all the way across the bridge to the gatehouse at the front. It made the crowd waiting ahead of them turn to see what made that guest so important, before whispers rang out at the sight of Prince Cylvan perched in his saddle behind where Saffron and Sionnach lead the group. Even if he wasn't so obvious, though, the royal crest emblazoned on everyone else's riding tack would have been a hint.

But then the collective gaze traveled from Cylvan—to Saffron. Looking him up and down, eyes lingering on his face as if memorizing him. As if they recognized him from somewhere, from something, dozens and dozens of faces that didn't bother trying to be subtle about their long looks.

Saffron just watched Aodhán at the head of the line. He silently begged them to *hurry*. He knew why those people looked at him, why they thought they recognized him. He'd been quoted in Alfidel's most popular gossip columns just that morning. Surely, most of them had those same leaf of paper tucked in their bags, the pockets of their cloaks. *The high fey deserve what happened to them at the Midsummer Games.* He could practically see the printed letters passing like bold marquees behind their eyes.

By every blessing of Ériu and Danu and perhaps even Lugh, Aodhán rode back with a handful of gold-tasseled paper tokens before anyone could confront Saffron to his face. He nearly melted out of his saddle for a second time from the relief.


IT WAS NO WONDER THERE WAS SUCH A LINE OF FOLK waiting outside the gates, as the streets of Ailinne were packed edge-to-edge with other patrons hurrying this way and that. Because of the overcrowding, horses and carriages weren't permitted past the gatehouse, which meant after leaving their animals at the stables, the group was forced to move on foot. It made it easier to blend into the crowd, in some ways—but the ability to blend didn't matter once Cylvan was recognized, and gossip spread like a bloody cough through the congestion. Saffron practically saw the movement of the news with his own eyes, knowing exactly where the ripple had stretched by how far ahead people turned to look for themselves.

*"He must be seeking alleviation for his own ashen state,"* came one of many whispers within Saffron's range. *"I hear he was so kind to those in Erelaine."*

Saffron bit his tongue. He adjusted his grip on the luggage in his hand, turning his eyes back down and focusing again on just following Saoirse's broad-shouldered lead through the crowd. Parting bodies like a steel-tipped boat through lake ice.

*"I'll tell you if I sense anything,"* Taran ghosted in his mind, a welcome offering just like back in Erelaine, allowing Saffron more focus on his feet. On the cramming walls of people on every side.

With the rabble of spring-goers making it hard enough to breathe, let alone navigate, Saffron eventually reached out to hook his fingers under the bottom lip of Saoirse's back plate in order to keep her within reach. The shiny silver surface was blurred beneath a thin layer of humidity from the myriad of hot springs that belched steam into the air, various signs and arrows pointing in various directions between Ailinne's building to indicate the paths to reach them. Some were available right on the other side of the buildings, while other signs warned of the distance required to reach one or another, located a little further out in the trees.

Of the buildings themselves, there was nothing of particular note that stood out to Saffron as any more unique than the shops he passed in Avren, or those in Erelaine—restaurants, clothing shops, innumerable apothecaries and other storefronts that promised all sorts of charms and salves and potions to cure any ailment a high fey could think of. Copper had been right, when he guessed the springs were overrun with fey from Avren seeking respite.

Still, his eyes lingered on those medicinal-charm shops the longest as they passed by—until he spotted a particularly large cluster of patrons huddled around a little shop window, and he recognized the attendant serving through it. The same one he'd spotted in Erelaine, selling opulent silver. Somehow, still, knowing exactly which way the prince's entourage headed and even beating them there.

As Saffron clung to Saoirse's armor to ensure he didn't get lost, the massive fey guard occasionally glanced over her shoulder to double check for herself. When the crowd grew even more untenable, she'd slow her pace some to ensure no tangling feet or elbows to the ribs would result in him losing his grasp. With his other hand, Saffron grasp the handle of his luggage, sharing it with Sionnach, who went bright red and whipped around to bark at Copper when the fox-fey teasingly grabbed their tail in the same sentiment. Perhaps without thinking, after yanking their tail away, Sionnach gripped Copper's hand in their own, instead—before turning back to Saffron with wide eyes like they only then just realized the irreversible thing they'd done. They didn't let go, though. Neither did Copper, who just furrowed his brows and went silent, like he wasn't exactly sure how to react, either.

They passed through a series of gates along the road, stopping at each where a beantighe checked the legitimacy of their golden tassels, one by one, by plucking one of the narrow threads and dipping it in a shallow bowl filled with cloudy water. Each time, the golden threads turned green as if left in saltwater for a decade, and the group would be waved through to the other side. And each time, despite knowing they were legitimate, Saffron still held his breath as he watched the process. The growing need to pass through to the other side, where the crowds gradually thinned, and thinned, and thinned, until they could all walk without bumping into every stranger on the street—was simply too strong, making him paranoid that they'd be forced to return to the throng.

King Ailir was a regular patron of the hot springs, enough that the royal family had a private guest house in the golden-tier quarter of Ailinne, and Saffron nearly shed tears when they finally reached the end of the drive and left any semblance of a crowd on their heels.

Nestled within a wide circle of trees, steam curled from a private pool in the back yard of the house, while the building itself was simple, but stunning in its construction. With toothy, natural-wood shingles on the sloped rooftops, and open-air sliding doors and windows on every side, Saffron wasn't sure there was a single pane of glass to separate the inside from the out. Only sheer curtains, or woven lattices of pine needles delicately sewn together with silk string, though he overheard mention of silencing charms for each room, not unlike the one that once dampened the noise of the Aon Adharcach suite. The floors were polished and smooth on the bottom of his feet, though they, like every other surface in the house, were kissed with the smallest sheen of humidity from not only the private pool in the back yard, but the constant cloud of natural spring air that coated all of Ailinne.

Perhaps sent ahead the moment Aodhán made their arrival known at the front gates, a handful of beantighes hurried throughout the house as the prince's entourage made their way up, opening windows and racing back and forth over the slippery floors with rags to dry them. When Saffron and the others arrived, the servants only briefly halted their rush long enough to offer a greeting and a bow, to ask if they would like anything particular brought to them to improve their stay, before listing off everything that was already prepared and at their disposal. Bath-wraps to wear both while soaking and while strolling the main thoroughfare; reed-woven shoes for the same; Ailinne's specialty of steamed wines and sap-seared fruit platters, though they would have a proper meal delivered within the hour. All offerings made to Cylvan, who just waved them off without requesting anything in particular. Clearly exhausted, himself, from all the attention, from the crowds. It was dismissive, the way he did it, in a way Saffron hadn't seen of him in a long while.

Changing out of their traveling clothes into Ailinne's more common bathing robes, Saffron was admittedly grateful for the flowing, even borderline-revealing nature of the barely-opaque shawl of fabric that hugged his body. A single, long piece of cloth that came with an illustrated instructional parchment for wrapping oneself properly, lilac-purple fabric hanging to his mid-thigh and leaving his back and arms bare to the warm air. A welcome relief from the constricting, protective gear he wore on the road. It reminded him a little too much of what he'd been chased through the woods wearing at the satyr party.

Despite Saffron's own exhaustion, and how badly he wished to throw his things on the floor and walk straight into the steaming, bubbling natural bath right on the other side of the back porch—he found it difficult to let his guard down, even once the beantighes excused themselves and it was just Cylvan's party left. As Saoirse and Aodhán circled the perimeter of the yard to check for anyone who might be hiding, whether it be gossip writers or—someone else. Someone else who, the mere thought of, was likely the reason Saffron couldn't seem to stop pacing back and forth. Why he couldn't stop checking every room, himself, or pushing the pine-needle shades aside to look out over the yard. Even though he was sure Ryder wouldn't come early, in the middle of the day. He wouldn't perform another veil event that didn't align with his already-established schedule, if he was following the exact same timeline as the queen's coronation route. But that didn't mean the man wasn't already somewhere close by. Already in the town. And if he was—he likely knew Saffron and the others had just arrived, too.

"Do you guys want to go walk around some more?" He finally asked as everyone else slumped over the cushions and blankets spread out in clusters in the main sitting area, snacking on Ailinne's treats and sipping at streaming goblets of wine. Most of them groaned at the thought of going back out again, including even Sionnach—but then they noticed how clearly antsy Saffron was, biting their lip and getting back to their feet.

"Sure," they said. "I wouldn't mind walking around. This is my first time in Ailinne too, anyway."

"Are you sure that's such a good idea?" Maeve asked, though the argument wasn't made particularly strongly. "Considering the reason we're here, and all."

Saffron wrung his hands together. "According to what Sionnach and I know—Ryder won't likely cause a scene until at least tomorrow. More likely, even tomorrow night, according to how many days passed between the queen's visit between Ailinne and the Fall Court on her coronation route, assuming he's following the same schedule like already demonstrated—"

"But he might still be in the area," Aodhán muttered, though they didn't lift their head from where it was draped over the back of a particularly round cushion.

"I think it best you stay where you are, Saffron," Cylvan added. He, took, didn't look up from the tray of food he lazily observed. "For the sake of everyone."

Saffron didn't know what that meant—but something told

him it was a needle at his tendency to find trouble. There wasn't anything teasing about his tone, though, which only made Saffron prickle all over again.

"I don't want to just sit around and wait for him to come," he argued. "The least we can do is walk around and try to figure out where he might be when he comes tomorrow—"

"Somewhere significant to Queen Proserpina, as you've theorized," Cylvan said, cold-purple eyes cutting upward and meeting Saffron's.

"Well, yes," Saffron answered. Flushing with a sudden frustration and, admittedly a bit of embarrassment. Cylvan looked and sounded so exasperated.

"I'll come, along," Copper interjected suddenly, despite having been the one most spread-out over the cushions only a moment prior. He got to his feet and smoothed down the bottom of his fabric-wrap that had hiked up over his bare ass. "C'mon, I'll show you both where to get the best grilled pheasant in this place. Gotta brave the green-tier shops again, though, if you don't mind."

Saffron didn't. He just turned on heel and made his way for the exit before Cylvan could think of something else to say, first. Perhaps realizing no one else was going to stop him, even Saoirse sighed and got to her feet to join them, too. Saffron didn't object. Saffron didn't care. A part of him even hoped Ryder might show himself while they were out. There would be nothing more goddamned delectable than bringing him back trussed up like a pheasant of their own, to thrown in Cylvan's face.

## 22

# THE QUARREL

Saffron reprised Taran's offer to keep an eye out for Ryder at least a dozen times, particularly once he had a few drinks in his system. As Copper showed him and Sionnach around the green-tier shops of the city, with Saoirse on their heels at all times. Even indulging in a drink, herself, at one point, but only at the start. After just an hour of stopping wherever the sights and smells carried them, even she knew she needed every faculty at her disposal to keep Saffron, specifically, out of trouble. He was hungry for trouble. For rebellion. For a way to get his frustrations out, come what may. A dangerous predicament to be in, as a beantighe who could hold a grudge.

Instead, he just ate anything and everything Copper put in front of him. Grilled pheasant, honey crystals like beads on strings, river fish drizzled with a sweet sauce on skewers, apple-cinnamon croquettes, then candied apple slices, then apple pie in a clay cup, then apple-spiced beer by the mugful. Just because he could. His own wildly misplaced sense of rebellion, considering how careful he normally was when it came to allowing the fruit anywhere within Cylvan's vicinity.

They visited a handful of the natural springs within walking-distance, soaking in some that smelled of wildflowers with thousands of petals floating on the surface; others that were cram-packed with visitors in a wide spectrum of undress, the special water promised to give their skin a permanent perfumed aroma; another that was nearly empty and set behind one of the dozens of Ailinne's apothecaries, where the water was thick with natural minerals to the point of reeking like eggs. Saffron didn't mind one bit, though Copper complained more than he didn't. Claiming his heightened sense of smell, as a fox-lord, made it particularly torturous. Saffron just hooked an arm behind his head and dunked him.

They drank, ate, and wandered between springs until the moon reached its highest point overhead. Until all three of them were stumbling, slurring, sloppy and easily distracted. Until Copper was too drunk to stand up straight in one pool long enough to follow the steps out, having to drag himself over the edge to lay in the dirt like a fish on a dock, claiming he was going to pass out from the heat. Only to then complain about being too cold and bodily sliding right back in. All the same, not too drunk to catch Sionnach as one of their hooves slipped on the wet stone steps, sweeping them into his arm as they both blinked in confusion at one another—before he dunked the satyr with a splash and elicited screech that got them kicked out.

After visiting one of Ailinne's innumerable apothecaries, with expensive tobacco and cannabis leaves in bags in both his hands as they exited, Saoirse had finally had enough and shepherded Saffron and the others back in the direction of the king's private house. And even then, with the remnants of the sweet sting of apples still on his tongue, he made certain to rinse and gargle multiple times with the city's sacred mineral water whenever they passed a public fountain. Each and every time, stretching the journey back to double what it should have been, but in such a state of inebriation he wanted to be absolutely certain he didn't accidentally poison his raven. He only wished to rebel—not actually harm the heir to the throne.

Once safe and sound back in Ailir's private house, Saffron's choice in smoking leaves was unexpectedly effective—and it wasn't long after they returned that he was spread out on the pillows in the main sitting room, staring up at the rafters while certain flower sprites buzzed back and forth between the gaps. Any time he tried to point them out, though, the Sionnach claimed to not see anything while Copper insisted they weren't sprites at all, but hundreds and hundreds of spiders, which only made Sionnach squirm before telling him to *stop talking.* Saffron was just certain smoking made it so high fey could lie more easily.

HE DIDN'T KNOW EXACTLY WHEN CYLVAN WENT TO bed, only that the prince appeared in the corner of Saffron's view to bend over and offer him a kiss on the cheek, then a wish good-night. At least—Saffron thought so, as everything felt a little too floaty to know for sure. The longer the night wore on, he was certain he'd only imagined it, determined even to stumble his way through the house and find where Cylvan slept to demand to know the truth—but he didn't make it off the pillows. In fact, the few hours of sleep he was able to claim came to him right there on the floor, wrapped in blankets and around Copper, who was as soft and comfortable as a fine mattress the more Saffron's mind swirled in circles.

When morning came, Saffron woke to the sound of beantighes shuffling in and out through the front door and down the hallway, past the main room where he and his friends slept like a pile of pixies in the center. Trays of covered food paraded by, as well as more carafes of wine to drink, armfuls of clothing and bushels of aromatic flowers, as well as a small stack of letters. Saffron thought nothing of them, even content to curl back up under Copper's bare arm to try and sleep a bit longer—but then he recognized the sound of Fiachra chittering in the backyard, joined by the raspy crowing of Cylvan's one-eyed raven, Balor.

Sitting up, Saffron yawned, rubbing his eyes and adjusting the fabric wrap that'd fallen off his shoulder and revealed his bare chest to the world. He left behind Sionnach and Copper within the pillows—making a mental note to tease them both to death about how Sionnach slept draped over Copper's chest, as Copper's arm wrapped snugly down the curve of the satyr's back, where his hand cupped the round of their ass like holding a cat in place. Later. There would be plenty of time to tease them later.

Following the hurried line of beantighes into the eating area, someone already sat at the round table by another wide-open gap in the wall overlooking the trees and hotspring in the back. The fresh air tousled Cylvan's hair like a needy lover as the prince sipped at a cup of juice, two slices of seed-sprouted bread spread with butter and jam in front of him. He'd only taken a single bite of one of them, clearly distracted by the letter in his hand. Saffron didn't have to ask who it was from as he approached—he recognized the wax seal of King Ailir snapped in half on the upper edge.

"Good morning," Saffron said. Cylvan didn't jump—in fact, he barely reacted, except for his eyes. They flickered to meet Saffron's, before returning to the letter.

"Good morning," he answered simply.

"Is that a letter from the kings?" Saffron asked as the silence between them was like needles pricking under his tongue.

"Yes," Cylvan answered. He took another bite of toast, before returning it to the plate and sliding it away. Toward Saffron, silently offering it to him. Saffron hesitated only a moment, before approaching to claim a seat next to him.

"What does it say?" He asked, not expecting Cylvan to sigh when he did.

"Father is asking why we've extended our journey to Ailinne."

"Oh." A longer silence, that time. Saffron took a bite of the toast, crossing his legs and appreciating the view on the other side of the opening in the wall. Birds chittered endlessly in the trees as the sun rose over them, thinning a blanket of nighttime mist until there was only the steam of the pools billowing in the light.

Saffron wanted to say something. It would have sounded like, *'well, we'll be heading back to Avren in the morning, so they won't have to worry much longer...'* but he couldn't bring himself to speak it. Because—he wasn't sure. He hated that he wasn't sure, but—there was no way to be. He didn't know what would come that evening, or later that night, or whenever else Ryder might act. He wished he could vocalize *those* things, instead—but something told him uttering anything except certainty would only sour Cylvan's mood further.

"Have you seen today's gossip column?" Cylvan surprised him when he spoke again, next. His eyes flit upward once more, over the edge of the paper, holding Saffron's gaze before returning to the king's letter. He must have been reading it for the third or fourth time, considering how long his focus lingered.

"Er—no. Not yet?" Saffron answered, unsure how else to.

"They brought some with breakfast this morning. You can find them on the entryway table."

Saffron lingered where he was, though. He took another bite of toast, watching Cylvan the whole time. Watching his amethyst eyes skim each line of the written letter—before, sure enough, they slid all the way back to the beginning again, starting over. He almost asked if there was something wrong because of it—but then Cylvan's eyes flickered to him a third time, and Saffron realized—he was waiting for Saffron to leave. Pretending to read, because he didn't wish to speak.

Scoffing, Saffron tossed the piece of toast back onto the plate, roughly shoving it back toward Cylvan and pushing his chair out. Cylvan muttered something as Saffron left, but Saffron didn't hear it. Something told him it might have been for the best.

Making his way to the entryway, Maeve and Aodhán were already there, clearly for the same reason as they each had a different gossip leaflet in each hand. As Saffron approached, they gave him a look that chafed him even worse, snatching the one closest to him in Maeve's grasp.

*PRINCE CYLVAN'S HOLIDAY CONTINUES IN AILINNE AFTER SPENDING QUALITY TIME WITH MASTER RENARD DÉ BRICRÍU AND LADY MAC DELBAITH IN THE FALL COURT; Sources Say Most Likely Discussing His Future Reign In One Final Attempt To Earn Allies. Lady Mac Delbaith Arrives In Ailinne Hours Before Prince Cylvan—Is He Keeping Her Trail On Purpose? Has The Young Head Lady And Priestess Of Dagda Won The Affection Of The Cold Prince?*

*THE FLOWER OF ALVÉNYA TURNS HEADS ON THE ROAD AFTER RECENT OUTBURST AT TRAIN STATION OUTSIDE OF TYARA; Mairwen Peers Of Alfidel's Visitor Claim He Was 'Unpleasant' And 'Discourteous' To Professors In Class; One Fey Lady Who Attended A Suitor Gala For The Prince Comes Forward To Claim The Alvényan Once Attacked Her For Chastising A Beantighe Who Spilled A Drink On Her; It Begs The Question Why Prince Cylvan Continues To Associate With Someone So Incorrigible...*

"What's this word?" Saffron asked sharply, venomously, even though he practically knew.

"'Incorrigible'?" Maeve asked.

"Undisciplined, unscrupulous," Aodhán answered sooner. "Impulsive, malfeasant, improprietous..."

Maeve threw them a look of exasperation that clearly said *don't use more big words to explain another*—and it nearly sent Saffron over the edge. He shoved the paper back into Maeve's chest. He turned to storm back into the kitchen—but stopped short. He turned to stomp his way back to where Copper and Sionnach still slept amongst the pillows—but stopped himself that time, too. Finally, the errand-beantighes hurried by and out the front door—and he followed them, instead. Wanting nothing more than somewhere to hide, where he could crouch down and scream into the grass until the tangling thorns in his chest were broken enough to breathe again.

.  .  .

THE REST OF THE MORNING PASSED WITHOUT FINDING the relief Saffron sought after. He wandered the yard of the king's guesthouse in silence, though there wasn't much to it apart from the trees and small patches of manicured grass and places to sit and appreciate the surroundings.

He didn't want to go into town again. He didn't want to get into the pools. He didn't want to go back to sleep. He didn't want to see or speak to anyone, for as long as he could manage.

But worse of all—he didn't want to let his guard down. He couldn't. Not when they anticipated Ryder appearing anytime that same day, that night, somewhere in that damned city so crammed-full of visitors it was impossible to tell a living fey from a carved statuette outside a restaurant.

They still didn't know *where* Ryder would appear. The veil hadn't told him much. A part of Saffron had even hoped it might tell him more as soon as they arrived in the town. He thought he might be able to sense it, or it would just jump out as something obvious. A specific pool dedicated to Danu, or the veil, or Lugh, or even the Dagda for god's sake, somewhere as significant as all the other locations Ryder had gone—but there was nothing. There were no pools dedicated to any gods, only those that cost more money to buy privacy in.

Saffron wasn't familiar enough with Ailinne's security to know if someone like Ryder could get into one of the more isolated pools without a golden-tasseled token. He didn't know if Ryder would continue his pattern of not drawing attention to himself, therefore avoiding large crowds of people. Saffron— didn't actually know, for certain, that the man was following the queen's coronation route. Or that, even if it started that way, that he would continue to do so. Especially if he realized Saffron had caught on, and was following him.

By late afternoon, Saffron resided on the edge of the back

walkway that stretched the length of the house. He absentmindedly fed blueberries to Fiachra who nibbled greedily on his fingers. Through the open wall of the sitting room at his back, Maeve and Copper played cards. Sionnach restlessly flipped through a book. Saoirse and Aodhán chatted by the trees a few yards from him. And Cylvan—kept to himself. In his room, somewhere in the house. Balor was still scuttling around, which meant he hadn't sent a response to the kings yet, but that didn't necessarily make Saffron feel better.

The longer the hours dragged without even a stir in the veil— the more uncertain Saffron grew. The more embarrassed he felt, the more mortified he was to think he'd dragged everyone that way, possibly for nothing. Heavier than anything else, though, was the feeling of pure—*abandonment*, but by who, exactly, he didn't know. Abandoned by Cylvan, who wouldn't linger in any room where Saffron did. Abandoned by the veil, who Saffron wished had shown him *anything else*. Abandoned, even, but Ryder, himself, for not appearing when Saffron actually needed him to.

When the sun started to set, and beantighes arrived to begin preparing dinner, Saffron felt more lost than ever. Lost and humiliated and—nauseated with anxiety, thinking that he did not, in fact, know where Ryder would go next. He did not, in fact, have any idea where that man could be found, let alone still, what he was doing. He didn't know. The witchhunters didn't know. Even the veil didn't know. Which meant—Saffron had failed, once again, to get any closer to bringing Asche and his friends back home. If it hadn't already—the hope and excitement he'd witnessed in Cylvan's eyes in Erelaine would surely soon turn to resentment.

THE SUN WAS BELOW THE HORIZON WHEN DINNER WAS ready to be served, and Saffron blankly followed the others to the meal table. When Cylvan wasn't there, though, he stopped. He stared at the prince's empty seat for a long time, until Saoirse nudged him from behind.

"Cylvan has decided to take his dinner later," she said, before lowering her voice to whisper: "I believe he's in the private pool behind the house, right now. But don't tell him I sent you."

Saffron said nothing, just turned and hurried away. Saoirse didn't let anyone follow after him.

"Cylvan?" Saffron asked the growing darkness of the backyard as he made his way down the compressed-dirt pathway toward the house's private pool, finally spotting the prince sitting alone in the water once he rounded a bend in the trail. Cylvan turned just as Saffron approached, offering him a little smile at first—before it slipped away again just as quickly. Like he'd done it on instinct, before realizing and pulling back. Saffron swallowed against the nerves lodged in his throat.

"Already finished with dinner?" Cylvan asked as Saffron approached and stood on the edge of the raw-stone steps leading down into the water. Saffron shook his head, wringing his hands together before kicking off his shoes. Perhaps he should have asked first, but—a part of him was afraid of hearing Cylvan command him away if he did.

"I haven't had a chance to speak to you all day..." Saffron said, trying to keep his voice light. The water rose to his chest, and he sank a little deeper until the surface kissed the skin below his ears. He waded closer to where Cylvan leaned against the far edge, but resisted the urge to get any nearer than that.

"Is there something you want to talk about?"

Saffron swayed back and forth in the hot water, allowing a moment to pass as he gathered his thoughts. Any of them, anything that might break through the awkwardness between them, just for things to feel normal again.

"When reading through one of Sionnach's books the other night, there was this map of Alfidel, and I realized Morrígan isn't all that far from here," he said with a weak smile, trying to just make casual conversation. To summon anything at all to appear on Cylvan's flat expression. "I was thinking how nice it would be if we'd have time to stop by, so I can visit—"

"You wish to extend this journey even longer?" Cylvan interrupted. He wore a stiff smile that time, and Saffron immediately clamped his mouth back shut. It struck him like an icicle to the heart.

"Well—I wasn't meaning—I don't know, not really... Although I guess it would be nice if it were possible, since I haven't been able to visit in months. With everything going on, maybe it would be nice to check in on—"

"And how do you think something like that would be portrayed in a gossip leaflet?" Cylvan asked, voice calm as ever, but Saffron felt as if it raked down the back of his throat. "Or—you hadn't considered that, had you?"

"No, but..." Saffron looked this way and that, hating how badly he wished to meet Cylvan's eyes. Knowing it was best he didn't. His face felt hot, trying to convince himself it was only from the warmth of the pool—but Cylvan's immediate refusal of such a little comment made his whole world spin. He tried to justify himself: "But—I mean, there could be more reason for us to visit, too, I guess. Professor Adelard is there, and he definitely knows more about the veil than he lets on—"

"You must be mad."

Saffron finally looked up, driven by disbelief. Sure he hadn't heard those words, exactly—but the way Cylvan looked at him in return, the certainty wavered.

"What?" He asked softly. Cylvan's frowned twitched downward.

"Think about it a moment," he said with a sigh. As if days, weeks of pressure were finally building up the back of his throat, too far to push back down again. "First you wish to visit your old beantighe friends, without considering how that might be perceived—and then you suggest visiting Morrígan's human professor to ask what he knows about the veil." Not bothering to include any clarification to why that was preposterous. Not needing to. Saffron's face swelled hotter. He couldn't blame it on the water, that time.

"Or did you dream of Ryder Kyteler visiting Lake Elatha?" Cylvan went on. "Perhaps drinking from Quartz Creek, or having a meeting with Headmistress Elding—"

"What's gotten into you?" Saffron interjected, mouth hanging open slightly in further disbelief. Caught so off guard by the aggression, he almost wondered if it was a mimic who stood in front of him, rather than his prince.

"Nothing has gotten into me," Cylvan answered, before pausing, then shaking his head and adding: "Don't you think we've chased this ghost long enough?" He let the words hang between them for a long moment, as if counting how many times Saffron's pounding heart made the water ripple. Finally, with a notable, bone-deep exhaustion, he concluded: "I think it's time we give this up, Saffron."

"We..." Saffron trailed off. He didn't know exactly what he wished to say—until he did, and the words rushed out of him like a winter wind. "What in god's name is wrong with you?"

"Wrong with me?" Cylvan asked. "Perhaps I'm not the one—"

"You've been acting miserably ever since you got back from the dé Bricríu estate yesterday!" Saffron argued.

Cylvan's eyes bore into him for what felt like an eternity, tongue pressing into his cheek and between his teeth as he clearly swallowed back what he really wished to say.

"Nothing is wrong," he finally uttered. "I simply don't understand why we continue this wild goose chase, after a man we don't even know we can catch."

"We don't know that—"

"Where is he, then!" Cylvan snapped, making Saffron jump as he threw out his arm and whisked water across the pool. "You were certain Ryder would be in Ailinne *tonight*—but he isn't. He isn't here, Saffron! He may never have meant to be! Maybe there is no pattern to his madness after all. It was an outstanding theory, púca, and the reality is disappointing, but—we now have to reassess how else to make ourselves useful. To Alfidel, to finding Asche. I think this was all a very good effort, but—but it's not needed, any longer."

"But—"

"We've made enough fools of ourselves already, don't you think?"

"Is—!" Saffron bolted up, making water splash around him. "Is this because of those things in the gossip papers this morning!"

"Far more than just *things*, I'd say," Cylvan replied flatly. "They should act as a warning to you, Saffron—that eventually, you're going to have to stop acting like a *beantighe*, and start acting like someone who knows they're being watched."

"It doesn't matter to me what those godawful people write in their stupid papers!" Saffron exclaimed.

"You've made that evident."

"You—!"

"The kings asked us to investigate the veil event at *Erelaine*," Cylvan went on tightly. "Nothing more—and nothing less. The fact we've continued on this long outside of those orders is questionable enough. You must, at the *very* least, understand that."

"Is that what Ailir said in his letter this morning?"

"It does not matter what exactly my father wrote—"

"Clearly it does!"

"No!" Cylvan shouted back, rising to his feet and towering over Saffron in a way that made him steal a step backward. "My father wrote asking to know what exactly happened between you and those gossip writers. Wishing to know what other careless things you may have blabbed for them to publish—because, apparently, even members of Avren's high council are beginning to show concern for my *motives*. Because that's what every gods-damned person is starting to wonder, with something so simple —! And they will only *continue* to wonder, to question me, until I am able to return to Avren and address the rumors properly!

Until I am able to return to my duties as crown prince of Alfidel—"

"When has that ever done anything to change their minds about you!" Saffron shouted back, reclaiming the step forward he'd lost.

"It nearly did!" Cylvan's voice boomed, making Saffron's ears ring. "After my due diligence in Erelaine, it nearly did! For once, in my entire life, a single string of favorable words were disseminated to the masses about me—but of course I should not have expected it to last, with such an incorrigible partner by my side! How can you not understand!"

"How can I—!" Saffron choked. "You're acting like all of this was just—! Just some kind of stupid game, to keep myself busy! To make me feel useful, or—!"

"Hasn't it!" Cylvan exclaimed. "Are you sure chasing after this man isn't just some misguided attempt at feeling useful for you! Even if we catch him—he's not going to give me my sibling back, Saffron! Catching Ryder Kyteler now is not going to absolve you of what you've already done!"

The sound echoed across the trees, summoning a cold wind to whistle back over them in return. Stealing steam from the air, making every inch of Saffron shake. It was only the wind. It was only the chill of the wind that made him shiver, made his eyes burn, made it feel like he was suffocating despite breathing so heavily.

"We must return to Avren," Cylvan continued, though his voice trembled that time. "Where we can *actually* be useful. Where we are *meant* to be, prepared for the moment a path through the veil is found."

"When have you ever been any use to Avren?" Saffron said, hating how his voice wavered, betraying the hot emotions roiling in his stomach and threatening to swell up the back of his throat. Hating the words he chose, knowing there was no use trying to explain what he really meant. *Avren hates you, they think you're cursed, they've never appreciated you; Avren has never asked for anything of you because of it, they don't need you—but I do. I do.* Beneath the hot water, he clenched his fists tight enough to dry the skin of his palms.

"How dare you," Cylvan whispered, shaking his head. Clearly wishing to say more—but swallowing the words back, replacing them with others chosen carefully. "We will not be visiting Morrígan. Or anywhere else, for that matter. If you wish to consult with Professor Adelard, he will be invited to join us at the palace. We will be returning to Avren in the morning, as we should have done already. And you will simply have to accept—you've already done enough. Don't you think?"

Saffron still didn't speak. He couldn't. He'd forgotten how; he felt nothing but the cold breeze on his face, and the boiling-hot water against his stomach. Neither caused him as much pain as the sharpness of Cylvan's words.

Rather than answering, Saffron lowered his eyes down, then away. He turned and made his way back to the stone steps, and out of the pool, to follow the path back to the house. Cylvan called his name, suddenly, with a sharp inhale of breath—but Saffron ignored him, and continued on his way.

## 23

## THE GHOST

" Is everything alright?" Sionnach asked as Saffron returned to the house, wearing only the thin covering that clung to his wet skin underneath. "Saffron?"

"I think I'm just going to go to bed," Saffron told them with a practiced smile, hoping they couldn't see how it trembled on his lips. He just wanted to be alone. He wanted to find somewhere to hide, somewhere he could sit and fester in his own confusion, his shame, his guilt.

Since he hadn't slept in his own room the night before, Saffron didn't know exactly where to find his things without peeking into every guest room along the way. Finally recognizing his luggage on the other side of the last door in the corridor, he let himself into the darkness with a quiet sigh, closing the door behind him with hardly a sound.

*Saffron, there's someone—!*

Taran erupted in the back of his mind—but before hearing it, Saffron saw what was drawn on the floor.

A magic circle, exactly like the one he'd seen reported in the Tapestry Hall. Broken in Morrígan's temple. His dream of the stripped henge. A nest of yew twigs and an apple in the center.

He barely had a chance to gasp before something rushed from

the darkness, slamming him back against the door with a hand over his mouth. Saffron thrashed in return, throwing out his fist and striking flesh, though it did nothing to halt the attack.

Ryder hooked an arm around Saffron's middle, lifting him off his feet with a hand still covering his mouth, twisting to throw him down on the nearby bed. Crushing him, knocking the air out of him.

"I heard everything, your highness," Ryder said, practically cooing. "That prince of yours is bent on choosing the cruelest words he can muster, isn't he? Shh, shhh, Saffron, it's alright—*be still.*"

Saffron stiffened. He hadn't noticed, in the struggle, the moment Ryder stole the engagement ring off his finger. Making him vulnerable to compelling intention. The emptiness of his finger was stark and horrifying, even beneath the blanket of controlling enchantment.

His body went limp, sinking back onto the bed as Ryder gently clucked his tongue before slowly removing his hand, then his arm from Saffron's middle. He hovered over Saffron for a moment, tucking some of the wet hair from Saffron's forehead, before pulling back and looking him all over. Saffron couldn't move, head tilted toward the wall, but his heart pounded as he knew exactly what Ryder saw. The thin fabric of his covering, clinging to the wetness of his skin until practically translucent. He wanted to scream—and when Ryder's hand gently trailed down the outside of Saffron's exposed thigh, he almost broke through the enchantment and did.

"If you wished to follow me across Alfidel, Saffron, you could have just asked. I would have answered right away, and come to you in a moment." He spoke in a breathy whisper, fingers traveling up Saffron's leg, over the bottom hem of his covering; tracing the indent of his navel, then up the center of his stomach. "We could have enjoyed ourselves much more than your prince allows you, now."

A hand tucked beneath Saffron's jaw, turning his head from

the wall toward the rest of the room. Ryder remained partially on top of him, leaning down to speak directly into his ear.

"Did you know it was me, from the start? I'm flattered. You must think of me often. *Be still.*"

Saffron whimpered. Ryder must have felt how hard he fought against the constraining command, enough to twitch his fingers.

"Have you figured out what it's meant for, yet?" Ryder went on, petting the side of Saffron's face before leaning close again. Hanging over him. Saffron squeezed his eyes closed, before forcing them open again. Refusing to be caught off guard a second time. "The magic of it is older than anything written in any high fey book. Would you believe it? Does that interest you, Saffron? Let me show you."

Saffron remained motionless as Ryder jumped off him, planting both feet on the floor in the very center of the drawn epithet. Saffron fought to move, fought to break the enchantment as his heart pounded in terror, on the verge of ripping through his chest. Ryder extended his hands over the circle, and closed his eyes.

Saffron braced to be swallowed. To be devoured by a sudden knocking tear in the floor, through the veil—but the air never shifted. His soul only rang with fear in the silence, heart pounding loud enough to bang against his sternum.

A shriek from the window, like Fiachra, suddenly struck Saffron's ears. Loud enough to make him flinch, gasping as his eyes watered as it grew louder—louder—deafening, bright, sharp like tearing metal. Splitting Saffron's ears, nearly tearing his mind in half, vibrating his bones. *Find me! Come for me! Help me—! Please, find me—! I need you, I need you!*

Even Taran flinched, whimpering like a wounded animal and stirring madly in the back of Saffron's mind. Pulling at the seams of both of them at once, until Saffron thought he might die. Until he was sure his eardrums bled, until he felt the heat of his blood boiling; *find me! Find me! Come for me! Please! Please! I'm here! I'm here, my love!*

As quickly as the sound pierced him—it faded. Not fully at first, still clamoring in the back of his ears, but—Saffron was no longer in his room. No longer paralyzed on the bed. He was—back in the hot pools with Cylvan.

No, not Cylvan—someone he didn't know. But at the same time, a face he knew too well. Taran mac Delbaith, whose lap Saffron straddled, features slightly warped, slightly older, his hair long and clinging to the tan skin of his chest. Smiling up at Saffron like he was the most infuriating, delightful thing he'd ever seen, with hands cupping either side of his bare hips. And Saffron, whose own hands tucked around the back of Taran's neck, pulled closer. Hands that were perfectly manicured, slender, donning rings of bright jewels that shone even more so after a bath in the mineral water.

They pulled Taran into his chest, where Taran's hot mouth kissed him up the center between two pale breasts, to his throat, as hands trailed around Saffron's thighs to his backside—and as Saffron tucked a hand up the side of his neck to pull his hair away and allow the roaming mouth more room on his skin, long tresses of golden blonde spilled into his vision, down the front of his body.

He jolted back—back to where he laid numb on the bed in the dark room. The shrieking in his ears petered off, but Ryder remained where he was. There was something else approaching, he didn't know, he couldn't hear it, he could merely sense it—and then a knock came at the door. A light, polite rap of knuckles, followed by Sionnach's voice. Asking if Saffron was alright. If they could come in.

"Sionn..." Saffron attempted, but Ryder interrupted.

*"Be still,"* he hissed, rich with vitriol for more than just being interrupted. As if—whatever he was looking for, once again hadn't answered him. Did he not hear the shrieking? Did he not see the vision Saffron did? There was no time to question as Ryder stepped from his magic circle, toward the door, pulling a knife from his belt as he did.

He opened it—and grabbed Sionnach by one of their horns. They barely yelped, yanked inside and thrown over Saffron on the bed—but not before Ryder's blade slashed a line up their forearm, drawing enough blood to spill over the bedsheets as Sionnach threw their hands out to catch their fall.

Ryder attempted to close the door in the same motion—but Copper was suddenly there next, slamming into it and knocking Ryder backward.

It all happened too fast to see every moment—Saffron only knew Sionnach whimpered while clutching the gash in their arm, before whirling back again to where Copper stormed in. Where he slammed the door shut behind him, looking Ryder up and down, having only a few inches over the man but seeming suddenly massive.

"Oh, it's you," he said, and even Ryder took a step backward. Copper's eyes flashed over every corner of the room—the window where the man had crawled inside, the magic circle on the floor, Saffron limp but wide-eyed on the bed, and lastly—to Sionnach who only just realized Saffron was beneath where they'd stumbled. Still clutching the weeping cut in their arm, spilling like red paint down their elbow and staining the sheets. Copper stared at them for a long moment, saying nothing else—before snapping back to Ryder, and lunging. Arms outstretched, ready to tear the man's head off.

Ryder dodged out of the way, slamming a heel into Copper's broad back and sending him flying into the bed, landing with arms caged on either side of Sionnach's body as Sionnach yelped and threw their hands up in fear of being crushed. But Copper just met Sionnach's eyes, before turning and pushing off into Ryder one more time, snarling like an animal. As if—the sight of Sionnach's bright red blood sent him into a frenzy. Summoning animalistic, feral noises from the back of his throat, body tightening and muscles swelling until the threads of his tunic popped under the pressure—culminating suddenly when the fey lord suddenly buckled forward, tearing through his skin into the form of a growling fox. Shredding through his ashen state by the sight of Sionnach's fear.

Sionnach cried out, throwing themself over Saffron as Ryder and Copper tore about the room. They took Saffron's face, forcing him to look at them, begging him to respond, to move, to say something, anything—and Saffron managed to squeeze his eyes shut, clenching his jaw, barely twitching his fingers with the effort. Sionnach finally realized what had happened, making them clamor in another rush of panic while pulling Saffron close.

"Copper, his ring!" They cried. Copper heard it, his giant head turning to look for the briefest second, and Ryder attempted to slice him with the knife. But Copper's foxlike instincts were undeniable, opening his jaw—and snapping his teeth down on the man's hand, which Ryder raked back out again with a bark of pain.

The bedroom door flew open with Maeve on the other side, all heads turning in a flash—just enough time for Ryder to stumble backward, clutching his bleeding hand, before leaping through the window at his back. Copper took off after him, tearing through the pine shade and landing in the grass on the other side with a muted thud, before tearing through the soil in chase.

"Go get Cylvan—!" Sionnach started, but Saffron clawed weakly at their arm.

"No—" he croaked, before slumping back against the bed. "No—don't..."

"But—!" Sionnach demanded, attempting to lift Saffron back up again, but Saffron had finally given in to the enchantment paralyzing him. Allowing it to do as it was meant to, no longer owning the strength required to fight back. He didn't want to know how it felt to experience the crashing disappointment that would have devoured him, otherwise. Ryder had been right there. Taunting him within arm's reach—and Saffron still failed to grab him. To stop him, to do anything. Maybe Cylvan was right—and all of Saffron's attempts to be useful truly were for naught.

. . .

Copper returned to the house a few hours later —still in fox form, leaping through the window and summoning a shriek of surprise from Sionnach, whose arm Saffron was busy wrapping with bandages. Whimpering as his paws were swollen from the chase, the beast hopped onto the bed, opening his mouth to drop two wet circlets into Saffron's open palm. Saffron stared at them in the low light—his engagement ring, and one of Ryder's pixie rings.

"Good boy," he whispered, unable to think of anything else.

Maeve had already brought them tea and something to eat, before leaving again to find Saoirse and inform her of the trouble. Saffron begged her not to tell anyone exactly what happened, and Maeve had agreed, but he wasn't sure she'd keep the promise. Especially as, when prompted to *why,* Saffron hadn't been able to give her a good reason. *I feel humiliated* wasn't a very good excuse.

Even as he and Sionnach sipped at tea in silence, as Copper laid on the pillows next to him, a part of him kept expecting Cylvan to come knocking. To storm into his room and demand what happened—but he never did. Saffron thought he might, at the very least, come to tell him goodnight—but his prince never did that, either.

Petting Copper's head, his fur was soft and thick as Saffron remembered from the first time, ears velvety and sensitive as they flicked every time his fingers brushed some of the longer, inner hairs. Standing upright, the points of those ears might have reached Saffron's ribs, so lying on his side and stretched out, the fox nearly commanded half of the wide bed. Especially with such gangly, skinny legs that stretched and dangled in every direction.

Even Sionnach reached out to hesitantly scratch under the orange beast's chin, making Copper purr and stretch out long, yawning and showing off rows of sharp teeth. At first Saffron wondered why he didn't change back into himself sooner, but considering all the affection he was receiving in animal form, perhaps it wasn't actually any surprise at all.

"Do you think he knew we were here?" Sionnach asked once Copper had settled again, his head tucked snugly into the bucket of Saffron's crossed legs. "At least, at first..."

"I don't know," Saffron breathed, eyes flickering back to the floor where he'd already scrubbed all the charcoal of the magic circle away. His hands still itched from picking up the apple and stinging yew twigs to burn them in the private furnace in the corner of the room. A small price to pay in exchange for no veil event swallowing him. "I do think he planned Ailinne all along, like we figured out—but I don't know if the king's guesthouse was his target all along. I think he must have decided to come here only once he learned we'd come, too. He just wanted to fuck with me..." Saffron trailed off, pressing his lips together before glancing up at Sionnach again. "Thank you, Sionnach," he said. His friend flushed, shaking their head, but Saffron insisted. "I don't know what he would have done with me if you hadn't come. Thank you."

Copper whined, pressing his snout into Saffron's palm. Saffron couldn't resist a little smile, petting the fox on the nose.

"You, too," he whispered. "Though I don't really understand why you're still trotting around like this."

"He just likes the attention," Sionnach mumbled. Copper's thick tail smacked them on the thigh.

Saffron chuckled weakly, taking another sip from his cup. The warm tea meant to calm him burned all the way down. Even as he tried to distract himself, tried to find any semblance of calm, the memories of his vision kept knocking at the back of his mind. Bright and terrifying and as vivid as the moment they came.

The crying, pleading voice; his vision sitting perched on the lap of a fey lord who looked like Taran, but wasn't. In the body of someone with such beautiful hands and long blonde hair. Was that what Ryder had been looking for? Did he really not see it himself? It had to be from one hot pool or another, there in

Ailinne, but whatever he was actually trying to find—apparently was not in that place. Which meant Ryder would continue to his next location, to try again.

Saffron put his face in his hand, holding his breath as he forced himself to think. Of the vision, of Ryder's strange magic circle, of what in god's name the man could be looking for.

"I assume he'll continue to Vjallrod, next," Sionnach whispered, like they read Saffron's mind.

"In the Winter Court?" Saffron asked, cracking open his eyes. He gazed down at the tea set on the tray between them. "Is that the next place on Proserpina's coronation route?"

"Yes. Technically where it started."

They sipped their tea in silence for a long moment, as Saffron considered it. Sionnach gave him all the time he needed, never nudging to ask what else Saffron was thinking, like even they could sense his growing apprehensions. The itch that there was something he wasn't considering, something he should know before deciding what he wished to do next. Meanwhile, Copper licked at crumbs that fell from the teacakes they chewed on, before sniffing at Sionnach's bandaged arm. Wrinkling his nose slightly without a sound, before returning his head to Saffron's lap.

In the silence, Saffron's mind swirled. Spinning and spinning, until—he realized something, and it was obvious. The missing note that had briefly escaped him, ringing in his ears the moment it swirled back. So obvious, he didn't dare speak out loud until everything had clicked into place.

Those people in his vision weren't random. He wasn't sure he ever assumed they were, just that he didn't personally recognize them—though he also never anticipated figuring out *who* they were so suddenly, either, despite never knowing what they had looked like in life. But it really was obvious.

More than once, Saffron had heard Taran described as *resembling the wolf king*. It had been one of the driving inspirations behind bestowing Clymeus' silver bones upon him.

Beneath her black veil, Queen Proserpina was described with long, beautiful golden-blonde hair; with pale skin and a slender figure. And while any other details hadn't been visible to him from that perspective in the vision—the fey lord who resembled Taran, and whose lap she straddled with gold-spun hair spilling over her chest, told him plenty enough.

But placing names didn't bring him any relief. His mind just returned to spinning, that time saturated with a new rush of anxious nausea. He gazed at the pixie ring Copper had brought back from his pursuit of Ryder, stored in one of the empty teacups between them.

What in god's name was Ryder Kyteler trying to do? What was he trying to find with visions of Queen Proserpina and King Clymeus while performing that spell—in addition to Saffron's vision of the crow statue in The Morrígan's temple the night Ryder did the same in Erelaine. Where Proserpina had once prayed, where she'd left that note begging the queen for protection over her loved ones. What in god's name was Ryder looking for—and *why was Saffron seeing visions with him?*

Further—what in *god's* name was *Saffron* supposed to think after witnessing such a vision up close? After witnessing Ryder perform that spell on the floor right next to him, after describing it as *older than anything in any high fey book*—the same spell the veil had once described as '*from the Dagda's own book.*' Something old, ancient, and, without question—dangerous.

Knowing all of that—was he really expected to just go back to Avren? To give up on catching Ryder, as the man continued north for whatever it was he sought? Was Saffron really meant to just let Ryder continue how he pleased, because it was futile trying to get ahead of him? Was there really any chance he was hunting for something Saffron needn't worry about—something he could risk turning his back on to return to Avren? Cylvan made it sound so simple—but how much of his contention stemmed from his own fears, rather than genuine belief that all their effort was a lost cause, and time was better spent elsewhere?

If Saffron went back to Avren, to sit and wait for oracles to find a way through the veil, putting all his faith in someone else to do that for him—he would go mad. He would tear all his skin away in the foreboding miasma that hung over Avren. Waiting for something to happen. Waiting. Waiting. *Waiting*—the first rowan witch in centuries, forced to *wait* while he had no way of helping; while the man who had once been his promised mentor roved over Alfidel in search of something Saffron didn't know, but didn't trust.

Copper's spindly legs jolted as Sionnach teased some fluff between his back toes, knocking the tea tray askew and spilling the teacup containing Ryder's pixie ring. Saffron sighed, taking it from the blankets and reaching over the side of the bed where his shoulder bag was in reach. He dug through an inner pocket to find a chain he'd kept with all of his access rings from Morrígan Academy, briefly running his fingers over the bands in a moment of sentimentality. He threaded the pixie ring on with them, while his thoughts raced.

Perhaps visiting Morrígan was more than just a spur-of-the-moment proposition he'd made to Cylvan. Perhaps his subconscious, in all its growing uncertainty and doubt and shame— knew, before the rest of him did, why his instincts turned that way. Perhaps visiting Professor Adelard, to beg on his knees for *anything* the man could tell him, either about the veil or about Ryder's ancient circle, even about his visions, or anything, *anything else*—was in fact what Saffron was meant to do, next. Even if it wasn't following Ryder straight to Vjallrod—it also wasn't returning to Avren. By Proserpina's own coronation route, and the number of days that passed between her time there and arriving in Ailinne, Saffron would have a few days of peace from Ryder's chaos, anyway.

Even if Cylvan didn't agree. Even if Cylvan would despise him for insisting—Saffron just gazed down at the pixie ring dangling from the chain with all the others, those circlets that used to clutter every one of his fingers as a beantighe. A trembling emotion tightened his hand over them.

Saffron would make himself useful. He had to. Even if Cylvan didn't agree with his ideas—Saffron was not going to sit around and fucking *wait* for someone else to save them. Not when he knew, if anyone could stop Ryder, and rescue Asche, and rescue everyone else taken through the veil—it was the first rowan witch in centuries.

## 24

### THE SPLINTER

Their tickets to Avren were already purchased by the time everyone sat down to breakfast in the green-tier quarter of Ailinne. The restaurant where they ate overlooked one of the many natural spring falls that fed into Ailinne's sacred pools, where high fey drank from cupped hands and stole bottles of the cloudy water to take with them. Saffron wondered how many of the visiting fey actually had been cured of their ashen states after soaking in the pools—but the persistently solemn atmosphere even there in the restaurant implied none had found the divine healing they'd been looking for. He actively avoided the thought of how different everyone would have acted that morning, had Ryder opened and closed the veil again the night prior.

The train they would take back to Avren was a one-way, nonstop route, highly expensive and seats sold out to the point they would have to send their horses on a secondary train later that afternoon. Nearly three days on board, all the way back to Avren, no stopping for any reason. Saffron bristled at the thought.

He endlessly reprised his argument with Cylvan the night before, then his conflict with Ryder, as everyone else enjoyed their meal as if nothing had happened. Apart from him, only Cylvan on the other side of the table didn't speak much. Saffron felt the constant prickle of amethyst eyes regarding him as he just looked down at his food. Petting Copper's still-fox-shaped nose where it perched on the bench next to him under the table. Thoughts turning, over and over, churning and curdling until his ears rang.

The heavy pit in his stomach told him being useless in Avren was worse than being swallowed by the veil. Cylvan could curse him all he liked—but forcing Saffron back to Avren to sit and wait for news was practically a death sentence for his sanity. Even if he couldn't catch Ryder, he could still be useful. He could still have a purpose.

Teeth nipped at his fingers, and Saffron jumped. He scowled down at the golden eyes looking back up at him, bopping Copper on the head and wondering for the hundredth time if he was being stubborn and purposefully remaining that way. But all their attempts to shift him back only proved—he may have been truly stuck. Some sort of unique curse by the ashen state, punishing him for breaking through it through sheer will. Despite all the attempts to startle him back to normal. Feeding him hot mineral water just like those fey who bottled it for the trip home. He and Sionnach had even stopped by one of the hundreds of apothecaries on the way to the station, telling Cylvan and the others to go ahead as Saffron didn't want to cause any kind of scene. Only for Cylvan to insist, turning heads like Saffron anticipated—as if the prince didn't want to let him too far out of his reach.

Soon it was clear there was nothing they could do about Copper's state in Ailinne, and he would have to make the journey back to Avren as a fox. Despite everything else, Saffron managed to find humor in having to buy Copper an 'animal companion' ticket at the bursar, no different from the one he bought for Fiachra. Even Sionnach smirked as a leashed harness had to be tucked over Copper's head, though Copper didn't complain. He mostly just lolled his tongue happily and rubbed his face all over Saffron's lap, begging to be pet like a common dog.

Cylvan never commented, though he occasionally threw them a look of disgust. He never asked what had happened, how it happened; he must have assumed they'd just been up to no good in their rooms, getting drunk and getting into trouble. Maybe he thought Saffron had done something with his magic. Saffron didn't know, he didn't ask. He mostly tried to avoid Cylvan's eyes all morning, as every time they met, even for a moment, he was overcome with the urge to be sick. Still not sure how to mention what had happened with Ryder.

As the meal wound down, there was the briefest moment when Cylvan excused himself to imbibe in his last aromatic clump of tobacco from a pipe outside the restaurant, as there was no smoking allowed on such a crowded, multi-day train. Saffron watched him for a moment from where he sat at the table, heart pounding loud enough in his chest to make his throat tighten in and out, finally rising stiffly to his feet and excusing himself as well.

He didn't want to board the train without trying again. He wanted to express his thoughts about Professor Adelard again, if possible. He didn't want to board the train without trying at least once more to explain how physically nauseating it was to imagine returning to Avren under those circumstances.

"Cylvan, can I—"

"Oh, your highness!" Someone else rushed up from behind, bumping Saffron out of the way. They were joined by a few others, who all seemed to notice the prince accessible and lingering outside. All with the same quills, the same pads of parchment floating alongside them and scribbling notes as there was no pinch of ashenness that far north from Avren. Cylvan, all the while, just smiled politely at every single one of them, hardly even giving Saffron a glance.

Saffron didn't know if it was on accident, or if Cylvan really was outright ignoring him—but embarrassment consumed him whole in an instant. Embarrassed to be seen even trying to speak to Cylvan alone, embarrassed knowing Cylvan likely cringed at the thought of Saffron acting up again when surrounded by all the wrong people to see it. So Saffron just bowed his head, turning stiffly to go back into the restaurant. To reclaim his seat, as Cylvan talked up the people outside.

He could only guess what they must be asking him—but the way a few kept glancing his way through the windows gave him a good enough hint of some of it. Saffron's face went hot, turning away and biting back the bile rising in his throat. Knowing he would get no more chances to speak to Cylvan again before boarding the train. Knowing to return to Avren was to go mad. Knowing, perhaps, he'd been left with no choice.

Saffron rose from the table a second time, finding the bartender at the drink counter and asking if he could have a piece of paper and pen. As quickly and clearly as he could, even as Copper bumped against his leg in question and his friends watched from their table, Saffron scribbled out everything he thought Cylvan needed to know:

> *Attend to your dueties in Avren. I am going to Morrígan to visit Professor Adelard. I know no writers will bother following me if you go to Avren. I will have Taran with me. I didn't tell anyone else I was leaving, so do not be angry with them.* ~~*I don't know how long*~~

He scribbled out those last words in frustration. Not caring if Cylvan worried or wondered. An immature way to do it, but— Cylvan seemed to only expect bratty pettiness from him anymore anyway, so he didn't care. He was just a beantighe, after all, like Cylvan had said during the satyr party.

"Bastard," he mumbled, forgoing everything else he thought to write, and instead ending the letter through his teeth.

> *Stay safe. Enjoy the journey. I will see you again soon.*

Saffron's hands shook as he handed the pen back to the bartender. As he folded the paper once, then twice, then clutched it in his clammy palm and rose just as the rest of his friends did to head for the door. For their train back to Avren, that three day journey where Saffron would not be joining them. Where he would go to Morrígan by the urging twist in his gut that if he couldn't stop Ryder, he could at least find another way to help. He would deal with the fallout, with Cylvan's anger, afterward.

Outside, Cylvan was still chatting with the writers, but managed to excuse himself as the arriving train on the platform rang its bell to invite passengers to begin boarding. Saffron wasted no more time, hurrying up behind the prince and pretending to bump into him, in the same motion tucking the note into Cylvan's doublet pocket. Cylvan didn't notice, just put his hand out to grab Saffron's arm and steady him, meeting his eyes for the briefest moment that—at the same time, felt like an eternity. Saffron almost thought Cylvan was reading his mind, that he would reach straight into his pocket and find the note, summoning the fallout before Saffron ever had the chance to go —but then Cylvan turned, releasing Saffron's arm just as the others caught up, and the moving crowd swelled around them.

Cylvan might as well taken Saffron's heart with him; it wasn't until that moment he realized, there was a part of him that wished Cylvan had actually read his mind. Found the note. Begged Saffron not to go. But he didn't—so Saffron would.

There were at least a few hundred high fey gathered on the platform, bustling around the train doors waiting for them to open so the sea of bodies could flood through. In the chaos, it wasn't hard to linger back slightly. Still within reach of Sionnach, who turned and gave Saffron a little smile like they'd seen the awkward interaction between himself and Cylvan moments prior. Saoirse turned and did a quick head count from where she stood at the front of the crowd with Cylvan, keeping most of the people out of reach of him. Copper pressed himself between Saffron and Sionnach's legs so he wouldn't get trampled between all the feet, and Sionnach kept swatting at him as he constantly nudged the bottom hem of their skirt with his wet nose. Saffron lifted Fiachra's cage to his chest, holding it close so no passing knees would bump into it and knock her off her perch.

He'd released Copper's leash, seeing as he wasn't actually any other normal 'animal companion' that needed to be shown around. Copper would follow Sionnach and the others onto the train, too. None of them would notice Saffron was gone in the crowd, until the train doors had already closed and the journey was already started. Cylvan would find the note in his doublet, and then they would all know Saffron hadn't been accidentally left behind, or grabbed at the last second, or anything like that. They might be angry with him too, but—he didn't know how to draw Sionnach, Copper, Maeve, any or all of them away with him, without Cylvan immediately noticing. He didn't want to take any of Cylvan's friends from him suddenly, either. As if they'd planned on abandoning him all along. Despite it all—that was not something he wished Cylvan to think he was mentally, emotionally capable of doing to him.

The train doors opened, and the excitable crowd rushed forward. As they did—Saffron locked his legs, and didn't move. He just stood there, clutching Fiachra's cage to his chest, allowing the other passengers to crest around him like waves around a stubborn log lodged in the sand of a beach.

The rest of the group had managed the crowd well enough to board the train swiftly, leaving only Sionnach on their heels. And at one point, the satyr did actually turn to look for him. Saffron threw up a hand with a weary smile to imply he'd only been separated, he'd catch up, don't wait. Sionnach had no choice but to continue as the surging mass of bodies forced them toward the train. With such uneven footing on their hooves in such a tight crowd, if they tried to push back, they would be knocked off balance anyway. Knowing that much, they obeyed the tide all the way to the train doors, where they threw Saffron one more look, then had to hurry out of the way. The last one of his friends who would turn to look, and notice him lagging.

Saffron pivoted suddenly, pushing against the crowd. Away

from the platform. Before he lost his chance, or his courage. Knowing if he didn't go in that moment, he may still be too much of a coward to make the commitment.

There was still a crush of a hundred people pushing their way onto the train once Saffron made it into a bubble of open air, having to lean against one of the platform awnings to clutch his chest and catch his breath from how claustrophobic the effort felt. His thoughts raced once he regained his composure, searching for the steps down to the road, picturing in his mind the station stables where Boann and the other horses were being kept until the later train came to take them.

He only made it a few steps that way, before a whine and the sound of scattering feet caught his attention, making him twist around just in time to watch Copper's massive body wriggle and writhe its way through the crowd, knocking more than one group of fey passengers to their ass on the platform. Harness long gone, like a wild beast.

"Copper—!" Saffron gasped, lowering to one knee with Fiachra's cage in one hand as his friend rushed to meet him. Copper head-butted him, knocking him backward and making stars flash in his eyes. "What—are you doing, damnit! Why didn't you get on the train!"

But Copper just bit at Saffron's sleeves, attempting to drag him back into the throng, bright golden-brown eyes demanding to know what *his* problem was. Saffron nearly heaved the animal into his arms and threw him into the crowd, hoping the surge would carry him all the way to the train doors like a sponge in a bath—but then he heard the chittering whispers of a group of people watching him, and he turned to see the same handful of gossip writers from outside the restaurant watching him in curiosity. His blood ran cold, breath catching as his instincts immediately shifted. Knowing more than anything he wanted to get out of their sight before they could ask questions. Before they could write anything about what he was doing.

"Gods, alright, just—come on. Come on!" Saffron hissed,

grabbing Fiachra and jumping back to his feet, motioning for Copper to follow as his bird screeched and angrily flapped her wings from all the jostling. Copper yipped and barked in bewilderment, still biting at Saffron's hands, his ankles, like he thought Saffron was just confused—but Saffron focused only on leaving the platform and making his way to the stables.

Only when Copper realized the direction he was heading, did he seem to finally understand. His snapping urges trickled away. Replaced with uncertain whines, small yips of frustration, constantly trotting faster to try and get ahead of Saffron and meet his eyes. But Saffron just looked ahead. Toward the stables. Knowing if Copper noticed him lagging behind, he might not have escaped as seamlessly as he hoped.

The stable-keeper recognized Saffron from earlier in the day, barely managing a greeting and a nod as Saffron hurriedly stepped inside and motioned to his horse. Boann, in the stall farthest in the back, had had her saddle removed, with all of Saffron's traveling things still in the bags as the worker made his way down the row. Saffron quietly thanked Ériu for the blessing, hurry to his horse and through the stall door.

It took all his strength to heave the saddle from where it hung over the barrier, but Boann was patient as ever as Saffron managed to pin it against her side, then shove it upright onto her back. He was just tightening the first belt around her belly when the steam train released a deafening whistle, making him jump. He leaned toward the stall window, peeking as the train doors closed to passengers. There was no one else coming for him, after all.

His heart pounded harder, faster, as the same part of him that hoped Cylvan would find his note and stop him all the way on the platform, also hoped he might notice Saffron missing and still chase him down. But he didn't—he didn't, and he wasn't coming. Saffron was going to go to Morrígan. He was going to continue trying to find a way to get his friends and Asche back. Even if Cylvan thought he was mad, or a fool, or hated him by the end.

Knowing there would be no way to keep Fiachra silent as they fled, Saffron opened the flap of her carrier and released her, then flattened the foldable cage and tucked it into one of his saddle-bags. The bird swept over Copper, claiming a talon-full of fur from his tail and summoning a snarl from the beast, who chased her ahead of where Saffron hurried Boann to the exit.

But outside, just as Saffron pulled himself into the saddle—something grabbed the back of his cloak, choking him as he was wrenched from his lift in the stirrup. Thrown to the road with a breathy grunt, Boann reeled backward in alarm as Copper snarled, but Saffron heard none of it—suddenly pinned beneath pale hands and the sharp glare of icy eyes.

Despite Saffron's first instinct, though—it wasn't Cylvan who'd grabbed him.

"Th-the train!" Saffron exclaimed, and a bitter smile split Aodhán's face.

"Oh, think you're funny, do you?" they said with venom, shoving Saffron down and knocking the air from him. They kicked Copper away as the fox attempted to bite their hand, grab-bing Saffron's face and squeezing until Saffron flinched. "Run-ning away to meet with your rebel leader, hm? Finally had enough pretending? That true nature of yours, I see, to lie—"

"Oh, fuck you!" Saffron snarled back, making Aodhán raise their eyebrows. "I'm not going to find Ryder, goddamnit—I'm going to Morrígan!"

"What is gods' name is at Morrígan that's so important?" Aodhán growled back, grunting when Saffron slammed a knee up between their legs and made them buckle.

"None of your business!" Saffron shoved Aodhán off, scram-bling for Boann's reins to pull himself into the saddle before he could be grabbed again, but Aodhán was faster, grappling for Saffron's ankle and yanking him back down. From the platform, the train's whistle blew again, followed by a cloud of dark smoke as the coal engine roared and the weight of all its cars crept forward. Even Aodhán lifted their head to look, furrowing their brows in annoyance like they really thought they'd be able to grab Saffron and drag him back in time.

"Did Cylvan send you to get me?" Saffron asked, kicking Aodhán away. "I guess it shouldn't surprise me—that he wouldn't come after me himself!"

"I came for you myself," Aodhán grumbled, clearly realizing the futility of their chase and releasing their grasp on him. Sitting back, they brushed themself off, before glancing over their shoulder as the cluster of gossip writers still watched from the corner of the platform. Saffron noticed them, too, heart leaping into his throat and propelling him to his feet.

"I'm sorry," he said breathlessly, pulling himself into Boann's saddle. "I have to go—but I'm not going forever. It has nothing to do with Ryder—well, not directly. I promise. I'm not trying to —hey!"

He barked as Aodhán approached, moving faster than Saffron expected, heaving themself up into the saddle behind him. He attempted to elbow them in the stomach to knock them back off, but they just growled at him, jamming fingers into his side and making him choke.

"I'm not about to let you go anywhere on your own, witch," they hissed. "Not when you're leaving in secret like this. If it really is nothing to be worried about, then you won't mind me joining you. Since you've made me miss my train, and all."

"There will be other trains," Saffron attempted to argue, accidentally yanking on Boann's reins as he fought to meet Aodhán's eyes over his shoulder, turning the horse in circles. "Get off!"

"Go on, my lord," Aodhán insisted otherwise, sneering as they uttered the title. "Wouldn't want people to think you were up to no good, fighting one of the prince's guards in the dirt on the road. You said you were going to Morrígan—so let's go."

Saffron glanced back toward the gossip writers, who continued to watch him. Biting his lip, he swallowed back everything else he meant to say. He tightened his grasp on Boann's reins, then swallowed the nerves growing in his stomach. *Alright,* he thought to himself, rather than speaking it out loud. It seemed he really had no choice.

# 25

# THE RIDER

Boann may not have noticed much of a different in weight once the majority of Saffron's luggage was removed and replaced with Aodhán. The fey gentle wasn't much broader than Saffron once they were pressed so closely together, he realized, wondering if it was simply their imposing energy that made them feel so *large*. He could have sworn they were at least as tall, as broad as Cylvan, though perhaps only because they shared so many other features. And not just physically, as their temperament grew more and more bitter and sour as they continued on. Annoyed with how Saffron held Boann's reins, annoyed with how people looked at them as they passed on the road, even annoyed at how Copper trotted silently alongside them. When rain began sprinkling the road, it was as if they'd been insulted straight to their face.

"I think he's actually stuck like that," Saffron attempted to explain at one point, but Aodhán just scoffed. He almost turned to look, sure it was actually Cylvan seated behind him in the saddle. They sounded exactly the same.

"Your doing, witch?" they muttered, and Saffron really did throw them a look.

"Excuse me?"

They mumbled something else, but didn't repeat it. Saffron wasn't sure if the heat in his face was from anger or annoyance, but he made sure to elbow the other rider in the stomach while adjusting Boann's reins.

"I think because he shifted despite being ashen," he explained anyway. "He couldn't change before, but somehow shifted despite that, but—is still ashen. So he can't change back."

"The veil must have quite the sense of humor. Are we sure it isn't punishment for how his brothers acted at the satyr party?"

Even Copper glanced over his shoulder with narrow eyes in warning to Aodhán, and Saffron felt the resentful, electric buzzing between the two of them. He almost asked if Aodhán and Copper had met before, but decided against it. He was already getting too many skeptical looks from his unwelcome riding companion, not to mention the comments under their breath. Saffron didn't actually care to know anything more about them.

When Saffron wasn't keeping an eye on the fox, his attention drifted toward the edge of the trees on the side of the road, where a familiar black wolf stalked just out of sight. Saffron had tried to convince Taran he didn't need to wander out in the world if Aodhán would be joining them, not to mention Copper, but the wolf had insisted. Saffron knew it was because he personally considered every member of that tiny traveling party to be idiots —but a part of him wanted to think it was because he genuinely wished to keep Saffron out of harm's way. Whether or not he had any choice.

Copper constantly lifted his head to look, too, either to see if the wolf still followed, or like a part of him was tempted to trot a little closer. Perhaps a shared animal instinct—perhaps because it was only the second time he'd seen Taran out in the open like that, and was curious to see what his old friend was like after so many years.

Saffron adjusted his grasp on Boann's reins again, wondering, if Aodhán knew of Copper's fox form—how much did they know of Taran, too? Seeing as they were clearly aware of Saffron's arid tendencies, his biggest secrets, likely shared by Saoirse so they knew what they were getting into. But had they also been around long enough to have known all of Cylvan's friends as children as Saoirse had? He almost wanted to ask. But he wouldn't. At least not yet.

THEY PASSED FROM THE FALL COURT INTO THE SPRING without any fanfare, except the little flutter of excited anticipation in Saffron's stomach. Riding until the sun lazily sank toward the horizon, the darkness deepened the rainy chill in the air and made Saffron shiver, though seemingly had no effect on the passenger behind him. Who only huffed and constantly adjusted their hood with a small curse every time.

Passing through Connacht just as the light fully dipped into night, Saffron's stomach growled, and he pulled Boann to the side of the main street outside a bakery. Aodhán hissed complaints as he did, exclaiming that the roads would only get more dangerous in the dark, but Saffron just rolled his eyes.

"There's nothing that could surprise me in the Agate Wood," he said. "Never was. Just wait here."

Aodhán scoffed—again, exactly how Cylvan would have— and kicked their feet over the saddle to stomp into the bakery behind him. Saffron said nothing, just greeted the attendant inside and went about his business. He ordered a box of warm pastries, a mix of both sweet and savory, before hesitating—then requesting an extra, of all the same things.

He hoped Baba Yaga would be in Wicklow Cottage once they arrived. He hoped she would be awake. He hoped the other beantighes wouldn't mind receiving a little gift of Connacht treats from someone they assumed to be a stranger—the reminder, too, which made his heart sink.

His mood quieted while finishing the transaction with the attendant, having to clear his throat before handing over the handful of chaplets to pay. Aodhán watched in curious silence the whole time.

"You're taking pastries to someone on campus?" they figured on their own while stepping back out onto to street, newly illuminated with lanterns that flickered against the darkening sky. "Who, the headmistress?"

"No," Saffron muttered, ignoring the question a moment longer as he reached into their personal box to dig out a honeyed bacon and salt croissant, which he tossed to Copper waiting patiently next to Boann. His friend caught it mid-air with a squeal of delight, tearing into it like a prey rabbit. Handing the boxes to Aodhán to hold, when Saffron did respond, it was in hardly more than a whisper. "They're for my henmother. And the people who used to live in my cottage in Beantighe Village."

Aodhán clearly didn't anticipate that, which meant they didn't argue. They just looked at Saffron with the same curiosity mixed with frustration they always did, before shaking their head and pulling themself up into the saddle one-handed. Saffron followed, careful not to kick the boxes from their hand with his leg.

Returning to the road, they barely slipped through the town's gates as they closed for the night, the guards giving Saffron a funny look as he smiled and nodded while passing. They were even more perplexed at the sight of Copper, the giant orange creature three times as big as any normal fox, clearly a wild thing on the heels of the very normal-looking fey folk on the back of a royal horse. Saffron tried not to think about it too much, how the sight would likely stay with them, how they would be able to easily identify them to any leanan sídhe princes who might pass through next, demanding if Saffron had been spotted.

"I thought you said there was nothing in the Agate Wood that could surprise you?" Aodhán muttered as Connacht's gates disappeared behind them, only the dark road ahead.

"I did say that," Saffron muttered, digging into the side-bag of the saddle to pull out the handheld lantern inside, striking a match and letting it fester before hanging it off a loop on his belt.

"Why did you stiffen the moment we left the town, then?"

Saffron scoffed, that time. "Not because of anything we might cross on the road."

"Then what?"

Saffron scowled at Boann's flicking ears, the tiniest puffs of steam emerging from the horse's nose with the absence of the sun's warmth. The chill of the rain gently pattered against Saffron's hood where Fiachra also huddled, playing like a thousand plucked instrument strings on the earth and leaves in the trees.

"It's nothing," he mumbled, pausing before adding: "Cylvan is going to be so angry with me."

The silence between them puckered with the relaxed clopping of Boann's hooves, the pattering of Copper's paws, crickets in the grassy gutters of the road and the sound of heavy, crunching feet a little further than that. Off in the distance, other wolves howled; owls hooted and made Fiachra stir under Saffron's hood, poking her head out from where she'd drifted off to sleep.

"He most certainly will be," the fey gentle finally answered. "But sometimes Prince Cylvan needs to be made angry, to remind him what he could lose. He's quite spoiled in Avren."

Saffron turned to look at them, never expecting such blatancy. But Aodhán just gazed down at the printed shop name on the top of the boxes they held, swirling letters drawn in ink and dusted with sparkling powder.

"Have you known him for a long time?"

"Oh," Aodhán smirked like they had a secret, averting their eyes like they hadn't meant to imply that. "A while yet, yes. He's been a pain in the ass the entire time, too."

"Yeah," Saffron couldn't help but chuckle. "I've heard that a lot."

"You two met at Morrígan Academy. Where you were a beantighe." It wasn't a question.

"Yes. He was a mean, bitter, brooding raven back then, too," Saffron answered. Unable to keep a little smile off his face. His hand sank to his waist, where the dagger made from Cylvan's horn hung from his belt. Absentmindedly cracking open the sheathe to rub his finger over the root of the glasslike blade. "I think he's lightened up at least a little bit since then, though."

"You may be right."

Aodhán said nothing else, Saffron said nothing else. The brief exchange had quelled the smallest part of Saffron's nerves, but the rest remained. Storming in his chest, terrified of whatever consequences he might have to face from what he'd done. Hoping Cylvan would understand. If not at first, then eventually. Hoping he would understand, Saffron only did it because he thought it was best. He just wanted to keep Cylvan safe. He just wanted to chase after any and all threads he could to save the people taken from then.

Even if oracles did manage to get back through the veil—even if they somehow managed to retrieve Asche and Saffron's friends—that didn't mean Ryder was going to stop. Saffron had to do everything in his power to learn. To know how to stop him, once and for all. He only needed Cylvan to understand that.


THE FAMILIARITY OF THE AGATE WOOD DIDN'T FULLY strike him until, out of the corner of his eye, he spotted the shimmer of pixies buzzing around the last blooms of an apple tree. Until he swore he heard voices calling out on the breeze, until Copper paused to lift his head and look. How even Taran emerged from the undergrowth to walk a little closer to Saffron's side, like he could sense the growing energy of the wild woods, and the wilder things that lived there. Copper had said the Fall Court's woods were the oldest, filled with the strangest things— but perhaps only because he'd never had to pass through that patch of the Spring Court once the sun went down.

Passing a sign pointing toward Morrígan Academy, everyone

else seemed to breathe a quiet sigh of relief, while Saffron felt the opposite—a new sense of dread. Not sure if he wanted to go through campus, or head straight for Beantighe Village for the night. Eager to see his henmother, his old home, his friends—despite knowing they weren't really his friends anymore. Not as much as they knew, at least; not since the royal oracles unthreaded him from their memories.

Saffron lost himself easily in those sinking feelings, especially wrapped in such encompassing darkness of the wood, the white noise of the rain, his muffled senses beneath the hood, the silence of the road. He only emerged again when Taran's ears suddenly perked, and then Copper's—and then Saffron saw what caught their attention, far ahead in the darkness.

Something floated over the middle of the road, bobbing lazily up and down, glowing from three holes on its front. Eyes, a mouth. Carved into a gnarled gourd that grinned an uneven little smile at them.

"That something you're familiar with too, witch?" Aodhán asked, reaching around Saffron to tepidly grasp at Boann's reins. Saffron didn't answer, just scrutinized the unusual sight, swallowing against the growing uncertainty in the back of his throat. Was it a will o' the wisp? A púca? A brownie? What else would play such a strange little trick?

Reaching to touch the scar on his arm, Taran twitched like he felt it, offering Saffron a brief glance. But Saffron didn't give the wolf a command, instead focusing on the magic in his blood. Summoning it to his eyes, into his vision, wanting to see if the strange totem glowed red with arid magic, or white with opulence. When the object didn't glow at all, he wasn't sure if he should be relieved or even more suspicious. Even wild things usually had a halo, tinged pink in their natural mix of opulence and aridity—whatever it was floating in front of him, even his rowan magic couldn't see it.

He nudged Boann forward, and the horse obeyed, though snapped her head back and forth a few times with snorts of protest. Saffron just patted the side of her neck with whispered words of reassurance, before speaking up a little louder and directing Taran to go ahead and get a closer look. Taran obeyed right away, ears flattening against his head as he darted forward. Copper followed suit, without having to be asked. Curious as any other fox like him.

Both beasts reached the floating object, and Saffron pulled back on Boann's reins once more when the gourd immediately drifted away from the fox and the wolf observing it. First it bobbed up and down, then circled them, spinning on an invisible axis and even flipping over itself as if sentient and playing games. Only then did Saffron fully recognize its shape as a butternut squash, and he might have laughed if he wasn't so confused.

"What in Cailleach's name..." Aodhán muttered, nudging Saffron in the shoulder again. "What's going on?"

"It must be a fairy trick," Saffron chuckled. "Just a plaything—"

The words caught in his throat when something else appeared further down the road, accompanied by loud, echoing clopping of horse hooves before slowing to a stop. A sight that made Saffron's blood run cold in an instant, the hairs standing on the back of his neck. Boann sensed the same shift in the air, whipping her head back and forth once more and stomping backward. Ahead of them, Copper's tail bushed out, claiming a feet steps back of his own, though Taran remained exactly where he stood. Head low, back flat and tail swishing in warning.

"What is it?" Aodhán demanded again in a hiss, but Saffron still didn't know. He knew—but he didn't. He'd read about *dubh-lachan* in books; Baba Yaga used to tell stories of them as human-made horrors. He never thought one would stand face-to-face with one on an Alvish road. But the silhouette of it, with its dark cloak, massive black drafthorse, were enough to make his mind spin. It was too dark to tell if the creature really was as headless as all the myth claimed—but the glowing-faced gourd teasing his wolf was enough to make Saffron's breath lock.

The distant rider's horse pawed a broad hoof against the road a few times, before stamping its feet in agitation—and breaking into a bolt toward them. Saffron choked on a gasp, reeling back on Boann who threw her legs up in a panic. He barely threw his arms around her neck, but Aodhán wasn't so lucky, tumbling off the back with a grunt to the road, the boxes of pastries on their lap crunching and skidding away. Saffron wasn't far behind as Boann bucked one more time, throwing him and knocking Fiachra free of his hood as they hit the road. He scrambled to grab the bird before she could be trampled, pulling her into his chest and clambering backward. Boann clearly wished to bolt, herself—but clearly didn't want to leave her riders behind.

Circling him in agitation, she jerked away once Saffron scrambled back to his feet and desperately chased her. Meanwhile, Fiachra wriggled free of his grasp, taking off into the sky just as Copper raced back to Saffron and skid to a halt in front of him. Up ahead, Taran remained where he stood, lowering into a striking hunch as the gourd continued spinning and taunting him. Only once the horseman approached at full-speed, the wolf lunged and slammed into the rider, attempting to knock him off. But even with the weight of the beast attacking him—the rider remained in the saddle, and Taran was flung back to the road with a yelp and a bounce.

"Taran—!" Saffron shouted on instinct, before fiery blood boiled up his veins, into his chest where it swirled like a torch. Moving, allowing his instincts to drive him, he threw back the edge of his cloak and pulled the obsidian knife from his belt. He cut the tip of his finger deep enough to bleed, grabbing the lantern hooked on his hip.

Using his blood, with only mere moments allotted to him, Saffron drew a sloppy arid stele for *fire, burst* on the glass exterior —and lobbed it against the earth, just as the rider came within reach of him. An explosion of light and flame erupted from the seed of the candle inside, hot and blinding enough that even the dubhlachan reeled back on his horse.

The rider indeed still had a head, clearly illuminated in the light. And while the bottom half of his face was covered with a cloth mask—Saffron swore he recognized the person's eyes. No one he could name—but someone he was sure he'd seen before. The feeling was mutual, it seemed, as the rider's own eyes widened before pulling back on the reins.

The massive horse stumbled back to the road, stomping back and forth in irritation, both from the flames and the sudden forced halt. The rider never took his eyes from Saffron—until his gloved hand lifted, and he pulled down the bottom of his mask, calling out:

"Have you heard the music of the moon's harp?"

Saffron's mind reeled as he tried to make sense of the words. The rider just watched him, still holding the edge of his mask, like he wasn't certain. Perhaps because of Saffron's glamour, perhaps because his own recognition was barely a pinch, as much as Saffron felt. But the only place such a thing could have been possible there in the Spring Court—was at Morrígan Academy.

It struck Saffron in an instant, mortification churning in his gut at how obvious it was.

"P-Professor Dullahan?" he called back. Behind him, Aodhán made a noise like *'seriously?'* at the irony of the name.

The rider cocked an eyebrow, pulling back on his horse's reins with a little more strength. Saffron scrambled for the amethyst pendant down the front of his tunic, yanking it off to reveal his human face. Thankfully, the rider seemed to finally understand, and he yanked more firmly on his horse to calm its stomping agitation.

"You're Adelard's student," Dullahan stated, rather than a question. Saffron nodded. During the two months he spent waiting for Cylvan's call from Avren after Ostara, Saffron had spent as much fleeting time as possible with Professor Adelard as he did wandering alone in the woods. Learning every little thing he could squeeze out of the man, mainly focusing on his Gaeilge spell-vocabulary as Adelard was hesitant as ever to dive any deeper.

Occasionally, Saffron had brushed past Professor Dullahan on his way in or out of Adelard's office, though the man's handsome face never met his eyes a single time.

"We're trying to get to Morrígan," Saffron said, putting his hands up slightly as a sign of peace. As he did, the flames of his spell began to putter under the rain, making it harder to see Dullahan's expression. "We're not here to cause any trouble."

"This is a *professor* of yours?" Aodhán growled, re-emerging from their own pocket of darkness to grab Saffron's shoulder.

"Who is this?" Professor Dullahan asked in the same tone.

"A royal guard traveling with me," Saffron answered. "Gentle Aodhán."

Aodhán's hand on his shoulder tightened in protest, and he shoved them away.

"That fox there is my friend, too. He's stuck like that because of Avren's ashen state. And that wolf—he's my familiar. I have an owl somewhere nearby, too, but—ah, there she—*Fiachra, no!*" Saffron choked as the bird's ghostly-white form suddenly dove from the dark sky, talons flared and tearing into Dullahan's dark hair. But the professor didn't snarl or attack her in return—his hand swept out with precision, grappling Fiachra's middle with the same ease of grabbing a cat off the fireplace mantle. Fiachra screeched, flapping her wings and flailing her feet, biting relentlessly all over the man's gloved hand.

"Easy, *a bhobain,*" he said in a low, calming tone. Fiachra wriggled free again as he loosed his grasp, flapping away and landing on Saffron's head, instead. Dullahan's attention returned to him as Fiachra did, reaching out to pat his horse's neck before tilting his head down the road. "Come, then. Adelard will be wanting to see you."

Saffron finally released the lungfuls of air he'd been holding, nodding and turning to search for Boann, who stood nervously at the edge of the trees. Dullahan said nothing else as Saffron worked to regain control of his skittish horse, barely casting extra glances down to Copper, then Taran, as they slinked past him with skeptical looks. Even Aodhán was less-than-thrilled to continue down the path on the heels of someone who'd nearly attacked them, especially after muttering curses beneath their breath while gathering the dented, but still intact pastry boxes from the road. But Saffron felt only relief, despite the still-racing of his heart.

Boann wanted nothing to do with the dark rider who'd rushed them, complaining each time Saffron attempted to nudge her closer so that he might ask the professor what, exactly, he was doing on the road, and with so much theatricality. Especially as they passed the hovering, carved butternut-squash, which just bobbed and twirled in place as if wishing them goodbye. It didn't follow, even as its master rode away. Keeping watch for any and all who wished to approach Morrígan Academy. Saffron was both eager to ask—but afraid to know what must have happened to earn it.

# 26

# THE PROFESSOR

Rain continued to soak the earth, and while King Tross' gifted cloak did its best to protect him, the Spring Court's familiar chill infiltrated Saffron's bones as they approached campus. Traveling down the main road for some time, Dullahan eventually veered off into the woods, and Saffron followed without question. Even as Boann and Aodhán both protested with grunts and scoffs of continued skepticism. But Taran walking slightly ahead of them didn't alert to anything astray, and even Copper, who, as far as Saffron knew, had never been to Morrígan, seemed more curious than nervous.

Approaching campus from the shadows, not needing his access ring after all while following Dullahan's lead, Saffron summoned Taran back into his mind. Not wanting to draw any unnecessary attention—especially since, the last time a massive wolf had stalked that place, it took a rowan spirit to come and banish it.

Even keeping to the edge of the treeline, Saffron felt wave after wave of familiarity wash over him, from all the times he'd walked to and from the Grand Library at night during his geis with Cylvan; those trees, hidden paths, underbrush he knew as well as he knew the interior of every one of Morrígan's buildings. As intimately as he knew Beantighe Village. Even in the darkness, far from the road, Saffron knew exactly where they were. Needing only a peek toward the school and its flickering lantern-light. The silhouettes of its buildings. The sound of the fountain in the center of campus. And—the occasional whisper of night-shift beantighes going about their chores.

Even as the strange traveling party emerged onto the paved walkways from the shadows, those same beantighes barely paid them any mind, except the briefest of glances. Some of them offered a greeting, nodding to Professor Dullahan specifically and reigniting Saffron's curiosity that told him something had gone amiss to earn the professor's behavior on the road. For more reason than that, Saffron had to resist looking back at those they passed, wanting see if he recognized any of them who had their veils pinned up. Having to remind himself that, with his glamour back in place, he was just another fey lord. And a fey lord wouldn't pay nighttime beantighes any mind. A fey lord wouldn't have noticed—how few actually wandered between the buildings, compared to when he'd been there only months prior. A sinking thought, that even those so far from Avren were falling for Ryder's promises, too.

The Administration Building was dark except for ambient light of lanterns lining the walkway outside, and one window illuminated from the inside. Saffron knew that window better than any other, too—he'd once been lifted inside by Hollow's hands, after Adelard offered his office as a safe refuge while Saffron performed as the rowan spirit for the beantighes on campus. Where he slept curled up on a bedroll in the corner, where Taran came to threaten Hollow to tell him where Saffron was hiding. Ironic, the dynamic they returned with, after all of that. Saffron felt Hollow's absence more than ever in that moment, exhaling a small breath and praying once again his friends were safe on the other side of the veil. Unsure how he felt to think they may have been joined by familiar faces of Beantighe Village since then, too.

Rather than approaching the front doors of the building,

Professor Dullahan led his draft horse through the decorative brambles alongside the exterior, to that one illuminated window of Adelard's office. Saffron dismounted his horse as Dullahan did, approaching the glass as the man knocked a gloved knuckle against the pane. On the other side, a familiar form shifted from where he'd clearly fallen asleep at his desk, lifting his head with a piece of parchment stuck to his cheek.

Professor Adelard adjusted his glasses, glancing blearily around the room before stopping at the window, a sleepy smile growing on his lips as he spotted Dullahan's shadow on the other side. He quickly pulled the parchment from his face, ran a hand back through his wild curly hair, then smoothed the wrinkles of his vest before getting up to push the window open.

"It appears a wild wraith of the night has come to tempt me into someth—*SAFFRON!*" Adelard exclaimed, hand flying out in surprise, nearly slamming the windowpane against the building had Dullahan not grabbed it, first. "Oh, Saffron, child, look at you! Wh—what in god's name are you doing all the way here! You as well, Prince Cylv—oh, hold on a moment..."

Adelard adjusted his glasses as Aodhán wrinkled their nose—admittedly very Prince Cylvan-esque of them—as Adelard adjusted his glasses, studying them longer than was really necessary. His eyes then traveled to Copper, who sat like a patient dog at Saffron's feet. Then to a ruffled-looking Fiachra on Saffron's shoulder, before his eyes traveled back to Saffron.

"My, what a curious band of wild things you've brought me, Cormac. Alright, all of you, come inside and warm up before you catch your death out there. Through the window, Cormac, if you don't mind—probably shouldn't leave any trace of opening the front door, considering the nature of this company..."

Cormac must have been Professor Dullahan's first name, Saffron realized, once the man turned to him. Without warning, he scooped Saffron around the waist and heaved him in through the window, catching him off guard so that his foot caught on the sill and he tumbled in face-first. Adelard yelped, rushing to help him up as Copper was tossed inside like a bag of sloppy wet pota-toes next, followed by a stern *'don't you dare'* from Aodhán as they pulled themself up on their own with one arm, the other hand still protectively balancing the pastry boxes.

Dullahan hovered by the window as Adelard scurried around the room to stoke the fire and hang a kettle of water over the flames. Copper loped lazily to the hearth, shaking off his thickly-soaked fur and making Aodhán pull his tail as they were splashed. Fiachra perched on the skeleton in the corner of the room, preening her feathers as Adelard hurried back to the window where they exchanged whispers. Saffron barely caught the essence of their conversation—Adelard asking if Dullahan was returning to the road for the night, Dullahan confirming so, before tucking something into Adelard's palm and telling him to call if he needed anything. Adelard then threw a quick glance over his shoulder, checking to see if anyone was watching, and Saffron looked away. Adelard quickly leaned out to give Dullahan a kiss and wish goodbye.

When he finally closed the window and turned back to the room, he placed something on his desk before speaking, and Saffron saw it to be a palm-sized acorn squash carved with another wonky smile like the gourd on the road had. The object shud-dered slightly, making Saffron jump, before it rolled around a few times on Adelard's desk, then righted itself, rocking back and forth until it fully turned to observe the room. Saffron bit back a smile.

Professor Adelard's office never changed in all the time Saffron knew him, from their earliest secret meetings to their weeks spent while Saffron waited to hear from Cylvan. And while it was hardly different that night, Saffron sensed right away some-thing was—*off* about it at the same time. The smallest shift in the air, like all of Adelard's belongings had been tucked slightly one way or another. Askew enough to feel but not enough to see. Saffron tried to ignore it, especially when everything else about the professor seemed perfectly fine, especially as he puttered to hurry and clean off the scant chairs around the room, shoveling armfuls of books and stacks of papers onto any available surface so Saffron and Aodhán had somewhere to sit.

Saffron claimed the chair he normally did when visiting, as the man hurried to address the whistling kettle for tea. Right after settling, his eyes caught on something sticking free of a stack of parchment on Adelard's desk—and Saffron's heart thumped nervously. A rowan-red corner of thick paper, the shade of it just a little too familiar.

He reached for it. He shouldn't have, and he tried to resist at first, especially with the acorn squash shifting to watch his movements—but the sudden anxiety was overwhelming. He wanted to prove himself wrong—but the moment he pulled it free and saw the words printed on the front, he knew there had been no point in trying to convince himself otherwise. He already knew, just by observing how few night-shift beantighes passed by on campus.

Saffron sat back in the chair with the card pinched between his fingers, only for Adelard to practically leap across the length of the room. He snatched the card from Saffron's grasp, grabbing a handful of the parchment stack and slamming it back between the pages with a flurry of panic. Saffron attempted to reassure him not to worry, that he already knew what it was, but Adelard had suddenly gone serious. He spoke in a tone Saffron had never heard before—one that chilled his blood to the bone.

"You will not touch such things of mine so freely again, Saffron. Do you understand?"

"I—" he gulped. "I'm sorry, professor."

Adelard's looming boldness lingered barely a moment longer, before he slumped again with a small exhale. Saffron couldn't help but continue: "It's just—I've seen that card before. I know what it is. God, I know more than I'd ever care for."

While his intensity diminished, Adelard didn't fully relax again. Still, his gaze shifted into something more like concern rather than fury, and Saffron swallowed back the lump in his throat.

"I—I saw many things in Avren, having to do with... with, erm, cards like those," he went on. "I know the man behind them, even—the same one who opened the veil at the summer games..."

Adelard put a hand up, and Saffron closed his mouth in an instant. Behind him, even Aodhán and Copper were stiff and wide-eyed. That was a familiar motion, too, from when Saffron had been just a beantighe begging for any information Adelard would be willing to give him. That lifted hand to *wait, be patient*, before he'd normally hurry around the room to ensure everything was fully closed; the rug was lodged into the crack beneath the door and the floor, the window was pulled shut and latched; the air vents were shuttered. That time, though, Adelard didn't leap up to address such tasks, as if already in place before Saffron arrived.

"Are these companions of yours trustworthy, Saffron?" He asked, and Saffron's raised his eyebrows.

"Yes—"

"I know all there is to know about this witch already," Aodhán interjected, clearly trying to establish their authority, even with pink, scuffed pastry boxes on their lap—but even they chilled slightly at the narrowed, dark look Adelard shot them.

They awkwardly adjusted how they sat as Adelard took a seat at his desk. He fished a black-stone wand from a locked box in a chest by the foot of his drawers, pausing only a moment to glance between everyone in the room one last time.

"They're safe," Saffron reiterated, throwing Aodhán a look that dared them to try and speak up again. They didn't.

Adelard still said nothing, getting to his feet and proceeding to use the stone point to draw an implied, uninterrupted line around the edge of the room, followed by adorned arid hatch-marks. It was then that cold sweat dripped down Saffron's spine, unsure what to expect next. Only knowing that it must have been serious for Adelard to perform human magic right there in front of him, in front of Aodhán, in his own office only a few doors down from the headmistress'. Empty or not—performing such things in that building posed a dangerous risk.

"You say you know the man who opened the veil?" Adelard only started once he finished and returned to his desk. By then he appeared pale, forehead beneath his dirty-blonde hair shiny with a thin layer of nervous sweat. "How well? What sort of things did he tell you, Saffron? About these cards, specifically."

"Not much," Saffron admitted. "Only that he used them to recruit beantighes wishing to join him, to be trained as witches."

Adelard looked him over a moment longer, like a part of him still wasn't sure how much he wished to share. His finger tapped the book where the card was stuffed, as he considered it.

"The first four lines printed on that card were once used by actual human rebels, during the War of the Veil," he finally said. "Hence why it is so dangerous for you—or *anyone*, for that matter —to be found carrying one."

Saffron nodded. He hated feeling like he was being scolded, while Adelard's tone was merely informative.

"That random thing your lover said on the road, then, is fair game?" Aodhán interjected, both Saffron and Adelard throwing them a look. Adelard frowned, eyes flicking back to Saffron.

"What did Cormac say to you?"

"Um—he asked, *'have you heard the music of the moon's harp?'*"

He expected Adelard to groan, like he would be disappointed in even Cormac for uttering something else that might be risky if overheard by the wrong folk—but Adelard only nodded.

"And you didn't know how to answer?" He asked, surprising Saffron. "A wonder he let you pass."

"I sort of... pulled off my glamour, to prove I was human," Saffron admitted sheepishly. Adelard narrowed his eyes, but Saffron added before the scolding could finally come: "How should I have responded? To that phrase, I mean. Is it also something from the war?"

Adelard, once again, let his consideration pass in silence, only shifting his eyes to Aodhán, then Copper, then Fiachra a few more times. Finally, he answered: *"'I've heard it close, and learned the song myself.'* It references the harp of Ériu. Who you know well enough is a human goddess. Plenty of old rebel musings revolved around her, understandably."

"Sure," Saffron nodded. Adelard tapped his finger against the book again.

"Back to my original concern with your dealings, Saffron. The man who has been passing these out, the one you say you met and got to know well—what sort of dangerous things did he tell you, exactly?"

Saffron bit his lip. His eyes lingered on the stone pointer in Adelard's hand, clutched so tightly it rattled against the side of the desk as the professor hovered too close.

"Is that a hematite wand?" he asked before answering. Adelard somehow grew paler, practically fainting into his chair with his hand over his face.

"Oh, god help us," he whispered, voice shrill. "God help you, god help me, god help—"

"He calls himself Ryder Kyteler," Saffron went on before Adelard could fully spiral. The professor's pleas for heavenly mercy petered off, before lifting his hand from his eyes just enough to look at Saffron again. That sharp intensity had returned, making Saffron shift where he sat. Afraid to speak more too soon.

"He does, does he...?" Adelard asked. He finally sat back up, staring down at his desk before carefully lifting and placing the black-stone wand in front of him. Saffron wished he could read every new, sudden, wild thought racing behind the professor's eyes. Did he recognize Ryder's name? Its relation to the red card he'd snatched from Saffron's grasp? Or perhaps because of their proximity to the old Kyteler school?

But something old, something ancient churned in Adelard's countenance with the same intensity as moments prior, to the point Saffron barely recognized the man sitting in front of him.

Even as Adelard lifted his eyes back to Saffron again, blue in the firelight, hair wavy and still clinging to his nervous forehead. He released a long breath through his nose, before placing the stone rod on the desk in front of him with a small, glasslike sound.

"This is a hematite wand, yes. Used by practiced arid witches to cast spells without having to write them down. I take it Ryder Kyteler shared such things with you."

Saffron nodded. "Ryder Kyteler once gave me a hematite ring to do the same. I practiced with it a few times, but... stopped as soon as I realized he wasn't who I thought."

He thought Adelard might look relieved to hear that, that Saffron had given such a thing back; then he expected Adelard to ask for more details, about who exactly Ryder was, or who Saffron first thought he was, then who he ended up actually being—but the professor did neither of those things. He just shook his head, gazing down at the wand a moment longer. Seemingly in disbelief, then in silent consideration.

"News of what happened during the summer games traveled to Morrígan quickly, of course," he said, instead. He met Saffron's eyes again, expression soft. "I'm sorry to hear what happened to Daurae Asche. As well as all those innocent people. How is Prince Cylvan doing?" His eyes flickered to Aodhán as he asked, who remained in their chair sipping silently at their tea. Avoiding Adelard's eyes, like it was actually the first time anyone had ever mistaken them for the prince. Like they'd never noticed the resemblance, themself, and were embarrassed by it.

"He's doing alright, all things considered," Saffron answered, before grimacing and wringing his hands together. "Cylvan, he... he doesn't know I'm here, actually. Erm, well, maybe he does. I technically left a note. I'm sure he's figured it out. But he didn't know I was... planning on coming here, without him."

"Why *are* you here, child?" Adelard asked, the familiar sound of his voice breaking through again. "Is something wrong?"

"It's... complicated," Saffron said, eyes remaining lowered on his hands over his lap. "But... professor, there have been more veil events. I'm sure you've heard of them. More than just the one in Avren, there was one in Erelaine, then another one in the Fall Court. There would have been one in Ailinne last night, but—" His eyes flashed to Aodhán, then back to Adelard. "But we were lucky. We've been trying to chase him down, we realized he's following Queen Proserpina's old coronation route, so I thought I would be able to do something if I found him, but... that's proving too difficult. Cylvan wanted to go back to Avren, but... but I couldn't stomach it. Going back there to just sit and wait for news. I thought... I was hoping... you might finally be willing to help me with more than just my arid vocabulary, professor. Ryder has more than just Daurae Asche, he also took my friends—"

"Your friends?"

Saffron's hands wrung together harder in growing agitation. He nodded. "Yes," he said hoarsely. "Before the Midsummer Games ever happened, Ryder took Hollow, Letty, and Nimue through the veil. I think he did so to try and trap me. He—he wanted me to partner with him in this attempt at a human rebellion, I think, and I was slow to agree—"

"Good," Adelard said firmly, and Saffron finally met his eyes again. The intensity had returned—that time, as proof Adelard knew more than he shared. Saffron went on, hoping the professor might finally explain. He went on about how Taran had been his intended familiar all along; he talked about Sunbeam, and how she was there with Asche during the games; he reiterated every promise Ryder had ever made to him, about controlling his magic, offering him a witch's mark. Lying the entire time, purposefully keeping truths from Saffron because, in reality, he wanted Saffron's magic as wild as possible to ensure he would be the one to wreak havoc at the games. And by refusing to be that tool for him—Ryder had resorted to opening the veil, instead.

The words spilled out of him like blood from a desperate cut. Adelard never interrupted, just nodding, resting his chin against intertwined fingers on his desk. All the while, Aodhán gazed at Saffron in the same way, eyebrow slightly raised in curiosity. It wasn't widely known exactly what happened in those final moments of the games, after all. Saffron couldn't blame them for being intrigued.

"I thought you might be able to help me because, paired with his trail of veil events—" Saffron hurriedly yanked his sketchbook from his bag, flipping through the pages to where he'd kept the leaflet of illustrations Cylvan provided him when the high keeper first reported the circles to the palace; on the page alongside it, he'd re-drawn the Tapestry Hall's strange circle larger, with accompanying notes.

Adelard adjusted his glasses as he leaned forward—before reeling back with a choked sound, nearly knocking his chair over backward. He stared at the drawing with wide eyes, paler than ever as Saffron gently questioned his name. He could practically hear the pounding of Adelard's heart, especially once the man opened his mouth to clear his throat and speak.

"M-my apologies," he said, voice shaking. "You only startled me with that one, Saffron, ahaha... Ah, there, I see it now, you left your drawing of the circle broken so it wouldn't activate. Good lad. Let me—let me take a closer look, hm? Thank you."

Saffron gave him plenty of time to skim every marking on the page, before quietly continuing.

"Before we knew it was Ryder doing it, I—I kept having these nightmares. Someone calling out to me, begging me to come and find them. To save them. At first I thought it was Asche, but..." He glanced to Aodhán again briefly. "But recently, realized the cries only come to me when Ryder performs this spell. I think they're related."

Adelard nodded along. He adjusted his glasses once again, as if paranoid they'd slipped off and he wasn't seeing correctly.

"*Proclaim self, shelter soul, disgrace,*" he read under his breath. Saffron nodded.

"Do you know what it means?"

"Unfortunately, I may have an idea, yes," Adelard finally answered after what felt like a century of bated silence. He smiled wearily at Saffron, pressing his glasses into his nose yet another time before gingerly closing the sketchbook and sliding it back across the desk. "Not here, though, lad. God above, not here. This really is none of my business. In fact, I think you would be better off doing as Prince Cylvan said, and returning to Avren once you've completed your social visits here."

"Then—"

"I'm sure you're itching to get to Beantighe Village before the sun rises, hm?" Adelard said, getting to his feet and brushing the wrinkles from his sweater. "Best start making your way, so no night-shift beantighes spot you and start asking questions. Ériu knows, with those rebels sniffing around, they've been nagging your poor henmothers for information on human magic they keep hearing about. Ah—best you keep this from Nora for now too, hm?"

"Professor, please—!" Saffron begged, leaping to his feet as Adelard shoved the sketchbook closer. "Professor—with all due respect, damnit, I'm not leaving until you help me! I'm not going to be polite anymore, not when you might be THE ONLY ONE WHO CAN HELP ME!"

Saffron didn't expect to shout—but even Aodhán jumped. Adelard stared at him, standing stiffly on the other side of the desk as Saffron's breaths came in hard and fast.

"I—" he croaked. "Professor, I'm sorry, I—I'm just—" Defeated tears rimmed his eyes. "I'm begging you, Adelard. I need you. My friends, Daurae Asche—we all need you."

Adelard said nothing for a long time, again. Long enough that Saffron's shoulders slumped, and he finally lowered his eyes. He reclaimed the sketchbook from the desk, tucking it into his bag.

"You've grown quite bold, after spending all that time in Avren," the professor finally spoke.

Saffron winced, looking back at Adelard—surprised when the professor looked at him more in fatherly exasperation than full disapproval.

"I never would have imagined someone so polite would raise

their voice at me in my own office," he went on, finally removing his glasses to wipe the lenses as the ear-chain dangled around the back of his neck. He gazed down into the glass pieces for a long moment, as if regarding something only he could see in the reflection. "Are you asking as a beantighe, or as a prince?"

"I'm asking as your friend," Saffron said weakly. Adelard's movements paused, and his eyes flickered up to him again. Saffron swallowed against his tight throat. "I'm asking—as a stupid human who's gotten too far in over his head with all of this. The veil is relying on me, and I can barely even string an arid stele together. I desperately—*desperately* need someone who can help me."

"You tried to set Cormac on fire on the road. Seems you can deliver arid steles well enough."

Saffron grimaced. "Well—someone very dear to me once taught me a long list of arid vocabulary. But, as much as I would enjoy it—I don't think setting Ryder Kyteler on fire is going to solve all my problems."

"A thought," Aodhán muttered.

Adelard smirked, too, then sighed. He tucked his glasses back in place.

"I will come to Beantighe Village after sunset, where we can speak a little more openly." He looked at Saffron pointedly, that time, and Saffron straightened up. "I'm sure your henmother will like to know what sort of ideas I'm planting in your head this time around. I am not promising to teach you anything, but—is that at least acceptable to you, for now?"

"Y-yes!" Saffron exclaimed, holding his bag close to his chest, before sinking into a deep bow that made Aodhán grunt in disapproval. "Thank you! Thank you, professor! I'm really sorry! I'm really so, so sorry—!"

"Don't bow to me, your highness, I'll blush," Adelard answered with a new, weary playfulness as he sank into his desk chair.

Saffron gathered himself again. His heart pounded in excitement, at the mere thought of Adelard finally, finally being willing to speak openly about even some of the things he knew, his long lifetime of experience with magic.

Adelard continued to gaze at him as the others got to their feet as well, before lowering his eyes to where the hematite wand sat on his desk. He turned it in a slow, considerate circle with his finger, before flicking it faster then sweeping it into his hand.

"Hold onto this for me, will you?" He asked, extending it to Saffron. "It's much more effective than a mere ring; much less painful than pricking your finger to draw with your blood, as well."

Saffron's cheeks went hot, unsure what to say as he slowly reached to take it. Cold and smooth in his hand, it was hardly no thicker than the sticks of charcoal he used for drawing, barely longer than his fist with every finger curled around it. He didn't get his chance to offer Adelard proper thanks, before the professor was shuffling all of them on their way out.

# 27

# THE HISTORIAN

Making their way from campus, still keeping a low-profile, following the well-trodden footpath into the woods made Saffron more emotional than expected. Even with his eclectic mix of companions, the wolf residing in the back of his mind, the horse whose reins he carried behind him, even the owl companion he'd sent ahead to notify Baba Yaga of his surprise visit—he kept absentmindedly reaching up to touch his hair, expecting to feel the tug of veil pins whenever the breeze came through.

He found himself smiling at little landmarks he'd memorized after so many years passing them by, like a gnarled oak tree right off the path, a place where the road had sunk away after a heavy rain, the creaking wooden bridge that spanned Quartz Creek swollen with water from previous rains. The sights, the smells of the rich woodland surroundings, the mud, the persistent magic in the air that wasn't as intense as that in the Fall Court, but still saturated enough to make him buzz. All of it was so familiar, and brighter than ever on his senses after being away for so long. A few months by the calendar, but an eternity by how he felt like a stranger in that place he once memorized down to every step.

In addition to those comforting, familiar things, there were additional improvements he hadn't expected. Small, earnest attempts at making things easier for the beantighes who made that long walk morning and night, efforts by Cylvan who simply wanted to do what he could, where he could, while all of Alfidel was still out of reach of his power.

While the bridge over Quartz Creek still creaked beneath their weight, actual support beams had been nailed over the width of the water. Lanterns spotted the walkway every hundred feet, flickering with the same flames as those on campus. Small things—the smallest, most unnoticeable things, that anyone else might scoff at. But Saffron knew. And more than ever—he was learning exactly what lengths Cylvan was forced to go to in order to accomplish even those tiny things, in such an inconsequential place, for even less consequential people. For the first time since leaving him, Saffron squeezed his amethyst pendant. Wondering if Cylvan felt it on the other side, unsure if the prince even still wore it after all that happened.

They crossed paths with no other humans on their way, chatting lightly as they went but otherwise appreciating the silence of the morning. As they approached the gates of Beantighe Village, Saffron spotted a familiar figure waiting right at the gates. An undeniable sight, draped in her knitted shawl and donning two long, silvery braids, the same chicken-foot necklace namesake bouncing on her chest with every step. Her appearance flooded the backs of Saffron's eyes with emotion, and he whimpered slightly like a lost child finally spotting home. Baba Yaga paced back and forth across the entrance, one hand grasping at her cane while the other held a clinking lantern. Impatient, but seemingly eager.

Fiachra perched on the iron fence and preened under her wing all the while. She only perked up once Saffron and the others appeared at the end of the road, too far yet for the old henmother to see for herself. Still, Saffron couldn't help himself, throwing up waving hand and yelling out her name. He finally burst into tears the moment his henmother turned and smiled at him, calling his name back.

He ran to embrace her, never let down by the strength of her legs as she bolstered them for an incoming hug. Wrapping her arms back around him, she squeezed him tight, cooing and patting the back of his head while welcoming him home. *Home,* the word that made held-back tears finally spill from his eyes as he buried his face into the comforting shape of the crook of her neck. Breathing in a familiar perfume of herbs and sweat and spun wool and creek water from washing, before pulling back to litter her face with a hundred kisses that made her laugh in surprise.

"Oooh, I've been waiting for you to come see me again, little spice. I know you must have so much to tell me about your time in Avren." She said, reaching up to tuck hair from Saffron's eyes, like he was a lost cat finally finding its way home. "Your highness, you look—ah, wait..."

Aodhán grumbled just like the first time. Still, they approached with a look of uncertain curiosity, before offering Baba Yaga a bow with an exaggerated sweep of the arm and a little flick of their foot, as if trying to show off. Followed by an extension of the pastry boxes, that barely kept themselves together after all the abuse.

"A pleasure to meet you," they said. "I'm Saffron's personal guard, at least for the time being. Gentle Aodhán."

"Well, how charming," Baba Yaga chuckled. "I see your taste in companions has improved, Saffron. Oh, and who's this handsome creature?" she went on before Saffron could correct her, letting it go as Baba Yaga knelt down to scratch Copper all over. The fox, soaking wet from the rain all over again, practically purred, seemingly the second lost cat eager for a warm welcome.

"That's my friend Copper," Saffron said. "He's normally much taller. And dryer. The ashen state has been hard on him."

"Oh, I bet you're just as handsome as a fey lord, aren't you?" Baba cooed, rubbing under Copper's chin. "Though I much prefer Saffron bringing home something furry again, like old times. His choice of lords has been *questionable* lately, to say the least. Ah, come, let's get you rain-wet things inside before the others make their way home. I have to help the morning-shifts get ready for the day, but you and your friends are welcome to sit in the parlor. You remember how frightful mornings can be."

"Do you need help with anything?" Saffron asked, taking Boann's reins again to lead her through the village gates, toward the side of Cottage Wicklow. His home, as much if not more than Luvon's estate in the Winter Court. The same size, shape, color as he'd left it only a handful of months earlier.

Removing Boann's bridle once sure she wouldn't wander far, Saffron left her to graze on the dew-rich grass of the cottage's front yard, making his way to Cottage Wicklow's open door where the others had already been invited inside. Where it smelled of breads and breakfast foods, fire crackling in the parlor hearth and warming the entire bottom floor; with its repaired staircase and glass panels in the windows. Many things fixed even while he was there over the summer—but things still foreign to him, things so small, things that again reminded him of Cylvan and made his stomach flutter with a whisper of guilt.

The morning rush came in as much of a flurry as Saffron always remembered, seated toward the back of the parlor with Aodhán alongside him, Copper at his feet, and cups of hot tea between them. On the other side of the wall, beantighes decimated the pastries brought in offering.

As unexpected visitors, they did their best to not stand out too much, to cause any alarm—but of course the others would notice two strangers and a giant, wild beast in the house with them. Especially when Copper wasn't even the most awkwardly-placed creature there, as Aodhán sat stiffer than a statue as they sipped their tea and looked at the floor, the ceiling, commenting on the colored glass in the parlor window before ever meeting eyes with the dozen of beantighe chicks who came down the stairs. Perhaps Cylvan wasn't the only person the guard resembled, Saffron suddenly saw so much of Asche in them, too.

Eventually, the investigative looks from the clustering beantighes grew inescapable, and Saffron couldn't stop himself from glancing up to meet the constant, lingering eyes. Only to jump, spilling the hot drink over his hand when it was Fleece who looked at him with a raised eyebrow, or Silk peered out from the corner into the kitchen. Appraising him like they were sure they knew him from somewhere, but couldn't quite place it. Saffron could only turn his eyes down again, holding his breath and placing a hand against his chest as his heart pounded hard enough to make his scar ache.

"Everything alright?" Aodhán asked between sips of their drink.

Saffron nodded. "When I left Morrígan to join Cylvan in Avren... they sent royal oracles here to p-pull memories of me from everyone in the village." He hated how he stammered, how his voice trembled slightly despite his best efforts. "It's my first time being back since then. I don't think I realized... how bad it would feel."

Aodhán considered that for a long moment, watching where Fleece and the other familiar faces hurried into the kitchen to ask for something to eat.

"You gave up many things to be a prince," they stated.

"Not to be a prince," Saffron corrected, "to be with Cylvan. I couldn't care less about any titles like those."

"Hey," someone else approached, and Saffron jumped to his feet in an instant. It made the beantighe jump, and Saffron quickly smiled and set his tea down to try and soften his intensity.

"Good morning," he said, having to resist calling Thread by name. "Can I do something for you?"

Aodhán cleared their throat, but it was too late. Even the corner of Thread's mouth twitched like they weren't expecting Saffron's eagerness, let alone such a beantighe-esque string of words.

"Are you here on behalf of the prince?" They asked, eyes

flashing briefly to Aodhán like they'd also confused them for Cylvan.

"Not exactly, but—I can pass any message you need, yes," Saffron drew their attention back.

"It's not a message—more of a question."

"Then I can try to answer it, if you'd like."

"I was hoping he'd be able to tell me what exactly he wants us to do."

Saffron blinked, blank smile swelling with confusion. "What he wants...?"

"Well—those humans keep coming from Avren offering us ways out of our contracts, right?" they said outright. "But then witchhunters follow right after them. The people with the red cards claim they're here on behalf of the rowan spirit—but anyone who worked at Morrígan when the rowan spirit *actually* haunted this place knows it was once a friend of Cylvan's, and he was the one to give it peace in the end... So are the red cards being sent by him or not? Why's he trying to trick us to take them, only to send witchhunters right after? Kind of evil, if you ask me."

Saffron stared at them, the smile still stiffly plastered on his face. Other beantighes clearly watched, too, like it was a common point of discussion.

"What?" he rasped at first. A little dumbfounded by how blatant the question was. Thread paled slightly, like they realized they'd completely misinterpreted everything happening. But when they bowed in apology, turning to hurry away, Saffron's hand lashed out to grab their arm.

"No, wait, sorry!" he said, before cringing, then having to move past it. "I didn't mean to confuse you. I simply wasn't expecting anyone to be so upfront when they asked. Can you actually tell me—what exactly have the humans with the red cards told you about the rowan spirit?"

"They... said the rowan spirit would save all humans like it saved us here at Morrígan," Thread answered, slightly less bold that time. Saffron waited for them to continue—and when they didn't, his nerves ground into one another in agitation. Ah. He smiled, but his jaw clenched through it. Insulted that Ryder and his witches would feel so emboldened to continue using that moniker without fully understanding what it ever meant.

"The humans passing out the red cards, claiming to be messengers of the rowan spirit, have no real understanding of what happened here at Morrígan," he said. "I'd advise you to be careful who you follow into the woods. That's not to say the real spirit won't come one day soon, but—until it does, there will be people who make promises similar to what was done here, when they are actually the wolf in disguise."

Thread didn't look frightened, or even anxious—in a way, they almost looked relieved, like there had been something bothering them about those who came to Morrígan looking for people to take.

"Prince Cylvan is not sending the witchhunters to come for you, either," Saffron added with certainty. "I swear to you. They are acting on their own—and may even be hunting the people who are claiming to be rowan messengers in the first place."

"A lot of us here have been hesitant to believe anything they say," Thread said quietly. "After what the actual rowan spirit did for us—and then the things Prince Cylvan has tried to do afterward—it's hard to believe some of the things those false messengers claim. Someone from Cottage Dublin actually punched one of them because she hated how they were using the spirit's name... they haven't come by in a while since then. Maybe got tired of wasting time on us."

*Not to mention the dubhlachan blocking their way in,* Saffron thought, biting back a smile when he understood.

"Will you tell the others what I said?" he asked. "Also, tell them that—when the real rowan spirit comes, you'll know. The beantighes of Morrígan will know better than anyone else—and they should say so, when the time comes."

"Alright," Thread answered with a little smile. They offered Saffron a nod of thanks, before giving one to Aodhán, then turning to hurry back into the kitchen. Saffron watched them go, unable to reclaim his seat for a long while as something petrified his insides. Turning him to stone as he watched night-shift beantighes saunter in from their exhausting chores, and day-shift beantighes scurried out in the opposite direction.

Rage—that feeling locking Saffron's joints and filling him with clay was rage. That Ryder would continue to claim the rowan spirit's name as his own, that he would still pretend like Saffron had anything to do with him. To take that crimson veil and parade it around like a false prophet, when he had no idea exactly what Saffron gave in order to don that mantle for himself.

Saffron wouldn't lose his chance on Ryder Kyteler again, the next time it came. He would face the consequences worthy of a false prophet.


ONCE THE HOUSE SETTLED DOWN AGAIN, WITH NIGHT-shift beantighes asleep in their beds and all the others long gone down the road, Saffron couldn't sit and wait any longer. He carried the tea tray into the kitchen, asking if there was anything Baba Yaga needed done while he was there. If he didn't do something about his itching bloodlust, he might just tear his own skin off.

Baba Yaga, as it turned out, had a similar idea—but not for the same reasons. She pinched at Saffron's cheek, then his ear, tugging on it.

"Enough of this, now. Take this glamour off, child, let me really look at you."

Saffron grimaced, knowing with certainty, it wasn't going to be a particularly pretty sight, considering how little he'd slept in the past week. He'd been able to get away with it on the road with Dullahan due to the darkness, but his henmother would spot every inch of him in an instant, thinking of the confrontation with Ryder in Ailinne. All of the traveling they'd done, falling off his horse, being thrown to the ground by Aodhán outside the train station...

"I don't know if that's such a good idea, Baba, considering anyone could come downstairs—"

Baba Yaga pinched his ear harder, a threatening look sharp as a knife in her eyes. Aodhán wandered in a moment later, crossing their arms and leaning against the wall. Like they wanted to see, too. Saffron's grimace deepened.

"God—alright. Just a warning though, that I haven't slept in a while, and we've run into some trouble on the road, but everything is alright, and I'm fine, so—"

"Oh, Saffron, if you don't show me your face right this second—"

"Alright!" Saffron exclaimed, tucking his hand down his shirt and yanking the amethyst over his head in one motion. "Anyway, about those chores—"

"Saffron!" Baba cried out, staring at him. She grabbed his face again before he could pull away, looking him over more aggressively than the first time, turning him this way and that. She pressed her thumbs into the bags under his eyes, the bruises on his face, the scuffs under his chin, then took his hands to do the same. Saffron finally managed to pull free with a groan, about to reassure her everything was fine, but she whipped around to look at Aodhán, first. "What in god's name have you allowed to happen! *Personal guard*, my wrinkled ass!"

"Baba!" Saffron attempted—but even Aodhán just stared at the state of him, looking a little paler than normal. Like even they were shocked at how well the glamour worked to hide all of Saffron's slow, exhausted withering. "I said it was alright! It's just been a rough couple of days. How about you mix me up one of those pastes you used to put on us after falling off rooftops? I think it would feel really nice. You can brew me a sleeping tea tonight, too, if you want. I would like that a lot."

Baba Yaga muttered something, clearly frustrated by Saffron's attempts to brush it off, but she knew better than anyone that was exactly how Saffron had always responded to bruises being found somewhere on him. Grabbing her cane from next to the door, she hobbled past him and started angrily yanking down dry herbs from the bundles hanging over the sink.

As she worked, she tried to insist Saffron go upstairs and get some sleep, instead, like she could see the exhaustion emanating off him no different than Luvon with his aura-glasses. But Saffron just shook his head, making up a lie about how he'd slept all the day earlier, despite the henmother knowing better. Knowing he was as impossibly stubborn as she was, she listed off a handful of chores he was welcome to do around the cottage, and even around the village, if he so badly wished to work himself to death. Saffron said nothing to deny that—he just turned to Aodhán with a tiny nod, and excused himself to start.

SHOVELING DIRT, PULLING WEEDS, CLIMBING UP ONTO the roof to hammer-down loose shingles while once-fellow beantighes slept in the rooms beneath him, Saffron disappeared into the movement of it. He turned off his thoughts, he turned off his emotions, he just did the work asked of him.

Work that used to be grueling, but came with open arms that morning. He'd spent too long sleeping in beds that were too soft, eating foods that were too indulgent and rich, reveling in pretty luxurious things he didn't deserve. Working himself to death felt right, at least for a few hours. He even nodded off alongside the water wheel with Copper in the afternoon, while Aodhán helped Baba Yaga around inside. Even they didn't call him lazy, as if equally shocked by the exhaustion on his unglamoured face.

When morning crept into afternoon, then evening, then sunset, Saffron was in the middle of scolding Fiachra for harassing Baba Yaga's orange cat in the rafters when a knock came at the door, and his heart pounded for a different reason. On the other side, Adelard stood with a apprehensive smile and greeting, wearing a cloak pulled over his head. Behind him, Saffron was more surprised to spot Cormac Dullahan, who looked handsome and stoic as ever as he followed the smaller man inside.

After pleasantries were finished exchanging, Cormac sat in the parlor with Aodhán and Copper while Adelard made himself at home there in Cottage Wicklow's kitchen. He sat at the table across from Saffron, eating a piece of Baba Yaga's pound cake like it was the true source of his youthfulness. He and the henmother even bickered back and forth some, hinting at a sense of growing closeness while Saffron was gone. Saffron had to hide his amusement. Anyone who didn't know any better, who didn't know the giant, frighteningly intimidating man in the parlor was Adelard's paramour, might think them an old married couple. Perhaps a grandmother and her stubborn grandson. Strange to think that Adelard was, technically, a few centuries older than Baba Yaga, even if he hardly looked or acted like it.

As they ate, Saffron undid the tight ribbon keeping the satchel of his emotions at bay, allowing them to spill out at a controlled pace. As Adelard asked him to start from the beginning all over again, that time sharing even the littlest details he never would have thought important, without any reservations at all. And Saffron did—he started at the very beginning, when Ryder first visited him in the hospital in Avren.

Only when Saffron recalled his contact with Ryder at the Beltane festival, and how he thought that was the first time a memory was taken from him, did things become complicated to try and keep track of in order. To explain why he suspected memory manipulation, he had to explain how he later learned Ryder was only half-human, and according to Taran, must have been oracle-trained in threadweaving. He described how Ryder could also manipulate the veil using veil circles—at that point producing the man's pixie ring stolen by Copper—and adding how one of Ryder's own accomplices once implied he wasn't even oathed to the veil. The veil wanted nothing to do with him, yet he could still somehow cause so much destruction through it, seemingly with just the rings on his fingers. It was around that time

Aodhán appeared in the entryway to the kitchen, crossing their arms and looking more perturbed than ever as it was the first time they were hearing about Ryder's attack in Ailinne.

Saffron continued on tangents about how Ryder was intent on trying to make Saffron doubt Cylvan every time they were alone together; how he spoke endlessly about how he was exactly what Saffron needed to understand his rowan magic, even promising him a way to get his witch's mark, though whenever they were together he always insisted Saffron try and find it all for himself, first. Which, eventually, made sense once Saffron actually had a chance to peruse the man's library in the ruins and realized there was nothing there of note.

He talked about the portrait he and Cylvan found in Avren National Library archives, that painting of Acacia Kyteler that so closely resembled Sunbeam; he then described what Asche had once told him about how Sunbeam used to be the one in Ryder's position in the Finnian Ruins, trying to help displaced beantighes, keeping them safe when they no longer wanted to be owned by their high fey patrons. How Ryder came in and took that from her—and how Saffron wondered if her place in the hierarchy wasn't the only thing he took, in whatever happened between them. How he might've even been holding someone close to Sunbeam named Chandry hostage on the human side, which was why she was in Morrígan at all, looking for the Kyteler School ruins to try and get through the veil that way—and it was then Adelard cleared his throat, urging Saffron back on track.

Halfway through his diatribe, Adelard began scribbling down notes. Quick, few-word notes, though he never interrupted. Each time Saffron paused to watch him, waiting for a word or a question, Adelard just motioned for Saffron to continue. And Saffron did, growing more tangled in his voice, forgetting what he'd explained and what he'd forgotten, voice growing hoarse by the end of it all.

"Last night you said he's following the night queen's coronation route, didn't you? Opening the veil along the way?" Adelard clarified while jotting down another note. Saffron nodded. "Do you mind showing me that epithet of his again?"

"Be careful—" Baba began, but Adelard threw her a smile.

"Your chick is quite clever, left the circle incomplete and all so as to not perform anything he doesn't mean to."

Baba Yaga smiled like a proud parent, and Saffron blushed as he hurried to remove his sketchbook. Once he did, Adelard dragged the book closer to himself, gazing down at the page for a long while. Just like the night before—except that time, his eyes lingered for a long time on each and every stroke. He skimmed Saffron's notes off to the side, considering the yew branches, apple, and other objects included within the circle. All the while, the tip of his pen hovering over a hair's breadth from his notepaper.

"Professor?" Saffron eventually whispered, but Adelard only shook his head, sitting back slightly. He adjusted his glasses, again like the night before, a little more pale than when he started as he adjusted how he sat.

"I didn't imagine it, then," he breathed. Cormac suddenly appeared, as if he could sense the shift in Adelard's demeanor even from the other room. "He's trying to contact the dead."

Saffron gaped at him a moment. Baba Yaga made a small noise, too, before hurriedly shuffling over to get a look at the epithet for herself.

"Oh my," she whispered, barely audible. "Such a thing is..."

"Very old," Adelard whispered with a small nod. That time, he reached out to gently pass his hand over the drawing, like he couldn't believe it himself.

"Contacting the dead?" Saffron asked, a mix of confusion and disbelief.

"That's right." Adelard sat forward slightly. "Nora recognizes it, too. This is a very old spell for calling out to someone in the mounds. You said the veil once described it as being 'from the Dagda's spellbook'? I'm not one to confirm whether or not that specifically is true, however—*'proclaim self, shelter soul, disgrace,'* with these objects, and in this arrangement, it's quite undeniable. Nora, would you like to explain?"

Baba Yaga sighed, restlessly stroking one of her silver braids. At her feet, her fat orange cat meowed and rubbed against her ankles, like it could sense her nerves as well as Cormac had sensed Adelard's.

"There are three parts to any formal fey deal," she finally began. "At least, there used to be, when such things were taught to keep humans from being fooled. All fey deals come with terms —I suppose unless you make a *geis* with a prince, in which case the rules seem to be a little looser."

Saffron grimaced. Adelard grinned. Baba Yaga continued.

*"The request, the offer, the consequence.* The request, understandably, is what the person proposing the deal wishes; the offer is what they're willing to give for it; and the consequence is what the secondary party will face if they break the terms. In this spell —the request: *proclaim self;* the offer: *shelter soul;* the consequence: *disgrace...* which is quite bold of him, considering he's trying to wake some poor slumbering soul to listen to his inane demands..."

"What could he mean by *'shelter soul'*?" Aodhán asked, still leaning against the wall. "Assuming he's really trying to contact someone long in the mounds."

Adelard adjusted his glasses, gazing at Aodhán in consideration. Before Baba Yaga could answer, the professor steepled his fingers together, pressing them against his lips. Saffron swore he saw Cormac smirk, just for a moment.

"How old are you, Gentle Aodhán?" Adelard asked.

Aodhán scoffed. "Older than you, human—"

"With all due respect—I doubt that," Adelard smiled, before chuckling. His anti-aging ring, a simple gold band on his thumb, shined in the candlelight as if choreographed. "This man's first attempt at calling out to his chosen deceased in Avren's Tapestry Hall, specifically, does not escape me. All these other arid circles reported around Avren are pure nonsense, aren't they, Saffron? You knew that already."

Saffron nodded. "I assume to confuse the high fey who found them. I told Cylvan I thought as much, too."

"That's right. Now—to communicate with someone who has passed, you generally utilize something of personal value to them; something that could ring through the veil between life and death. However, he clearly does not possess such a thing, so one can only guess why he continues the way he does."

"Maybe he thinks he does?" Saffron asked. "The apple, or the yew branches, or... maybe something he picks back up before leaving to try again at the next place."

"Did you see anything when he performed it in Ailinne?"

Saffron thought about it, before shaking his head. "Not that I remember, but, it was dark, and he had me compelled, so I don't know..."

"It's possible, too, that he is not calling out to the lost soul itself—but rather to its memory tapestry," Adelard went on.

"Then why use a spell for summoning the dead?" Aodhán asked. "Surely you witches have spells for finding lost things."

"What makes a soul, Gentle Aodhán?" Adelard asked, eyes flicking up to meet theirs. "Perhaps high fey believe differently, but humans, witches especially, *oracles especially*, believe memory tapestries contain genuine pieces of a person's soul, enough to make them viable. It's the only way they can explain how some tapestries simply refuse to weave, or go blank after a time."

"So he's not trying to talk directly to someone who's dead," Saffron clarified. "He's just trying to find their memory tapestry. And using a very old spell to do it. What for?"

"You will have to ask him yourself, if you ever get the chance again," Adelard smiled wryly. "Who can say why a madman does anything."

"Do you know who he might be trying to find?" Baba Yaga asked Saffron, who bit his lip.

"Well—I assume someone important, if one of his first places to check was in the Tapestry Hall. But whoever it was, clearly wasn't being stored there."

"He's following Queen Proserpina's coronation route," Aodhán muttered. "Is it not obvious?"

"Queen Proserpina?" Saffron asked, turning to them in disbelief. Even Adelard made a small noise like he'd been kicked in the stomach. Perhaps on the surface, that answer made the most sense—but even with someone like Ryder, Saffron could hardly fathom it. What purpose would he have, to seek the veiled queen in that way? When everything he claimed to be doing in favor of liberating humans was in direct opposition of everything she ever did?

"Saffron, you said you've been hearing voices, seeing visions, whenever the spell is performed. Could any of those provide any insight?" Adelard asked, like he was just as eager to figure out something else. Saffron pressed his lips together, nodding. The reminder did nothing to settle his confusion.

"I once... in Ailinne, that is, I... well..." his cheeks went hot, shifting in his chair. "I saw a vision of who I later realized—might have been the queen and Clymeus. I was sitting on a fey lord's lap in the pools; he resembled, erm... well, he resembled Taran mac Delbaith quite a bit, which I know is something people have said before. Er, that Taran resembled Clymeus, that is."

"That doesn't necessarily mean—" Adelard attempted, but Saffron shook his head.

"She—erm, I... in my vision, I had breasts. And long blonde hair. Just like... she did."

Adelard stiffly adjusted his glasses.

"Is that so?" He asked. "Well—have any other visions been so clear?"

"No," Saffron answered right away. "No, nothing as vibrant as that one."

"Why would Saffron be receiving visions when the spell is performed?" Baba Yaga asked, next. "When that man is the one performing it."

"Well—I do wonder if that could also be a clue as to who Ryder is trying to find." Adelard gazed at the drawn arid circle again. "The specific epithet he's chosen to use in this search makes me think... he considers himself somehow significant to the tapestry, which may give us a clue."

"The veil once told me..." Saffron trailed off as all eyes turned to him, eyebrows raised. He cleared his throat. "Erm, it said—that Ryder *'thinks himself a ghost's most precious thing'*... so whatever— erm, *whoever* he's trying to find, maybe he knew them when they were alive?"

"Perhaps," Adelard considered. "He may also think himself significant to them as an ally. Perhaps as the leader of these human rebels. Considering you are also witnessing the visions he summons, perhaps we should not disregard your rowan witch status in that regard, either. Further considering who exactly you witnessed in your visions, and their historical significance, perhaps Ryder is trying to call out to—"

"Another rowan witch?" Saffron blurted, heart fluttering in what he could only describe as a rush of protectiveness.

"You say the veil has refused to oath with him," Adelard said with a nod. "Perhaps this is his attempt to circumvent that. To steal the tapestry of a rowan witch and try to learn their techniques that way. A foolish, insulting effort of perverting the sacred oath... it will only come back to bite him, I can assure you."

"Even if he can manipulate memory threads, it doesn't mean he'd be able to read them in a way that's useful," Aodhán commented, that time with a sprinkling of sincerity.

"Ah—that brings me back to why I asked your age, Gentle Aodhán," Adelard said. "I was curious if you were familiar with the old practice of *woven surrogates.*"

Baba Yaga inhaled sharply, catching Saffron's attention. She paled slightly, staring at Adelard like he would dare speak of something so wicked in her cottage.

"I'm vaguely aware of them," they answered, though something about their tone made it sound like an attempt to hide how much they actually did know. "Woven surrogates fell out of practice with King Elanyl."

"But memory tapestries did not. Ah—that look on your face. You're understanding my concern."

"What are woven surrogates?" Saffron finally asked, and Adelard turned back to him, looking grim.

"An ancient practice no longer observed, as Gentle Aodhán said. Made more controversial than ever once Queen Proserpina died by Verity Holt's hand. Woven surrogates are the bodies of people, given consensually, to be unwoven of their own memories and re-woven with the memories of someone deceased. A form of necromancy, if you will." Adelard sipped his tea, as if biding his time before continuing. "Queen Proserpina, specifically, had nearly a dozen woven surrogates at the time of her reign—at least that we know of. A cloister of volunteers willing to give their lives and bodies to her, should anything happen to her during her great work. They were her first priestesses, in fact—and soon became her first witchhunters. Like a baptismal in her ideals to prepare for when she would need them. Hence why, once Verity Holt killed her, King Elanyl and Queen Una were coronated less than a moment later. Kneeling in the fresh blood of his mother—so no woven surrogate could be made into a new queen to continue the war."

Saffron's ears rang. He pushed past the horrible images, shoving forward to remain in the moment. "Then—then you think Ryder is trying to find a memory tapestry, in order to put it into someone? To bring someone back to life?"

"A rowan witch?" Baba Yaga rasped. "Since the veil will not respond to him? And Saffron has refused as well?"

"Perhaps. From what you've told me, it sounds like the man is in desperate need of some guidance in his cause, after all."

"But who?" Saffron sat forward. "Could he—Verity Holt? Virtue Holt?"

Adelard stiffened, shaking his head quickly. "No, no, neither of those. Verity Holt insisted her memories be left intact when she died. There was no tapestry made for her."

"And Virtue?"

"Who knows where Virtue Holt has gone, in all this time," Adelard answered simply, adjusting his glasses again. "Once King Elanyl was crowned, and after some time to ensure as peaceful a transition of power as possible... well, Virtue took his leave. Perhaps back to the human world, perhaps hoping to find a quiet life somewhere else in Alfidel, considering what the war had done to so many like him. He'd just lost his sister, after all..."

Saffron sat back in his chair again, letting all of the information weave in and out of him like a thousand pricking needles embroidering his skin.

"If Ryder is following the queen's route, then it surely must be someone related to the war," he said. Considering Ryder's motives for freeing humans from beantighehood, or perhaps simply his greed for power being refused by the veil, it made sense.

Adelard's eyes suddenly lingered on the gold pixie ring still on the table between them, slowly reaching out to pinch it. He turned it over in the candlelight, appreciating the detail of the wings, the band.

"Who, indeed..." he whispered, but something about it was heavy, like he knew. Like he had an idea. Rather than sharing it, he just gazed at the ring, brows furrowing the longer he stalled.

"Professor?" Saffron asked, hardly a whisper.

"You know—these rings are no more than veil-touched pixies," Adelard spoke, casual, informative, as if his own mind didn't turn over like Saffron's did. Saffron had to force himself to pay attention, rather than snapping at him to *focus*. "Pixies have such a unique relationship with the veil, including how they are the only known wild-fey things that can create micro-tears for passage between worlds. Some say they are even physical embodiments of the veil, itself, due to their mischievous nature... the way their colors reflect every shade of the light-spectrum... the fact you will never find any explanation for where they come from, how they are born... The Dagda's freckles, or perhaps their tears... jewels from their crown, given life by their innate magic..."

Adelard returned the ring to the table, hardly making a noise —though it sounded like crashing glass in Saffron's ringing ears.

"After getting them drunk on wild fairy fruits, you pluck their wings," he went on. "Then, with a little fire, and a little luck, you can forge their veil-magic into rings like these. To force the veil to bend to your whims, whether oathed to it or not. That is, until the veil realizes what you're doing, and responds. You said the veil refuses to commune with Ryder Kyteler, didn't you? It's no wonder he's resorted to such old tricks to fool anyone who doesn't know any better."

"Old tricks?"

Adelard tapped a finger against the table, through the loop of the ring.

"Pixie rings were first used by rebels during the War of the Veil. The means of forging them was kept a well-guarded secret, knowing there would be consequences for anyone who used them without the veil's consent."

Saffron's heart lifted and spun. In the back of his mind, where he was certain Taran had sat listening, the wolf let out a breath like he'd been holding it all along. Even Copper had long wandered into the kitchen, ears perked as he sat by Adelard's feet to listen.

"Did the rebels have consent?" Saffron asked, barely a whisper.

"Oh, yes," Adelard sighed with the weight of a thousand years —and Saffron's heart thrummed, like he was only just making a connection that should have been obvious from the start. "Verity and Virtue were the first human-human bridge oathed through the veil. They had quite the unique relationship with it, too. Verity, especially. Just like two mischievous pixies themselves..."

Saffron wanted to ask—he wanted to know more. He wanted to know exactly how well Adelard knew all those things he explained, personally, even first-hand—but the professor continued before Saffron could, wiping any and all whimsy that dared tease the back of his thoughts.

"From what you've described to me, Saffron, there is only one thing I can say with near-certainty." He flattened his hand over the paper donning his scribbled notes, and took a deep breath. "Virtue Holt made sure every pixie ring used by humans fighting in that war were destroyed once it was done, with a promise to the veil that they would never be used to twist it up ever again." He pointed at the ring, and Saffron's heart thudded. "For this man to know the significance of the Kyteler name enough to steal it for himself; for him to know how to ally himself with witchhunters once only loyal to the queen herself; for him to know how to both make and use pixie rings to rip open the veil to his will... for even the veil to know better than to oath with him despite his practice —I can say, with certainty, he is much, much older than any of us could have ever guessed. Much older—and far more powerful, more *dangerous,* than simply a rebel sowing havoc in Avren."

28
———

# THE REMAINS

Saffron managed a few hours of sleep that night—only to be wide awake again the moment the sky lightened through the attic window.

At least that night, there had been no screaming to wake him. His restlessness was his own; he couldn't even blame the hard floor of the attic under his back, or the dusty rafters overhead, or the occasional chatter as night-shift beantighes woke their day-shift counterparts and stole their pre-warmed beds in the early morning. Saffron's restlessness was bone deep, only sinking its teeth with more fervor after the conversation with Adelard the night before.

Not even considering Saffron's constant, low-burning worry of what Cylvan must be thinking since he left. What he would think once they found one another again, and Saffron told him everything he'd learned. Specifically—that there was no way under Ériu's plucking harp Saffron would be going back to Avren again anytime soon, after what they'd determined of Ryder's intentions.

Fresh air wafted through the attic window cracked open over the back yard, and Saffron finally lifted his head from the patch-work pillow when he heard the distinct sound of buzzing wings hovering around the gap. Three shimmering spots hummed inside, going first to Fiachra perched and tucked into her wing, to Copper lying on his back between Saffron and Aodhán on their bedrolls, then lastly to Saffron. He had to bite back a laugh as they immediately crawled into his hair, pulling at the gem in his engagement ring and the amethyst in his pendant. Peeping and squeaking and pinching his cheeks, they attempted to tug on his eyelashes to steal for themselves, artfully dodging every one of his swiping hands to try and knock them away.

Kicking himself free of the blankets, Saffron moved silently as to not wake Aodhán or the fox lying like a motionless corpse on the bedroll alongside him. Gathering his doublet and cloak, he paused upon spotting a familiar sight resting on a box in the corner—his old roaming boots, still caked with mud around the bottom soles from the last time they'd been taken into the wood. Biting his lip, he left his fancy fey-made boots in favor of the others, holding them in one hand while pulling up the hatch and slipping through with only his newest pixies companions to see him go.

Sitting on the bottommost step of the main stairs, Saffron pulled on his boots, then his doublet, shaking his head when Baba Yaga offered him something to eat. He just kissed her cheek like he used to every morning, telling her not to let Aodhán worry when they woke up and he was gone. Asking she keep Copper close by as well, as he wasn't sure how much actual survival instinct the beast had. He was only going for a walk in the woods, he'd be back soon enough. He'd have his best guard dog with him, anyway.

That made Baba narrow her eyes, but she decided against arguing, just sighing and muttering about how she'd put Aodhán back to work the moment they came down the stairs, and would even think of something for the fox to do if Saffron really wished to be left alone in the woods. He hurried out before the old witch could think of any more tasks to assign to him at the last second, too.

Finger-combing his hair as he left Cottage Wicklow, Fiachra swept down from the attic window with a number of complaints to him for leaving her behind. He scratched under her beak in apology, before throwing her back into the sky where she tumbled before catching the wind and soaring. Meanwhile, Saffron double-checked his shoulder bag for his sketchbook and the pouch stuffed with wild fairy fruits from the satyr borough. Feeling only a little bad for lying to his henmother. It hadn't been an *entire* lie, at least—he did technically have to *walk* to the Kyteler Ruins. It would just take a bit longer than expected. He might be gone all day. He'd apologize profusely as soon as he returned back home.

Wandering up the length of the iron fence, Saffron appreciated the red rowan berries weighing down the trees right on the other side, smirking as he knew how the overburdened branches felt. The pixies followed him, as he went, making him laugh as they jumped from iron prong to prong ahead of him, wings fluttering as they turned to see if he was watching.

He didn't recognize them as ones he'd named in the past, but they seemed to recognize him all the same, either as the impatient human who used to tromp around while waiting for his prince to call him to Avren, or maybe even further back when he was the human who brought honeycomb in exchange for rifling around in their stolen treasures.

*Daffodil. Chartreuse. Cherry. Copper,* he named them one by one, out of old habit.

"Don't tell my friend you share his name," he said to the golden-orange creature perched on his finger, attempting to pry the emerald jewel from his engagement ring. "He might eat you out of jealousy."

Rather than taking his normal path down the fence straight to the nearest gate, Saffron took the long way around, allowing him a chance to see every part of Beantighe Village he'd missed so much while away. First passing the celebration field, then appreciating the new paint on the exterior of the gathering hall, smiling to himself at how the number of individually-painted accents had grown since he last saw it. Some beantighes drew flowers, others butterflies and bugs, others pixies or unicorns or other wild fey. All signed in scraggly attempts at their own names, many drawn in flowing cursive by one of the henmothers who knew how to write. A bittersweet sight, a bittersweet reminder that he'd always made excuses for why he didn't ever have time to add his own to the wall. At the time, not knowing how to tell anyone that, within a few more weeks, none of them would remember he existed once he vanished off to Avren.

*"Icarus, come."*

Saffron knew the Agate Wood inside and out, but not what went on while he was away. He didn't know if something shadowy had moved in, he didn't know if something dangerous crept around because there was no longer at least one beantighe wandering around in the daylight.

Never would that same beantighe have thought that, one day, he'd be back there with the wolf of the Agate Wood by his side, either. A wolf who perked up and stretched his legs with a yawn like a cat in the sun as soon as his paws touched the fresh earth. But Taran made it easier for Saffron to relax, even in a place he knew so well. To not have to continually glance over his shoulder or jump at every unexpected noise, especially with Ryder on the loose. Especially not knowing where, exactly, Ryder would be until his next anticipated event in Vjallrod. Especially after what Adelard had told him the night before—that Ryder Kyteler *might be someone older and more powerful than any of them could have anticipated.*

God—Saffron wished he knew what that meant. He wished he had more time to speak with the professor about it, maybe even in private, in case there were things the man didn't wish to discuss in front of Aodhán, or even Baba Yaga. He fiddled with the hematite wand from his bag as he thought about it, rubbing his thumb up and down the side, pressing it into the slightly-flared tip.

"Do you have anything to say about that?" He asked, speaking aloud for the first time since summoning Taran to his side. Taran perked up, glancing over his shoulder, eyes like dark rubies in the dull morning light. Not yet raining, but the smell on the air told Saffron it would be soon enough.

"No," he answered. "But I have been thinking about it."

Saffron rolled his eyes. He should have expected no less from such a proud beast.

"What about anything else Adelard shared?" he went on, following the wolf over a downed tree, enjoying every moment his hand pressed into the soft moss growing on the bark, or when the heels of his familiar boots squished into the loamy earth on the other side. He never expected exactly how much he'd miss wearing those old leather boots, formed so perfectly to his feet it was like being held in the embrace of a life-long lover.

"I think it's interesting how much Adelard seemed to know about human practices during the great war," Taran answered after some consideration. "Perhaps he thinks he's keeping his secret well, but it's obvious, isn't it?"

"That he may have been involved, somehow...?" Saffron asked with a little nod. "I thought about that too. Though I can't imagine someone so meek and, well—*anxious* being anything more than, I don't know... a messenger, maybe? Or just a rebel on the side? I guess I don't know much about the goings-on of the war, or what exactly humans were doing while fighting in it."

"That's on purpose."

"Wouldn't want any current-day humans getting ideas, I suppose," Saffron chuckled bitterly. "But the joke's on them—humans are figuring it out all on their own."

"Maybe asking the professor for a little more information wouldn't hurt, in that sense."

"What's this, Taran mac Delbaith encouraging me to engage in treasonous behavior?" Saffron gasped with a dramatic lilt, and the wolf growled in exasperation. Chuckling, Saffron went on: "Maybe. If we get another chance before..." he trailed off, unsure. Before *what?* He pushed the thought away. He'd worry about that later.

They made their way through the overcast wood in mostly silence, only the occasional comment passed between them, though otherwise Saffron just tried to enjoy himself. He breathed in as much of the familiar air as he could hold in his lungs; he watched as Fiachra swept in and out of the trees, seeming to feel none of the same apprehension in such an open sky as she normally did in Avren. The pixies flit this way and that closer to earth, either trying to steal beads off Saffron's doublet or bringing him wild berries in attempt to trade. He just traded berries back, though, plucked from bushes as he passed without the pixies noticing. They always squealed and threw tantrums when they realized.

Approaching the outer gates of the Kyteler Ruins was familiar enough from all the trips he'd made on his own in the months waiting for Cylvan's call, but that time there was the added irritation of the beast walking ahead of him. Taran, who was tangible but incorporeal, who was weak to yew branches as much as Saffron was, whose thick fur still twitched in irritation as they approached the iron gates surrounding the old school. Who snorted in agitation and rubbed his nose against the ground like the air burned to breathe, ears laying flat against his head the entire time Saffron walked down the length of the iron fence to the same gap in the bars where he'd once snuck in and out with Sunbeam.

When Taran was too large to pass through in his wolf form, Saffron had to command him away, then summon him back on the other side, which was a clear hit to the dog's ego as he walked ahead with his head bowed and snout wrinkled in annoyance.

Following the same trail through the trees he'd also learned from Sunbeam, they emerged on the edge of the clearing on the other side, able to see where the buildings stood clustered together in a blanket of mist. By then, Saffron had gone quiet; Taran had gone quiet. The pixies had fluttered off to mind their business elsewhere, leaving the abandoned grounds silent except sunsingers and robins and crows that clustered on the sinking beams of the old buildings. Even Fiachra soon lighted down on Saffron's shoulder, like the openness of the clearing was finally too broad for her to comfortably explore.

Taran was the one to break the silence as they reached the perimeter of the buildings, voice like a shout despite spoken normally. Saffron would never get accustomed to constant, ringing silence of that place, even after visiting so many times.

"I'm surprised any of it still stands, even after Asche burned more."

"Asche mostly burned down the library," Saffron said. "But maybe the fire just made all the stone stronger, like after the first time."

*The first time*, words that struck him more than he expected. It was different that morning, and not because Saffron had brought the wolf as his companion by his side. That morning, Saffron understood better than ever what it meant to open a veil in the middle of the library where students could flee for safety. He could imagine exactly what they may have been running from, witchhunters draped in black veils and carrying bottles of silver liquid that would burn them from the inside.

"That's where I broke my leg," Saffron said, attempting to lighten his own mood as they passed the queen's collapsed chapel. "Remember when Asche dragged me out of the ruins and you left me on the side of the road?"

Taran exhaled with a sharp sound.

"I recall no such thing."

"You were definitely coming back to kill me. Because you were tired of my shit. But Cylvan reached me first, so you couldn't."

"Oh, if only."

Saffron chuckled again, and Taran gave him a wary look, before flattening his ears.

"There are many things I look back on that I…"

"Regret?"

"Am ashamed of," he growled. "But not out of guilt for my cruelty—only because it's embarrassing, to be reminded how mad I'd gone during it all. Trying to maintain my control on Cylvan, I would have done anything. Even make a futile deal with a stupid beantighe… Danu strike me down in all my arrogance."

"Who, me?" Saffron really laughed that time, hurrying to catch up as Taran stalked off in irritation. He put a hand on Taran's back, petting him like a dog needing comfort, and Taran snapped teeth at Saffron's hand before hurrying up ahead. Saffron hurried after him, until they were both running full-speed down the center of the ruins, Saffron practically howling with laughter as Taran easily outpaced him.

REACHING THE DOORS TO THE BURNED-OUT LIBRARY, Saffron breathed in the smell of the charred wood and stone with the same familiarity as the woods all around them. Even with the ceiling gone, the interior gutted, the shelves along the walls hardly more than skeletal bones after Asche's fire ate away at them, that place still brought Saffron a sense of peace.

"I know this has been your problem from the start," Saffron said as they climbed the creaking stairs to the upper floor of the building. Fiachra took off from his shoulder again to explore the burned shelves, wings swirling up black dust whenever she swooped too close. "But do you think you could try and sniff out any wild fairy fruits amongst the bushels here?"

Taran's upper lip curled, but he said nothing, just turning his nose to the floor to do as he was asked. Saffron, meanwhile, breathed in another lungful of the acrid air, before approaching the wide circle in the floorboards. Partially destroyed by the daurae's flames, though even the parts swallowed beneath charred wood were just barely visible. Saffron spent a long moment studying every arch of the massive circle, like hundreds of times before. That time, though, he specifically scouted for the knock-rings that should have been at the bottom of the epithet, like Ryder once told him was required for all veil circles. The one at his feet lacked anything like that.

Removing his sketchbook, he crouched down on the balls of his feet, snapping away a piece of long, burnt wood fibre from a nearby floorboard, and used it as his drawing utensil.

Taking his time, he walked the perimeter, drawing every line one after another. Some areas were easier to transcribe, others took a little more focus, some were so deeply burned he had to guess a few hatchmarks over others.

"There are no fruits anywhere in this library," Taran informed him flatly an hour later, approaching where Saffron was crouched alongside another heavily-burned section.

"Alright," Saffron said without looking away from his page.

"Isn't this where you made your oath as a rowan witch?" Taran asked. "Perhaps it's not a circle to pass through the veil at all, but to oath with it."

"Maybe," Saffron mumbled in consideration. But would Sunbeam have spent so much time working on it if that was the case? Wouldn't she have been able to tell the difference? Even the ghosts of the ruins, the beannighe-headmistress herself, said it'd been used to send students to safety—so what was the truth?

Saffron swallowed back against the lump in his throat. Another thought occurred to him, as he reached out to trace his fingers down the charred lines. Technically, it had been that burnt when he made his oath. The circle wasn't entirely destroyed. Could he beseech the veil again, like he did the first time, or like he did at the satyr borough, to ask for its help? Would it listen to him if he asked from that same place they once shook hands?

Saffron closed his eyes, pausing a moment before tucking his sketchbook away. In the same motion, he pulled the small collection of wild fairy fruits he still had in his pouch, dumping them into his hand.

It was worth a shot.

He followed the same order of movement as in the satyr borough; eating the berries, closing his eyes, allowing them to infiltrate every inch of him. Imagining their natural veil magic kissing the rowan in his veins, combining with it, flooding him quietly and smoothly until it traveled from his heart out to his feet, his fingers, up the back of his neck, and finally—into his eyes. Blinking them open, he knew right away the halos of undulating color meant he was fairy-drunk, just as much as in the stripped henge.

In front of him, though, there were no clear remnants of a brutal tear through the veil had been in the Fall Court; there were no shimmering cracks in the air, no buzz of poorly-stitched gaps repaired by the veil itself after being rent apart. There was nothing, except the slightest glow of pink magic in the edges of the epithet burned into the floor.

In his drunkenness, Saffron could hear the voice of the bean-nighe speaking to him, instructing him on what to do next. To beseech the veil, to hear its voice. To call out to it.

Rising to his feet, Taran observed him in silent question as he began unbuttoning the front of his doublet.

*"Into the mounds the way you came; stripped of your magic, both the same..."* He mumbled to himself, recalling that spell with more clarity than anything else he'd learned before or since. Stripping off his doublet, he kicked off his shoes, next, then his pants, though left his undershirt on against the chill. *"Devour the flesh, the root of the other; breath to breath, exchange your charter..."*

He stepped over the outer edge of the circle, moving with an uneven, drunken gait into the center, where he stood staring down at his feet.

*"Exchanging a look, a hand, a kiss; whichever you choose, share in your bliss..."*

The last time, he'd touched himself. Drawing himself to climax, his bliss, on his own, as Cylvan wasn't there to help him. Cylvan was the reason he did any of it, trapped in Avren at Taran's side. Saffron had done it all by himself once before, and the understanding that he was there all by himself, a second time —made his stomach sink. Made hot tears threaten to drip over his eyes as the emotions inside him swirled untethered in the buzz of the fruits.

"I'm not here to make another oath," he said out loud instead, lifting his eyes again to search the rim of the epithet. "I just want to speak with you. I don't know any other way."

To his surprise, the air shifted in response. Even Taran took a slight step away from the edge of the circle, hairs on his back standing up like he could sense it.

*You always go to such lengths,* the veil hummed, but it wasn't teasing. It sounded—agitated. *You only call to me when you need something, witch. What is it this time?*

The harsh tone made every plea halt at the back of Saffron's throat. Suddenly confused, even embarrassed, to be standing there in only his undershirt, not exactly sure what he wished to ask for. If the veil could take him straight to where his friends resided in *London*, would it? But then what would he do—half-naked, in a place he'd never been?

"Where did this circle once lead?" he asked instead. "I know it's where I made my oath with you, but I've also been told it was—"

*A place called Dùn Èideann, in Alba. This circle was delivered by two bridgekeepers. Only they can revive it.*

Saffron didn't know what he was expecting, but the clear Gaeilge sound of those words piqued his interest.

"Is *Alba* anywhere close to a place called '*London*'?"

The veil shifted; it swirled around him, circling him like a fox circling prey, trying to decide if it was worth the effort to catch. It made Saffron's heart pound, chills racing up and down his skin as the sensation burrowed and plucked at a deep-rooted human fear inside of him.

"What's wrong?" he asked. "Have I done something wrong?"

*Are you so daft?*

Something within his shoulder bag moved, catching Saffron's

attention. From the bottom of the leather sack, the hematite wand suddenly rolled out—then bolted upright, shuddering before sliding forward. The tip of it carved a line in the wood floor as it moved, emitting a shrill sound as it approached then circled around Saffron once, twice, three times.

*You nearly had that man in Ailinne. I told you right where to find him, yet where is he now? Who knows what he may do next. Who knows where he may tear me open next!*

*You know how to pass through the veil,* it continued, harsh and cold. *You have been told. You have the tools to do it yourself. Why must you continue to bother me for answers? Are you such a coward? If I'd known my only witch was so useless, I would have chosen someone else to help me.*

Saffron stared at the floor, where the hematite wand had come to a sudden halt in front of him. There was no more air in his lungs, like he'd been hit in the chest. The words rang in his ears, loud and echoing, only made worse as the veil used his own voice to utter them.

*You know what to do. You know how to do it. You wish to go to 'London,' do you?* The wand stiffened again, before circling Saffron once more, but that time with two knock-circles at the bottom. Saffron gasped, tripping backward, out of the center in an instant.

*Coward!* The veil shrieked, loud enough that Saffron threw his hands over his ears. *Beseech me for nothing else, bumbling malingerer! Arrogant charlatan! You promised me so much, you promised me protection! I promised you all you ever needed—and yet you hesitate! You watch as I am torn apart, too frightened to do a thing! I will brook no more false promises from you! Selfish! Arrogant! Impertinent witch!*

Saffron stumbled fully out of the circle, crashing to the floor and kicking away from the edge of it as the hematite wand dug trenches into the wood again, tearing in fast circles around and around as the veil shredded all that remained of the ancient epithet. And all Saffron could do was watch in horror, in shame, in confusion—in gut-wrenching heartbreak, as the insults thrown at him repeated endlessly in his fairy-inebriated mind.

Only once the hematite wand bounced off a piece of the uplifted floor, thrown across the room and out of the circle, did Saffron finally snap out of his agonized trance.

He hurried for his clothes. Saying nothing, keeping his eyes low. He pulled on his pants, his boots, his doublet, not bothering to button up the front before throwing the bag over his shoulder. He nearly left the wand behind, but in a final moment of uncertainty, swept it off the floor before hurrying toward the exit.

Taran followed closely behind, asking what happened, what was wrong—but Saffron felt like he was being turned inside out. The fairy fruits made it hard to think. Hard to walk. Hard to know what was real and what wasn't.

He just wanted to go home. He wanted to go *home*. To his bed in Cottage Wicklow. Where Baba Yaga would brew him some tea, where he'd be able to lie down and sleep, to disappear beneath the blankets where there was nothing, nothing, nothing, except the smell of linen and baked bread and the Agate Wood and nothing, nothing, nothing else—

He heard his name called. As soon as he stumbled through the iron fence around the old school, he heard it loud and clear— someone calling out to him, like all those times before, loud and echoing off the inside of his head. He didn't know how much more he could take of it. Especially when, that time—the voice was Cylvan's.

29

———

## THE BEANTIGHE

"Saffron, slow down—!" Taran attempted, having to squeeze himself through the bars of the fence as Saffron wasn't paying attention. He only hurried without stopping, heart pounding in his ears, vision humming in front of him from the remnants of the fairy fruits.

The sound of Cylvan calling out to him—was just his imagination. Just his drunkenness, just a trick of the old wood or the veil itself as it continued its cruel tirade against him. Calling him a coward, calling him a fool—but what did it know? Such an ancient, all-knowing, omnipotent thing—yet it could barely grasp the fear Saffron held for it in his heart. A fear he'd held since he was a child; since he'd been traded through the veil by his human parents when he was a baby, unwanted, exchanged in a deal between them and Luvon; those same parents that, the one time Saffron did return to the human world to see them, held a gun to his head and told Luvon to get Saffron out of their sight.

Saffron never actually wanted to go there—if Ryder hadn't taken his friends, Saffron would have been content to never think about the human world for the rest of his life. He didn't make his oath with the veil in order to be able to pass through it—he made it to become powerful and cunning enough to keep Cylvan safe.

What did the veil know? What did the veil know about him, about anything at all?

Despite the spinning of his vision, Saffron managed to find his way to the overgrown road leading up to the ruins—just as a black horse galloped by, nearly crashing into him as he stumbled from the underbrush at the same time. Reeling back, the horse did the same, eliciting a shout from its rider—followed by another exclamation of Saffron's name.

Saffron met Cylvan's eyes, staring at him in disbelief, or—anger. It may have been anger, pure fury, Saffron didn't know, he wasn't seeing clearly, he wasn't thinking right, everything was glowing and undulating, his thoughts were thick like syrup and he could see every flutter and sparkle of the crackling veil and opulence in every direction. All he knew was—that look, on the rider's face, made his heart stop. A rush of fear—knowing it couldn't be Cylvan. Knowing it had to be a trick of the wood. Some wild fey that could glamour itself with a familiar face; it wouldn't be the first time. Beantighes had often gone missing at night, claiming to hear the voice of a friend calling to them. Lost, in the darkness.

"Saffron!" The rider shouted again as Saffron tripped back-ward, leaping back into the woods— *"Saffron, be still!"*

His movement ceased. Mid-step, making the muscles in his legs tremble. Behind him, Taran growled, circling around Saffron impatiently before turning back to the person who left their horse and approached.

"I'm not in any mood for this," Cylvan announced in exasperation, reaching for Saffron's arm—only to step back again when Taran snarled, ears flattened and baring his teeth. "Out of my way, Taran!"

The way he knew the wolf's name—perhaps it really was his raven prince, come to find him.

"Keep your hands off him," Taran growled in return. "Not until you've calmed down, Cylvan."

"Calmed—!" Cylvan barked. *"Me!* Do you have any idea—!

You will not tell me what I *can and cannot* do with *my own harmonious king,* you dog!"

Taran moved and snarled again, standing between Saffron and Cylvan, as Saffron was forced to stare into the woods while the exchange happened behind his back. Then—maybe it really was Cylvan. Maybe Cylvan really had come to Morrígan looking for him, it wasn't a trick of the wood, it was—his prince. His prince, who was furious—who said Saffron's name with such thick venom, like Saffron was a thorn in his flesh he wished to pull.

He knew Cylvan would be angry when they met again—Saffron had anticipated, from the start, that Cylvan would not be thrilled to see him when they crossed paths again. And Saffron had been prepared to apologize, to explain himself, to do everything he could to reassure Cylvan to *why*—but never once did he expect his raven to compel him into stillness. Into silence. Just like Ryder had, so many times.

Bile turned in his stomach, up the back of his throat. Taran and Cylvan continued arguing at Saffron's back, as Saffron just fought to regain control of his body. Fighting for the feeling in his fingers, first, just like every other time. His fingers, his toes, his hands, his feet—until finally a wash of life tingled through his muscles, and he slumped forward into the step he'd been in the middle of taking.

*"Saffron—!"* Cylvan dared try again, but Taran lunged and rammed his head into Cylvan's chest, knocking him back and halting the command. The fact he would try it a second time made Saffron want to vomit. He wished to run again, to disappear between the trees, but instead—he turned. His entire body shook with a cocktail of embarrassment and a further brush of fear, something he'd hadn't felt while facing Cylvan dé Tuatha dé Danann in a long, long time.

Cylvan finally met Saffron's eyes, that time clearly seeing the pink glow of them, indicating Saffron's inebriation. But rather than catching his anger for Saffron's instinct to flee, understanding why he might have—instead, his handsome face only contorted into a further rage.

"Why would you do this?" he asked, voice harsh but flat, in a clear attempt to keep his anger at bay. "You agreed to return to Avren with me—why humiliate me like this instead? I had to demand they stop the train—in the middle of the godsforsaken Fall Court! I had to tell them—it was so I could chase down my disobedient beantighe servant!" That time, spoken through his teeth, between sharp breaths as he trembled with fury. Saffron's heart continued to twist in rhythm, with every gasp Cylvan had to take in order to keep his composure. Whatever he had left. Had he ever seen the prince so angry?

"I—" Saffron attempted, but Cylvan continued:

"And here I find you! By yourself in the woods, wandering the ruins! Performing veil magic, eating wild fairy fruits! By yourself! Are you really so *careless*, Saffron! Do you have a death wish! Don't you think I've lost enough, already! If something had happened to you, who would have known! I would never have known where to even begin looking for you, gods*damnit! How can you be so godsdamned selfish—!*"

"How am I the selfish one!" Saffron shouted back, startling even Taran with the shrillness of it. "How dare I—? How dare you accuse me of being *careless*! Of being *selfish*! When all I'm trying to do is help! I'm trying to find my friends, too! Not just Asche! Or have you forgotten all about them! Ryder took them first—Ryder took them first just to control me, damnit, and you haven't brought them up once in all of this! And you call *me* selfish—!"

"Asche is more important than your friends!" Cylvan shouted, nostrils flared. *"The Daurae of Alfidel is more important than a handful of beantighes!"*

Saffron stared at Cylvan, who stared back, eyes wide and breathing heavily. Swelling hot with emotion, Saffron didn't know if he wanted to cry, or scream, or throw punches, paralyzed where he stood as his lip trembled.

He looked down at the fine fey doublet he wore, hands shaking as he suddenly wrenched it off over his head. Yanking the amethyst pendant with it, and throwing both in Cylvan's face. Cylvan swore at him, demanding to know what his problem was, but the words caught when Saffron next yanked the emerald engagement ring from his finger—and threw that at the prince, too.

"There," he said, voice cracking. "Now you have no reason to come looking for me again, either."

Saffron turned and rushed into the trees. Cylvan called out to him again, but Taran must have kept him at bay. Saffron ran faster than any enchantments could catch him; he ran blindly into the foliage, knowing he'd find his way home eventually. Just wanting to run, wanting to get away. Just wanting to go home. Where Baba Yaga would brew him tea. Where could lie down and disappear. Where there was nothing.

REACHING BEANTIGHE VILLAGE AS THE SUN WAS beginning to set, Saffron shivered from being soaked through in the rain, especially without his doublet to protect him. Saoirse's horse was visible in the front yard of Cottage Wicklow, but Cylvan didn't appear to be back yet. Saffron had the briefest worry that the prince had gotten himself lost—before it was overtaken with another bitter thought of *good*. He wouldn't be lost for long, even if he was. He hoped Cylvan was as cold and miserable as he was.

Sneaking in through the back door, he was silent as any other beantighe would be, though his henmother standing in the entryway to the kitchen still sensed him. Baba Yaga threw him a look as the sound of Aodhán and Saoirse's voices came from the parlor, and Saffron quickly shook his head to imply he didn't wish to be known.

Baba Yaga's lips pursed, but she nodded, before subtly tipping her head to indicate he could sneak through the back hallway.

There was nothing but her own bedroom that way, but he didn't question it. He just wanted to get out of his wet clothes, he wanted to hide away somewhere dark and quiet.

Stripping naked in Baba Yaga's quiet bedroom, Saffron scrounged around in his henmother's things until he found one of her old nightshirts, pulling it on over his head in favor of something dry to wear. He crawled into her old bed and burrowed beneath the blankets, still able to hear the low mumbling of the parlor conversation, though nothing of the specific words exchanged. Perhaps that was why he didn't cry—he worried they would overhear him. He didn't want to be known.

That was—until an incessant scratching came at the closed door, and Saffron had no choice but to crawl from his warm hole to open it, thinking it to be Baba's fat orange cat demanding entry. Instead, it was another similarly orange beast—Copper, who whined the instant Saffron appeared, throwing up his paws and planting them on Saffron's chest in question. Saffron hurried his friend into the room, where Copper leapt up onto the bed and sniffed around the tousled blankets, making room when Saffron returned to the place he'd carved in his shape. The moment Copper nestled down under the blanket next to him, warm and soft and whimpering more in question, Saffron couldn't stop the emotions from swelling until they spilled over—and he pulled his fox-friend close, silently crying into his thick fur.


Eventually, Saoirse and Aodhán's voices faded, and a knock came at the bedroom door. Saffron peeked his swollen, tear-stained eyes out from under the blankets as Baba Yaga opened it. She took one look at him, clucking her tongue and closing the door behind her. Approaching to take his face and push hair from his eyes, kissing his forehead, his cheeks. She asked what happened, but Saffron just shook his head. He didn't want to talk about it.

Preparing a bedroll on the floor for him to sleep through the night, Saffron never complained, glad at least to know he wouldn't take the old woman's bed from her. Baba Yaga brought him a warm cup of tea without being asked, charmed with an arid circle that read *peace* and *restful sleep.*

He curled up around Copper who spiraled under the blanket alongside him, like a personal hearth to keep him warm even as the rain continued on the other side of the dark window.

Knowing Saoirse and Aodhán had gone out to look for Cylvan, Saffron thought he'd be able to close his eyes and disappear. To let the magic of the cup, whether real or not, take him and do whatever it pleased until sunrise. He would decide what to do next, then. He wouldn't think about it until then. Nothing, nothing, nothing—that was all he wanted.

But then a loud, demanding knock came at the cottage's front door, and Saffron held his breath. He didn't otherwise move, just staring at the wall in the darkness and holding Copper close. Listening.

"I'm here for Saffron," Cylvan's voice came, clearly audible even over the noise of the rain. "I know he's here."

"Saffron will return to Avren if he sees fit," Baba Yaga responded, firmly. Saffron tried to imagine Cylvan's expression in response to that—but he couldn't. For the first time, he wasn't sure what Cylvan would do, how he would react. Like every impression he'd ever had of his prince had been wiped, warped, with that one look of seething resentment he'd worn.

"You tell him to come out here and speak for himself, like the proper fey lord he promised to be for me." Cylvan's response finally came, cold and cutting. Saffron's heart thumped painfully, and he pressed a hand to his chest. He didn't want to.

"I've already told you my peace on the matter," Baba replied. "Now, get out of my house. Before I show you exactly why your great-grandmother was so afraid of people like me."

Even Copper shivered slightly.

"How dare you speak to me like that," Cylvan hissed, clearly in disbelief. "After everything I've done for him—!"

The sharp, distinct sound of a hand striking flesh rang out through the cottage, and Saffron petrified in an instant. His chest ached. His heart pounded in his ears, making it hard to hear. Worried tears burned in the backs of his eyes, terrified of what might come next—

"You will not darken my doorstep again, you vile thing," Baba Yaga hissed, the air in the house shuddering. "You dare come making demands for that poor boy to bend himself backwards further than he already has, for the sake of your ego—but when was the last time you looked at him? He comes to me bruised, beaten, exhausted, on the verge of collapse, after everything he's already sacrificed for you. Worse than I've ever seen him—after I trusted you to take care of him in Avren. Worse than after years of slaving as a beantighe. A handful of months away, and your darkness has already consumed him practically to the bone. Ériu curse you for taking someone so soft and patient—someone who cared for you so much, and breaking him like you have. Get out of my house, or there really will be no heir to the damned throne once I'm finished."

Saffron pressed his hand into his mouth. Suffocating himself as the emotion ebbed in and out of his body, agonizing and leaving trenches where needly fingers scraped through his insides. Hating the feeling of wishing to keep Baba Yaga from saying such things—too scared to go out and stop her. Wanting to remain hidden, not wanting Cylvan to know where to find him. Just a little bit longer. He just wanted to be alone, for a little bit longer. Alone beneath the blankets, on the floor of his henmother's bedroom, curled up tight with the warm, protective body of his friend pressed into his back.

A long, distinctly silent pause followed Baba Yaga's voice. Saffron almost thought Cylvan had turned and left without a sound, barely pulling his hand from his mouth, just a moment before an answer came.

"Alright," Cylvan said, sharp and in finality—before breaking slightly, with the words the followed. "Then—keep him here.

Where I know you will take care of him. At the very least—just—tell him I didn't mean what I said. And keep him out of the woods on his own. It isn't safe."

There was another pause, joined by the softest whispering Saffron couldn't make out. Baba Yaga said nothing else after, followed by the sound of the door closing. The old henmother sighed quietly, before the sound of the creaking floor followed her into the kitchen, where she sank into one of the chairs in silence.

Saffron couldn't hold it back any longer. He cried, curling up tighter on himself as he did everything he could to suppress the noise. But Copper surely heard; Baba Yaga surely heard. Even the beantighes lying in their beds upstairs might have heard him, crying into his hand. Unsure where the sound came from. Likely assuming it rattled from some sad ghost haunting their cottage. One of many lost human souls that wandered the Agate Wood—left there by centuries of the same hubris what had just stormed out.

*"Cylvan is a fool,"* the beast in the back of Saffron's mind whispered.

Copper tucked his head into the dip of Saffron's side. Fiachra purred and chirped softly, nipping at Saffron's hand once again pressed tightly to his mouth.

For the first time in what felt like ages—Saffron fully allowed the miserable emotions to storm in and out of him, until there was nothing left to ravage. Until, finally, he was cursed to sleep as deeply as the dead.

# 30

# THE ANIMAL

Baba Yaga's spell worked. Saffron slept until he ceased to exist, dreaming only faintly and briefly of the sound of knocking doors. Knock knock, knock knock, melting in and out each and every time, until Saffron didn't know which was the sound of a fist on a door, or the veil being torn asunder.

The thing to finally, fully rouse him, long after the sun had already risen on the other side of the window—was a familiar voice speaking assertively from the other side of the bedroom door.

*"I mean no disrespect! But I really must insist! I just want to know he's alright!"*—followed by the sound of Baba Yaga's door opening. Sionnach stood looking pale and apprehensive on the other side, staring as Saffron lazily lifted his head, hair wild and an impression of the pillow printed on his cheek. Next to him, Copper perked up as well, stretching his legs long before yawning with a broad array of sharp teeth.

"Saffron!" Sionnach exclaimed, racing into the room. They shoved Copper out of the way, throwing their arms around Saffron who was still trying to reattach his ghost to his bones. He at least had enough wherewithal to hug his friend back. "Gods, I've been worried sick! About *both* of you!" They grabbed Copper by the snout next, making the fox writhe and roll around in protest. "How could you just leave like that! And then Cylvan threw such a fit on a train, scared everyone half to death! It's only because Saoirse thought to tell us anything just before she left with him that we even knew how to come find you! God*damn* you, you—! You *witch!*"

Despite every other emotion coursing through him, summoned back to the surface by the mere mention of Cylvan's name—Saffron still smiled weakly. He hugged his friend again tightly, stealing their warmth, their liveliness, their energy.

"I'm sorry for worrying you," he said, and Sionnach's tense body loosened. They slumped back into his arms, holding him again and sighing.

"Don't do it ever again," they whispered. "Or I'll never forgive you."

"Alright," Saffron breathed. "I promise."

Pulling on his dried clothes, he followed them from Baba Yaga's room out into the kitchen, where Saffron was surprised to find Maeve also sitting at the kitchen table with a cup of tea— only to be more caught off guard at the sight of Aodhán sitting with her. Saffron had fully expected the fey gentle to have gone back to Avren with Cylvan and Saoirse, but instead they sat looking more irritated and brooding than ever while glaring down at an herb-and-seed scone. When he and Sionnach stepped into the kitchen, Aodhán barely turned to give Saffron a look, before sighing and grabbing the scone to bury into their mouth.

"Good morning, Maeve," Saffron said as Maeve sipped her tea. "Sorry for making you worry."

"No apologies," she said. "It was thrilling to watch Cylvan go completely mad on the train in front of all those people."

Another mention of his prince, another twist in Saffron's gut. He nodded, but averted his eyes. A part of him wanted to know exactly what had happened—a part of him wished it would stop being mentioned.

Before any further conversation could be made, Baba Yaga

made Saffron and Sionnach sit down to eat something. A welcome offering, as Saffron's stomach growled, but surreal all the same. Especially as Maeve made perfectly polite conversation with his henmother like they'd known each other for ages, though perhaps that was only her mastery of high fey manners coming through.

When Aodhán's eyes on him were finally too much to ignore, Saffron gave them an exasperated look. They smirked in reply, but something about it seemed awkward, like even they weren't entirely sure what they were looking for. Clearly they wished to say something, though, more than just the pleasantries passed around between the others, and Saffron raised a pointed eyebrow at them to go ahead and break the ice.

"Are you alright?" They asked, and Saffron raised his eyebrows in a different way. Surprised, as it was the last thing he expected.

"I'm fine," he said, though not with any real persuasion. "Thanks to Baba Yaga, I finally slept through the night, at least."

"Must have been a pretty strong spell."

Saffron swirled the coffee in his mug, watching as the rough grounds at the bottom settled. Everyone else had gone quiet, too, also watching him. He hated that. But he also shouldn't have been surprised.

"Thank you all for coming to get me," he said. "I... wasn't expecting it."

"We weren't about to go back to Avren all alone with his highness," Maeve muttered, sipping at her own mug. "We passed him on the road last night as he was leaving Morrígan, too. Wouldn't even look at us."

Saffron's hands wrung together under the table.

"I'm sorry for causing so much trouble," he whispered. "But it was the only thing I could think to do."

"Did you find what you were looking for?" Sionnach asked with a sense of reassurance. At the very least, Saffron was able to nod at them.

"Yes—I was able to speak to someone who knows more than they let on, here." Everyone glanced to Baba Yaga, who gave them a wicked grin, and Saffron laughed before shaking his head.

"What did this mystery person say?" Maeve asked. Saffron tangled his fingers together a little more, picking at frayed pieces of his cuticles and scratching at the nearly healed-over scrapes on his palms.

"They said... Ryder is most likely hunting down a memory tapestry. One he thought would be in the high hall, but obviously wasn't."

He let that reveal settle amongst them, waiting for any more questions to come. When none did, he realized it was because everyone sat in a state of nauseated uncertainty.

"Yeah," he grimaced. "That's how I feel, too. What's more, after looking at some of the things I had to show him... specifically, the arid circle Ryder has been using, and the pixie ring Copper took from him in Ailinne... my friend said Ryder Kyteler is more likely not who we think. For reasons other than the obvious. He—he may be a lot older and know a lot more than we anticipated. Which makes him even more dangerous than we originally thought."

"Have anything stronger than coffee, Ms. Nora?" Maeve groaned, but Baba Yaga was already gone to work digging some scotch out from her hiding place in the spice cabinet. Saffron took it from her before anyone else could, drinking straight from the bottle. He felt like he deserved it.

"So should we continue following him?" Sionnach asked. "He'll be in Vjallrod, next, according to the queen's route..."

Saffron didn't answer right away. He let the alcohol hook into his soul, watching as Maeve dumped two fingers of the drink into her mug, before passing it to Aodhán, who added a splash to theirs.

Saffron—didn't know. Adelard had told him many very helpful things, yes, but—none of them solved the issue of *catching* Ryder. Let alone provided him any immediate insight into ways he could help the oracles get through to Asche and the others, like he'd hoped. Not that Saffron was eager to beseech the veil for anything again anytime soon, but—that had been the entire reason he'd abandoned Cylvan and the others from the start.

"Oh, god," he moaned, snatching the bottle back and taking another swig. He didn't want to be reminded of what came of his visit to the ruins. Or after.

Everyone else was back to speaking, allowing him a moment to gather his thoughts. To listen, to see if they had any better ideas than they did. Discussing the pros and cons of following Ryder to Vjallrod, or returning to Avren to try and work with the oracles. Saffron took another drink at that.

"I don't think I want to go back to Avren yet," he said with a grimace. "I doubt Cylvan wants anything to do with me at the moment. It might only make things worse if I go back now..."

They all looked at him like he was the most pitiful thing in the world, but at the same time, with eyes that swam with curiosity. Wanting to know what happened, what was said. Saffron didn't answer out loud, but glanced down at his hand on the table— only then realizing part of the reason why they kept throwing him so much pity. Without his amethyst pendant, every one of Saffron's friends saw his human exhaustion right at the forefront. Not only that, they saw how his scarred, ugly hands—lacked the prince's engagement ring, any longer.

"Oh, gods," Sionnach gasped with a hand to their mouth. "You two—did you...?"

"I don't know," Saffron groaned, shaking his head. "No, no, I —I didn't break off our engagement or anything, I don't think— not really, at least, I was just—I was just emotional, and he was driving me mad, and he wouldn't leave me alone, and I just snapped..."

"Explains his mood on the road," Maeve commented. Saffron groaned again, planting his face in his hand.

"Seems like a good time to go, if you did mean it," Aodhán

added. "Cylvan has been acting like a real bastard for some time, now—"

"No!" Saffron exclaimed, voice cracking. "No, I don't—I don't want to go! I mean—I don't want to go for *good*. I—I love him, I still love him, I only... I only wish..." he hated how his eyes burned, but he refused to cry. "I only wish things were easier. For the both of us."

"He's been making it hard all on his own—" Aodhán started, but Saffron shook his head again.

"No, it's... it's complicated, isn't it?" He asked, like they would be able to answer. They just raised an eyebrow at him. "I mean—I know why he's angry! Why he's acting like this. I understand why he's so upset and stressed out and—*bitey!* I even understand why he resents me, even if he won't admit it. And I don't blame him!" The words poured out of him, motivated by a single good night's rest and lubricated by scotch on an empty stomach. "I think I resent some things he's done, too! Considering what this goddamned world has put the both of us through, it all makes perfect sense, doesn't it! But I promised him a long time ago—I promised I wouldn't leave. Especially when things stopped being so sunny and bright and perfect. That's all anyone has ever done with him! Once the darkness creeps in, whether his fault or not, they leave! Because, yeah! He can be a bit of a bastard! But I promised to stay with him. Even when things felt impossible. I promised I would always try to understand him, and support him. And I will. I'm going to. I've done more for him in worse—and he has always been there to catch me when I needed him most, too, I..." a few tears dripped, and Saffron scrambled to smear them away in embarrassment. "I'm in love with him. I still am, obviously. I agreed to be his king, but more than that—I agreed to love him. No matter what came. I'm the only one who knows—exactly how warm and bright he can be. So I'm not leaving him, even if he resents me for that, too..."

Sionnach's hand found Saffron's on the table, and the tension in Saffron's body deflated in an instant. He shook his head, wiping his eyes one more time.

"Sorry," he whispered. "I think I'm a little drunk, already."

"Don't apologize," Aodhán answered first. Thoughtfully, but also like they'd just been blasted with a cold wind they weren't prepared for.

"So, should we go back to Avren?" Sionnach urged quietly.

"No!" Saffron exclaimed again, before biting down on his tongue. "Sorry, I mean...! I don't know, god, I just don't know...."

"Maybe slow down on the scotch for a bit," Maeve said. She put out her hand, and Saffron handed it over willingly, watching as she dumped another finger-full into her mug. That was when Baba Yaga finally stepped in, snatching it back and corking it with a definitive squeak.

"That wicked prince of yours cares for you as well, Saffron," the henmother interjected, as she tucked the bottle back into its hiding place. Turning back to the others, she reached into her apron, extending her hand. Dropping Saffron's ring first, then the long chain of his amethyst pendant second, into his open palms. Saffron's breath caught. "Last night, after I cursed him to the bone, as satisfying as it was to see him looking like a kicked puppy in my doorway—he still paused to make sure to give that to me. He asked me to give it back to you. Then—he asked that I allow you to stay here, as long as you'd like. He said you don't have to return to Avren until you're ready, and he'll wait, no matter how long it takes."

Saffron stared down at the purple stone, that matched Cylvan's eyes. Shiny, polished, but not with a soft rag or expert hands. As if Cylvan had anxiously rubbed his thumb over the face of the gemstone like he did the wooden hair pick Saffron had gifted him.

"Oh..." he whispered, before carefully returning the ring to his finger, where it belonged. "I didn't hear any of that."

"He whispered it," Baba assured him. "Like it suffocated him, to have to turn and leave without you."

Saffron pressed his lips together. Before the emotions could grapple for him again, though, his henmother's hand found his chin, tipping his face up to look at her.

"That prince of yours is a nefarious thing," she said. "His capacity for cruelty is—well, perhaps there is more to it than simply rumors. I believe he has been treating you poorly lately, and I made sure he knew it. I do not think you should forgive him just because he is as pathetic as he is wretched. However..." she sighed, brushing a thumb under one of Saffron's eyes, where the glamour once again hid his exhaustion. "I agree with what you said—that things are complicated, aren't they? You both have much to learn, about what it takes to be in love in a world without a single friend. Well, apart from this peculiar little band." She scratched between Copper's ears as she said it.

"Your henmother is right," Maeve said. "As someone who's known Cylvan since we were children—she's absolutely right. He's like a wild animal that's never known love, suddenly offered a sweet little rabbit to keep him company. Wanting to care for it, but unable to help when the environment makes him snap. That's not to say the rabbit is obligated to stay if it feels unhappy, or unsafe, but... but it was never the rabbit he despised."

Saffron nodded. He squeezed the ring on his finger.

"I know that," he whispered. "Cylvan is inherently—kind. He's soft. He just wants to love—and be loved. And I want to love him. Even if no one else does."

"He's grown on me a bit, since you and I met," Sionnach admitted, going red when everyone turned to them in surprise. They put their hands up with a nervous laugh. "I mean! I still don't quite care for him, either, but... I can see how having someone to care for has changed him."

"Agreed," Maeve said. "If I were you, Saffron—I would leave him in Avren, for now. Let him go into hiding, if that's what he needs. Like when Daurae Asche has to sneak away during fetes. Let him stew and think about what he's done. Reflect on his behavior and all that. He'll realize his mistake—though by what

Ms. Nora already explained, it sounds to me like he already has. Even if his pride wouldn't let him admit it last night."

Saffron chuckled. He reclaimed his pendant in his hand, rubbing a thumb over the top before squeezing it. A subtle, uncertain warmth radiated back. Like Cylvan on the other end wasn't sure Saffron actually meant to call out to him.

"You're right," he breathed. "You're right. All of you. And I think..." he squeezed the pendant a little tighter, closing his eyes. He inhaled a deep breath, before looking up again. "I think we should continue north, to Vjallrod."

**31**

———

# THE PASS

Saffron went to check on Boann as the others finished their breakfast, grabbing a brush to try and wick away the wetness of her fur before returning the saddle to her back. Aodhán approached to ask if he needed any help. It caught Saffron off guard, but he offered them the brush, nonetheless. He watched as they reached to stroke the horse's back where Saffron couldn't reach on his own, stomach fluttering more than ever at how much they resembled his raven.

"I'm surprised you didn't go back to Avren with them," he said after the silence nibbled a little too deeply. "I hope it wasn't out of some sense of obligation—"

"Cylvan is a real piece of work," Aodhán interrupted flatly, reiterating their sentiments from the table. They didn't look at Saffron as they said it, but their movements with the brush intensified a little more as their clear annoyance grew. "Despite the conclusions you came to about him—I still can't believe the nerve of that spoiled little prick. I'll be writing a harshly-worded letter to his damned father the second I'm back home."

"His fath—you mean the king?" Saffron couldn't help but laugh. Aodhán said nothing else, just pressed their lips together like they were on the verge of splitting apart. Saffron wondered how they'd react if they knew just *exactly* how many of their mannerisms reminded him of the prince he knew so well—especially when trying to keep their composure against the ruthless swell of their own emotions.

"I made sure he knew how disappointed I was in his behavior, when we crossed on the road last night," Aodhán said with a sense of finality. "It won't mean anything to him now—but soon enough, may it cast ice in his heart."

Saffron wanted to ask what that meant, but hesitated as Aodhán pursed their lips, slowing the motion of the brush while clearly anchored to a coming thought.

"Again, those conclusions you came to earlier... I mean, the things you said, about how... you'll love him, no matter what. No matter how cruel he is, or how hard it gets. Knowing as well as the rest of us, all of Alfidel will do everything it can to ruin the both of you once you're revealed... do you really mean that? You'll really love him forever, no matter what?"

"Yes," Saffron answered. Quickly enough that Aodhán huffed, like they thought he was exaggerating. "I mean it. And the things we've been arguing about lately aren't even the worst of what he's done to me—worse things he's apologized for, already. Genuinely. Baba Yaga is very protective of all her beantighe chicks, sometimes to a fault, so it makes sense for her to demonize him so much, but... I think even she can understand the kind of pressure Cylvan is under."

"You as well."

"Yes, me as well," Saffron smiled, though grimaced toward the end. "I don't normally take any of Cylvan's attitude to heart—in fact, I usually tell him off right back. I don't just submit to whatever he wants, either—but maybe that was obvious, considering where we've found ourselves... Hence why I threw my ring at him. Or why I turned on heel and came to Morrígan on my own, even when he *expressly forbade it.*"

"I suppose you also insulted Renard dé Bricríu to his face, too," they mumbled, shaking their head like they still couldn't believe it, before adding: "I'm glad Cylvan found you. I only hope he truly understands what he'll lose if he continues navigating such precious relationships like this..."

The look on their face after saying it was one of surprise, like even they hadn't expected it. Before they could circle back, however, a sudden heavy *thud*, then the clatter of dishes and a bark of surprise from Baba came from inside Cottage Wicklow. Saffron turned in alarm—but then heard a familiar voice laugh a little bit, followed by: *"Oh. Nice to properly meet you, granny."*

*"Granny!"* Baba Yaga hissed, followed by the clang of a tin dish against a skull, and Copper's sharp laughter. Saffron's heart leapt, racing to the open door and rushing inside to find his friend crouched on one knee, naked, messy-haired, flushed as Baba Yaga puttered over him.

"Copper!" Saffron exclaimed, summoning his giant friend to turn with a massive grin, sweeping him up into a hug and squeezing him hard enough to push all the air from his chest. "Oh, thank god! I thought you might be a beast for the rest of your life!"

"Kinda miss it already," Copper laughed, shaking Saffron back and forth like a ragdoll. "A lot warmer with all that fur."

"I'll fetch him some of Hollow's old things," Baba Yaga sighed, slipping past them and up the stairs as Saffron just laughed and clung to his friend in return. Not bothering to wonder how, or why, Copper had seemingly, suddenly, regained dominance over his sídhe magic in the face of the ashen state—though he could muster an idea, once Sionnach appeared in the kitchen doorway. Squeaking in alarm, before covering their eyes against Copper's nakedness. Summoning a booming laugh from Copper, who knocked Saffron away in favor of stalking toward the satyr, who shrieked at him to stay away, to put some damned clothes on, to find even an ounce of dignity—but even Sionnach, caught in Copper's arms and powerless to stop it, eventually sighed and offered Copper a bashful hug back.

"I know you missed me, goat," Copper grinned, swinging

Sionnach back and forth. Sionnach didn't respond—but didn't pull away, either. Hugging Copper just a moment longer, until Baba Yaga appeared to offer him something to wear.

HIS FRIENDS WHO'D BOARDED THE TRAIN IN AILINNE, only to de-board suddenly in the middle of the woods when Cylvan demanded it, had managed to barter for horses in the next town they reached on-foot—but while they had steeds, they still lacked most of their other traveling essentials, especially considering their upcoming traipse into the Winter Court.

Arriving in Connacht, Maeve and Aodhán walked the shops to purchase winter clothes for the rest of the party, while Copper went to procure a carriage for them. If there was any benefit to most of their belongings being sent to Avren—it was that they would no longer travel bearing the crown's sigil emblazoned on the sides of their saddles. Even with Boann's, Saffron could cover the motifs with bags, at least. To disappear into as much anonymity as any other group of travelers making their way north. Something about that was reassuring. Something about it was unexpectedly harrowing.

Saffron and Sionnach, meanwhile, were tasked with finding some food to take on the trip with them—only for Saffron to lose his focus as they wandered a general store, and a stack of that morning's gossip pamphlets caught his attention with big, bold letters:

*AFTER FLOWER OF ALVENYA SEEN ABANDONING HIS HIGHNESS' TRAVEL PARTY, PRINCE CYLVAN DEMANDS ONE-WAY TRAIN HALTS IN MIDDLE OF FALL COURT; Raving Mad About Lost Beantighe Servant. Is The Prince's Perfect Facade Finally Starting To Show Cracks?*

"This is overdramatized, right?" Saffron asked Sionnach weakly, and Sionnach grimaced. That was answer enough. Saffron nearly tucked the paper back, not wanting to know—before biting his lip, and adding it to their pile of things to pay for. Feeling like he wished to know what those people wrote about Cylvan, especially if he wasn't there to see what really happened.

From Connacht to Ailinne, then north to Turias, then Ceilt, they traveled the remainder of the day and into the evening, when Saffron felt the first kiss of chill on his skin.

With new clothes to help keep the cold at bay, and a little bit of steamed rum in his stomach to quell his nerves—Saffron had officially turned his back on Avren. And, therefore, Cylvan.

That far away, though, there was an easier sense of accepting what he'd done. He could settle in the back of the carriage with Copper and Sionnach, knowing it was too late to turn around.

Maeve rode alongside them as Aodhán drove from the seat on the front, helping lead the horses through a growing layer of snow, chatting lightly between one another as the sídhe lady attempted a few times to summon her ice-magic with the help of the natural elements.

Inside the cab, Sionnach sat on one side while Saffron and Copper occupied the other, the once-again-fey lord's head resting in Saffron's lap as Saffron attempted more than once to draft a letter to Cylvan on a pad of letter parchment. Fiachra watched from her carriage perch, waiting for him to finally finalize something and give it to her to deliver. Like even she would be willing to traverse the distance in those circumstances. Not knowing that Saffron was quickly realizing there wasn't a combination of words in his limited vocabulary to properly express how he was feeling, especially after the conversations earlier that morning.

Finally crumpling up the fifth sheet of paper in a rush of frustration, Copper's giant hand whipped up to snatch the whole writing stack away from him, tossing it to the floor before locking his arms around Saffron's middle to imprison him where he sat. Saffron huffed, but didn't fight back. He opened the carriage window enough for Fiachra to wiggle out if she felt like she needed to get her own jitters out, but instead the bird seemed relieved in her own way when it became clear she would be delivering no messages at any long distance anytime soon.

Saffron tried to study instead. He tried to read his books. Then he tried to play a card game with Sionnach on a plank of polished wood balanced between the satyr's knees and Copper's broad shoulder. He watched as Sionnach went to work knitting a scarf with hand-spun wool yarn gifted to them by some satyrs at the borough, showing Saffron the unique type of stitching satyrs always used that could be stretched wide for cooler days or squished together to brace against the cold.

Saffron did everything he possibly could to simply distract himself from looking out the window. From reckoning with exactly how far they traveled in the opposite direction of Avren, even at such a slow pace as the snow on the road slowly steadily deeper.

When nightfall came and they opted to continue riding through the night, Saffron hunkered down in the back of the carriage with Sionnach and Copper, who had returned to his fox form to act as a shared, furry heater. Having apparently healed his own ashen state, though it was still unclear exactly *how*.

Saffron just buried himself beneath the blankets, under the pillows, forcing his eyes to remain shut. Knowing that, as soon as morning came, they would be on their way into the Hoarcliff Pass, and by the end of it, fully crossed over into the Winter Court. Where there really would be no turning back.

SAFFRON COULD TASTE THE COLD ON HIS TONGUE before ever opening his eyes to see it. In the low light of morning, he knew the shade of blue-gray in the air. It made him close his eyes again, digging fingers into the thick fur of Copper's neck and making the beast grumble in his sleep. Sionnach was already awake, themself, wriggling around beneath the shared blanket and attempting to use a small bag of charmed fire-stones to warm up some tea to drink.

When they whispered Saffron's name to offer him some, Saffron finally emerged from the warm burrow to take it, forcing himself to look out the window and accept there was no going back. There was only one way through the Hoarcliff Pass into the Winter Court, which meant no changing one's mind. Not until the next town, where an entirely separate road would take them back south again.

He'd made his choice. Eventually, when Saffron never returned to Avren—Cylvan would know it, too. He could only hope the prince had meant what he said to Baba Yaga—that he would understand, and he would wait. No matter how long it took. Even if he never anticipated Saffron choosing to leave Beantighe Village to continue north on Ryder's trail without him —the prince had still promised.

Sionnach sipped at their tea while gazing out the window, absentmindedly petting the thick fluff of Copper's tail with their opposite hand. Saffron cast his own occasional glances outside to the familiar landscape blanketed in white, distant horizon hidden behind a wall of snowy mist. It didn't alarm him at first—but then a heavy wind whisked through the pass, making the carriage sway and causing the horses outside to whine and stomp their feet. He pressed a hand to the cab wall to steady himself, glancing out the window again, before throwing a brief look to Sionnach, who did the same on their side.

Unlatching the window, Saffron slid it down just a crack to ask Aodhán if everything was alright—but the carriage suddenly jolted, knocking everyone inside on top of one another. Groaning, Sionnach kicked Copper off their lap as the fox scrambled to return upright, finally shifting back into his fey form—resulting in him straddling Sionnach naked. It summoned a screech of disapproval from the satyr, followed by a flail of their hooves into Copper's chest. Saffron barely dodged the chaos, grabbing Fiachra to keep her from being flattened in the commotion as he called out through the window a second time to ask what was going on.

"Someone on the road!" Aodhán called back against the wind. "Look like they lost their horse. Maeve is going to check them out."

"Someone on the road?" Saffron asked, detangling himself from Sionnach and Copper's squabble as Copper fought to pull his clothes on, throwing open the carriage door and jumping out.

The wind whipped Saffron's hood over his head in an instant, nearly knocking him off his feet as the road beneath his feet was compacted with more snow than he expected. Fiachra attempted to follow after him, and Saffron yelped just as the wind hooked on her wings and nearly sent her flying into the abyss. Throwing out his hands, he grabbed her from the air, cursing before stuffing the owl under his cloak. She writhed and squirmed upward until she could settled on his shoulder, within the curve of his hood instead.

"Saffron, come back into the carriage!" Sionnach called, before snapping, *"Copper, no, damnit! Both of you get back in here!"*

"I just want to look for myself!" Saffron called back, already making his way slowly through the wind, barely able to see through the thick snowfall as Maeve approached a shadow with its hands raised further up the road. The stranger's own dark cloak whipped against the constant gusts, dusted in a thick layer of frost to prove they'd been out there a while. Not so long to succumb to the cold, at least, as Saffron's mind turned over the possibility of picking them up to take them into the next town— but then Maeve suddenly reeled back on her horse's reins with a shout, and Saffron choked at the sight of the stranger leaping forward in an attempt to grab the horse before it pulled out of reach.

"Hey!" he exclaimed, just as Aodhán leapt from the driver's bench, racing to where Maeve shouted at the figure to let her go, kicking them in the head with her boot.

Hands grabbed her foot with one of the thrusts, yanking her free of the saddle just as Aodhán skid through the snow to reach them. Maeve hit the ground with a heavy thud, and Copper grabbed Saffron's arm to pull him back. But Saffron moved on his own instinct, reaching for the obsidian knife in his belt. He raced down the snowy road toward where Aodhán put themself between Maeve and the stranger, and Copper kept close on Saffron's heels the whole time.

Maeve drew her sword, white-silver and bright in the reflecting snow. Her horse reared back against the stranger attempting to mount it, who had to throw their hands up while stepping backward so as to not get their head smashed open. As they did, the wind suddenly shifted direction, slamming into Saffron's front and whipping his hood off, practically blinding him with snow like a thousand needles. Crossing his arms over his face, he squinted through the gale toward the conflict only a hundred feet ahead from him, finding the stranger's hood had been blown back, too—and they were looking right at him.

"Your highness!" Ryder Kyteler shouted with a grin, as if not realizing who exactly he attempted to rob until that moment. Saffron just stumbled backward, nerves bright as Fiachra dug talons into his shoulder.

"I wondered when we would cross paths again!" Ryder continued, barely audible over the wind, though Saffron heard each word like fired crossbow bolts. Before the man could say more, before Saffron could respond—Maeve lunged through the storm with her blade ready, moving for Ryder's throat and matching the man's instantaneous footwork even in the loose snow and ice under their feet. Clearly even Ryder didn't antici-pate the fey lady's fluidity with the blade, as the arrogance twitched on his face, reaching under his cloak for his own blade to crash against Maeve's with an earsplitting ring.

*"Summon me!"* Taran snarled in Saffron's mind, but Saffron wasn't sure, moving as quickly as he could over the slippery surface with his own dagger still drawn. No—it might only be a

distraction, for Maeve or Ryder, or both, especially with two blades drawn and crashing against one another. Especially on a road so narrow and icy, only a weathered wooden fence indicating where the edge dropped off over the cliffs on the other side. And when it came down to it—Saffron didn't want Ryder dead. At least, not yet. If Ryder died, he might never learn how to get his friends back; but with the ferocity Maeve unleashed upon him, Saffron wasn't sure how many chances he'd get to call her off before she did something irreversible.

"Maeve, wait!" He still attempted, but Aodhán grabbed the back of his cloak before he could get any closer. Helpless but to watch as Ryder and Maeve slammed into one another, blades clashing with white sparks, knocking one another off balance or shoving them across the slippery road, more than once losing their footing and having to roll out of the way of a blade coming down on them. Ryder wouldn't hesitate to kill Maeve, either, if he didn't think he had any reason to avoid it.

The very moment the man spun on Maeve and caught her off guard, hand gripping her wrist and twisting her around, blade lifting to her throat, Saffron's magic snapped and flooded him.

Extending his hands pin-straight toward them, the pink glow of Ryder's inherent aura burning bright in Saffron's eyes as he focused, summoning the power to the surface. Gripping Ryder without touching him, like Saffron once did the vines grasping at Fiachra. Holding the man in place where he stood, as if pinning him by the wrists. As if uttering the enchantment to *be still*, without needing such words.

Not again, not again—Saffron would not let that man hold a blade to anyone's throat that way again, he would not allow him to threaten someone that way, ever again. Especially not in a place like that, so remote, where no one else would see what Saffron was capable of to stop him.

Ryder should have known better—and Saffron was sure he did, as the man realized his mistake the moment Saffron buried fingers into his being like he once buried them into those rowan vines wringing around Fiachra's struggling body at Ériu's shrine.

Hot blood crept up the back of Saffron's throat. It found the rim of his nose, dripping over his lip, from his chin, as every inch of his body shook in concentration. He dug through Ryder's magic until he felt every shuddering mote, until he thought he could scrape fingers through the light like digging his hand through a bag of rice. A vein swelled over Ryder's temple, muscles straining in his neck as he stared at Saffron in return, unblinking, unmoving. Saffron held him firm, held him in place, paralyzing him by hooking himself into the man's magic.

"Maeve, come," Saffron said with a shaky breath, puffs of steam thicker than ever with the effort coursing through him.

Maeve hesitated, moving one toe of her boot, realizing exactly what Saffron had done—but it wasn't enough. The blade remained too close to her windpipe, that she could barely shift before a line of bright crimson formed on her skin.

It wasn't enough to just pin Ryder in place, Saffron would have to control him, to move him bodily. But he didn't know how—he didn't know if he had the knowledge, let alone the strength, the will to do something like that—and worse, he knew the moment he let up his grasp, Ryder would certainly kill Maeve just to punish him for trying.

"Please," Saffron attempted, wishing to utter, *please don't do this* as if it would make any difference to Ryder—but the words never came, as a massive gust of wind crashed down from the sky, unexpectedly hot and sulphuric. On its tail, a sound that paralyzed Saffron down to his core, the only thing in the world that could possibly break his concentration in that moment.

A roar, a resounding, gut-churning cry of something titanic and death-defying—and it was plummeting straight for them, from the cloudy sky.

Ryder managed to turn in Saffron's brief distraction, the blade in his hand slipping away just enough for Maeve to shove free. But she only made it a few steps before another gust of hot wind crashed against the road, knocking every one of them off their feet and sending the horses scattering. From the clouds, a winged, black-scaled dragon swept downward in an arch, blasting a line of fire along the edge of the road like a warning. Another roar emanated from the depths of its throat that froze Saffron where he stood. A dragon—a Winter Court dragon, like Saffron had only ever heard of in stories.

The beast turned back upward, rotating wing-over-tail in the sky in order to swing back down over them a second time. Saffron's hands remained extended, though his concentration was long-shattered—until the sound of rushing feet and someone shouting his name brought him back to earth.

He couldn't react fast enough, as Ryder lunged at him. Throwing his arms out, slamming into him—and sending them both careening over the edge of the cliff into the white unknown below.

# 32

## THE WARMTH

Saffron hit the snow at the bottom with a thud softened only by the thick blanket of powder. It was enough to stave off death, but not nearly cushion enough to keep the wind from being knocked out of him.

Buried almost instantly beneath the blanket, he couldn't grasp which way was up until the feeling of fingers hooked into the fabric of his sleeve and yanked him upward. They unearthed him back into the cold, air, the cutting wind, and he almost wished to sink back beneath the frost in comparison.

"You alive?" the gruff voice asked, still pulling Saffron upward, though Saffron just sank back into the deep snow every time the grasp on him was loosened even a little bit. Saffron didn't know—he didn't know if he was still alive. But the pain of the freezing air on his skin gave him a clue, and all he could do was roll his head. "That's a good boy. C'mon, up you go."

The man bent his knees to heave Saffron onto his back. Saffron sank into him, arms draping over his shoulders and head hanging forward. Only then did actual thoughts finally poke through the frozen haze—and he realized who it was that carried him.

Jerking backward, he tumbled off Ryder's back, inadvertently taking the man down with him. He crushed Saffron into the snow, making Saffron groan as the brief air he'd reclaimed in his lungs was instantly knocked free again. Focusing instead on kicking his legs and throwing his hands out, Ryder grunted in response, finally grabbing a hold of one of Saffron's arms to shout at him over the howling wind.

"I'm not takin' you anywhere except out of the snow, Saffron! Unless you want to freeze to death, I suggest you stop being so difficult!"

"Get your hands off me!" Saffron snarled back, attempting to yank his hand away, but Ryder just audibly groaned in exasperation. He bent forward again, that time throwing Saffron over one shoulder and getting back to his feet. Saffron could only shout, kicking his legs and pounding his fists against Ryder's back, but Ryder seemed to feel none of it.

Saffron didn't know for how long he was carried—he didn't even know if Ryder was taking him somewhere on purpose, or just wandering aimlessly in that snow-blinding landscape, though the man's slowly deteriorating movements hinted at one more than the other. Eventually even Saffron was too cold to kick, to pound his fists, just shivering and attempting to pull his body into itself as much as he could. As he did, he tried to take stock of what he had with him, what he didn't; his cloak was still tied securely to his shoulders, by the grace of Ériu. His shoulder bag dangled heavy across his chest, though he had no idea what still remained inside. Fiachra wasn't following them. Neither was anyone else, it seemed. Perhaps they all thought him dead, just like that. So easily.

"Fuck—thank the gods," Ryder finally groaned, and Saffron managed to lift his head. Through the ice-frosted ends of his hair, he spotted what Ryder meant—the silhouette of a cabin in the distance, perhaps for hunting, perhaps a witch's trap for lost travelers just like them. Saffron didn't care. He was a witch, too. He could reason with some old crone if he had to.

The door was locked as they reached it, remaining firm even

as Ryder attempted to shoulder his way inside. Finally, he set Saffron down beneath the eaves that offered minimal protection from the snow, where Saffron promptly collapsed against the wall and sank to the snow. Ryder scolded him through clenched teeth, but focused on reeling back to slam himself into the door. Again and again, until the wood cracked, then split, and he threw himself inside and crashed to the floor. Saffron wished he was warm enough to laugh. He just dragged himself to his feet, using the wall of the cabin for support as he stumbled inside after the man who was just pushing himself up to his knees.

"What, couldn't close the door behind you, your highness?"

"F-f-fuck you," Saffron chattered through his teeth, going straight to where the moth-eaten bed was located on the opposite side of the room, bumping into the table and chair on the way. Collapsing on top of it and summoning a cloud of dust, the mattress was hardly more than wool-stuffed linen, lumpier in some places than others, the pillow in no better shape—but it reminded him of Beantighe Village. Of his own bed back in Fern Room, before Cylvan's demands had everyone's sleeping conditions improved. He'd long moved on to plush high fey silks and thick cushions by then.

At the thought, Saffron buried a stiff hand into his shoulder bag, mentally taking stock of everything inside. Relieved when he'd lost nothing of note, particularly when his fingers trailed over the cold stone of the hematite wand. He pulled it from the bag in a flash, tucking it up his sleeve before Ryder could notice.

Meanwhile, on the other side of the cabin, Ryder had managed to pin the broken door back in place using the wooden table, though the sound of the whistling wind remained deafening as blustering snow spilled in through the gap where the latch had broken away. Saffron nearly piped up about the fireplace hearth in the wall—though the distinct lack of joined whistling, flurries down the chimney told him it was likely too clogged with debris to be useful. He collapsed back to the bed again, closing his eyes in defeat.

When Ryder turned to approach Saffron on the bed, Saffron didn't even look at him.

"Don't come any closer," he said. Ryder's footsteps stopped.

"We'll freeze to death otherwise."

"Speak for yourself," Saffron hissed. "I grew up in the Winter Court. I can keep myself warm."

"I did too, unless you already forgot," Ryder answered flatly. "But that only means you know as well as I do, it's no chilly Winter Court night outside. I'm not going to do anything to you but share my body heat."

"Yeah, right," Saffron muttered. "Keep away from me before I break both your hands."

"Don't think you could. Maybe back when you were a beantighe, but not anymore, highness."

Saffron knew he only kept using that title because he'd once insisted he didn't—but Saffron did not correct him. He did think himself higher than Ryder Kyteler, or whatever the fuck his real name was, even freezing his ass off in the middle of nowhere after falling from a cliff. He pressed the base of his wrist into the tip of the wand tucked in his sleeve at the thought, wondering if he could just stab the man instead.

Fighting the urge, Saffron instead just ignored him, pulling the near-rotten blanket off the bed and over himself, hardly bothered by the smell of mothballs, the holes eaten through the fabric. He barely thought to strip off his wet cloak first before curling up as tightly as he could, ears remaining sharp as Ryder sighed and paced the room.

He even approached to pick up Saffron's discarded cloak, draping it over the back of the lonely chair before taking a seat in it for himself.

"You sure?" he asked one more time. Saffron could practically see the smirk on his face. "I promise you I run warm. We'd both be feeling better in—"

*"Icarus, come."*

Taran manifested from the shadows, head low and ears flat

against his head. Ryder said nothing, only exhaling a small breath, though Saffron didn't know if it was through a smile or just exasperation.

"I could always wear your prince's face for you, if you'd like. How are things between you and him after Ailinne, anyway? Noticed he wasn't there earlier—"

"Taran, kill him."

Taran's snout wrinkled over a growl, and Ryder put his hands up again with another smarmy grin.

"Alright, sorry."

"Do you ever shut up?" Saffron asked, crossed his arms over his face, attempting to block his ears. "Don't think about coming anywhere near me. My dog will tear you apart."

"You two are on good terms, then? Been a while, Taran. See you've finally grown into those bones of yours."

Taran snarled again. Saffron didn't want to—but Ryder's words caught his attention, and the man grinned in satisfaction when he peeked over his shoulder.

"Curious, your highness? C'mon. Don't you remember anything I've told you? Taran and I spent some time in Fjornar together as kids, didn't we, my lord? You were such a favorite of those oracles there."

Saffron didn't want to listen. He'd already assumed all of that, after learning about Taran's past, after what Ryder had told him during that brief dance on Beltane. But for Ryder to admit it so casually while Saffron felt like he was on the verge of freezing to death—was infuriating in a way.

"Is that where you learned to weave memory threads?" He decided to ask outright. Taran's ears perked, and in the back of Saffron's head, his voice warned him not to fall for Ryder's charms. Saffron rolled his eyes, cursing Taran back. He wasn't falling for anything. He had a right to know—considering the man's fingers had once dug through his own mind, to take things Saffron didn't even realize were missing until the end.

"If you want to ask me questions, your highness, I would prefer if you met my eyes."

Saffron scowled, but he sat up. He turned on the bed, leaning back against the drafty wooden wall. Between him and the man in the chair sat Taran, hardly more than an intimidating shadow in the darkness. Ryder wasn't much more, himself.

"Answer me."

"Yes," Ryder said with ease. "And also where I learned some of my veil tricks, if you're curious about that as well."

"Are they the reason you're doing all of this?"

"Doing all of what?"

"Taran—"

"I'm doing all of this for my own reasons, I can assure you," he answered with a charming smile. "The oracles of Fjornar taught me what I know—but I think even they were surprised with what I did at the games."

"Your witchhunter friends, too."

"Isn't that what I just said?"

Saffron pressed his lips together. He'd never been sure exactly how much crossover there was between modern witch-hunters and the oracles of Fjornar, but assumed it to be at least some. Ryder's words implying them to be one and the same, though, made Saffron heart twist in panic. Thinking of Cylvan back in Avren, where all of the oracles had gone to try and find Asche.

"Are all Fjornaran oracles also witchhunters?"

"No; but all witchhunters are from Fjornar."

"That's where they originated, when Queen Proserpina started training them to hunt down humans."

"Ah—see, why do you keep wasting my time when you already know everything?"

"Were you trained as a witchhunter, too?"

"Not specifically, no."

"Then how do you know so much about them?"

"Well—they raised me. One big happy family."

Saffron swallowed the lump in his throat. "So you were an orphan?"

"Of sorts."

"Just fucking tell me."

"My stepfather sent me there."

That admittance paused Saffron's insatiable frustration. He raised an eyebrow, tilting his head slightly in a moment of genuine curiosity.

"You just said you were an orphan."

"I said I was something *like* an orphan."

"... Why did your stepfather send you there, to be raised by oracles? Did he want you to train as one?"

"Not particularly," Ryder sighed, but never took his eyes from Saffron. Like it was a thrill, even for him, for Saffron to be so interested. To hold Saffron's attention so doubtlessly again, after losing his trust at the games. "After he killed my father, my mother wanted nothing to do with me. I don't think he really cared what they decided to do with me."

Saffron's breath caught. "Your stepfather killed your father?"

"Yes."

"Why?"

"Who knows," Ryder smirked. "I'm the only one who knows he did. Even mother never found out, I don't think. I wonder if she would have cared, anyway—she hated him as much as my stepfather did. Perhaps that was his work too, though."

"Why not kill you too?"

"I don't know that either," Ryder answered. His eyes flickered warily to Taran for a moment, then back to Saffron. "I never got the chance to ask him."

Saffron shifted where he sat.

"Why are you telling me this?"

"Because you asked."

Saffron rolled his eyes, and Ryder chuckled.

"You've never asked, before."

"I'm certain I did."

"Well—maybe I'm just in a good mood tonight. You know seeing a dragon so close is said to bless you with long life? Maybe that's why we survived that fall together. I'd gladly do it again for another night alone with you."

Saffron scowled, shifting how he sat, averting his eyes toward the shuttered windows that rattled on their old hinges. He hadn't taken any time to think for himself about that dragon they saw up on the ridge. Its black scales, the frightening size of its wings and snout. It could have swallowed Saffron whole if it wished, and only gagged a little at the size of him on the way down. Shaking his head, he forced himself back into the moment.

"What were you doing on the road by yourself like that?" Saffron went on, before deciding he already knew. "Heading to your next *location*, I suppose."

"That's right. Horse got spooked by the storm, threw me off. How lucky, for the crown's traveling party to pass by."

"You had no chance of ever getting a horse from Maeve dé Bhaldraithe."

"Oh, is that her name? A sídhe lady, then."

Saffron clenched his teeth—why did that simple comment finally make him snap? He jumped to his feet, moving on instinct and attempting to kick the man in the chest—but Ryder just grabbed his foot mid-air, twisting it and sending Saffron tumbling to the floor. Taran leapt forward and snapped his teeth at Ryder again, as Ryder also got back to his feet—and Ryder just put his hands up, slowly returning to the chair.

"I've had enough of you!" Saffron shouted, untangling himself from his cloak. "God—*damn* you! *Fuck!* I should just fucking kill you right now, after everything you've done! After everything you've taken from me—and yet you still have time to be so goddamned—*sarcastic!* So fucking *arrogant!*"

"Why haven't you killed me yet?"

*"Because you took them!"* Saffron cried. He pushed past Taran, shoving Ryder back. The chair tilted onto its back feet, but the man righted himself again before he could fall backward. "Because

you took my friends from me—and I have to get them back! All while you're being so goddamned reckless! Putting so many other people in danger!"

"And here I thought I was being so careful with my latest antics."

"You—!" Saffron barely resisted throttling him. "Tearing open the veil—! Even if it doesn't swallow anyone up, it—!! The veil told me itself, if you keep shredding it like this, it's only going to end up worse for everyone! For the high fey, and for humans, both!"

"What does it matter to me if a few more high fey are left ashen?" Ryder asked calmly, leaning back in his chair.

"It's not just—! Humans might lose their aridity too!"

"Humans only devised aridity to protect themselves from opulent fey."

Saffron gaped at him. "What in god's—What are you even saying? That's not even close to true—The Dagda, they—"

"And how would you know, beantighe?" Ryder asked, smooth and infuriating. "Did your prince tell you that?"

Saffron wanted to hit him—to hit him hard enough to actually kill him, that time. It was a wonder he remained on his feet, fists held at his sides and clenched tight. Perhaps only because he knew someone like Ryder Kyteler would not die so easily, no matter how infuriated Saffron was.

"Beantighes are suffering more because of how careless you're being," he said angrily. "They're being forced to clean up after your messes! They're being threatened in the gossip papers, they're being abused by their patron fey because people are scared—!"

"More motivation for them to come join my red coven then, hm?"

Saffron couldn't stop it—his hand lashed out, slapping Ryder across the face. Ryder stared at the floor for a long moment in silence, in disbelief, before slowly turning his attention forward again.

"I see you... have strong feelings about that."

"*Ugh!*" Saffron snarled. Tangling his fingers in his hair and pacing back, then turning on heel again.

"Why didn't you destroy the Tapestry Hall after performing that spell? Like all the others that came after. With a veil spell. Or all the other false ones you planted around Avren."

"I did not plant all those other ones without help—or do you really think I can be in so many places at once?" Ryder smirked. "A handful of defecting beantighes helped me out, actually, in exchange for helping them through the veil. I hoped to throw the fey, their oracles, off my scent—but clearly not you. I never once thought I would be able to throw you off, Saffron. You're too smart. Have you figured out what I'm looking for, yet? It should be obvious by now."

Saffron almost responded, demanding Ryder answer his question first—but forced himself to pause. Just for a breath, to catch it, to think about his priorities. Especially with someone so insufferable and prone to word-games.

"It's for finding lost things, isn't it?" he conceded, choosing his words carefully. Not wanting to imply he knew more than he did; let alone exactly how much Adelard was able to share with him. *He's trying to contact the dead.*

Ryder hummed thoughtfully, tapping a finger on the table like, despite Saffron's effort, he knew better. Like he could tell when Saffron was lying; like he really did hold Saffron to a higher standard than that. Saffron bit his lip, but added a bit more: "You're looking for a memory tapestry. One you first thought would be in the Tapestry Hall, but wasn't."

"Have you figured out who exactly it is I'm looking for?"

Saffron bit his lip, and Ryder cooed after it took him longer than a moment to respond.

"Come on, your highness—you've figured out where I'll be going next, but you haven't thought any deeper than that? Maybe you're not as impressive—"

"It's someone to do with the war," Saffron blurted, unable to help himself. Ryder cocked an eyebrow, before smirking again.

"Very good, Saffron, but that doesn't answer my question. You're making it far more complicated than it really is. Don't make me tell you, that's no fun."

Saffron's mind whirled, forcing himself to think more simply —and the answer slammed against him like an avalanche. Visions of blonde hair and straddling the lap of a high fey who resembled Taran; The Morrígan's temple with a notorious history; the queen's coronation route.

"Queen—" Saffron choked, the word vomiting out of him at the exact moment he made the connection. "You really are trying to find—Queen Proserpina's memory tapestry?"

"Good boy."

"Why?" Saffron croaked. Unable to believe it. Having been so certain in his conversation with Adelard that such an idea was simply too—outrageous, even for Ryder Kyteler. "What could you possibly want with...?"

Ryder chuckled. "I'll tell you, but only if you help me warm up a little."

"Oh—fuck off," Saffron snapped. But Ryder got to his feet, even as Taran's ears flattened again in threat. Saffron could still only see the man's silhouette as he paced the edge of the room, finally coming to a halt by a row of hooks on the wall by the door. When he turned back and took a few steps toward Saffron, Saffron snorted at the sight of rope looped in his hand.

"Are you serious?"

"If it makes you feel better. C'mon, Saff, I'm shivering my ass off here. I know you are too. I can hear your teeth chattering every time you speak."

Saffron clamped his mouth shut again, before scoffing. He approached, snatching the rope from Ryder's hand. The man said nothing, just turned and bent his arms behind his back for Saffron to bind. And Saffron did—gladly, willingly, tying the rope as tight as Baba Yaga would truss a wild turkey on Mabon. Ryder huffed and grunted a few times from the roughness of it, but said nothing, never attempted to fight back.

Once Saffron was done, he grabbed Ryder's bound arms and yanked him back, summoning a sharp laugh as Ryder stumbled and landed on the bed.

"Easy, your highness—don't you have a fiancé?"

"Another word and I'll throw you out into the snow."

Ryder considered that, closing his mouth but continuing to smile. Saffron pointed at the wall in instruction, and Ryder did as he was told, lying back on the bed and turning to face it. Only when his eyes were finally moved away could Saffron breathe again, giving Taran an uneasy look before approaching the bed, crawling onto the lumpy mattress and silently pressing himself into Ryder's back.

The man was not nearly as warm as he tried to claim, but god help him, anything was better than shivering until his fingers snapped off. Saffron was even desperate enough to shove the bottom of Ryder's shirt up a few inches, just enough to press his hands directly against the man's skin, making him writhe and laugh in discomfort. Saffron just bit back another threat for him to be quiet.

"Now answer me," he grumbled once they both settled down. "What do you want with the queen's memory tapestry? Are you even good enough with memory threads to be able to read it?" Playing dumb on purpose, despite everything Adelard had explained about *woven vessels* churning in the back of his mind. Not wanting to give Ryder any ideas to mislead him, to lie and trick with his silver tongue.

"Even if I'm not," Ryder breathed, "I know people who are."

"Answer my real question."

Ryder's body bounced slightly as he chuckled.

"Her majesty destroyed all of her journals and missives just before Verity Holt brought her down. Surely even you know that much, with how often you stick your nose in places it doesn't belong."

"Watch it."

"Is it so outrageous to simply—want to know? To want to know why she did what she did, what made her finally snap. Her first lover was a human, after all; she even lived amongst humans for many years, never thinking she would end up queen. So what changed her mind?"

Saffron stared at the broadness of Ryder's back, how the fabric of his shirt strained slightly every time the man took a breath.

"What good would it do?" Saffron asked quietly. Ryder lifted his head like he hadn't heard, but Saffron went on without repeating himself. "How is that supposed to help you help the humans trying to find better lives? Just make your own choices."

"There may be things in her memories that can *help me help the humans trying to find better lives,*" Ryder argued flatly. "I only have to find them, first. I know there's good reason why they were hidden away so well, but—I'm going to find them, no matter how many tries it takes. I know they'll respond to my call soon enough."

"Maybe you need to try a different spell," Saffron muttered. "Seeing as this one isn't giving you anything worthwhile to go off."

"And what makes you think I'm not getting anything worthwhile?" Ryder asked. Saffron almost rolled his eyes, to reiterate how every vision he'd personally received had only reflected memories of the location where the spell was performed, rather than where the tapestry itself was—but something told him to pause, first. To notice how Ryder's muscles tightened slightly as he said it; to recognize the slightest twinge of defensiveness in the man's voice.

Was the spell—not showing Ryder the same visions it showed Saffron?

He held his breath. Even Taran perked behind them, ears twitching like he shared Saffron's sudden intrigue.

Ryder was not a foolish man; he was stubborn, but he did not like to waste time. Especially his own. If he'd realized how useless the visions were from the start, he would not have continued with the same epithet over and over again, especially with the added trouble of traveling north. The fact he even knew that ancient spell to start with made Saffron think he'd have access to others that would work better in his favor—but then he recalled once more what the veil had once told him about that epithet, specifically. *He thinks himself a ghost's most precious thing.*

Adelard had assumed Ryder was searching for a rowan witch's memories, hoping they would respond to him as the new leader of a new human resistance. By that standard, there was no way for Saffron to know what exactly Ryder thought made him significant to *Queen Proserpina's* memories, especially in that same context—but still, Saffron's heart pinched, then thudded as he lifted his head an inch. Just enough to glance over his shoulder to where the dark wolf sat at the ready behind him. Close enough to feel the beast's warm breath on the back of his neck.

Saffron might never know what sort of delusions motivated Ryder's ego enough to make him think the queen's tapestry would respond to *him* in that capacity—but he *did* know why she might call out to her wolf king's silver remains, instead. The spell wasn't calling out to Saffron because he was a rowan witch—it wasn't even calling out to Saffron at all. It pleaded with King Clymeus' bones, which belonged to Taran, which belonged to Saffron. So desperate to be found by him, crying so loudly her voice reverberated across all of Alfidel even when nowhere near the epithet beseeching her.

Ryder had no idea Saffron witnessed the visions at all. He might not even know there were visions to be had, with how his desperation clearly grew with every attempt to summon *any* response from the missing tapestry—and it struck Saffron like a punch to the chest.

"She learned so much about the veil from opening and closing tears as much as she did, you know." Ryder went on after Saffron didn't reply, as if he believed Saffron to be intrigued by his last attempt at mystery rather than swallowing back the rush of thoughts making it hard to make sense of anything. "Her work pushed the understanding of veil magic farther than even the most practiced rowan witches like you understood. We actually have her to thank for many—"

"Her 'work'?" Saffron sneered, snapping out of his fog in an instant. Incited by those words enough to burn every other distraction away. "You mean ripping the veil open and sewing it shut as she pleased, never caring what damage she did to it or the people living nearby."

"Sometimes you have to understand history so you don't repeat—"

"I understand enough!" Saffron jolted upright, making Ryder turn to gaze up at him in the dark. "I lived it, damnit! I don't need to know Queen Proserpina's intentions to see exactly how, even with Verity and Virtue Holt kicking her off the throne —humans still never fully regained their autonomy. Not even with their magic, but just the ability to *live!* Because Queen Proserpina didn't convince high fey to hate humans all by herself— they've always resented us. So that once humans fell even an inch on the hierarchy, high fey never gave them another chance to climb back up again. Even with Elanyl, Verity's friend, in power."

"Do you think if he'd lived a bit longer, he would have had the chance to change things back to good for humans?"

"I don't know!" Saffron shouted, shoving Ryder on the shoulder. "Don't patronize me, asshole."

"Where do you think Virtue Holt has been in all this? Verity died, yes, but her brother? Why did he immediately refuse a position in the king's court to vanish into obscurity?"

"How should I know that?"

"And Harper, Verity's lover, why did she go back to the human world as soon as they were finished? When her condition would have been more easily treated here, with the fey."

"Her 'condition'?" Saffron asked, before screwing his face up and shaking his head. "You—! Harper *Kyteler*, you mean! The woman whose name you stole—!"

"Who said I stole it? Maybe I'm her son."

"Oh, sure, you resemble her exactly," Saffron sneered, grabbing Ryder's pale face with one hand and taking a handful of his blonde hair in the other. "A spitting image of dame Harper Kyteler. Do you actually think I'm stupid?"

"Not even a little bit."

Saffron wanted to squeeze until he ripped the blonde hair from Ryder's scalp, or broke his jaw beneath his grip; he wanted to sneer and reveal that, actually, he knew exactly who Harper's real descendant was, as a matter of fact—but he kept his mouth shut. Ryder likely knew all of that, too—and maybe it was dangerous for Saffron to continuing sharing everything he'd learned. It might only put Sunbeam in more danger on the other side.

That was, assuming Saffron ever let Ryder go. Even once morning came and the storm petered off. But from the moment he bound the man's hands as tightly as he could, Saffron had ideas of leashing him like a dog of his own and dragging him to the nearest town, where Aodhán or Maeve or *someone* could properly put him under arrest, to be taken back to Avren where he'd never be able to tear open the veil again—until Saffron forced him to.

# 33

# THE COLD

Saffron never fully drifted off—a part of him wasn't sure he knew how to anymore, at least not without Baba Yaga's tea —but he still sank just enough beneath the surface of drowsiness that when the sound of the wind shifted, he was the last one to notice.

Taran lifted his head. Ryder lifted his head, then turned to gaze toward the door with the broken latch that rattled and whistle against the wind. Only when the shift in direction was followed by a ground-shaking *thump* of something heavy colliding with the earth, did Saffron bolt upright, too.

Heart pounding in his ears, Ryder asked what it was, but Saffron shushed him. *Thud, thud, thud, thud,* the ground trembled with every rhythmic fall to the ground, crunching snow beneath something broad and *weighty*. It paired with heavy, but steady breaths, and all Saffron could picture was a bear, or a moose—until an impossibly dark shadow slowly blocked the gap in the door, followed by the whistling sound of an ear-piercing hiss. The moment he realized, it was already too late.

Long claws pierced the cabin's sagging rooftop, hooking into the wood and slowly tearing the ceiling away like the peel of a frostorange.

Snow and whipping wind crashed instant, hard and fast enough that Saffron had to throw his hands up to cover his face. On instinct, he lunged for his cloak still draped over the back of the chair, catching it just before the torrent carried it off into the pre-dawn sky. Still dark, except the slightest shift of light from the distant sun through thick clouds—which was more than enough to see exactly what tore the roof away. The black-scaled dragon, with indigo-blue eyes that searched inside once enough of the rafters and roof had been sheared away.

"Jesus *Christ!*" Ryder shouted before Saffron had the chance —and the dragon snorted in what could only be described as *disgust*. It then reached inside to scoop Ryder into one sharp hand, before flinging him over its shoulder. Into the air, before he vanished into the distant snow with a far-off grunt. Saffron had no time to react, to even scream, as his instincts shouted at him to *run*—but it was Taran's snarling command of the same that finally moved his body.

Shoving the table out of the way of the door, it whipped open in an instant, nearly smashing Saffron in the face from the wind. Even if it had, he wouldn't have felt it—he just barreled out into the storm, choked by the cloak around his throat and running in the first direction available to him. Not sure exactly which way Ryder was tossed, still with his arms tied behind his back; not sure which way the dragon had come from, or which way the cliffside was, or if he was headed for another—all he knew was, he wanted to get as far from the titanic beast as fast as he could, else he end up pitched into the snowy ether all the same. Else he end up a meal, or, perhaps most inconveniently—as its sacrifice, its mate, whatever it wanted to do with him.

Saffron ran into the whipping wind, pulling his cloak close and cursing the bright red color of the fabric against the white snow. He went straight for the naked trees, hardly more than dark, spindly branches with all their leaves long whipped away, knowing they would at least mask his movements better than wandering out in the open.

A dragon—a *godforsaken dragon!* Finding them not once—but twice! *Searching for them!* Cylvan wouldn't let Saffron live it down once he found out. Saffron had never doubted they were real—but at the same time, always assumed them to be long gone. That first random encounter on the road should have been the end of it, considering how they were said to be such solitary beasts —but that one seemed intent on making a meal of him.

A rumbling of wind whooshed overhead again, and Saffron ducked in a panic, bracing for claws or teeth to grab him, or giant back feet to flatten him. When nothing did, he caught his breath, and pressed on further. Deeper, into the snowy landscape. Into the white nothingness, where he would either find Ryder, find another cabin, find a town, find the dragon, or—he wasn't sure what else. Any other idea filled him with cold, aching dread. All he could think was—he hoped to live long enough to tell Cylvan what he'd seen.

Morning came and went, as far as Saffron could tell by the smallest shift in overhead light. His hands, his feet had long gone numb, but that wasn't anything he wasn't used to. He'd wandered too far plenty of times during the harsh winters at Luvon's Estate. He wasn't nervous, yet.

But then morning slipped into afternoon, then evening—and as the landscape never changed with the setting sun, Saffron felt his first rush of panic. He did his best to keep it out of his mind, just focusing on himself; on his feet, on Taran walking ahead of him as a lead through the abyss. Having to constantly remind himself to keep his cloak pulled close.

The sun set—and soon Saffron was too frigid to feel anything but the frost collecting on his hair, making his teeth chatter.

He didn't realize he'd collapsed to one knee at first, until he tried to take another step forward and his boots dragged through hip-deep snow beneath him. Frost gathered thickly on his eyelashes, though he didn't notice that at first, either; there was only snow. Whiteness. His eyes burned when he closed them for too long, and something about it only made him colder. He kept wasting his breath on his hands, fighting to keep them warm by clutching the fabric of his cloak, though even the thick underlayer of the covering had grown wet and cold. Ahead of him, Taran's dark form was the only thing he could focus on, so starkly black against the white earth. Even passing through the trees, the beast was hard to lose, as wind whipped the sides of trees and left snow like white icing on a log cake. But even with that constant proof of his continued walking—even Taran couldn't seem to find their way out of the storm.

Maybe Saffron should have let the dragon take him. At least the dragon's roost would have been warm. Its cave would have been fire-lit and its belly would have swirled with hot flames that Saffron could cling to. Was it really so bad to be nested as a dragon's mate when it was so bitterly cold outside?

When his knees finally buckled beneath him in exhaustion, he fell face-first into the snow, cloak instantly caught by the wind and bundling over him. His shoulder bag spilled over the snow, immediately vanishing into the powdery blanket of frost and blown over by the wind, summoning what might be his last cry of desperation as his sketchbook, the pouch of fairy fruits, his chain of rings, Cylvan's knife, and other belongings disappeared into the whiteness. If he'd had the strength, he might have burst into tears that very moment, but instead just collapsed back into the snow and curled up in on himself in defeat.

*"Come on, get up,"* Taran ghosted in his mind, followed by a dark snout prodding at the side of his face. Saffron didn't have the strength to push him away, arms already locked in place with frozen fingers tucked into his chest. His body didn't have enough heat left over to keep them from freezing through much longer.

"I—I c-can't," he managed to chatter, though it came out more like a withered sob. "God, it—it's so c-cold."

"You're willing to die like this?"

"Oh, fuck—fuck off-f," Saffron whimpered. Every time he

opened his mouth to speak, biting cold air rushed over his tongue, down his throat, infiltrating his chest and sucking the heat from him even faster.

"Come on, beantighe. The most powerful witch in centuries and you can't even hobble your way through a snowstorm?"

"What's that got to d-do with—with being a witch, you mutt?" He chattered, before groaning and dragging himself forward to where a imprint in the snow indicated one of his lost items. Plunging his purple hand into the depths, he dug around for the pouch of fairy fruits. Taran's words echoed in the back of his mind, while the wind blew strong enough to whip the tassels cinching the bag shut. Saffron's trembling hand tightened on it, before closing his eyes and stiffly pulling the bag into his body. Realizing—perhaps there was at least one other way out.

"T-Taran," he rasped. "Will—will you—find my th-things. In —in the snow. My sketchb-book, Cylvan's kn-knife, my ch-ch-charcoals... any—anything else that f-fell out of my bag..."

"Don't hurt yourself," Taran muttered, but turned to trail his nose through the deep snow despite the tone in his voice.

Saffron took another moment to catch his breath, to search his body for any strength that remained, before forcing himself to sit up with a pathetic, frozen sound. His cloak had already frozen to the earth, peeling up behind him like stiff wallpaper from plaster.

He managed to untie the knot on the bag, not caring to tap only a few into his palm at once and instead dumping the contents straight into his mouth. A few bounced out the sides, disappearing into the snow, but most of the bigger morsels made it to his tongue. Bright and fruity, they warmed his mouth in an instant, and even more all the way down.

One by one, Taran returned his things clamped between teeth, snout and paws thick with matted snow. Saffron's sketchbook came first, perhaps because it was easiest to sniff out. As Taran returned to uncover the rest of Saffron's trinkets, Saffron went to work fighting the wind to flip the pages of his sketchbook to where he'd drawn veil circles and accompanying notes in the past.

The berries took longer than normal to infect his frozen blood, but he felt every moment of the ice crystals in his veins slowly thawing as the sparkling magic infiltrated them. Crawling slowly from his stomach into his chest, his hips, down his arms until he could even, barely, feel the texture of the paper beneath his fingers. Until he could turn the pages one at a time.

On the page of veil circles and instructions scribbled down the side, Saffron did his best to skim what he could, before deciding. Two knocks; *two knocks for passage.*

Taran dropped the knife made from Cylvan's obsidian horn, and Saffron clutched it to his chest with a shaking hand. With his other, he slipped the hematite wand from the cuff of his sleeve, blinking through the wind and appreciating the smooth canvas of snow in front of him.

"Will you c-come here, and b-block the wi-wind," he asked, and Taran obeyed.

With the giant wolf protecting the patch of snow in front of him, Saffron stabbed the wand into the smooth whiteness, and drew his outer circle slowly. As close to perfect as he could manage, though his wobbling, discolored hand made the lines far from as pretty as the ones the veil itself had drawn around him in the ruins.

*I don't mind,* a voice cooed, and Saffron whipped around in alarm, but found nothing behind him. Goosebumps trailed down his spine, and he closed his eyes to catch his breath.

"Please h-hear me," he said out loud, voice shaking as much as his hand, terrified to even dare ask considering the last conversation he and the veil had had. Terrified it would whisk him away into nothingness, just to be done with him. "P-please help me go where I w-want to go. Please don't tr-trick me. Please take me some-somewhere s-safe."

*So now you wish to trust me? Don't I frighten you?*

"Yes—so p-prove me wrong. Please. I want to—to tr-trust you. I want to be—allies."

The presence considered that, circling him a moment longer.

*Show me where you wish to go, then,* it answered.

Saffron finished the outer circle, closing his eyes again to focus on the spelling of his destination, then how to transcribe it into Gaeilge. Amber Valley. Should he translate those words literally, or would Gaeilge spelling of the Alvish words suffice?

*Knocking is about intention. I will know you.*

Saffron swallowed back his nerves. He did his best, choosing the Gaeilge spelling of the Alvish words.

*Where, in this place?*

Saffron's hand hovered weakly over the circle, still clutching the wand, on the verge of tears as the frustrated desperation hooked into him.

"I..." he trailed off. "L-Luvon's Estate."

*Where, in this place?* It repeated.

"I..." he muttered again. He wasn't sure how to explain, or even how to picture it. What if the interior had changed since he'd last been there? What if the decor was different, what if they'd put on new wallpaper or changed the rugs? Would it matter if his memory wasn't exact? What if Luvon had guests over, like he always did—what if Saffron suddenly appeared in the entryway in front of a dozen high fey drinking wine and eating dinner? What then? It would put Luvon in danger, wouldn't it? He would have to speak for Saffron to explain it away, wouldn't he?

*Calm your mind, witch. Show me your intention. I will know you. You can trust me. As your ally.*

Saffron squeezed his eyes closed. He shoved all of those thoughts away, instead searching for someplace else. It came to him effortlessly, as soon as he allowed it to. Luvon's servants' quarters, located behind the estate house. Alongside the front half of the vineyard. Built from the same wood as the main house, though the support beams, the windows, the doors were all original while the house's interior and exterior had been updated.

Saffron imagined his old bed where he'd slept first as a child, and then for every year after. The one Luvon promised would always be there for him if he ever needed time away from Avren. From his high-fey life. He pictured the woven wool plaid blankets, the cozy linen sheets, the hand-sewn pillow under his head. He picture the fur-lined slippers he wore in the dormitory, because outdoor shoes weren't allowed past the entryway. He pictured the fireplace on the wall, burning bright and hot, the vineyard dog sometimes curled up on the rug in front of it when she wasn't sleeping in the parlor on the first floor.

Every detail of that place where he'd lived and slept since his earliest memories as a changeling child came to him more vividly and sharper than he knew possible, as if the veil's fingers coaxed even the smallest details, textures, smells, colors, sensations from the deepest recesses of his memories, so minute that only the most skilled of threadweavers would ever be able to pull the fibers of.

Before he gave his mind any chance to be distracted, Saffron's eyes snapped open. Pulling the sketchbook tight into his chest, he slammed his hand into the center of the circle, like he'd once watched Ryder do outside the palace dorms—and the frozen earth rushed to meet him.

He fell.

Past the snow and through the earth, igniting his blood with electric magic and fiery, sugary heat, whipping past his face and drawing all breath and thought and life from him. He fell and fell and fell through everything and nothing, faster than blinking and slower than incoming storm clouds—until an image split through the darkness, and he collided with it. Bouncing off and crashing to the floor with a grunt, then a groan.

The contents of his bag spilled across the same hardwood floor he once spread stolen books over—and he was home.

34

___

# THE GUARD

Luvon had Saffron wrapped so tightly, in so many blankets, it left him paralyzed in front of the fireplace in his patron master's study. Luvon's daughter, Agnea, wrote the words Saffron dictated in a letter he wished to send to Sionnach, refusing to close his eyes and sleep, to eat, to tell Luvon anything about how he ended up there until a bird was already on its way to his friend who was likely losing their mind with worry.

When Luvon asked if Saffron wanted to send anything to Cylvan as well, Saffron just groaned—and shook his head. It earned him a curious look from both his patron master and his patron's daughter, like they both wished to ask why not. Neither did. Agnea just continued writing what Saffron asked, while Luvon perched on the arm of her chair at the desk.

Sionnach—I'm safe. I've made it to Luvon mag Shamhradhaín's estate in Amber Valley. If you continue following the mountain pass, you will find the sign on the road. Luvon will send someone to meet you. I will explain everything as soon as you get here. Please be safe and don't rush. Do not worry. That uninvited guest who met us on the road is still somewhere in

the mountains. I left his ass there to freeze (if he isn't already dragon food! P.S. WOW!) I'll tell you everything soon.
    —Saffron

Sionnach would know Saffron hadn't written it, himself, by Agnea's swirling cursive handwriting and the perfect spelling of every word, but they would recognize Saffron's voice behind it. That was relief enough for Saffron to finally close his eyes and sink into the pile of blankets crushing him, the moment he watched as Luvon's bird flapped off through the window. Just before he drifted entirely, Luvon tucked the messenger token into Saffron's bundle, and Saffron managed a weary *thank you* just before sinking into the heavy darkness behind his eyes.

He did not sleep deeply, or for any length, constantly jolting awake whenever he thought he heard horses coming up the snowy drive, or voices in the hallway. Each time, he checked the messenger token that kept getting lost in his pile of blankets, until finally, the third time, the gem on the front had changed color to indicate the letter had been successfully delivered.

He sighed, smiling to himself and slumping back into the blankets in relief. That meant Sionnach and the others were also still safe, wherever they were. Safe enough to accept the message and indicate as much. If the snow storm didn't keep them stuck on the road, even at their slowest pace, they would make it to Amber Valley by morning. Thank god.

A GUST OF WIND STRONG ENOUGH TO RATTLE THE glass in the windows brought Saffron out of another restless haze. He nearly squirreled right back down into the blankets to ignore it—but the rattling of the window continued, until something in the back of his mind questioned if it was more than just the wind. Lifting his head from the warm pocket he'd made, he turned to look—gasping aloud at the sight of Fiachra flapping her wings and clawing at the window in agitation.

Throwing the blankets off, he nearly tripped over himself while hurrying to the window to yank it open, allowing the bird to crash into his chest. She squirmed and squalored, attempting to right herself in his arms, before biting endlessly at his chin and hands as if to scold him. With his opposite hand, Saffron managed to shove the window back closed again—only to notice through the thick haze of the storm, a dark silhouette parked on the cobblestone drive.

He turned on heel, hurrying barefoot from Luvon's study into the corridor outside, heart pounding as he recognized the sound of the front doors opening. Then—Sionnach's voice, shrill and trembling as they greeted the servant at the door, within a breath of asking Saffron's name before Saffron called out to them first.

Sionnach turned to look just as Saffron raced down the stairs, face flushed and hair wind-whipped from the storm. Their body slumped instantly in relief, running to hug him with a praise to the gods.

"I was so worried, gods, gods above, all of them—! I thought we'd lost you for good, when even Aodhán couldn't find you—!" They squeaked suddenly, pulling back with brown eyes wide as tea saucers. "Oh my gods, Saffron, you'll never believe— Aodhán—"

Before they could continue, Luvon swept through he front doors and erupted into a cry of fury, waving his cane over his head.

"What have you done this time, you beast! I can hear it clearly, the grinding of your damned claws on my drive! You've cracked them again, haven't you! No, don't bother trying to stick them back in! Those damn talons don't have the dexteri—I said STOP IT!"

Sionnach released another high-pitched sound, clinging to Saffron's hand and hurrying him toward the doors. Saffron stumbled after them, flinching against the sharp winter wind blasting through the entryway and bringing flurries of snow with it. He expected to find Copper and Maeve on the other side with the horses, both looking as windswept and miserably chilled as Sionnach was—but what waited for him, instead, summoned a shriek from the back of his throat.

It was—the dragon. The same one from the road. The one that tore the roof from the hunter's cottage, where it reached in a claw and scooped Ryder out, throwing him into the white abyss. That same, black-scaled dragon stood with its head lowered in Luvon's drive, looking smug as Luvon smacked it on the nose and declared all the ways it would be paying him back for the damage.

"That's—!" Saffron resisted screaming—but even over Luvon's griping shouts and the moaning wind, the beast heard his voice. Its jewel-toned, amethyst eyes flashed to where he stood in the doorway, before lifting its giant head to regard him fully. Saffron stiffened, grabbing a handful of Sionnach's sleeve as his own frightened squeak escaped him.

"That's..." Sionnach rasped, like even they couldn't believe what they were about to say. "That's Gentle Aodhán."

"Aod—!" Saffron wheezed, snapping toward Sionnach, then back toward the dragon, who extended its long neck into the covered entryway. It summoned more furious shouting from Luvon, who pounded fists against the creature's neck in protest, but the dragon just peered Saffron up and down, the heat from its skin emanating like smoldering embers after a wildfire. The breaths exhaled from its nose were as hot as steam, reeking of sulphur and the smell of burning trees.

"Get that snout out of my doorway, you brute! I will not have you stinking up my entry hall with your breath, Naoill, or may Cailleach pluck your scales for teeth!"

"*Naoill!*" Saffron's voice cracked. The earth tilted beneath him. "No, Luvon, that's—!"

But a low, rumbling sound emerged from the dragon's throat, and Saffron realized—it was chuckling. He clamped his mouth back shut again, thoughts racing in disbelief. In confusion, as he was certain—someone would have told him. If they had really been traveling with Cylvan's progenitor mother the entire time—surely, surely, someone would have told him! But then he thought of how much Aodhán and Cylvan resembled one another—more than just physically. The scoffing, the sighing, the attitude. But Aodhán didn't have horns, Aodhán and Cylvan never exchanged any pleasantries that might hint—

Unless, perhaps even Cylvan never knew it was his mother the entire time.

"Really?" Saffron asked hoarsely. The dragon's head lowered to the floor again, eyes narrowed in delight like he was reacting exactly how they hoped when he finally learned the truth.

Biting his lip, Saffron slowly extended a hand to press it against the smooth, polished scales of the dragon's snout, before jumping back again when it exhaled a wave of fire-hot breath over him.

Luvon finally got the dragon's attention back, thwacking them with his cane before yanking on one of Naoill's horns as big as he was. He flailed his legs when the dragon raised its head, lifting Luvon right along with it. The beast let out another chuckling breath, before in a wave of sweltering air, scales and claws and wings vanished. They melted into the shape of a person standing naked in the entryway.

They resembled Aodhán still in their actual appearance—or, more accurately, Aodhán's glamour had simply resembled them more than Saffron expected—though Gentle Naoill dé Fianna had black hair longer than Cylvan's, hanging straight and draping over their chest and back, ends nearly tickling the tops of their thighs. They donned the same curling black horns as their children, the same impish grin, with bright amethyst eyes and ears slightly longer and more sharply-pointed than most high fey Saffron knew. As if they were a little wilder than those who lived in Avren, for more than just their dragon-shifting.

They had strong, angular features like their oldest son, but a slightly narrower frame like Asche, though every inch of them shifted with obviously trained strength. Saffron assumed the strong cuts of muscle in their shoulders and back, especially, were from the wings they used to fly.

"I did not mean to scare you so badly in the mountains, witch," Naoill said with a sly smile, approaching to curl a finger under Saffron's chin. They were easily as tall as Cylvan, and having to look up to meet their eyes made Saffron's heart race. "I never intended to eat you, either—though after all the time we've spent together, I think I understand why my son certainly does."

Saffron's cheeks went hot, quickly averting his eyes to where even Sionnach stood in shock alongside him. Naoill proceeded to smile and purr and tease Sionnach a bit, too, rendering Sionnach paralyzed in embarrassment.

Before Saffron could ask any of the growing questions on his tongue, Luvon shuffled all of them fully inside, asking the nearest servant to bring Gentle Naoill something to wear. As if he already knew how naked the fey gentle was after shifting back, a common occurrence for Naoill to never mention it, themself. Saffron couldn't help but wonder how many times before they had wandered Luvon's house fully nude before someone finally mentioned it, Luvon never having had a second thought.

Saffron asked how far behind Maeve and Copper were, and Luvon's eyes lit up at the thought of dinner plans as Naoill answered they were moving swiftly up the road with Luvon's messenger. Saffron found comfort in that thought, relaxing a little more with the reassurance—though all thoughts of his friends were then quickly swallowed back up by everything he wished to know of the dragon-fey in front of him.

"Why were you wearing a glamour?" he asked, following as Luvon motioned them to join him in the sitting room for some hot tea by the fire. "Did Cylvan know it was you? He told me his mother returned to the Winter Court after visiting Avren—"

"Well, I did return to the Winter Court, didn't I?" Naoill asked with a smirk over their shoulder. Saffron's heart thumped at the sight, reminded so much of Cylvan—though even if he wasn't, he would have been floored by how handsome and beautiful and *thrillingly intimidating* the fey gentle was just in their smile. "Just not when Cylvan thought."

"Why?" Was all Saffron could manage, wishing he could be a little more clear with his feelings on it. But even he wasn't sure. "Were you ever planning on telling him?"

"I'm sure Saoirse has informed him by now," they answered simply.

"Saoirse knew?" Sionnach was the one to balk.

"Of course," Naoill smiled at them, next, and even they weren't immune to their icy charm. "As Saffron said, I was meant to return to the Winter Court after visiting Cylvan and the kings in Avren—never expecting another veil event to coincide with my departure. While Cylvan thought I'd already left, I tagged along with the rest of you. Curious to know..." their eyes floated back to Saffron, gazing at him a long moment. "Exactly who had sacrificed my youngest through the veil, and why my oldest insisted I couldn't eat them in retribution."

"Oh," Saffron wheezed. His feet came to a sudden halt beneath him, but Luvon was right there, sweeping him forward again as if even he knew Naoill would never do such a thing. He couldn't see the sharp-toothed grin on Naoill's face as they said it, though.

"Don't worry, witch," they continued teasingly. "You've proven yourself to me. I understand much better now, everything that happened—and why my son was so *viciously* protective of you when I first threatened. I have no interest in eating you any longer. At least—not in retribution."

"Oh," Saffron rasped again. Luvon chuckled, squeezing him, before shushing their conversation until the tea was prepared and the fire was stoked, as he wished to be fully comfortable to hear it all.

As a robe was brought to Naoill to cover their nakedness, Saffron offered to find something warm for Sionnach to change into, not to mention a pair of shoes for his own bare feet. Taking his friend's hand, he hurried Sionnach up the stairs, where the satyr secretly told him everything once out of earshot of Saffron's gossip-loving patron master.

"What did Copper and Maeve think?" Saffron asked regarding Aodhán's reveal—actually giddy at the thought of being there when they eventually learned Aodhán's *true* true identity as Cylvan's mother, once they arrived in Amber Valley.

"Copper was completely surprised—then horribly jealous that Aodhán invited me to ride on their back to get here. Instead of him."

"And what was that like?" Saffron asked with wide eyes. He had to resist asking, *'do you think they'd give me a ride on their back, too, if I asked?'*

"Cold. Windy. Terribly miserable, I must admit," Sionnach answered right away, like they could read Saffron's thoughts. "I'm sure the old dragon-riders were much better dressed than I was. Even Fiachra wasn't too thrilled, though she did stay nicely tucked in my cloak the whole way."

Sionnach reached out to pet the fluff of the bird's breast at the thought, and Fiachra affectionately nibbled on their fingers before chittering lightly. The owl could barely keep her eyes open as she perched on the back of the couch by the fire, exhausted by all the excitement. Still, as Saffron and Sionnach made their way from the study, she opened her wings and swooped out after them.

Returning to the parlor, the rest of the afternoon was spent gossiping—that time, mostly about Saffron. Mostly about Cylvan. To Saffron's horror, Luvon had collected every single gossip column that mentioned either of them in the previous weeks, having already laid them all out in chronological order on the coffee table with Naoill's help by the time Saffron and Sionnach returned. He asked Saffron to go through every single one, individually, to give him the context. The fey lord didn't need to take notes as every detail was relayed to him, even when Saffron explained why one random column waxed on and on about how surprising it was for Copper dé Bricríu to be spotted travelling with the prince's party; or why Anysta mac Delbaith kept being teased as Cylvan's secret lover. All the while, Saffron could practically see the quill scribbling letters to King Tross behind his patron's ghostly-white eyes.

When Saffron wasn't explaining the gossip columns, he sat back and drank his tea as Luvon and Naoill chatted between one another, proving they too had an old friendship not unlike Luvon did with King Tross. Eventually, Sionnach was the one to ask, and Luvon confirmed that they'd studied at Ambegun there in the Winter Court, together.

No matter how many times Luvon and Naoill tried to coax information from Saffron about his time at the bottom of the Hoarcliff Pass, he didn't want to share anything until Copper and Maeve were there to hear it, too. They would be involved with what he was thinking, next, after all.

He needed everyone who might travel with him further to hear it first from him—though he wasn't sure how any of them were going to take the news. Copper, especially, Saffron worried about, after the way his friend reacted to the first time King Ailir asked if he would proclaim loyalty to Saffron as the future king. Saffron better understood why after visiting the Fall Court and witnessing Renard dé Bricríu for himself, but—he hated not knowing how Copper would respond to anything Saffron might ask going forward. He was almost afraid to. The smallest part of him almost wanted to ignore all of it, and just enjoy his time in Amber Valley, for who knew how long of a chance he would get—

But then Maeve and Copper finally arrived in the front court-yard, and Saffron's heart beat out his fears. He leapt to his feet, racing to throw his arms around Copper, who hugged him back hard enough to make his spine pop. Maeve didn't hug back nearly as firmly, but even her embrace came with a reassured sigh, commenting how glad she was to find him alive and well.

Learning Aodhán's true identity was what actually made the sídhe lady pop, practically shrieking before clamping a hand over her mouth in disbelief. Then—an undeniable sheen of adoration draped her expression, like knowing everything Naoill had seen of Cylvan's behavior was akin to a spiritual experience. Something for Maeve to dwell on for years to come—and to humiliate Cylvan with for the rest of his life.

Rather than disturbing the comfortable, casual energy in the parlor by moving to dinner in the dining hall, Luvon had their plates prepared ahead of time and brought to them by the fire. Saffron, Sionnach, and Copper sat crossed-legged on the floor at the table while the others remained in their chairs and on the couch, enjoying the hot meal of roast beef and root vegetables, apple frostwine—which Luvon was thrilled to finally be able to serve without Cylvan there to worry about—and more sweet treats than any of them knew what to do with. Well—anyone but Naoill, who devoured plate after plate of the entree, the side dishes, clearly starving after shifting into such a great beast and then back again. It made Saffron wonder exactly how much they'd been holding back, all that time previous.

Saffron especially indulged in the apple wine, until his words slurred slightly, and the nerves in his gut were drowned beneath sparkling inebriation. When he finally had the confidence to do so, he wobbled to his feet, shuffling to stand in front of the fire and get everyone's attention.

"Hello," he announced. "I have something to say. I'm going to regale you with the story of how I fell off a cliff and was almost eaten by a dragon."

Naoill grinned while the others laughed under their breaths—and Saffron began. He wove a wandering tale of survival and intrigue, too drunk to even lower his volume when he started talking about sharing a bed with Ryder, and the things Ryder said to him. No one else hushed him, though, too captivated by what he shared. Even as he talked about his miraculous escape through the veil, there was no pause for waiting questions, no hesitation to choose his words wisely. A part of him didn't care if anyone else heard—it would only be Luvon's beantighes, anyway. Maybe they had a right to know.

"So he really is seeking a memory tapestry," Naoill spoke first once Saffron finished. "Like your professor said."

Saffron nodded, taking a long, gulping drink from his wine glass. Luvon extended the bottle to pour more for him right away, like he wished to keep Saffron's lips flapping loudly and liberally.

"What in gods' name could he want with the Night Queen's, though?" Luvon asked next. "Does it have something to do with his connection to the witchhunters?"

"Actually," Saffron started, and Luvon looked toward him with bright, anticipatory eyes. "I have it on good authori—authorititty that the witchhunters are not happy wi—with Mr. Kyteler at the moment."

"What good authority?" Maeve asked.

"My infallible gut instinct."

"Saffron," Sionnach chuckled.

"No, no, I mean it," Saffron said, waving his wine glass a little too enthusiastically. "I've thought it since they stopped the train on our way to Erelaine. I cannot remember any of ways I came to those conclusions, exactly—they're buried beneath a bathtub full of apple wine at the mo—moment—but I can assure you, they are not happy with him. They also don't know where the fuck he is either—so we have had that leg up on them all this time. We guessed it a while ago, on the train—oh, I said that already, didn't I?"

"Sorry, who is 'we'?" Luvon asked.

"The big dog in me."

"... Ah. Lord Taran."

"Yes. Like I said," Saffron grinned.

"But if the witchhunters aren't loyal to Ryder anymore, what else could he possibly do with the queen's threads? He can't read them himself, can he?" Sionnach asked.

"We don't know if they're *unloyal*," Copper interjected. "Maybe they're just pissed off like the rest of us that he's causing so much commotion. Witchhunters have never been ones for drawing lots of attention, unless it's on purpose."

"But there were witchhunters are the Midsummer Games, right Saffron?" Sionnach went on with pursed lips. "They knew what he was doing."

"Maybe some of them," Saffron said, waving his glass a little more. "Or maybe—none of them knew the *extent* of what Ryder was planning on doing, seeing as him opening the veil was his second plan if I didn't let my dog loose on everyone there." Saffron took a long drink at the reminder, wiping his mouth as Naoill graciously refilled his cup. "And—there are a lot of witchhunters, you know? Perhaps they don't *all* love what Ryder's doing. Especially considering—he's not exactly using them for what they're meant for, you know. Catching witches and—and *et cetera.*"

"So it's safe to assume Ryder Kyteler has not yet found the queen's memory threads, then," Naoill brought the conversation back to the main point. "And by the way he was traveling north, we should assume he'll continue his search here."

"I think so," Saffron grinned, pointing at them in confirmation. "Good. Beautiful *and* smart. I see where Cylvan g-gets it."

Naoill smirked.

"Where do you think he might look next? Master Luvon, Gentle Naoill?" Sionnach asked. "What places are known to be significant to Queen Proserpina in the Winter Court?"

Luvon and Naoill looked at one another, grimacing.

"Plenty," Luvon answered. "Seeing as King Clymeus was from the Winter Court, and Proserpina's coronation route originated in Vjallrod; not to mention the Fjornaran Oralcry located a little ways out of the city, which is know for its connections to the veiled queen."

"Her—her woven coven," Saffron said, before furrowing his brows. "I mean—her cluster. Her woven clams."

"Her cloister of woven vessels," Naoill whispered in correction, quoting what Adelard had told them. Saffron pointed at them in agreement."Perhaps the king's church in Vjallrod? Though if they actually had such a thing, I doubt they would be able to keep it quiet... have you heard anything, Luvon? Considering you know all of the Winter Court's dirtiest secrets."

"No mention of any royal memory tapestries in the King's Church, no," Luvon said, sighing with a bone-deep disappointment as he did. "I imagine another potential location may very well be the mac Delbaith estate."

*"No,"* Taran insisted in a growl, but Saffron audibly shushed him.

"Hold on, are we looking for Ryder or this memory tapestry now?" Copper asked, mouth full of meat as juice dripped down his chin. "'Cause I can't beat the snot out of a memory tapestry."

"Both," Saffron said. "Whichever comes first. If we find Ryder first—we can leave the tapestry wherever it is for now, to worry about later. If we find the tapestry first—we make sure Ryder doesn't get it."

*And*—Saffron halted the words from escaping his mouth before speaking them aloud—*if we find the tapestry first, maybe we could even use it to leverage Ryder into giving my friends back.*

"Well, nothing we can do about it tonight," Luvon said as a contemplative silence festered over his parlor that was only ever meant to boom with laughter and amusement. He raised a glass to Saffron, cheering him without word, before throwing it back and clapping his hands together. "How about a game of blindman's bluff, hm? Come on, everyone have a little more to drink. We'll continue this sorry conversation in the morning."

Saffron gulped back the rest of his wine. Gladly. He even had some more, laughing as Luvon picked Copper to wear the blindfold, and the rest of the players scattered around the room to be searched for. Each time he felt the pinch of Cylvan's absence, Saffron drank more. Until he could hardly see straight, until he could hardly feel the twist of disappointment that he would, eventually, climb into bed alone to prepare for what would come next.

He hoped, at least, whatever he was doing in Avren—Cylvan was warm and safe, too.

# 35

# THE LETTER

Saffron had only ever slept in the guest beds of Luvon's estate a handful of times as a beantighe, even his favorite one. It felt strange, like he didn't belong on that perfectly soft mattress between so many thick layers of fur and wool, breathing in the warm air of the crackling fire that never died thanks to charmed birch wood in the hearth. Feeling like he didn't belong, but at the same time—he slept like the dead. As if the familiar taste of frostapple wine, the smell of burning birch logs on the fire, the whistling of winter wind on the other side of the window, the feeling of woven-wool and fur-lined blankets, all combined into the same magical effect as what Baba Yaga did to charm her sleeping teas.

The following morning, it was surreal to wake to the sound of beantighes knocking on doors and ringing the waking bell, inviting all the mag Shamhradhaín guests down for breakfast. Saffron stumbled from the nest of blankets where Sionnach remained nestled somewhere inside, though soon followed behind him with their hair a mess and eyes groggy with hungover exhaustion from the wine-fueled entertainment of the night before.

Breakfast was a spread of grilled white fish on toast, soft-boiled eggs, egg and bacon ragout, apple pancakes, and all the champagne and frostfruit juice they could drink. Most of the others opted out of alcohol so early in the morning, especially after how late they'd been up playing parlor games the night prior, but Saffron helped himself. Maybe people in the Winter Court drank more than all the others combined, in their efforts to keep warm in the bitter chill.

When a beantighe approached Saffron from behind to offer him two letters in their hand, he thought it was a mistake, motioning for them to take them to Luvon—but the beantighe just cleared their throat and quietly insisted. Taking them, Saffron saw the way his name was written on the front of the top envelope, knowing exactly who had sent it—and his heart fluttered. Unable to wait, he used the nearest clean butter knife to slice it open.

ARE YOU STILL AT MORRÍGAN? I KNOW I SAID I WOULD NOT DO THIS. PLEASE COME BACK TO AVREN SOON.

Saffron's insides twisted in regret—before the alcohol in his blood sparked, and frustration mixed with it. Unsure exactly how to describe the unique emotion swirling in his chest—worried for his prince and missing him; still sore about how they'd parted ways. Even after declaring to all of his friends that Saffron had no intention of leaving Cylvan for good anytime soon—there was still so much of their argument that stung.

Excusing himself, he hurried from the dining room into Luvon's study nearby. Grabbing the nearest quill, he wrote a response directly beneath Cylvan's request:

*I am not ready to return to Avren yet, but I am glad you arrived safely. I hope you are able to rest.*

He folded it up exactly the same. He crossed out his name on the front, and wrote Cylvan's beneath it. Seeking out the beantighe who'd delivered it to him, Saffron asked them to send his reply as soon as the messenger bird had some time to rest. The beantighe just looked at him with eyebrows raised, like no one in that house had ever sent a response to anything within minutes of receiving it. Regret further mixed with frustrations in Saffron's chest—but he pushed it down, especially when he was reminded, there had been a second letter handed to him at the table. Forgotten in the rush of emotions.

Returning to Luvon's study, he spotted the extra letter where it'd slipped to the floor, picking it up with an eyebrow raised in question by his name written on the front of a black envelope, in silver ink.

"*Oh,*" Taran whispered suddenly, and Saffron knew in an instant, long before he saw the wax seal pressed into the back. The same motif that had followed them from city to city, from Avren, to Erelaine, and beyond. The mac Delbaith wolf.

*Lord Saffron mag Shambradhain,*

*Prince Cylvan informed me you are spending some quality time with Master mag Shambradhain; I would be honored if you would join me for a fete at my family estate, tomorrow night. I'm sure you would love an opportunity to become acquainted with members of the Winter Court's high society, during your continued stay in Alfidel.*

*Lady Anysta mac Delbaith.*

Saffron's insides clenched, before letting loose again.

Cylvan hadn't told Anysta a thing—the prince did not even know Saffron had left Beantighe Village. It meant Anysta had eyes in even more places than Saffron ever thought—or, perhaps less maliciously, had simply pieced her own conclusion together once news of Cylvan's sole return to Avren spread through gossip channels.

Had they not just had the conversation about the mac Delbaith estate the night prior, in regard to possible hiding places for the queen's tapestry, he might have even *eagerly* refused such an invitation—but instead, he just gazed down at the fine hand-written letters.

*"The queen's memory tapestry is not being held anywhere in my family home,"* Taran reiterated yet again. Saffron still couldn't tell if it stemmed from a sense of self-consciousness, or defensiveness, or a genuine wish for Saffron to not waste everyone's time—but Saffron still was not convinced.

Besides—the way he saw it, even if the queen's tapestry, itself, was not located somewhere in the belly of the mac Delbaith estate —that didn't mean there weren't other secrets he was interested to learn. Considering their relation to King Clymeus; Anysta's status as a Dagdan priestess, where she'd surely spent some time of her own studying in Fjornar. Saffron didn't know for sure, he didn't know enough about the sect of worship—only that it left plenty of opportunity for things that might interest him.

He took up his quill, penning a response.

*Dear Lady Anysta,*
> *I am flattered to be invited. I will be sure to attend.*
> *Until then,*
> *Lord Saffron.*

*"Surely you don't intend on going alone, at least,"* Taran grumbled next, stirring as if preparing everything he wished to argue if Saffron were to confirm it. But even Saffron wasn't that reckless— not to mention, a fete at the mac Delbaith estate wouldn't be nearly as fun without his friends to join him. Whether or not Anysta expected them.

Luvon was not thrilled at the thought of Saffron attending a mac Delbaith fete—but once his horror wore off, a mischievous grin took him over, and suddenly he was whispering to himself, planning exactly what Saffron would wear the following night. Within a few hours, and a handful of birds sent and returned, he even had a guest list compiled of all the others who would be attending. No one of particular note, according to him—only that, a handful of them specifically mentioned their eagerness to 'greet the mac Delbaith's special guest.' Saffron's first instinct was to assume that was in reference to himself, somehow —but by Luvon's details, it was clear the dinner party had already been planned as early the night before Saffron met with Anysta. Someone else was on her roster—and his thoughts spun endlessly in consideration.

His was not the only one, as Taran stirred endlessly in the back of Saffron's mind. Endlessly muttering to himself and circling round and round, resulting in Saffron constantly confusing the wolf's whispers with overhearing voices in Luvon's house. Until Saffron himself paced back and forth past the tall windows of the library, while Sionnach sat in one of Luvon's chairs with a book, Copper and Naoill played a game of cards, and Maeve appreciated the golden-blade rapier displayed over the fireplace.

When Saffron finally couldn't take Taran's agitation any longer, he slammed his hands to his head as if it would knock the wolf off his feet, before exclaiming he would be outside if anyone needed him. Sionnach snapped their book shut and followed, which meant Copper followed, then Naoill, and even Maeve who threw her head back with a sigh and trudged along behind.

*"Icarus, come,"* Saffron said, once draped in his thick cloak and wearing his boots, standing in Luvon's snowy back garden, tucked in the trees where no peeking beantighes would be able to see. The beast emerged in an instant, and only then did Saffron realize it was many of his friends' first time seeing the wolf that was once a fey lord.

"Oh, Lord Taran, aren't you handsome!" Naoill said first,

sounding almost exactly like Cylvan and earning a curled lip from Taran who just swung his giant head away.

"He's driving me mad," Saffron said. "He's more agitated than anyone else at the thought of going home—Taran, why don't you go for a run in the woods and give me a damn break from all your pacing?"

"You'd be more agitated if you had any idea what you're getting yourself into," Taran grumbled in response, pawing at the earth in a mix of annoyance and embarrassment. Especially with everyone watching him like that, the fur on the back of his spine prickled in self-consciousness.

"I never expected him to be so... big," Sionnach whispered, shuffling a little closer but never fully emerging from behind Saffron's back. Intimidated by the massive black wolf that, at full height, could press his snout into Saffron's sternum. Saffron glanced over his shoulder at them, just as Copper made a noise, then scoffed, crossing his arms.

"He's not that big," he muttered. *"Big* doesn't mean anything, anyway, where it matters..."

"Like I haven't already run circles around you once, fox," Taran growled back. Copper's nose wrinkled, his next response to unclip his cloak and begin stripping off his clothes. Saffron couldn't help but laugh, throwing out his arms to catch his friend's discarded pants until Copper was fully naked in the snow. He shifted into his fox form, landing on all four feet before bounding back up again to leap at the wolf. Taran let out a sharp bark of surprise, stumbling backward before catching his footing and snapping his teeth in warning, only for Copper to release a shrill laugh as he hopped back, side to side, then pounced again to bite at Taran's tail.

That was the end of Taran's stoicism, as he lunged back, then took chase as Copper darted away. They disappeared into the trees in a volley of upturned snow and topsoil, the sound of yipping and breaking branches following quickly behind.

"No different from when they were kids, hm, Maeve?" Naoill

chuckled, crossing their arms as they gazed toward Maeve who pinched the bridge of her nose.

"A lot less fur and teeth, back then."

"I don't know about less teeth."

"Cylvan was the only one who ever bit first."

Naoill threw their head back with a laugh, and Saffron couldn't resist grinning the same.

"Did you all spend a lot of time in the Winter Court together?" he asked, and Maeve sighed again like an exhausted mother.

"Mostly during holidays; it wasn't unusual for Copper to be passed off to Naoill rather than spending it at home with his family, and the kings always brought Cylvan to the Winter Court for Yule. My family has a house up here as well, so my parents would drag us along to join them. And Taran's family already lived here, so you can imagine it was easy for us all to be tossed into the same room during fetes." She glanced briefly at Sionnach. "Sionnach too, occasionally. Though they mostly just clung to Lady Étaín's hand or hid behind her skirt all night long."

"I never knew what the rest of you would do to me," Sionnach said with a weary laugh, shaking their head.

"Copper spent Yules with you?" Saffron asked Naoill, who nodded.

"Sometimes. I knew his mother during our school years, and before she left, she... asked me to keep an eye on him."

Saffron wanted to ask what that meant, especially since it was the first time he'd ever heard mention of Copper's mother—but the sound of snarling and shrill fox-laughter from the snowy wood distracted him.

"Meanwhile, Taran's father hardly let him out of sight for longer than an hour at a time," Maeve went on thoughtfully, a pinch of sadness tingeing the words as she gazed into the woods like Saffron did. "I wonder... if a part of him prefers the way he is now. None of those people even know he's alive anymore. They can't bother him, like they used to..."

Saffron's heart squeezed. He followed her eyes into the trees, where only the noises of the playing beasts and the occasional shadow or flash of bright orange showed where they tumbled over one another. He'd never thought of that—but was struck with a sudden, unexpected wash of protectiveness. Over the same beast he once hated, a beast he once would have wished death upon at the first chance he got.

But while Taran had done many horrible, terrible things—not unlike like the veil being torn open to serve those who had the right keys, Taran mac Delbaith had been torn open and forced to accept magic he never wanted; magic that would be turned loose against his friends and anyone else who got in the way of what the mac Delbaiths wanted. Through the removal of his own body, his bones, to be replaced with those of a stranger. And just like Saffron couldn't blame the veil for causing so much harm when it was torn against its will—for the first time, he thought he couldn't fully blame Taran for all the wrongs he'd done, either.

"Well," he whispered, responding to Maeve's comment. "He belongs to me, now. No one will be bothering him again anytime soon, as far as I'm concerned."

Maeve watched him for a moment, before the corner of her mouth lifted into a tiny smile.

"Considering the mood he's in—I think he knows that, too."

Saffron almost asked what she meant, considering Taran was never in a mood other than *bitey* and *hostile*—but then came the sound of Copper's beastly trilling and more breaking branches, the barking and snarling of a wolf, heavy bodies chasing and ramming into one another. Never once was there any cry of pain. There was no wet sound of teeth sinking into flesh. There was only the wild playfulness of two beasts chasing one another between the trees, and that told Saffron exactly what he needed to know.


CYLVAN'S BIRD BALOR ARRIVED AGAIN ON THE TAIL OF the following sunrise, that time tapping his beak directly against the glass of the window and drawing Saffron from sleep. Arriving just as the sun did, a sign that Cylvan had sent his response in the earliest hours of the morning.

Fiachra flapped to the windowsill, angrily tapping back at the raven, squaloring at him in a way that crossed language barriers as the blackbird just croaked right back and flared his wings. Fiachra flared hers in return, until they both showed off their very impressive wingspans. Relentlessly clacking their beaks and causing enough of a ruckus that Saffron finally kicked his thick blankets away to break it up. He held Fiachra under his arm like a clamoring farm hen and opened the window for Balor to hop inside, where the bird shook off the snow collecting in his dark feathers.

Saffron pulled Cylvan's note from the envelope, but a second piece of parchment slipped out and to the floor with it. Stooping to grab it, he read the headline before ever seeing what Cylvan wrote—and his heart stopped.

*VEIL EVENT REPORTED IN FALL COURT AROUND TIME OF PRINCE CYLVAN'S VISIT; Folks Beginning To Wonder If The Dagda Is Trying To Speak Through The Veil. High Councillor Demands Precipitous Court Of Expectations While Fjornaran Oracles Remain In Avren...*

"What?" Saffron rasped in surprise, hurrying to open Cylvan's letter with shaking hands.

Please come. I need you, Saffron.

Saffron sank back onto the edge of the bed, staring at Cylvan's words as his heart pounded in his ears. But—a Court of Expectations, the ceremony to determine whether the next ruler would have a Morning, Day, Evening, or Night Court, was only ever meant to happen once the coming ruler had chosen a Harmonious Partner. Only once they were preparing to be crowned. Not so far away. Not while the current kings were still in such good health, and may still have another hundred years of their reign to go. Was it a threat on King Ailir's life? Or were the people really just so terrified of all the things Ryder had done—and blaming Cylvan for it, still?

The papers wrinkled in Saffron's hands as fury and fear and worry saturated him. Wasn't Cylvan dealing with enough, already? Hadn't he already done enough for every damned soul in Alfidel?

Saffron leapt to his feet, prepared to pull on his shoes and start preparing to return—but he caught his reflection in the mirror, first. Since arriving in Amber Valley, he'd finally been eating well again. He'd finally claimed a few good nights' rest, as Ryder hadn't yet performed the summoning spell that always woke him to screams.

Saffron *looked* better, even almost looked back to normal, but —there was an emptiness in his eyes. Deep enough that he recognized it in himself—an emptiness he couldn't explain, one he didn't know how to fix. One he was certain wouldn't fill again if he returned to Avren prematurely. He had to find Ryder one last time, first. He had to find the queen's memory tapestry, first. He had to at least try searching one last place, the same place he was set to have dinner that very night.

Closing his eyes, Saffron inhaled a deep, uneven breath. Rather than rushing down the stairs to prepare to leave, he instead walked silently to the writing desk against the wall. That time, he used a brand new piece of paper, and properly addressed it.

*Cylvan, I will leave first thing tomorrow morning. Everything will be alright. You are in my thoughts, always.*

His hand hesitated a moment, nib dangling so close to the paper a rogue drop of ink kissed the surface, spreading like a dark web between the fibers. Saffron swallowed against the lump in his throat, slowly adding: *I love you,* and hating how his heart raced in the worst way. Like he wasn't sure—that was still a thing that would bring Cylvan comfort.

AN HOUR'S CARRIAGE RIDE FROM AMBER VALLEY SAT Vjallrod, the largest city in the Winter Court accessible by road. Built into the embrace of a half-moon cliffside, buildings and spires made of metal and stone reached up to meet the piercing peaks of the snow and ice-capped mountains behind them, marking the end of any hospitable plains for miles and miles past. Saffron knew that place well enough, at least along the route Luvon used to travel to sell his goods or meet with friends for a drink, but he'd never travelled into the city much deeper than the exterior rim where things weren't so cramped, crowded, bustling in every direction with pedestrians and carriages.

Morrígan Academy dressed itself in humble iconography of the great queen; Avren deified Lugh; and Vjallrod, Luvon had once told him, paid tribute to Cailleach Bhéarra. The goddess of winter, bringer of frost and storms, decider of life and death in the darkest months of the year. She who determined when winter came, when it ended; a crone who rode across the sky during Samhain on the back of a dark wolf as large as a horse, when she wasn't herding her prized deer across the countryside. But only on that frigid morning, as they approached the gates of the city, did Saffron realize why the goddess' name was so familiar compared to all the previous times he'd visited and thought about it—it was similar to the Gaeilge word for *veil*.

The very same was illustrated by the crone carved from stone, standing protector over Vjallrod's gates with a hand extended toward the road as if to strike down any who meant her people harm. Depicted with long, wild hair that spilled out from beneath the back of the veil she wore, her aged face showed weathering from the very storms she was said to bring, eyes closed with a third painted on her forehead to see without seeing.

Stuck in the stone pedestal by her feet was a staff as tall as she was, and behind her, stood the unsettling form of a wolf that resembled Saffron's own a little too closely.

When he was younger, Saffron used to stand beneath that statue clutching the reins of Luvon's horse while the man made conversation with other travelers on the road. He'd gaze up at her towering form and wonder why the high fey would ever worship someone who they depicted to be so frightening—only to later return to Morrígan after the holidays, to hold Baba Yaga close and kiss her aged cheeks even as she hollered at others walking into the house with muddy boots. Perhaps there was simply something comforting about being on the good side of an old witch.

The crone's name wasn't the only thing that rang with familiarity that time he visited, and Saffron's grip on the wine glass in his hand tightened as they passed beneath the old woman's gaze in the carriage. The veiled one; patron of wolves; she who decided the cycle of death and storms that brought it. Proserpina—Aryadna—the veiled queen, and Clymeus, the wolf king, had their fated first meeting there in Vjallrod, according to stories. The significance of what would come after was not lost on Saffron that evening, making it hard to meet the gaze of the eye painted on the statue's forehead.

No matter—he wasn't there for the old crone. He wasn't there to pay respect to the queen, or the king, or anyone else for that matter. He was there to find Proserpina's memory tapestry before Ryder did—whether or not Anysta mac Delbaith would be able to show him in the right direction. And even as Taran continued to insist there was no such thing in his family home—even he, eventually, admitted Saffron's instinct was right. The mac Delbaith estate had secrets, as deep as the family's own ran. And while Saffron might not find the tapestry, specifically—even Taran would admit, there were plenty of other things he could steal that could force even Anysta to bend a knee as he needed.

36

—————

## THE DINNER

The mac Delbaith estate was located outside of the city, up a winding road through the frozen mountains where even the Winter Court horses pulling the carriage snorted and protested as snow fell in thick clumps from the sky. Through the windows there was only a wall of frost-laden pine trees on either side, steeped in darkness prickled with orange light from the carriage lamps that swung to and fro on either side of the cab.

Inside, each passenger huddled close to one another, particularly Sionnach and Copper who weren't used to the cold of the Winter Court, even thick layers of wool doublets and cloaks barely enough to keep their warmth in.

A few times, Saffron turned to gaze nervously through the window between himself and the back of the driver, wondering if it had all been a trick. If there really was no mac Delbaith estate that far out into the dark wood—but surely Taran would have said something if that were the case. Still, Saffron had both his knife and his wand tucked away in the inner pocket of his doublet, down under the cuff of his sleeve, just in case. He wouldn't be caught without either of them ever again.

When the house did finally come into view, Saffron was

strangely emboldened to know it wasn't anything bigger or grander than Luvon's estate on the outside, though he could tell the age of it from the off-color of the glass in the windowpanes, the stonework, the metal shingle work supporting centuries of ice and snow on the peaked rooftops. A garden of winter roses and frozen fountains decorated the front side, and by the glowing light of lanterns in the back, Saffron knew it likely extended further in the rear. Perhaps even all the way to the base of the mountainside.

*"If you look closely, there, toward the northwest side of the cliffs... you may be able to see the glow of Fjornar's belltower,"* Taran mumbled as Saffron stepped from the carriage, and chills unrelated to the temperature kissed his skin. He searched the dark mountainside carpeted with centuries of snow as Taran suggested, until he thought he saw the faintest glimmer of light within the trees.

None from the mac Delbaith family greeted them at the door, though the human servant that requested an invitation wrinkled their nose slightly when Saffron produced Anysta's letter over anything else more formal. He braced to be kicked in the ass right back out into the snow, but the beantighe motioned them in, though the dirty look on their face remained as all of Saffron's group followed along on his heels, Copper especially shoving his way inside in need of warmth. Sionnach, more politely, hurried past the rest right on his heels.

The beantighe who greeted them wore finer clothes than Saffron expected of a family who despised humanity so much—but perhaps it shouldn't have been a surprise, either. If there was anything the mac Delbaiths hated more than humans, it was looking cheap.

While expecting to go straight to the dining hall for dinner, Saffron was once again only partially surprised to learn the dinner itself was already in progress—and he'd only been invited to attend the fete afterward. His instinct was to be insulted—Cylvan definitely would have been—but instead, Saffron just grabbed a glass of champagne from the nearest tray, throwing it back and entering the room where a few-dozen other high fey mingled.

Clearly more half-invited guests, all looking far too thrilled to be there despite being hardly more than filler, not even invited to the main dinner. Dressed in their finest clothes, some older Winter Court traditional garb while many other had clearly purchased their own recently. Saffron wondered who would be so important that high fey would travel so far north to meet them at Anysta's offer, before internally rolling his eyes and himself and taking another drink. Anyone. High fey would cross open seas and vast prairies at any fete invitation, no matter who sent it.

Ultimately, it was no matter to him who those people were or where they came from, how far they traveled, even who exactly they were all so excited to meet. Once the main dinner was over, and the remainder of the guests joined them in the ballroom, Saffron would have a better idea of where everyone was. He could better figure out the means of slipping away, to begin his search to perform Ryder's own searching spell. A broom closet. The back gazebo. It didn't matter. He paused his considerations to make room for Taran's repeated promise he would find nothing with it —but the wolf didn't comment, that time. Like he had finally accepted, even he wasn't sure what was possible any longer.

When the time came for the dinner guests to join the rest in the ballroom, Saffron was unsurprised by the sort of high fey who appeared, instincts confirmed by Taran in the back of his mind as he lazily listed off names of any face he recognized. A handful of sídhe family members, court nobility, local businessmen, patrons of the biggest gossip papers in Alfidel, a handful of foreign diplomats that even Taran was perturbed to see coming out of dinner with his sister. But those surprised Saffron least, once the final guest emerged—wearing the mask of a stag, the only one in the entire room who did.

It must have only been a beantighe, put on display in a more visibly demeaning way than just a veil. Saffron tried not to think about it, instead searching for another drink to imbibe on while keeping a close eye on his friends who mingled around the room on their own, especially once the remaining dinner guests arrived and some recognized particularly Copper and Maeve.

"The dinner wasn't anything better than they serve in the palace, I can assure you."

Chills raced down Saffron's back, going stiff as his heart thumped loudly in his ears. He hadn't noticed anyone sidling up alongside him—but it wasn't only the unexpected presence that startled him. It was the owner of the voice.

Saffron turned just barely, just enough to see out of the corner of his eye. Standing alongside him, not a beantighe, but a fey lord wearing the mask of the deer. The lower half of his face was pulled into a bitterly familiar crooked, but tight-lipped smile that would have given him away if his voice hadn't already. Even in the fine doublet he wore, objectively handsome in that shade of dark red and accentuated with black beading that spilled from the collar down the front. But even dressed more regally than Saffron could have ever imagined—he would know that voice, that uneven smile, anywhere.

He had to resist grabbing the knife from his belt. From moving on instinct and slamming it into Ryder's chest if that would truly be his last, and only, opportunity—but something else caught his eye, first, and his body stilled again. Familiar silver cuffs glinted from beneath the man's red sleeve cuffs. Two hands overlapping a dagger. A lump formed in Saffron's throat.

Ryder noticed Saffron's eyes lingering on them, making his smile slump as he lifted his hand into view. Turning it over in the light, he observed them as Saffron did.

"Quite pretty for a pair of shackles, don't you think?" He mused, making Saffron's skin crawl. Ryder had no idea, Saffron was more than familiar with how pretty those shackles were. He didn't know how Saffron could feel the weight of them on his own wrists at the mere reminder, let alone the tightness of the collar that was meant to be paired with them.

"Anysta keeps me right where she wants me, at least for now.

That bitch," Ryder went on under his breath, before swallowing back half of the wine in his glass at once. "You have nothing to worry about from me tonight, your highness. This is not a party I will be disturbing, as much as I would like to lock the door and set it all on fire."

"What..." Saffron attempted, but he couldn't speak. The lump in his throat, the tightness in his chest, he could hardly inhale a breath. He subtly scratched at the underside of his wrist, before rubbing the back of his neck. He had no reason to believe such an empty promise from the man who never told the truth— but the silver cuffs on Ryder's wrists were shocking. Those were not something he could falsify—and even if he could, *why?* Still, Saffron strained the magic in his blood, just for the briefest moment. A white halo glowed around the opulent shackles, blending into the light pink of Ryder's own half-human, half-fey existence. "What are you doing here, then?" he finally managed to rasp, before clearing his throat and taking a sip of his wine.

"Anysta found me nearly frozen to death in the mountains on her way back to Vjallrod," Ryder answered, that time with a newly wry smile. "She was kind enough to pick me up and give me a ride the rest of the way."

"How does she know you?"

"Don't ask stupid questions, Saffron."

Saffron snapped to him in shock, nostrils flaring. Ryder just raised an eyebrow and shrugged. Worst of all—he wasn't wrong. Saffron could guess. And while that guess wasn't anything definitive, he knew it likely had something to do with Ryder and Anysta's joint connections with the witchhunters. If not that, then certainly due to the history between Ryder and Fjornar, and Taran in Fjornar, even if Taran couldn't recall any specific memories of Ryder's presence there. Ryder had confirmed as much, himself, while they were snowed-in in the cabin.

And if not that, then—it didn't matter. Saffron didn't have to know the specifics to question whether it was a good or bad thing for Ryder Kyteler to be under house arrest by the mac Delbaiths.

"Why are you still traveling alone, anyway?" Saffron asked, next. "Where's your normal entourage?"

"You mean Breton and the others?" Ryder mumbled. "On the other side. Keeping an eye on things while I'm away."

Saffron kept the rush of adrenaline from showing on his face. Ryder's eyes lingered on him all the same.

"What does Anysta want with you?" Saffron asked, next. Taran's presence shifted in the back of his mind, like a quiet warning to '*choose your words carefully*.' Saffron knew that much. "Or does she plan on just keeping you as a pet?"

"It doesn't matter what she plans," Ryder answered over the rim of his wine glass, swallowing back another mouthful. "I'm only playing nice for now. Until I can figure out what the hell is going on with all of them, myself."

"All of who?"

"What did I say about stupid questions?"

Saffron glowered, turning away again in frustration.

"Your witchhunters still aren't very happy with you right now, are they?"

Ryder's smile twisted in agitation. "What makes you say that?"

"It's obvious. You're traveling alone, they're following your every movement. Are they still trying to find you, Ryder? Are you still avoiding them on purpose?"

Ryder just smiled at him. That same tight, aggravated smile that repeated his words a thousand times over. *What did I say about stupid questions?* A wry smile and pregnant silence were answer enough, as was the man's growing annoyance the more Saffron prodded at what was clearly a sore subject.

Saffron sipped his wine, giving Ryder a moment of peace to gather himself again. Minutes passed with silence between them, watching the crowd of high fey guests, dancing and drinking wine and indulging in the buffet of food on the banquet table across the way. It made him feel like he was back at another of Cylvan's suitor's galas, watching as the handsome prince socialized around the room with a smile as empty as the laughter he summoned from those who stood and listened. Who always turned from the conversation with an immediate drop of their expressions, whispering quick gossip to one another when they weren't quickly beseeching a day with their hands.

Something brushed the back of Saffron's neck, and he turned to realize it was Ryder's fingers. Ryder looked at him with silent appreciation, appraisal, a softness in his expression Saffron wasn't expecting.

"Don't touch me again," he muttered, rubbing his neck where the contact had been made.

"You really are beautiful, Saffron," he said. "You do belong on the arm of a king, whether or not it's Cylvan's."

A chill raced down Saffron spine, and he threw Ryder another look. But Ryder didn't meet his eyes, just gazed instead at Saffron's mouth, then down his neck to where his collarbones peeked through the deep-cut neckline.

"Stay with me," Ryder said, and Saffron threw him a fully sharpened look that time. A familiar, sarcastic smile finally found Ryder's mouth, replacing the furious one. "I mean, just for tonight. This place holds many secrets you won't learn otherwise. And I know you're here for a reason—even if that reason is just getting in my way. Perhaps we can help each other, once the party dies down."

That told Saffron everything he needed to know—that the queen's memory tapestry may in fact be somewhere in that house, and Ryder knew it. It was the only explanation for why he was being so polite. A well-behaved dog. Leashed or not. Saffron knew even opulent cuffs couldn't neuter someone like Ryder unless he allowed it.

"Doing alright, Saff?" Copper asked as he approached with a plate full of food, one mouthful already stuffed into one of his cheeks. Saffron had never been more relieved to see him coming, even with crumbs on the front of his tunic. "Making friends?"

"Ah, you've actually already been acquainted," Saffron said

with a tight smile, stepping back so Copper could get a closer look at the deer-masked guest. "You met him at Ailinne's hot springs. Don't you remember? He and Sionnach got into a little tiff."

Copper raised an eyebrow in confusion, before his eyes traveled to Ryder, lingering for a long time before his mouth dropped open.

"Oh, *this* asshole!" he snarled, shoving his plate of food into Sionnach's arms as the satyr barely approached behind them. "Oh, yeah, I'm *well* acquainted with you, but I sure would like to get to know you even better."

"It was nothing personal, you brute," Ryder snapped back, but still put his hands up in defense. "Your little animal friend just got in my way."

"They're a satyr, jackass," Copper said back, managing to keep his voice low despite the rising emotion. Knowing it would only draw attention from the other guests, and clearly wishing to keep Ryder all to himself. His eyes briefly flickered to the healed, pink scar on Sionnach's forearm from where Ryder's knife cut them. "Why don't you come over here and apologize, while I've got you? C'mon. I'll break your legs if you won't bend them yourself."

"Copper, please," Sionnach rasped from behind, putting all the pieces together on their own and going pale. "I don't want any trouble—"

"He's not going to cause any trouble," Saffron assured them. "He's wearing a pair of the queen's silver cuffs. Lady Anysta's got him leashed like a good dog."

"You'd know plenty about *good dogs*, considering the company you keep," Ryder muttered back—only to grunt and buckle forward when Copper grabbed him by the shoulder and slammed a closed fist into his gut. Smooth and silent enough that no one else in the ballroom noticed, but Ryder looked like he was on the verge of vomiting beneath his mask.

"You're lucky I'm domesticated," Copper told him in a low voice. "Otherwise I'd do much worse, even on this shiny floor.

Now," he grabbed the scruff of Ryder's collar, shoving him around to face Sionnach and knocking the man's mask askew. "How about that apology?"

For some reason, Ryder threw a look at Saffron, as if silently begging for mercy—but Saffron just sipped his drink, then tilted his head toward Sionnach, who was bright red in disbelief for a myriad of reasons. Perhaps more than anything else, for Copper's insistence, and not for the reason of teasing them about it later.

"I do apologize for behaving so poorly in Ailinne," Ryder finally sneered, grunting when Copper's grasp on the nape of his neck tightened to the point of leaving welts.

"Don't kill him yet, Copper, I'm not done chatting," Saffron finally said, knowing his giant friend would gladly spill first blood of the night if he didn't. Copper muttered something, but shoved Ryder away, who stumbled a few steps before straightening up and rubbing the back of his neck with murmured insults.

"Copper, why don't you take Sionnach to get something to drink?" Saffron went on. The fox-lord gave him a reluctant look before sighing and throwing an arm around Sionnach's shoulders, making Sionnach squeak in surprise and stumble away with him. Saffron watched them go, noticing how stiff Sionnach's movements were even as Copper grabbed a glass for them and handed it over. Taking it with careful movements, like they thought he might throw the drink in their face at any moment.

"What else, exactly, do you think I'd be interested in in a place like this?" he finally asked Ryder, as Ryder finished smoothing down the wrinkles of his handsome tunic and adjusting his mask.

"What?"

"You said there were secrets here that I might be interested in. While I'm not focused on getting in your way, that is."

"Aren't you curious? As the future king of this place," Ryder answered, snagging his own drink from a passing beantighe waiter.

"You think they're keeping Queen Proserpina's memory tapestry somewhere here, don't you?" Saffron finally said. Ryder's body snapped around to face him, grabbing Saffron's arm and nearly spilling his drink as he suddenly stood close.

"Keep your godsdamned voice down," Ryder hissed. "Or are you really stupid after all?"

Saffron yanked his arm away, fighting the urge to throw his drink in Ryder's face.

"I don't know how you ever think you're going to win me over if you continue talking to me like that."

"Like your prince treats you any differently? I thought you liked being degraded."

"Cylvan doesn't speak to me like you do."

"Not from what I overheard at Ailinne," Ryder scoffed. "Or was that a *rare* occurrence for him? No wonder you're so poorly behaved. Maybe he should assert himself over you more often."

Before Saffron could offer his retort—an old fey lady and her wife suddenly approached. He straightened up, thinking they might have recognized him as a member of Cylvan's inner circle, but to his surprise, they instead went to Ryder. Where they said nothing, only offered him a small bow, followed by a moment of direct eye contact and a few whispered words Saffron didn't catch. He wasn't sure Ryder caught them, either, with how softly they were spoken—as if uttered in a ritualistic sense, for some intangible force to hear. Ryder didn't react as they did, even looking annoyed, just gulping back another mouthful of his drink when the two fey ladies wandered off again.

"What was that?" Saffron asked.

"You haven't asked about my mask yet, either," Ryder said, tugging at it in agitation. "Aren't you curious?"

"I assumed it was a way to *degrade* you in front of all these high fey. Don't you like being degraded, Ryder?"

Saffron couldn't see exactly how Ryder sneered, but he could sense it.

"Cailleach had her wolf—and she had her deer," he muttered, taking another drink. "Anysta sure thinks she's funny, pulling this outdated stunt to make everyone obsess over me."

"Oh, so it is a form of degradation," Saffron bit back his amusement. "Maybe Lady mac Delbaith actually does have a sense of humor. I never would have thought of something like that."

"I'm sure your way of degrading me would be much more enjoyable, your highness. If you stay the night with me, perhaps I'll even find out."

"I'll show you something, alright," Saffron answered flatly. Ryder glanced back his way, and Saffron could picture the look on his face beneath the mask again. An eyebrow raised in curiosity.

"So you do plan to take me up on my offer?"

"I'm not taking you up on anything," Saffron assured him. He swirled his wind as Taran stirred in the back of his mind again, though still said nothing to argue. "But perhaps a night in this giant estate would answer some questions I have, like you said." *If it really is here, maybe I'll find the tapestry before you do. Maybe I'll tie you to a bedpost and leave you there for the next century.*

"And your friends?" Ryder asked, nodding toward where Copper, Sionnach, Maeve, and a glamoured Naoill all lingered by the buffet table, doing a terrible job each at pretending like they weren't watching Saffron like hawks. "Will they be joining us as well? I doubt Anysta will be thrilled to have so many guests clogging up her rooms, considering how many of these other courtiers will be getting too drunk to leave, either."

"Maybe I won't wait for an invitation, then," Saffron said. "Maybe I'll just... blend into the crowd, and follow you when you go to bed."

Ryder grinned. "I promise to keep you warm, wherever we do end up."

Saffron rolled his eyes. He sipped again at his drink, searching the ballroom for Anysta at the thought. She was on the far side, conversing with the same two fey ladies who'd just approached Ryder to offer that strange exchange. She paid Saffron no mind at all. In fact, when she did glance up again—she only had eyes for the man wearing the deer mask by his side.

37

---

# THE MAP

Not one of Saffron's friends were thrilled to be told to go home while Saffron remained overnight at the estate, but he had been expecting that. He reminded them of the beast that lived in his head; the one he could summon with two words, not to mention the size and brutality of whom they'd all witnessed firsthand that morning when Saffron had summoned him into the woods alongside Copper.

"Why should we trust him to protect you? Especially in a place like this," Copper argued, speaking low as they all crowded in the hallway outside the ballroom, holding their drinks and all equally a little bit buzzed.

"Taran hates this place," Saffron said. "And he hates his family. I think he'd save Ryder's ass before he ever chose his family first."

Taran grunted in the back of Saffron's mind, neither confirming nor denying that idea.

"He has a point," Maeve said. "Honestly Taran might even be eager for Anysta or someone else to try something, if it means he gets to gut them."

"Maeve gets it," Saffron said, only slurring his words slightly, but definitely spilling a little bit of the spiced wine in his glass.

"It's only for one night. And it's the only chance we'll get. And I don't think I can sneak all of you in with me."

"I thought we were going back to Avren in the morning?" Sionnach said, clearly more concerned than they let on. "You said you promised Cylvan—"

"We still are," Saffron answered. "It's not like I'm going to stay for breakfast. If I can get away with it, Anysta won't even know I never left."

"Because you'll be sneaking into wherever Ryder is staying the night," Copper said with narrowed eyes.

"Yes. But don't get the wrong idea."

"I'm getting the wrong idea," Naoill muttered.

"Why in god's name would I fool around with Ryder Kyteler when I have Cylvan waiting for me back in Avren?" Saffron cut that sentiment off at the head.

"Humans are prone to fucking anything that moves."

"Um, alright," Saffron wrinkled his nose, pointing a finger at them. "That's a satyr stereotype, actually."

"Hey," Sionnach hissed.

"*Beantighes,* then," Naoill corrected.

"I'm not staying the night to fuck Ryder Kyteler," Saffron said. "And you know what—even if I was, that's my business. But I'm not, so I need all of you to stop thinking that. He would be insufferable in bed anyway. God, I can't even imagine."

"Probably couldn't even last that long," Copper said. "I know Cylvan can probably last a long time, right Saffron?"

"Ew, Copper, what are you saying?" Maeve hissed, elbowing him.

"I—" Copper stammered. "I don't know. I'm a little overwhelmed."

"Just—!" Saffron cut back in again. "Can we focus, please! I'm not actually here to have a discussion about whether or not I'm staying or not. Or what I'll be doing while I'm here—*not* in the way you all think. I'll be back in time to leave first thing for

Avren. You know what—find a room nearby in Vjallrod. To be close. Just in case."

"Alright," Naoill said. "There's a bit of sense."

"But what if something happens?" Sionnach asked. "What if you need help?"

"I can send Taran to get you."

"How far can he actually go without you there?"

Saffron stared at Maeve for a long time in considerate silence, until her face finally twisted up and she scoffed. "That's not making me feel any better!"

*"Let me talk to them,"* Taran growled. *"Call me out."*

"Absolutely not," Saffron answered.

"Absolutely not what?" Sionnach asked.

"I think he was talking to the dog."

"What's Taran saying? Bet he hates the idea, too."

"Alright!" Saffron finally snapped, throwing his hands up and spilling a little more from his glass. "You all, find a room at the nearest inn. Wait for me to come back. If something happens, I'll send Taran. Or, you know what? I'm sure there's a nightjar roost somewhere in this godforsaken house. Why don't I just send a bird at midnight and another a few hours later? To reassure you all."

"Oh... a messenger bird. That makes a lot of sense, actually," Copper nodded, before looking at Sionnach. "Why didn't you think of that?"

Sionnach stomped their hoof, and Saffron downed the rest of his drink. He was going to need it.

As the fete stretched long into the night, guests grew progressively drunker the closer to midnight the time drew, including Saffron and his own. Partially to better blend in, partially to ease their collective nerves, as, despite having a plan, even Saffron was beginning to feel apprehensive about staying there by himself once the chance came. But it would be fine—he would have Taran. He might even be able to count on Ryder to keep him from getting into too much trouble, at least when it came to Anysta. And if Ryder tried to start trouble of his own, Saffron knew what to expect from him. Something even told him Ryder wouldn't have any opportunity to open any veils there in the middle of the house, too, considering how tightly Anysta kept him on her leash during the nighttime fete alone.

Saffron really might be able to use all that to his advantage. To incapacitate Ryder first; to sneak through the house using Taran as a guide; to either perform the summoning spell like he originally intended, or take his time searching. To find the queen's memory tapestry, or to return and throw Ryder on Taran's back to take all the way back to Avren. One way or another, Saffron would not be leaving the Winter Court empty handed.

When guests began trickling out, some returning to their carriages in the courtyard, others retiring to the block of rooms in the estate, Saffron made sure to stumble through the front door and climb into the carriage with his friends, putting on the front of leaving alongside them—only to yank his shoulder bag out from where he'd hidden it under the seat, then scurry through the opposite door of the carriage and into the bushes along the edge of the courtyard.

Ryder had already described to him where his own room was, promising the window was unlocked, and Taran knew his own home well enough to direct Saffron there once he had a chance to sneak through the darkness.

The entire time, Saffron's teeth chattered. His heeled boots slipped on the ice of the drive, but he only fell and cracked his head once. He barely felt it, having done the same an infinite number of times growing up in Amber Valley.

Ryder wasn't lying about the open window, thankfully, and Saffron was able to shove the pane open before heaving himself inside. He tumbled into a pile of his own cloak on the other side, untangling himself from his cloak and hurrying to re-latch the window, before scrambling over to where the fireplace burned low to keep the otherwise dark room at a comfortable temperature. Holding his hands toward the flames, he exhaled a low breath of relief, before patting the breast of his doublet for his knife, and checking beneath the cuff of his sleeve for his wand. Both remained where he'd stored them.

"Icarus, *come*," he whispered, and his shadowy companion emerged with hardly a breath of sound to join him.

"What's your plan, exactly?" Taran asked. "Do you really intend on trusting Ryder this much?"

"Hardly," Saffron answered back, rubbing his hands together as the feeling slowly returned to his fingers. "I'm going to wait at least until Anysta lets him leave the party; I assume that'll be proof that all other guests have also left or gone to bed."

"And then what?"

Saffron thought about that. "I admit—there's a part of me willing to ask you to just kill him on the spot," he muttered, and even Taran chuckled darkly. "But I don't think that's the right thing to do. You say the memory tapestry definitely isn't here, but I'm curious to know why Ryder thinks so. I'll ask him, and depending on his answer, maybe you'll realize something he doesn't."

"Fair enough," Taran said, lowering himself to rest on the floor. He crossed large paws in front of him, but otherwise remained upright and alert with ears pointed. "Do you think Ryder will assume you're also looking for the tapestry? To find it before he does."

"He'd be the stupid one if he hasn't already figured that out," Saffron muttered. "And honestly, I don't know if I care if he thinks that. He wouldn't have told me what he was looking for if he didn't also think I'd also look for it, especially something so dangerous..."

"Maybe he hopes you'll find it first, in order to take it from you. To save himself the trouble."

"That's fine," Saffron said with a frown. "He must really be desperate, to risk that though..."

"Or he truly underestimates your ability to keep things from him."

"Oh, I know he does."

"He's a bit of a prick, isn't he?"

"And the sack."

Taran chuckled again—a sound Saffron might never get used to, one that still made a little chill race down his spine, as even in wolf form there was the smallest hint of familiarity to it.

"You really will keep me from getting hurt, right?" he asked before realizing the feeling had turned into words. Taran's bright red eyes turned to him, regarding him for a long moment, before gazing back toward the fire.

"I don't have any choice," he answered simply. Lacking any sentimentality, until he adjusted the overlap of his paws, and stretched out his neck in order to nudge Saffron on the shoulder with his nose. "Don't do anything stupid, and I won't have to."

"When have I ever done anything stupid?" Saffron asked— just as the bedroom door suddenly slammed open, and the stench of burning yew flooded his nose.

Leaping to his feet, Saffron barely made it upright before he was shoved back to the floor again, pinned beneath gloved hands that clawed at the ring on his finger, his engagement ring, that would make him prone to enchantment.

*"Icarus—!"* he attempted, but yew was shoved into his mouth first, burning and making him gag as the wolf vanished into the shadows beneath the weight of the assaulting tree.

Dragged from the room, the corridor on the other side was too dark to see, Saffron's insides burned too brightly against the yew to think clearly, to consider any possible way to free himself. He didn't know who had their hands on him, only that it wasn't Ryder, himself. They towed Saffron too roughly, grunted their commands too bitterly, where Ryder had always handled him with such possessive ease and care. But it didn't matter who exactly carried him through the halls of the mac Delbaith estate,

Ryder or not—Saffron knew the man was not innocent in any of it.

A door was kicked open in front of him, and Saffron was dragged through on his knees, before tossed to a carpeted floor. Inside the room was warm, smelling of burning birch logs and candles, ink and paper, leather-bound books.

When he finally managed to push himself up just enough to see for himself, Saffron deciphered the inside of a old study, where only two other figures waited for him to be delivered.

Anysta mac Delbaith sat at the large desk in the center of the room, writing something calmly on a piece of parchment. In the chair facing her—Ryder sat stiffly, one leg crossed as he looked down at Saffron with an unreadable look on his face. But whatever it was didn't appear directed at Saffron, specifically—rather, like he was furious to be forced to betray him at all.

"Here he is," Ryder said, addressing Anysta flatly, but with a sense of urgency. "Now tell me what you promised."

"The queen's memory tapestry is not here," Anysta answered, with such simplicity Saffron almost didn't realize the implication of the words. "It vanished with Virtue Holt at the end of the war. I believe Verity entrusted him with it."

"Virtue—!" Ryder exclaimed, leaping to his feet. Anysta's eyes flickered up to him for a moment, before sliding to Saffron, then to the group of people who'd dragged him there from the guest room. Saffron finally turned to look, too, stomach sinking at the sight of three veiled witchhunters hovering at his back. Blocking the doorway.

"Take Master O'Daire back to his room," Anysta continued calmly, before smirking with faux apology. "Ah, my mistake. Mister Kyteler, I mean."

"You bitch—" Ryder attempted, stumbling backward as the same witchhunters who once obeyed him flared forward, grabbing him by the arms and shoving him to his knees. One of them hissed *'restraint,'* and Saffron jumped at the familiar sound of two silver cuffs snapping together behind Ryder's back.

"Should one of us wait here with you, my lady?" Another asked before dragging Ryder out. Anysta just waved them away, focused on finishing her letter as the contentious group left with the door closing on their heels.

She paid no mind to Saffron in the meantime, even as he forced himself all the way upright, reaching into his mouth to scrape as much of the yew from his tongue and the back of his throat as he could. Even cleared of the offending taste, Saffron still couldn't hear Taran in the back of his mind. He could still feel the disconnect from his magic. He knew it would return, it was only a matter of time—he only needed to prolong his life a little longer.

"I assume there's a reason you—" he started, but Anysta raised a hand to him. A sign to *wait* as she finished what she was writing. Saffron stared at her, struck first with a rush of beantighe-tinged embarrassment, before it was quickly overtaken with annoyance.

"There's a reason you brought me here!" He insisted. "Rather than have those witchhunters kill me on the spot. Why take Ryder away? I think he could have made our conversation much more entertaining."

"Ryder won't be kept long, I'm sure," she said. "I knew from the start he was only behaving because I had something he wanted. Now that I've told him, it's only a matter of time before he shakes free."

"Aren't you worried the witchhunters might betray you? Seeing as they were loyal to him first—"

Anysta barked a laugh, sitting back in her chair. She tipped the end of her quill into the inkwell, allowing the writing on the parchment to dry as she finally turned to meet Saffron's eyes. Resting her chin on overlapping fingers, she smiled at him, appraising him up and down. Looking far too much like Taran, though lacking the same brooding misery that fey lord always had hanging heavy under his eyes.

"Those witchhunters are loyal to only one person in this life

—and that is their queen. Ryder Kyteler made them promises in her name, but I made better ones."

"Like what?" Saffron asked, but Anysta just continued smiling at him.

"You really are quite bold, considering whose floor you are currently kneeling on."

Saffron clenched his jaw. "I'm not afraid of you."

"Why would you be?" Anysta tilted her chin slightly. "The first veil-oathed rowan witch in centuries... I should be more afraid of you, shouldn't I, Saffron de Patron de Luvon mag Shamhradhaín?"

Saffron's blood ran cold, lips parting slightly as the air slipped from his lungs, leaving him empty.

"... Ah. My mistake," she said, with the same amused curl of her lip as when she uttered the same to Ryder. "The Flower of Alvénya, I meant. Lord Saffron mag Shamhradhaín of Lelfe, of Alvénya. Is that right?"

"You..." Saffron meant to threaten something in return, but managing that single word was almost too much. And Anysta mac Delbaith—just kept smiling, like the look on Saffron's face was her favorite taste of wine.

"You look surprised," she cooed. "Though, not nearly as surprised as Cylvan was when I shared it with him. For a second, I thought maybe even he'd been tricked by you—but no, he knew all along, didn't he? You were the wild, red-veiled witch who killed my brother at his own engagement party, weren't you? What a shock, that Cylvan knew all along..."

She rose to her feet, taking the parchment from her desk and folding it over, once, twice, three times, before tucking it into an envelope. "I'm saving those details for after the prince's court of expectations, though—when I'll really need them most. Thankfully, Cylvan's own reputation is propelling the rest as it is. I think the final call for it will come tomorrow night, at this rate, which means we'll have our coming Night King declared by next week. So much to do, still, so many things..."

"You—!" Saffron attempted again. He leapt to his feet—only to stumble, tripping back to the floor as something long and thin, silver and sharp, shuddered on Anysta's desk before lifting and darting toward him.

He didn't have to see the companion quill in Anysta's hand to recognize it—Elluin's quill, her silver needle, the same one that carved words into Saffron's back. The one that killed Kaelar, the one Saffron himself used to claim Taran's silver bones. In the chaos of what he'd done on Ostara, he'd assumed someone else had picked it up. Cylvan, or Adelard, or someone else, to put it away to never see the light of day again—but that was wrong. Right in front of him, he could see how wrong he was—and Taran's warning from Cylvan's bedroom the night of the games rang like deafening church bells in his ears.

*I can assure you, they are not as isolated as you may think.*

*They do not need to attend galas in-person to know exactly what goes on at them.*

Even back then, Saffron had asked if there was any chance the mac Delbaiths were working alongside Ryder in all of that man's destruction—and Taran had reassured him it wasn't likely. *My family wants to* rule *on the throne, not overturn it.*

The needle hovered mere inches from Saffron's eyes as Anysta went back to her business, opening the latticed window and allowing the wintry nighttime air to waft inside. She whistled something, summoning a great horned owl to clasp at the edge of the window with flexing talons. She scratched under its beak, before tucking the envelope into the sash attached to its back, and sending it on its way.

"I don't wish to kill you tonight, Saffron," she spoke again, closing the window with a small flurry of snow rushing through the crack between the panes. "In fact, I think you're more important to my cause than Prince Cylvan himself—considering how easily you'll bring his undoing. More than anything I could have ever dreamed up, myself. You really are a gift to the people of Alfidel, and I intend to treat you as such."

"I'm not doing anything for you—"

"You don't have to," she said, turning to him with an excited shine to her warm hazel eyes. "The fact Cylvan chose you secured his Night Court already, don't you understand? He was doomed the moment he thought a human better suited him than my brother. Or any other high fey, for that matter."

"I told him as much first," Saffron sneered. The tip of the needle followed his slightest movements, making his heart pound harder than the wind against the window.

"No matter," she said, sweeping back to her desk. "I promise to take good care of you until Cylvan's Court of Expectations has come and gone. After which, you're free to return to Avren. I already have a room prepared for you."

"And then what?" Saffron asked. "After Cylvan's Court, then what will you do?"

She practically fluttered her eyelashes at him. "I can assure you, Flower of Alvénya, you'll know in due time. The people of Alfidel need someone they can turn to for the promise of a rising sun after such long darkness—and I intend to deliver them exactly that. One who resembles the veiled queen herself. Ambitious just like she was—and bright enough to devour Cylvan's impending darkness as they were always meant to, with a little guidance." She glanced at the table behind her for a moment. "Just you wait and see, the warm Day I will deliver to the people of Alfidel."

"*Saffron!*" A voice tore through the back of his mind, and Saffron didn't waste a second.

"Icarus, *come!*"

The wolf tore from the shadows, summoning a sharp gasp from Anysta, who stumbled backward from her chair at the desk. The needle collapsed to the floor as she stared at him—at her brother, at the wolf king, who pawed at the ground with a lip-curling growl emerging from the back of his throat. Like Saffron would have to command him to hold back on killing her, instead of the other way around.

Saffron turned for the door, only to be knocked back when it suddenly slammed open, and one of the witchhunters stormed back inside with their veil askew, nose bloodied. Nearly tripping over his feet, Saffron rushed backward, out of the hunter's reach while they were distracted by the sight of Lord Taran glaring down Anysta on the other side of the room.

Stumbling backward into a wide table pressed into the wall beneath the rows of books, the glasslike sound of wind chimes rang up in protest—and when he turned to look, his already-racing heart slammed harder against the inside of his ribs.

A drawn map of Alfidel, curled edges weighed down with silver blocks on each side. Hovering over the parchment, more than two dozen small, silver points loomed, some bobbing up and down slightly, others shifting as their tips slowly traced along a minuscule road, a river, within various cities across the map. The largest cluster hovered over *Fjornar* at the highest point of the map, unmoving except whenever Saffron's thighs bumped the table. One barb trailed up the edge of the mac Delbaith Estate—before suddenly jumping ahead, whisking into the cluster floating over Fjornar and colliding with the group already there. Saffron knew without having to ask—it was Ryder, tracked somehow by the needle hovering over the parchment. That was Ryder—and he was going to get away, again, if Saffron didn't hurry.

Taran's confrontation nearly brought Saffron back—but something else caught his attention. A smaller handful of points scattered over Avren—one of them indicating the place where Saffron knew Lugh's Altar to be. Where Cylvan spent so much of his time praying for the recovery of his lost sibling. Just like Ryder—Anysta was following his every move, too.

"Cylvan—" Saffron choked, recalling the prince's opulent silver horn. Placed by Anysta, herself. Claimed to help the missing horn grow back, but instead—Anysta had used it to track Cylvan's location. Explaining how she always met them wherever they went. Explaining how she knew Cylvan had already returned to Avren, why her invitation to Saffron didn't bother including his name.

Throwing out his arm, Saffron swept it across the map, knocking every piece of silver away with a sound like a bag of coins spilling across the floor—but the needles just shuddered where they rolled to a halt, before lifting upright again and, like a choreographed dance, returning one by one to where they belonged. That same barb once again indicating exactly where Cylvan stood. Where he lingered on the edge of the cliffs. Alone. Waiting for Saffron to return.

Of course Cylvan was eager to return to Avren after Anysta confronted him at the dé Bricríu Estate. Of course he'd acted strangely toward Saffron, knowing someone so powerful knew Saffron's most dangerous secret—god damn him, he should have just said something!

"Damnit!" Saffron exclaimed, inadvertently drawing the witchhunter's attention back and compelling them to rush him. Rammed back into the edge of the table, the silver points clattered against one another a second time as Saffron's hand struck his attacker's chest. Shoving them away just enough to roll back onto the table, bending his knee and slamming his heels into the witchhunter's chest to send them flying back into the bookshelf.

Only as the witchhunter caught themself on their hands and knees, pushing themself upright, did Saffron see the silver ring on their finger—the same one Kaelar once wore to command Saffron's silver cuffs in Danann House. That time, used to control the ones Ryder wore. Perhaps even the very same.

Saffron summoned the rowan magic in his blood to flare—to fill and overflow in his veins, to swell up into his eyes until the glow of opulence and aridity filled his vision and haloed around every living thing in the room. Seeing the bright white glow around the ring on the witchhunters hand, it was the last confirmation he needed, before pushing off from the table and lunging at them.

Grabbing the back of their veil, Saffron tore it off, revealing a feral fey lady underneath, baring her teeth and snarling like a wild animal. Saffron bared his teeth right back, slamming a knee into her stomach, before shoving her into the books and pinning her against the floor. He clawed at her hand, fighting against her defensive fists that found his chest, the side of his face, until he was able to wrap his fingers around the ring and rip it away for himself. In the scuffle, he didn't notice her opposite hand fly to her waist, removing something from her belt—and liquid silver was thrown across his face, setting his skin on fire and sending him reeling back with a cry of alarm.

Collapsing onto his back, Saffron threw his hands up to smear the silver away, fighting to rub it out of his eyes, to spit it out of his mouth. He barely managed to look up through blurry vision again when the witchhunter leapt on top of him. That time, she bore down with a knife, pinned just barely out of reach of Saffron's throat as he held her back with his elbows.

In a rush of panic, he did the only thing he could think of— and summoned all his magic into his chest. Down his arms, into his hands, he forced it into the witchhunter's body. Just like outside the beantighe dorms at the palace—but that time, he was prepared. He would kill her, before she killed him; he would kill anyone, anything, if they dared get in his way again.

Flooding her pink-tinged halo with red, with crimson arid magic as bright as fresh blood, there was no fear in him that time —only fury. Anger and a burning wrath which flooded that pink glow with his own merciless, burning magic, hotter than any silver that seared his skin or might burn him from the inside out. The veil once said he was too scared to use the magic given to him— and he was going to prove it wrong. He would use his magic, as wild and untenable and dangerous as it was, to carve his way back home no matter what it took.

The witchhunter guttered with wet gasps, blood spilling from her mouth across his chest, before finally collapsing onto her side with a choking death-rattle. Saffron kicked her off, scrambling back to his feet, searching the room for where Taran still had Anysta pinned against the wall.

Saffron didn't wait—he just called out for the beast to follow, and threw himself into the corridor to run.

38

# THE PASSAGE

*Not again—I won't let Ryder Kyteler escape from me again.*

Saffron's thoughts raced like ribbons in a whipping wind, in and out of his mind, not knowing which Taran heard and which he couldn't have possibly caught. Thinking only one thing—Ryder was already fleeing. He was on his way to Fjornar, if not already there. Perhaps through a veneer, or hopping through the veil—but Saffron was not going to let him go. Not again. *Not again.*

*"There are tunnels beneath the estate,"* Taran informed in Saffron's mind as they ran down the length of the corridor, adrenaline alone allowing Saffron to keep any pace with the beast. *"Old ones, barely used—but they lead into Fjornar."*

*I should have known,* Saffron thought back. *Take me there.*

Ahead, Taran rounded a corner, only for his claws to tear against the marble floor as he came to a sudden halt and spun back, slamming into Saffron and shoving him in the other direction. Saffron barely had a chance to see why, spotting a cluster of family guards and a witchhunter at the end of the hallway.

When his chest ached, that old wound over his heart throbbing, Saffron clung to a handful of Taran's fur in an attempt to keep pace—but when even that wasn't enough, clutching at his chest and gasping through the pain, Taran finally came to a halt, buckling forward into Saffron's momentum, effectively tripping him into falling over the wolf's back. Grappling for two handfuls of fur as the wolf immediately took off running again, Saffron clung to him in disbelief, before rasping out a little laugh, and a *'thank you.'*

Taran only grunted in response, tensing every muscle as his speed steadily increased further, moving faster than the a whistle through the winding hallways. Leaping down flights of stairs and through doorways, he finally leapt through a narrow window to slam all four feet in the snowy back-garden before turning and tearing off again toward a secluded section of the yard. Just like in the house, Taran moved with all the familiarity of someone who'd grown up in that place—and Saffron couldn't help but tighten his hands in the wolf's fur. Though whether out of compassion, or merely a sense to keep upright, he didn't know. He would let Taran decide.

Embraced on both sides by snowy pine trees as they raced ahead, Saffron shivered against the brisk wind whipping past him from the animal's speed, keeping himself low and his face pressed into the fur of Taran's back.

*"There,"* Taran announced as they raced through the snow, summoning Saffron to lift his head again. He spotted a small collection of stone cenotaphs clustered on the other side of a modest lichgate, the clearing surrounded by snowy-laden trees all around. At the furthest end, beneath the thickest row of trees, a stone doorway with steps leading into the earth. The entrance to catacomb, or perhaps a family ossuary—Saffron knew he was about to find out. But that wasn't what made his stomach leap. Hurried footprints crossed through the snow ahead of them, the silver bars over the front of the entryway thrown open and creaking in the winter wind.

Taran leapt through the entrance, grinding against the stone wall that immediately curved downward on the other side, though he moved with clear familiarity of that place as nuanced as in his childhood home. All the way to the bottom, where darkness swallowed them in an instant, and Taran finally came to a halt. He lifted his head to search for anyone else who may be lurking in the shadows, only the sound of his heavy breaths and Saffron's pounding heart evident in the darkness.

When no one jumped out at them, Saffron sat up slightly, finally allowing himself to breathe as hard as the beast did beneath him.

"Ryder isn't here," Taran said, like a reassurance. Saffron nodded, carefully sliding a leg over Taran's side to return his feet to the floor. "Not anymore, at least."

"Can you find me a torch? Or a candle?" Saffron asked. Taran lifted his head to sniff, before shuffling toward one of the walls. His fingers left trails through the frost on the walls as he searched, finally discovering a small shelf that clattered with thick altar candles. Claiming one for himself, Saffron slipped the wand from his sleeve an used the tip to carve the same arid spell into the wax that he'd once seen on the candles in the Kyteler Ruins. As soon as he placed the final mark, a perpetual flame spawned to life on the wick, instantly illuminating and warming his hand. Standing closer than he expected, Taran had watched him the entire time, and even he wouldn't be able to deny the curiosity that reflected in his red eyes once the light came to life.

With the candle raised to observe the antechamber, Saffron kept his opposite hand on Taran's back, gripping the wolf's fur in order to steady himself. And then—in order to ground himself, when he realized what, exactly, he was looking at.

Indeed a family ossuary, a tomb of bones burnt on Winter Court pyres, bones gathered into morbid bouquets of femurs and ribs and pinned with pouches labeled *fingers* and *teeth*, wrapped in a garland of their own vertebrae on twine. Saffron grimaced at first, glancing at Taran, then back to the gruesome display, only softening to his own curiosity when he noticed how every bone shimmered with the slightest sheen of silver. Stepping in for a closer look at the nearest stack, he read the name and label carved into the deceased's skull. A pattern that continued on every forehead that came after.

LADY KRYST MAC DELA, KNOWER OF LIES.

LORD SEABH MAC DELA, CALLER OF BEASTS.

LORD AINDREAS MAC DELA, WEAVER.

LADY SORCHA MAC DELA, ASHEN.

GENTLE MUIRE MAC DELA, KNOWER OF THE DEAD.

LADY ISBEIL MAC DELA, FINDER OF LOST THINGS.

LORD UALAN MAC DELA, ASHEN.

GENTLE MORA MAC DELA, HEALER OF WOUNDS...

"A funny take on *headstones*, huh?" Saffron asked with an amused little smile, risking the briefest touch over Mora mac Delbaith's carving between her eye sockets. Taran looked at him for a long, silent moment, before rolling his eyes and turning away.

"These are... your family members," Saffron went on after clearing his throat. "Their bones. And these describe their abilities in life, right?"

"And what their silver might be charmed with," Taran muttered. "Gods, I hate this place. They used to lock me in here when I misbehaved."

Saffron looked back at him in surprise, but Taran was already making his way forward, through the mouth of a never-ending ossuary corridor Saffron hadn't noticed in such a thick darkness. Overhead, a carved wolf-bust loomed at the peak of the arched ceiling.

"This way, beantighe. The entrance to the tunnels is this way."

"What does it mean when it just says 'ashen'?" Saffron couldn't help but ask, still following Taran's lead. "I mean, other than the obvious, I guess."

"They were born and died while Verity Holt's ashen curse was in place. No oracles have observed what their inherent magic is, yet."

"Why not?"

Taran sighed. "Who knows."

"What if someone has some kind of extra unique inherent magic that could solve all our problems? But your oracles haven't bothered observing them yet."

"What if?"

Taran clearly didn't wish to discuss it further, despite Saffron's hunger for information. So Saffron just followed, keeping his questions to himself for the time being, though unable to resist shining the light of his candle over the infinite number of skulls they passed on the way. Column after column of at least a dozen bone-piles high, some reaching even taller than Saffron stood. Crowding the already narrow corridor on both sides, barely wide enough for Saffron to walk straight ahead and only receive the occasional brush of something on his cloak. Taran wasn't so lucky, as his skin constantly twitched every time something kissed the finest tips of his coarse fur.

"Your..." Saffron started without thinking, before trailing off.

"It's going to annoy me, isn't it?" Taran asked, clearly referring to whatever Saffron had on his mind.

"Are your own bones here?" He asked, so softly the words had no chance to bounce off the narrow walls. "Your original bones. Before they were replaced."

"Who knows."

"You don't know what they did with them?"

"Who knows."

"I wonder what your inherent magic would have been."

*"Who knows."*

Saffron let his interest wane, tucking it away for another time. Sending Taran's continued agitation, enough that it made his own skin itch. He went back to reading the names of the deceased piles of bones they passed, soon enough surprised when the mac Delbaith names soon gave way to other sídhe family names, or so he assumed, as he didn't know the Old Alvish names for the others.

"Other families donate their loved ones to the mac Delbaiths?" He asked. "To make silver out of."

"They used to," Taran answered, clearly wishing to encourage that line of questioning rather than the other that were so personal. "Most of these bones are very old, even older than Queen Proserpina. King Elanyl prohibited the forging of opulent silver from non-mac Dela sídhe bones when he was in power."

"But your sister has been hawking opulent silver all over Alfidel—"

"Most common fey don't know the truth about it, and never have; most ancient fey, including sídhe fey, pretend they don't know, because the benefits outweigh the morbidity of it. The kings pretend they don't notice. Or they like to assume the silver on the market was forged before the ban. They tell themselves such, at least."

"Why?"

"To keep the peace. No differently than how they navigate the likes of Renard dé Bricríu. It's not worth the potential fallout, should they step on the wrong toes. For King Ailir, especially, whose reign is already so tenuous."

"Oh," Saffron muttered. "I guess that makes sense." *There are an awful lot of things they pretend not to notice, for the sake of keeping the peace. But peace for whom, exactly?*, he thought with a stubborn frown, intentionally knocking one precarious pile of bones to the floor with a deafening crash. Taran whipped his head around in surprise, but Saffron just shrugged like it was an accident.

Even as they continued ahead, Taran must have been able to sense the constant turning of Saffron's thoughts, how they even festered into agitation of their own, because he soon sighed through his nose and offered: "There is some argument of the validity of this, but Ancient mac Delas were said to be the first to traditionally burn the deceased on pyres, here in the Winter Court

—because it was the easiest way to clean the silver bones, once they realized there was opulence stored in them. The tradition then spread across the Winter Court, as you know now."

"Your family must be the oldest ones from the Winter Court, then," Saffron said.

"One of them. Gentle Naoill dé Fianna's family line may be the only one to challenge the age of mine. Unsurprising, considering their lineage."

"From dragons."

"Yes. Though neither are nearly as old as the Tuatha dé Danann, who descend from the Dagda and Danu, themselves," he let the idea settle, before his ears flicked like a part of him preferred the casual chatter to the unsettling silence. "The dé Fianna are the ones who argue themselves the first to burn the dead, by the way. Once again, considering a dragon's propensity for... burning."

"I think it's fascinating," Saffron said, earning a narrowed look from the wolf over his shoulder. "I mean—the theory of it all. Silver in your sídhe bones, being able to forge them into objects that could, again, theoretically, actually help people... If only they hadn't fallen into the hands of people like your family." He grimaced. Taran rolled his eyes. "It makes me wonder if rowan witch bones were discovered to become hematite by the same theory, or totally on accident. Maybe your family even took the idea from the first rowan witches, hm?"

"Unlikely. But an amusing thought."

Saffron chuckled. He reached out to pat the back of Taran's haunches, earning a smack of the wolf's tail against his stomach.

"Maybe opulent silver isn't inherently evil," Saffron went on, observing another line of named skulls they passed. "Just like how hematite-bones aren't inherently *good*, I suppose. If the sídhe fey —or rowan witch—consented in life to their bones being forged into useful tools, why not?"

"You sound like Magnin," Taran said, sounding almost amused. "He used to wax poetic about the exact same thing."

"I remember he forged my silver leg cast." Saffron said.

"Yes. From the bones of my aunt, Lady Murva. I went and collected them from the pyre myself, while you were all in Connacht. Do you remember?"

"Oh, yes!" Saffron said, genuinely surprised. "I—I never made that connection. I guess I should thank you, for doing that?"

"I didn't do it for you. I did it for the sake of our deal."

"Right," Saffron chuckled. "Well, even so. It did help a lot."

"Magnin is very talented. If you and Cylvan manage to survive to your coronation, you might consider requesting Magnin for your inner court."

"Oh..." Saffron said with interest. "I hadn't thought of that..."

Silence returned. Saffron nearly asked how much farther they would have to travel down the seemingly endless corridor of silver bones, the chill of the subterranean ossuary nearly reaching his own rowan-bones the longer it took them to go. He was just on the verge of his teeth chattering when Taran finally came to a halt, and Saffron lifted his candle to look where the wolf's attention caught.

It was the painting of a snowy landscape, one Saffron recognized as the mountains overlooking Vjallrod. Near the bottom left, stark against the white-painted snow, a black wolf gazed at the viewer, eyes bright red and reflecting the light of Saffron's candle as if inlaid with jewels.

"This is the passage into the tunnels. I don't know how to get through, myself," Taran admitted, ears flattened when Saffron gave him a look of confusion. "I only ever passed through here an handful of times, and when I was, it was always blindfolded with an oracle. They'd make me drink weaverthistle tea afterward, and I was only a child—"

"I wasn't judging you," Saffron reassured, sensing another uptick in the beast's anxiety as he justified himself. "The fact you brought me this far is more than I ever would have gotten on my own. I appreciate you."

Taran mumbled something, pawing at the ground before pointing his nose back at the painting.

"Whatever the trick is, it's something Ryder knew. Something he was capable of doing, himself, that didn't require a lot of time or any special tools, seeing as he's clearly already long gone inside..." Saffron recalled watching that needle skirt across Anysta's map. Certain it had been following Ryder's opulent cuffs, if they were also tracking Cylvan's opulent horn in the same way.

Shaking his head to focus, he used the candle to search the frame around the painting, then the ground, the ceiling, the shelves of silver bones that continued in both directions.

"Do you remember anything at all from when they'd take you through here? Even blurry memories."

"I do not."

"That's alright," Saffron repeated, trailing off when he realized the wooden frame was carved with more than just floral elements—there were figures present.

Bands of trouping fairies crossed over the top amongst lush flowers and trees, the sun with bright rays extending across the length of it; down the sides, roots crawled downward and intertwined with bones, before upside-down trees grew in the opposite direction. Leading the eye to the bottom, where a secondary landscape was illustrated, as detailed and lovingly carved as the one on top, except illustrating a snowy horizon with white-capped mountains, snow-laden pine trees, and tousled, thorny blackberry bushes.

The attention to detail reminded him of something similar he'd once seen, in the bookshop in Connacht. That tall mirror that lead into Pimbry Scott's secret room, once Saffron understood it to be representing the story of Narcissus and the pond. Even the door into the Kyteler School's crypt could only be opened because he knew the word 'Cerberus' to answer the riddle that unlocked it...

He searched up and down the frame one more time. A sunny, welcoming, warm landscape on top; a cold, but beautiful, northern landscape after passing downward through the earth. Was it the otherworld? Tír na nÓg, the spirit world, beneath the mounds? Anysta was trained as a Dagdan priestess, the god associated most with the mounds. The painted wolf looking directly at the viewer from the painting told Saffron it had to be something related to King Clymeus, the wolf king, considering Fjornar was also home to the King's Keep. What had Taran first told him about that place? In their shared dreams, before Saffron fully understood what they meant, who he was speaking to…

*"Does it ever snow like this in the Mid Court?"*

*"Not like this. Aryadna hated the cold in Fjornar, so her king built her a Keep in Avren. This is—"*

"The King's Keep…" Saffron reiterated out loud, letting the thoughts drape over him.

The wolf king; the cold, dark place of the Winter Court; Queen Proserpina, and her preferred warmth in Avren. Queen Proserpina, nicknamed such by the humans she hunted, named after Persephone; Persephone and her Hades; the warmth of the land of the living, and the cold darkness of the underworld where she was forced to reside for months out of the year…

Saffron's mind spun. Was he overthinking it? Squeezing his eyes closed, he exhaled a long breath, fogging up the glow of his candle with the chill of his breath.

Something Ryder would know, half-human and half-fey. Something Ryder would be able to do in the moment, without special tools, and without requiring a lot of time. Something all half-human and half-fey oracles would be able to do. Something that would have been silent, if Taran as a child never overheard an audible charm to pass through.

Hades and Persephone; the land of the living, the land of the dead; the warmth of Avren in the Mid Court, and Fjornar in the Winter Court. The warmth of the sun, the chill of the moon. The light of the day, the dark of the night.

"Day court, Night court," he whispered, dragging fingers down the side of the painting again.

Holding the candle and his wand in one hand, with the other, Saffron made the motion of beseeching a Day court. He formed a circle with his thumb and fingers, drawing a high arch over his head from shoulder to shoulder. When nothing happened, he frowned, trying again. Then he sarcastically beseeched a night court like Cylvan had once taught him, forming a crescent shape with his hand and doing the same motion.

"They—" Taran suddenly yipped, making Saffron jump and turn to him. He gazed at the painting for a long moment, then back to where Saffron still held the crescent-shape in one hand. "They held my hand the entire time we walked—except for one moment, while passing through the painting."

Saffron considered that, then offered the candle and wand to the wolf. Taran wrinkled his nose, but gently separated his sharp teeth to clamp down on the wax and hematite rod, careful not to scorch his whiskers with the perpetual flame.

"Two hands, then," Saffron said, as if alerting the painting to his next move. He formed a singular circle using both hands, and formed the arch. When nothing happened, he made two crescent moon shapes and did the same—though that was hardly any different than forming the single circle.

"Oh, damn you!" He hissed, stubbornly forming a crescent moon with one hand and a circle with the other, piecing them together and arching over his head—jumping when the faintest sound of shifting wood undoubtedly emerged from the painting. He did it again, still only earning that single scratch of a response —until he realized, he'd only performed half of the motion. From his left shoulder, he moved his hands in a full circle, to his opposite shoulder, then back around again over his chest—mouth hanging open in shocked satisfaction as the painting scratched against the stone wall, then bent inward.

"Well!" Saffron exclaimed with a grin. "I wonder what they'd think, knowing a silly little beantighe figured out their trick? Come on—"

He extended the candle through the frame—only to jerk

backward when something cold and sharp bit down on him. It yanked the candle clean from his hand—but the flame never clattered to the floor on the other side. There was only blackness, made heavier with the sudden lack of light.

"This isn't just another tunnel to walk all the way to Fjornar," Taran's voice ghosted through the darkness. "It—swallows you."

"It's a veil passage," Saffron whispered. His voice trembled slightly with understanding that struck him like a lightning bolt. If he'd known to look for it—he suddenly wondered if he'd find a veil circle carved into the ornate illustrations around the frame.

On instinct, he claimed a step back—but stopped himself from fleeing any further. Recalling what the veil had said to him in the Kyteler Ruins. Recalling what it had promised at the base of the Hoarcliff Pass, where he begged to be able to trust it. Where it encouraged him to draw his first veil circle—and passed him through safely. Landing him exactly where he wished to go.

"I trust you," he whispered. To the veil, to Taran. Even though his voice cracked as he did. Even though his hand shook as he extended it one more time to skim the darkness he knew was right there on the wall behind the painting.

"I'm not afraid," he whispered in finality—before stepping through, and allowing the passage to take him where it pleased.

# 39

## THE KEEP

It was a surreal, unsettling reminder that Saffron had once already crossed through the center of the King's Keep courtyard. Previously had also been on the heels of Taran leading him, though Cylvan and Copper had also been alongside him. That night Ryder first tried to overpower and take him away, and would have, had Cylvan not invaded the Finnian Ruins to steal him back just in time. Where they'd sought shelter in that one stone building, where Taran showed them the veneer through the back door that would take them through the King's Keep in the Winter Court, then back to Avren again through the cold woods on the other side.

Saffron squeezed his amethyst pendant at the thought. Warmth responded. Another reminder—that when the time came, he may still be able to return to Avren through the exact same way.

He emerged from the veil passage in a frozen stone corridor, barely within reach of the mouth of it. Leaving him breathless, frost crystals forming on the inside of his lungs as in a snap, he stood within the arms of the coldest mountain peaks of the Winter Court. Of the oracle monastery of Fjornar, where folk like him were never supposed to step foot.

Walking to the end of the chilled corridor, Saffron paused at the top of a set of snowy steps left unbrushed as most of Fjornar's oracles were still gone to Avren. He gazed across the snowy monastery in front of him, unable to help but hold his breath, as if the thick steam on every exhale was as loud as speaking.

The buildings in front of him were not the same ones he'd once crossed through with Taran into the veneer, leaving him wondering where exactly he would have to go to find it. Deeper into them, at the very least. His heart thumped apprehensively.

At least, once he found it—he would be back in Avren by morning. Just like he'd promised Cylvan. In an instant, hardly any different than passing through the veil of the mirror at his back.

It was the only thought that could possibly bring him comfort, standing there in a place he was not welcome. A place he would be executed on sight for crossing, even if he wasn't a human. Even if he wasn't a witch, a rowan witch. Even mere common fey were prohibited from crossing those boundaries meant only for appointed oracles and their pupils. It made him wonder—had oracles spotted their footprints the night they passed through the king's keep? How they crossed through the untouched snow in the direction of the woods, where they vanished through the veneer? Had they ever found out who left them? Had Ryder told them, before or after he destroyed the passage in the Finnian Ruins, where Saffron had escaped him that night before the Midsummer Games?

"Me first," Taran said as Saffron took a step down, passing him to float his nose over the top layer of still-falling snow to sniff.

Saffron kept close as they walked, breathing quietly, walking silently, straining his ears to listen. It was deathly silent there, the same sort of liminal silence that fell over Luvon's estate when thick cloud paired with a blanket of mist, muffling every living thing. Until there was only the ringing on one's ears and the sound of tufted snow kissing the earth.

"Was it always like this?" Saffron asked. Taran huffed a little crater into the snow.

"No," he said. "There was never a lot of raucous noise, but, there was always someone within earshot. While I was here, at least."

Saffron bit his lip, but nodded. "When you were a child."

"Yes," Taran answered shortly, clearly wishing to end the swelling string of questions at the back of Saffron's throat. Of all the times Saffron would take the hint, it would be that one. It felt wrong, it felt strangely blasphemous, to speak in such a silent, sacred place. Even if nothing about it was sacred to him, specifically. He would have preferred to burn it down.

They followed a paved walkway barely visible beneath the snow, as the remainder of the grounds were buried beneath countless previous storms that had rolled through. In some areas, the snow reached nearly up to Saffron's shoulders, walls of the cleared corridor carved with long, icy genre illustrations down their lengths. Depicting scene after scene of myth, or what Saffron assumed to be other moments in history significant to that place. To the Winter Court. To the veiled queen.

Cailleach and her staff striking the earth; the old crone passing over a Samhain festival on the back of her wolf; who he assumed to be Queen Proserpina nursing a baby fawn in a circle of mushrooms; depictions of the queen and King Clymeus dancing in a circle of cheering high fey, outside what Saffron thought to be an ancient church. He tried to resist—but *accidentally* stumbled and dragged his hand through those illustrations, ripping off a thick layer of polished ice on the surface and crunching the queen and her little fawn under his boot. Taran said nothing, only snorted in response.

"If Ryder is still here, where would he be hiding?" Saffron asked after they passed another collection of stone buildings, dark and weathered and icicle-adorned.

"We'll start in the chapel," Taran said. "It's the same place they kept me when I was a child, the sacristy at the back of the chapel. There are false doors, false rooms—if he's trying to find a place to disappear for a while, it'll be there."

"Eias studied here too, right? Did they stay in the same place?"

"No. There were separate dormitories for oracle apprentices." The wolf tilted his head toward a building as they passed, and Saffron understood by the rows and rows of latticed windows set within more stonework, though far less ornate than that on the chapels and other practice buildings.

"Queen Proserpina liked this style of architecture," Saffron said, as if Taran didn't know. So when the wolf actually glanced his way, he was surprised. "It's no wonder all of her buildings are designed this way. I wonder if Clymeus designed it to purposely match her preferences, too."

"It's a human style of architecture, isn't it?" He muttered in response. "Ironic, how comfortable they are bringing human aesthetics to this side of the veil before kicking humans back out again."

"'*Ironic*' is being generous," Saffron said first, before frowning. "I'm surprised someone like you would be able to utter all those words in that order, without dying instantly."

"Hush, beantighe," Taran snapped. "I don't hate humans any more—or less—than anyone else. You should know that by now. The amount I despise all living things has nothing to do with opulence or aridity."

"How equitable."

The wolf sneered, but something about it was humorous. Like even Taran thought it was funny.

All the way to the back of the monastery sat the king's cathedral, similar in its structure to the queen's in the Finnian Ruins. Saffron could tell there was a little more further back, through a metal lichgate in the stone barrier around the proximity, and hidden behind the width of the massive church—something telling him it was the inner sanctum of the king's keep, where he would find the veneer. Soon. Only when he needed it.

Before Saffron could speak again, Taran came to a halt and gazed at where the grand front door to the cathedral hung open a crack. Saffron held his breath, then searched the ground below his feet. Sure enough, half-covered footprints hurried up the path and into the building.

"Let's go," Taran urged under his breath, starting forward. Saffron followed, though the sensation in his chest was no longer full of hopeful butterflies. Instead, he reached into the front of his doublet, and pulled out his obsidian knife.

That time, Saffron went ahead, as he would be able to slip through the open door without needing to creak it open any further than it already was. He poked his head in first, searching the empty rows and rows of pews on the other side, holding his breath to listen but hearing only his own heartbeat in his ears. On the stone floor leading from the door, compacted snow in the shape of heeled boots hurried up the center of the nave, and Saffron knew exactly who they belonged to.

Saffron's boots lightly echoed off the stone walls, the interior of the cathedral not nearly as ornamental as the one in the Finnian Ruins had once been, but still impressive in its own right. Meticulously-woven tapestries hung from the clerestory bannister on either side of the wide aisle, muffling Saffron's footsteps as well as a thick wall of mist would. To his disappointment, they only depicted the same scenes as those carved into the icy walkways outside; Cailleach and her staff, riding her wolf; a portrait of Proserpina clutching a fawn to her chest, as if posing for a royal painting; her and King Clymeus hand in hand donning crowns on their heads as a bright moon and starry landscape spread out far behind them; the queen in her black veil, posed on the back of her wolf king with a bloody crimson circle beneath them, giving birth to hundreds of little flowers. Saffron wished to accidentally trip and tear each and every one of them down as easily as he tore the face off the snowy carvings of the walkway.

"Who is the fawn supposed to represent?" Saffron asked once Taran slipped in through the doors behind him. "Ryder's mask at your sister's fete was shaped like a deer, as well. Though technically a stag."

"I was always told the fawn was a symbol of hope," Taran said. "Take that what you will."

"Hope for *what*," Saffron mumbled bitterly, not actually wanting an answer. Mostly, it made him question why in god's name Anysta would put Ryder Kyteler in a mask that clearly symbolized something so deeply rooted in the veiled queen and her old lore. But then something else tugged at Saffron's mind, clearly tangling enough that even Taran sensed it.

"What's on your mind?"

"It's just..." Saffron paused, trying to piece it all together. "Back in Morrígan's temple, in that plea from Proserpina we found, it specifically mentioned someone named *Deimne*."

"And?"

"Deimne was another name for Fionn mac Cumhaill, who married Sadhbh, a lady cursed to take the form of a doe. Later, they had Oisín, whose name means *fawn* in Gaeilge, and maybe even Old Alvish... I'd forgotten about Proserpina's letter to The Morrígan until now, thinking it meant nothing, but now I'm... confused."

"Perhaps her *Deimne* was a mere pet," Taran mumbled. "What does it matter? She wrote that note centuries ago."

"Then why would they still be depicting her with a fawn even all this time later?" Saffron hissed in response. "Clearly it meant *something.*"

"If it *meant* something about a fawn, why wouldn't she have used the name *Oisín* in her plea, then?"

"How in god's name am I supposed to know why she would or wouldn't do something?"

Taran suddenly shushed him. Saffron kicked him in the back of the leg, making the wolf snarl and snap around to him, before Saffron heard it, too. Muttered curses. The sound of scraping, clinking metal from the end of the nave.

Saffron held his breath, refocusing himself. He met Taran's eyes a moment, offering the wolf a brief nod and grasping at his knife a little tighter. Walking together, they crossed the remaining length of the aisle to an open door at the very back, a plaque reading *Sacristy* over the top. Saffron noticed how Taran's fur prickled the closer they went; he sensed the ebb and flow of anxiety, then anger, then, even, *panic* as they approached closer, though every taste of it felt as old as the stonework overlooking them.

Tastes of Taran's childhood memories, striking him sharply enough that they reverberated even through Saffron's body. Making it hard to focus, hard to keep his eyes looking straight ahead. Overcome with the constant urge to reach out and touch Taran's back. To place his hand between the wolf's ears. To comfort him, as if they weren't on the verge of confronting someone right on the other side.

Even as Saffron peeked around the edge of the open door, though, where Ryder was on the other side fighting against the cuffs on his wrists—Saffron barely saw him at first. His eyes instead went straight to the silver-inlaid feretory uplifted on an altartable in the center of the room. Painted with detailed imagery of the wolf king, both as a beast and as a fey king; a vessel for storing sacred parts, shaped like a coffin.

Just to the side of it, in a glass bowl far less ornate, even left dusty and unkempt, a pile of young white bones dropped in once and forgotten. Saffron knew without knowing—Taran's instincts told him in an instant.

Those were his bones—his fey bones, before they were replaced with those made of silver.

Saffron wanted to be sick. His world spun, despite knowing it wasn't his own reaction to the sight. It was Taran's, reverberating off him like trumpets and thunder and an avalanche, silent as the bones abandoned in the glass dish, like refuse from an uninvited guest.

Ryder noticed Saffron in the doorway, then. He turned fully, exposing the red marks and bloody scratches on his wrists from where he fought to remove the cuffs by force. On the altartable next to him, the silver ring that controlled them, just like the one

Kaelar used to wear to dominate Saffron's own in Danann House. Perhaps even one and the same. Ryder had taken it, not knowing the wearer of the cuffs could not also command them off.

"A little help, your highness?" He asked, voice cracking beneath the weight of his unweaving sanity. "Aren't you curious how they work? I'll show you. Come here, Saffron. Put this ring on."

Ryder scraped the silver ring off the table with a heavy hand, extending it out. Not knowing that Saffron knew more about them than he did.

"Where are they?" Saffron asked, instead. "Asche. My friends."

"What?" Ryder asked, verging on shrill. "What—Why in gods' name would I tell you that?"

"This is the last chance I'm going to give you, Ryder. I'm done playing games, and playing nice. *Tell me where my friends are.*"

Ryder barked a hoarse laugh, thrusting the ring out again. "Take the fucking ring, Saffron, and I'll tell you whatever you want to know!"

Saffron did, but only after extending his knife in warning. He took the ring without a word, and slid it right on.

"Now, I want you to command the cuffs to *release*—"

"Where's the daurae?" Saffron repeated, interrupting him. By his side, Taran stood stiff as ever. Crashing waves of his emotions continued to slam against Saffron's mental fortifications, anxiety and fear and repressed terror, again and again as he stood in that same room where his bones were taken. His very bones just within reach.

"The fucking—*daurae!*" Ryder snarled with a wide, exasperated grin. "Is exactly where I *fucking left them!* Even Anysta can't fucking find them! *Now,* do as I say, you *worthless—!*"

*"Restraint."*

The cuffs slammed together with a ringing crack. Ryder

stared down at them in a long, frozen state of disbelief, before slowly lifting his eyes back to Saffron.

"You—"

"Tell me where they are," Saffron commanded, holding the knife out again. Making sure Ryder saw exactly how the light passed through the blade, and how expertly Saffron held it. Without a single tremor in his hand. "My friends, too. Tell me where all of them are."

Ryder attempted to lunge, but Taran snapped out of his distraction, leaping in front of Saffron with snarling teeth. Ryder stumbled back into the feretory, making the king's coffin rattle on the table.

"Funny we should meet here again like this—" he said, that time to Taran. "You know—these are your bones, here? Useless and ashen—I could hear you screaming the entire time they pulled them out and put the new ones in, years ago. It really was a miserably long night for all of us, wasn't it?"

Taran's nose wrinkled, baring his teeth. Waiting for Saffron to make the call, but Saffron was fighting against the surge of frayed memories cresting over him from every direction. Frayed images from Taran's time spent there, where his bones were replaced, where he was taken as a child and made into what the mac Delbaiths wanted of him. Saffron felt the ache in his being, he felt the stretching of muscles—he felt the briefest snap of a moment where his bone was taken, and then replaced. In the fringes of the recollection, he even knew they used veil circles to do it. One at a time, for every single piece.

"Good thing I pulled all those memories out before you left for Avren, huh? Would've recognized me right away, otherwise," Ryder went on breathlessly. "Sorry your engagement didn't work out. Much prefer you like this, though. Much prefer Prince Saffron to you, too—"

*Keep talking*, Saffron thought. Taran claimed another snarling step toward Ryder, who pressed himself back against the altartable again, nearly kicking the wolf in the nose in appre-hension.

"You were such a cute kid, too—a shame you turned out so ugly. Not to mention—a lapdog to a rowan witch. What would mother think, to witness her king obeying every word of—"

*"Restraint!"* Saffron exclaimed the moment Ryder's wrists parted. He'd been attempting to burn time, clearly, not expecting Saffron to have anticipated that—and the man was instantly flooded with rage the moment the cuffs locked back into one another.

"Enough, Ryder," Saffron said. "You're going to tell me where my friends are. Where Asche is. Or I really will let Taran tear you apart."

"Your guard dog is a coward, your highness—"

"I've seen what he can do," Saffron answered. "He's far from afraid to kill someone standing in his way. Or mine."

Ryder's eyes frantically flashed between Saffron and Taran, back and forth, before the weakest of smiles twitched on his lips.

"Alright—alright, fine. You got me, your highness. They're in London. In a place called England. Got them a nice shared flat and even jobs to keep them busy. Y'know it's only been a few days there? Hardly enough time for me to do anything worse than make Letty cry. 'Bout as easy as making you cry, you know. I'll take you right to them, if you'd like." He extended his hands, still clasped. "I'll show you how. I'll even let you take me prisoner that way, if you want. You still have that pixie ring your fox-pet stole off me? I'll show you how to use it."

*"Restraint."*

"Oh, for gods' sake!" Ryder shouted. "Careful you don't really piss me off, highness—I'll have Hollow and Letty both tied up and tossed into the Thames. I'll have that mermaid slit up the tail and thrown in after them, if I don't boil it into a fucking stew first! I'll throw everything you've ever loved into places you'll never find them, on that side and this one—your dear prince, first and foremost. How many apples will it take for him to choke on his own vomit?"

Saffron moved before he processed it—suddenly only a few inches from Ryder's face, staring at him, unblinking, as something hot and thick bubbled out over his fingers. Between them, Saffron still gripped the handle of his obsidian knife—the blade buried inches into Ryder's stomach.

He knew where to find them, with those threats. Exactly where to look once he passed through the veil to the other side—no longer needing Ryder even for that. Capable of it himself. No longer needing Ryder for anything, ever, ever again—especially not threats on his raven prince.

"You won't lay—a fucking finger on him," he said, breathless. Ryder only stared at him, eyes wide and bulging. Like he truly hadn't believed Saffron was capable of such a thing—but Saffron had taken lives to protect the people he loved before, more than once. And he would continue to do so, as many at it took, until every living soul knew better than to take what was his ever again.

Yanking the blade out again, Ryder grunted, buckling forward as his clasped hands flew to the wound. Pressing hard against it, though blood still gushed out between his fingers.

"Rowan—bitch," he choked, sinking to one knee. Saffron took another step back. Ryder's blood dripped from the end of the knife, trailing behind him. "I'll kill—all of them, and then—I'll make you mine, whether you like it or not. I won't give you any choice, ever again, you goddamn—moon-eared—"

"You can try," Saffron told him. That time, his voice trembled slightly. "I dare you to try, Ryder Kyteler. Ryder O'Daire, whatever the fuck your name really is. But only if you don't bleed to death, first."

He turned. Ryder reached out to grapple for his cloak, but Taran's teeth clamped down over his arm, hard enough that bone crunched. Ryder shrieked, throwing himself back and slamming his heel into the side of Taran's head, kicking him, shouting and cursing even as he slumped onto his side, writhing in his own growing puddle of blood. Saffron left without glancing back.

———

———

———

THROUGH THE GATES AT THE BACK OF THE MONASTERY, Saffron crossed into the private sanctum of the wolf king. A familiar sight, though it filled him with no relief. He'd been there once before; he knew it would take him back home. Back to Avren, where he could fall into Cylvan's arms, and plead for his forgiveness for failing to find Asche despite it all. To find a way through, despite it all. At least, at least—he could assure his raven that Ryder Kyteler was dead.

The oracles of Fjornar must have once seen the unexplained footprints through the snow of the king's keep, because they put up a stone fence around the cluster of buildings to keep access to the veneer in the woods closed-off. It didn't matter—through another metal gate, leading into an arched stone tunnel, Saffron could see the snowy woods right on the other side. It took no more than a simple arid spell to unlock the latch, and step through.

Saffron would walk back into Avren with nothing gained— except Ryder's blood on his hands.

# 40

# THE CRONE

Saffron moved swiftly between the trees, branches whipping his face and leaving stinging marks on his cheeks as his pace remained steady despite the exhaustion in his muscles. Icy fingers tugged at his cloak as he passed, when they weren't pulling his hair. His thoughts raced, heartbroken and ashamed and heavy, loud, enough to block out anything Taran might have said in warning, in instruction. Just focused on getting *away*.

If Saffron just kept walking, eventually the veneer would spit him out somewhere on the outskirts of Avren. It didn't matter where or how far away. He could walk. He could perform the same veil spell he did to get to Luvon's estate. He only needed to get past the snow on the ground, to Avren's warm greenery.

He shoved his way through low-hanging branches, leaping over fallen logs and doing everything he could to keep his feet from getting tangled in roots and flattened brambles beneath the weight of the snow. He still tripped more than once, landing roughly on his stomach, but the snow was a welcome cushion each time.

Only when he lost his footing for the third time, falling face-first into the earth, did he first realize the snow beneath his feet was thinning. Its blanket remained on the earth in every direction, weighing down boughs of pine and yellowed fern tendrils, but sharp rocks met his palms as he crashed into the frozen whiteness. Proof he'd finally reached the boundary of the veneer. He was so close. Only a little farther, and he would be in Avren. He would be close to Cylvan again.

The clumps of snow long-gathered on fans of pine needles and piled like white nests between forked branches thinned. They dripped, striking his head and the back of his neck like pinpricks before slithering down the back of his high collar and making him shiver. He kicked his legs over a fallen log, practically crying out in joy when his boots splashed in a puddle of mud on the other side. Just on his heels, the snow remained patchy in places, a worn-through quilt with cotton bursting between seams—but in front of him, he knew Avren's woods were reaching out to embrace him.

A deep, velvety green soon painted every leaf, fern, long grass; white mushrooms clustered in bouquets at the heels of tall birch and oak trees, all dripping with a chorus of raindrops to the loamy earth below. As he inhaled a chestful of air, it was rich with verdant smells he didn't recognize at first; there was no low hum of magic on the air. It reminded him of the energy of the Kyteler Ruins, or the Finnian Ruins—which was a welcome sensation as well. The Finnian Ruins were so close. Even if it wasn't the abandoned Queen's Keep where he stumbled out of the trees into, even if it was somewhere else long-abandoned by humans and surrounded by protective iron, he didn't care. He was just happy to find the snow long gone. He was happy to be anywhere in Avren's forests. He would smell the salt of the sea soon enough.

Moving in as straight of a line as he could manage, Saffron still constantly checked over his shoulder to ensure no one followed behind him—only to suddenly trip over something tall and hard jutting out of the earth, sending him sprawling into the mud for a second time. Groaning, he pushed himself up, scowling at his scraped knee before searching for the perpetrator, and catching his breath when the familiar stone tablet caught his eye.

It took only a moment to recall where the resemblance stemmed from—a lecture he'd sat in in his earliest days at Mairwen. He could recall the lecture hall, all of the students crowded around him, the light-projected image on the wall, the sound of the professor's voice.

*Celtic knots... Also called knotted stones, this form of ancient epithet is older than any high fey records...*

"Huh..." he mumbled. Getting back to his feet, he shucked off as much mud as he could from his stomach and legs, realizing he must have indeed stumbled out of the veneer along some sort of old human ruins. Maybe even a branch of the Finnian Ruins, considering how many little cottages were scattered around that place, only accessible by following winding trails into the trees. If he couldn't find the ruins themselves, if he could find that lake where Letty's cottage had been, that would be enough to supply his bearings to make it back to the city, at least...

Before turning to search again, though, Saffron's curiosity got the better of him. He stepped closer to the carved stone idol, crouching on the balls of his feet to get a closer look. The sculpted edges were weathered down, porous and infiltrated with patches of moss burrowed in the textured sides; carved in the front, lines overlapped one another in a symmetrical, circular pattern, and Saffron exhaled sharply through his nose in indignation. That professor had scolded him in front of the whole class when Saffron insisted he'd seen knotted memory threads donning the same overlapping pattern, telling him *'common memory thread manipulation was taboo'; 'only the highest of oracles in Alfidel were allowed to manipulate memory threads'; 'whatever he thought he saw certainly wasn't a memory thread, but a tourist scam'*—but crouching in front of that Celtic knot right there, Saffron knew he'd been right all along. He wished he could drag that professor by their nose to come and see for themselves, then to apologize to Saffron for calling him a fool in front of everyone else.

"I never thought meddling in your memories would come in handy even after all this time," he said out loud, speaking to the wolf lingering silently in the back of his mind. When Taran still said nothing, Saffron frowned, but pushed the annoyance away. The beast always had his reasons.

Rising back to his feet, it was as soon as he lifted his eyes back ahead of him that Saffron spotted another Celtic knot only a few yards away. Biting back another curious smile, he approached, appreciating its slightly different pattern.

A third totem emerged from the ground a few yards further from that one. Then a fourth, then a fifth, before the sound of chimes in the wind caught Saffron's attention, making him perk up. He held his breath, listening for a moment, then carefully making his way in their direction. A rumble of thunder and sprinkling rain combined into a light chorus as if summoning him closer, and he gladly went. Curious to know what he'd find on the other side; eager to get out of the rain and back to the capitol as soon as he could. Cylvan would be waiting for him, after all, with the sun already risen.

Through the curtain of trees and thick undergrowth, he finally spotted the edge of the wood, a broad clearing spreading like a stretched green blanket on the other side. He hurried his pace, thrilled to finally have a chance to see exactly where the veneer had spat him out. Imagining what he might see once he passed through the edge—only to stop right at the treeline with a frown, and an uneasy thump of his heart.

Ahead of him, there were only rolling hillsides. Green as the forest he'd stumbled from, dark and velvety under the overcast sky where they didn't vanish into a thick fog draped over the landscape. Spots of white-wooled sheep grazed within a wide fence, the only sign of life apart from what he was certain was a silhouette of a building a little ways into the mist. It would have been enough to make him snap—had that partially-obscured little house not been the exact size of the cottage Ryder had once shown him. He really was somewhere on the edge of the Finnian

Ruins, then. That little cottage may have even been the very same one Letty had stayed in, alongside the lake hidden beneath the mist. He nearly cried out in relief.

More chimes sang out to him as he emerged from the thickness of the trees, and he searched up the edge of the treeline to find them—surprised at exactly how many dangled from every branch. In both directions the trees ran, disappearing into the mist both ways and adorned with the jingling chimes for the entire length.

He shuffled between two thick bushes to continue his way toward the house—only to trip over yet another stone, that time at least catching his footing before crashing all the way down. Cursing, he yanked on his cloak where it caught on yet another— but that time, his heart thumped again.

More Celtic knots than he could count cluttered that area where he emerged, most hidden by the thick bushes and ferns that swallowed them, but obvious once he really looked. Like the chimes in the trees, more carved stones lined the edge of the forest in both directions. Wooden posts of various sizes poked out from amongst them, hammered into the earth in sporadic intervals and adorned with upside-down horseshoes and capped with bushels of long-dead rowan branches wrapped in ivy and pinned in place with gnarled iron nails.

A signpost stood out within in the thick grass a few feet away, and Saffron went to read it out of curiosity, only knowing a few of the Gaeilge words.

*Warning... fey folk*
*Do not...*

"Huh," he repeated under his breath with a little smirk, wondering if one of Ryder's witches had planted it, or perhaps someone from far earlier in time. He would have to come back to search for more points of interest when he had the chance again, he told himself, turning back to the issue at hand.

The nearest path was a sloppy, muddy mess, but the slippery decline was at least pitted with white stones to help keep one's balance. He made his way to the mouth of it, slowly navigating down with two fistfuls of his cloak to keep it off the ground and help his balance. Not wanting to be caked in yet another layer of mud before returning to his prince.

Thankfully he didn't have to go far to reach the cottage by the lake, squinting into the rain as the faded shadow materialized a little more clearly with every dozen steps. Just as the rain finally soaked through his hair, though, did Saffron suddenly stop. Standing in the middle of the muddy pathway, water spilling down his cheeks and the back of his neck as he realized with another sweep of his nerves—the house was not the one Letty had once stayed in.

Swallowing back the lump in his throat, he still took another handful of steps toward it, growing more certain as he went. Still— that didn't mean anything. He was certain it was one of the scattered cottages outside of the Finnian Ruins, either way. There was no other explanation for the tongue-in-cheek stone knots and signs along the edge of the trees. Only other humans would have placed those. Considering their age, it may have even been rebels during the war. Saffron had simply stumbled out on the far side of the Finnian ruins, and just had to keep walking. Eventually he would find where he was going. He would find a familiar landmark to guide him back home.

His feet came to a halt again as he came within shouting distance of the cottage—realizing with a tight squeeze of his lungs that smoke billowed from the chimney of the cottage. There was —someone inside.

*What do you think?* He posed to Taran, secretly desperate for even an ounce of guidance. When the wolf still didn't respond, Saffron silently cursed him for being so stubborn, but at least took it as a sign that Taran didn't sense anything *dangerous* nearby. Perhaps some of Ryder's witches had merely lingered behind. Perhaps it was some lost traveler taking shelter from the rain, no different than how he and Ryder had taken shelter in that hunter's cabin from the snow. If anything—they might at least be able to give him some idea of where the veneer had spat him out.

The only question was whether or not to approach while wearing his glamour. Depending on who exactly stoked a fire inside would determine which would earn him a warmer welcome. He pulled up his wet hood in the meantime, hiding his ears until he could decide for the better.

None of the cottages outside the ruins were particularly fancy or ornately built, but that one was particularly worn-through nearly to the bones. Any ornamental carvings in the facade's wooden beams had long worn away beneath centuries of rain; the thatched roof was in desperate need of replacement, dark and discolored where it absorbed rain and mildew like a sponge in muddy water. The entire thing leaned slightly to one side, propped up with beams of wood in an attempt to keep the slump at bay. Even those beams appeared older than Saffron was, nearly eaten through and leaving trenches in the earth where they'd slowly bowed beneath the gradual inevitability of the house's demise.

Outside, more horseshoes were hammered over the doorway. Bowls of sour milk and honey were left to rot or kicked over along the base of the exterior walls, and had the rain not splattered into the congealed white liquid, diluting it, the stench might have made Saffron gag. For a brief moment he wondered if he'd only imagined the smoke through the chimney as more fog, leaving the house actually abandoned—but then one of the shuttered windows suddenly slammed open, and he nearly leapt out of his skin. Searching for the source, he met the bright green eyes of a wild-haired crone, who looked him up and down with narrowed, suspicious eyes.

"Where'n ye come from, then?" She asked, voice rough like it'd been a few days since last speaking.

"Um," Saffron said, unsure how to answer. He glanced over his shoulder toward the distant trees, where the wind chimes continued twinkling in the breeze. The crone followed him with her eyes, before nodding that way herself.

"Show me yer ears, lad," she said like a warning, voice thick in an unfamiliar accent and speaking in an equally strange form of Alvish that made it hard for Saffron to process at first. His mind raced when put on the spot so suddenly, looking back at her one more time, trying to decide which role was best to play. Deciding he would rather risk being outed as human, than anything else. He reached down into his doublet while pulling down his hood, subtly removing his hood and showing the round of his ears. To his surprise—and body-melting relief—the crone grinned wide at him with yellowed teeth.

"I see!" She exclaimed. "Which way ye come from, lad?"

"Erm—" Saffron bit his lip. Deciding to take another chance. "The veneer, through the trees."

Her grin softened into clear surprise, raising her eyebrows.

"The king's keep?" She said in a whisper, like it was a secret. Saffron nodded. She looked him over a moment longer, before narrowing her eyes again.

"Have ye heard the music of the moon's harp?" She posed, next. Saffron's heart pounded.

"Oh, yes!" He said with a little too much enthusiasm, scrambling to recall what Adelard had told him about that phrase. "I've—I've heard it close, and learned the song myself."

"And how'd ye hear it, with the veil stitched as tight as it is?"

Saffron nearly mentioned the veneer again—before realizing, she wouldn't have asked if that was already the answer. Staring at her a moment, his mind spun. His hand moved slowly, reaching into his bag. He removed the chain of access rings, separating the pixie ring from the others.

"I... became as slight as a pixie," he said. A guess, by everything Adelard had told him of rings and pixies and the veil's secrets. A bead of cold sweat dripped down his back.

"Oh, *a chara!*" The crone suddenly exclaimed, smiling broader than ever. "I was wonderin' when ye'd come!"

Leaving the shutter hanging open, the cottage-hag hurried for the door, and Saffron caught a brief sight of what awaited him inside long before he was greeted face-to-face. A clay fireplace burning brightly, a cauldron tucked deep in the flames; sparkling crystals lining the mantle; a ram's skull hanging from the chimney; an unfathomable number of horseshoes and other iron totems nailed into the sagging walls and support beams. In a flash, his mind whirled through every possible kind of wild fey the crone might be, though he came to no conclusion before the door swung open as forcefully as the shutter had.

Before he could think to return the chain of rings to his bag, Saffron was grabbed by the arm and yanked inside. Yelping, he stumbled over his feet, landing directly into one of the uneven chairs of the crone's kitchen table. Barely righting himself before he tipped all the way to the floor, Saffron finally looked up again just as the woman quickly shut the door, then proceeded to latch at least four different locks down the side. Saffron swallowed back the urge to shout at her to stop, fearing he was about to become some wild thing's dinner—voice only catching the moment he noticed arid steles and circles scattered throughout the house, despite being so worn it was clear they hadn't been active in some time. He forced himself to relax, settling slightly back into the chair while pinching at the hematite wand tucked in his sleeve.

Inside, the house smelled of herbs and butter, soda bread, beer, even a little bit of humid peat. It was one main room, with a single door leading into a small bedroom on the opposite side. The inside was packed to the brim in every space available, whether it be the floor or the walls. Bushels of twigs, herbs, flowers dangled from wire across the sagging rafters; salt and scattered leaves dusted the table next to where Saffron sat, a loom draped in a project in-progress crowded the corner alongside the fireplace.

Even the old woman kicked footstools and woven baskets out

of the way as she shuffled around, going straight for the nook of cupboards and shelves to peek into a dented copper kettle on one of them. She wrinkled her nose, popping the lid to scoop loose tea inside, then filling it with water. Hooking it on the same bar her cauldron hung over the fireplace, she finally turning back to Saffron while adjusting the round glasses on her nose. Only then didn't Saffron spot rounded ears through her wild hair, and his tense muscles relaxed slightly more. He couldn't help but imagine how long that old woman had been there by herself, wondering if she was as old as Baba Yaga, or perhaps even Adelard, considering where she lived on the edge of the ruins, her knowledge of the veneer. Had she been there since the war? Had Ryder known about her? Perhaps she'd even kept herself hidden during all of that time, too.

"Dangerous of ye to come knockin' at my door with that ring in your bag and not on yer hand, you know? Put it on where it goes, so ye don't get caught up in any trouble ye can't pop out of," she winked, before grabbing Saffron's hand without warning. He smiled awkwardly, nodding and using his other hand to unclip the chain of rings. They all tumbled loosely into his bag, making him groan internally, but if anything—swapping the circlets gave him a chance to remove the opulent ring he still wore as well. Letting it drop to the floor with a small sound. No longer wishing to be reminded of it.

He shakily produced the pixie ring next, though, actually setting it on his finger made bile rise up the back of his throat. The crone seemed determined to watch him slide it on. Only once he did, did she smile and pet the back of his hand, shuffling back to her pot over the fire.

"You bein' here tells me Master Deimne won't be comin' again anytime soon, will he? Damn him, how long's it been now?" She rambled while preparing the tea—and Saffron barely heard what she said next. Ears ringing at the mention of that name.

"You tell him to come soon, I'm missin' him sorely," the crone went on. Unaware of how the earth turned beneath Saffron's feet in a rush of alarm, evident by how she poured hot tear into a clay cup and handed it to him casually as ever. She had to be mad—didn't she? Truly mad? "Got plenty to tell him 'bout the folk comin' around askin' for him, too. Gonna put me in an earlier grave than I'm meant, shufflin' them all off without suspicion, 'specially with this brat he's foisted on me. Reminds me too much of he himself whenst he was a bairn, when I think about it much."

Saffron wished to say something, but he had no idea what. He opened his mouth, dry and numb, hoping some words might spill out.

"And—when was the last time Master *D-Deimne* came to see you?" he asked. Her answer would tell him what he needed to know—whether or not, in her clearly long-term isolation, the crone's mind had been lost to the rain and the mist. He didn't know what exactly he hoped to hear. "Was it when he brought the —the *'bairn'*?"

"Aye," she sighed, scraping the edges of the cauldron over the fire and filling the room with the rich aroma of meat stew. "Don't think the thing's eaten more than a bowl since they was brought here. Always goes for my fingers when I try, a'course... Young master won't be thrilled to hear I wasn't able to get close enough to take those unsightly horns off 'em, either..."

Saffron stiffened. His dry mouth clenched on itself, throat tightening up until hardly a raspy exhale could escape him.

"Oh?" he managed, voice tight. His hand gripping the clay cup squeezed hard enough to turn his knuckles white and make his fingers tingle. The fire in the hearth was suddenly deafening; the scraping of her spoon along the edge of the cauldron was enough to make his bones vibrate. Surely, through her strange accent, like modern Alvish rolling over a Gaelige tongue, he'd only misheard. "Their—their *horns,* huh?" He had to pause, attempting to drink some of the tea in the cup, nearly choking on it.

"Aye, ugly little growths. Tried to tell him to find someone else, his mother won't appreciate havin' those to worry about when she comes, but he insists. He always insists, even when I know I know better. Hardly even knew his mother before he went through the veneer, himself. Perhaps for the best, seein' all what went and made her mad... Havin' horns to worry 'bout will only make her madder, I know..."

The crone rambled. She dumped a splatter of meat stew into a shallow bowl, offering it to Saffron. He took it without thinking, moving numbly to accept whatever she gave him.

"Go on, eat some, then," she said, and Saffron obeyed, tilting the hot stew into his mouth. "Most goin' to waste since I ain't botherin' to offer any to those folk always comin' 'round lately. Glad to see a face not hidden b'neath one of those dreadful veils. You wanna talk about what's truly *unsightly*, it's them veils."

Saffron choked, before forcing himself to chew. The hot hunk of potato melted in his mouth and burned all the way down.

"The folk who keep coming around looking—looking for— Master Deimne—they're witchhunters?" He croaked. His hands began to tremble. His thoughts clicked together, before being frantically snapped apart again in an instant. He didn't want them to piece together. He didn't want to follow those connections as they slipped into place, one after another, and another, and another, a long and fast-moving chain he soon could not keep up with.

"Callin' themselves *priestesses* again lately," she muttered bitterly. "Thinkin' I'm just some ancient thing that can't remember when my dear princess first called 'em to her cloister. Not botherin' to know I was the very first one of 'em, too. Nothing now like they used to be. Just shells of what they once was. New ones're plum-stupid, too, think I can't tell when they're usin' that dirty-human itch and lyin' to my face. But I kept the bairn secret, even from them. Just like Master Deimne told me. Don't know if they even know they're here, in his mother's cottage. New witchhunters always just askin' 'bout the young master, askin' if I know where he is. Not knowin' by usin' that new name of his I can tell right away they ain't any folk I could trust."

"Right," Saffron said, shrill, sharp like a blade slicing up his throat. His heart pounded faster than should have been possible, making his body tingle with heat, about to lift out of the seat of his chair with the pressure. Speaking in a rush, barely aware of each wore as it tumbled from his mouth. "Foolish of them to think they can get away with that—especially trying to trick you like that—which name are they calling him by now? He's so clever with the ones he picks, isn't he? To keep Avren folk off his tail." Saffron yammered through his teeth. He had no idea what he was saying, but—he had an idea. A horrifying, terrible idea weighed down beneath the perpetual and insurmountable realizations his mind forced on him like a hot-white brand to the nape of his neck.

*Witchhunters asking about him. Using that new name of his.*

*Master Deimne. Dear princess. Priestesses, cloister.*

*My dearest Adone and Deimne, and those who watch over them...*

"Some call him *Master Finn O'Daire,* actin' so smug when they do," she scoffed. Saffron's ears rang louder, deafened as if the distant chimes rang just behind him. "But the real new ones—the ones who don't know any better, who wear their veils pinned in their hair with shiny trinkets like it's some fete accessory—" she scoffed, "—come knockin' on my door thinkin' utterin' *'Ryder Kyteler'* will get me to tell 'em anything. Wonderin' why utterin' that name makes me snarl and spit at them. The nerve, speakin' the Kyteler name on my doorstep after everything that one moon-fevered bitch did to sweet Arya. Even Master Deimne knows better than to repeat it when he comes by."

Finn O'Daire. Ryder Kyteler.

*He is much, much older than any of us could have ever guessed.*

Deimne. Master Deimne. *Proserpina's Deimne.*

Saffron's ears knelled; they crashed with the sound of rushing blood, as everything flooded his mind in an attempt to remain upright. To remain in his body, to string thoughts in one piece. Loud, deafening, keening sounds that marched in rhythm with his heart. Pounding so hard it made the tea in his held cup ripple.

Ryder Kyteler was Queen Proserpina's son. Half-human, half-fey. Perhaps even hers and Adone's. Her human lover.

"'Nough chatter now, let me show you the wee bairn since that's why you're really here, ain't it?" The crone puttered around the kitchen a moment again, her voice dull and muddled as if speaking underwater. Perhaps it was Saffron who was beneath the surface. Sunken deeply, buried beneath snow and ice, mud and lichen, far beneath any surface of any air to breathe. Silently suffocating, unable to think, hearing only the sound of his own heart and the ringing shrill of understanding.

"... Will have to only peek through the slider, though, since they still try to claw out any eyes that look too long. Had to tie 'em up recently 'cause they kept threatenin' to cut their pretty hair off, and you know how disappointed the queen would be if she woke with horns *and* her new hair chopped off."

The crone laughed, the sound of it echoing through the thick mound Saffron's mind layer prone beneath. He forced himself to hear it. He forced his bones upward, to hook around the sound and pull himself upward. Into the air, again. To be there, fully, entirely, to witness this horned bairn the crone spoke so possessively of. As if they already belonged to her Princess Aryadna. To Queen Proserpina.

Still, when Saffron attempted to stand, he nearly tumbled straight back to the floor. The old woman didn't notice, just shuffling her way toward a door at the back of the kitchen, grabbing a lantern as she went. The smell of crisp rain washed through every hole needle-pricked through him in that brief conversation, striking him with a breath of clarity as bright as the tip of his obsidian knife. As sure as the point of his wand, still tucked beneath the cuff of his sleeve.

He followed without any more questions. He heard only that name spoken again and again in the crone's unique voice,

*Deimne, Deimne, Deimne.* He wished Taran would say something. He wished Taran would confirm—or deny—the terrible, astounding, impossible thing Saffron had just realized of the man he'd chased across Alfidel. The man he'd once trusted to help with his magic. The one Saffron thought could only possibly betray him as deeply as being half-fey while telling no one. The one who always knew too much, without explanation. The one who the veil refused to make an oath with.

Into the fog, the crone went without worry. Saffron trailed on her heels. She said nothing else to explain where exactly they headed, just hummed a song Saffron didn't know, though it didn't make the atmosphere any more pleasant.

If the thick fog wasn't unsettling enough, the sound of chimes from the distant treeline within the fog made his nerves flush and chitter nervously. He hadn't been able to ask where exactly the veneer had lead him, in all the old woman's ramblings —but learning what he did about Ryder, and her relation to him, Saffron was certain he did indeed stumble out somewhere in proximity to the Finnian Ruins. Where else would Ryder allow someone like her live? Where else would witchhunters know to go and ask her about Ryder's whereabouts? About Deimne's whereabouts. About Queen Proserpina's firstborn son's whereabouts.

Saffron was going to be sick.

Eventually a second cottage appeared through the mist, and Saffron let out the nervous breath he'd been holding. More chimes dangled from the house's eaves, interspersed with crossed pieces of iron and bells, garlands of protective herbs and flowers woven into one another, more iron horseshoes and nails hammered into the hard mud exterior. It made Saffron's nose and throat burn, lifting his hand to his mouth as several shiny silver talismans interspersed with the iron flashed in the lantern light, next. There was nothing to indicate they were made of opulent bone ash like all of the silver in Alfidel was, and Saffron was certain he hadn't seen any floating barbs over the Finnian Ruins on Anysta's map. He didn't spare a thought for *why*. He had no strength left for curiosities like that.

"Lemme take a peek first, see if they're where they should be," the crone said, putting a hand up for Saffron to wait, before reiterating yet again: "Last couple'a times they tried to claw out me eyes when I moved the slider."

Saffron rooted his feet in place as the crone walked unevenly down the rest of the path to the door. Using the staff carrying her lantern, she banged it against the door, making Saffron jump when she roughly called out: "Ye better not try your claws on me again, fiend! I'll happily cut off more than your nails this time if ye don't show me a bit of respect, hear me? Behave good and nice like you're s'posed to."

No response came, but Saffron was back to holding his breath. The old woman waited another moment before grabbing the knob of a viewfinder hidden amongst the markings and nails on the door, peering inside before turning back to Saffron with an approving nod.

"They're where they should be in the back, come'n see for yourself. Perhaps finally learned to behave so'n they don't get the lash again."

Saffron said nothing. He stiffly moved forward, keeping his eyes first on the crone in case she was attempting to entrap him herself, only sliding his gaze toward the viewfinder when the door got in his way of passing.

Inside the cottage was dark, with all the windows boarded closed beneath the weight of the herb garlands and protective iron tokens. It smelled of humid sweat and mildew through even the slight opening of the gap, and he nearly covered his mouth again. He ran his eyes over the dark shadows inside, trying to find exactly what the old woman spoke of as being 'where they should be in the back'.

His eyes found the one she called 'the bairn', and his lungs filled with agony as deep and burning as a long inhale of fresh yew.

Even from the distance, he knew Daurae Asche's long, corn-silk hair; their curling horns; even the whiskey-gold color of their eyes that looked right back at him through the slit in the door. Full of hatred, disdain, a threat to anyone who dared come closer to where they hid in the darkness.

"Even in such a state, and with those loathsome horns—they look so much like Princess Aryadna, don't you think?" The crone asked, voice soft but giddy. "Only a matter of time 'fore Master Deimne brings her threads back. Just ye wait and see how well I know they'll fit."

One final, incomprehensible realization clicked into place in Saffron's mind. The last one he wished for anything but to recognize, to accept. But staring at Asche through the gap in the door, he knew. Ryder Kyteler—Deimne—sought his mother's memory tapestry, with Daurae Asche as her intended woven vessel.

# 41

# THE VESSEL

Saffron didn't know how long he stood there and stared. Until the rain overhead broke a little harder and soaked through his hair and down his spine all over again. Once again unable to breathe, but smelling every moth-eaten, mildew-rich stench of that prison where the daurae was hidden.

Comprehending too much at once, that it only dug him deeper into uncertainty. Too many shrill, striking warnings and understandings crashed into him all at once, slamming against his back, wailing directly to his face. Forcing him to shove through each and every bit like cleaving a shrieking wraith, allowing himself only one absolute truth to ring through.

Saffron was not going anywhere without Daurae Asche by his side.

Glancing back to the woman, his thoughts raced again as, in a flash, he reconsidered every strange thing she'd uttered since he arrived. Piecing together the exact lie he needed.

"You said the bairn keeps trying to pull out their hair, yes?" He asked with new authority, voice smooth and sure of itself, even if his insides continued to roil like water in a pot. The crone nodded with a wrinkled frown. "Let me approach them to make sure they haven't done any other damage to themself. I want to be thorough in my report back to Master Deimne." Uttering the name almost made Saffron's teeth clamp down on his tongue to sever it.

"Oh, I really don' recommend it, sir—"

"I insist," Saffron answered, that time with the practiced authority of a high fey. A rowan witch. Whichever would convince the crone first. "That person will know better than to do me any harm. I can assure you."

The crone gave him a wild, hesitant look, before pressing her lips together and nodding, Digging around on the belt strapped against her wide, beneath her tattered shawl, she produced an ancient key easily older than King Ailir himself.

"I'll be lockin' the door behind ye while you're in there, just a warning," she said while posing the key into the latch. "Don't need to risk them gutting you then runnin' out."

"No problem," Saffron answered. He knew more than enough arid epithets to unlock a damn door. He didn't care, he just wanted inside the goddamned cottage, and the old woman moved like syrup on a winter's day.

Finally stepping inside, Saffron practically slammed the door shut behind him. The crone didn't protest, as the sound of the locking door came quickly after.

The thick miasma of the closed-off prison was worse once on the other side of the door, and Saffron had to resist covering his mouth. His heart continued mercilessly pounding in his chest, ringing in his ears—only interrupted by the low, animalistic growl of the fey crouched in the back corner. A low, rumbling warning of something once demure and proper, reduced to their most innate instincts in order to survive, practically back to their wildest roots. A creature that once crawled with claws out of the earthen mounds where all fey were born.

Saffron raised a hand, yanking the view-piece shut to keep the old crone from watching. He turned back to Asche one more time, breathing in a deep lungful of the thick air, forcing himself to endure what Asche had been subjected to for days and days on end. Saffron didn't want to think about how long the daurae had actually spent in the human world, before being brought back to the Finnian Ruins where time would have dragged on as long as it did for Saffron. Ériu above—Saffron could barely stomach the thought of the daurae having been there the entire time, as they searched the Finnian Ruins a week and few days prior.

"Asche," he finally said in a low, calm voice. He put his hands out slightly. "It's me, Asche. It's Saffron."

Asche hissed, then scoffed, tangled blonde hair shifting over their face.

"I'm not falling for that trick again, you bastard. I suggest you heed the old woman's warnings and get out of here before I take your godsdamned eyes for something to eat."

Saffron forced himself to remain calm, as well as to remain where he stood. The last thing he wanted was to scare them, when they were already clearly frightened enough.

"It's really me," Saffron said. "Let me prove it, alright? Someone glamored to look like me wouldn't have all the same memories I do."

"Try me."

Saffron swallowed the nervous lump in his throat. He mentally scrambled for anything, anything, that only he would know. "The morning they snuck me out of Avren, after what I did at your brother's engagement party on Ostara—you snuck a beaded bookmark through the carriage window just as it was leaving."

Asche visibly shifted.

"It was beaded with a white unicorn on it."

"That doesn't convince me of anything," Asche insisted, but a flicker of their resolve had softened.

"It..." Saffron glanced back over his shoulder, nerves ringing hot as he considered his next words. He shared them in a whisper. "It was Sunbeam who held you at the Midsummer Games, wasn't it? Dressed as a witchhunter. She was the one who carried you through, wasn't she?"

"What?" Asche asked, but not out of confusion—rather, real surprise that someone might know that. Saffron only nodded.

"I saw her aura. Her red halo, meaning she was rich with magic from eating rowan berries right beforehand. That's the only reason I didn't intervene. You recognized her too, didn't you? You met my eyes for a moment, like you were trying to reassure me."

"I wanted you to choose Cylvan," Asche's voice cracked, and Saffron's heart ripped with it. He nodded more, taking a few steps forward.

"Yes—and Cylvan is fine. Everyone, Cylvan, your fathers, everyone made it out of the veil event fine. And they're all worried sick about you. Cylvan spends most of his free time praying to Lugh at that family altar, the one on the cliffside that overlooks the sea. They've got every oracle in Alfidel trying to find you. We've been tracking Ryder across the country for weeks, too—"

"But how did you find me?" Asche asked desperately, sitting upright. The blanket draped over their shoulders shifted, revealing their narrow wrists bound roughly together with rope. Bile raced up the back of Saffron's throat.

"I—I don't know exactly how I got here, or why that woman thought I was here to see you, but—" Saffron had to catch his breath, lungs too tight to inhale fully. "—but it doesn't matter, because we're going to get out of here. I'm going to take you back home. There's a veneer nearby, just into the woods, that leads into the Winter Court."

"What?" Asche croaked again. Saffron was close enough to see their face by then, though it only made it harder to keep his composure. Asche, who looked exhausted, the bags under their eyes so dark it was impossible to know if they weren't actually bruises. Whose bright gold eyes were rounder than ever against their pale skin and sunken cheeks. Staring at Saffron with wild abandon like all they wanted in the world was to believe it really was him standing there.

Saffron nearly stepped close enough to embrace them—but

they suddenly thrust out their bound hands, eyes going dark and cold once more. Saffron reeled back in surprise, just as Asche searched for something on the dirty floor. They picked up a sharp rock, tossing it to Saffron's feet.

"P-perform some arid magic, for me to see. The Saffron I knew was rowan blooded. He made his oath with the veil in the Spring Court."

Saffron obeyed without question. He bent down onto one knee, but rather than taking Asche's rock, he pulled the hematite wand from down his sleeve.

"Professor Adelard, from Morrígan, gave this to me," he explained as Asche narrowed their eyes. "What do you want me to do?"

Saffron pressed the tip of the wand to the fraying floorboards. Asche thought about it for a moment.

"Summon a flower," they said. "An iris."

Saffron couldn't resist a little smile. "Cylvan's favorite."

Those two words made Asche's tense body relax slightly again, allowing Saffron to do the same.

With ease, focusing on his hand to not let it rush the movements, he drew a simple arid circle surrounded with ogham markings that read *'grow/flower/iris/violet'*. After returning the wand to his sleeve, Saffron placed his hand at the circle's contact point, closing his eyes and shifting his energy to magically deliver for the spell. Such a simple thing, it wouldn't take much.

But when the sensation of magic coursing through him didn't come right away, he cracked open his eyes, thinking perhaps the task was so small he simply didn't realize it'd happened—but his nerves twinged when the circle remained empty in front of him. Perhaps he wasn't focusing enough, perhaps it was the stress of the moment blocking his ability to do something so simple—but no matter how hard he tried, his magic refused to obey him. Just like how the wolf once pinned in the back of his mind refused to stir no matter how he tried to rouse it.

"I don't understan—" His frustration escaped, cut short

when Asche suddenly lunged from their spot and slammed Saffron to the floor. He braced for fingers to dig into his eyes—but the daurae didn't attack him. They embraced him, bound hands looping over his head and grasping at him. Clinging with a tight desperation, before collapsing into gasping sobs and burying their face into Saffron's chest.

"Thank the gods!" They wept. "I knew you would come, I knew! But I didn't know when, I didn't know if you knew—what they wanted to do with me! Gods, I was so afraid! I was so scared I would be here forever, Saffron...! I thought they would unravel all my memories and it would be too late...!" Asche wept until their words were no longer sensible, just clinging to Saffron until he was sure their clawing hands left bruises on his skin.

Saffron held them back just as securely, locking his arms around Asche's slender frame and pulling them even closer when he felt the bumps of their spine through their dirty shirt. He held them as tightly as he held Cylvan, as tightly as Cylvan would have had he been the one to find them first.

"It's alright, Asche," Saffron whispered, voice cracking as the sound of the daurae's sobs choked him. "It's alright. You're safe now. I'm so sorry it took so long. I swear we've been trying to find you from the first moment they took you. I'm going to take you back home, alright? I'm here. I'm here."

"H-how are we supposed to get back home?" Asche stammered wetly into Saffron's shirt. "Especially if—if you can't do any magic."

"What?" Saffron asked with a weak chuckle. "What makes you say I can't... You mean the iris I couldn't summon? Well, that's nothing, it was probably just—"

"No!" Asche exclaimed, pulling away with a new look of panic. "I thought—you once told me the veil wouldn't let you do magic in the human world!"

Saffron stared at them. His ears rang with those words, loud and bright and deafening.

"What?" He asked. His voice sounded a thousand miles away.

Asche just stared back at him, realizing as he did, exactly how little he knew of where they were.

"You're... in the human world, Saffron," Asche whispered, choking on a few of the syllables. "In—in a place called *Ire-land. Daire*, I think, the town is called..."

"The human—" Saffron choked, grabbing Asche's arm with wide eyes. His mind raced again, barely managing to tear a thought free of the gale to speak it out loud. "We're not—outside the Finnian Ruins?"

Asche shook their head, eyes searching him with brows cinched in a panic.

"Then—the others," Saffron blurted. "Letty and the others, are they close—!?"

"I don't think so," Asche shook their head, speaking softly, but it was still enough to knock the wind from Saffron's chest. They sat back, unlooping their arms from behind Saffron's head without every pulling their eyes away. "They blindfolded me the whole time they brought me here. I think it took a few hours from where they first had us. Maybe even a whole day. I think we crossed some borders along the way, too, because I think the language changed—but only in whispers. Like everyone suddenly spoke an unusual sort of Old Alvish, but never out loud. Maybe we even crossed the sea, I don't know, I don't know, Saffron—"

"It's alright," Saffron insisted. He shoved the adrenaline down, forcing himself to return to the moment at hand. Forcing himself to swallow the disappointment like a shot of searing poison that burned all the way through. If Asche was right, what they thought to be unfamiliar, whispered Old Alvish was more likely human Gaeilge. If Asche was right—then the veneer really had carried Saffron into the human world, where Ryder once lived. Where Queen Proserpina once lived. Connected to Fjornar through that veneer. Saffron really hadn't emerged anywhere close to Avren, or the Finnian Ruins, at that.

Closing his eyes, he swallowed every one of those truths like thorn-tangled knots. Having to understand and accept that—

even if he couldn't find and take his friends home with him that time—he could at least rescue the daurae. Even without his rowan magic to help him, he could get Asche back through the veneer. He didn't need magic to beat his way out of a rotten old house, to overpower the old crone keeping watch on the other side of the door, to carry Asche on his back the whole way if he had to. He only had to get back through the veneer, back into the Winter Court. Taran would be able to hear him, then. Taran, who wasn't ignoring him, who was simply—out of reach, as Saffron had unknowingly passed—through—the veil. *Into the human world.*

His existence, his very being, spun until he through he'd be sick.

"It's alright, it's alright," he repeated, pressing a hand to his face and fighting to grapple his bearings. After catching his breath again, he sighed, tucking a piece of tangled hair from Asche's face. He closed his eyes, inhaling in the murky, tepid air of the house.

"I'm going to take you back to Alfidel. Back to Cylvan, alright?" He promised again. "Once we get back through, we'll take the train all the way back. I'll buy you as many treats as you can eat. I'll send Fiachra to let Cylvan and the kings know you're coming. It'll be alright; you're going to be alright."

Helping Asche to their feet, Saffron's simmering anger boiled a little hotter at the reminder of how weak the daurae had clearly grown since being trapped there. At least, it really hadn't been the same length of time as in Alfidel. Only a fraction. Still—Saffron didn't want to think about what might have happened if he'd waited any longer.

The most reassuring thought came next, that once the daurae was safe—Saffron even knew how to return. He'd leave Asche safe in Avren, and turn right back around. He'd return to the Winter Court, to Fjornar, to pass through the veneer in the woods. He would find his way through *Daire* in *Ireland*; he would find his way to London, whatever that took. He'd find his friends, he'd find Sunbeam. He'd bring them all home—and only then would he finally demand to know exactly how Sunbeam had allowed

Asche to fall into such a dangerous predicament, when Saffron had trusted her with their life.

Until then, though—he would just cling to Asche's hand, and walk them home.

RIFLING THROUGH THE CLUTTER OF THE MOTHER'S cottage—*Queen Proserpina's cottage*—Saffron forced himself to remain calm. Even as the crone on the other side of the door constantly called out to ask if he was alright, or if the daemon inside had gotten free and gutted him. Each time, Saffron just called back that he was fine, he was nearly finished looking the bairn over.

Eventually the crone would stop believing him and drag the slider open to look for herself, and Saffron felt every minute that passed knowing that. But Asche wore only a thin shirt and pants, without even a pair of shoes on their feet, perhaps to discourage attempting to run. He had to find something warmer for them to wear, especially once they returned to the Winter Court.

Settling on a ratty cloak, Saffron yanked it off a hook on the wall, grimacing when a tower of other dusty belongings crumbled from the movement. He braced for the crone to call out again, frantically trying to manufacture a convincing lie—surprised when she didn't. Surprised when there was only silence, enough that he crept to the door and nudged the slider away. The old woman was gone from the other side, both a relief and a frustration, as she'd locked the door behind him. No matter—he couldn't use arid magic to open it, perhaps, but there were plenty of non-magic ways to break down a door. Especially one comprised of rotten wood as old as the queen herself.

Draping the old cloak over Asche's head, they wrinkled their nose against the strong smell of mothballs, but didn't complain.

"I assume you can't use your fire to burn it down, 'else you would've tried that already, huh?" Saffron asked, returning to the door to drag his hands over the wood, the knob, the lock, the hinges.

"Too much rowan—" Asche answered, "—and other anti-fey shit around here. Gods, I'm looking forward to being able to breathe again."

"I can't blame you," Saffron said, searching the floor until he found a broken stake of metal, lining it up with the edge of the lock bolt and slammed it into the old wood with a dull sound. "You know—I met your mother, Naoill. It's suddenly occurred to me why you were born with fire magic, and Cylvan with wind—" *Thud.* "Seeing as you both really are descended from dragons."

Asche wrinkled their nose again. "You thought that was a lie?"

"No, just—Cylvan exaggerates everything, so I assumed the same for that claim. Consider me fooled."

"I'm surprised mother didn't eat you."

"Almost did. Thought they were going to, after I fell off this cliff..."

"What?"

"Nothing—I'll tell you everything on the way home."

Asche laughed weakly, the sound of it twisting up Saffron's heart. "I missed you, Saffron."

*Thud. Thud. Thud.* Saffron slammed the end of the metal spike into the wood, slowly chipping away at the edge of the lock like taking bites from a frozen apple. But pulling back for the next hit, thinking it might be the one to finally break through— Saffron's body petrified the moment he heard voices approaching. Two of them.

"What in gods' name were you thinking, Fidelma, gods*damnit!*"

"*Shit,*" Saffron hissed, glancing back to Asche, then to the door. He pulled the slider open an inch—but there was no time to do anything else. Ryder was only a few yards away, and approaching fast. Looking wild, furious, red-faced and stalking like an animal toward the cottage.

Saffron put his hand out, grabbing Asche and pushing them

to the side of the door. Asche clung to him from behind, holding their breath as the slider was shoved open, and Ryder looked inside to find it empty. Saffron could hear how heavily the man breathed, angry and desperate. He tightened his grasp on the metal bar.

The assault on the door must have jammed the lock, because Ryder tried twice to unlatch it with the key, before stepping back and ramming his shoulder into the wood. It split the rotten fibers with a deafening sound, and he stumbled into the cottage.

"Where are you, little mouse—!" he snarled into the darkness. Around his waist, a black witchhunter veil was cinched tight over the knife wound Saffron had left him with, though blood had already soaked through the fabric. The cuffs from his wrists were also gone, only swollen bruises left behind—possibly only getting his chance as Saffron hadn't thought twice about dropping the opulent ring in the crone's kitchen.

Ryder turned in his search of the cottage—freezing the instant his eyes met Saffron's, metal bar raised between them.

"I believe that was your mother's door, Master Deimne," Saffron said, voice shaking. "I'd say she'd be angry with you—but I think it'll be a long while still until you get to talk to her again."

"You—!"

Saffron slammed the metal bar into the side of Ryder's jaw, sending him to the floor in a heap of curses. Behind him, Asche bolted for the doorway, slamming into the crone on the other side and shoving her down with a small cry of alarm. Saffron wasted no more time, swinging the bar against Ryder's arm as the man reached for his leg, stumbling backward before throwing the metal piece at him, then turning to take chase after the daurae.

"Asche, this way!" he cried, grappling for their hand once in reach and running as fast as his legs would carry him. Straight into the thick wall of trees a hundred feet from the queen's cottage. On their heels, Ryder called out after him, voice exploding with fury. Saffron didn't look back. He just clung to Asche's hand and ran.

42

———

## THE FAWN

Coursing through the trees, Saffron smacked low-hanging branches and tall ferns out of his way with one hand, while the other kept an unyielding grasp on Asche who followed close behind. Despite their clear bodily exhaustion, the daurae moved fast; despite their gasping for air, they managed to keep up with him, all the way until the chill of the Winter Court through the veneer nipped at their skin, and Saffron stopped short to scoop the fey gentle onto his back. Not wanting them to have to tread snow with no shoes. Never once did Asche ask where they were going, or how they were going to get home—they just clung to Saffron in return. Trusting him with everything they had. He was not going to let them go again.

As if his blood reached ahead for the first taste of magic he could grapple at, Saffron felt the exact moment it tingled in his veins. Recognition crashed forcibly into him, nearly losing his footing as if crushed beneath an ancient oak tree. Clutching at his chest as it ached, he shook off the initial shock, reaffirming his grasp on Asche and pushing forward—but not a moment later, something rushed up behind them.

Spinning so fast he lost his grip on Asche, the daurae tumbled to the cold earth as Saffron thrust his hands outward. The crone slammed into them, nearly snapping one of his wrists as she ricocheted right back off and crashed on her heels. The force knocked Saffron backward into the mud as well, nearly crushing Asche beneath him as the daurae yelped and scurried out of the way.

They barely leapt away as the crone clambered for them. Saffron grabbed her first by a fistful of wild hair, only for her to reel and pit her assault on him, instead. Clawing at him and raking grimy nails down his cheek, she snarled and snapped her teeth within an inch of his cheek, his eyes.

Clenching his teeth, Saffron could only attempt to summon whatever thin ribbons of magic were within reach of him, but finding nothing, nothing to pull on and use against her. It soon didn't matter—when Asche appeared over her shoulder, swinging a heavy branch to smash over the back of her head. Enough to make the crone slump over Saffron's chest, where he quickly shoved her off again.

"C'mon," he said quickly, already knowing by the gargling of her breaths. Not wanting Asche to linger, to see. He scooped them onto his back before they could argue, not allowing himself even a second to catch his breath. He just had to get Asche back home.

The moment a presence stirred in the back of Saffron's mind, the words were already leaping from his mouth, summoning Taran into the thin carpet of snow replacing the mossy forest floor of Ire-land. Saffron had already offered Asche his cloak, still carrying the daurae on his back, breathing heavily as his throat ached against the growing chill in the air.

He practically shouted Taran's command to *come*, and the wolf slammed into the ground with such force his snout nearly crushed against the frosted soil. He then turned so fast his back feet tore the earth from beneath the snow, baring his teeth at Saffron to demand what in gods' name had happened—only to go stone-still at the sight of Asche on Saffron's back. His bright red eyes stared, unblinking, at the daurae, before flickering to Saffron in disbelief. Saffron offered him a tiny nod of promise. Confirmation. *It's them.*

Taran bowed his head slightly, still in shock, approaching slowly with wide eyes. Foot over foot, he softly sniffed at the young high fey on Saffron's back.

"Hello, Taran..." Asche said in uncertainty, and Taran's ears flattened, before he audibly whined. Like an overwhelmed dog, he stamped backward, before rushing forward again, whining and nipping at Asche's leg, then throwing his muddy paws up to plant them on Saffron's shoulder and lick Asche's face all over. Saffron stumbled beneath the beast's weight, cursing at him, but was unable to resist the weak chuckle that escaped him.

"Give me some help with them, will you?" he asked, and Taran immediately planted his feet back in the snow. Saffron carefully transferred the daurae to Taran's back, where Asche grinned and ran their fingers up through his thick black fur. Taran's giant head continued to twist backward, over both shoulders, trying to get a better look at Asche like he still couldn't believe it. Craning his neck one way then the other with every attempt. When he was sure it wasn't a trick—he even turned and leapt at Saffron again, licking his face in gratitude before howling in joy and bounding around in a circle. It made Asche laugh, which made Saffron laugh, which made Taran yelp and yip all over again.

Continuing through the last traces of the veneer, the air grew colder, the snow deeper, and Saffron realized beyond the overcast sky that the sun had risen overhead faster than should have been possible. He was reminded why, just as Taran spoke to confirm.

"You've been gone hours. Your friends are probably worried sick."

Of course—he'd been in the human world, even just for that small amount of time. A small amount to him, at least. It couldn't have been more than an hour or two he'd spent recovering Asche —but in Alfidel, that was nearly five. Sunrise had already come and gone. Saffron was supposed to have returned to his friends hours ago. He was supposed to be on a train back to Avren already, and his stomach sank when he thought about Cylvan. Saffron had promised.

He pushed away the twist in his gut, forcing himself to look at Asche again. Knowing Cylvan would understand, once he saw who Saffron returned him.

"I was in the human world," he answered, reaching up to touch Asche's back. Taran's head whipped around so fast, Asche nearly lost their grip on his scruff. "I know, just—I'll explain later. Let's get the daurae somewhere safe, first."

Taran didn't ask any further questions, though Saffron could feel him digging around in their shared mind. Trying to get into Saffron's memories, trying to find out for himself exactly where he'd gone, how he'd gotten there, how in gods' name he'd managed to stumble across Asche in the midst of it all. Saffron wouldn't have known where to start, even if there was time to talk. He wasn't sure he'd have any better of an idea even with extra time to think. He wasn't sure Taran would be able to keep his composure once Saffron told him everything else he'd learned, too. Still, he couldn't stop the ghostly thoughts from trickling through his mind, more as sensations than actual explanations. Allowing Taran a taste, without going into too much detail. The wolf stared straight ahead as they crested over him.

*Ryder Kyteler is also Finn O'Daire, is also Deimne, is also the first son of Queen Proserpina and her human lover, Adone...*

*I think—no, I'm certain he intended on using Asche as a woven vessel for the queen's memories, in an attempt to bring her back to life...*

If Saffron hadn't stumbled through that pocket veneer into the human world, if Ryder had at any point actually found the queen's memory tapestry first—he couldn't form the thought. He just pressed his hand to Asche's back again. Protective, as much as the wolf that carried them.

"Ah," he realized, stopping short and turning. "We can still use the veneer. The one that actually leads to Avren from the king's keep. Don't you think? Which way to Fjornar, Taran?"

Taran lifted his nose to the air, sniffing—but a metal bar suddenly whisked from the trees, slamming into the side of his head and making him yelp. Asche nearly toppled from the wolf's back as the beast stumbled, had Saffron not thrown out his hands to catch them. He whirled around in alarm—just in time to witness Ryder bursting from the trees in a flurry of snow and ice.

A swelling gash flared on the side of his jaw where Saffron had struck him with that same metal beam in the cottage; the stab wound in his stomach remained open and weeping into his shirt, bright red and unsettling. The man's eyes were wide and searching, hair tangled with snow and pine needles as his attention snapped between Saffron, the wolf, the daurae. He lifted a hand, pointing at them.

"That's mine," he said. "I took it fair and square, your highness. You've robbed me. And I'm taking it back."

"Over my dead body," Saffron answered.

"Don't tempt me."

"*Let me,*" Taran growled, but Saffron put out a hand to stop him.

"Take care of Asche," he whispered, in the same motion slipping the wand from under his sleeve. It nestled into his palm, the length of it fitting perfectly between two of his fingers—and gently clinking against the band of the pixie ring he still wore. His heart thrummed. His eyes returned to Ryder, where sure enough —the man had a series of rings on his own fingers. Two on one hand, four on the other.

"Go," Saffron whispered. Taran snarled in protest, but Saffron whispered the same as a command, next. Growling, Taran bowed his head as if resisting as long as he could—before turning and tearing through the snow. Saffron knew he wouldn't be able to run all the way through the veneer on his own, he would vanish as soon as there was too much distance between them—but

Ryder didn't know that. It was obvious, by the way his nostrils flared at the sight.

He moved to get a better view of Taran's trail—but Saffron followed. He raised his wand, making Ryder pause.

"Enough of this," Saffron said. Every word was trailed by a puff of steam on his breath. Overhead, thick bundles of snow began to fall, again, making his skin pucker beneath his rain-soaked tunic without a cloak to keep him warm. "You're badly hurt. I've taken Asche back. I know where to find my friends, and I know how to get to them without your help. I know who you really are—and soon so will everyone else."

"You know nothing, your highness," Ryder said, but it lacked the same intimidating venom he clearly meant. He knew it, too, as his teeth visibly clenched.

"What's the purpose of bringing her back?" Saffron asked, risking a moment of sincerity. His eyes flickered to Ryder's hand as it twitched. An intangible presence swirled behind Saffron's own back, breathing against the nape of his neck, sparkling and warm. "In the cabin, you said—you said you were only trying to find it to better understand her. You could have done that without using Asche as a vessel. Without—without killing an innocent person. A *child*, Ryder—"

"There are some things I can only understand of my mother by speaking to her face-to-face," Ryder answered, head tilted down and watching Saffron like an animal. A wolf eyeing a rabbit in the snow—no matter that Saffron had long already become a master over wolves.

*The band of the ring acts as a knock in itself. To inform a veil epithet.*

Saffron jumped. He nearly turned, but locked his muscles, first. It was his own voice. Spoken in a clear whisper, as if by something hiding behind him. Making his blood tingle and shimmer like fairy wine. The veil was beseeching him.

*With only one, you allow me to decide where you go when you pass.*

"Don't—" he whispered, not wishing to be whisked away so suddenly.

*I will obey your wishes. I will know you.*

Saffron swallowed against the lump in his throat. His eyes returned to the six rings on Ryder's fingers. He recalled the same six he'd worn at the Midsummer Games, before renting open the earth in that horrific display. The same number he wore there in the snow.

*Do not let him touch you*, the veil warned, and something compelled Saffron's eyes to flick to Ryder's left hand, specifically, donning four of the rings. *I will not be able to help you, then.*

Saffron wanted to ask—but there wasn't time. Instead, he exhaled a shaking breath, squeezing his hand around the narrow length of his wand. It pressed the band of the pixie ring into his skin, and he was reminded of what Adelard told him of how such cruel rings were forged.

"I'm sorry," he went on softly. "I don't mean to hurt you."

*You have my consent, rowan witch. I am your ally; and you are mine.* Ghostly fingers trailed from the nape of Saffron's neck to his shoulder, down his arm, to where the wand in his hand tapped against the band of the ring. *Form a circle with your fingers. Show me where you want to go. Remember—it's about intention.*

Saffron inhaled deeply through his nose. He searched where Ryder stood, mind racing—but before he could move, Ryder did first. *Knock, knock*—he vanished from where he stood, and Saffron barely ducked out of the way as an instant later, the man manifested behind him.

Ryder clawed at him, barely grabbing a handful of the back of Saffron's doublet—but Saffron twisted, slamming a boot into Ryder's chest and knocking him away, while simultaneously curling his fingers into a circle like the veil had instructed. Instantly, the earth gave way beneath him, overwhelming him with the sense of falling, squeezing, flying—and he materialized again on the other side of the small clearing, where Ryder had just been standing. Exactly where he'd imagined appearing, just before Ryder surprised him.

"Alright," he wheezed with a clutch of his chest, understanding immediately what it meant to *knock once,* allowing the veil to move him as it wished. Suffocating, chaotic, and nerve-wracking—but at the same time, flooding him with hot adrenaline; with a sense of wild, untethered deliverance from all the rules that'd ever kept his feet on the ground.

Ryder knocked twice again, but that time Saffron was prepared. He rolled out of the way, knowing the man would appear alongside him yet again; and the moment Ryder did, Saffron knocked once, and clapped into existence behind him, instead. Where he pulled the obsidian knife from his belt, swinging it in a long arch and slicing across Ryder's back.

Ryder shouted, tripping forward, then whirling around—but not before Saffron knocked again, throwing himself out of the man's reach. That time, the whiplash knocked him off his feet and he rolled through the snow, barely lifting his head again as Ryder came crashing back through thin air to slam a foot into Saffron's wrist, knocking the knife away before kicking him in the chin. Saffron's teeth cracked against each other, spitting blood into the snow—but knocking again just before Ryder's hand could grab him around the throat.

Re-emerging a dozen feet away, Saffron landed on his hands and knees, spitting more blood to the ground before searching the whiteness for his knife. Lost in the wide expanse, gone beneath the surface of the cold blanket only growing deeper as the snow fell over them—but then the veil tickled the backs of his eyes, and a myriad of weblike cracks shimmered in his vision. Tears in the veil, fresh and raw, left behind each time he or Ryder passed through. Torn and reaching in the direction the person had passed—and telling Saffron exactly where he'd just been, and where Ryder had thrown the knife away.

Ryder saw him searching, his own head snapping around to do the same. He threw his hands out, tearing through the snow in search as Saffron knocked again and crumpled to the ground just within the man's reach. Scrambling for the knife barely visible in its crater left in the powder. Within another second, Saffron snapped away another hundred feet away—but that time, he collapsed to his knees, spitting blood unrelated to Ryder's boot to his mouth. It swelled from deep down inside of him, filling the back of his nose and making his eyes burn as his vision swirled.

*You're still weak!* The veil cried.

"Fuck off!" Saffron snapped back, practically feeling the veil claw at him for the disrespect. He just wiped his mouth and the fresh blood dripping from his nose, rising to his feet and searching the clearing yet again—but Ryder was nowhere to be found.

"Where did he go?" He asked, turning in every direction—until the distant sound of two knocks echoed through the trees, and clumps of snow thudded to the ground from the reverberations. Saffron whipped around to follow it, stomach sinking when he realized they came from the direction of Taran's racing footprints.

"Take me there!" He demanded. The veil shouted back a warning—but Saffron was already circling his fingers, swallowed in an instant.

He wrecked into the snow at least a mile away, trampled by something that snarled and lost its footing, thrown into the snow over his back. Teeth clamped down on his arm as he threw it up, shoving Taran away as the wolf immediately reeled back with a panicked, apologetic whine. The beast then turned and raced to where Asche gathered themself in the snow, crawling back onto Taran's back before shouting Saffron's name.

Saffron managed to rise back to his feet, though he swayed under the weight of his growing debility. Blood spilled freely from his nose, drops gathering in the corner of his eye and partially muffling his ears. Even with Taran nearby to cushion the demand of the magic again—it wasn't enough. Even with a familiar to absorb some of the trauma, Saffron was still a valley witch, as Baba had once described. Without a bridge-partner to properly balance him. He knew it—and he was sure Ryder did, too, as the man snapped into existence a few yards from where they stood. Hunched and spitting blood, Saffron crossed the obsidian knife in front of him.

"You're killing yourself," Ryder said with an arrogant smirk. "Is this all worth it, Saffron? You know if you die—so does your dog. And then it's just me and the daurae out here."

"Eat shit!" Asche shouted, and Ryder's smile split wider.

"Why don't you come closer and say that, you little rat?" He said tightly, moving his hand as if to knock again—but a massive gale suddenly tore through the trees from the sky, whipping ice and snow in a whirlwind that blinded every inch around them. Saffron stumbled backward, knowing Taran was only a few feet behind him. He grappled for Asche, searching for the veil's presence in the chaos, desperate enough to beg for a way for them both to pass through at the same time—

*Wait!* Taran barked in Saffron's mind, a mere moment before Saffron formed the circle with his fingers. Lifting his head, Saffron searched for the reason, and his breath caught as a titanic shadow dove from the sky, sweeping over them and churning up more snow and mist, before crashing to the earth and nearly knocking Saffron off his balance.

"Naoill—!"

"Mama!" Asche cried out, and a pillar of fire tore through the mist in an instant. Ripping through the snow at Saffron's feet, clearing the air in a pocket around them. Someone rushed from where the shadow landed, and Saffron quickly realized—it was Maeve.

"Saffron!" She called first, before stopping short at the sight of who Saffron clung to. "Oh—oh *gods! What—!*"

"No time!" Saffron shouted back. He grabbed Asche from Taran's back, shoving them into Maeve who wrapped her arms around the daurae. "Take them! You and Naoill, take them back to Avren! Now!"

"But—!" Maeve attempted, but Saffron shoved her.

"Hurry, before he—!"

*Knock, knock*—Ryder's passage rang out through the mist. Saffron whipped around to search, but he hadn't found them yet. It was only a matter of time. The snow and ice in the air would only float for so much longer, blinding Ryder's hunt. Maeve seemed to understand in that moment, as well—still, she hesitated, before rushing to throw an arm around Saffron. Embracing him tightly, shaking as she did.

"Come back home," she said. "Don't leave us."

"I'll—" Saffron started, words catching as Maeve pulled back, and Asche had tears in their eyes. "I'll... I'll meet you there," he said, offering the most reassuring smile he possibly could. "I promise."

Maeve wasted no more time, turning and rushing into the swirling mist toward the crouching dragon in the snow. Saffron wished he could have seen Naoill's reaction to the fey lady emerging with their missing child—but he would have to wait and hear about it, later. So long as they made it into the sky, out of Ryder's reach, that was all that mattered to him. Just buying time for them to go. He would meet them back in Avren. He would make sure of it.

The might of Naoill's wings to lift from the earth sent another gale of wind whipping across the snow, that time flattening the mist and leaving the view gaping wide over the landscape. Saffron barely uncrossed his hands from his face in time to see Ryder approaching, forming another finger-circle in a flash and crashing into the snow a few feet away from where he started. That time, barely moving at all—as blood flooded the back of his throat, and he bent over to vomit the crimson across the charred ground eaten by the dragon's fire. As if, with the daurae finally out of Ryder's reach—he could no longer pretend to have the strength to knock through the veil more than a few feet at a time.

Even Taran no longer lingered behind him—and Saffron didn't have to ask where he'd gone, the moment he attempted to return to his feet, only to sink back to one knee. Struggling to inhale even a single full breath; ears ringing from the deafening wind and constant knocking echoing off the trees, the distant mountains, dislodging snow to the earth where it collected in boughs on ancient pine trees.

*Don't let him touch you,* the veil's warning reiterated in the back of Saffron's mind, and he stumbled backward as Ryder appeared within reach of him. That time, walking slowly. No longer needing to chase, his rabbit left exhausted and trembling at his feet.

"You still need me, more than you think," Ryder said. Saffron shook his head, stretching out his arm and dragging himself away. "I know arid tricks older than my mother; secrets once offered to humans by the Dagda themself, when the veil first formed. Even if it refuses to speak with me—you've seen with your own eyes, how I can still force it to my will. Or should I demonstrate for you one more time, Saffron?"

"No," Saffron coughed, spitting more blood to the ground, kicking at Ryder's knees. That time, the man slowed to a halt. He watched in silence as Saffron dragged himself away a little more, before collapsing.

*Get up!* The veil shrieked, begging. *Get up, damn you!*

Saffron groaned. He rolled onto his side, then onto his knees. The world spun beneath him, and nauseous bile mixed with the overwhelming blood that choked him.

Somehow, Saffron clambered back to his feet. He swayed on his balance, but managed to remain upright—just in time to watch Ryder smile wearily at him, before lifting both of his hands to form a circle over his chest—a circle with all size rings.

Six knocks rang out, just like at the Midsummer Games. The air shifted, then plummeted.

The earth cracked beneath Saffron's feet. The veil wailed in his ear, begging him—and Saffron threw out his hands.

With everything he had left—he raised his hands. He clutched Ryder's being between his fingers, holding him. Just like on the edge of the Hoarcliff Pass; just like he'd once torn at the vines strangling Fiachra.

Ryder didn't fight back. Ryder didn't writhe or curse or even grin wickedly—he just watched Saffron closely. Knowing, as well as Saffron did, that it would not last. Saffron had reached the limit of what a mere human body could do, what a valley witch could do, without anyone to balance him on the other side. Still, though —Saffron tried. Even as his hands shook, and his vision ebbed in and out, he hooked his magic into Ryder's and claimed him. *Be still, be still.*

Saffron might never be able to overwhelm Ryder Kyteler physically; Ryder may have more experience with magic; but Saffron had no choice—and he'd promised Cylvan he would be there with him. Back in Avren. He promised to never leave Cylvan's side. It was what drove him to making his oath in the first place—and it would continue to be the reason he fought to return safely by his side, every time.

*Let go, witch.*

Saffron clenched his jaw, closing his eyes. His own voice beckoned to him through the ringing in his ears. Coiling around his mind like a shimmering ribbon. The veil, beseeching him still, even as weak and pitiful as he was.

"*No,*" he rasped, shaking his head. Jolting as Ryder suddenly attempted to wrench himself free. Saffron put a foot back to keep from tumbling backward. His vision blurred, colors rimming the edges of his eyes. He tried blinking through it, but it made no difference. "He's—going to tear you open—again."

*There is nothing more you can do to stop him.*

"I can—"

*If you die here, I will stand no chance.*

Saffron whimpered softly.

"If I let go—it'll swallow me."

*It won't. I will carry you to safety.*

"It won't be far enough—"

*I know exactly where you can go and rest peacefully.*

"Won't that kill me all the same?" He asked miserably. Tasting only blood in his mouth.

*I will bear the burden.*

"But—"

*I am your ally*, it practically begged. *You cannot hold him forever. This is inevitable. You are weak. Accept it, and let me help you.*

Yes—Saffron was weak. He knew that. He'd spent too long avoiding his rowan magic, whether afraid of it or unsure how to learn, and it had left him weak. He knew that, he wouldn't deny it, but hearing it in his own voice from the veil yet again twisted like a knife in his gut. Because—if he, of all people, couldn't stop someone like Ryder—then who would? What would stop Ryder from going straight to the palace, next? Opening a veil beneath the beds of everyone who slept inside? What would stop him from taking Asche a second time, knowing right where they would be? That time ensuring no one would ever be able to find them again, until it was too late? Unless Saffron could do—*something*. Anything. He just had to do—anything.

*If you linger, the strain will kill you before—*

"Then help me!" Saffron demanded, choking as blood splattered from his mouth. "You insist I'm—useless until I learn—so *teach me*, damnit!"

The veil said nothing for a moment, but Saffron could feel it. Like it considered him, like it hadn't expected him to argue. How much easier it would have been to drop his hands and let it whisk him away, so Ryder could continue with what he wished—but Saffron had never done anything easily. It wasn't easy to learn how to read on his own; it wasn't easy making the geis with Cylvan; it wasn't easy navigating Danann House with no words and no agency; it wasn't easy becoming a rowan witch. It would continue to be impossible until someone taught him—and there was no teacher like the veil, itself.

*Gaze at the center of his body.*

Saffron blinked through the strain blurring his eyes. When

there was nothing to see, he squeezed them closed, blinking again and summoning whatever strength he had left to scavenge for any magic he had to spare. Over and over, churning through what remained of him—until the faintest glow shimmered around Ryder's being, pink and dull. Half-arid, half-opulent. Could Saffron overwhelm him like he did those other witchhunters? Whether to kill him or not—would it even matter, with the six-knock veil tear already locked beneath his feet?

*Slow down,* the veil encouraged. *Let your magic settle. Let it continue its search.*

"Its what?" Saffron croaked, but the voice didn't respond. Saffron focused on his hands, on clinging to Ryder's being, keeping him from moving; he focused on the glow surrounding the man, static and familiar—before the glow throbbed, slightly. Thrumming like a slow-beating heart, flashing brighter, then cooler, trickling upward—and gathering behind Ryder's head. Like a crown. Like—a glowing halo. Like the ones Saffron had seen on all the courtiers at Cylvan and Taran's engagement party on Ostara. But if he could see those halos again, that meant, maybe—

His breath caught; his focus flickered, and the earth warped beneath Ryder's feet as he was allowed the briefest moment to continue his destruction.

In the center of Ryder's chest, dim at first, but slowly growing brighter—Saffron saw the faint shape of hatchmarks. Feda lines on a red ogham stele. A true name.

*"Icarus—come."*

His balance faltered, nearly collapsing to one knee as the additional draw on his magic hit like a knife to the chest. Tasting blood on his tongue, in his lungs.

"I need you... to get closer to him," Saffron begged hoarsely. No strength left to even compel it. "Show me what's on his chest."

Taran took off like a shot. Not waiting for an explanation, not bothering to try and push Saffron back. Running as fast as he could to where Saffron barely contained Ryder, unsure how much longer he could last with every wisp of his being spread far too thin.

Taran's thoughts materialized in Saffron's mind, first as unintelligible sounds, then a warping mental image. The glowing name was fainter through his familiar's eyes, barely discernible—but just enough.

*"Eoghan,"* Saffron mumbled. His fingers twitched, hands tingling with creeping numbness. His eyelids sank, growing heavy as the rest of his blood turned icy. *"Eoghan—be still."*

He couldn't keep himself upright any longer. His vision faded, body collapsing to his knees, then forward onto his stomach. The earth turned beneath him, stinking of burnt sugar and snow and soil. Ice cracked as the echo of six ringing veil knocks crashed across the distant mountains, disrupting centuries-old facades of snow and making them shift. Saffron hadn't been quick enough. He hadn't managed to stop Ryder soon enough to cut his assault short—

But none of that mattered, as Taran bound back to him. As the wolf vanished, and invisible hands embraced him, coiling around Saffron's body and lifting him from the earth just before it swallowed him whole. Pulling him into the ether, into the space between worlds, realities, holding his face and whispering reassurances. *You did well. You did well, my brave witch.*

Saffron floated—until he fell. Like plummeting from the sky itself—air suddenly warm and rich with the salty scent of the sea.

He hit the earth with only half his weight, crashing over a stone altar. Colliding with golden bowls of wine, burning candles, pots of incense, trays of food, scattering every oblation to the ground that weren't flattened beneath the heavy *thud* of his body. Too weak to catch himself, to move, to even lift his head as a scream tore out from nearby.

*"Saffron! Saffron, my gods—!"* it shouted, before hands grappled for him. Different than those of the veil—tearing at him in desperation. Strong and familiar in the sharpness of their nails.

Searching him, taking his face and turning it, gasping at the sight of blood still spilling from his nose and mouth. A trembling hand sloppily smeared the crimson away, begging his name, then grabbing him under the shoulder to drag him from the altar. Not prepared for how limply he slumped, sinking to the ground while pulling him closer.

"Saffron, púca—gods, oh gods, what's happened? What have you done? Please, my love, wake up, look at me—"

Saffron searched for his eyes, scraping at the darkness behind them with all he had left. Prying them apart, heavier than two slabs of stone, he searched the overcast, rainy light of the sky on the other side. Upon finally, blearily meeting Cylvan's eyes, Saffron's racing heart unclenched slightly. His ringing ears diminished, until he could hear distant waves. The wind in the trees. The desperate breaths of his prince hanging over him. His prince, who looked terrified, eyes wide and creasing the perfect skin of his face. No—that was all wrong. That was not how Saffron wished to see him again, for the first time after returning home.

He managed the smallest, weakest smile, as his raven shuddered over every inch of him. He lifted a hand, cupping the side of Cylvan's face, as Cylvan grabbed and squeezed it.

"Sorry," Saffron said, managing a pathetic chuckle, then a groan. "I must look—like shit."

"Púca—"

"I'm alright, Cylvan—trust me," he said, before grimacing, knowing the words likely wouldn't convince even the calmest of folk considering the state of him. "You'll be—so impressed, when I tell you all about it."

"What happened, Saffron? Please, please, gods, tell me what's happened—"

"I think—I'm going to pass out," Saffron went on, offering Cylvan one last wobbly smile. Cylvan pulled him closer, demanding Saffron keep his eyes open, but Saffron felt it coming. The cold tingling sensation in his fingers. He gently patted Cylvan's cheek, shaking his head, closing his eyes.

"Asche—will be here soon," he whispered. "I'm sure—they'll tell you everything, before I wake up. I promise... I'll wake up, so don't worry. I'm just—tired. But—I'm here. I'll be back. You haven't—lost me."

Cylvan's breaths, fast, sharp, horrified, hitched once, then slowed slightly.

"Alright..." he said, like it was all he could manage. "Alright, Saffron—you promised. You promised me. You'll wake up soon. I'll keep you safe until then. I'll never let you go, ever again."

Saffron smiled. He sank into Cylvan's chest, releasing a long breath, and dipping beneath the surface of his exhaustion. Safe, in a place he could rest peacefully. Just like the veil promised.

43

———

# THE PRINCE

No dreams plagued him. No pleading wails of Daurae Asche to haunt him. No screaming cries begging for rescue. No veiled queens demanding Saffron find her.

Nothing stirred Saffron for what could have been a century. But even if hundreds of years had dripped by while Saffron rested—never once did Cylvan leave his side, where Saffron slept in the prince's own bed. On those black sheets he knew as well as his own; in that room the with the constant scents of a myriad of sweet and sharp perfumes, where Saffron could hear the distant ocean with the ceiling-high windows propped open. Allowing the late-summer air to waft inside.

Occasionally, sharp-tipped nails would gently brush a piece of hair from his eyes, and Saffron would twitch. He would mumble just enough to prove life, and Cylvan would sigh softly in a way Saffron could perfectly imagine a weary smile accompanying it. Cylvan would gently kiss Saffron's forehead, each time whispering *'I love you,'* and *'rest more if you need.'* And Saffron did. Every time, as badly as Saffron wished to finally wake, he continually sank back down again as if sedated by Cylvan's mere presence. The song of a handsome leanan sídhe, singing to lull Saffron's thoughts back into a buzzing tranquility, where he lost his grip on the threads of wakefulness and returned under the surface.

Occasionally, otherwise, Saffron could discern when someone else entered the room. Either bringing something to eat, or to deliver a message, or to check if Saffron had woken, yet.

*"It has been confirmed that a veil event caused the avalanche in Vjallrod. It's still unclear how many lives were lost. Fjornar's monastery remains buried beneath the snow; the kings have extended offers to the visiting oracles to remain in Avren for the time being."*

*"I will send them my regards."* Cylvan answered.

*"You've received another letter from Anysta mac Delbaith. Would you like me to put it away with the others?"*

*"Yes, with the others."* Cylvan told them.

*"The Danae of Alvénya sent a bird, expressing their relief that Daurae Asche was brought home safely."*

*"I will respond to them soon."* Cylvan said.

*"More flowers and gifts have been delivered."*

*"You can take them to the daurae's hospital bed—"*

*"Oh—they aren't for the daurae, but for..."*


"Saffron?" Cylvan hummed, near but far from where Saffron bobbed in his heavy slumber like a pinecone in a pond. Calling out to him. Prompting him to emerge, perhaps that time for good. Beckoning him to return to the land of the living, the earnestness of it hooking Saffron under the chin and lifting him upward. From his comfortable, dark pool of sleep, wishing to know the mouth that urged him so ardently.

Releasing a long exhale through his nose, Cylvan inhaled slightly in response. A warm hand once again tucked hair from Saffron's eyes, before gently cupping his cheek. A breathy, musical laugh escaped and danced through Saffron's ears, drawing him nearer. He found his limbs, his muscles, his skin, sighing again wearily and shifting to press a little closer into Cylvan's body, who reclined on the pillows alongside him. Fingers combed his hair once more, before trailing over his eyebrow, down the length of his nose, tracing over his bottom lip.

"Come back to me, púca. I cannot stand to be without my treasure much longer."

"You didn't give me a choice," Saffron mumbled through the haze. Without thinking, without any real intention, but it summoned Cylvan to slide his hand to the nape of Saffron's neck, then over his back to pull him closer. Until Saffron was pieced perfectly into the shape of Cylvan's body, face tucked sweetly into the crook of Cylvan's shoulder. Allowing Saffron to breathe him in, the sweet oils of his hair, his skin, the fabric of his light tunic.

"That's not what I meant," he whispered, pressing his face flush to the side of Cylvan's neck before touching his lips to bare skin. Cylvan still held him close, dragging his hand up and down Saffron's back.

"I know what you meant," he answered just as softly. "I deserve for you to mean it, however, with how monstrously I treated you."

Saffron reveled in that closeness once finally awake enough to appreciate it, that quiet intimacy he'd almost convinced himself he'd lost forever. It nearly brought him to tears, swallowing the emotion back and finding his arms to wrap around Cylvan in return. Cylvan responded by holding Saffron closer, squeezing him, as if relieved Saffron had embraced him back at all. Worried, perhaps, that Saffron might have pulled away instead.

"I missed you," he said, sighing, before finally forcing his eyes to open. His lashes brushed the side of Cylvan's neck with how firmly, tenderly Cylvan held him in place.

"I missed you," Cylvan answered. His arms around Saffron flexed slightly, before his head dropped and he pressed his forehead into Saffron's shoulder. "Gods—there are not words for how deeply I regret leaving you the way that I did—and curse me for ever thinking you would stay there in Beantighe Village as I did. Lugh and Danu and Ériu have all conspired to make sure I felt every agonizing moment I spent alone without you in this place."

"Even Ériu?" Saffron whispered with a little smile. Cylvan grimaced, barely tilting his head in order to meet Saffron's eyes. They were rich and deeply colored in the blue light of early morning through the open windows. Saffron's heart fluttered, and he couldn't resist another smile.

"Especially she," Cylvan whispered. "Wracking me with guilt, suffocating me with nightmares of a long-plucking harp every night I could bear to drink myself to sleep at all. No amount of alcohol or artificial fruits or tobacco or oracle-brewed teas made any difference, as if your goddess conspired with the veil to ensure nothing could sedate me. Even when I outwitted them—she came to me in scolding voices that followed wherever I went."

"Ériu is not known for sending legions of scolding voices."

"Perhaps only because no one has ever infuriated her as rightfully as I have." He tucked a piece of hair from Saffron's forehead, eyes trailing over every inch of his face as if it had been years, rather than only a handful of days they were apart. "I don't know what you must think of me, and how I acted," he went on softly. "But—despite how impossible it might be to believe, especially all the times it broke through my lips for you to hear—it was never *you* who I despised so much. It was..."

He pressed his lips together, before closing his eyes and furrowing his brows. As if Ériu still plucked the strings of her harp to ring in his ears, with every reminder of the things he'd said and done.

"That night, after the dé Bricríu dinner—Anysta invited me to share a private dessert with her. It was either that or join Renard in his smoking room for another eternity while the man rambled on about himself and his sons—so you can understand why her company was preferable. Or so I thought—as she proceeded to threaten me. A thing that wouldn't have unsettled me so much—until she mentioned you. But not *you,* my glamoured high fey Alvényan flower—*you,* my treasure. The *you* I have been able to selfishly keep all for myself until now. You, the beantighe who I made a geis with; who disrupted my engagement party with Taran, and cast him away; you, the human witch turned rowan-blooded. The first in centuries. She—knew *everything*, Saffron, and I... I simply..."

His voice cracked, growing hoarse. He took Saffron's hand, kissing the back of his knuckles with furrowed brows and a clenched jaw. Like it took everything in him not to unravel all over again.

"She threatened to reveal you to all of Alfidel, before we would ever have a chance stop her. Before I could make you my public fiancé, which would have split the share of the scandal's burden on both of us. But it isn't the scandal that frightened me so much, it was—the understanding, the *instant, gutting realization* that someone so influential within my own court knew exactly how to take you from me. When I've already lost so much, and you are all I have left—to be faced with the threat of losing you as well, I—I became something I didn't recognize. I only wished to come home. To return to Avren. Where I could hide you from her, from *them*. But you..."

Cylvan finally opened his eyes, red from how hard he'd squeezed them closed. Searching Saffron's face again, a mix of admiration and incredulity. Like he couldn't believe Saffron was real; like he couldn't believe he'd ever thought he could subdue someone as wild as a rowan witch.

"But you—weren't afraid. You weren't afraid of any of it, of anything at all. You weren't afraid of falling through a veil tear; you weren't afraid of what lies they spread about you in papers; you weren't afraid to talk back to the most terrifying sídhe of all of us. You hunted the man who tore open the Midsummer Games, despite knowing what he could do. You *attended a fete at the mac Delbaith family estate,* then *demonstrated your ownership of Anysta's own fucking brother against her.* Gods! And all while I *hid.* I was a coward, and I thought I could force you to be a coward with me—but I should have known, I should have *known,* as the Prince of Alfidel who has never once managed to assert any sort of authority over you—you were not going to hide from the world with me.

"You, who've survived worse things than any threats a privileged, pompous high fey like me could ever suffer. Gossip articles, scandals, *blackmail*—Ériu made sure I felt the rake of every second that ticked by while I cowered in my glistening palace, as you fought tooth and nail for what had been taken from us. To bring my sibling home to me. To bury Ryder Kyteler beneath a mountain of snow. To have allied with the veil, that we may easily step into the human world, hand-in-hand, as simply as walking into class, while even the Fjornaran oracles failed to find a single crack.

"When I say you are my treasure, Saffron, whom I wish to spend every one of my long days appreciating, falling madly in love with more and more, for eternity—I mean it, with my entire, ancient being. Even when the wrath of my soul breaks free, lashing over you—you are the reason I fear what I cannot control so much more than a fey who had nothing to lose. But you, who persist even in the face of losing it all—my wrath will grovel at your feet every day it wishes to flare, from this day forward. If I ever come to speak to you that way, ever again—let my heart come to a cold, dead stop. Because if I lose you by means of something I can control, my own self—I deserve to choke on dirt beneath the mounds for as long as I would have been allowed to cherish you, otherwise."

Saffron could only gaze at him in adoration, in a melting overwhelm by his raven's words, speaking as if pleading for Saffron to *stay*. As if he believed Saffron would still leave the moment he had his strength back, and that was his final chance to explain. To change his mind.

Without pulling his eyes away, Saffron carefully sat up. Cylvan pulled out of the way to make room for him—but Saffron slid a hand behind his ear and drew him back. Kissing him despite the dryness of his lips, the taste of stale iron-blood in his mouth from all that had spilled over his tongue. And Cylvan kissed him back, also despite it all. He kissed Saffron with all the delicacy of pressing his lips to someone made of snow, afraid they might crumble away if he was too rough.

"I'm sorry it took me so long to come back," Saffron whispered, and Cylvan's hand gently pressed against the nape of his neck firmed suddenly. "Anysta told me what happened at the dé Bricríu estate—but even before then, I never blamed you. I only wanted to protect you, too—even if it made you hate me."

"No," Cylvan said, pressing their foreheads together and shaking his head. "No, you don't dare utter those words to me— not with what you've done for me. Not with—what you've brought back to me, Saffron. To all of us. But even if you hadn't, even if you'd returned to me empty-handed despite it all—never, in my entire being, would I ever find anything but devotion to you."

Saffron kissed him again. Taking those words, and the bright light they bloomed with in his heart; wishing it was so easy to take the relief and elation and send it back to his darkest moments alone.

"Asche made it home," he reiterated with a happy sigh through his nose. "Thank Ériu."

Cylvan's hand on the back of his neck trembled as he nodded. "They did, only a handful of hours after you crashed over Lugh's altar. On my mother's back. A dragon—my mother, the *dragon.*"

"Oh, yes—!" Saffron perked up again, making Cylvan pull away slightly in surprise. "Gentle Naoill is a dragon! You weren't lying all along, when you always said—!"

"I was descended from them," Cylvan finished with a strained laugh. "Gods, but I never thought my mother could take the form of one! Let alone that they'd come crashing down from the sky like a thunderstorm, with my little sibling on their back!"

Saffron kissed him again, grinning between their mouths as Cylvan finally laughed with more heart. Overwhelmed again with the rich joy in Cylvan's voice; having feared he'd never hear it again. All while Cylvan held Saffron's face and kissed him back—before forcing himself to pull away again.

"I hoped you might let me grovel a little longer—" he attempted, but Saffron just grabbed and kissed him again, and again, and again.

"You can grovel later," he said. "I want you to grovel until your knees bleed, to win my forgiveness—but do it later. Right now, I just want to have you again. My raven, Cylvan—just let me have you right now, for a moment longer. While we can still pretend."

Cylvan kissed him back; Saffron sank into the pillows with Cylvan on top of him, between his legs as Saffron held him, pinning their mouths against one another, chests pressed flush together and allowing Saffron to feel every inch of his prince on top of him. Sensing his pounding heart beneath his hands, tasting his breath and his skin, tangling fingers in his hair and pulling on his horns. Yanking off the silver cap that still donned the broken one, throwing it across the room before demanding Cylvan back again without any explanation. Just refamiliarizing himself with Cylvan all over again—feeling far too much like a stranger even after only a few days. Not knowing how else to survive the crashing emotions inside of him, except to press skin-to-skin with the daemon, the Night Prince, for whom he would forgive and do anything.

SAFFRON DIDN'T REALIZE EXACTLY HOW HUNGRY HE was until he sat at the table in the palace kitchens, shoveling warm potato and meat stew into his mouth. He did so circled by his friends around the cramped little servants' table, all of them insisting on joining him rather than waiting another hour for him to get something to eat first. Cylvan was none too happy to be smashed by Copper on his opposite side, constantly elbowing the fox-fey in the ribs as Copper just pelted Saffron with questions while Saffron ate.

They'd all heard the events from Asche's point of view already, but Saffron had other, more exciting, more infuriating details to share. Not only about Ryder and the identity he'd been hiding from them all that time—but what he'd really intended on doing with Proserpina's memory tapestry should he have found it. Saffron quickly followed that sequence of information with chattering all about how he'd hopped in and out of the veil using the pixie ring, how he'd clutched at Ryder and halted his veil event in the middle of it tearing apart, and most importantly—how Saffron had witnessed the man's most vulnerable secret just before the veil whisked him away. His true name, glowing in an arid stele on his chest.

"You can see people's true names?" Copper asked.

"They're on the sternum?" Maeve asked right after, eyebrows raised in curiosity. "Arid spells, too?"

Saffron nodded. "It's sort of like how I gave Taran a new name that controls him. Oracles do the same to all you high fey as babies, so you can only be compelled by people who know that name. It's technically a name given to your opulence, rather than your body, but—same concept. It's why ashen folk can be compelled as freely as humans, because they don't have any opulence to stitch a true name to, to protect them."

"Taran's family ring used to be charmed with an anti-enchantment spell," Cylvan added, clearly eager to appear like a united front with the rowan witch at his side. "Even while we attended Morrígan. Which, I might add, is also a form of arid magic."

"Why don't you let Saffron finish before you blabber nonsense, huh, Cylvan?" Copper asked, but Saffron, with his mouth full, shook his head.

"He's right," he said, nearly choking on the lump of meat between his teeth. "Patron rings have arid circles on them. Hard to see unless you know what you're looking for, but it's true. Here." He popped off his engagement ring, handing it over to Cylvan so the prince could do the honor of pointing out where the arid marks were hidden amongst the overlapping leaves of the band. He smiled so smugly the entire time.

As the prince and Copper quickly found something else to argue about, Saffron's attention was caught through the narrow kitchen window overlooking a piece of the back gardens. Three strangers clad in all black passed by, clearly caught in a focused conversation with how stiffly they moved and turned to one another. Saffron let the initial rush of panic drain from his heart before he spoke, not wanting to show how alarmed the reminders made him.

"Those are the oracles from Fjornar, aren't they?" he asked once his mouth was empty of food. Cylvan glanced for himself, before nodding.

"It looks like a few of them, yes. I believe there are a total of twenty currently residing in the palace, since their monastery is currently under a mountain of snow. Amongst other reasons..." he trailed off through his teeth, sipping bitterly at his coffee.

Saffron grimaced. Not only was Fjornar buried—but so was the veneer he'd hoped to eventually return to, in order to pass back to the human world. To Ire-land, to begin a proper search for his friends. At least—he'd learned far more effective ways, in his time traveling across Alfidel.

"Lingering for your court of expectations...?" He asked with the same venom, shoveling another spoonful of stew into his mouth. "Here I hoped bringing Asche back would get people to drop that idea. I wonder if those oracles know their little fawn is the one who swallowed half the king's keep and buried their shit under twenty feet of snow..."

"I'm sure they're aware," Cylvan muttered. "Perhaps they'll save us the trouble and do away with Ryder themselves."

"Are we sure he's not also under all that snow?" Maeve asked.

"It would be quite a poetic way for him to go," Sionnach noted flatly, stirring sugar into their cup. The motion soon slowed, as the lighthearted conversation fizzled again. As if everyone already knew the answer to that question—or, at least, what was most likely.

"Do you think he'll come back again?" Sionnach asked next, quieter that time. The table remained quiet, the only sounds around them being the banging of pots and pans and chatter amongst beantighes preparing lunch for the rest of the palace.

"Yes," Saffron was finally the one to answer. "He will."

Everyone shifted where they sat—but no one tried to argue. There was no point; they all knew it as well as he did. Saffron stared down at his stew, chewing on the inside of his cheek, before exhaling hard through his nose.

"His true name is '*Eoghan.*'"

Everyone's heads snapped back to look at him. A chill draped over the table, but no one reacted. Saffron just inhaled another breath.

"His true name is Eoghan," Saffron reiterated with a breath. "Use it, the next time you see him. Don't hesitate. He's only going to grow more unpredictable, I think, the more often we get in his way. We have to start acting like every time we cross paths with him will be the last, for either us or him. And—I don't need him anymore. There's no point in letting him live, either, assuming he really did make it out from under the snow..."

Cylvan's hand found Saffron's leg under the table, offering a reassuring squeeze. Saffron regretted dulling the lighthearted mood, but—he didn't know how else to say it. He didn't want to lose anyone else. He didn't want to ever give Ryder the chance to try, without all of his friends having the same advantage he did.

Whatever came next—Ryder Kyteler's true name sat primed and ready on Saffron's tongue. Ready for whenever he showed himself again, where Saffron would be ready to use more than just a knife to finally do away with him. For good.


SAFFRON SPENT THE REST OF THE AFTERNOON IN THE royal infirmary with Asche, who was in good health apart from some bruises and scratches, a little malnutrition, and difficulty resting like they needed to—but even as they begged Saffron to break them out, as they were going mad with boredom, Saffron pretended not to hear it. He just pointed at the beadwork in progress on their lap and asked about it.

Asche's miraculous deliverance through the veil had been announced and spread far and wide across Alfidel, resulting in feasts and dancing in the streets, an ungodly number of gifts being delivered to their hospital bed, and even more purported to altars of Lugh around the country. Thanking the sun god for the return of their golden child.

None of that was surprising in itself—what shocked Saffron most, was how widely it was shared that *he* had been the one to rescue them. Lord Saffron mag Shamhradhaín, the Flower of Alvénya, had somehow saved the daurae from an unknown fate at the hands of the human rebels. And while the palace never revealed any details as to *how* exactly Saffron had managed it— that wasn't even his biggest concern.

"There is nothing under Danu's grace we could do to keep the people from reacting how they choose to the news their next king will be a human witch," Tross had calmly explained when Saffron went to him after learning he'd been the one who decided what the palace shared. "But the goodwill earned through your deeds will, at the very least, soften the blow when it inevitable comes. Not to mention..." he winked. "Your good grace will reflect kindly on Cylvan as well, once you're announced as his fiancé."

Saffron turned those words over endlessly while sitting in the hospital with Asche, as the daurae taught him how to crochet-bead. He thought of them whenever he passed the throne room, the ballroom, the back gardens, clusters of Fjornaran oracles in the hallway, as the palace was prepared for Prince Cylvan's Court of Expectations. Where he would, almost without a doubt, be declared Alfidel's next Night King. Declared far ahead of his time. The first to ever receive their court while the previous kings still ruled.

And all Saffron wished to know what—what then? When the people knew, what then? Would they feel better? Would they use it to justify their fear? Their hatred? Did they truly wish to know —or did they only wish for someone to blame and abuse for everything and anything they wished, for centuries to come?

Or would it be simpler, but more vile than that, like Anysta mac Delbaith had teased—that as soon as Cylvan was declared the coming Night King, powerful sídhe like her or Renard dé Bricríu would step forward to offer a better replacement for king? Her first choice was gone, possibly buried beneath a mountain of snow—but Saffron had not forgotten what Taran had told him prior. What Cylvan had feared, prior. That Asche was always meant to be the replacement, to be used by those who wished to gain power in Alfidel. Asche, who was so young, who was praised and loved from the beginning, who those same people thought they could so easily manipulate to usurp the throne from their very own brother.

Saffron didn't know what would come next—but he knew exactly where he would be throughout all of it. Walking beside Cylvan, his prince, his raven, even in the most suffocating darkness that might come.

"I want you to announce our engagement at your Court of Expectations. No matter how it goes," Saffron told him that night, lying face-to-face in Cylvan's bed with only the sparse light of a single candle to illuminate them. "Before Anysta can do anything first. Before Ryder can try and separate us again." He cupped the side of Cylvan's face, overwhelmed with every feeling imaginable. Apprehension, fear, confusion, vulnerability—but above all, one thing shouted louder. He wanted to be with Cylvan through it all. No matter what came their way. Saffron would promise all his days to that fey prince on the pillow across from him. And he wanted everyone to know it. He wanted every single fey in Alfidel to see and know, without question, Cylvan dé Tuatha dé Danann would always have at least one person who cared for him.

Cylvan took Saffron's hand, pressing a kiss into his palm, then closing his eyes and breathing him in.

"No matter what comes," he said, lips brushing Saffron's skin. "I will always have you. You will never be without me. Day or Night."

"Day or Night," Saffron repeated with a smile, before leaning in to kiss him. Another geis between their lips, another in a long eternity.

**44**

---

# THE REBEL

"*Saffron... Púca, wake up.*"

Saffron stirred, waking into the gentle touch of Cylvan's hand against his cheek. The prince held a single candle, fully dressed in a dark green tunic adorned with golden thread and beads in the shape of wheat stalks down the collar and button seams.

"What's wrong?" Saffron asked wearily, sitting up as Cylvan's hands remained on his shoulder, helping him balance.

"It's time to beseech the old king. I want you there with me."

Saffron followed Cylvan's request, crawling quietly out of bed to join him. He dressed in a dark green doublet that matched Cylvan's, missing only the golden embroidery. Starched and subtly shimmery with a forest-green brocade, the buttons were made of polished silver shaped like the Celtic knots he'd passed on the edge of the trees in human Ire-land. Even his slacks were new and stiff, hugging his waist and cuffed at the bottom over a pair of new shoes.

More than once, he almost asked what exactly they were doing in the middle of the night, with no servants to help them dress, with only the light of a single candle to guide their move-ments—but each time, kept words to himself. Something in the air was solemn, something that was neither nervewracking nor reassuring. Cylvan moved with intention, but lacked any panic. A stoic certainty guided his hands as he buttoned the front of Saffron's tunic like any beantighe would, before smoothing his hands across the collar, and settling on his shoulders. His eyes lingered on Saffron's for a long moment in the darkness, before he leaned forward to press a kiss to Saffron's forehead.

"Come," he whispered. "They'll be waiting for us, I'm sure."

"Who?" Saffron asked softly, but Cylvan just took the candle in one hand, and Saffron's in the other, leading him from the bedroom into the dark corridor on the other side.

Saffron knew the path they followed as soon as they left the warmth of the palace and made their way through the back garden, through a golden gate manned by a single guard, up a winding trail laid with stones in the earth to form steps up the hill. Between the trees scarcely lit by lanterns, illuminated only slightly more with the candle Cylvan still carried ahead of them. Saffron never released his hand, all the way to the top, where he knew Lugh's altar would be waiting for them, overlooking the sea.

The 'others' Cylvan mentioned were the kings, Gentle Naoill, and Asche, who stood tucked into Naoill's side under the protective warmth of their cloak. As Cylvan and Saffron came into view, Asche bounced a little bit on the balls of their feet, but Naoill held them back. On Lugh's altar, a spread of offerings reflected the golden light of an array of candles, fresh fruits and bowls of wine, a thick sheaf of freshly-harvested wheat, a scatter of incense sticks lazily spilling smoke from the dishes they dangled from. The altar itself had been long cleaned of the carnage from Saffron's return, reverent totems replaced and blessed so that members of the royal family could return to praying there as normal. But that night, every object, from the wheat to the altar cloth, was slightly different that Saffron remembered, and he realized each had been newly brought and laid there by the hands of those who stood at Lugh's feet. Evident by the wheat grains clinging to Asche's sleeves, the smell of incense thick on Tross and Ailir's fine clothing, the carrying basket set to the side of the altar.

Cylvan walked Saffron to where Asche and Naoill stood a few steps behind the kings, kissing the back of his hand with a lingering pause before turning to join his fathers facing the altar. Asche's hand slipped into Saffron's the moment it could, and Saffron smiled down at them wordlessly. King Ailir reached out to cup the nape of Cylvan's neck as he stood alongside them, pulling him close and pressing their foreheads together in a quiet moment of affection. It made Saffron's heart race, biting his lip as emotion swelled within him.

The prince and the Primary King stepped forward, then knelt to one knee together at Lugh's feet. King Tross knelt next, and Saffron followed suit as Naoill and Asche knelt last. Something tickled the back of Saffron's neck, and he turned to look, expecting a leaf to have fallen into his collar—but there was nothing, except the tiniest sparkle in his blood. Even the veil had come to bear witness.

"Our beloved Lugh Lámhfada, king of kings, and kings of us Tuatha dé Danann—we beseech thee to hear the plea of one who came after you, in the favor of his son—" Ailir's strong voice hitched, just for a moment. Saffron cracked open his eyes, gazing at the grass beneath his knee. "My son, Crown Prince Cylvan dé Tuatha dé Danann. His people demand a Court of Expectations, to anticipate what fate his reign may bring—a fate long thrust upon him in all the unkindness of his youth, and even now as he has only just come of age. My king—" Ailir paused again. Tross extended a hand, gently touching Ailir's back in comfort.

"My first born son faces a Night Court, despite the benevolence of his heart, never allowed a chance to share it." Ailir said, maintaining his composure, except for the slightest twinge in his voice at the end.

Next to him, Cylvan kept his head bowed—but Saffron noticed how he began to tremble. His hand, clenched into a fist and pressed into the earth alongside his bent knee, flexed in and out in clear, growing nerves. Perhaps broken only by the wavering voice of his normally-unshaken father, who had to pause another moment to gather his words. No one else seemed to notice, or perhaps they knew better than to react—but Saffron didn't. Saffron didn't know this god, he didn't know this ceremony, he only knew Cylvan knelt before the royal family's king of kings, shaking, anxious, vulnerable. Head bowed low in shame, like he didn't dare lift his eyes to the same king he pleaded with for guidance.

Saffron didn't know that king—only all the promises he'd ever made, to never leave Cylvan's side. And with them, he released Asche's hand, and rose to his feet.

He passed King Tross kneeling just behind Ailir. He briefly—and intentionally—met eyes with Lugh towering over them, before turning his gaze down again and lowering onto both knees alongside his raven. He took Cylvan's hand, Cylvan's head snapping to him in instant disbelief—before his hand tightened around Saffron's, and he released a tightly-held breath. He relaxed again. Alongside him, King Ailir's golden eyes had lifted to regard Saffron as well, before turning back to the king. As if he thought the same thing Saffron did—that Cylvan had, actually, been allowed to share his secretly benevolent heart at least once. It was the reason Saffron knelt alongside him at all.

Squeezing Cylvan's hand in return, he bowed his head and closed his eyes once more as King Ailir continued his humble plea for guidance, for clarity, for protection. All while Saffron knew, no matter what came of the court of expectations that coming night—he would be Cylvan's Harmonious King, Day or Night. And King Lugh Lámhfada would know it, long before any oracles declared it for the rest of Alfidel to hear.

THE REST OF THE DAY WAS SPENT IN A FLURRY OF preparations, both for the court itself, and for the feasting and celebrations surrounding it. Saffron thought it ironic, how the same people who feared their fates enough to call for an early court could stomach a fete amidst it all—but at the same time, he'd never known the fey to pass up an opportunity to celebrate any event. Even those on the declaration of their destruction.

Cylvan was sent to be spiritually and physically cleansed by the royal oracles—and Saffron only let him go once he was reassured there would be no Fjornaran oracles with hands in that part of the process. It left him alone in Cylvan's room, supposed to wait for his time to be dressed and prepared. In any other circumstance, Saffron would not have been about to *sit* and *wait* for anything—but whatever outfit they'd prepared for him was kept far out of his reach. Somewhere he wouldn't be able to find it, to dress himself prematurely. King Tross may have planned it on purpose. He only wished there was something, anything—to keep his hands, his mind busy, from turning over and over in endless, apprehensive circles.

Night or Day. Night or Day. Saffron didn't care what they declared Cylvan to be. He didn't believe reading the stars or scrying a basin of wine or whatever it was they were going to do would determine the next few centuries of life in Alfidel. But the people of Alfidel believed it—so he would have to pretend. He would have to act properly in regard to that, even if he didn't respect it. Even if he thought them all fools; even if he hated every single one of them for the torture they put the person he loved so much through for such archaic beliefs. It was those same archaic beliefs that made him a beantighe from that start, anyway.

"Your highness?"

Saffron jumped, turning at the familiar voice. A grin spread over his face, though he wasn't sure if it was out of excitement or body-melting relief. In the doorway, Professor Adelard meekly poked his head inside, smiling back and inviting himself in as Saffron battled the piles of clothes on the floor that congested the feet of the stool where he sat. Nearly trapping him against Cylvan's vanity, finally kicking himself free to greet the professor properly.

He tripped into the man near the doorway, where Adelard laughed and righted him again. Behind him, Professor Dullahan stood, and Saffron noticed how nicely both of them dressed— wearing all black each, as was apparently traditional both for periods of grief *and* for guests of a Court of Expectation. Adelard's normally stiffly-oiled hair was even coiffed handsomely over his forehead, wearing a little eyeshadow and blush on his cheeks that brought out the warm brown color of his eyes. Saffron apologized right away for knocking the man's glasses askew, offering Cormac a nod of greeting before stepping back and holding the door open to invite them both inside.

"Sorry for the mess," he said, grimacing when he realized he should have tidied up rather than just sitting and stewing. He'd learned to find a sense of comfort in the endless garments and blankets and shawls left in piles and draping over the back of the sitting couches, though. That time, stemming from Cylvan madly stress-changing into every outfit he owned in the interim between that morning's prayer at Lugh's altar and when he'd be dressed for the formal ceremony. Adelard, however, might have been the last person to ever care, instead adjusting his glasses and looking over Saffron's outfit. It was nothing special, all things considered—but compared to the worn-through travel clothes the professor had last seen him in, not to mention the years of beantighe uniforms before that—even Saffron knew he was dressed like a shimmering little doll.

"I'm still waiting to get dressed for the ceremony, myself," he said, trying to sound lighthearted. "They know I would do it all myself at the first chance, so I've been imprisoned here until they're ready for me. This is apparently the biggest party the palace has seen in centuries, erm—understandably, but with so much of the human staff defecting with Ryder, they're spread a little thin, so I have to wait my turn..."

"You're going to look beautiful, Saffron," Adelard said with a genuine smile, making Saffron blush. "Even now, I think so. Far from the Morrígan beantighe who used to accost me after class during the week, begging me to identify the scribbled images in his sketchbook. More often with dirt on his face and twigs in his hair than not."

"Th-thank you," Saffron said, laughing weakly. He hurried to clear off room on the sitting couch, searching for the cart of tea and snacks that had been brought to him an hour earlier. The tea in the pot had gone warm, and he glanced over his shoulder, before shaking his head and readily pulling the hematite wand from a pocket in his blouse to draw a circle around the base of the pot that read *'steaming hot'*. The pot's ceramic lid rattled with a little puff of heat.

Pouring cups for Adelard and Cormac, the two of them looked both like they belonged there on the prince's couch, while also wildly out of their element. Even Cormac, in all his stoic grace, held the hoop of the teacup like someone who'd only ever known drinking whiskey from a hip flask.

"Is that really only a passive outfit for you here? All of the palace can surely here exactly where you are, at any time, with all those beads and—ah, then little bells on your cuffs," Adelard teased further, sipping at his tea and smiling down at it when the rich flavor far exceeded what he brewed on his own at Morrígan. "Charming, though, I'll admit."

"Don't forget the heels," Saffron exhaled, plopping down in the seat across from them and extending one leg to show off his heeled boots, as ornate as the gold collar of his blouse and the matching, pointed ear-cuffs on the tips of his ears. "King Tross insists we always look more than presentable, even when stalling before a party... Er, thank you both for coming today—I assume Cylvan invited you?"

Adelard nodded, pulling a dark-green enveloped from the inner pocket of his jacket, donning Cylvan's personal wax-seal on the back. "Yes, on his personal letterhead, even," Adelard said with a wry smile. "Informing me, without so many words, I was not allowed to refuse."

"Oh—"

"He insisted my presence might help ease your nerves," he went on, returning the envelope to his jacket. Saffron flushed in embarrassment again, mentally cursing Cylvan for it, but Adelard continued before he could apologize. "And, I admit, Saffron, I... was disappointed in how our last meeting ended off. Erm—disappointed in myself, that is." He passed a brief glance to Cormac, who met his eyes, and returned the sentiment with a little nod. Adelard inhaled, and held the breath. Saffron could practically feel the nerves growing under the professor's skin, making him straighten up.

"It is actually Cormac who convinced me to come and speak with you before the prince's court tonight," Adelard continued. As he did, Cormac's hand silently reached out to touch Adelard's leg, and Adelard's hand found and squeezed it. Hard enough to strain the skin over the backs of his knuckles, betraying his real nerves. "You see—I wasn't entirely honest with you, while you were at Morrígan. About—about myself. About the things I know."

Saffron held his breath. It took everything in him not to interrupt.

"I'm sure there are things you've already figured out on your own—you've always been very smart, to a fault, which I'm sure had everything to do with how you've found yourself in this position," he chuckled, shaking his head, then inhaling another slow breath. "But—there are reasons why I was able to share so much about—well, about pixie rings, for example, and their use amongst rebels during the War of the Veil."

Saffron nodded, clenching his jaw to keep from exclaiming. He'd wondered such things. He'd assumed them, but never thought he'd get the chance to ask. It took everything in him to swallow back the urge to leap to his feet.

"I see it on your face—you know what I'm about to say," he said, that time his smile weary. Cormac's hand visibly squeezed Adelard's, and the professor sighed. "I know, I'm stalling—lord help me, it's been some time. I've kept my secrets well for centuries, give me a moment."

"Take your time," Saffron rasped, feeling like he was being squeezed from the inside out. Then he couldn't stop the next words from coming, unable to find the patience: "You were a rebel during the war, weren't you?"

Adelard grimaced, but nodded. "Er—yes. More than just a rebel, even, I... I..." his mouth opened, then closed, a choked sound escaping the back of his throat. "I... knew Verity Holt personally, I suppose I'll say. It's all I can stomach to share, right now. Ah, I suppose I should—you should know—well, you see, that hematite wand I gave you, is actually—*was*, actually, hers."

Saffron stared at him, stomach sinking, before swelling up the back of his throat so fast it emerged as a shrill *'oh, fuck!'*

Thankfully, Adelard laughed in response—though it sounded equally like a wheeze—putting up his hands as Saffron instinctively looked down at the wand he still held in his hand from warming the teapot.

"Don't look so nervous, Saffron, there's nothing special about it other than that—nothing to be worried about, just a standard arid wand is all—"

"But Verity Holt—! She's the one who—! Who—!" Saffron choked, extending the wand as if Adelard didn't realize what he was saying. "She—killed—Queen Proserpina—!"

"Yes, she did," Adelard managed to chuckle again. "I took the wand for myself after she died, for sentimental reasons, but, ah... it's better suited for a rowan witch, you see, and I had no more need for such a thing by the time the war ended..."

Saffron wanted to ask what that meant, specifically—*no more need*. But instead, he remained silent, gazing down at the wand in his trembling hand. The same one Verity Holt, human witch, rowan witch, once carried throughout the war. Possibly even the same one she carried when dealing the final blow on Queen Proserpina, bringing the fighting to an end.

"Virtue..." he breathed, speaking before his thoughts caught up. Across from him, Adelard paled slightly. He adjusted his glasses, like a nervous tick, like that name summoned a different twist of emotions for him. "Erm, Verity's brother, Virtue, he—" Saffron didn't know how to explain. Was he getting ahead of himself? "Erm—! The man who has been opening the veils across Alfidel, Ryder Kyteler, it turns out he's been looking for Queen Proserpina's memory tapestry this whole time! He was going to implant the threads into Daurae Asche, as a woven vessel, like you once told me about, but I found Asche before he could—"

"And thank god for that—" Adelard attempted, but Saffron couldn't halt the momentum of his words.

"But while we were in the Winter Court, at the mac Delbaith estate, Anysta told him—told him Virtue Holt had taken the queen's memory tapestry after Verity died. If you knew Verity, then did you also know—"

"I don't wish to speak of Virtue Holt at this time," Adelard interrupted that time, a tight smile spread thin across his face, pale as a ghost. Cormac's hand on his leg flexed again, but that time, Adelard ignored it. "But I will tell you what I know about Ryder Kyteler."

"He's—he's Queen Proserpina's son," Saffron said first, and Adelard nodded, stiffly. "He's the son of her and her human lover, Adone."

"That's right," Adelard said. "I didn't make the connection at first, and I apologize for that. When I knew him, he called himself Finn O'Daire."

Saffron's stomach turned over. Words that struck him deeply, but came as no surprise. The crone had mentioned witchhunters attempting to use that name to trick her into sharing where Ryder was, after all. Perhaps it was simply hearing it spoken by the last person Saffron ever expected, that made goosebumps flush his arms.

"He must have thought himself so clever," he mumbled to himself. Ryder's birth name had been *Deimne*, after all, another name for Finn mac Cumhaill in myth. For him to use the name

*Finn* while pretending to be someone else during the war—it was painfully ironic, but Saffron knew, also entirely intentional. He must have really thought himself so *cunning*. Saffron could imagine the smugness of his grin when he'd introduce himself with that name—wishing to reach back in time and smack it off his face.

"Did you know he was Proserpina's son, during the war?" Saffron asked.

"No," Adelard insisted. "No, he glamoured himself as a human while I knew him. He—he lied to me. To all of us. He lied to Verity, too. He was nearly the reason Proserpina found her, near the end, that absolute bastard..." Adelard's fists on his knees clenched tighter, trembling in the effort, matching the growing intensity of his voice. "I'm—I'm terribly sorry that I did not realize it sooner, Saffron, I... I think of it now, and it's obvious, but I... I have intentionally avoided any manner of recalling details of my time during the war, for my own sanity, but also for the sake of protecting myself and the simple life I've been able to make for myself at Morrigan—"

"I understand," Saffron said right away. "Professor, you don't have to apologize. I understand."

Adelard looked like he wished to share more, like something buried deep within his being crawled at the back of his throat to be spoken. Another secret, another hidden part of his life he wished to share, but fought to keep down. Whether he was afraid to share it for his own safety, or perhaps for Saffron's, Saffron might never know—and while that frustrated him to the bone, he could understand. He, more than most, knew the importance of keeping one's true identity a secret in order to protect oneself and the people they cared for.

"Thank you for telling me," Saffron added, squeezing the wand in his hand and lifting a reassuring smile to Adelard. "Please believe me, when I say I will keep your secrets safe. As one of the first people to keep my own secrets—I owe so much of my current happiness to you and your discretion, professor. All those times you helped me read in your office, or shared information about the wild fey with me—not to mention how you hid me while I was passing as the rowan spirit."

"I think I've always known there were great things in store for you, Saffron," Adelard said with a gentle smile, shoulders finally relaxing from how tensely he held them. "I only hope I can make up for all the things I wasn't able to teach you back then—and for the cowardice that kept me silent. If you'll let me, I'd like to remain here in Avren with you, for now. To teach you all I know about rowan magic, veil magic—"

"Oh!" Saffron exclaimed, that time leaping from his seat in excitement. "Of course! Of course, please!"

Adelard laughed again, getting to his feet and shaking his head before gazing at Saffron in long, quiet consideration. He lifted a hand, touching Saffron's cheek, still wearing a tiny smile, before his fingers trailed up to gently trail over Saffron's hair combed back with aromatic oils, then down to the golden tips on his ears, before plucking his hand away in embarrassment.

"You look beautiful," he whispered. "Like a rightful king."

"Not quite yet," Saffron chuckled. "Hopefully someday still, though, if these high fey will allow it."

"I am certain of it," Adelard said, like a promise. Like an ancient creature declaring a premonition. "I have seen kings and queens come and go many times; I have nearly seen the veil undone, then haphazardly stitched back together again for the sake of regaining a tenuous balance. But those stitches were never going to last—and in order for true balance to return, they must all be torn open again. No matter what these oracles declare of yours and Prince Cylvan's court, tonight, we are far from any peace on the horizon..." he trailed off, eyes lingering on the amethyst pendant Saffron wore around his neck, polished bright down to the silver moon charm dangling from the jewel. "But you and Cylvan know that as well as I do, which gives me more hope than I've had in a very long time. Hope that we may soon see actual change in Alfidel. A change for the better, for both sides.

These high fey will not listen, yet—but even they will bow and kiss your feet in thanks one day, Saffron. I know it."

Saffron blinked back tears, before reaching out to wrap his arms around Adelard. Hugging him, his professor, his mentor— his *friend*, who had been there to encourage him when he was nothing more than a veiled beantighe scrubbing floors at Morrígan. Saffron, who'd lived only the smallest fraction of time as Adelard, yet that ancient man had still given Saffron a weak smile and invited him into his office to chatter on and on about all the wild things Saffron had seen in the woods that morning. Who offered Saffron a place to sleep while he roamed the campus drenched in red rowan berries; who never once turned Saffron away, even though it could have lead to disruption of the simple, quiet life he protected so closely.

"Thank you," he whispered. "Thank you, Professor. I won't forget your kindness, no matter what comes next."

Adelard held Saffron in return, embracing him tightly, like Saffron was something precious. Like he meant it, when he said Saffron was the first thing to give him hope in such a long time. Saffron swore he would not take such a delicate thing for granted.

## 45

# THE COURT

S affron wore all white, with gold beading and stitched filigree up the line of his sleeves, across the square shoulders, and down the back of his spine to spill and trail along the fabric on his heels. Only a tissue-thin, sheer panel covered his back, displaying his skin and trailing like beaded constellations that sparkled with every movement; from the peaks of his shoulders, a similarly-delicate cape draped out behind him, blending with the layers of chiffon that made up the skirt. It was apparently customary to wear white to a court of expectations, a blank canvas, a pale void in which to invite any and all possibilities. Even if they already knew what would come. Even if there was no possibility of anything else. Mostly, while the dress was beautiful as ever—it just reminded him of the veil he used to wear at Morrígan, to hide his face. Where being a blank canvas was a force of submission, not a call for possibilities to find them.

Pinching at the fabric, Saffron stood in the dimly-lit corridor located behind the ballroom, waiting for the courtiers to find their places on the other side. The air smelled humid and sweet like a mountain lake, mixing with the light smoke of what he imagined to be oak-sap candles and incense. He hadn't been told what exactly to expect during the court's ritual, he didn't know what he would see when he was finally able to step through to the other side, but all he could imagine was opening the door to step straight into the middle of the woods rather than the elegant ballroom. Perhaps they'd placed a temporary veneer right there in the palace, to take all guests somewhere within the heart of Avren's wood. He smirked, he grimaced, sarcastically wondering why no one had thought to ask for his help, considering he was now a master of the veil.

"Ah, excuse me, beantighe, I seem to be—oh, dear, my mistake~" Cylvan's voice made Saffron jump, and he turned fast, caught in a sharp laugh when a mouth was suddenly pressing to his. Saffron wrapped his arms instinctively back around his prince, practically tasting the trepidation emanating off of him. Cylvan kissed him for a long, drawn out moment, hands finding Saffron's waist and holding him there, allowing time to slow to nearly a stop before finally pulling away and pressing their foreheads together.

"I didn't mean to startle you," he said in an exhale. "I'm actually not supposed to be here, either—"

Saffron touched his face, pulling back just enough to meet his eyes. He meant to reassure him—but Cylvan's appearance caught him by surprise. His dark, brooding, haunted raven was dressed in pure white vestments just as his own, contrasting beautifully against his dark hair and jewel-toned eyes.

"Oh," Saffron breathed like the air had been knocked out of him. "You look..."

"Like a little doll," Cylvan smirked. Saffron cupped his face, chuckling too.

"Yes, but—a handsome one. White suits you. It's making my heart race."

"Has it not been racing before now?" Cylvan asked, a little rattled at the thought that he may be the only one who was nervous. Saffron kissed him again, drawing his nerves back to where he could gently hold them in his hands.

"Everything is going to be alright," he whispered. "If anything —there will be no surprises. I will be right there with you when we announce our engagement—then for you the entire time after, if you ever feel uncertain, just turn and find me. God knows I'll stand out like a spotlight in this outfit, too."

"I'll look for you," Cylvan said, taking Saffron's hand. He pressed his mouth into his palm, breathing him in a moment before leaving a kiss in the center. "I'll find you again the moment it's over. I'll think of nothing else but leaving with you when it's all over."

"Leaving for good?" Saffron teased. "We could still run away together, never to be seen again."

"Gods, do not say such things. Did you just feel me twitch? I nearly took your hand and bolted."

Saffron laughed again. He tucked a piece of Cylvan's long hair from the corner of his eye, where it draped down in long, luxurious waves over his shoulders. He hadn't realized how much longer it'd grown since they first met. Hardly enough for anyone else to notice—but Saffron knew everything about his raven, down to the shifting emotions behind his eyes, how his lips were slightly less full because he clenched his jaw tightly in apprehension.

"I love you," Saffron said. "Even before, and even after a Night Court, I've always loved you. No matter what comes."

"Day or Night."

"Day or Night," Saffron repeated. He touched his forehead to Cylvan's one last time, closing his eyes. "I love you, Cylvan."

Cylvan exhaled a long breath, as if drawing those words in to wrap over himself like a comforting blanket.

"I love you, Saffron," he whispered. "I will never love or cherish anyone, or anything else more than you. And finally, tonight—all of Alfidel will finally know it, too."

Saffron's heart leapt for the first time, though he didn't know if it was out of nerves or affection. He only nodded. He was ready. He would bravely face whatever came next, with his hand clasped tightly in Cylvan's. To prove to any and all who ever doubted—that there was at least one person who cared for the Night Prince of Alfidel. Someone who commanded power none of them would ever anticipate, in order to protect him.

THE KINGS WOULD ENTER THE BALLROOM FIRST; THEN Cylvan would follow them, then Saffron would be introduced formally as the prince's fiancé, to follow them in last. But until then, Saffron watched from the back corridor with Sionnach, who joined him once Saoirse arrived and forced Cylvan away. The moment Saffron had to release Cylvan's hand, Sionnach was there to claim it for themself, smiling in reassurance.

Behind them, Naoill approached in their Aodhán glamour as well, offering Saffron a flourishing bow and a compliment, before showing where a piece of the carved floral design stretching over the wainscoting could be slid to the side and offer a view into the ballroom. Saffron instantly pressed himself close, barely hearing as Naoill indicated a second one for Sionnach's view, then took a third for themself.

On the other side of the wall, at first, was only darkness. The ballroom normally swathed in the warm, bright light of crystal chandeliers and candelabras and what he assumed to be a bit of charmed magic—was nearly pitch-black, like a moonless night. Only as his eyes adjusted properly, was he able to make out the undulating groups of shadows that were Avren's highest-ranking courtiers. Wearing all black, from their outfits to their head-coverings, no different from the Fjornaran oracles who oversaw the ritual. It explained why Adelard and Cormac had been dressed the same.

"Traditionally, Courts of Expectations are held in the oldest woods of one of the four courts," Sionnach whispered, as if reading Saffron's mind. As if even they had just finished bingeing a textbook about it, before getting dressed and arriving at the palace. "King Ailir's was held in the Summer Court, I believe. Perhaps there wasn't time to decide, with Cylvan..."

"Perhaps they didn't want to get their suede boots muddy," Naoill muttered a little further down the wall.

Saffron said nothing, just blinking through the darkness. Attempting to make out a more detailed view, only growing frustrated when his humans eyes did him no favors.

"Icarus, *come,*" he whispered, and even Sionnach snapped back from their viewing spot in the corner of Saffron's eye. Saffron still said nothing, until the wolf appeared alongside him. "Go offer me a better look. Don't let them see you."

Taran grumbled something, but seemed intrigued at the task, trotting off down the hallway. Just like in the mountains, when Saffron summoned the wolf to witness Ryder's true name for him, he was able to tap into Taran's vision in the back of his mind —perceiving without it blocking his vision.

That time, as Taran slipped in through the doors of the ballroom, Saffron even felt the few inches of water blanketing the floor; he smelled the rich scent of shifting lake water and oak wood incense; he could feel the chill in the air as all the windows had been thrown wide open, and the nighttime breeze gently wafted inside. None of the guests clustered amongst themselves noticed the beast moving past like a silent shadow, except the slight brushes against skirts or tailcoats. Amongst them, Saffron recognized the occasional attendee from Cylvan's suitor galas, or Saffron's occasional time spent in the palace—but from them, other more familiar guests appeared in the darkness, and even Taran hesitated before keeping his distance.

Renard dé Bricríu stood with all seven of his sons, appearing harsher than ever in their all-black ensembles while exchanging the lowest whispers between one another. Except for one, who remained silent—Copper, who stood slightly off to the side, appearing so out of place amongst his family members despite sharing so many similarities. All sets of their foxlike eyes focused on the center of the ballroom where the altar stood, waiting for Cylvan to arrive.

Alongside them, but not near enough to imply any sort of close ties, Saffron next recognized a cluster of elegant, icy-blonde fey, two of which held the hands of Maeve in the center. Her parents, the dé Bhaldraithes, appeared both apprehensive and humming with pride, clearly aware of how close their daughter had been with the prince in recent weeks. Even if Cylvan was not expected to leave that ballroom with anything more than a curse of Night, even if Maeve was not intended to be his Harmonious Queen like once considered, even they found it in themselves to stand tall with pride.

Anysta Mac Delbaith hovered toward the back of the crowd on the opposite side, silent and upright. The barest light in her eyes indicating her excitement; enough to summon a fiery, angry rush of blood to fill the back of Saffron's throat. He forced it back down again, instead focusing on the undeniable silhouette of Carce a few yards away from her, standing with Étaín held in his arms with her back to his chest. Protective, defensive, surrounded by all of those high fey who'd once spurned her. Looking like an intimidating wild fey in his all black clothing.

Of the other courtiers gathered around, none uttered a word. For the first time in perhaps all of fey history, Avren's palace ballroom was crowded with people, but not a single word was exchanged. There was only the light splashing and rippling of water on the floor, and the near-imperceptible sound of Taran's paws as he passed by.

In the center, the water lapped at a wide ring of muddy, grassy sod, encircling a shallow bowl on a stand made of roughly-stripped posts tied together in what Saffron thought to be rather haphazardly thrown together. He had to resist mumbling something in frustration, reminded of what Anysta had said in her study. He had to keep reminding himself that the odds of any part of that ritual being genuine were slim, considering how premeditated every other aspect of it had been.

The moment a low, chanting hum emerged from the Fjornaran oracles standing around the outer rim of the sodden grass, one at the head of it gently plucking the strings of a wooden harp, Saffron whispered for Taran to return. Rather than sneaking all the way back, the wolf merely vanished into the shadows already engulfing him, and Saffron felt the moment his intangible weight nestle back into his mind.

*What do you think?* Saffron asked. Not sure why—though knowing he was far more restless than he allowed himself to admit.

*"I think they are going to get the court they've been hoping for,"* Taran said venomously. Saffron knew that much, as well. There was no doubt.

The doors at the head of the ballroom opened, and while Saffron could not see who entered first from his vantage point, he knew by the wave of bowing courtiers that it must have been the kings. Ailir and Tross, who walked so elegantly alongside one another they barely disrupted the water glazing their ballroom floor, soon passed into Saffron's line of sight. Asche walked on their heels, also donning all white as they watched their feet pass through the water. The kings reached their thrones, Asche positioning themself to the side of Ailir's out of view—when King Tross' eyes met Saffron's through the pinhole, and Saffron's heart thumped. They way they lingered, he couldn't shake the feeling the king was trying to tell him something.

"... When in all of this do they intend on sharing our engagement?" Saffron asked. "Cylvan said I would be announced before the ceremony began."

Naoill gave him a look, before grimacing.

"At the last moment, the head oracle of Fjornar thought it better to wait—*ah*, good, I was hoping you'd disagree," they grinned as Saffron immediately pulled away from the gap in the wall. Naoill even put out a hand for Saffron to take, sweeping him out of the corridor as Sionnach hurried along behind in surprise.

It wasn't a far distance to where the main entrance to the ballroom was crowded with more black-clad guards, oracles, lower-tier courtiers—but despite the small throng blocking most of his view, Saffron spotted Saoirse over all of them. He spotted Cylvan's horns, the broken one newly replaced with a black cap that contained no hint of opulent silver at all.

"Your highness," Saffron said as they approached, compelling everyone crowded around to turn in surprise. He couldn't see the expression on the head oracle's face beneath their veil, but Saffron knew it must have wrinkled in annoyance. Cylvan, meanwhile, looked at Saffron with a rush of pale relief, like even he had only been told a moment prior that there had been a change of plans.

Saffron was not going to allow that to happen, and he made sure of it by pulling away from Naoill to go straight for where Cylvan stood, hooking an arm through his. Cylvan's arm tightened around his in return. Refusing to let him go. The people of Alfidel wouldn't need a long speech to announce their engagement, then—they would simply understand the moment Saffron entered the prince's court with arms woven protectively around one another.

In Cylvan's opposite hand, he held a single lit candle with a trembling flame that indicated his barely-subdued nerves. Saffron offered his hand while still wrapped in Cylvan's, and Cylvan passed the candle over. Holding it between them, at the same time. Allowing the dancing light to settle, flame stretching long and tall on its unflinching foundation, supported between the both of them. Together.

Entering the ballroom arm in arm, into a sea of darkness. The shallow lake of water instantly soaked through Saffron's shoes and pulled on the train of his dress. They entered into a dreamlike sphere of whispered chanting song and a plucking harp, soon joined by the surprised, muted gasps of courtiers as they recognized Saffron walking tall and arm-in-arm with the prince. Saffron felt the weight of the reveal on his shoulders. He felt the sharp, vitalizing squeeze of satisfaction knowing he and Cylvan had decided for themselves what would be written in gossip columns the following morning, despite the oracles' attempts to hide Saffron away just a bit longer. They should have known. If they'd ever shared a single word about him with the witchhunters they claimed to no longer be associated with—they should have known better. Saffron was not the witch to snub; Saffron was not the Rowan Witch to leave his Night Prince to face the darkness alone.

Passing through the crowd, Cylvan would have never bowed his head or hid his face in that circumstance—but Saffron felt how even he moved with a swift confidence, a renewed sense of authority, arm interwoven with Saffron's as they carried the candle between them with an infallible flame.

The courtiers, despite resorting to silence at the start, began to whisper—and some even reached out to gently brush fingers through the white chiffon cape at Saffron's back. As if unsure he was real; wishing to see if they could feel him, or if he was merely a ghost. *Lord Saffron, who rescued Daurae Asche from their horrible fate—is the chosen fiancé of Prince Cylvan of Alfidel.*

At the circle of sodden grass, Saffron followed Cylvan's lead. He bowed toward the altar bowl in the center, before releasing the candle for the head oracle to take and place in a small cup on the rim of the bowl. Then, Cylvan turned—and bowed to Saffron, eliciting another muted gasp from the crowd. The prince bowed, then took Saffron's hand to kiss the back of it, meeting Saffron's eyes.

Time froze around them one last time, hand-in-hand in the darkness, a thousand words passing between their eyes, never having to be spoken to be known. A thousand promises, a thousand certainties for the future—all stemming from one single geis made in the Aon Adharcach suite of Morrígan Academy.

Saffron's emotions stirred. The backs of his eyes burned, and despite his wish to remain stoic and intimidating in front of all those people—he couldn't help but offer Cylvan a small, reassuring smile. *Everything will be alright. I'll be right here if you need me. Just turn to look.*

Cylvan knew it. Saffron could see it in his eyes, as he smiled back so minutely that only Saffron would ever recognize it. Even as he straightened up again and extended an arm for Saffron to turn and join the kings by their thrones, Saffron could see that shift in Cylvan's demeanor. Sure of himself; almost optimistic in his unwavering presence. The next king of Alfidel stood in front of Saffron, and all those people, even draped in darkness—and they all would know it.

Saffron joined the kings at the head of their thrones, smiling and nodding at Asche alongside Ailir as he offered all three of them a deep bow, before finding his place at Tross' opposite hand. A thousand eyes followed him his every movement, meaning they also saw how King Tross reached out to take and squeeze Saffron's hand for the briefest moment. As if to compliment him, for recognizing something was amiss. Saffron squeezed back before letting go, a silent thank you for the hint.

In the center of the room, the head oracle crossed the grass circle into the center. They took the shallow bowl in their hands, raising it over their head as the rhythmic chanting continued. They beseeched the Dagda in a language Saffron only recognized to be Old Alvish due to its similarities to Gaeilge, even recognizing a handful of the chosen words. *God, welcome, bless, protect,* they invited the god of the mounds to join them, before the chanting died down, and the harp music slowed.

Cylvan stepped into the circle with them. He leaned over the surface of the bowl containing a dark liquid, seeming to breathe it in a long moment before straightening up again.

"May the Dagda draw the stars as we are meant to read them," the oracle spoke aloud. "May they counsel our sights, and address our shortcomings. For the coming reign of Crown Prince Cylvan dé Tuatha dé Danann, of Day King Ailir and Harmonious King Tross, and Progenitor Mother Naoill dé Fianna dé Tuatha dé Danann—we beseech the Dagda to concede what they know."

The head oracle threw the contents of the shallow bowl in an arc over their head. But rather than raining down across the attendants—the ink hovered in an opaque bloom, before spreading. Crawling in every direction until it formed a broad, black cloud of nothingness, even darker than a moonless night sky.

Saffron held his breath. He nearly took a step forward in anticipation, waiting for something to come, waiting to see what the gods would say—only for his heart to stop the moment a deep, crimson-red moon appeared through a split in the darkness.

## 46

# THE BOUGH

*Crimson tears the moon shall weep.*

Saffron could only stare. Unmoving, unbreathing, as the ringing silence of the ballroom suddenly split like a swollen thunderstorm, crashing open and tearing through the air with a resounding uproar. Shrieking and crying, shouting words of calamity and destruction, the wrath of the gods, punishment for what wicked thing the people of Alfidel would allow to step onto the throne.

The crowd oscillated as courtiers stumbled into one another, some clambering for the closed doors to demand release, others shoving against one another in an attempt to rush the grass circle where Cylvan stood frozen. With his head tilted back, craned toward the undeniable, bright red moon floating overhead. A blood moon. A rowan-red blood moon, declared over his coming court.

When he did finally move again—it was to gaze toward Saffron. Saffron, who met his eyes in an instant. Who nearly leapt back into the water to race for him, had King Tross' hand not lashed out to grab his wrist and keep him back. Saffron didn't turn to look at him, to demand to be let go. He could hardly think. There was only the red moon, the crowd growing in its uproar, but most unsettling of all—was the calm disbelief on Cylvan's expression. Gazing at Saffron from where he stood, there was no sign of panic in his own demeanor. His eyes were still, even a layer glazed over, as if stripped of his ghost. As if only his body remained where it stood, like every last hope had been unraveled from his bones, leaving him empty. Saffron swore he mouthed something for Saffron to read—but it was too dark to see. Saffron's human eyes weren't sharp enough, even in the unnatural red glow of the blood-moon displayed overhead—but it didn't matter. In a voice as ancient as the mounds where the Tuatha dé Danann first emerged, a voice spoke in the back of Saffron's mind, matching Cylvan's lips.

*They who forsake the veil—are forsaken by me.*

A rush of air crashed into his lungs the moment Cylvan broke eye contact, even he stumbling back a step and pressing a hand to his head. Just behind him, Adelard was visible in the front of the crowd, illuminated by the crimson light—and also staring straight at Saffron. Knowing the symbolism of a blood moon as well as anyone else who'd ever read the poem on the red cards passed by Ryder's witches. Anyone who had ever walked the path of Verity and Virtue Holt during the war, or stood against it.

Just behind the professor, another familiar face stood, staring wide-eyed and astonished at the red moon glowing in the void. Anysta mac Delbaith—as if even she could have never anticipated exactly what sort of Night Court was promised of the Prince of Alfidel.

As the vision began to fade, the redness of the moon dissolving away into a brief moment of clear, bright white light, the ink suspended in the air turned into a trickling rain, first only a sprinkle before releasing into nearly a downpour. Rippling across the water carpeting the ballroom floor, staining the shoulders of Cylvan's pure-white tunic and pants. Soiling every courtier who stood too close, until black ink slithered in trails down arms and faces and soaked through Cylvan's dark hair.

When the cloud fully dispersed, the chaos only rang louder

and more frenzied. Saoirse and the other palace guards fought to keep the crowd at bay, spitting and cursing and throwing out their hands to grapple at the prince who remained motionless in the center of the circle. Just staring at where the shallow bowl had been dropped, floating in the water—until even it was swept up by the head oracle, who swung and slammed it against the side of Cylvan's face with a shriek of contempt.

Saffron jolted forward, but Tross still had a tight grip on him. That time, he snapped around to demand the king release him—but Tross wasn't looking at him. Neither was Ailir, both of them sitting stiff and motionless in their thrones, unable to do anything but stare at the unraveling of the court in front of them. Even in the dim light, Saffron witnessed silent tears filling Ailir's eyes and slipping down his cheeks, into his beard.

"Gentle Aodhán," Tross said, barely audible over the noise. "Take Saffron away from this."

"No!" Saffron snarled, tearing his wrist from Tross' grasp. The king didn't react—he didn't turn his head from watching Cylvan in the center of the room, where Saoirse had already gone to his aid. Tross didn't even lower his hand from where it newly grasped at air where Saffron had been. Even Naoill struggled to pull their eyes away, clearly torn between what they wished to do and what they knew would be best—finally turning and stiffly placing a hand to Saffron's back.

"You should go," they said. Their voice shook. "Cylvan wouldn't want you to see this."

"I can help—" Saffron attempted, but cut himself short as he understood as well as Naoill didn't that *no*, he couldn't. That was not the time to reveal his magic to all of those people. Not when he'd just been revealed as Cylvan's fiancé, not when the prince had just received an unprecedented message from the gods. Cylvan did not need Saffron to jump to his rescue at that moment, to risk making everything worse. Hating that anything could be *worse* still than what unfolded in front of him.

But Saoirse was there with him in the center of the room; the other guards were keeping the rest of the crowd at bay. Ailir had finally turned to speak in fast, hushed whispers to Tross, preparing what he wished to say in the next moment when he would stand and command his court to silence. Saffron had to go.

"Stay with him," Saffron said, gently tucking Naoill's arm away. "Tell him he can find me in his bedroom. I'll be waiting for him, alright?"

"I can't let you go alone—"

"I know all the secret passages," Saffron said with a weak smile, eyes flashing to where Asche stood alongside Ailir, white-knuckling the king's hand as they visibly fought against tears welling in their eyes. Fighting to keep their expression flat, stoic, while forced to witness the vicious backlash against their brother. "The daurae made sure to show me, a while ago. No one will see me."

Naoill searched Saffron's face, but it was clear how badly they wished to do as he asked. Saffron knew it. He offered them a bow, then turned to slip behind the kings' thrones, where he knew there to be a beantighe passage through the wainscoting. He would go straight to Cylvan's bedroom. He would wait for him there. And Cylvan would know it.

Saffron didn't want to go—he didn't want to leave Cylvan, not in that state. He wanted to rush to meet him, to take his hand and threaten anyone else who dared step close, but—there were eyes on him. And Cylvan was keeping his composure. Even against his will, he was forcing himself to remain calm so no one would have anything to say the following morning. There would be nothing to write about, except his astounding calm in the face of a warning from the gods.

He must have felt so lonely, standing there in the middle of that crowded room, surrounded by hungry wolves waiting for any reason to bite him. He must have been so lonely, and—Saffron had to leave him there, to suffer it in silence. He had to.

Saffron would wait for Cylvan in his room, to be there the moment he returned. To hold him. To tell him everything would be alright, just like the last time. To wash the ink from his face and clothes and hair, to hold him tightly. To kiss every inch of him and tell him everything would be alright. To tell him how much he loved him, how Saffron would be there with him for whatever came next. To hold his hand, endlessly, no matter how dark the night that came.

Slipping through the wainscoting hidden behind the kings' thrones, Saffron barely closed the panel behind him when something grabbed his arm, twisting it backward and shoving him roughly into the wall. Grunting, he attempted to shove off on impulse—but something cold and metallic clasped around his throat. Two sharp prongs bit into his skin.

"Easy, your highness," Ryder growled, as amused as he was furious. "I only came to wish you congratulations on your engagement."

The grip he held on Saffron's forearm pressed into the small of his back was harder than steel, breathing heavily as he tucked his chin into the curve of Saffron's shoulder. Pressing his nose to the side of Saffron's neck and breathing him in.

"I wanted to give you your gift. Something just for you. I've got it out in the back garden. Come on, before something else finds the poor thing and pounces."

Saffron threw his weight backward, managing to break free of Ryder's grasp just long enough to twist and slam an elbow into the man's jaw. Ryder spit blood into Saffron's face, grabbing and slamming him back against the wall a second time. That time knocking the air from Saffron's lungs, making his world spin as the silver collar squeezed around his throat. Filling him with an incomprehensible dread; sending him all the way back to Danann House's attic, where he sat in silence. Nothing more than a ghost.

No, no, no—he wouldn't become a ghost. Not again. He had to be there for Cylvan, he had to be there when Cylvan finally emerged from the fray. He wouldn't let Ryder get his way again, he wouldn't—

"There will be no fox fey to help this time," Ryder hissed.

"And you and I both know—I'll kill that satyr if you don't behave like I expect you to."

Saffron's blood froze in his veins. He stared at Ryder with wide, panicked eyes, only bringing the man to grin.

"That's right," he whispered, cupping under Saffron's chin with one hand as if briefly appraising him. "Come on, then."

Saffron thought Ryder might let up on his grip once he submitted to walking down the hallway, but it remained domineering. Even as they passed beantighes hurrying by, who gasped and jumped back, but remained silent. Staring at Saffron, glancing at Ryder, then shying out of the way as Ryder hissed at them to *move along*.

"*Summon me,*" Taran whispered. Even he sounded panicked, distressed, like he knew as well as Saffron that he couldn't. Saffron didn't know how to, without a vocal command. He could only roll his tongue over in his mouth, which had gone dry in his focus to remain upright. His desperate fight to remain calm.

*As soon as I can*, he offered in return.

"*I will be here,*" Taran responded, as if there was anywhere else he could go. "*I am right here, the moment you can.*"

Saffron could barely breathe as it was, spit building in the back of his throat and choking him with every sharp breath. Fighting the hot, icy panic rising and falling in his chest. Forcing it back down, screaming at himself to keep his wits. He had to keep his composure. He had to make sure Sionnach was alright. He had to get back to Cylvan. He had to do—*something*.

He knew exactly how far the palace gardens were from the ballroom. He practically knew how many steps it would take to get there, but the distance had stretched into eternity as they went. As Ryder's hand bruised the skin of Saffron's wrist, as fresh drips of blood slipped from the prongs of the silver collar around his throat.

Through the back door into the gardens, the air outside was icy. A storm brewed over the distant sea, as if ringing out for all to know exactly the result of Prince Cylvan's Court of Expectations.

It brought a chilled wind with it, whipping through the wisteria trees and scattering petals across the path Ryder forced Saffron to follow.

At the end of it, within a thicket of trees and right alongside the creek ribboning down the center—Saffron choked at the sight of Sionnach on the ground. Arms and legs tied behind their back, a bloody gash soaking through their pale hair. They gazed at him with half-lidded, blurry eyes, lips parted slightly as if desperate to call out for someone to help.

Saffron reeled with a flood of rage, slamming himself backward into Ryder, throwing his feet out as the man's arms wrapped around him in return. Gripping him with enough strength to nearly snap Saffron's ribs, attempting to sedate him, finally kicking Saffron's feet out from under him and pitching him to the earth. Saffron landed with a heavy thud, rolling immediately onto his stomach and scrambling to where Sionnach remained unmoving on their side. He reached for their face—only to be grabbed by the collar and wrenched back just before he could.

"Draw the circle," Ryder told him, throwing a tin of charcoal to him. The lid popped open as it bounced against the grass, a cloud of black dust staining the front of Saffron's fine clothes. "The summoning spell. Not with your wand, either—I want to exactly what you do. Then you're going to tell me what you see, when you perform it right fucking here. Tell when what I want to hear, and we'll leave your friend in peace. But either way—you're coming with me."

Saffron lobbed the charcoal back at him. Ryder swiped it out of the air, then reached into the back of his pants, pulling a pistol that reflected the stormy moonlight and set Saffron's nerves alight. Making his heart pound hard, in a different way—in the same way it once did when he was first taken back to the human world. With Luvon, where he was meant to be re-introduced to his parents. When his father pulled a gun just like that one, threatening to put a bullet in him if Luvon ever tried to bring Saffron back again.

Saffron raised his hands slightly, on instinct. They trembled, caked in black charcoal as his mind raced. He couldn't remember the markings, for a moment. There was nothing in his mind except cold, paralyzing fear. Begging it to only be a dream; a horrible dream he'd wake from soon enough, safe in Cylvan's bed. In his arms.

"Enough of this, Finn."

Ryder whipped around, and Saffron flinched behind his hands. From the darkness, someone stepped from the path with their own hands raised—and Saffron recognized Adelard, just as a second pair of feet hit the earth on the other side of the creek a few yards away. Saffron barely turned to look, seeing only the silhouette of Cormac. Standing tall and intimidating, eyes glowing a pale yellow with broad wings like those of a bat furling in behind him.

Ryder held the gun pointed at Adelard for what felt like an eternity, as he clearly looked the human professor up and down. Saffron wished to tell Adelard to *run*, knowing Ryder wouldn't hesitate to kill him of all people, as unimportant as he was to everything Ryder wanted—but then Ryder turned a little more, to better face Adelard head-on. He never lowered the gun, but he tilted his head slightly. Curious.

"Haven't heard that name in a bit," he said, trailing off as the wind whistled around them. Thinking. "Only a handful of folk used to know me by it. Why don't you come a little closer? Let me see you clearly, hm? Refresh my memory."

To Saffron's horror, Adelard obeyed. He threw his hands out, attempting to cry out to him, only for the collar to tighten and choke him. Ryder barely twitched, just watching as a nearby lantern better illuminated Adelard's unassuming demeanor. Another torturously long moment passed, despite only being a few seconds. Saffron glanced back to Cormac, silently demanding to know why he didn't do anything while Adelard stood in such danger—

Ryder clucked his tongue. Saffron turned back slowly, noticing how, that time—Ryder's grip on the gun quaked slightly.

"Take that glamour off, friend. Let me see you honestly."

"You already know who I am," Adelard asserted back, voice firm. In the low light, something about him was off; there was nothing meek, sheepish about him. He nearly made chills race down Saffron's spine. "Do as I say, Finn, before you do something you regret."

"I've already done plenty of things I regret. What's a little extra?" Ryder asked. Saffron knew he meant it to be playful, but even his words carried the smallest jitter. His thumb moved on the pistol, clicking a piece of metal at the end of the barrel. Saffron jumped; behind him, Cormac shifted his feet. But Adelard raised a hand to both of them. "Tell me who you are, or I'll pull the trigger."

"You really don't recognize me, Finn? My glamour isn't even particularly elaborate," Adelard insisted. That time, he smirked. Goosebumps raced down Saffron's arms. "Come on. You're still an embarrassment, even after all this time."

"You shut your mouth," Ryder said, but he still didn't answer. His grip on the pistol flexed, knuckles white as a vein popped beneath his skin.

"Last one to figure out Harper's secret; still too stupid to figure out mine. I hear you've been searching high and low for something I took from you, too, tearing up the veil just like the veiled bitch," Adelard went on. Saffron no longer recognized his voice. Angry and threatening and—completely unwavering. "Like mother, like son. Oh, if only Verity were here to see you. The things she'd have to say would make you cry—just like all those times before."

"Take off your fucking glamour!" Ryder exclaimed. His finger flinched on the trigger, firing a round into the trees over Adelard's shoulder. Tears filled Saffron's eyes, overwhelmed, confused, desperate for Adelard to turn around—

But Adelard remained where he was. He said nothing else,

just reaching up to pluck off his glasses. He pulled the chain entirely from his head, folding the ear pieces and hooking them over a nearby branch.

Even in the darkness, Saffron saw how the the man's glamour fell away. Professor Adelard, the short, timid, nervous human who taught anthropology at Morrígan Academy—suddenly gained a few inches of height. He lost the roundness in his face, gaining freckles that dotted his cheeks. His brown eyes shifted into a pale blue, blonde hair growing dark and taking on a curl, lengthening into a short ponytail at the base of his neck. Handsome, but ordinary in every way—except a look in his eyes that made Saffron's blood chill. An ancient, formidable look that cut straight through Ryder like he were made of rice paper. Even the wind whistled louder through the trees, thrashing the branches; even the veil suddenly surged to life amongst the falling wisteria petals, swirling along the earth and circling Adelard like he was an old friend it'd lost track of.

Ryder barked a shrill, fractured laugh, louder than glass breaking.

"You really haven't changed a bit!" he cried with crackling amusement, pulling back the hammer on the pistol. "Just like I remember you, Virtue. With your hair that long, I could almost confuse you for your sister—so sorry about her, by the way. I don't think I ever had the chance to apologize."

Cold hands gripped Saffron's lungs as tightly as the queen's silver squeezed his throat; the prongs burrowed deeper against his windpipe, dripping more blood into his collar.

Professor Adelard—had been Virtue Holt, brother of Verity, and redeemer of humans during the War of the Veil, the whole time Saffron had known him. Living his simple life as a human professor at Morrígan Academy, where every day he'd skirted Saffron's pleas for information in order to protect himself and an attempt at a quiet life. Saffron didn't know if it was hot betrayal that filled him to the brim—or despair, to think it was his fault the man had instantly lost all of that in exposing himself.

"You know I am not someone to trifle with, Finn," Adelard—Virtue—responded, voice as piercing as his gaze. "Put the gun away. Leave these poor folk alone."

"Funny—you used to *love* trifling with me, after everyone else was asleep," Ryder cooed. "Does your new boyfriend know that? Does he know all the things we used to do? All those times I had to cover your mouth, to keep the others from hearing how you moaned?"

For the first time, Virtue's expression twitched. Ryder smirked, nudging the end of the gun toward where Saffron remained on the grass behind him.

"Tell me where you've put my mother's memory tapestry, and I'll consider letting this all go," Ryder said.

"There's nothing she can tell you that I cannot," Virtue answered. "She doesn't wish to have anything to do with you, *still*, even after all this time—why else would she have ignored your efforts, and called out to a beantighe instead? I hope her soul writhes in humiliation, knowing a rowan witch has been hearing every pitiful cry she's made."

Ryder glanced at Saffron over his shoulder. Saffron glared back at him, wishing he could speak. Wishing he could confirm everything Adelard said—to tell him exactly how the queen's tapestry had indeed preferred to call out to him, rather than her own son. He, who owned her beloved king's bones.

"Well... that changes things, doesn't it?" Ryder said. He kept his eyes on Saffron as he did; the calm in his voice, that time, made Saffron's breath catch. "Seems you really are as special as I always thought, Saffron. No wonder your prince is so obsessed with you, despite having no idea how to best use you. But I do. I have so many uses for you, even now. Even if you refuse, even if I have to force you..."

He trailed off, turning back to Adelard. To Virtue Holt. Ryder's opposite hand flexed at his side, as if picking at a hangnail. Turning something over between his fingers—but Saffron's eyes quickly flashed away, back to the gun as Ryder lowered it.

"Virtue—be sure you tell the prince, to his face, that your refusal to give me what I want is the reason I've done this. Send him my regards—and Saffron's."

*"Adelard!"* Cormac shouted, pushing off from the grass with wings flared. He slammed into Virtue, shoving him away—just as Ryder turned on heel, lunging for where Saffron instantly threw himself over Sionnach, clinging to them.

In the light, four pixie rings glimmered on Ryder's fingers. The same number the veil had warned him to avoid being touched by while they fought in the Winter Court.

*Knock, knock, knock, knock*—the veil swallowed them whole. With it, all that remained—undone, flaring across Alfidel like a lesion in skin. Butterflied open and ringing through every inch of Saffron's being—telling him exactly what it meant, the moment he crashed to the wooden floor on the other side, an instant before all of his own magic left him.

Ryder had finally plucked the last seam, stealing Saffron through against his will—and with it, the veil was no more.

# EPILOGUE

Three days behind a locked door. A ghost no one knew existed, except for Sionnach who sat on the edge of the bed and cried, when they didn't gaze blankly out the window with only a brick wall visible on the other side.

Three days slamming his shoulder into the door. Screaming from the moment someone pulled the collar off him; clawing at the wood, feeling every single second that passed.

Three days in the human world was nearly a week and a half in Alfidel—if time even passed how it used to. With no veil to weave through—there was no way to know. It could have been years. Decades. Centuries.

Saffron should have stayed in the ballroom. He should have made a scene. He never should have left, no matter how much Naoill encouraged him, or however hard Ryder gripped him right on the other side of the wall. He should have been there to take Cylvan's hand. To hold him. To show him exactly where his feet would remain planted, despite the cries of dissent and demands for explanations. He should have been there. When Cylvan needed him most—Saffron had been nowhere to be found. Just like Cylvan once told him he feared so much.

He screamed, he cried, he clawed at the door, and then at his hair, his face, his clothes, screaming in such agony and unable to do anything about it. He couldn't stop time from passing, he couldn't go back and stop himself, he couldn't do anything except scream and tear and beg for mercy, until Sionnach's hands found him and pulled him close, petting his hair despite even they being unable to speak. There was no comfort to give. Even if there was, Saffron didn't want it.

Saffron wasn't with Cylvan. He wasn't with him. He wasn't there. He should have been there. *He should be there.*

Despite so many promises made, despite swearing to cling to Cylvan's hand no matter what came, no matter how dark the night that swallowed them, when the blackness finally found them—

Saffron hadn't been there. He'd left Cylvan to wander it alone. Lonely and silent in a crowd of wolves. Bracing to be torn apart with nothing to fight back. His only comfort would have been knowing Saffron waited to hold him when it was all over. Where the sun would rise and the palace would go quiet again. But Saffron hadn't been there, when Cylvan finally turned to look. Again, and again, and again, how many times did Cylvan turn to look for him, and Saffron never appeared again?

And every additional day that passed—would be three more gone by in that darkness where he'd left Cylvan to wander alone.

Saffron screamed and lobbed himself, wild and deranged in his desperation, at the door for every hour of sunlight and darkness that followed. Until strangers rammed the door from the other side, shouting back at him in familiar and unfamiliar languages to *shut the fuck up*. Once, the door even opened as someone attempted to threaten him to his face—but they didn't get more than a single foot through before Saffron's nails raked through their cheek, ripping away fingerfuls of skin as he fought to escape. Blood that stained the door and smeared over the knob once it slammed shut in front of him again.

Two more days passed before a second body attempted to open the door and subdue him—and Saffron sank teeth deep enough into the man's arm to taste blood, before realizing who it was. Hollow, who gazed down at him with such pity, with such a heavy heart that even he looked on the verge of tears.

"Saffron," he said weakly, voice cracking. The weakest sound Saffron had ever heard his friend utter. "Please, Saffron."

Saffron pulled away. His friend's blood stained the corners of his mouth as he stared up at him. Behind him, a patch of curly blonde hair bobbed in the hallway, and Saffron lunged for it, too. He didn't know if it was to attack, or something else—he didn't know anything else by that point—but Hollow's big, strong arm swept Saffron up around the stomach and bodied him back into the room.

Rather than shoving Saffron away and hurrying back out, though—he followed inside. Behind him, Letty also stepped in, looking pale. Avoiding Saffron's eyes. She did, however, meet Sionnach's, who shied away and attempted to cover their horns, their ears, in shame. Letty smiled gently at them, approaching carefully while Hollow wrestled Saffron onto the edge of the bed.

"Saffron, I said *STOP IT!*" Hollow boomed, loud enough to shake the walls. Saffron finally went still. Staring at his friend who knelt in front of him, Hollow had his wrists gripped, one in each hand. Saffron's fingers twitched from the strength of them, stained under the nails with old blood and splinters.

Hollow stared at him, breathing heavy, expression warped in fury and something else unreadable—before it all crumbled down, and he released Saffron's wrists to embrace him. To wrap his arms around Saffron's writhing body, squeezing him with his own desperation, as his own body shuddered. Hollow—was crying.

On the other side of the room, Letty sat at the foot of Sionnach's bed, wringing her hands together with her eyes turned to the floor. Dark, wet dots appeared on the canvas pinafore she wore as she silently cried, too.

Saffron couldn't breathe, and not because of Hollow's grasp encircling him. Saffron wanted to scream more, he wanted to claw at Hollow and race for the door, to throw himself out it. He had to get back, he had to get back, Cylvan needed him, Cylvan had been left all alone—

But the moment he was embraced by someone familiar, someone he found such immediate comfort with—Saffron's resolve buckled. He collapsed into Hollow's arms, pressing his face into the crook of his friend's neck where he sobbed. He cried like he'd cried every moment before then, but that time it felt different. He'd cried into Hollow's shoulder so many times before, that even without any words to speak, Saffron felt like he could give up control for just a moment. He could be useless, desperate, pitiful, just for a moment, where nothing would be able to come and hurt him. Where he could fool himself into thinking time stopped passing, to allow him a single moment.

He clawed at Hollow's back, straining the fabric of his shirt. He cried until there was nothing left, until he trembled over every inch and felt every bruise and welt left on his skin from assaulting the door without end.

"I'm so sorry," Hollow whispered, cupping the back of Saffron's head to tuck him closer. "That bastard—that evil bastard, maybe it was only a matter of time..."

He pulled away, smearing his calloused thumbs over Saffron's swollen eyes to wipe the tears away. It did no good, as more replaced them in an instant. Saffron just clung to Hollow's hands, anchoring himself there.

"If there is anyone in this world who can find a way home, Saffron, it's you," Hollow said. Saffron shook his head, blubbering disagreements, but Hollow just took his face again. "There is no one in this world who loves you more than Prince Cylvan," he went on, and Saffron's insides shredded into nauseating ribbons at the words. But Hollow kept holding his face. "And between the first rowan witch in centuries, and a fey Night Prince who would tear the world apart for him—I know you will not be here for long."

"I can't," Saffron sobbed, shaking his head. "I can't—I don't have any magic here, Hollow, I can't do anything, I—can't—do anything..."

"You've spent more of your life with no magic than you have with it," Hollow told him, wiping more tears from his eyes. "You are more than your magic, Saffron. I know it. I've seen it. Even Prince Cylvan devoted himself to you long before you ever had any magic of your own—and I know he'll do anything to get you back."

Hollow reached into the pocket of his patchwork jacket, taking Saffron's hand and pressing something into it. Like white-hot metal, making Saffron attempt to jerk away, but Hollow kept him where he was. Only when he slowly removed his hand, did Saffron see what burned him so intensely. It was his amethyst pendant.

Despite what he was certain had been irreparable damage to the veil—heat kissed his hand. Someone was calling to him, from the other side.

Exhaling a shuddering breath, Saffron closed his fingers over the crystal. He pulled it into his chest, hunching forward and giving the stone everything he had. His heat, his breath, the heavy beating of his heart. Cylvan would feel him. Cylvan would hear Saffron calling back.

"I'm here, I'm here," he cried softly. "You haven't lost me, I'm here—..."

The pendant burned brighter, hotter and hotter until the tiny sound of snapping glass rang out. Holding his breath, Saffron shakily opened his hands to look. A hairline crack stretched through the center of the crystal, overwhelmed by the charmed magic coursing through it. It kept its shape in his hands, though. It did not crumble. It remained hot enough to leave red, flushed kisses on his skin.

Saffron closed his eyes again. He clasped the necklace between his hands, squeezing it again. He forced himself to breathe, inhaling his first lungful of air since arriving in that place.

He raised his eyes back to Hollow, who watched him with so

much worry. His gaze then traveled to Letty, who finally looked at him, too, green eyes wet with emotion. Finally, he looked at Sionnach, who remained curled tightly in on themself, watching him as every inch of their being trembled.

Saffron released the poisonous breath he held, and turned back to Hollow.

"Where are we?" he asked, voice hoarse.

"A place called London," Hollow answered. The confirmation nauseated him, but Saffron nodded. He inhaled another shaky breath, then released it.

"Is Sunbeam here?"

Hollow glanced over his shoulder to Letty, who sat up slightly.

"Yes," she said. "Still pretending to be a witchhunter. It's hard to talk to her much, since Ryder keeps all of them busy, especially since the others... Well, the other witchhunters, they..."

Inhale. Exhale.

"I know," Saffron whispered. "Where's Nimue? Is she alright?"

"Yes," Letty straightened up slightly more. "Yes, she's fine. She spends most of her time in the bathtub in our shared flat. She isn't able to walk around very easily because I haven't been able to find any more seaweed to make a charm for her."

Before Saffron could ask his next question, a tiny voice emerged from where Sionnach sat on the bed.

"Are you a witch as well, miss?" they asked. Letty turned to them with a smile.

"A little bit," she said. "Nothing like Saffron, though. Well, human magic works a little differently here than in the fey world, so maybe I'm even better than him at it right now... What's your name?"

"It's... Sionnach."

*Inhale. Exhale.* Saffron squeezed the pendant again. For the first time, the heat faded slightly, before swelling back. It told him what he hoped—that Cylvan truly was on the other end. The charm wasn't just overheating from being on the wrong side of the veil.

*The wrong side of the veil.* Saffron's stomach turned. Inhale, exhale. He gazed down at the pendant again, rubbing his thumb over where the crack in the middle was embedded deep within its purple heart.

"You haven't lost me," he whispered, pressing the smooth face of the pendant to his lips and speaking directly into it. Injecting as much strength into the words as he could, like when he used to flare the magic in his blood. *"I'm right here. You haven't lost me."*

Inhale, exhale. Except that time, his nostrils flared. His teeth clenched. A hot, bitter anger filled him, flooding the gaps in his veins where magic had once resided.

Saffron would learn to bend light. He would learn to bend shadow. Whatever he had to do, he would not let Cylvan walk alone in darkness without a hand to hold.

Ryder Kyteler thought stealing Saffron through the veil would leave him defenseless—but Saffron had spent his entire life defenseless, and it had never once made him weak. Ryder thought taking Saffron from Cylvan would break his spirit—never thinking it would only make Saffron more determined than ever, to take ownership of any and all obstacles that ever threatened his rightful place by Cylvan's side. He was the first rowan witch in centuries. He was oathed to the veil. He was the future Harmonious King of Alfidel. But by stealing Saffron to the human side of the veil, Ryder had made his biggest mistake. By taking away everything Saffron had ever known—he suddenly had nothing to lose.

Ryder had made him desperate—which was a stupid thing to do.

*I'm right here.*

"Alright," he said, exhaling the word with a tremble. He sought Letty once more, holding her gaze as the fire in his stomach ignited, sparking against blood he knew had to still harbor rowan magic, even if he couldn't reach it. It didn't matter.

Rowan magic or not—the blood in his veins was still hot and alive. "You said human magic on this side works a little differently?"

Letty nodded. Saffron nodded back.

"Teach me."

# ABOUT THE AUTHOR

Kellen Graves (they/them) is a queer indie writer and artist from the Pacific Northwest, where they live with their partner, two cats, and crystal collection. They also enjoy digital illustration, photography, collecting planners, and disappearing into the ocean.

You can find more info about this release and upcoming releases, see their art, and connect by following Kellen on social media or checking out their website.

SKELLYGRAVES.COM

SKELLYGRAVES.CARRD.CO

 bsky.app/profile/skellygraves.bsky.social

 instagram.com/skellygraves

 tiktok.com/skellygraves

# ALSO BY KELLEN GRAVES

**ROWAN BLOOD**

PRINCE OF THE SORROWS (VOL. ONE)
LORD OF SILVER ASHES (VOL. TWO)
HERALD OF THE WITCH'S MARK (VOL. THREE)
THE FOX AND THE DRYAD

———

A BONE IN HIS TEETH